Chicago Billionaires

A Contemporary Romance Series Boxed Set

By Aria Hawthorne

Paperback edition
ISBN: 978-0-9968364-5-6
Published by French Kiss Press LLC

TABLE OF CONTENTS

Closer

Aria Hawthorne

Closer – Book Summary

Famous Dutch architect, Sven van der Meer, has just completed the greatest achievement of his professional life—the design and construction of The Spire. But a shameful secret threatens to destroy his prestigious career—he's losing his eyesight. Now, he's run out of time and the only woman qualified to help maintain his charade of invincibility is also the one woman who despises him and The Spire. And he's fairly certain she's hiding something as well. Will the fiery, but enchanting Miss Sanchez be the right woman to play the role of his pretend girlfriend? Or will the temptation of getting too close, too fast jeopardize their business arrangement and the future of his entire career?

When twenty-eight-year-old, woefully unemployed, Inez Sanchez, arrives to her interview with hotter-than-hell billionaire architect, Sven van der Meer—mastermind behind Chicago's tallest, most controversial skyscraper, The Spire—she quickly realizes his job proposition isn't what she was anticipating. He's hiding a life-changing secret, one that could ruin his career as the most influential architect in the world, and he's willing to pay her five thousand dollars a day—just to help him keep it. Will she accept his offer to become his "pretend girlfriend" for the next four days in order to ensure the success of the most important week of his life? Or will her sassy flair for independence and smartass sarcasm keep her from submitting to his stern authoritative commands, no matter how sexy his European accent might be? And what will happen when he discovers she's hiding a secret, too—one that could threaten the stability of their arrangement and prevent her from getting too close to the one man in the world who might be capable of gaining her trust…

Chapter One

THE ONLY THING THAT INEZ was told about this interview was that it would be different. Very different. It had the potential to pay three, maybe four times more than the usual ten dollars an hour temporary assignment. Plus, Inez's temp agency recruiter, Beatrice, told her it offered flexibility. Inez wasn't assured as to what kind of flexibility exactly, but she had made it very clear to Beatrice that the reason she was seeking temp work—and not a real job—was because she had obligations and she wasn't able to re-prioritize her morning commitments for some meager, nine-to-five office job, regardless of how great the benefits. Flexibility, Inez repeated in her mind. Flexibility with amazing pay. It sounded too good to be true, and it probably was. Beatrice hadn't told her much about where she was going or who she would be meeting, but she had told Inez that five girls from the agency had already interviewed for the position and all five girls had been turned away as "unsuitable."

Inez was the final temp to be sent by the agency, likely because she had the least office experience: a few jobs at law firms and a recent poor performance review from an owner of an auto repair shop. She dared to offer "car advice" to one of the customers.

"Sounds like an idle air controller," Inez said, cracking her gum from behind the plexiglass of the service counter. "I had one of those, and I got it cleaned and readjusted for about thirty bucks." Then, she rang up the six-hundred dollar charge for the "tune up" to his credit card.

The auto repair shop owner quickly took Inez aside during her dinner break and made sure to let her know—in no uncertain terms—that women should answer phones and men should stick to fixing cars. Inez fixed her black eyes on him and let him know—in no uncertain fucking terms—that she quit. That's how Inez became known as the temp with the "attitude" problem. From that point on, Beatrice always reminded her before her interview: "Don't mention you're a college graduate. Men don't like women who are smarter than they are. They like women who smile and nod a lot and make them feel like they're doing you a favor by hiring you."

Barf, thought Inez.

She peered up at the skyscrapers as she rode the elevated train through downtown Chicago and considered all her other employment options. *Zippo*. She needed money—a lot of it and badly—and this job was her last hope. The train came to a stop at the Randolph station and Inez exited onto the platform as she mentally rehearsed her standard interview spiel.

Why was she interested in the job?

Well, for starters, she wanted the job because she loved being part of the team.

Internal eye roll—cue, *silent gag*. The truth was Inez usually hated all the other office staffers because they were full-time office employees and she was just "the temp"—a notch down from the receptionist and two notches down from the pizza delivery guy—and they always made sure to let her know it.

She jaywalked across the busy street. *God, how she loved downtown Chicago*. The noise, the energy, the vibe. She even loved the taxi drivers who honked at her for darting out in front of them rather than waiting for the pedestrian light. She had traveled to the "Loop" hundreds of times and it never got old. Hurrying along the broad sidewalks, she scurried past the meandering crowds. *Move over, tourists…this was her town*. She had somewhere important to be and she knew exactly how to get there.

When she came upon the address—88 North Michigan Avenue, she pushed through the revolving doors and into the sleek modern lobby.

Pressing the elevator call button, the security guard greeted her. "Going up?"

"Suite 6600." She knew the drill and passed into the elevator cab.

"Lucky girl. Floor 66 is all the way at the top…enjoy."

All the way at the top? She had interviewed in dozens of downtown office buildings, but none of them were as fancy as the top floor of a skyscraper along Michigan Ave. The elevator doors closed and Inez quickly felt it flutter upwards.

"It's gonna be a bit different," Beatrice had warned. But Inez had dismissed her. How different could it possibly be? A pop quiz in proper filing etiquette in which Inez would be forced to color code the CEO's secret condom jar?

She didn't know what "different" meant, but Beatrice had told her in the past that she should be prepared for anything and she always was, including the time she was asked to serve morning coffee to the president of the company on a silver platter.

Douche bag.

The elevator stopped and the doors chimed open. She stepped out and into a private glass-paneled lobby. Beyond their doors, she saw a large empty business suite with a sweeping view of Lake Michigan.

"Okay, you win, Beatrice," Inez muttered to herself. "This is certainly different."

She slowly slipped through the doors. There was no receptionist. No waiting area. There were only walls and walls of panoramic glass, stretching in both directions along the suite's pristine hardwood floors and open floor plan. Then, she noticed something else—eerie silence. At the end of the corridor, she thought she spotted an entertainment bar and several tables and chairs. Perhaps it was some sort of weird, underground night club for business men—closed during the day, but teeming with macho executive bravado at night. Inez imagined a fraternity of suited businessmen, breaking out the Jameson and grooving along the hardwood floors to the beat of the Bee Gees under the illumination of a disco ball. If there was one thing she had learned from all her temp jobs it was that men—especially wealthy, powerful businessmen—were also painfully repressed assholes who did all sorts of bizarro things whenever they thought everyone was so plastered that nobody was going to remember any of it.

But Inez rarely drank. And she knew all the settings on her camera phone.

She moved to the floor-to-ceiling windows and reached out to touch their cool glass. She shivered, as if she could feel the stark wind rushing across the lake. It was one of the most beautiful vistas of the lakeshore she had ever seen—an expansive view of its endless crystal waters, lined by sandy beaches and the miniature highway of Lake Shore Drive. Peering out across Monroe Harbor with the tiny toy sailboats moored in its bay, she settled her gaze on the unobstructed view of the historic lighthouse, just south of Navy Pier. She always loved seeing that lighthouse, wishing she could disappear into its isolation and ignite its single blinking light every night for the seamen who needed it. Inez wished she didn't need a lot of money so badly. Instead, she wished she only needed a tiny place to call her own to protect herself from all the rigors and hardships of the cold, cruel world—her own private lighthouse where she would take on the responsibility of maintaining a constant flame.

Inez paused, sensing that something—or someone—was watching her. She glanced up and saw a series of small tinted black bulbs, spaced along the ceiling every six to ten feet. *Security cameras.* Then, a metallic click at the opposite end of the corridor caught her attention. She stared at the two shimmering nickel-plated doors, realizing they had just automatically unlocked. She waited for them to swing open and reveal whoever was watching her, but not before glancing back up at the security cameras.

What was her favorite part about being a temp? Her routine interview questions ran through her mind while she moved towards the door. Showing up to weird, messed-up interviews like this…

She pulled the door ajar and slipped through it. *Just barely.* It was heavier than she expected, and she thought for a moment she would be trapped within the jaws of its steel doorjamb. After jumping forward, securing her escape, she stopped and surveyed the dimly lit executive suite. Decorative lights hung above the immaculate mahogany desk and the silver blinds were drawn down past the middle of the floor-length windows.

Too stupid to live, she suddenly thought. If she was watching a horror movie, that's what she would be screaming at herself right now. *Too stupid to live, chick.*

Taking in the lack of furniture and the minimalistic décor, her eyes flicked across the room. Much better than a moldy basement or rat-infested garage. At least her ax murderer had some sense of style.

"You should have knocked to announce yourself."

She flinched. The masculine voice behind her echoed off the hardwood floors. Its reprimanding sternness dared her to turn around and its owner's unusual accent made her wonder about his country of origin. *Sweden? Norway? Liechtenstein?* She swallowed and held her ground, lifting her chin slightly, adding an extra inch to her height when she sensed his presence closing in on her. He passed by, brushing his arm against her own, as if he sought to push her out of his way.

Tick, tick, tick... The silver tip of his black cane tapped along the floor as he skulked through the shadows towards the desk.

Oh frick. Another geriatric geezer who expected her to spoon feed him his soft boiled eggs every morning while she soaked his dentures in mineral water from the Fiji Islands. *No, God no.*

Tick, tick, tick... His cane clicked with menace against the floor as he circled around his desk. But to Inez's surprise, he wasn't an old geezer at all. He was young, not more than forty, and undeniably attractive in his tan sharkskin suit that complemented his fair complexion and slick, golden hair. Okay, she would even admit it—but just to herself—that he was not just attractive, but *ride him hard H-O-T.* And Inez wasn't even that kind of girl. Tall and commanding, he gazed at her with an intensity that disarmed her and revealed something she hadn't anticipated—he was wearing a black eyepatch over his left eye. Anyone else would have looked ridiculous or vulnerable, but not him. On him, it only served to sharpen the chiseled features of his angular face. *A masculine force of elegance*, she acknowledged, as if his beauty had hypnotized her.

Then, he opened his mouth. "You are smaller than I expected. The rest of the girls were taller."

"And you're weirder than I expected," she shot back. "What kind of an employer cares about the height of his potential office temps? I can only think of one kind."

"I'm not that kind," he replied, almost amused.

"Good. Because I'm not looking for that kind."

He stroked his clean-cut jawline. "And you are not easily intimidated, are you?"

"As a general rule, no," she retorted, realizing she had nothing to lose.

"Hmm." He exhaled through his nostrils, as if to insinuate that he didn't believe her and he intended to prove it.

He held out his hand, inviting her to take a seat in the lone chair in front of his oversized desk. She hesitated and considered walking out. She so desperately wanted to walk out. But then she heard Beatrice's voice in her head. *Flexible schedule and amazing pay.* She felt herself involuntarily pulled towards the chair. *Ugh…too stupid to live.*

"I have my résumé here." She dug into her purse for her file folder.

He dismissed her with a wave of his hand. "I've already reviewed it. You know…you would look a lot taller if you wore heels."

"I hate heels."

"Yes," he mused. "And by the tone of your voice, I suspect you hate a lot of things."

"Just things worthy of hatred," she slung back. Forget his too-damn-perfect-to-look-away-chiseled face. She definitely hated this guy and wanted him to know it.

It didn't work. Instead, he seemed invigorated by it. In fact, she was fairly certain she saw him smirk.

"Please take a seat."

She stared down at the white leather chair. "On that?"

"Don't tell me you are a vegan, too, and you are opposed to sitting down on leather chairs."

"No, I'm opposed to sitting down on chairs that cost more than an entire year of my rent."

He eyed her with interest and rubbed his chin. "How do you know that?"

"Because that's a Mies van der Rohe Barcelona chair. I'm fairly certain I saw that exact chair on exhibit at the Art Institute."

"Yes, it's true. I lent it to them for that exhibition. It's one of the two originals that Mies van der Rohe produced for the Barcelona Exposition of 1929. So more precisely, it cost me more than a decade of your rental expenses." He gazed at her, as if she had unexpectedly impressed him. "None of the other temp girls who interviewed for the position knew that."

"One point for short girls then."

He muted his smile and held out his hand, insisting that she take a seat. Closing her eyes and cringing like he was scratching his nails across his mahogany desk, she sank into the chair, barely able to fathom the fact that her ass was being supported by something that cost more than her entire college tuition.

He rested his cane against the edge of the desk and reclined in his black executive chair. "So tell me…why is a smart Northwestern graduate, who knows the worth of a Mies van der Rohe chair, seeking an office job through a temp agency?"

"Because Northwestern didn't do their job training me to do anything else."

"I find that hard to believe."

She shrugged and fell silent. He was fishing for something and she didn't feel like making it easy for him. Crossing her legs, she tested him, wondering if he would shift his gaze away from her face. She had been told by the temp agency to wear pantyhose and a skirt. Her experiment failed. He didn't flinch.

"And you haven't walked out of the room—yet. Perhaps because the temp agency told you that this was a special interview for a significantly higher wage than usual. Which means you need the money. More than usual. Why?"

She shrugged. "Doesn't everybody need money?" He was being a nosy bastard and she *definitely* wasn't going to make it easy for him.

He threw his weight back into his chair. "Okay, I'll guess."

Inez rolled her eyes—*big time*. She wanted him to see it, but he ignored her.

"By the manner in which you disrespected your own alma mater, you seem to realize it's a cut below true Ivy League universities."

He paused and waited. Inez suddenly worried he had fallen asleep.

"And...?" she pressed him, seriously annoyed.

"And your silence confirms that I am right, which tells me you don't need money to pay off student loans since you most likely received a full scholarship to attend Northwestern, despite the fact that I'm sure you would have preferred to attend Harvard or Yale."

"Princeton."

He nodded. "Of course. Harvard is...

"For nerds."

"Too traditional," he overrode her. "And Yale is..."

"For trust fund babies."

He smiled slowly, as if he had recorded the exchange in his mind and was now replaying it for entertainment. At least she was amusing someone.

"You failed to list your college major on your résumé. Which means it's something unemployable like drama or dance."

She smirked at the thought of herself in a ballet tutu. "Art history."

"Ah, yes...your knowledge of Mies van der Rohe and the fact that you visited a somewhat obscure architectural exhibit at the Art Institute. I should have gotten that one. An oversight on my part."

"Next time, Billions," she sassed back.

It just came out. Inez couldn't help it. She didn't want the job—whatever the hell it was—so at this point, she was free to insult him as much as she thought she could get away with.

"And so, you don't need tuition money because Northwestern gave you a free ride to study whatever you wanted, so where does that leave us?" He tapped his fingers along the sleek surface of his desk. "Credit card debt? However, you sound far too exacting to have frivolously gotten into credit card debt. Wedding?"

She snorted, then covered her nose and tried hard to compose herself.

"Ahhh, I see. No boyfriend." He registered her silence with a smug smile.

"Maybe I just need a job, like everyone else."

"I'm sure that's true." He said it as if he had finally figured her out.

"You're kind of acting like Hercule Poirot, aren't you? You've even got the same quirky accent."

"Poirot was Belgian. I'm Dutch."

"Ah, I assumed German."

He huffed, like she had finally succeeded in insulting him. "Hercule Poirot—that's another unusually obscure reference for a young woman of your age. Agatha Christie isn't something most girls read widely anymore."

"Maybe I'm older than you think." Inez shifted in her seat. He hadn't moved his gaze from her since she sat down in his two hundred thousand dollar Barcelona chair.

"You're twenty-seven. Perhaps twenty-eight."

"You're good," she conceded.

He nodded and continued with his interrogation. "What are your table manners like?"

"I generally try to eat with my hands as much as possible."

He ignored her. It unnerved her.

"What about your cursing?"

"My what?" For a moment, she was certain she misunderstood the lilt in his accent.

"Cursing," he repeated. "Right now, you're on your best behavior because this is an interview. But in your real life, how much do you curse?"

"Never."

He shifted his unpatched eye onto her. They both knew it was a lie.

"Okay, a whole fuck load." It was the first honest thing she had said all interview.

"Yes, that's more likely the truth," he mused. "And what about your posture?"

"Worse than Quasimodo."

"That will have to change."

Inez started to sit straighter in her seat, and then realized she wanted to do the exact opposite of what he wanted. A whole fuck load of opposite.

"First tell me whether or not I've got the job."

He fell silent and leaned back in his chair. "I'm not sure."

"About what?"

"About you."

"Yeah, I got that, but which part?"

"Well…you're clearly…verbal."

"Geez, thanks."

"And sufficiently intelligent. Certainly smarter than the last five girls that the agency sent me."

"Somehow I doubt that's saying much."

"But you're sarcastic."

"Can't handle it?"

He stared her down. "Sarcasm is a sign of weakness."

"I like to think of it as my best asset."

"No, it means you don't have the confidence to say what you honestly think."

"Trust me…get me going, and I'll be more than happy to tell you."

He leaned into the edge of his desk and folded his hands across its gleaming surface. "And you're a bit too cocky and I'm not sure why."

Inez tempered her urge to smile and slouched deeper into her seat—her two hundred thousand dollar Barcelona chair. "Because I know whatever job this is…whatever weird fetish office tasks you need me to perform, like balancing your coffee mug on my head because you like watching me take orders, or taking dictation while you're getting your nose hairs trimmed, or reading aloud pages and pages of painfully boring legal memos while you ignore me and then ask me to re-read them again, but this time, in Pig Latin, I know I can do it. I can do any of it."

He abruptly called her bluff. "I need you to pretend to be my girlfriend."

Busted. Inez felt her sassiness slide off her face.

"Yes, I'm not sure you're up for it either."

As a general rule, Inez never let anyone tell her they didn't think she couldn't do something without serious ramifications. But this time, she had to admit it: Billions had pegged her.

"On the other hand, you may have a certain…potential." His unpatched eye scanned the details of her face.

"You mean I'm not ugly."

He reclined in his chair. It was exactly what he meant; she didn't need him to confirm it.

"You do realize it's kind of illegal," she said.

The suggestion caught him off-guard. "What? Hiring you to pretend to be my girlfriend?"

"Yeah, it's kinda an awkward form of prostitution, right?"

Billions laughed and swiveled in his chair.

"Don't worry. I don't want to fuck you. You're far too opinionated for my tastes. I prefer women who—"

"Have one brain cell?"

His mouth spread into a sly smile. "Talk less and obey more."

"Sorry for them."

Billions eyed her, silently gauging whether or not to proceed. It was a familiar moment during all her interviews—the moment when the man across the desk was sizing her up, calculating whether or not he wanted to hire her to be his whipping girl, and whether or not she would happily go along with it.

"So why do you need me to pretend to be your girlfriend, anyway?" It seemed like the most natural question in their whole interview.

"Because the fact of the matter is… I'm losing my sight."

"Well, you are wearing a pirate patch."

"You're right. That's an obvious confession. I've already lost my sight—in my left eye, my *pirate* eye," he clarified with subtle amusement. "The eye beneath my patch has nearly zero vision. I can register shades of light, but not much else, so I wear this patch to cut out all light and reduce all distractions. It helps me focus all my attention on my right eye—my good eye—*good* being highly subjective because 'good' implies a relatively high level of functionality. And unfortunately for me, that is not the case at this point in my life."

"But you knew I wasn't wearing heels?"

"Because I heard how quietly you crossed the room. All the other girls clicked like exotic dancers. You were silent as a mouse."

"Or a ninja."

"Preparing for my execution," he confirmed, almost charmed. "But now, the problem is that I'm fighting a deadline. I'm losing my sight in a way that I never expected. I can see you now, but not very well. I can see that you're young, younger than me by almost ten years. I can see that you have long black hair and red lips. I can make out that you're fairly well-dressed. Conservative, like an uptight Northwestern graduate, but still well-dressed. But I cannot see much else, although I did make out the way that you scowled at me when I confessed I did not want to fuck you."

"Indigestion."

"Of course." He confirmed with a nod, betraying a hint of amusement. Then, he hesitated, the first time the entire interview. "But the reality of the situation is that the doctors cannot tell me my fate. They cannot explain why I am losing my sight in my right eye. Unlike my left eye, it was not damaged in the…incident. And so, they tell me it is a problem with the way that my brain is receiving the optical image—or rather, choosing *not* to receive it. I could fully regain my sight tomorrow or I could awaken and find myself completely blind. And while everyone knows that I'm sightless in my left eye, no one suspects that I am losing my vision in my right eye as well. I am an architect. My sight and my ability to design buildings are paramount to both my career and my reputation. Complete blindness is not something I can endure without severe consequences. I've become quite proficient at maintaining this extraordinary charade, but now I must admit that I need…" he paused and hesitated again.

"A seeing eye dog?"

He nodded.

"Basically a really attractive, but capable bitch."

"Crudely put, but yes."

Inez peered down at his hand. *No ring.* "Why can't you just get your real girlfriend to help you?"

The expression on his face hardened like stone. "You have your reasons for interviewing for the job, and I have my own reason for offering it. Let's just leave it at that."

She had dug into him so many times before, but this time was different. This time was the first time that Billions betrayed discomfort. "This is all kind of weird…you know that, right?"

"Unfortunately, I do. We will have to work together as a team. I'll have to…depend on you. And I'm not used to that dynamic in my life. I'm used to being the boss and getting exactly what I want whenever I want it."

"Boy, you really know how to sell a job, don't you?"

He paused, underscoring the gravity of the situation with the intensity of his gaze. "I am willing to pay five thousand dollars a day for the next four days, including the opening night of The Spire. It's one of the most important buildings of my career and one of the most important new additions to Chicago's cityscape."

"The Spire?" Inez heard the question escape from her lips.

"Yes," he confirmed.

"Are you telling me that you're Sven van der Meer?" It wasn't a question. It was a revelation.

"Yes." He mused, as if he enjoyed the fact that she obviously knew exactly who he was.

"Well, then…this is impossible. We can't work together."

He arched his brow. "Why not?"

"Because I hate that building."

"Well, that's not particularly original. Most of Chicago hates The Spire."

"Because it's a garish eyesore on our skyline."

"That sounds like a stolen quote from *Architectural Digest*."

"Urban Art Gazette."

"Yes," he said with a faint smile. "Chicagoans don't like it when you change their city. Especially as a foreigner. Nor do they like it when you change their city's history. The Spire is thirty stories taller than the Willis Tower, which makes it the tallest building in the country."

"Chicagoans also don't like it when you refer to the tallest building in their city as anything other than the Sears Tower."

"It's not the tallest building anymore," he corrected her.

Inez pursed her lips. Clearly, he was the kind of man used to living an ambitious life of achievements and having the upper hand whenever possible. *Bastard.*

"So you're offering to pay five thousand dollars a day for the honor of being your fake girlfriend, just so nobody finds out you're going blind. That's the deal, right?"

"Yes. I will hire you officially as my office assistant through your temporary agency, but everything else is between you and me. I will pay cash at the end of the work day and our agreement remains one hundred percent confidential."

"That sounds almost criminal."

"Which is why I haven't confirmed you have the job."

"Oh, yes you have." Inez laughed, reveling in the fact that she was now the one with the upper hand. "Because I can guarantee you—I'm your best and only option."

He fell silent, as if he had no interest in affirming what they both knew was true. "You'll have to make yourself available to me every day this week, including Saturday night—the opening night of The Spire."

"Only until midnight. Then I'm off the clock."

"Does your carriage turn back into a pumpkin at midnight?"

She ignored his condescension. "I've got places to be in the morning and I need my beauty sleep."

"Then you'll have to be available every day by noon."

"Four."

"Two."

"Deal."

He nodded. She nodded. It was the first thing they had agreed on and it felt like an unexpected peace treaty.

"So…should I just show up here tomorrow?"

"No, I would prefer you to start immediately."

Inez floundered. She wasn't expecting "immediately," but she sure as hell wasn't going to turn down her first chance to make five thousand dollars.

"Stand up," he directed her, as if he knew he was making the decision to permanently alter their fates.

Inez obeyed, absorbing the surreal absurdity of possibly earning twenty thousand dollars in one week. Slowly, he circled around from behind the broad desk and approached her.

"Don't move," he said in an even tone, edging his intimidating build into her personal space.

It was her first test. Twenty thousand dollars, twenty thousand dollars, twenty thousand dollars…she chanted it over and over in her mind. She told herself to take a deep breath. It would only be four days. Suck it up and do what he wants…

Cautiously, he held out his fingertips to her chin and angled her face towards his good eye, like an appraiser examining a fine painting. *It was the only way he could see her*, she told herself, *from this close of range*. Inez parted her mouth to speak, overwhelmed by her need to diffuse the awkward silence until he spoke first.

"You're Caribbean."

She stared at him. Almost everyone assumed she was Mexican.

"Yeah, my father was from Cuba."

"Was?"

"Yeah. He's dead now."

"And your mother?"

"Irish. But dead, too."

Sven shifted his unpatched green eye onto her. It arrested her with its clarity. There was zero hint that it was failing him except for the way that it lingered on her, longer than normal.

"Come closer," he commanded.

She didn't want to obey him, but the authoritative magnetism in his voice edged her forward. The seam of his suit coat grazed against the curve of her breasts. He was even more attractive than she thought. *Absurdly attractive*. Strong jawline, Alpine nose, chiseled cheeks and dimpled chin. And that European accent—with a lilt of aristocracy beneath his smooth pronunciation—charmed her into submission.

His fingers tilted her chin, coaxing her to straighten her posture while he gauged her true height. He was tall, so much taller than she had expected. The oversized mahogany desk had made him seem average in size, but now, his domineering build overpowered her. His unpatched eye traced an invisible line across her neckline down to her waist. She tried hard not to indulge in the scent of his cologne, but it was one of her favorite blends—musk with a hint of cedar.

"Five foot, five inches tall. Size eight."

"Six," she whispered, flustered by the tender pressure of his fingertips on her chin and his ability to tame her.

"Eight," he reiterated.

Damn, he was good.

His lingering green gaze shifted onto her mouth. Inez suddenly remembered her lipstick shade—"Roxanne Red." For a moment, she feared, then anticipated the sensation of his lips against her own.

"Average," he finally said, dropping his hand from her chin and moving back around his desk.

The weight of a frown sagged the corners of her mouth. Then, a flare of aggressive anger inside her chest replaced the ridiculous way he suddenly made her feel inadequate. *Twenty thousand dollars...twenty thousand dollars...asshole.*

"Gather up your things," he snapped at her. "We'll need to get you properly dressed.

Chapter Two

INEZ STOOD ON THE PEDESTAL and gazed at herself in the three-way, full-length mirror. The seamstress tugged down her measuring tape from around her neck and curled it around Inez's bustline, hips, and backside. As she worked, Inez noted the seamstress' black backless top, revealing the massive dragon tattoo snaking down her neck and across her shoulder blades.

"I expect that you'll be able to do something with her, Ebony," Sven said to the seamstress. "She's smaller than I would have liked."

Inez glared at Billions in the mirror. With his legs crossed at the knee, he leisurely reclined on the black leather reception sofa positioned along the windows of the clothing boutique. He occasionally tapped his silver-tipped cane against the white tiled floors. Tick, tick, tick…like the impatient click of a pendulum clock.

"Just pretend I'm one of your other dolls that you keep stashed away in your secret fetish cupboard, and I'm sure you'll be just fine," Inez said.

The seamstress snorted past her nose ring.

"Small," Sven insisted again. "But her attitude clearly makes up for it."

"I'm in the room, you know," Inez shot back at him.

Ebony smirked and slipped the measuring tape around the girth of Inez's cleavage again, checking her measurements. "Hips—36 inches. Waist—30 inches. Bust—43 inches which translates into about a 38DD. Hardly small, Sven. Much more like the perfect figure to me." She winked at Inez in her defense. "Besides, you're almost completely blind. I doubt you're the best judge of these things, anyway."

Surprised, Inez shifted her attention to the seamstress. "So you know, too?"

But Sven answered for her. "Ebony and I have known each other a long time. She's my own personal tailor and the only other person who knows I cannt see as well as I should. I trust her implicitly."

"Why don't you make her your girlfriend then?" Inez challenged him in the mirror.

Ebony snorted again and measured the vertical lines of the back of Inez's thighs. "Because I already have one."

Flashing her a smile, he waved his foot like an anxious dog. Ebony's cheeks flushed pink, a sign that she wasn't as tough and edgy as her dragon tattoo suggested. "Trust me though," she mumbled under her breath. "He's tried plenty of times. Sven always tries."

"Most men will," Sven asserted, reminding both women that his hearing was impeccable.

Ebony flipped her long braided ponytail over her lithe shoulder and exhaled a *boys-will-be-boys* sigh. Amused, Sven lifted his sharp chin, as if he was still calculating how to get his lesbian seamstress into his bed—someday.

Inez rolled her eyes. How the hell did she get herself into these messes?

"She will need a full wardrobe as soon as possible," Sven directed Ebony. "Spend at least a hundred thousand, but if you need more, we can discuss it. And make sure you include Parisian fashions as well. She needs to be...presentable if anyone is going to believe we've been dating more than twenty-four hours."

Inez felt like she *should* have been insulted, except she was too busy trying to keep her mouth from dropping open. *A hundred thousand dollars? On clothes?* She barely could bring herself to spend forty dollars on new underwear at Target.

Absorbing the challenge, Ebony crossed her arms and pressed the point of her black high-heeled boot on the edge of the podium. "And what about for tonight?"

"An evening dress," Sven confirmed. "We have a cocktail engagement tonight."

"Tonight?" Inez repeated, as if she was a child being ignored by her parents.

"Yes, you're coming out of my cupboard," he mused, twirling his cane. "You sound worried." He said it to taunt her. She could hear the tease in the softened lilt of his accent.

Inez scowled at the triple reflections of him in the mirror. Did she really agree to pretend to be the girlfriend of some arrogant bastard wearing a designer suit and a black pirate patch? *Actually, yes...yes, she did.*

"Well, let's see...what could I find for you to wear by tonight?" Ebony's thoughts trailed off as she assessed Inez's face and figure. "You know, I think we should try to do something to match your eyes," she finally proposed, gazing at Inez with keen interest, as if she was an art student admiring a statue in a museum. "They've got this fiery red highlight in them, hard and glossy like cherrywood."

"Sven said I was average," Inez replied.

Ebony sighed. "Sven doesn't always appreciate unconventional beauty."

"It's true." He nodded, adjusting his cufflinks. "My style is more classic."

"Which generally means blonde and boring," Ebony tossed back.

He smirked and wagged his foot again. He definitely enjoyed the negative attention.

"Don't let him fool you," Ebony whispered to Inez. "His last girlfriend wasn't blonde, and she certainly was far from boring. And I'm fairly certain she broke his heart."

Sven's expression hardened with severity. He stopped twirling his cane and slowly rose from the sofa.

"Let's focus more on her wardrobe, please," Sven warned her. It was obvious she had struck a nerve and he wanted her to know not to repeat the offense.

Inez watched him through the mirror. It was hard to imagine Billions with a shred of a sentimental heart, much less imagine the woman capable of breaking it.

Ebony fell silent, but a glint of rebellion remained in her dark eyes. She gazed at Inez and hid her smile. "Very well, Sven...here's my opinion about tonight's wardrobe. You don't normally let me dress your dates in striking color, but with Inez's coloring—her hair, skin and those eyes—it would be a sin to make her wear black."

"Let's not go overboard" Sven cautioned her.

"Would you like to make a statement or not?" she pushed back.

"Of course. Always."

"Then, I'm thinking...scarlet."

"You mean, red," he corrected her.

"No, I mean scarlet," she asserted. "Dark red with a hint of magenta. C'mon, Sven. You're an architect. Close your eyes and imagine scarlet."

"I design buildings, Ebony. Not pick out the curtains."

"*Tsk*," Ebony clucked, ensuring that he would hear her displeasure even if he couldn't see her expression of annoyance.

"Bee," he said her nickname sternly. "I want to make a statement, but I do not need people thinking that I picked her up in the red light district."

"Well, you *are* Dutch," Inez interjected.

Ebony released a laugh. Sven cocked his jaw and pushed towards them with a *tap, tap, tap* of his cane until the tip struck the base of the pedestal with a firm whack. He edged himself into Inez's personal space. His tall form and freshly-shaved face met her eye-to-eye and she noted the trace of a menacing scar, peeking out beneath the rigid eyepatch.

"No," he said, lowering his voice, controlled and steady. "You are not my whore. I can find plenty of whores. I expect you to present yourself as nothing less than my loyal and attentive girlfriend. Are we in agreement?"

Holy hell. Giving him a blow job would be easier than this...

"Whatever you say," she replied. "Pookey."

"Don't worry, Sven," Ebony said, coming to the rescue. "She's going to look stunning. I promise." She guided Inez off the pedestal and away from Sven, breaking the tension between them.

"Thanks," Inez mouthed to her.

"You're welcome," Ebony mouthed back before turning her attention to Sven. "Now stop being such an intimidating bulldog and get up here. It's your turn to be put on display like a little doll."

Sven resisted. "I already have more suits than I care to wear."

Ushering him upon the pedestal, she said, "Trust me. You don't have a suit that can compete with a chic scarlet cocktail dress."

Escaping with relief, Inez flopped down onto the leather sofa. It was her first moment of relaxation since arriving for the interview two hours ago. The future of her life had just been changed for the next four days and she barely had been granted a chance to even process it.

She watched Ebony take Sven's hand into her own as if she was preparing to remove a splinter from the paw of a roaring lion. It was hard not to admire how Ebony handled Billions with confidence and grace. She removed his suit jacket and carefully hung it on a nickel-plated wall hook. He adjusted his diamond cufflinks while she rolled a lint brush along the seams of his tan pants. His broad shoulders accentuated his athletic build and tapered waist beneath his pin-striped white business shirt, tucked neatly into his slacks. With his rigid demeanor and threatening eyepatch, he had attempted to intimidate her like a ruthless bulldog. But now, his European mannerisms and Dutch facial features softened his appearance like a runaway model.

"I think we will need to do something more contemporary," Ebony offered.

He eyed her with skepticism. "*That* sounds intimidating."

She smiled and measured his neckline. "I have something special in mind in the back. Imported today from Luxembourg. It's going to make you feel like the admiral of a war ship."

"Luxembourg is a land-locked country. They have no business designing naval-inspired fashion."

"Which is why you're the perfect man to pull it off, Sven. Trust me."

He fell silent, as if he was absorbing the sensuality of her husky voice and the scent of incense on the surface of her mocha skin. "Implicitly," he whispered.

Inez was certain he would be more than willing to kiss Ebony if she would let him. "*Ack, hmmm*," she cleared her throat, intentionally obnoxious. "So I need to get home—at least for a half an hour to pick up some of my personal things."

Sven barely acknowledged her presence. He didn't appreciate the interruption.

"Ebony will arrange for all of your clothes tonight, including your undergarments."

"My undergarments?" Inez mocked him, openly. She couldn't help it.

"Bra and panties," Ebony clarified. "You'll need the perfect match for the cocktail dress."

"She will need heels as well," Sven cut in.

"No heels," Inez shot back. "And really, I need to go home to pick up a few... you know, personal items."

Sven finally shifted his full attention to her. "There's no reason for you to leave. Our agreement was for you to start immediately, and so you're committed to me until midnight. In the meantime, I will pay for any of your expenses today if you need to purchase something specific."

"No, really," Inez insisted. "I need to go home for just a brief—"

But Sven would not relent. "Ebony will send your entire wardrobe to my penthouse this afternoon and you will dress there."

Inez held her ground. "Tampons, Sven. And yes, a shower...but in my own home."

It was juvenile charade and a total lie. But it was also none-of-his-freaking business why she needed to go home, and she wasn't prepared to be his submissive prison bitch—yet.

Sven fixed his gaze on her, as if he heard the tremor in her breath, but chose not to challenge it. "Then my driver will take you home. That will be the fastest way. I expect you back at my penthouse within the hour."

He pulled out his phone from his pocket and called in the request to his driver.

"Don't worry. I'll be there—ready to wear all the necessary undergarments."

She let the sarcasm seep out of her voice. Sure, it would have been a lot easier to follow Ebony's lead and pretend to be a deferential employee. But being a sly, cocky, confrontational smartass was *way* more her skill set.

"Good," he confirmed. "Because plain little dolls usually need flashy accessories to make them look more impressive than they actually are. Heels, especially." He said it with a click of his back teeth, reminding her who ultimately had the upper hand.

But Inez didn't need the reminder. She needed money—a lot of it—and he was the only prospect she had for getting it. She stared at him, mulling over the disparity between his smooth complexion and his intimidating black eyepatch, and bit her tongue with subservient silence. *Jackass.*

Chapter Three

SHE CHANTED AS SHE JOGGED up the dingy stairwell within the apartment building. *An hour, an hour, an hour*...she felt like a fugitive escaping from her captor, except with a twist—he had placed a ticking time bomb on her life and threatened to detonate it unless she returned to him within an hour. Hyperventilating, she stopped on the top landing in front of the door and leaned against the wall to catch her breath. *God, just blow her up now.*

She clicked open the locked door and pushed into the one-bedroom apartment of her best friend.

"Sarah?" She barely called out, in case she was napping. Inez surveyed the messy heap of dank clothes dangling across the blinds and strewn across the couch. Clearly, the basement dryer was broken again.

She stepped over two crushed cans and an empty pizza box, still on the floor in the exact same place as when Inez had been there earlier that morning. *Bar boys*, Inez thought, knowing Sarah's weakness for picking up stray men during her night shift as a bartender and bringing them back to feed and pet them like alley cats. She tried not to judge. At least one of them was getting some.

Inez crept down the corridor and into the bathroom where she had left her personal belongings—*hairbrush, toothbrush, perfume, make-up bag.* She glanced around the bathroom. What the hell else did she need to get her through an uptight fancy schmancy dinner with a bunch of rich arrogant snobs? *Hello Kitty Pez Dispenser*? Check.

She looked at herself in the mirror. Billions had been right. She did look like an uptight Northwestern graduate. She quickly stripped off her interview clothes and slipped into her favorite jeans and off-the-shoulder T-shirt before stuffing everything she owned into her oversized crochet purse.

"You're back already? That can only mean failure."

Inez turned towards the whimper in the doorway. Weary and exhausted, Sarah rubbed her eyes while cradling a baby in her arms. She noted Inez's purse stuffed to the brim. "Correction—you look like you're leaving and never coming back?"

"Actually, I got the job," Inez confirmed.

"Really?" Sarah yawned through her surprise. "Do they know that you got fired from your last two jobs?"

"Three. And no, I'm absolutely certain they've hired the wrong girl, but apparently I was the only one who could walk and talk at the same time. They expect me to start immediately… Hey, can you keep Luna until dinner time? Nana usually naps in the afternoon and it's getting harder and harder for her to care for Luna all day."

Sarah handed off Luna to Inez who embraced her daughter like she hadn't seen her for weeks.

"Of course…I don't go to work until nine. What else am I going to do here during the day besides cat nap and experiment with non-dairy kale smoothie recipes?"

Inez kissed her daughter's soft black hair and savored her baby scent—fresh diapers and shampoo. Her fuzzy flannel onesie made her whole body soft to cuddle. Her black jelly eyes fixed on Inez, as if she recognized her mother's voice. It had been only three months since Luna's birth, but already Inez couldn't imagine her life without her. Luna had become her guiding light. No matter how angry she was at the world for all the injustices in her life—the unexpected death of her parents, her embittered years in foster care, her grandmother's debilitating illness—she could simply cradle Luna and remember that nothing else mattered except for the well-being of her daughter.

"Is she hungry?" Inez lowered herself to the covered toilet seat, testing whether Luna wanted to nurse.

"Maybe." Sarah nodded, yawning again. "I gave her a bottle right after you left, and then we hung out and listened to Broadway show tunes while I painted my fingernails." Sarah held up her hands, proudly displaying the vibrant neon blue nail polish.

"Bitchlicious," Inez agreed. "Oh, and one more thing. Can you please tell my grandmother not to wait up for me because I'm not going to be home until midnight?"

Sarah arched her brow. "Please tell me you didn't take a job as a lap dancer."

"Yeah, definitely…because you know how much experience I have looking sexy while dangling from a pole."

Sarah eyed Luna sucking from Inez's breast. "Well, you are a triple D these days. And pretty shameless about it."

"Ugh, that reminds me. My pump."

"It's here," Sarah said, disappearing and reappearing with the heavy black bag slung over her shoulder. "You left it on the kitchen counter next to the half-eaten carton of Oreos."

"Naturally."

"Naturally. So c'mon on. What is it?" Sarah pressed her to dish. "More practicing English over dinner with wealthy Japanese businessmen?"

"No." Inez shivered. "And I'll never look at butter the same way again."

"One pat or two," Sarah joked, repeating the phrase Inez was forced to pronounce over and over.

They both laughed. It had been one of the many horrible jobs that Inez had endured and it seemed like there was no end in sight. "No butter etiquette, but it does involve spending the next four nights with an extremely rigid businessman."

Inez paused, suddenly remembering her agreement with Sven was supposed to be kept confidential. Sarah spotted her hesitation.

"Hmm..." she pondered, admiring her neon blue fingernails. "That sounds almost...indecent."

"It does require me to wear heels."

"Well, whatever it is, make sure you keep your legs crossed at your knees and smile with your eyes, not with your lips. Otherwise, men think we're easy, and just because we are, doesn't mean they shouldn't have to work for it."

Inez gazed at Sarah. Her long auburn hair always looked amazing, even thrown up into a tousled ponytail, and her waif figure and unblemished porcelain skin made her look like one of those Swedish magazine models. *She* was the perfect person to play Sven's girlfriend, not Inez who suddenly felt nauseous with doubt and uncertainty.

Twenty thousand dollars. It was the only thing motivating her to leave her daughter again. Inez wanted to confess to Sarah that she was going to make more money in a week than she had made in an entire year, but she also knew Sarah would assume the worst.

"Let's just say that I'll be able to pay you double what I'm paying you now every time I need you to watch Luna."

"Pay me whatever you want. Luna is the only person I know who doesn't mind me belting out the high notes of *Memory* like the faux soprano that I am."

"Thanks, Sarah. I don't know what I'd do without you," Inez said, feeling Luna release her latch and nestle snugly into her arms.

"You'd probably go onto welfare and be better off."

"Clearly, they taught me nothing at Northwestern."

"Community college was way more fun. I guarantee you."

They both fell silent. It was the moment that Inez dreaded—the hand-off. Reluctantly, she stood up from the toilet seat and passed Luna over to Sarah who accepted her with a soothing bounce.

"You know, things might be easier if you let 'you-know-who' back into your life."

Inez looked away. "I'd rather just struggle." She gathered up her purse and breast pump bag and headed for the front door.

"He came here looking for you today."

Inez stopped cold in the doorway. "Did you tell him to go flush his head in the toilet?"

"Noooooo, I'll leave that precious honor to you. Instead, I told him you'd be back soon, but that was before I knew you were officially employed as a woman of the night."

"What did he want?"

Sarah smiled slyly. "What does he always want from you?"

"Money."

"No, the other thing."

"Cigarettes?"

Sarah flopped onto the couch and held up Luna like a trophy. "I think he genuinely misses you. And I think he wanted to see Luna."

"Too bad. He should have thought about that before he slept with all his tango partners in Argentina."

"Well, in his defense, you didn't exactly tell him you were 'el preggo' before he left."

"In my defense, I didn't exactly realize it until a month after he was gone. And he didn't exactly tell me he had every intention of sleeping around while he was away."

Sarah shrugged like it was no big deal. She treated the ideal of monogamy like an expensive car or a fancy house—something completely unobtainable in her own life. "Well, he's back now and he wants to see you. Maybe you should give him a chance to try? He is your baby daddy."

"Sperm donor," Inez corrected her. "And the perfect example of a man who got me too easy. I'll never make that mistake again."

Inez failed to suppress the resentment in her voice. It was hard to acknowledge that her heart had been broken; it was a lot easier to pretend that she had always been tough and bitter—even from birth.

"Okay, well...don't shoot the babysitter. Just pointing out the fact that we're both examples of girls who grew up without fathers, so...there's still plenty of time to not screw up Luna's life."

"I'd rather just stay on the pill forever and not get knocked up again."

Sarah shrugged again, like there was no winning the conversation. "Say goodbye to Ma-Ma," she said, waving Luna's chubby little hand. "And don't worry. We'll only binge on organic ice cream and public television."

"I'm jealous." Inez stared at Luna in Sarah's arms, yearning more than anything to trade places with Sarah rather than leaving Luna in the care of a babysitter—again.

Without saying goodbye, Inez forced herself out the door and down the stairwell. When she exited into the courtyard, she spotted the silver Rolls Royce, idling along the curb and strode towards it.

"Do not run away before you give me the chance to say, hello."

His powerful voice surprised her. *Enzo*. She glanced at his backlit body, bathed in the mid-afternoon sun.

"I'd much rather say goodbye," she asserted, turning towards the Rolls Royce. Without warning, his strong hand encircled her wrist before she had a chance to look up into his playboy face and dark, devilish eyes.

"It has been over a month since I've been back. You should forgive me by now." He lowered his voice, deepening his strong Latin accent. She struggled against his unforgiving grasp and the familiar way he pivoted his pelvis against her own, attempting to greet her with a kiss.

"You went back to Argentina for six months to screw other women. Maybe it's just a cultural thing—but here in America, that's pretty hard to forgive and forget."

"It was not my choice to leave and you know it. They forced me to return because of my VISA."

"But it was your choice to invite every tango partner of yours into your bed."

He spread his hands open like he had nothing to hide. "It was a year, Inez. You cannot expect me to be a monk."

She crossed her arms and glared at him. "You could have tried."

"Impossible," he said earnestly. "And I did not lie to you about it, not the way you lied to me about our daughter."

"I never lied. I just didn't bother to inform you that I was pregnant. And just because you *told* me you were sleeping with other women doesn't make it honorable. Unless you expect a medal for not infecting me with the clap."

Uncertain, Enzo gazed at her. "I do not think I understand your meaning?"

Inez sighed with disgust, just to ensure he would understand her meaning. "We were together a year, Enzo. A year. And you act like that meant nothing to you."

"I thought about you every minute that I was gone."

"Oh really? While you were fucking them?"

"After," he admitted, like it was a confession. "Because none of them satisfied me the way your cruel words and passionate heart satisfy me."

Inez rolled her eyes. "Oh, geez…well, just wait. Because my cruel words haven't even had a chance to flame out of my mouth yet."

As if he was enchanted by her hatred, he grabbed her and pulled her firmly against his chest.

"I remember the feeling of that fire in your mouth. *Te echo de menos*, Inez."

Did he really miss her? Inez stared into his fierce black eyes, softened by his long eyelashes. His scent relaxed her like a favorite memory. He smelled exactly like he always smelled—like an artist. Clove cigarettes scented his black ponytail and olive skin, and the unmistakable aroma of oil paint varnish wafted from colorful smudges on his forearms and baggy white painter's pants.

"I will not let you go. You're stubborn and proud and vengeful, exactly like me. You are determined to punish me and I know that. I accept it. But I also know that you miss me. Miss us. Because I can hear it in your voice—and in your pain."

"That's called sarcasm, Enzo."

He edged his lips closer to her ear. "No. That is your armor. Your protection. And I am the only one who has found a way to remove it." He drew his fingertip down the hollow of her throat, stopping it just above the crease of her cleavage, as though he expected her to dismiss everything except the sexual tension between them.

"Miss Sanchez?"

Inez turned towards the voice. James, Sven's driver, had exited the Rolls Royce and opened the passenger door. Now, he beckoned her towards him.

Enzo scanned the Rolls Royce. "This is a very expensive car."

"My new boyfriend owns it," she informed him, savoring how his smug confidence withered away into confusion. She strode towards James who assisted her into the car before closing the door and sealing her inside like a priceless possession. Buzzing down the tinted window, she gazed out at Enzo.

"You are seeing someone else?" Enzo insisted.

"Six months is a long time to wait, Enzo. A girl's got needs. I'm sure you understand."

He did understand, but his macho pride wasn't happy about it. Abruptly, he yanked open the door and pushed himself inside the car. She slid across the leather seats, away from him, but he snagged her by the hand and squeezed it until she betrayed pain.

"You are making a mistake. We have a child together."

"Yeah, and it would have been such a precious fairy tale if you had gone away and come back, still in love with me and our daughter," she asserted sarcastically, flinching only for a moment before twisting out of his clasp. "But since I don't believe in fairy tales, try not to miss me too much. Unlike you, I won't be thinking about anyone else while I'm in bed with him."

Their eyes locked. This time, her meaning was clear to him. Reluctantly, he backed out of the car and slammed the door with fury.

Inez rubbed the burn on her wrist and hugged her purse like it was Luna. She suppressed her urge to cry; she had already shed all her tears months ago, and now, there was nothing left except bitterness and exhaustion. Yes, they had a child together, but she didn't need a reminder because it was the first thing she thought about when she woke up every morning and the last thing she agonized about when she went to sleep—how on earth was she going to raise Luna by herself? The only thing she thought about more was the fact she had been so dumb, so foolish, so ridiculously naïve to have fallen in love with a man who had conned her into believing that true love existed in the first place.

As they sped away, the driver's eyes watched Enzo in his rearview mirror before buzzing up the interior tinted window between them. With the rare moment of solitude, Inez sighed with relief and nestled herself comfortably into the luxurious leather seats, smooth and creamy like vanilla bean ice cream.

Yes, it was true. Well, sort of. She did have a new billionaire boyfriend. Too bad for her, he was just a fake one and an even bigger asshole than Enzo.

Chapter Four

SVEN SETTLED HIS UNPATCHED eye on his favorite painting in the penthouse—*Water Lilies* by the nineteenth century impressionist painter, Claude Monet. It was a priceless painting, smuggled out of his grandmother's estate in Amsterdam when she fled the country during the Nazi invasion and occupation.

He sank lower in his black Bugatti sofa and counted. *Eleven, twelve, thirteen…* He strained his eyesight onto the canvas. *Where was fourteen? There, yes, there…and fifteen?* He squinted again to make out the individual water lilies within the cluster of soft green, white, turquoise, and pink feathered strokes. *Such cruel irony*, he thought, giving up for a moment and dropping his head back against the sofa's sleek leather. Monet had painted his *Water Lilies* series at the end of his life while almost completely blind. It was a fleeting attempt to console himself and press on. *Sixteen, seventeen, eighteen...* Yesterday, there had been at least twenty. He had to find at least twenty.

He scanned the lily pad cluster again before succumbing to the demoralizing sensation of defeat. Just last week, he had easily found thirty—thirty distinct water lilies. Now, dread overwhelmed the inner core of his being. Someday soon—sooner than he was prepared to accept—he would attempt to count the water lilies and fail to find even one.

How would he continue to design buildings without his vision? The question terrified him, then filled him with bitter injustice. He was man of only thirty-eight who had made his first billion by the time he was thirty, and yet nothing could restore the one thing he desired most—his ability to perfectly see the world. Yes, he was a designer and an architect and a businessman. But at the core of his soul, he was an artist who loved *seeing* the world—all its beauty and all its imperfections. He loved noticing every detail of every event that passed by him, and he loved absorbing all the nuances of life through his own keen observations of them.

Not long ago he had been a man determined to leave his mark on the world through the designs of his buildings—buildings that almost defied the laws of gravity and challenged the social standards of decency. But now, as he sloshed his Holland gin around in his tumbler, he felt nothing except the oppressive shadow of despair darkening his soul. He had become a man trapped in a tunnel, reaching out for the flickering light at its end, knowing that if he did not escape, he would be rendered useless and irrelevant to the world once everything fell completely black.

His phone rang. Slightly drunk and despondent, he sat up straighter, glancing around as if he had forgotten where he was. He fumbled to remove his phone from his pocket.

"Yes?" he answered.

"Miss Sanchez to see you, sir?"

"Yes," he confirmed to the doorman. "From this point forward, always send her up."

Sven rose from the sofa and called into his phone. "Time?"

The robotic voice answered back. "Five fifteen. P. M."

Five fifteen, he considered with a frown. *She was late.* Sven paced unevenly around the spacious living room. Tonight's dinner commenced at eight, and Ebony hadn't yet sent over their wardrobe. There would barely be enough time for them to dress—much less familiarize themselves more with each other—before he thrust her in front of the most important people in his life.

It all suddenly felt like a grave mistake, a gross miscalculation of judgment by a man who was accustomed to the flawlessness of his own strategic decisions influencing the successful achievements within his life. Despite his attempts to appear otherwise, he was no longer the same Sven van der Meer he had been—ruthless, fearless, uncompromising. Instead, he felt like a thin shadow who was desperate to keep up the facade of being the indomitable version of him.

The front door buzzed.

"Door—open," he said aloud, his stern voice booming off the sleek marble floor. The front door vibrated ajar and Inez's blurry figure strode through it.

"You're late," he stated, as if it was a fact rather than an accusation.

"It's not my fault that your driver navigates the slow lane like a cadaver."

Sven muted his smile as she approached him. *It was true.* James did often drive in the slow lane like a cadaver.

"It's a new Rolls. I'm sure he was just being extra careful."

"Well, next time, let me drive that thing myself and I'll get back here when you want me back."

"Hopefully, with the car in one piece."

"Optional." She shrugged and brushed past him towards the panoramic windows. "Wowzas…that's some view." Pressing her nose and forehead against the glass, she peered out across Lake Michigan, tinged pink and orange by the withering rays of twilight.

"It's a bit of a commute," he said, yielding to the strange desire to make his lifestyle seem more modest and accessible to her.

"Why? Because your office is downtown?"

"No. Up and down the elevator."

He heard her snort, amused by him. *It was a start.*

His gaze lingered on her clothes. Jeans and a wide neck T-shirt, slung to one side. He strained his vision to make out the curve of her exposed bra strap. *Orange.* Then, he looked down at her feet—sneakers.

She gazed down at the tiny dots along the bike path. "It must be nice to be constantly reminded that we're all just tiny ants in this cruel, cruel world."

Normally, he would seize upon a remark like that and belittle it. But there was an edge of sincerity in her voice that made him refrain from provoking her.

"And there it is...The Spire," she proclaimed, her voice trailing off as she cast her eyes onto the twisting silver spindle of reflective glass and steel, cutting like a spear through the cityscape. "I suppose it says something about you that you can see it directly from your penthouse."

"Only that it's the most important building in my career," he asserted. "I designed it, built it, and financed it from ground zero. Every part of it represents me. It is my most accomplished achievement—as an artist and as a man."

"Too bad it's the most hated building in the city."

He paused, uncertain whether to be annoyed or charmed. *She had that effect on him.* It was hard to take himself so seriously when she refused to.

"Shall I make you a drink?" he asked, like a peace offering.

"I'm not certain I should be drinking on the job."

"For both our sakes, I'm fairly certain you will need to. Wine?"

She shook her head. "French Martini. Vodka, pineapple juice, Chambord. Shaken not stirred."

He flinched, absorbing the complexity of her order. *She was challenging him, obviously.* And he would be lying to himself if he didn't admit that he enjoyed it.

He turned towards the kitchen, silently counting his steps. Three months ago, when his vision had started to degenerate, he completely re-designed his penthouse to help him navigate with ease. Six steps to the contemporary handwoven floor rug. Six steps across it. One step to the base of the half flight of stairs up to the entertainment bar. Four steps up to its landing.

"So...how much help do you need these days?" she asked.

Perhaps he had counted too loudly, or perhaps he was moving too slowly. *Like poor James, the cadaver.*

"Do you see that painting with the water lilies?" He pointed across the living room, seeking to divert her attention away from him. "Today, I can only see twenty of the lilies."

"Um…you mean the Monet painting on the wall?"

"Yes." He fumbled around the liquor cabinet, searching for his mixer and martini glasses.

"The friggin' *real* Monet painting on your wall?"

He stopped to consider her slang. "You mean as opposed to a cheap print from art.com or something?"

"Don't be a jackass. I'm serious."

Confused, he fell silent. That time, he hadn't actually intended to be an ass. *Art history major*, he thought, feeling through the cabinets for the vodka and the Chambord. Then, he considered reprimanding her for disrespecting him as her boss; he couldn't allow her to do that tonight—not during dinner. But truth be known, he rather liked the way she so flippantly called him a jackass.

"It's an original, I assure you," he confirmed and let the rest slide.

She crossed her arms and challenged him. "Sotheby's just auctioned off one of those paintings from his *Water Lilies* series for forty million dollars."

Sven grimaced. He couldn't help it. Forty million dollars was an insultingly low sum for a Monet original, especially one of his later works. "Well, then…I guess it's a good thing I didn't get rid of it at my garage sale last week."

"With all your billionaire friends?" she sniped before releasing an unguarded laugh. *Like a mischievous child*, he thought, as if the idea of a garage sale put on by a bunch of billionaires was the funniest thing in the world.

"Attempting to get rid of all our unwanted Degas ballerinas," he said, playing along.

"And girlie pastel Renoirs."

"And boring Pissarro landscapes."

"And erratic van Gogh self-portraits, especially those imbalanced ones with only one ear."

Sven eyed her. Most Americans mispronounced it as "van Go." But she said it exactly as it was meant to be pronounced—"van Goth." It was a Dutch name, after all.

"Have you been there?" She nodded to the painting.

"Where?" He questioned her, shaking up her martini.

"Giverny."

Sven smirked. Although he knew exactly what she meant, it still surprised him. He wasn't used to conversing with women who knew about Monet's studio sanctuary just outside of Paris. *A Northwestern girl who could have gone to Harvard or Yale*, he remembered.

"Of course. Have you?"

“God no, but I’d love to…” her voice trailed off as she pushed closer towards the painting, replacing her scorn for a private moment of indulgence. “So…you can only see twenty water lilies?” she finally asked before attempting to count them herself.

He waited for her to realize that there were far more water lilies than twenty.

“There’s at least twenty little ones in the dappling beneath the bridge’s shadow,” she confirmed. “You can’t see them from there?”

Sven didn’t glance up. He didn’t need to. “No…not anymore.”

“Hm.” She surveyed him like she was assessing how that directly affected her—and their arrangement.

He topped of her drink. “Vodka, Chambord, and fresh lemon juice, which will have to substitute for pineapple juice.” He started down the half-flight of stairs, but forgot to count the steps. Stumbling on the final one, he lost his balance and a bit of his dignity.

“Damn it,” he cursed at himself. The drink splashed across his hand and seeped into the cuff of his sleeve, the raspberry Chambord immediately staining it pink.

“Here, take it off so we can run it under cold water,” she offered.

Skeptical, he peered at her.

“The quicker the better,” she insisted, taking the martini glass from his hands and setting it down on the end table. She reached out for his wrist and started to unfasten his cufflink.

“I have a hundred shirts like this one. Let’s not make a production of it.”

She firmly placed the diamond cuff link into the palm of his hand. He winced as she dug it into his flesh. “Please don’t tell me you’re one of these billionaires who just throws dirty shirts and towels and sheets away instead of laundering them. Please tell me that’s something they make up in celebrity magazines for us plebeians to snicker at because it makes us feel better, not because it can possibly be true.”

He didn’t respond. There *was* truth in it, but he didn’t have the energy to deny it. He hated stained clothes, towels, and sheets.

“Busted,” she sassed and deposited the second cufflink into his palm. Without permission, she tugged his hands out of his sleeves before drawing off his shirt completely.

The cold air pricked his skin and his muscles flinched under her gaze. He heard the hesitation in her breath, as if she had just realized what she had done—she had just undressed him and they both knew it.

She was close enough now that he caught the scent of her detergent, or shampoo, or deodorant—something scented like lilacs and mint.

“Alright, let’s see some of this plebeian magic,” he quipped.

She dropped her gaze and turned away. “Bloody noses,” she said, traveling into the kitchen and guiding the conversation away from the fact that he was half-naked and rather enjoying it. “I used to get bloody noses all the time, and my grandmother used to soak my clothes in cold water. 'Straight away,' she'd always say. 'No time to waste if you'd expect to wear it again.'" Her voice faded behind the rushing spray of the faucet.

"She sounds like a sensible woman, your grandmother."

"Tough as nails, too."

"Like her granddaughter," Sven confirmed.

Inez didn't respond. She either didn't hear him or chose to ignore him. It was a test, but she avoided it. She was always sidestepping him, and he liked the challenge.

She shut off the faucet and held up the wet silk, inspecting it in the clarity of the overhead lights.

"I think we can salvage it. But just in case, I'll let it soak for a bit." She plugged the stainless steel sink and filled it with water before drowning the shirt beneath it.

"Your drink," he lamented, nodding to the half-empty martini glass. "I apologize for ruining it."

"You substituted pineapple juice for lemon juice, Sven. It was already ruined."

"Touché." He sunk into the sofa and fell quiet.

She followed his lead and didn't force him to talk. Thank God she wasn't like most American girls who needed to keep the silence filled with aimless babbling. He liked that about her.

After another minute of reflection, he finally spoke. "It's starting already. I thought I had at least another week. Certainly a few more days."

"What?" she asked, slipping onto the bar stool.

"My dependency on you."

She shrugged. "You're paying me five Gs to be here. You might as well use me."

She stood up and approached him. "Where are your clothes? Why don't I go and get you another shirt—"

"Let's not treat me like an invalid in my own home. I'm paying you to pretend to be my girlfriend, not my bed nurse."

The moment he said it, he regretted it. He bowed his head and cursed under his breath, waiting for her to retaliate. Instead, she simply scooped up the martini glass and dumped it into the miniature sink beneath the bar cabinets. He swallowed hard, listening to the lonely silence between them. *Such a pity*, he thought, scolding himself. They had connected so briefly only to be torn apart again by his own elitist pride.

Then, his phone rang. "Yes?" he answered, firmly.

"A delivery from Miss Ebony Walsh, sir," the doorman said.

"Send it up." Sven glanced sidelong into the bar. "Your dress is here."

"Thrilling," she replied. He saw the daggers flinging out of her glare, attempting to sear a hole into his bare chest. He understood. He deserved it.

The door buzzer rang. Rising from the sofa, he exhaled and crossed the living room, striding down the corridor towards the front entrance.

"Door—open," he called out into the air. The door clicked ajar and swung open, allowing the delivery man to roll the clothing rack across the gleaming black floors.

"Thank you, leave it there." Sven nodded, pulling out a handkerchief from his pocket and offering him the one hundred dollar bill. American dollar bills were the cruelest game on his senses. It was impossible to see or feel the distinction between a one dollar bill and a twenty dollar bill, or a one hundred dollar bill without holding it directly in front of his unpatched eye. And so, Sven had decided long ago not to bother with discerning the difference.

"Sir?" The delivery man gazed down at the tip in disbelief.

Sven shook the hundred dollar bill, encouraging him to take it.

"Th-a-n-k you, sir." The delivery man stuttered out his appreciation before shutting the front door behind him.

Sven waited. "Aren't you going to come see what she's sent over?"

"You're the one without a shirt. I'm still wearing my clothes."

He smiled. *Fair enough.* He investigated the leather clothing bags, zipped up tightly like precious cargo. "I will need you to assist me. I'm terrible with zippers." It was enough of a command that it did the job.

She appeared behind him, surveying the deliveries. She picked out the longest clothing bag. He heard her drawing down the zipper almost all the way to the floor.

"Holy hell."

A flash of glitter and fire caught his good eye. Rhinestones and sequins trimmed the strapless notched neckline of the scarlet cocktail dress.

Peeling back the clothing bag, Inez dug through its contents and slipped out a strapless black corset and matching G-string panties.

"She must be joking?" She held up the flimsy lingerie set, dangling off the hanger, like she had caught a strange species of underwear.

"Cinderella cannot wear white cotton panties to the ball. Try it on."

"And what? Just strip down right here? In front of you?"

"Well, I'm already half-naked. I don't really see the problem."

"Wow…Ebony wasn't kidding. You don't stop trying to get laid any chance you can get, do you?"

He flashed her a cavalier smile, but only because he wasn't intentionally trying to get her naked. If he actually wanted to bed her, she'd know it. "I cannot see you clearly, so it's hardly a proposition."

"You can see blurry shapes and colors," she tossed back. "And at least twenty water lilies."

"Interesting," he said, noting the edge of discomfort in her voice. "I didn't suspect you were the shy, awkward type in the bedroom."

Without warning, a searing pain spread across his chest. She had found one of the few chest hairs along his pecs and plucked it out without mercy.

Speechless, he covered his heart with his hand. He tried, with great difficulty, to keep his composure and not to raise his voice in fury, but it climbed an octave anyway. "What the hell did you do that for?"

"You're right. You never saw that coming," Inez replied. "And just so we're clear—there's nothing shy or awkward about me."

"No, apparently not," he agreed, backing away and adjusting his eyepatch, half-expecting her to go after another chest hair, just to prove it.

"And I'm certainly not shy about taking off my clothes. I just don't make a habit of doing it in front of my new boss. Where's your bathroom?"

"I have four," he replied, edging away from her, uncertain that her retaliation wasn't complete. "But the most spacious one is upstairs next to the guest bedroom."

He pointed to the black spiral staircase ascending to the private suite. "My maids clean it every day, but it's been untouched for months. The stairs are hard for me to navigate now and I rarely have guests anymore. You'll have the whole upper level to yourself."

He didn't wait for her to respond. It was late and they were pressed for time. "I'm going to take a shower now, but I will need you soon. So please prepare yourself as quickly as possible, then come downstairs." He turned and headed for his own master bedroom.

"What do you need me for?"

It was a fair question, but he wasn't sure how to answer it. "I'll need you to assist me with my own wardrobe," he finally admitted. "New suits are difficult for me to piece together, and I suspect whatever Ebony sent over from Luxembourg is going to pose a distinct challenge. Do you understand?"

Their eyes locked. He tried to bury the sound of his own wounded pride, but failed and he was certain that she noted it. Although he had brushed off her attempts to help him with his clothes, the fact of the matter was he needed her help—whether he liked it or not.

He waited to see if she would confront him with callous sarcasm. But she fell silent and nodded. "Yes, of course."

"Good," he replied, satisfied that they had moved beyond their confrontational differences into mutual agreement. "Oh...and by the way, the slender part of the G-string goes in the back."

"I have plenty of experience wearing G-strings, thank you very much," she slung back.

He smiled before disappearing through the private corridor towards the master bedroom, content with the fact that he was certain she didn't completely despise him anymore. *It was a start.*

* * * *

Inez stood in front of the mirror inside the guest bathroom, pumping milk from her left breast while attempting to finish her eye makeup. Since having a baby and breastfeeding or pumping at least eight times a day, she had become a kickass, ambidextrous multi-tasker. She surveyed the bathroom, noting how it was almost bigger than her own bedroom in her grandmother's house. The bathtub was definitely bigger than her own twin bed, and the adjacent glass-paneled standing shower was *far* bigger than her tiny closet. But it was the mirror that was the most intimidating—a floor-to-ceiling sheet of reflective glass, spanning the full width of the entire room and stretching upwards, curling like a decorative ripple of icing before spreading itself across the ceiling in delicious frosted waves. As she pumped, topless and pantyless, she had the pleasure of critiquing her full figure and every dimpled, cellulite pocket that puckered back at her. She had wide shoulders, wider hips, and a curvy ass—and the mirror certainly didn't pretend to hide any of it.

The reflection of the black G-string on the countertop glared back at her. She had lied to Billions. She had never worn a G-string in her entire life, and the suggestion that she should strut around in one tonight—like it was the most natural thing in the world—was the most hilarious joke the universe had played on her in a long time. Maybe if she actually *had* made wearing slinky lingerie a regular habit, Enzo wouldn't have cheated on her.

She dropped her mascara wand and watched the last bit of milk drip into the plastic bottle, filling it, and thought about all the different ways she had gotten to this exact moment in her life. *Yes, clearly the universe was having the last laugh.*

"Miss Sanchez!" Sven's reprimanding voice boomed up the spiral staircase.

Ugh. Inez rushed to unharness her breast from the pump and scrambled to finish brushing on her mascara.

"Miss Sanchez!" he called out again. "It's getting late."

"I'm shaving my legs!" she yelled back through the closed door and hurried to brush through her long hair. She glared at the G-string, glaring back at her.

"Inez!" he hollered with fury.

"You don't want a date with Sasquatch, do you?" she protested.

Silence followed. That seemed to shut him up.

Shutting her eyes, she picked up the G-string and shimmied it over her thighs. She slid it in place, and surprisingly, it did make her feel like she wasn't wearing any underwear at all. She quickly moved on to the black corset. Boned along the ribs. Loop fasteners to cinch the open seam. She inspected the breast cups. *Thank God...no fake padding.* Like her bad attitude, extra cleavage was something she didn't need any help boosting.

She reapplied her lipstick and studied her reflection like she was watching a stranger. The corset cinched her waist into the perfect hourglass shape, allowing her hips to flare out like a seductive tease while the French-cut G-string sharpened her curves into naughty forbidden lines. She unzipped the garment bag, took the cocktail dress off its hanger, and squirmed into the hip-hugging skirt and strapless notched bodice, beaded with crystal rhinestones and rouge sequins. Ebony was right. The proper underwear did make all the difference. And with her "Roxanne Red" lipstick, buxom cleavage, and cinched waist, she was almost disappointed that the night held no prospects for getting laid.

Billions.

She tried to put him out of her mind. And though she hadn't intended to undress him, after it had happened, she wasn't exactly sorry about it. She was more surprised than anything else, surprised that she had actually caught herself staring at his exposed sculpted shoulders, muscular biceps, six-pack abs and tapered waist. And now, she caught herself thinking about the sensation of his bare chest against her fingertips. Firm and unyielding, like he feared nothing except being pitied by her. *He was wrong*. She hadn't pitied him. She knew he wasn't an invalid and she had no intention of treating him like one. She simply wanted to get him dressed because she feared her own attraction to him, and the last thing Inez needed was to be attracted to her new boss. As she stared at her siren lipstick and considered how her naughty new G-string made her feel, she pinched herself with a vicious twist—a warning that nothing would be gained by turning into his paid prostitute. *Definitely not tonight.*

She quickly unzipped the second garment bag, revealing a crystal sequined clutch purse and a pair of translucent Cinderella slingback high heels, tagged with a note:

I know you hate heels, but Sven's right...you can't wear a high-slit dress with Mary Jane ballet flats. I spent three-thousand dollars on these beauties. I compromised—three-inch stilettos instead of five. I promise you won't even feel them. ~Ebony

Inez sighed, unable to stomach the note or the shoes. At least Cinderella was smart enough to ditch her heels. She held the strap of the slingback heels between her teeth, dangling them like a dog while transferring her belongings from her crochet purse into her new clutch. Searching for a safe place to deposit her clothes, breast pump, and bottles, she rummaged through all the seamless compartments of the vanity, before stopping when she uncovered something unexpected in its top drawer.

There, preserved like a precious memory, was a framed photograph. But not just any photograph. A recent photograph of Sven—handsome, smiling, and relaxed—posing for the camera on the deck of a yacht with his arms affectionately embracing a young, attractive woman. *And brunette*, Inez noted. Then, she studied the photo, noticing the one thing missing from Sven's face. It wasn't the glare of derision she had come to know so well in such a short time; it was the lack of his black eyepatch and the way he stared into the camera with boyish joy.

"Inez, please..." He groaned her name like it was his final plea for mercy.

“Coming,” she replied, her voice muffled by the heels as she stuffed the photograph back into the drawer.

Barefoot and disheveled, she shuttled down the spiral staircase, expecting to see Billions, fuming and enraged, at its base. Instead, she was only greeted by eerie silence. She crossed the living room and listened to the wind whipping along the penthouse’s panoramic windows; she shivered, as if the natural draft within the open floorplan chilled her exposed shoulders and neckline. She glanced into the exercise room and Sven’s study before pushing forward down a private corridor towards the master bedroom. She shivered again; the cool marble floor pricked her bare feet. Without a proper coat or shoes to protect her against the merciless Chicago wind, she was certain she would freeze to death. Not even a fancy scarlet dress and naughty lingerie could make hypothermia look sexy.

She approached the bedroom door. “Sven?”

She slid it open without waiting for his response, her gaze immediately falling on him. Fresh from his shower, he stood naked, with only a black towel wrapped around his waist, with his hands on his hips, scrutinizing the black suit lying flat across the king-size platform bed. Steam still wafted off his sculpted shoulders while water droplets flecked his pecs and biceps. As he ran his hand through his hair, slicking it back from his high forehead, she tried to ignore the way his towel barely clung around his tapered waist.

The exercise room. Inez had just seen it. Clearly, he used it. *Every day—without fail.*

“I’m sorry to be late,” she said loudly, announcing her entrance without a formal invitation.

He turned towards her, the menace of his eyepatch stopping her in her tracks. “It doesn’t matter,” he replied sternly. “I cannot make sense of these damn Luxembourg buttons.”

She started to slip into aggression as a form of defense, but then thought better of it. The edge in his voice told her that he had already lost his patience; now, he was fighting to keep from losing his pride.

“Well, it can’t be rocket science. It’s just a suit. That’s what I’m here for.”

He cast his gaze off the suit and onto her, as if the casual toss in her voice surprised him. The piercing glint in his unpatched eye relaxed into something softer—something unguarded and informal—something more like an unexpected gaze of interest.

“Is that the infamous scarlet dress?” He nodded to her with his chin, his voice low and husky.

“Yeah, pretty infamous.” She spread her hands across the form-fitting bodice, then rotated her hips towards him, granting him a clear view of the cinched curve of her waist.

Without smiling in return, he lifted his eyes from her waist to her neckline, deliberately scanning the forbidden contours of her cleavage. Then, he pushed forward and seized her by the hand, drawing her towards his hard bare chest. His grasp tightened around her wrist, pulling her closer. Like a moment frozen in time, he studied her face, as if he was taking in the fresh hue of her red lips, just as he had done earlier that morning during their interview.

"Ebony was right," he finally whispered. "Scarlet does complement your eyes."

He slid his hand down the curve of her hip, and for a fleeting moment, she thought she felt it testing the smoothness of her leg through the thigh-high front slit of her dress. But then she realized it was only the edge of the hem, brushing against her knee.

"But you're missing an important part of the ensemble." He looked down at the pair of high heels in her hands.

Maybe it was his calm voice, or the way he stood almost naked in front of her, as if it was the most natural thing in the world, but she suddenly was inspired to confess her biggest fear. "Please tell me you're not going to put me on display in front of all your wealthy snobby friends and let them ridicule me over the rims of their champagne flutes for my inability to strut around like a model in high heels."

"If I wanted a model, I would have hired one through a casting agency."

It was true, and they both knew it. Why he ended up hiring her she still could not fathom, but here they were—together now—and they both seemed resigned to the fact that there was no going back.

He lowered himself to the floor and unexpectedly encouraged her to slip her foot into the first heel.

She acquiesced, touching his bare shoulders with her fingertips to steady her balance. "You can unbuckle a woman's slingback heels, and yet you need me to help you figure out the buttons on your new suit?"

"I've had plenty of practice removing women's high heels."

She rolled her eyes. *Of course he had.*

He nudged her into the second high heel before rising to meet her gaze. Boosted by three extra inches, she stared straight at him, her mouth almost level with his chin. *Almost his equal.*

"See...? Heels have their advantages," he quipped, taking in the proximity of her lips to his own.

"That advantage cost you three thousand dollars."

"I would have paid one hundred thousand."

She could smell the scent of his aftershave—crisp and elegant—nothing like the edgy scent of cigarettes and painter's varnish that permanently stained Enzo's skin.

"You're still missing one more thing," he teased her. He turned away and she actually heard herself sigh with disappointment.

Approaching a small, square wall safe above the nightstand, he punched in numbers on the keypad and pulled open the door. When he turned back around, something glinted in his hands like diamonds and emeralds the size of ice cubes. Dangling it from his fingers by its clasp, he displayed a sparkling necklace for her to view. *Holy hell.* Those *were* diamonds and emeralds the size of ice cubes in an intricately-designed platinum choker setting.

"Turn around."

In a daze, she obeyed and whimpered the moment the cold prick of platinum slid down her neckline. Goosebumps tingled along the nape of her neck as he swept away her long hair to allow the necklace to settle around her throat.

"It must be nice to be able to buy anything you want," she whispered, touching the necklace like it had robbed her of her voice.

"I did not buy this," he replied, coaxing her to face him. "It's a priceless family heirloom from my mother. It was part of her historical jewelry collection that her mother—my grandmother—smuggled out of Amsterdam after the Nazis invaded the city. It was a gift from Prince Alexander of the Netherlands to his nurse who cared for him after he was almost killed by a tree during a storm. The fable says that Alexander's forbidden love for her was the reason why he never married."

He stared at her face and neckline with intensity.

"That story almost makes you sound like a hopeless romantic."

He smiled, as if it was the honest truth. "My mother knows that emeralds are my favorite gemstones. She would prefer I give it to my future fiancée, but very little in life works out as one plans."

He traced the square-cut emeralds with his fingers, admiring the way they glinted against her olive skin.

"And no...I don't believe that I can buy anything. In fact, when you have enough money to buy everything, you quickly realize that the most important things cannot be bought at all."

Like beads of sweat, water droplets still dripped off his firm pecs. He gazed at her, intently, daring her to be the first one who turned away. She challenged his gaze, wondering if his stern temperament and menacing eyepatch concealed more than just physical injury.

"I think it's your turn to get dressed."

"Likely," he agreed, but did not turn away.

Finally, she caved, sensing he was more than happy to remove his towel and test whether or not she was as tough and unshakeable as she pretended to be. *Clearly, she was not.*

Evading him, she drifted to the glass door leading to an open patio, realizing she could see his ghostly reflection in the window as he slipped on his black tight-knit briefs.

"So who's going to be at this dinner anyway?" she asked, watching his blurred reflection, waiting for him to slip on his pants before she rotated back to him.

"One of my business partners who financed The Spire."

She noted how he was holding his black dress shirt, inspecting its front seam, searching for a way to unbutton it. "Sounds like a dull dinner."

"And my younger brother and his new fiancée," he abruptly added. "Who also happens to be my ex-girlfriend."

She crossed her arms and stared at him. He avoided meeting her eyes.

"So the real reason you need me tonight is not to help you see. It's to make your ex-girlfriend jealous?"

He neither confirmed nor denied it. "There's going to be more to this dinner than you realize, Inez."

She absorbed his warning, but ignored its implications with silence. Instead, she moved towards him and took the dress shirt out of his hands. "Here," she said, encouraging his cooperation. "There's only four cross-over buttons at the top and a weird, European Metrosexual Mandarin collar. So you're right. You'll never get this on without me."

He sighed and sat down on the edge of the bed.

"Arms up," she ordered him.

Guarding his eyepatch, he obeyed, allowing her to slip the shirt over his head.

"You never take that off, do you?" she asked while smoothing out the folds of the shirt across his broad shoulders and firm chest.

"No."

"Not even when you shower?"

"Never."

She knew better than to press it. He lifted his sharp chin as she fastened the four black enameled buttons along the Mandarin collar. Finally, she pulled away and tried not to notice how handsome he looked in all black. *At least his eyepatch matched the whole ensemble.*

"You know, since this dinner is going to be our first test as a couple, don't you think we should establish a few ground rules?"

"Ground rules? What kind of ground rules?"

"Like how much we can touch each other. You know, like holding hands is fine, but not if your palms are sweaty."

He snorted. "What about if your palms are sweaty?"

She ignored him. "But no hugging, fondling, or touching of my ass."

Sven arched his brow, as if he hadn't considered it—until now.

"Oh, and this is an important one," she asserted. "No calling me, 'baby.' I definitely don't wear a diaper and I definitely don't suck anything except for chocolate milkshakes."

He rose from the bed and stalked towards her. "That's quite a list, Miss Sanchez," he said, his voice menacing and rebellious. "Do you give all your boyfriends that many rules?"

"Maybe." She pushed against his forceful chest, clad in his black dress shirt, crowding into her personal space. "Or maybe just blind billionaires paying me to act like their girlfriend in front of their ex-girlfriend."

"Well…let's review my ground rules, shall we?"

He drew her closer against his body like a punishment and traced the contours of her chin with his fingertip. "Tonight is extremely important for me, so the only thing that I expect from you is for you to support me in every way." He clenched his jaw and focused on her face—her lips, her hair, her eyes. "Do you understand?"

He peered into her eyes, holding her steady. His mouth hovered over her lips, emitting a faint heat, testing her willingness to accept or defy him. She absorbed his lingering gaze and unyielding embrace, and responded with a sigh. *No kissing*, she thought. She had forgotten that in her ground rules. Clearly, he didn't care about her ground rules.

Shutting her eyes slowly, she relaxed in his arms, expecting their lips to meet. But instead, like a cruel joke, he freed her and briskly pulled away with a smirk.

She glared at him, seeking out why she felt disappointed that he had released her. "You're a real asshole, Sven," she finally replied, a hint of dejection creeping into her voice. "I hope you realize that."

He nodded and lifted his suit coat from the bed. "Now you sound more like my girlfriend."

"An asshole. Truly."

"Come now," he directed her, waving his coat like he was luring a bull to charge him. "Help me put on this ridiculous Luxembourg suit coat so we can go get some drinks."

Chapter Five

WITHIN THE ELEVATOR, THEY STOOD side-by-side in silence as they sped up endless floors to the top of the Watercross Tower. Inez stared at Sven's reflection in the mirrored doors of the elevator cab. Dressed in all black, he looked austere and unshakeable—his fitted high-collar suit coat accentuating his black eyepatch and the severe angles of his Dutch profile. His hair was slicked back and glinted like gold under the elevator's overhead lights. He reminded her of a naval commander, mentally preparing himself for battle. *Was he preparing for battle?* They had hardly spoken during their drive there in the back of his Rolls Royce; instead, he encouraged James to speed through every yellow traffic light, as if the sensation of the car's acceleration released his own raging thoughts.

Inez had known him for less than six hours, but already she had learned that he was a man who was not accustomed to surrendering. Whatever professional and personal agenda he had for tonight's meeting, it was obvious he intended to obtain it at all costs. As the elevator rose, she eyed his stern expression and tolerated his punishing silence, noting his appearance walked a fine line between couture runway model and merciless executioner. In comparison, she gazed at her own ensemble—beaded bolero jacket, emerald and diamond choker necklace, scarlet strapless cocktail dress, and Cinderella slingback heels. No matter what protests Inez had made about her own wardrobe, Ebony had been right about one thing: she did look amazing standing next to Sven.

The elevator chimed and the doors rolled open. Without warning, Sven took up her hand into his own. *Like his possession*, she thought, until he waited for her to guide them out of the elevator. *Okay, maybe more like his equal*, she corrected herself. She led them into the seductive lounge, dimly lit by glowing red lanterns that reflected off the silver legs of the high-back black bar stools.

Red and black. A second point for Ebony. Sven and Inez blended right in.

The maître d' rushed into the reception area and greeted Sven with recognition.

"Good evening, sir. The Van der Meer party?"

Sven nodded. "Yes, thank you."

"Very good. Right this way." As they were ushered toward a long private corridor, Inez halted them in their tracks.

"Look at that view!" she exclaimed, gazing out the lounge's panoramic windows at the skyline, flawlessly twinkling like a tourist postcard. She involuntarily held her breath, almost certain she could see the curve of the earth.

"Just wait," Sven replied. "Our table will have an even better view."

He shook her hand, encouraging her to follow the maître d' down the corridor, lined with velvet walls and a coffered ceiling, each panel of glass churning with glittering plasma. The maître d' nodded with a smile and allowed them to pass into the private bar lounge. Anticipation pricked her skin and fluttered within her heart. Sven's relentless clasp of her hand was measured and controlled, signaling he wanted her by his side for their entrance.

"Well, if it isn't the man of the hour." The boisterous voice from the man leaning against the bar ricocheted off the polished nickel table tops.

Sven halted Inez. "How many guests are there?" he whispered.

"Three in total."

"Two men? And a woman?"

"Yeah," she confirmed, observing the other man and woman enjoying their cocktails at a broad table closest to the floor-to-ceiling windows. Their backs were towards them, but the table's magenta lamp shades cast a devilish hue on their profiles. The woman hardly glanced over her bare shoulder, as if the mere act of acknowledging Inez's presence might strain a muscle in her slender swan neck.

Sven nodded, confirming his blurry account with Inez's more reliable vision. He held out his hand to greet the tall, imposing man who approached them.

"And who is this stunning goddess you've brought with you tonight?" asked the man, pushing past Sven and sweeping into Inez's personal space. He was tall, tanned, and impeccably dressed in a trendy lavender shirt and metallic grey suit vest.

"Inez Sanchez…this is Eliot Watercross," Sven replied, providing the formal introductions. "His firm, Watercross Capital, built and financed The Spire, and about a half dozen other buildings in the city. Including this one."

Eliot lifted her hand and kissed it. "Let's give credit where credit is due. The Spire was a joint venture with Van der Meer & Associates. But it's true that this building, Watercross Tower, is all my own."

"Which is why you're one of the most hated men in Chicago," said Inez, watching his presumptuous lips slip off her hand with uncertainty.

"You're the man who infamously lobbied City Hall for the rights to fill the Chicago River with dirt and gravel to build the foundation for this skyscraper."

Eliot's tiger eyes seized on Inez. "Beautiful and smart. That's a dangerous combination. Where'd you pick her up, Sven? One of the architectural boat tours?"

His joke had a hint of mockery beneath it. She forced a smile, glaring at the smug grin that spread across his tanned face.

"Not since the nineteenth century, when the Chicago city bosses decided to reverse the flow of the river to send all the sewage waste downstream, has anyone attempted to alter the natural flow of the Chicago River," Inez sassed back. "Until you came along."

Eliot crunched down on the ice from his tumbler and rubbed his chin. Her direct challenge seemed to intrigue him.

"Beautiful, smart, and well-equipped with a sharp tongue that she'll happily use against you," Sven said, placing his own kiss on her hand like a subtle gesture to mark his territory. "Best to tread carefully, Watercross."

Inez shivered, disarmed by the warmth of Sven's lips against her hand and the sincerity with which he delivered his compliments.

"Always," Eliot agreed. "I'd offer to take your coat, but it looks like you might want to keep it. It's the sweeping vista that sends chills down your spine. It makes you feel like you're precariously suspended outside—seventy stories in mid-air."

Throwing back the rest of his rum, Eliot shamelessly dropped his gaze down to her cleavage.

It was more than just the vista, thought Inez, completely irked by Sven's business partner. "It's more likely the fishbowl walls," Inez replied, attempting to force Eliot's attention off her boobs. "You must be a Mies van der Rohe fan, like Sven."

"Miss Sanchez, you're such an architectural aficionado. Celeste…looks like you've got competition tonight." Eliot called out to the woman sitting at the dining table.

Celeste. Inez stared at the woman, remembering Ebony's hint about Sven's ex-girlfriend.

"Ladies first…" Eliot ushered Inez forward, but Sven kept her tethered by the hand. She understood. It was a new environment and she made a careful effort to seamlessly guide him to the table. The man and the woman sat in high-back metallic chairs on the outer edge of the table, forcing Inez to take a seat along the cushioned bench on the opposite side along the windows. As she slipped into her place, she glanced behind her, conscious of how the curvature of the glass wall accentuated the illusion of dropping seventy stories through a void of darkness to her death.

"We've been waiting for you before we let the drinks flow freely," said the unfamiliar man from across the table.

"Very generous, but unnecessary," Sven replied curtly.

Inez stared at the man—a younger, blonder version of Sven. *His brother.* Then, she glanced over at Celeste, purring over his lap like a cat. Inez immediately recognized her; she was the same brunette in the framed photograph buried within the drawer of Sven's guest bathroom. *The one that Sven had been embracing.* Now, she wore a gold cocktail dress that shimmered every time she crossed and re-crossed her slender waxed legs. Her French bob cut across her bony cheeks like arrows.

"You're wrong, Hans," Celeste said. "Eliot never makes his guests wait to indulge in their vices." Her crystal blue eyes flicked onto Inez—inspecting her hair, dress, figure, and even her emerald necklace—before glancing away and pretending Inez wasn't in front of her at all.

"Why pray in heaven with angels when you can party in hell with the Devil?" Eliot sneered with delight while refreshing Celeste's wine glass with the bottle resting on the side bar.

"I'm going to make that the next lead in my blog post," Celeste exclaimed with melodramatic laughter.

"No, it should be your slogan on your next investment prospectus," Hans chimed in.

"Make a deal with the Devil," Sven added morosely.

"There's a reason why I'm the only one with enough balls to build the tallest building in the city. And it ain't because I'm a saint." Eliot dug his hand into a glass nut tray on the side bar and popped almonds into his mouth with a crunch.

The waiter scurried into the salon and approached Inez and Sven. "May I get you something to start with?"

"A gin on the rocks," Sven said without a beat. "And she will have a French Martini. Shaken. With extra Chambord."

Inez smirked at him. He smiled unexpectedly in return.

"Sven," Celeste cut in, her eyes glinting like ice. "You haven't bothered to introduce us to your little friend?"

"Inez…" Sven conceded, as if it almost pained him. "This is Hans, my younger brother and business partner in our architectural firm. And this is his fiancée, Celeste Cartwright."

Inez stared at Celeste, then Hans who kissed Celeste's wrist like he was idolizing a queen. They seemed perfectly at ease displaying their affection for each other in front of Sven.

"You clearly know each other well since you already know her favorite drink," Celeste remarked. "I think it took you almost a year for you to remember mine."

"No," Sven replied dryly. "I knew it was Chardonnay, preferably Californian. But it always gave you a headache, so it seemed best for you to drink something else."

"Chardonnay gives you a headache?" Hans asked, like he had just entered the room. Inez noted how his boyish face and flaxen hair made him look like a college football star. But his accent was sharp and distinctly foreign.

Celeste fingered the stem of her wine glass. "Yes, dear. It's hard to remember everything about me, I know. Sven has an unfair advantage because he's known me longer."

"Plus, he's a genius with a photographic memory," Hans replied, popping the final baby shrimp from the shared appetizer into his mouth. "The rest of us are just mere mortals quaking in his presence."

Inez looked at Hans, wondering how much truth was veiled beneath his sarcasm. Then, she noticed Sven and Celeste gazing at each other, as if everyone else had disappeared.

"Which is exactly why Sven was the only architect able to engineer a modern-day vision of the tallest skyscraper in the country." Eliot leaned against the rail of the side bar. He shifted his tiger eyes out the window at the unobstructed view of the shiny metallic skyscraper rising above every other building like a glinting needle.

"Well, it is called The Spire for a reason," Celeste added.

"Because MightyGarishThing.com was already taken?" Inez tossed back. She wanted Sven to stop staring at Celeste and it worked. Instead, they both stared at her.

"Like most native Chicagoans, Inez hates The Spire," Sven clarified. "So if you're trying to impress her, Watercross, you're going to fail. Inez is rarely impressed by anything."

"And it's why you love me," she sassed back, knowing Sven would simply ignore her. But not Celeste. Exactly as Inez anticipated, Celeste's vicious glare narrowed onto her.

"Well, then…it seems that you were wrong, Eliot," Celeste suddenly announced. "Sven's little friend isn't much of an architectural aficionado after all because anyone who truly understands modern architecture knows that The Spire is a fearless feat of architectural and structural brilliance."

"Really? A fearless feat of architectural and structural brilliance?" Inez repeated and turned to Sven, desperately controlling the urge to openly flambé Sven's ex-whatever and her clown smile.

"Yes." He mused, clearly enjoying the fact that the two women at the table seemed to be catfighting over him.

"Hm. I had no idea," Inez said with fake ignorance. "Please enlighten me, Pookey."

Sven held her gaze, accepting her challenge. Taking up a cocktail napkin, he twisted it like a spiraling coil before balancing it on the surface of the table.

"The Spire is named after the four steel load-bearing beams, entwined in the shape of a corkscrew, narrowing in width as it runs vertically from its foundation to the very top floor. Three million tons of steel and glass evenly distributed along its center spire, not bolstering its massive weight upwards, but allowing gravity to evenly distribute each pound of steel onto the concentric circles of the interior spire, pulling its full weight down, down, down…It's the only reason the city agreed to build it in the first place—the cost to construct The Spire was made feasible by its simplistic solution to its load-bearing design."

Everyone fell silent, as if the complexity and ingenuity of Sven's design had hypnotized them, including Inez.

"Okay, you win. I'm sufficiently impressed," Inez conceded. It was perhaps the first honest thing she had said all night. "But that doesn't mean I don't have the right to believe it would have been better off being built in Las Vegas."

"And perhaps, more fitting," agreed Sven. "Especially since I've sold my soul along the way." His voice edged lower without hinting at irony or jest, and he touched his eyepatch like it was the physical manifestation of his submission to the dark side.

"Only half your soul…to be more precise," Hans corrected him.

Inez challenged him. "Why only half?"

"Because Watercross Capital owns half of The Spire," Eliot interjected like it was obvious. "Van der Meer & Associates owns the other half—at least, until The Spire formally opens at the end of the week and we all sell our entire equity interest to Harvey Zale."

"A small fortune to pay for your soul, Sven," Hans added. "Don't you think?"

"We shall see," Sven replied, forlorn and moody.

"Well, if it is only half your soul, Sven," Inez cut in, "then you can just cut off the rotting, blackened, gangrene half, and the new, regenerated half will just grow back. You know, like a liver or something."

The table fell awkwardly silent, but Inez didn't care. All this talk of souls and real estate deals and bank loans was boring her to tears.

Delivering a plate filled with Spanish croquetas, the waiter came to her rescue. She grabbed one before he had a chance to set down the plate on the table and stuffed her face with it. He placed her syrupy French Martini in front of her and she downed half of it, realizing it didn't matter if she spilled it on her scarlet dress because it would blend right in. *Thank you, Ebony.*

Then, the waiter set down a second plate of tapas onto the table.

"Morcilla, too?" exclaimed Inez.

Eliot arched his eyebrow. "It looks like you appreciate a good tapa when you see it." He threw back his rum and watched as she shoveled half the morcilla ringlet onto her own plate. "Sven, it's a shame to make her starve. Unlimited food and drinks are some of the many benefits of owning your own restaurant."

Eliot handed him the tapas menu. Sven paused and slowly pushed it over to Inez. She understood. He couldn't read it.

"What *are* those...exactly?" Celeste surveyed the black, bubbly consistency of each ringlet, as if she believed her approval mattered.

"Fried blood sausage. Yum. " Inez devoured two of them before closing her eyes and relaxing into her seat. When she opened her eyes, it was hard to decide which she savored more—something that reminded her of her father's cooking, or the look of revulsion that contorted Celeste's face.

"It's definitely an acquired taste," Hans said, enveloping Celeste's hand to soothe her.

"A taste for blood," Eliot mused and rudely reached through them to stab a full ringlet for himself. Like a brisk siren, his phone rang from inside his interior suit coat pocket. He pulled it out and scanned the screen. "Right on time. Harvey Zale—" he announced before calling into the receiver with obnoxious flare. "Just the man we were talking about." Eliot strode away from the table and into the privacy of the corridor.

Celeste took the distraction as an opportunity to shift the conversation back to Inez.

"I'm surprised to see she's wearing your mother's necklace, Sven. I didn't think you were the committed type."

They traded embittered glances.

"I suppose I've just been waiting for the right woman," Sven replied, cold and calculating.

"Ah, I see," Celeste tittered. "And how did you two meet...exactly?" She posed the question like an interrogation.

Inez glanced over at Sven. She had bothered to set the physical ground rules, but neither of them had thought to hammer out the fake details of their fake relationship. His steady unpatched eye gazed back at her. *Clearly, he was thinking the same thing.*

"At the Art Institute," she finally replied, as if it was the most natural answer in the world.

"Yes," Sven encouraged her and raised his glass of gin to his lips—a signal that he was as interested in hearing how they met as Celeste was.

"In the Impressionism rooms." Inez sat straighter in her seat and slipped off her bolero coat because she knew it accentuated her figure and cleavage and because from the very first moment they sat down, she had noticed that Celeste had none. *Bitch.*

"Apparently, Sven appreciates Monet as much as I do. He's even promised to take me to Giverny this month to celebrate our anniversary." Inez lifted her martini glass and gulped it down.

"Your anniversary?" Celeste repeated. "How long could you possibly have known each other?"

Inez gazed into Sven's eyes, wondering if he was going to come to her rescue. But he seemed more amused than alarmed, and it inflated her confidence.

"It feels like a lifetime." Inez sighed, feeling the relaxing effects of her martini spreading slowly down her neck and shoulders.

"So you just bumped into each other at the Art Institute?" Hans interjected.

"Well, I'm always there for work," Inez clarified. "I'm an assistant curator at the museum."

"At the Art Institute?" Celeste insisted, skeptically.

"Of course." Inez shrugged off Celeste's surprise like she was a total idiot and sipped again from her martini, wishing she could down the whole thing without having to pump and dump later that night.

Celeste narrowed her eyes. It wasn't the answer she expected. Neither did Sven.

"Which department?" Celeste grilled her.

"Nineteenth century European paintings."

"That's a prestigious position, and you're a little bit...young."

Inez glared at her. "Maybe Sven isn't the only genius at this table."

Sven hand squeezed Inez's hand. *Stop*, it told her.

Inez turned and smiled at him, sweetly. *No fucking way.*

"Celeste is an art critic for *The Chicago Tribune*," Sven clarified.

Inez peered at him, completely unfazed. "Really? I thought all the major newspapers went bankrupt eons ago, especially something as old-fashioned as *The Tribune*. I mean, it's almost as uncool as Facebook."

Sven stared at her with reprimanding silence. Apparently, *now*, she had just crossed a line. *Who knew Sven liked Facebook*?

"I just mean...you know," Inez said with a malicious smirk. "I'm a millennial. Not many things hold our interest."

"Well, do tell us...what *does* hold your interest," Celeste dared her with a laser shot from her robotic blue eyes.

Inez popped the final morcilla ringlet into her mouth and chewed politely while gazing back at Sven and making it absolutely fucking clear that she was not going to be thrown under the bus by his wicked witch ex-girlfriend.

"In terms of art? The new opening of the Klimt exhibit at the Museum of Modern Art in New York City. In the field of technology? They just 3-D printed a new nose for a patient in Boston and performed the surgical transplant over the weekend. How 'bout finance? The volatility in the stock market is unparalleled because there's so much oil being produced from fracking in

South Dakota that it's driving the world's oil market into a tailspin. Science? There's a Swiss company that's developing a new submarine to take private citizens down to the bottom of the Mariana Trench for the affordable rate of one million dollars—one way. Or how 'bout mindless Hollywood pop culture? I've heard that JLo and JLaw just wore the same vintage Versace dress to the Golden Globes and JLo won. Go Latina power." Inez paused and slurped down the last bit of her wonderful French Martini. When she sighed and looked up, she saw Sven gazing at her.

"Really, the Mariana Trench?" he asked. "Perhaps it's something we should look into."

"Deepest darkest place in the world's ocean," Inez confirmed.

He took her hand into his own, publicly and proudly, like he was sharing in her victory. "Why waste so much time building the tallest building in the country when you could simply pay one million dollars to travel to the bottom of the ocean?"

"My sentiments exactly," she replied, unexpectedly savoring the possessiveness of his hand, especially as Celeste's saccharin smile turned downwards with consternation, as if seeing them hold hands gave her as much displeasure as weight gain.

"I hope you haven't been having too much fun without me." Eliot's booming voice rattled the expansive glass windows as he swaggered back into the lounge. "Just finished talking to Harvey Zale. He wants reassurance that our deal is still in play."

Sven's expression darkened again and he released Inez's hand. She was starting to really despise Eliot Watercross.

"Which deal exactly?" Sven challenged him. "To sell The Spire to Harvey Zale in exchange for cash? Or in exchange for his contracts to build the Li Long Towers in Shanghai?"

"Come on, Sven," Hans pressed him. "It wouldn't be much fun if you just cashed out now without signing on to construct the tallest towers in the world."

"Not much fun for me?" Sven replied. "Or for both of you because you need me to design them?"

Eliot popped an almond into his mouth. "A design for which you'd be well-compensated."

"You make it sound like making billions from selling The Spire isn't enough?" asserted Inez. It was none of her business, but she couldn't contain herself. Her boiling hatred for The Devil spurred her sassiness.

Eliot's laughter thundered across the lounge as he stretched his long arm out across the silver edge of the bar, revealing his flashy gold watch accentuating his even flashier pinky ring.

"I'm an ambitious man, my dear. I don't wanna own the tallest building in the city. Or even own the tallest building in the country. I wanna own the tallest buildings in the world. And I expect your boyfriend to help me."

"And what if I prefer to simply retain my equity ownership in The Spire?" Sven flung back.

Eliot shrugged. "That's understandable. The Spire is the pinnacle of your career. You probably want to permanently hang it on your balance sheet like a trophy. Unfortunately, your equity ownership in The Spire represents a minority interest, and decisions about its sale are decided by a majority vote. And I own the majority." He popped several more almonds into his mouth and smiled slyly with a conspicuous crunch.

Sven's jawline flinched. "So you're saying that I'm trapped."

Hans cut in. "You make it sound like a prison sentence, Sven. We're talking about spearheading one of the most prestigious design projects in a decade. Maybe even a century."

Sven glared at his brother, as though he were the enemy. "Except you do not have a building without an architect who is willing and capable of designing it."

"Our firm is called Van der Meer & Associates for a reason, Sven," Hans asserted. "I spent three years working on The Spire alongside you."

"You worked under my direction," Sven seethed. "But it was always my design. My lead."

"Not during the time you took off after your injury and disappeared for months," shot back Hans. "Then it became my project. My lead."

Preparing for battle, Sven rose from the cushioned bench, asserting his commanding height and aggressive authority.

The room fell silent. He touched his eyepatch and peered over at Celeste, then gazed back at Hans. "You mean the injury caused by your betrayal?"

Hans' chair screeched as he pushed it backwards and rose to challenge Sven. "I took from you what you took for granted."

Inez watched each brother stare down the other, as if they were on the verge of throwing punches.

"Sven, please—" Celeste petitioned him with her sing-song voice. "You came up with the perfect architectural solution for The Spire. I have no doubt you'll be able to do it again for the Li Long Towers."

"You forget, Celeste, that when I designed The Spire, I had two good eyes. Now, I only have one."

Eliot slowly crossed the room and looked out across the skyline shrouded by nightfall. "Well, Sven...if you're not capable of designing it, then maybe Hans is right. Maybe the only thing the investors of the Li Long Towers are going to care about is the Van der Meer name."

"Which means what?" Sven challenged him. "You only need one of us to get the deal done and the other one is disposable?"

"There's always safety in numbers," Eliot conceded. "Better to come along for the ride than be left behind."

Inez slowly stood up from her seat. The Devil's veiled threat polarized the lounge like The Bermuda Triangle, threatening to imprison Sven and her within the magnetism of its menacing storm.

Sven shifted his attention back to his brother. "So not only are you scheming to transfer my ownership in The Spire into your pet project, but you're planning to steal credit for my designs as well?"

"The world is large and memories are short," Eliot answered for Hans. "History is only going to remember the Van der Meer brother who built the tallest buildings in the world, not the one who walked away from the challenge."

Sven glared at his brother whose silence confirmed his misplaced allegiance.

"I will remind you, Watercross—" Sven warned "—that you already went down this path with your own architect, Symeon Colovos, and failed."

The mocking glint in Eliot's green eyes turned cold and callous. He moved away from the window and stalked closer towards Sven.

"You went into a joint venture with Harvey Zale to construct the Li Long Towers using Colovos' design and it was summarily rejected by the Chinese officials as completely unstable and unfeasible for the proposed cost. Now, Harvey Zale wants out, but you still want to claim success."

Eliot chewed on Sven's words, the glow from the magenta lamp shades reflecting off his eyes. "I've never been a man to accept failure. And neither are you."

"Which means you can't return to Shanghai with designs produced by just any architect or architectural firm. You need designs that will be approved by the Chinese government. Which means, if you expect to successfully build the tallest towers in the world, you don't need more money, or more power, or more connections, or to spill brotherly blood...you simply need me." Sven swept up Inez's hand like he was rescuing her from a pack of wolves. "Talent can be bought and sold. Reputations can be fabricated. But true ingenuity cannot be stolen. And my cooperation is something you will never receive."

He led Inez away from the table and down the corridor. *Thank freaking, God*, she sighed with a deep breath. It had been the longest cocktail hour of her life and the only thing she enjoyed was her French Martini and how Sven's verbal swordplay dashed The Devil's smile off his smug face.

Eliot called after him like a warning shot. "The opening of The Spire is less than a week away, Sven. Don't end up on the wrong side of the deal."

Sven halted their pace and sneered back at him. "I may have sold half my soul to you in order to be a part of The Spire. But I still have my other half, which is just enough to make me want to do everything in my power to ensure your failure."

Chapter Six

AS HIS DRIVER CRUISED ALONG Michigan Avenue back to his penthouse, Sven rubbed his head, attempting to relieve his punishing headache, partly from straining his blurry eye throughout dinner and partly because he had come to hate everything about his bleak, uncertain life.

The Spire. He spotted its radiant spiral tip, glinting like a silver prism, higher than any other building in the northern sky. It was the crowning achievement of his professional career, and now, it filled him with nothing but vexation and dread. He had tried to sound unintimidated at the prospect of being forced out of his equity interest through the sale of The Spire as well as being excluded from participation in the construction of the Li Long Towers. But the truth was, after one tragic accident, one major eye surgery, and the slow debilitating decay of his other eye, Sven was far more vulnerable than he cared to admit. Just two years ago, he was confident everyone in his life revered him and he could conquer the world. Now, he only felt the cruel hand of fate working against him, wielding its vengeance for uniting himself with dishonorable men seeking dishonorable gain.

"Your friends are all assholes, Sven."

He glanced over at Inez, suddenly realizing he had rudely ignored her since they had left the Watercross Tower.

"It really was quite uncomfortable, wasn't it?" he acknowledged. "And at this point, I wouldn't categorize them as friends."

Her dark, challenging gaze was barely discernable within the shadows, but he knew she wasn't going to let him off easy.

Inez Sanchez, he mused to himself. Even she was karma's handmaiden. With her sarcastic wit and lashing tongue, she happily punished him—and all his asshole friends—for their offensive conceit and felonious aspirations. She considered The Spire a blight on the cityscape, a garish symbol of narcissism and ego, designed and constructed by greedy, selfish men who sought to openly mock the rest of Chicago with their superiority. And her scorn unnerved him because, deep down, he knew she was right. There had been very little dignity in what he had accomplished with The Spire. From the beginning, he had been motivated by the superficial allure of grandeur and ambition, which somehow made the threat of losing it all seem tolerable and even strangely fitting.

"How was your French Martini?" It was a pitiful attempt at consolation.

"Delicious. It was the only reason why I didn't stab myself with the prawn fork."

"You did quite well tonight, considering everything," Sven confirmed. "And I especially enjoyed the way you handled yourself with Celeste."

"You mean the way she dragged me into the mud pit by the hair before I body-slammed her with my cleavage?"

"Precisely."

"She's still in love with you. You know that, right?"

He shifted his gaze out the window. "No, I'm certain that's not true."

"She definitely gave me the stink eye most of the night, and you only do that to your ex-boyfriend's girlfriend if you're still in love with him."

"Are you speaking from experience?"

"I'm speaking as a woman," Inez insisted. "And all women know the subliminal signs behind 'bitch-don't-steal-my-ex-boyfriend-because-his-ass-still-belongs-to-me'. It's girl code. We're born with it."

"Really?" Sven raised his eyebrow. "That sounds quite sophisticated."

"It is. Especially the laser glares."

"Are you also born knowing all about The Mariana Trench?"

"Probably."

"And fracking in South Dakota?"

"What? You don't believe I'm naturally a genius?"

Sven squinted at her, gauging how to answer her honestly without offending her. "Not completely."

"That's because you're a cynic, like me."

As the lights from Buckingham Fountain danced off her face, he discerned her smile.

"But you're also clearly not…" he paused, struggling to find the right word.

"Average?" she tossed at him.

He looked away, avoiding her teasing gaze, and mulled through the strange mixture of shame and enchantment that she inspired in him.

"The truth is I'm a reader. I read everything I can find. Now you know my horrible dirty secret."

"Everything except for old-fashioned newspapers like *The Chicago Tribune*."

"No, that was a lie, too." She fiddled with the hem of her dress. "I read *The Chicago Tribune*. I just didn't realize your ex-girlfriend was *the* Celeste

Cartwright, art critic extraordinaire. But it dawned on me the moment she called The Spire a 'fearless feat of architectural and structural brilliance' because she was quoting from her own article, and I remembered reading that piece and hating every word of it. But there was no way in hell I was going to give her the satisfaction of letting her know it."

"Ahh, I see. More girl code."

"No. That was just flat out bitch anti-freeze."

Sven laughed and rubbed his good eye. It was late and his English was failing him. He felt both entertained and exhausted by their conversation.

"The fact of the matter is that I owe much of my success to Celeste. She's a well-respected figure within the community. She was the one who convinced me to design The Spire and she always supported my ambitions."

Inez didn't respond. She didn't seem impressed. She never seemed impressed and it made Sven feel strangely vulnerable.

"Until the day she didn't," Inez finally said.

Sven looked away. "Until the day that I pushed her away."

"So you're still in love with her, too?"

"No," he said quietly.

A fearless feat of architectural and structural brilliance. He had loved those words when Celeste published her first public review of The Spire because he had believed them, and perhaps he had thought he loved Celeste because she reinforced his shallow aspirations for greatness.

"I'm fairly certain I'm too selfish and egotistical to fall in love with anyone."

"Oh, that's right. You only own half your soul."

"Yes." He nodded. "And whatever part of my soul Eliot Watercross doesn't destroy, I'm certain no woman will want to claim it for herself," he teased with a self-deprecation that felt liberating. He was so used to taking himself seriously. It was refreshing to be around someone who couldn't care less about the fact that he was Sven van der Meer.

She smiled. It soothed him. She had a lovely smile.

"It's eleven o'clock, Miss Sanchez. One more hour until the stroke of midnight when your gown will turn back into rags and your carriage will turn back into a pumpkin."

"I'm fine with it. I've never been the princess type, but it's a good thing for you that I'm an excellent liar and damn good at pretending to be your girlfriend."

"Yes, you are," he conceded with a sidelong glance at her.

"And now that you're on the outs with the cool kids, you're going to need an ally more than ever."

The truth behind her playful jest dampened the mood between them. There would be repercussions for what had transpired tonight, and Sven had avoided contemplating them until that moment.

"You know," he said slowly, cautiously, as if he almost hated to admit it. "If I was an honest, honorable man, I would realize the folly of our charade and immediately release you from our arrangement."

"Shocker alert, Sven," she replied. "You're a conceited egotistical bastard who's paying me five thousand dollars a day to pretend to be your girlfriend. There's not much room there for vindication."

"No, I suppose not," he agreed, then paused. "But are you certain you're prepared to endure the consequences of becoming my ally?"

She fell silent within the darkness. The car rolled to a stop along the circular driveway of his penthouse building.

"I've only known you for about seven hours, Sven."

"Eight," he corrected her.

"Okay, eight. But in that time, I've learned one crucial thing about you."

"Really, what's that, Miss Sanchez?"

"It's way easier to be on your team than it is to fight against you."

Sven waited to see if he could hear her trademark sarcasm slipping beneath her compliment. But in the end, he only heard sincerity and it disarmed him. *Dangerous and unpredictable like a firecracker*, he thought. The moment he thought he knew how to handle her, she sizzled and popped and threatened to blow off his hand.

"So that means you won't be quitting on me?" He had feared it, especially after their dinner tonight.

"My last temp job was a week ago, and I only lasted for three hours. You've already beat that record and I haven't quit on you—yet."

"Hm," he pondered, rubbing his chin while wondering what made her tick. "That only tells me that you need my money."

She shrugged, pretending it was both true and completely irrelevant. "There are lots of ways for a woman to make an easy buck, Sven. And definitely easier ways than *pretending* to be your girlfriend."

A firecracker in the palm of his hand. And truth be told, he yearned to set her off, just to see what kind of explosive streams of color and light would illuminate his darkened sky.

"Yes," he mused, squinting at her with mischief. "Like coming upstairs to my private penthouse and helping me get undressed."

Chapter Seven

LISTENING TO THE STEADY CLICKS of Inez's high heels behind him, Sven passed through the shadows of his penthouse and through the private hallway leading to the master bedroom, encouraged by the fact that she was following him without distrust or protest. It had been a long day filled with conflict and antipathy, and he was grateful for the prospect of silence and peace. He moved to the foot of his king-size platform bed, its silky black sheets beckoning him like drowning waters. He stopped and heard her footsteps, narrowing the distance between them.

Here they were again, back in his bedroom. It had only been a few hours since they had been here together, passing through the unpretentious motions of preparing themselves for dinner. *Almost like a normal couple*, Sven thought.

But they were not a normal couple—or even a couple at all, and yet, that didn't change the fact that all evening he had suppressed his smoldering desires—desires kindled by the sight of her in that scarlet dress with her long black hair, pouty lips, and exotic face. He had felt her cinched waist beneath his fingertips, and the certainty that she was wearing a boned corset that accentuated her arcing cleavage made him yearn to remove it. And although her sassy tongue and acerbic wit fueled his attraction for her, it was her feminine sensuality tonight that lured him into a dangerous maze of wanting more. Unsettled by the consequences of their cocktail hour with Eliot Watercross, he had forced himself to suppress his arousal. But on the elevator ride up to his penthouse, he was consumed by his forbidden urges.

It had been the same during his interview with her, except at that time, he had concealed his attraction behind condescension. He was fully aware that he needed someone like her more than she needed him—or his money—but his ego and pride weren't prepared to let her know it. But now, after rolling through the flashes of tonight's conversation in his mind, it had become impossible for him to deny his good fortune: she had been the perfect choice because she refused to acknowledge her subordination to anyone. Not even to him. And he needed that now. Perhaps more than he needed anything else in his life.

The room was dark and silent. He considered calling out, "Blinds" in order to automatically open the vertical slats and allow the moonlight to stream in through the patio bay windows. But he decided against it.

"Here. You need to take this back before I get used to wearing it."

He heard the jingle of gemstones and platinum behind him. He turned and she held out the emerald necklace to him. Reluctantly, he accepted it. He had noticed during dinner how stunning she had looked in it, and he had caught himself fantasizing about seeing her wearing it—and nothing else.

She stood there, silently staring at him, waiting…

Of course, he realized. She was waiting for payment.

He counted his steps to the wall safe, pressed the keypad numbers to open its door, and deposited the necklace back into the velvet pouch. Reaching into the back of the safe, he removed a tidy stack of one hundred dollar bills, wrapped in the center with a paper band.

"Five thousand dollars. As promised." He handed it to her.

She stared down at it without accepting it.

"You can count it if you like. I won't be offended."

"I'm not certain I would know how to count up to five thousand dollars," she finally answered.

He smiled. He had only spent one day with her, but this was the first time he had rendered her speechless. "There's only fifty bills. Mint condition." He waved the stack of bills, encouraging her to take it.

She moved towards him and plucked it from his hands. "Are you sure you didn't rob a bank? They can trace serial numbers, you know."

"So you know about bank robberies, too?" He felt the urge to re-establish their lighthearted rapport.

She delicately flipped through the bills with her thumb. "They'll nab me the moment I try to buy hand lotion at the convenience store."

"That would be very expensive hand lotion."

"I have sensitive skin," she said quietly.

He stared at her, trying to make out her face in the darkness; she met his gaze and granted him a lingering moment of indulgence.

"Will you come here and help me undo these buttons now?"

She nodded and approached the bed, laying the money on the black silk sheets. She turned and reached up to unfasten the first button of his suit coat, just below the rigid Mandarin collar. He stiffened, attempting to keep her sudden touch from arousing him. But it was impossible. Her long black hair had fallen over her bare shoulder and the scent of her skin—a mixture of vanilla and baby powder—raided his inhibitions. Her proximity allowed him to study her Cuban profile and the sensuality of her neckline. He peered down at her, wondering if she could feel his heart pounding through his suit coat or if she could sense the only thing he wanted more than to remove all his clothes and crawl into bed was not to do it alone.

Her fingers diligently worked along the seam of his coat. *Freeing him.* She glanced up, studying his unflinching gaze.

"Your brother said…" she started before pausing to tread carefully. "He said there was an accident." She shifted her gentle eyes up to his eyepatch. "And that you were injured?"

"Yes." He replied without offering more. He understood her motivation. Within the secrecy and intimacy of the darkness, it felt natural to want to discuss everything avoided in the daylight. But in that moment, he was acutely aware that she was a stranger to all his personal conflicts and pain and he yearned to keep it that way. She wasn't a part of his hurtful past and it gave him solace. She didn't press him and he appreciated her all the more for it.

She unfastened the final button of the suit coat and slipped it off his shoulders. He exhaled deeply and sank down on the edge of the mattress. *That damn coat*, he thought. It had restricted his movements all night like a straight-jacket and now he wanted to burn it.

"Fireplace," he called out into the darkness. With a flash of bursting light, flames rushed up from the gas fireplace and illuminated the bedroom like the devil's lair before settling into a dim, methodical crackle. He expanded his chest, feeling the relaxing heat rush through the silk of his black dress shirt.

"Please—" he implored her, fidgeting with the shirt's Mandarin collar, the final constricting yoke around his neck. "I never want to wear this outfit again. Let's destroy it."

She came to his rescue and unclipped the collar. "The tailors in Luxembourg would be extremely disappointed to hear that."

Kicking off his dress shoes, he rolled up his sleeves. "Let them go out of business. They have no right to be designing suit coats and shirts."

She giggled and laid the suit coat over the back of his leather armchair. "I thought you rocked it."

He peered over at her with curiosity. "You mean like a rock star or something?" He sat up straighter, inflated by her compliment.

"Maybe more like a killer ninja," she tossed back. "Stealthy and menacing."

"Stealthy," he repeated, amused by her English. "Yes," he agreed, crossing his arms, considering how to draw her closer to him in the stealthiest way possible.

She seemed to sense his intentions and glanced over at the clock on his night stand. It was 11:38 PM.

"Well, it's getting late. I better go and get myself undressed—"

"No, wait—" he said in earnest. "Don't change yet. Not yet."

She stopped and narrowed her gaze at him. "Sven…a girl in a fancy red dress, with five thousand dollars in her purse, riding the 'L' train at midnight in downtown Chicago, is the beginning of a bad horror flick."

"Scarlet," he corrected her. "Scarlet dress. And you look lovely in it."

He was surprised by his confession. And so was she. She fell silent, watching him watching her.

"Thank you," she said politely, as if she didn't want to encourage more.

He paused, considering the implications of his compliment. It had been partially fueled by his desire not to be left alone and partially fueled by his need to let her know the truth. It was the first time he had allowed himself to conspicuously take in the full curves of her body, accentuated by the flickering flames of the fireplace. He didn't care anymore about being guarded or stern with her. He only wanted to keep her with him.

"And you won't ride the train. James will drive you home."

He said it like a protector. Perhaps he was yielding to his desire to protect her. But he knew she was not a woman who would be easily tamed, and she wanted him to know it.

"The Van Buren stop is two blocks from here. I'll be perfectly fine taking the train." She kicked off her heels and took them into her hands, a deliberate assertion of her independence. She moved forward, preparing to leave him.

"No." He rose from the bed, blocking her. "You're not going to travel home alone on the train at midnight. Not all the way to Northside. And not when I'm offering you a ride."

"I'm not going to remain Cinderella much longer, remember? My carriage will turn back into a pumpkin and my dress will turn back into rags."

Her trademark sarcasm, he thought. She was always hiding behind it, and it spurred him to get closer.

"Not if you stay," he countered, his voice deep and husky. "Stay."

He pushed even closer. Their eyes locked. She eyed him, holding her ground, as if she was granting him a rare privilege—allowing him the proximity to admire her fearlessness.

"That would complicate our employee-employer relationship, Sven. And I think I prefer our current arrangement."

He held her gaze, searching for any hint of weakness in her voice. "After midnight you're no longer my employee. You're free to do whatever you want."

His words dangled like a tease. He reached down for her hand, expecting to feel only resistance. Instead, her elbow slackened as he drew her into his body. He glimpsed down at the sensual crescents of her breasts and the tender slope of her neckline, wondering how she would respond if he kissed the hollow of her throat. Would she let out an audible sigh as he slipped his hand up the high slit of her dress? Would she drop her head back and moan while his fingers skated behind her thighs and massaged the fleshy cushion of her backside? Would she relax her stance and allow him to slide his hand between her inner thighs, granting him access to the silky crotch of her naughty panties which he had imagined her in all night? Would she acquiesce with a reluctant groan and submit herself to his invading caresses while he kissed the gentle curve of her collarbone?

"Stay," he requested.

He peered into her bold, cherrywood eyes. It was the first time since their interview that he had the chance to focus his good eye on their beauty—and the intensity of the woman behind them.

She did not look away or avoid his cautious advance towards her. His hand passed along the indent of her hip, just above the side seam of her dress. He fingered the cold metal tab of her dress's zipper and yearned to buzz it down to loosen her strapless bodice and reveal her cinching corset. He ached to drop his chin down her neckline and tease the buxom arcs of her breasts with his lips before nudging each one out of its satin cup, exposing her tits to his mercy.

All day she had punished him with her mocking wit and sarcasm—despite the fact that he was her boss and she was his employee. Now, he craved her submission by taking her lush body in his possession and dominating every inch of it with long curling flicks of his tongue and teasing nips of his teeth until she gave into him with breathy, uninhibited moans.

He edged his face towards her, lowering his chin and fighting his instinct to kiss her without her consent. He paused, hoping to feel the rotation of her pelvis and her soft warm breath against his lips—a sign of her surrender. He yearned for a sign—*any sign*—granting him permission to draw her down onto his bed, where he would smother her mouth with his own and kiss her with passion, aiding her to release all the anger and resentment she was holding against the world. He understood her anger because he had felt it, too—a scowl of bitterness permanently imprinted across his face, threatening to consume him with hatred. Hatred not only for his life, but for himself.

But she merely granted him a knowing smile, an enigmatic expression, barely discernable through the flickering shadows of the fireplace. It was as though she was silently acknowledging she had rescued him today, rescued him by helping to maintain the charade of being indomitable and unshakeable—at least for one more day. Perhaps it was the way that she had helped him to preserve his pride—as a man—that ignited his desire to seize her into his arms, spread her across his bed, and rip off the folds of her dress to expose her bare legs and black G-string that he knew was hidden there. He wanted to force her heel up onto his shoulder and make her shudder as his fingers slipped beneath the thin strip of her panties to fondle her clit and invade her wetness. With long, rhythmic strokes of his fingers, he wanted to make her gush until she fully parted her knees and begged for his touch. He wanted to bury his chin against her flesh and taste her wetness, unleashing her panting cry with every forbidden lick of his tongue while her fingernails pressed into the back of his scalp, urging him not to stop. She had bewitched his desires in a mysterious and incalculable way, and now, there was nothing to stop him from pursuing her except her own challenging eyes and the assumption that they would likely regret it in the morning.

He savored the whisper of her breath against his neck and the way the soft contour of her cleavage grazed against his firm chest. It was enough to grant him hope until she spoke.

"I'm going to undress now, Sven."

He exhaled and repeated her words in his mind, fondling the metal tab of her zipper on her dress.

"Upstairs," she asserted, covering his hand with her own. "By myself."

He closed his eyes and bowed his head against her shoulder, as if her rejection wounded him, despite the fact that he fully expected it.

"Good night, Sven." She softly touched the nape of his neck.

"Good night, Miss Sanchez." He inhaled her scent to commit it to memory before permitting her to escape up the spiral staircase to the guest bathroom where he heard the door shut and lock with finality.

Chapter Eight

SVEN SAT ON HIS SOFA, STARING at all the blurry water lilies within the Monet painting. Yesterday, he had strained his eye the entire day, and so it wasn't a surprise to him when he woke up with a headache and diminished sight. This morning, he only counted eleven water lilies before giving up completely. *Only eleven…* Things were deteriorating faster than he had ever expected. Shutting his eyes, he pressed the cold ice pack against the socket of his good eye and exhaled as it numbed him into relaxation.

He knew it could all change by tomorrow. If he rested his eye, he might be able to find at least fifteen or sixteen water lilies. That would be an improvement. *It could all change by tomorrow. Nothing was certain yet.* Some days were better than others, and not even the doctors were certain he would go completely blind. No one had any idea what was going to happen. *Nothing was certain.*

Buzzzzzz.

The front doorbell. He sat up straighter and removed the ice pack.

Inez? He thought.

It was a whisper of hope. When he had awoken this morning, alone and nursing a headache, he remembered how he had propositioned her last night and how reprehensible it had been. But she had not given in to him. She remained loyal to their arrangement and proved she was nothing less than the wise, self-controlled woman who he had hired to help him get through the week. *Yes, she had escaped from him last night.* But now, as the front door buzzer of his penthouse rang again, he wondered why the doorman hadn't rung his phone to announce the visitor before allowing her into the elevator. It had to be because the doorman recognized her. *It had to be because it was Inez.*

He rose from the sofa, motivated by expectation and anticipation. It was only nine-thirty in the morning. He looked down at himself and smelled under his arm. He was without a shower or shave and wearing only his silk pajama pants. He hadn't expected to see her again until this afternoon. Perhaps she had forgotten something. Or perhaps she had reflected on the evening, and now, she had come to tell him that she had reconsidered working for him.

A sudden pang of dread constricted his chest. He still needed her; there were still so many events this week he couldn't navigate without her assistance. He paced across his living room, summoning the resolve to make her change her mind. He would convince her to give him a second chance. He would promise her that he would be a better man. He would admit that she had seen a rare moment of weakness which had fueled his desire to keep her with him as long as possible. He knew he was a flawed man, and he wasn't as invincible as he pretended to be.

He counted his steps to the front door, vowing to himself not to lose her before he even had an opportunity to get to know her. Because the truth was when he woke up this morning, he hadn't regretted his actions last night. He only regretted not finding her sooner.

But when he whisked open the door, he felt his heart sink into the pit of his stomach. "Celeste?" His voice wavered before he had a chance to mask his disappointment.

She laughed awkwardly and brushed past him without waiting for an invitation to enter.

"Good morning, handsome. I know it's early, but you're a morning person, so I didn't think you'd mind the house call. Unless, of course, I'm interrupting..." Her voice trailed off as she cocked her head, listening for the presence of another person—another woman.

He closed the front door, tracking her blurry image sashaying across the black marble floor in her electric blue heels. In the past, Sven had always enjoyed watching Celeste's long sensual legs and tight secretary skirt follow an invisible tight rope whenever she entered his penthouse. But not this time. This time, he lowered his gaze and covered his eye with his hand, feeling the nagging ache returning with vengeance.

Celeste moved into the living room and spotted the ice pack on the leather sofa.

"Long night?" she asked.

"Before the cocktails or after Inez and I left?" He knew what she was thinking and he didn't mind letting her imagination run with it.

She scoffed. "If I didn't know you better, I'd think you were trying to make me jealous."

Silently, he turned away. There was more truth in that statement than he cared to admit. It was always a game between them. While he was dating her, she was one of the few women who kept him both sexually stimulated and intellectually interested. But now, it all seemed like too much work. And she had only been there two minutes.

"You're here for a specific reason, Celeste. What is it?" The edge in his voice made it clear that he was in no mood for games.

"Well, no need to sound so impatient." She glanced up the spiral staircase, again studying the silence. When she was certain they were alone, she untied her leopard-print wrap coat and draped it across the high-backed lounge chair. "I'm here to make peace with you." She said it simply, almost sincerely.

He strained his unpatched eye and focused on her face. Her sharp cheek bones, high forehead, and coral pink lips reminded him that she had paid her way through college working for a local modeling agency. *Beautiful...no, stunning*, he thought. But more importantly, she knew how to turn her good side towards the camera and use it.

He had taken too long to respond and she circled away from him, as if his silence made her nervous.

"I realized after last night that I'm tired of this...animosity between us, and I think it's time that we both try to reconcile the past."

"Reconcile the past? Which part of the past exactly?"

She avoided the anger in his voice and turned away to gaze out at the skyline.

"I'm not proud of the way things ended between us. But you make it sound like it was all a sordid act of malice against you. When you left for Shanghai, I was hurting, too, you know?"

Was he still hurt? It felt shameful and juvenile to still be hurt over her betrayal, and everything that had spiraled out of control after it. Shameful and juvenile because it had partly been his own fault.

"But you can't blame me for moving on after I realized you never had any intention of making a commitment to me."

"We were together for two years, Celeste. What more of a commitment would you have liked?"

She looked at him like he was the one playing games.

"You mean a proposal?" he replied.

She shrugged. "Your work always came first. And look at it...isn't it magnificent?"

Her gaze shifted out the windows onto the stunning view of The Spire. Her compliment softened the lump of bitterness in his throat. She had always supported his work. Even when The Spire had been defiled by the locals, Celeste had been one of a handful of influential voices in the media who openly defended his ambitions. And perhaps that was a large part of why he believed he had loved her.

He studied her now. The sunlight streaming through the windows sharpened the alluring lines of her navy suit jacket and matching skirt. She stroked the fox fur that trimmed the lapels of her fitted jacket, accentuating her long torso and slender waist. How many days—just like this one—had they spent together, here in his penthouse? How many nights had they spent together, naked in his bed like lovers, laughing, kissing, and plotting the roadmap of their own grandiose future?

Yes, he still hurt. He closed his eyes, as if he wanted to erase the past from his mind. But none of it mattered now. Perhaps that was the realization that hurt the most—so many visceral memories, so many private conversations, so many intimate emotions that, in the end, didn't seem to mean anything at all.

He touched his eyepatch. His head ached like his resentful soul.

"I was…am not a perfect man, Celeste. You said you came here to make peace, but the fact of the matter is that you are now engaged to my brother, and so I do not believe it is the past that we must reconcile, but our present situation."

"Can it be reconciled, Sven?" She pushed towards him. "We used to be so familiar and candid with each other. Don't you remember all those summer nights we used to spend out on your sailboat, just the two of us, alone and perfectly free with each other?"

His head flinched in pain. "I try not to think of sailing, anymore."

"Yes, of course." Celeste paused and stared at his wounded eye. "You must know, Sven…I want you to know that when I told you about Hans and me the last time we were together on your yacht, I never thought you'd react the way that you did."

"He's my brother, Celeste. And you were my lover."

"*Were*," she stressed, like she was asserting her innocence. "You made it very clear that you couldn't be bothered with making promises to me before you traveled to Shanghai because you weren't the marrying type. And it was at that moment I realized that our relationship was over." Her tone revealed the subtle grimace on her face. "Most girls believe in a certain type of fairy tale, Sven. And one of those fairy tales is that her Prince Charming will fall in love with her at first sight and love her more than anything else in his life. But on that day—the day you left for Shanghai—I realized you didn't love me. Not like I wanted you to…not like I had always hoped you would."

Sven fell silent, as if she was describing a stranger. *Had he been that cold and detached from her*? It was entirely possible that he had.

"And Hans," she continued. "Well…dearest Hans was more than willing to lend me a shoulder to cry on."

"He lent you more than just his shoulder," he replied.

She threw back her head with laughter. "Yes, perhaps he did." She closed the gap between them and reached out to toy with the waist strings of his silk pajama pants. "But you must know, Sven. I never meant to hurt you…it's just that…I was hurting, too."

She touched his bare chest, her fingernails skating down his flanks. He exhaled and looked into her smoldering eyes. She said she had come to make peace between them. But she wasn't a woman who inspired peace; she was a woman who inspired vices.

The sensation of her touch made his hair rise up along the nape of his neck. Celeste always had a knack for soothing his defenses, and after last night, his body was starved for attention. He noted the sophisticated scent of her perfume—something expensive and Parisian. For a brief, unguarded moment, he considered gathering her up into his arms and testing the sincerity of her innuendos. It would be the perfect revenge against Hans, and perhaps he would even be able to rekindle some of his attraction for Celeste. *Wrath and lust—two of the seven deadly sins.*

In the past, he likely would have done it. But not now. Now, the only thing ringing through his head was the sound of Inez's sarcastic voice. *Your friends are all assholes, Sven.* And the only emotion tugging at his heart was disappointment—disappointment that Celeste was the one who was there and Inez wasn't. Inez was right—*they were all assholes*—and something inside him made him want to prove himself different from them.

He confidently withdrew Celeste's arms from around his neck and pulled away from her. "Celeste, you're engaged to my brother now, and I have other obligations."

"You mean like speed dating younger women?"

He paused and glared at her. It was a petty insult—punishment for rejecting her physical advances, no doubt.

His cell phone rang out from the sofa where he had left it. Staring at her, he picked up the phone and deliberately answered the call. "Hello? Yes, of course. Please come up."

"How sweet. She's here now." Celeste's voice was filled with contempt.

He didn't correct her. Instead, he retrieved her coat from the sofa, offering to help her into it.

"She was wearing your mother's emerald necklace last night," she noted curtly while slipping her long elegant arms through the coat's flowing bell sleeves. "Something you never offered me."

Sven didn't feel compelled to answer. In fact, talking about Inez with Celeste seemed dishonorable. He draped her coat over her slender shoulders before she pulled away and sauntered towards the front door. Its buzzer rang.

"Open." Sven called out, triggering the mechanical click of the lock, allowing the porter to roll in the luggage cart.

"Oh, I see," Celeste said with a nod. "You're bringing her tonight, too?"

"Yes, of course. She's my girlfriend."

The comment rang untrue in his ears, but he didn't care. He liked the way it felt to say it, and he wanted Celeste to hear it.

She paused in the doorway, gazing at the two garment bags hanging from the cart's gold-plated rails.

"Let's hope she's better at influencing you than I was. Eliot Watercross is determined to have you onboard for the Li Long project, even if it means ruining you—just to ensure your participation. Be careful, Sven. I would hate to see you making choices that could hurt you or your career."

Without bidding him farewell, she brushed past the porter and strode out the door. Relieved, Sven watched her indistinct figure disappear into the private elevator before opening the door of a side closet, fishing through his coat's pockets, and retrieving a one hundred dollar bill, which he handed over to the young man.

"Thank you, Cyrus."

"You bet, sir!" the porter exclaimed, stunned by the tip as he exited the penthouse.

Within the privacy of his own personal thoughts, Sven edged towards the first garment bag, fumbling in his search for its zipper. When he finally succeeded, he buzzed opened the sheath and slipped his hand into it, savoring the silky fabric against his palm. He pulled out a swath of the dress and examined it in the light—shimmering iridescence like the interior of a sea shell. *Unconventional and flashy.* Clearly, Ebony was determined to taunt him, but perhaps not as much as his own imagination, as he stopped and wondered how much longer he would have to wait before he would have the opportunity to see Inez wearing it.

Chapter Nine

GROGGY AND DRAINED, INEZ ROLLED over in her bed, still wearing her street clothes from the night before. She peered over at Luna's crib. *Empty*. The comforting scent of homemade pancakes drifted into her bedroom. *Mmm…breakfast with Nana.*

Inez had crept quietly through the house last night, trying hard not to disturb her grandmother or Luna. Safely inside her bedroom, Inez had dumped her heavy purse and breast pump onto the floor, tore off her coat, and plopped onto her untouched bed. She didn't even remember the routine baby cries or the gentle movements of her grandmother, bringing Luna to Inez's bed to nurse. Through her haze of exhaustion, the only thing Inez remembered was her surreal dream—skinny dipping with Sven in the warm, crystal blue waters of the Caribbean, the sensation of freedom and fluidity overwhelming her subconscious. *Such an absurd dream, really*, she thought. Not only was she terrified of the water because she didn't know how to swim, but she certainly had no intention of letting Sven van der Meer see her naked.

Drained by her debilitating yawn, she attempted—and failed—to pull herself completely out of bed. She spread her arms out across her mattress like she was being crucified. *What had she gotten herself into?* Only in her messed-up life could Inez possibly believe that she was being paid to pretend to be the girlfriend of someone as prominent as Sven van der Meer. She exhaled a languishing sigh of surrender before unzipping her jeans and wiggling out of them. Last night's dinner was a faded memory now, but the final moments in Sven's penthouse within his bedroom still lingered with her. She had changed out of the black corset and back into her orange sports bra, but she hadn't removed the French cut G-string. *Why?* Because she liked how it made her feel sexier than just a struggling single mom.

She gazed down at the stack of cash, peeking out from her open purse lying on the floor. *Five thousand dollars*. The money stared back, taunting her. She had successfully escaped from him last night, but it had been surprisingly hard. And although she had refused Sven's advances, she felt like a whore for indulging in her own private fantasies of him this morning. *Touching her leg, kissing her throat, tugging up on her G-string while groping her backside.* Apparently, not even in her dreams could she avoid letting him see her naked. *Weak, weak woman.*

She dragged herself from her bed and lifted the stack of cash out of her purse. Yes, he had been a total prick to her during her "job" interview—if that's what you could even call it. But by the end of the night, it had been hard to resist the sensation that there was actually a meaningful connection between them. There was nothing pretend about the intensity in his gaze—and his touch—which hinted at something more than just forbidden sexual attraction.

And let's be real: Inez was officially on the rebound. It had only been a year since Enzo left for Argentina to renew his visa, leaving her accidentally pregnant and uncertain about their relationship and her future. After all that drama and heartache, she actually *felt* like she wanted to do something to get over Enzo, and yet, sleeping with Sven van der Meer—world famous architect who was paying her five thousand dollars a day to pretend to be his girlfriend—would easily score her a mention in the *Dumb Girl's Almanac* for "Most Desperate Rebound Options." Her life was already complicated enough and the last thing she needed was any more complications—much less engaging in anything illegal like an awkward form of prostitution. *Thank you, but no thank you.*

Simmering blueberries. The seducing aroma of berrylicious compote floated up the staircase and into her bedroom. Her grandmother was sending her a message: *breakfast time.*

She quickly slipped on a fresh T-shirt and yoga pants over her orange sports bra and G-string and slung her breast pump over her shoulder in case Luna wasn't interested in nursing. As she shuttled down the wooden-paneled staircase, she exhaled a sigh of relief. *Home.* Even with its unstable newel post staircase banister, drafty cracked windows, creaking foundation, and dusty floor rugs, she always loved being there in her grandmother's house. It was the same house her own mother had grown up in, and now that she was gone, Inez often took comfort in the framed photographs that lined the fireplace mantel. Her mother's portrait as a child. Her mother and father's wedding photo. Grandpa's vintage portrait as an army serviceman. *All remembrances of family.* Now, life was different and loved ones were gone. But that didn't change the way that Inez felt about living in that house, or her vow to care for her grandmother there for the rest of her life.

Inez immediately spotted Luna swaying in the baby swing, mesmerized by the chirping, rotating bird mobile above her.

"Aww, hi honey. I missed you so much." She swooped the baby into her arms and snuggled her chin against Luna's pink flannel onesie, kissing her soft black hair.

"She's waiting for the boob," Nana called out from the kitchen. "I tried the bottle, but she'll have none of it because she knows you're here. She always knows."

Inez carried Luna into the kitchen and sank down into the chair at the formica and chrome dining table, happily dumping the breast pump onto the floor. Her grandmother scuffed across the linoleum floor in her tattered bunny slippers, seamlessly delivering Inez a fresh cup of coffee before shuffling back to the gas range and flipping the last batch of pancakes like a gourmet chef.

"So what's this new job that has you skulking home in the middle of the night like a robber looking for a bullet between the eyes?" Nana interrogated her. "Your friend, Sarah, pretended like she knew zippo about it."

Inez unclasped her nursing bra, nestled Luna against her breast, and relaxed with her only cup of coffee for the day. It was a familiar morning routine and the main reason why she never accepted jobs that forced her to work in the morning. The morning was their bonding time—her only chance to spend an uninterrupted meal with both her daughter and her grandmother.

"Did I wake you?"

Her grandmother swatted away the insinuation with her spatula. "You know me. I'm a geriatric insomniac. I was already up, listening to reruns of Bonanza." Glaucoma had stolen her grandmother's sight years ago, but nothing could take away her love of watching TV. "Hey, did you know that Richard Simmons just released a new exercise video and it's only nine ninety-nine?"

"Please tell me you didn't buy it, Nana."

"It's called *Sweatin' with the Grannies*," Nana overrode her before placing the plate of pancakes squarely in front of Inez. "And I didn't. But I sure as hell wanted to. He's got seventy-year-old biddies out there on the dance floor, movin' and groovin' their false hips like the Hokey Pokey is their second language. Luna loves Richard Simmons, by the way. I think it's because he sounds like a Muppet."

Nana turned back to the range, stacked up two pancakes onto a second plate, and then took a seat at the table next to Inez. Inez suddenly was reminded of Sven. Just like her grandmother, he moved through his penthouse with a confidence and grace that impressed her. Within the familiarity of their own houses, Inez almost forgot how handicapped they both were by blindness.

As usual, Inez saw the copy of today's *Chicago Tribune* newspaper on the table, awaiting her.

"Which section do you want me to read first, Nana? Arts & Leisure? Or Business & Finance?" Inez stroked Luna's perfect little baby feet and settled into her seat for a long stint of reading aloud.

"Neither," her grandmother replied, shifting her glacial eyes onto Inez. "I want to know why you're being so coy about your new gig."

"Because there's not much to tell, Nana. I go to work. I make money. I come home."

"After midnight?" Nana folded her arms like a schoolteacher searching out the truth. "Are you involved with the mob?"

"You've been watching too many gangster movies, Nana."

"True. But only when you and Luna are gone, and I really want something to put me asleep. What about your clothes?"

"My clothes?"

"Are they making you take off your clothes?"

"Not unless I want to," Inez replied sarcastically. But then she paused, suddenly thinking about Sven and last night.

"Hm." Nana didn't sound convinced. "Are drunk men involved?"

"No, actually it's an incredibly demanding blind man."

"Really?" Nana replied, as if she suddenly approved. "Is he a widower?"

"He's not your type, Nana. Trust me."

"Ah…too old for me, eh?"

"A total grumpmeister."

"Hm. I hate grumpy." Nana stuffed her mouth with pancake and then offered her own solution. "Well, I heard yesterday from Phyllis that the church still has an opening in the office."

"Which barely pays five dollars an hour, Nana."

"And free BINGO on Friday nights," offered Nana, sweetening the deal.

Inez loved her grandmother, but she was clueless about inflation and even worse about managing her own finances. She didn't have the heart to tell her that her disability and social security checks barely paid the monthly bill to heat the entire house, much less anything extra like groceries, clothes, Luna's diapers, and the cost of Nana's glaucoma medication. Her earnings from her job as Sven's faux girlfriend would ensure them financial security for the rest of the year, plus the unexpected opportunity for Inez to spend more time taking care of Luna herself rather than relying on Nana and babysitters.

"Don't worry, Nana. I promise it's all legit and I only have to work three more nights. And I even get to use my *Tribune* factoids to impress my new boss and all his snobby friends."

"Well, see…? There you go. I never believed all this talk about that internet thingy replacing the importance of newspapers." Nana sat back in her seat in triumph. "So this morning, let's go with Arts & Leisure."

Inez flipped through the pages until her phone pinged from beneath the table. *Her breast pump bag*, she thought. She had deposited her phone in one of its pockets during the car ride home and forgot about it completely.

"Sounds like you're being summoned by Señor Grumpmeister."

Inez glanced down at the text.

Good morning, Scarlet.

Inez texted back. *Good morning, Mr. Van der Meer.* Without a beat, he sent back his reply.

My driver said he didn't return you to the same place last night as the apartment building where you returned in the afternoon.

Nosy cadaver, she wrote, shooting back her response. *Your driver needs to mind his own business.*

He usually does, except I asked him if you got home okay.

Inez dropped her phone into her lap. It was easy to be snarky and rude to someone who was spying on her; it was another thing to be snarky and rude to someone who was spying on her because he cared about her safety.

Shifting Luna to nurse on her other side, Inez relayed the text to Nana. "It is my new boss. He's checking that I got home safely last night."

"Oh, how dare he!" Nana cried out.

Inez tuned out her grandmother's sarcasm and watched her phone. Sven's text suddenly appeared. *He said he dropped you off at a mansion in West Ravenswood... If I didn't know you better, I'd think you were cheating on me with another billionaire.*

She marveled at the speed and shrewdness of his response. *Maybe you don't know me as well as you think*? She added the question mark at the last minute to soften the snark.

Definitely true. Which is why you're meeting me at the fart museum. Two o'clock.

Inez died. Clearly, he was using the speech-to-text feature. *You mean, the Art Museum?!?!*

Of course. What better way to better get to know my girlfriend than to visit the place where we first met?

A shiver of anticipation snaked down her spine. "He wants to meet me at the Art Institute," she said aloud.

"Is he some kind of art collector?" Nana sounded intrigued.

"Architect," Inez answered, lost in her own thoughts. There was no hint of cockiness or condescension in his text. There was only a serious attempt to be charming, and perhaps, even a bit romantic. She slouched in her seat, staring at his words, as if they were back in his penthouse, shrouded in darkness except for the intimate, kindling glow of the fireplace.

"Hmm," Nana mused, reading her silence. "Are you sure this architect isn't more than just demanding, blind, and grumpy?"

"Well..." Inez paused, on the verge of confessing everything. "He might also be wealthy, intelligent, and ridiculously...hot."

"Ah ha, BINGO!" Nana clapped her hands like she was the winner of her church's annual Sinners & Saints tournament. "So finally we have it. The real reason why you're working until midnight every night. Your new boss is a stud muffin." Nana stressed "stud muffin" like she was pronouncing a delightfully dirty phrase.

Inez eyed her grandmother's glee. "You've been watching reruns of *The Bachelor*, haven't you?"

Nana shrugged. "Apparently it's more fun watching it than living it."

Inez absorbed her amusement. Sometimes it was just better not to tell Nana anything.

Abruptly, Sven pinged back. *Come on, Miss Sanchez. We can stroll through the Impressionist suite and pretend we're in Giverny. It just might be enjoyable.*

Flustered, she texted back the first random excuse that popped into her mind. *I have nothing to wear and my dollhouse clothes from Ebony are all at your penthouse.*

What are you wearing now?

Considering the truth, Inez dropped her phone again and chewed on her fake fingernail. *Her orange bra and black G-string? No, wrong answer.* Instead, she got creative and texted back. *XL sweat shirt and fat girl sweat pants.*

There was a long pause before his follow-up text buzzed her phone.

Don't worry, Miss Sanchez. I apologize for last night. I won't try to overstep the boundaries again.

Strangely disappointed, Inez re-read his text. Then, he pinged her again.

But since we're meeting at the fart museum and it is our first date, I expect you to wear something appropriate.

Inez rolled her eyes and mocked his words aloud. "He expects me to wear something appropriate."

"Send him that dancing bird animation thingy," Nana replied.

"You mean the emoticon?"

"Yeah, whatever it's called. The one you said flips its middle finger up and down before spinning 360 degrees."

Inez stared at her grandmother, recognizing the origin of her own bad attitude. Instead, she opted for teasing sass and wrote back: *Is a Hello Kitty T-shirt appropriate enough?*

Inez couldn't help it. It was in her genes.

Awaiting his reply, Inez nervously twitched her foot and switched Luna to her other side. The last thing she needed was to meet Sven van der Meer at the fart museum with lopsided boobs.

There was a long pause, as though he was weighing her snarky response and all the possible ways he could assert his authority.

Finally, his text popped onto her screen and she read his words with his smooth Dutch accent in her head.

I trust you, Miss Sanchez. Just make sure you're not wearing sneakers. See you later at two.

Ugh. It felt like her phone had melted in her hands. She re-read the phrase again: *I trust you.* This time, the sound of his sturdy, masculine voice echoed in her mind, raising goose bumps on the nape of her neck. She started to perspire.

He trusted her. But did she trust him? *Ambivalently, yes.* She shifted her glance onto the kitchen clock. It was almost eleven, just enough time to grab a quick shower, change, and jump on the "L" to be downtown by two, but barely enough time to rummage through her closet and string together the sexiest outfit she could find. *Weak, weak woman.*

Chapter Ten

INEZ RUSHED UP THE MUSEUM'S imposing granite staircase, flanked by two bronze lions. She was ten minutes late and completely winded from running all the way from the "L" station. At least she was wearing comfortable Ugg boots and her long black dress coat shielded her legs from the freezing downtown wind. She had settled on a simple black spandex long-sleeved shirt, a short pink A-line skirt and black knit tights. Probably more bohemian artsy than sophisticated chic, but she didn't care. It was the fanciest thing she had worn in months. Besides, the last time she remembered wearing a skirt, she had been tango dancing with Enzo at a midnight *milonga*. And if she was truly on the rebound, it somehow seemed perversely appropriate to don the same clothes she used to wear to turn on her ex-boyfriend.

Inez sprinted to the ticket counter, paid the admission fee, and bounded towards the museum's grand foyer where she spotted him, bathed in sunlight beneath the atrium's glass skylight. His hair glinted with golden highlights and his artic blue dress shirt reflected the rays of sun like an immaculate sheet of ice. Patiently awaiting her arrival, he stared straight ahead, like one of foyer's majestic Roman statues. Like a stern schoolmaster, he had one hand stuffed inside the pocket of his charcoal grey dress pants while balancing his weight against his silver-tipped black cane.

European men, Inez thought. They never could just wear jeans and a T-shirt. Never.

"Sven?" she called out to him.

He angled his head toward her voice as a muted smile spread across his face.

"Finally, you've come to my rescue."

"I hardly doubt that you needed to be rescued."

He slipped his arm into the crook of her own and anchored himself against her body, as if she couldn't be more wrong.

"It took me nearly twenty minutes to navigate from the front entrance of the museum to this spot," he confessed in her ear. "I generally don't do well with unfamiliar open spaces, and I almost stopped to ask a young woman at the information counter to escort me here. But my pride got the best of me."

"Because she was hot, right?"

He smirked and declined to confirm it. "Because I already have an attractive escort."

His compliment made her heart race, but it was his steady gaze and the way that his strong, possessive hand snaked over her own that made her want to look away and pretend he didn't affect her. *She had her own pride to protect.*

"So tell me, Miss Sanchez—assistant curator of nineteenth century European paintings—which part of the museum was it that we first met?"

They stood at the base of the grand foyer staircase, considering their choices: they could walk straight ahead to the Medieval History wing or head upstairs to the second floor with all the European paintings. Inez knew the Art Institute better than any other building in Chicago. She would often come here, whenever she failed a job interview or after Enzo had left for Argentina, and find solace within the bright airy rooms decorated with the most priceless artistic masterpieces in the Western world.

"Well, I told Celeste that we met upstairs in the European paintings, but the truth is that we probably met right in there." She nodded ahead of them. "In the Middle Ages corridor with all the daggers, swords, and body armor. You know, your typical weaponry for drawing blood and inflicting incurable wounds."

"Then in that case," Sven mused, "I think it's best for my own personal safety that we stick to the script and head upstairs to the European paintings."

"Probably. I wouldn't want to scare you away. Not at least until our second date."

He lowered his chin to her ear. "Don't worry. I don't scare easily."

The confidence within his voice and the warmth of his breath against her cheek made her body tingle. While pulling her by the hand behind him, he shifted ahead of her to climb the massive white marble staircase, as if his domineering ego refused to give her the lead.

When they reached the top of the second floor, Sven stopped and stared through the glass doors onto Caillebotte's impressionist masterpiece, *Paris Street, Rainy Day.*

"Maybe it's a good thing that we're heading into the Impressionism wing," he said. "I won't feel so badly about only being able to see blurry brushstrokes."

He popped open the glass door, allowing her to pass through it. She noted how his protective body hovered behind her and how much she tried not to enjoy it.

Within the quiet, airy room surrounded by pristine white walls and soft lighting, she circled past all her favorite paintings by Renoir, Monet, Pissarro, and Degas—imprecisely-painted pastel scenes of country roads and flower girls and lively couples dancing in Parisian gardens. When she glanced back at Sven, she noticed he wasn't looking at the paintings. He was focused on her.

"You're not interested in any of these paintings?" she asked, unnerved by the intensity of his gaze directed at her.

"No, I am," he replied. "But watching you enjoying them is much more interesting because I've seen them all so many times before. Many of them are on loan to the museum from my mother."

"Ah, right. The great van der Meer empire." She tried hard not to sound condescending, but she couldn't help it. If she had even a sliver of his wealth, she would never have to leave Luna in the hands of babysitters again. "What was it like growing up as a kid in one of the wealthiest families in Chicago? Jewelry collections, priceless artifacts, original Monets and Renoirs decorating the walls of all fifteen of your bathrooms?"

He arched his eyebrow. "It was completely normal, I assure you. In Amsterdam, I was just a regular kid from a middle-class family. It wasn't until my mother brought me back here for high school that I realized we had money and that the world cared about our wealth."

"Yeah, your family is definitely a darling of the *Tribune*. I think I've read every article about your mother. She's like the Mother Teresa of the priceless art world."

"Yes, I learned a lot about her myself from those articles as well. She sent us away to attend boarding school in Amsterdam, and I never really knew much about her philanthropy until I was a much older man."

Inez stared at him. "You lived away from your own mother?"

"Of course," he said with a nod and circled the salon like it was his own living room. "She wanted to make sure that Hans and I learned proper Dutch. But for herself, she swore she would never go back to Amsterdam. And she never has."

"But why?" Inez asked, sensing that he was giving her a rare glimpse into his family.

"Because she escaped the city with her own mother during the Second World War when she was only a little girl. Her father stayed behind. He was the one who organized the delivery of their most valuable possessions out of Amsterdam during the Nazis invasion. The paintings and valuable artifacts escaped, but my grandfather did not. Waving good-bye from a train on her way to Paris was the last time my mother ever saw him."

"Ugh." A rock dropped into the pit of her stomach. "That's probably the saddest thing I've heard in a very long time."

They both fell silent and stared at Caillebotte's masterpiece of pedestrians carrying umbrellas and walking down the cobbled streets of Paris, sixty years before two major World Wars would permanently scar the city and the lives of its inhabitants.

"It's a common misconception that bad things don't happen to wealthy people," Sven added. "And sometimes, it's made worse by the irony that money cannot solve every problem. It's true that my mother owns priceless Renoir and Monet paintings. But in exchange, she lost her father forever."

Inez turned away from him. "God, Sven. I thought this was supposed to be a date. You're supposed to woo me, not make me bawl my eyes out." She never expected to be reminded of her own loss of her father and it rattled her tough guarded exterior.

"Woo you?" he said inquisitively, snagging her hand. He drew her into his body, as if he wanted the chance to see her face. "Ah, I see. You mean if we were on a real date, you already would be planning to abandon me in the cafeteria?"

She resisted his embrace, her hand pressing against his chest. But it was hard not to notice the way his muscles flexed beneath his ice blue linen shirt. "Yeah, but not before I made you splurge on some chocolate pudding."

Straining his unpatched eye, he gazed down on her. "Not vanilla?" he curiously asked.

She scrunched up her face. "God no, never. What fool picks vanilla over chocolate?"

He burst into laughter. "I do. Always."

Inez's cheeks tingled with a blush. She tried to pull away from him, but he refused to let her go.

"Come on, then…let's go find a way to woo you with some chocolate pudding."

Chapter Eleven

WITH HIS EYES CLOSED, SVEN SAT in the garden chair, allowing the bright sun to warm his face and illuminate the darkness surrounding him. There was a gentle autumn breeze that rustled the leaves of the miniature dogwood trees lining the perimeter of the museum's courtyard. Whatever expectations he had placed on his life, whatever goals or ambitions he had expected to accomplish and still intended to accomplish, strangely meant nothing to him in that moment. Within the simplicity of the garden and the serenity of its natural beauty, he felt at ease with himself and the world around him. In fact, he felt a sense of tranquility and satisfaction which had evaded him for months, maybe even years.

A surreal sense of peace, he thought, as he opened his unpatched eye and focused on her silence. She sat across from him at the white ornamental table while eating her chocolate pudding like it was the only thing she cared about in the world. Sipping his espresso, he noted how her black hair and black shirt framed her alluring lips and Caribbean profile. He rarely could get a clear glimpse of her, but in that moment, he thought he had seen the full force of her beauty, glinting like a rock in a stream. He dared not to disturb it, or else he risked losing the opportunity to simply admire its glimmer.

"You're staring at me."

Blunt and merciless, as always, he thought and lowered his eyes. But she was right, he had been staring at her. "I'm trying to figure out if you're a simple woman or an extremely complicated one," he finally confessed.

"Complicatedly simple."

He nodded and smiled, accepting her typical straight-forward answer wrapped up inside a sarcastic riddle. "Yes, I'm starting to understand that."

"Really? I'm surprised you're bothering to even think about me at all. I thought you already assessed my worth to the world as average."

She said it playfully, but his jawline flinched and he fell silent. Hearing his own words thrown back at him pained him. But it was a fair punishment and one he was willing to accept.

He cleared his throat, offering his own version of an apology. "Well…I'm fairly certain that I was quite wrong. And so, it certainly makes me wonder what kind of a girl, who is so easily pleased with nothing more than chocolate pudding and a trip to the art museum, would pretend to be my girlfriend for five thousand dollars per day?"

He was fishing and she seemed to sense it.

"Whatever, Sven. Who doesn't need five thousand dollars a day?"

"I'm not sure…perhaps only an extremely complicated woman."

He was testing her, cautiously, carefully, waiting for her to push back and assert that it was none of his business. It clearly wasn't, but somehow the chocolate pudding and courtyard scenery put her less on the defensive.

"You do realize your hypothesis is completely misguided."

He leaned forward against the edge of the cast iron table. "No, I didn't. Please enlighten me."

"There's no such thing as a simple or complicated woman," Inez confirmed. "There are only simple men who think that women are either simple or complicated. Really, we're completely indecipherable—sometimes even to ourselves. Isn't that exactly why women are the most beautiful, wonderful mysterious creatures that men can't get enough of?"

Amused, he gazed at her while finishing off his espresso and wagging his foot. "Yes. That is something on which we are fully in agreement."

"So?" she prodded him, clearly intending to divert his attention from her. "The real question is what painfully boring Sven van der Meer event are you planning on dragging this indecipherable woman to tonight?"

"A reception in my honor," he answered. "The Modern Architecture Society is bestowing upon me a 'Genius Award' for my work on The Spire."

"Hmm," she replied.

He fiddled with his espresso napkin, secretly enjoying how difficult it was to impress her.

"That sounds like another night of heels for me."

"Most certainly."

"And I suppose all your 'friends' are going to be there too, cheering you on."

He nodded. "Unfortunately, yes. My brother and Eliot Watercross are not going to relent until I agree to travel with them to Shanghai at the end of the week, after the public opening of The Spire."

Silence parted them. "I didn't realize you would have to leave at the end of the week," she said, lowering her spoon.

"Yes," he confirmed without looking up at her. "They need me in Shanghai to convince the Chinese officials that they're capable of designing and engineering the tallest towers in the world. The irony, of course, is that they're likely not capable of designing and engineering them *with* me either."

He touched his eyepatch and felt the seeping invasion of bitterness returning to his chest. "And even if I wanted to go in order to prevent them from usurping my name and reputation to claim my achievements as their own, there's certainly no possibility of me traveling to a foreign country these days without assistance."

He peered at her, conveying an unspoken message. *He meant her*. She slowly set her spoon down and stopped eating her pudding. He turned his espresso cup in its saucer in silence.

"How many water lilies were you able to see this morning?"

"Many less than yesterday morning."

The streaming sunlight flickered as the sun passed behind a cloud before shadowing the garden completely.

"More than half of my net worth is tied up in my equity ownership of The Spire, and the rest is tied up in my architectural firm that's half-owned by my brother—a brother who is willing to marry my ex-girlfriend and become business partners with the man who is trying to extort my participation in the Li Long project. And yet..." He stopped, letting his thoughts catch up with the sensation of warmth that glazed his cheek as the sun popped back into the clear blue sky. "I can honestly tell you that the only thing I am thinking about in this moment is how relaxed I feel, lounging here in the garden courtyard of the Art Institute, basking in the sunlight, enjoying my espresso, and sitting across from a very complicated woman who has been made extremely happy through the uncomplicated purchase of a cup of chocolate pudding."

He settled his eyes on her, making it clear that he was not mocking her.

"It is really good chocolate pudding," Inez offered quietly.

He nodded, containing his smile. "So you see...you are right, Miss Sanchez. It's men who are the simple ones because we are so easily enchanted by beautiful mysterious women."

Whatever connection had been uncovered between them last night circled back now. She had rejected his advances and he meant what he had texted her—he wouldn't attempt to intentionally cross the boundaries of their relationship again. But it was hard to deny the inexplicable effect she had over him—how uninhibited and unguarded he felt in her presence, despite the fact that she challenged him at every turn. *She was right*, he finally concluded. She wasn't simple or complicated. She was simply genuine and there was nothing else he needed to uncover about her, except perhaps the reason why she was willing to compromise her own authenticity for the sake of pretending to be his girlfriend.

* * * *

Ugh, she was falling for him. Well, maybe not *him*, exactly. But the romantic beauty and intimate atmosphere of the museum made her wonder if she would ever be able to stand on her own again. His casual posture and cavalier expressions had relaxed her in unexpected ways, and she tried hard not to enjoy the way the sunlight accentuated the golden highlights in his hair or the faint sheen of ice blue in his dress shirt. But it was his smooth accent and gentle voice that truly forced her to fight against the seduction of his physical charm, especially every time her sassy remarks inspired his smile and dimpled his chin. *She had succeeded*, she thought, sadly finishing her chocolate pudding without having another alternative to distract her from the temptation of his piercing gaze. She had succeeded in resisting the connection between them all afternoon until the moment his apology confirmed that he had been wrong about her. She was not as "average" after all—far from it, and although Sven hadn't been the first asshole to make that mistake, he had been the first asshole in a long time to openly admit that she was the exact opposite.

Leaving for Shanghai at the end of the week. That was a revelation. She hadn't expected him to drop that bomb on her and it was a cold reality check—one that confirmed the whisper of relief inside her. *Thank God, thank God, thank God*, she hadn't surrendered herself to his advances last night. The last thing she needed was to get her fragile rebound emotions wrapped up in another foreign playboy who was willing to fuck her in amazing ways before leaving the country without her. Only this time, through the intensity of his gaze and the plea in his voice, it almost seemed as though he wanted her to go with him.

Slowly, as if something subliminal had provoked her, Inez forced herself to break the unity of the moment and shift her attention over Sven's shoulder through the panes of glass encircling the courtyard.

"Oh my God," she heard herself whisper, barely registering the way Sven frowned in response.

She rose from her seat, hoping with all her strength that she was wrong. *Son-of-a-bitch, she had to be wrong—dead wrong.* And yet, she knew with painful certainty that she was not.

She approached the panes of glass and stared through them. Innocent museum patrons strolled down the interior corridors, but her eyes focused on the oversized black and white photograph, mounted on a nearby wall. It was a smeary artistic portrait of a naked young woman, peering out at the viewer with haunting brown eyes. The bottom edge of the portrait cut off just below her breasts, revealing more than it should while her lingering stare evoked an inescapable sensuality that turned the observer into both a perverse voyeur and the object of the woman's affection.

"Inez?" Sven called out to her with concern.

She barely heard him. Hypnotized by dread, she drew open the glass doors, slipped out of the garden courtyard, and drifted into the open gallery, as if she was being drawn inside by a magnetic force.

Unfazed by the anonymous faces and murmuring voices in the gallery, she pushed through the crowd to the center of the room and scanned the white walls. Dozens of oversized, overexposed black and white photographs stared back at her—all of them unmistakable images of *her.* She pivoted on her heel and surveyed each one. To the casual observer, they were a complex series of lyrical portraits—a mysterious, artistic commentary on the relationship between the woman and the photographer. But for her, they were a nostalgic depiction of her entire relationship with Enzo. Memories of their days together as a romantic couple, moments of intimacy and vulnerability captured in frames of exposed celluloid for eternity.

The blood drained out of her face. *So many intimate moments.* Moments at his loft, where they leisurely laid naked for hours on his mohair rug, planning for their future. Moments at his art studio, where she remembered a happier, more carefree version of herself—painting her toenails, showing off her bubble gum, or mimicking his pet goldfish through the concave glass of the fishbowl. Moments in his bed, where he inspired a sexier, racier version of herself—submitting to his seduction after he had set up the camera on a timer and promised only to shoot her face while he pleasured her with only his mouth from below the camera's view. *Private unguarded moments.* But now, they were all slung onto the gallery wall like cold distasteful hunting prizes, proving a camera truly could raid its subject's soul. Especially Enzo's camera.

"*Ciao, bella.* I am very happy to see you."

Inez turned towards his familiar gritty voice as Enzo approached her with his suave tiger gait. He nuzzled her for a kiss on the cheek. She shrugged off his affection and allowed her angry ice queen persona to kick in. Enzo greeted every woman with a "ciao" and a kiss on the cheek, and that was exactly his problem—*he was a Ciao Cheating Bastard.*

Enzo mimicked her scowl on his playboy face. "You don't look so happy to me." He eyed her with devilish charm. He was the only person in the world who relished the moments when she was pissed off at him.

"No, I'm not happy. I'm extremely unhappy, Enzo. What the hell do you think you're doing, putting all of these photographs on public display like this? All of our…memories?" Her voice trailed off as she forced herself into silence, trying to keep herself from causing a scene. Patrons ebbed and flowed through the public gallery, gazing at the photographs like they were worthy of serious contemplation.

She turned away to quell her emotions. Those images represented some of the most private and sacred moments of her life, and now he was exploiting them for his own gain.

"Because you are my muse, *mi amor.* You have always been my inspiration. Even our daughter is living proof of that."

"Which means what? You have the right to put up our pictures for everyone to see?"

"You say that like you are ashamed of them." Enzo reached out and ensnared her hand, drawing her into his personal space. "But I am not ashamed. I told you exactly what I wanted to do with them when I was taking them because they are a declaration of my love. You didn't believe me then. And you still do not believe me."

He pulled her against his smooth chest beneath the open neckline of his white painter's shirt. His sleeves were rolled up past his forearms, showing off his massive tattoo. *The one he got for her*. Two snakes entwined around an apple—a symbol of the Garden of Eden. *His primal, eternal love for her*. She closed her eyes and inhaled his seductive scent. *Painter's varnish and honeycomb candles*. He often burned candles in his studio while working late at night—the same candles he burned whenever they made love in the dark. Her mind flashed to all the times she had lain in his bed, entangled within his strong possessive arms, wanting nothing more in life than her time with him never to end. She caught herself missing him more than she should and attempted to push away.

"No, you're wrong," she whispered. "I did believe you then, but now I know that was a mistake. One I won't make again."

Her mind traveled back to those days. He *had* promised her that he would showcase the photographs in the most prestigious art galleries around the world. But that was when he was still a fledgling student at the School of the Art Institute, and back then, the possibility of viewing his work on display in the museum's temporary exhibits seemed like a romantic compliment, not a voyeuristic peep show.

"Now, I realize, Enzo, you're a bigger whore than I thought."

He swept his lips against her ear. "I love it when you say these things to me. Sarah told me you do not care about me anymore. But I knew she was wrong. You do still care about me—about us—and your anger proves it."

"No—" She pressed back on him, but he secured his forearm around the back of her waist.

"I still remember what made me take every photograph because I remember every single moment that I have spent with you."

She shut her eyes, pained by the familiarity of his touch and the tenderness of his confession.

"Let me go, Enzo." She whispered her plea, but he dismissed it.

"I cannot forget everything you mean to me, just because you have decided not to forgive me. Nothing has changed for me and these photographs prove it."

Without warning, Sven cut between them, flinging Enzo's arm away from her waist with a violent jolt.

"She asked to be let go," he asserted, shoving the full force of his palm against Enzo's torso, driving him backwards.

Enzo recovered and closed the gap again. Sven squared off with him, eye-to-eye—both men equal in height, prowess, and pride. Inez nibbled her fake fingernails. Her ex-boyfriend and her faux boyfriend wanted to murder each other while surrounded by half-naked photos of her. *God, how did her love life suddenly become an epic telenovela?*

She stared at Sven's threatening stance, realizing he intended to start a fight. He tossed down his cane, confirming her fear that he was more than capable of throwing the first punch than she thought he could be.

She reined him in by the arm. "Please don't, Sven. Not here. Not now."

"So this is the new, rich boyfriend?" Enzo said it like an accusation, as if he had already heard all about him. Then, he scanned Sven's business shirt and formal dress pants and sneered at Inez. "I do not believe it."

"Why?" she countered.

"Because you would never date someone who looks like a…dentist."

"Architect, asshole," Inez spat back. "Which means he's a true artist who actually knows how to build something useful rather than a fake artist like you who exploits smutty photographs of his ex-girlfriend without her permission."

"Without her permission?" He scoffed and pointed at the most seductive portrait in the room—a close-up of Inez's face, eyes closed, head resting on a pillow, chin tilted upward as her mouth slackened with arousal.

"Look at your face." Enzo's fierce black eyes flashed as he edged closer to her. "Do you remember how much you begged for me never to stop?"

He drew towards her and touched her cheek. In a brief moment of weakness, she acquiesced before brushing him off.

"*Claro, mi amor.* I had much more than your permission. I had your cooperation. But you do not want to admit it in front of your new boyfriend."

"How much do you want for them?" Sven challenged him.

"How much?" Enzo cocked a glance of interest at Sven.

"I'll pay you for them. All of them. Name your price."

Enzo laughed, his belittling amusement ending in a dry smoker's cough. "They're not for sale and neither is she."

Like his possession, Enzo seized Inez by the wrist and pulled her across an invisible line dividing the two men.

"No—" She fought against him and quickly reclaimed her position next to Sven.

"How much?" Sven insisted, sliding his arm around Inez. "How much for that one?"

Sven pointed at the portrait of Inez's full arousal, as if he sensed it was the photograph she wanted taken down the most.

Enzo ignored him and settled his dark, brooding glare onto Inez. "You are upset at me for what I did while I was in Buenos Aires, but that is unfair because I could have told you nothing. Instead, I told you everything."

Inez rolled her eyes. "Whatever, Enzo. I get that celibacy isn't the coolest thing when you're Rico Suave, tangoing every night. But I didn't expect you to become the Champion of Whoredom either."

"Inez," Enzo warned her, his accent turning sharper and more aggressive. "My life in Argentina has always been separate from my life here. You have always known that. But now, I am back and I want you back with me."

He held out his hand for her—his final attempt to bid her away from Sven.

Their eyes locked. She could feel Sven's possessive grasp, persuading her not to leave his side and she drew strength from it.

Sven slipped out the handkerchief from his pocket and peeled off endless one hundred dollar bills like disposable tissues. "You didn't name a price, so I will name one for you." He flicked them onto the gallery floor like he was dumping garbage at Enzo's feet.

Enzo's jawline flinched as he gazed down at the cash. He was counting the bills, just like Inez. *Eleven, twelve, thirteen, fourteen...Fifteen hundred dollars.*

"Here, even more." Sven tore off five more bills and tossed them into the air like worthless confetti.

Inez locked eyes with Enzo. *Had he meant what he said?* This was the test. Were the photographs an expression of his love for her? Or were they something he would easily sell off to another man for the right price?

Enzo glared back at her. When he seemed certain that she had made her choice, he turned to the seductive portrait of Inez and unhinged it from the wall.

"We were lovers every night of every day." He raised his voice, intentionally loud and brash, garnering attention from every spectator in the gallery before tossing the canvas at Sven who caught it by its rim. "And still, I could never make her come. Maybe you will be luckier with that than me."

"Bastard!" Inez shouted. Sweeping up Sven's cane, Inez charged at him until Sven restrained her into his arms. He cradled her body into his lustful embrace and kissed her with a ferocity that tamed every angry impulse flaring inside her. His wet hot tongue and supple lips entwined with her own, arousing the deepest part of her soul with burning, yearning desire. It wasn't just a kiss—it was a promise of more to come if she would have him.

As swiftly as Sven leaned her back for his kiss, he swept her up to face the man who had lost what he had gained.

"I already have been lucky," Sven punctuated, grazing his thumb over Inez's lower lip. "Many times over. And so has she."

Chapter Twelve

SVEN'S SOFT ACCENT INTERRUPTED her thoughts. "You are unusually quiet." She had been gazing out the window of his Rolls Royce at the children frolicking through the puddles of the Crown Fountain in Millennium Park. The children screamed with glee and darted merrily across the black granite pavement, glazed with water. *So happy and carefree.* It was one of those magical autumn afternoons, deceptively warm and sunny, as if the twilight chill in the air was nothing more than a cruel joke rather than the inevitability of colder weather. Inez had lived in Chicago her whole life, and never once had she pranced through the fountain's pooling waters like those children, barefoot and unrestrained while anxiously waiting at the base of the looming black towers for the cascading swell to crash down upon them.

"I don't have much to say." She shrugged because it was the truth. She didn't feel like talking after what had happened at the museum, and the last thing she wanted to talk about was Enzo.

"I should apologize to you…" Sven said, then paused.

Inez had only known him for two short days, and it was one of the few times she had truly seen him hesitate before speaking his mind.

"Apologize for what?"

"For what happened in the gallery. I took…liberties that I shouldn't have."

Inez peered out her window again. She knew what he meant, but she wanted to avoid the whole awkward discussion.

"I don't know what came over me. I suppose I became jealous."

"Jealous?" Inez's voice raised slightly in surprise. "Of what?"

"Of you, of course."

He cleared his throat and smoothed down the imaginary wrinkle in his shale grey dress pants. Silence lingered between them. "I still need your assistance this week, and I can't afford an ex-boyfriend coming into the picture and sweeping you away from me."

"There's no sweeping me away," Inez replied, nipping at her fingernail. "Trust me, Sven. I'm not a princess looking for my Prince Charming, and I don't believe in fairy tales anymore, so no one is going to be sweeping me anywhere. Especially not Enzo."

Her gaze fell onto the portrait of her—the one that he had bought for two thousand dollars.

"You realize you overpaid for that?" She nodded at the portrait, hiding the true pain it caused her to have to look at it.

"No," he countered, hoisting the canvas onto his lap and turning it towards her like a mirror. "I was willing to pay even more it—for all of them."

She dropped her fingernail from her mouth, realizing she was gnawing at it like a squirrel. "What are you going to do with it?"

"What would you like me to do with it?"

She stared at it, filled with rage and resentment. "Burn it."

"*Tsk,*" he clucked, as if her suggestion was unfathomable. "You are angry. I understand. But despite the fact that your ex-boyfriend is an opportunistic bastard, he does have an eye for lovely things."

"He used me, Sven. You're a man. You wouldn't understand."

"I understand you better than you think. You feel betrayed," he replied, letting her know that he recognized her pain. "But are you really so angry about the fact that your ex-boyfriend displayed naked pictures of you to the public without your permission? Or is it because you are still in love with him?"

His question echoed her question—the same one she posed to him after their dinner with Celeste.

She ignored his insinuation like it was a distasteful joke and glanced back out the window, avoiding his gaze. "Don't worry, Sven. I'm not going to quit on you and go back to hooking up with Enzo. If that's what you're afraid of."

He gazed at her sideways, as if he was deciphering the meaning of 'hooking up'.

"No, I'm not afraid of that. But I am afraid that you may choose not to accompany me tonight."

"Why?"

"Because Ebony has sent over your gown, and I am afraid that you are going to hate it."

She studied his smile, sly and baiting. "More ridiculous lingerie?"

He nodded. "Perhaps."

"And heels?"

"A certainty."

"You're right. I hate it already."

He grinned as their fleeting amusement evaporated into silence. Lowering his voice, he made a confession. "Inez…tonight is very important for me and my career, but there's no way I can attend it alone. There will be too many unfamiliar faces and wide, open spaces to navigate…" He paused, as if he wanted to ensure that she understood him. "There will be many real estate developers and investors there. And many of them are going to want to discuss future commissions. Normally, it would be one of the highlights of my career. But these days, it feels like I'm attending my own funeral, and I am certain that I would not be able to face it without you there to assist me."

She stared at him—the sharp angles of his profile, his threatening eyepatch, his crisp ice blue dress shirt—but she only focused on the rare whisper of vulnerability in his tone because it disarmed her.

"I understand," she whispered, wondering if she was imagining the sensation of his fingertips touching her own. She dared not look down to confirm the truth.

Suddenly, an unmistakable squeal of delight burst through the window pane.

"The children at the fountain," she clarified, noting how he squinted hard to ascertain the source of the noise.

"Crown Fountain?"

"Yeah."

"I know the architecture firm who executed its design. They won the commission over Hans and me."

"Really, why?"

"Because I wanted to erect a solar tower for recharging cell phones on that site rather than a fountain for screaming little children."

He unclipped his seat belt and leaned over her lap, reaching for the button to lower her window. Shrieks of excitement flowed into the car like an uncontrollable breeze.

"A solar tower for re-charging cell phones? That would have been vomit-worthy." Inez contemplated the horror of what had barely been avoided.

"Well, I never understood the trite proposition for another public fountain. Until now..." He closed his eyes, taking in the shrill sound of jubilation. Turning his attention to his driver, he said, "James, stop here please."

"Here, sir?" James asked. Inez shared his concern. It was rush hour traffic on Michigan Avenue and if they stopped, they would be blocking an entire lane.

"Here," Sven insisted to his driver who immediately obeyed him and pulled to the curb.

"Sven, what are we doing?"

"We're going to have some fun."

"Fun?"

"Yes, fun," he said before flinging open his door.

Inez cringed as the blurry streaks of speeding yellow taxis swerved and blared their horns. Disappearing around the rear of the vehicle, Sven re-appeared on Inez's side.

"You're kind of scaring me, Sven," she half-heartedly joked while peering out at him through her window. There was ferocity in his face. She recognized that look—it was stern with determination.

He didn't respond with words. Instead, he whipped open her door and grabbed her by the hand, dragging her out of the car with a physical strength that startled her.

"Go home, James," he called out to his driver. "We'll walk back to the penthouse."

James raised his hand in acknowledgement. Sven slammed the door and Inez watched the Rolls Royce tear away from the curb. Taxi horns bleated as it crossed into their lanes.

He took up her hand into his own and squinted past the streaming sunlight. "Let's go find some fun."

"You're acting like it's some kind of treasure hunt. Finding the fun."

"Yes, perhaps it is. But if we both fail to find it, then we'll know there's no hope for us."

"I'm pretty sure I already know the answer to that."

"Come on," he said with an encouraging shake of her hand.

"Okay, where?" She sighed, supremely annoyed that they were actually out of the car in the middle of Millennium Park rather than lazily cruising through traffic in his Rolls Royce. His hand felt like an anchor, willing to drown her at the bottom of the sea.

"Surprise me." He said it like a challenge—for both of them.

She acquiesced and led them towards the center plaza between a pair of towering glass brick fountains. Surreal video images of local residents flashed across their flat-paneled walls like a football Jumbotron,

"My favorite is when they pretend to shoot water out of their mouth, and it actually happens." Inez stared up at the goofy video image of a woman puckering her lips and blowing up her cheeks like a fish before a stream of water jetted out of her mouth. The cannon blast struck a trio of unsuspecting teenage girls who had been trailing their bare feet through the shallow pool of water. Completely drenched, the girls shrieked and shivered, pointing up at the offender who had changed to a video image of a young boy, smiling with the innocence of childhood, like he could do no harm.

"See? That's how you can tell who the tourists are," Inez snarked as her eyes lingered on the three girls.

She suddenly realized Sven had let go of her hand, abandoning her. She glanced back over her shoulder and spotted him on the edge of the pooling water.

"What are you doing?"

“I’m taking off my shoes.” He had removed both his dress shoes and socks, like it was the most natural thing in the world.

“Why?” she insisted.

“Because they are ten thousand dollar Crivellaro leather, and I’d rather not ruin them in the water.”

Inez watched him meticulously roll the hem of his dress pants up to his knees. “I’m not certain whether or not I’m more horrified that you’re wearing ten thousand dollar shoes or that you’re willing to make yourself look like a Dutch milk boy.”

He performed a surprisingly authentic barn jig, just to spite her.

She looked away, hiding her smile. “This isn’t fun, Sven. This is ridiculous.”

He submerged his foot into the pooling water, enduring the chill. “It doesn’t feel ridiculous. It feels…liberating.” He inhaled and swept his gaze across the skyscrapers along Michigan Avenue. “In fact, I feel like I’m seeing more clearly than I have all week. Come on. Your turn now.” He held out his hand to coax her in.

“Me? No, no way. This is how people get toe fungus, Sven.”

“You honestly expect me to believe that you have no desire to take off your shoes and wade through this water?”

“No, none.”

“I think you’re afraid to show me your bare feet. What’s the matter, Miss Sanchez? Is that why you despise heels so much? Do you have fat feet and stubby little toes?”

“I can’t believe you’re actually mocking my feet.”

He hiked his cuffed pants higher and performed his ridiculous jig again.

Inez crossed her arms and glared at him. “If you keep doing that, I’m going to pretend I don’t know you.”

“I think you’re secretly jealous that I’m having f-u-n and you’re not.”

“News flash, Sven… if you think *this* is the epitome of fun, clearly you’ve been hanging out with the wrong people for far too long.”

“Perhaps.” He splashed through the water with broad, scuba fin steps, intentionally circling closer and closer to her. “But I’m fairly certain that the epitome of fun is making you shriek like that.”

He nodded over at a little girl who wailed with ear-piercing glee. The cascading waterfall had just swelled over the top of the two-story tower and crashed down upon her.

“Our turn.” Without warning, he swept Inez into his arms and wrestled her like a flailing kite to the base of the fountain.

“No, please, Sven…Don’t!” But it was too late. Bracing her in his arms, he forced her against the side of the tower before a cresting swell of water surged over its top and shattered like a pane of glass, dousing them completely.

A shriek escaped Inez's throat before she recognized the sound of her own horror. Then, she recognized the sound of Sven's merciless laughter, enjoying every minute of it.

She peered through her black sodden bangs, plastered against her eyes, barely able to comprehend the sight of Sven, adjusting his black eyepatch and running his hand through his own drenched, disheveled hair.

"I—I—can-not—be-e-e-lieve you just di-i-iii-d that."

She was freezing and stuttering, and the only thing she could think about was the fact that every part of her body was soaked, right down to her panties.

He gazed at her with an obnoxious cocky grin. "Are we having fun yet?"

Shell-shocked, she pressed herself against his own waterlogged shirt. His hard chest shook with laughter as his strong, protective arm wrapped around her body and nudged her away from the gaggle of squealing children who had lined up behind them, signaling the next assault was about to crash upon them.

"Come on," he encouraged her, hugging her shivering body and trying to conceal his own sadistic amusement. "Let's go back to my penthouse and get you undressed."

Chapter Thirteen

UNDRESSED. There she was again, staring at her naked reflection in Sven's guest bathroom, trying hard not to think about the fact that he was downstairs doing exactly the same thing. She gazed into the mirror, thickening her long lashes with mascara.

Was he thinking about her the way that she was thinking about him?

She dropped her mascara wand against the countertop. *God, she hoped not or else she was freaking doomed. Doomed.*

During her shower, she had let the scorching stream of water flow over her hair and body, reflecting on how he had held her under the fountain's cascading waterfall, and how afterwards, he had embraced her when she was completely at his mercy.

Strong. Possessive. Dominant. He always knew what he wanted and exactly how to get it. *That stunt at Crown Fountain?* Had anyone else attempted that, she would have kicked him in the balls. But with Sven, she caved like a helpless little kitten—a helpless little kitten willing to lick milk from the palm of his hand.

Why was she so willing to submit to him? Was it simply because he was paying her?

"Yes," she resolutely answered, looking at her own reflection in the mirror while applying bright "Fuck Me Now" red lipstick. "Of course it was." It was five freaking thousand dollars and she was in desperate need of every cent. There was only one snag in that certainty, one complication that she had firmly dismissed from her mind until now—the kiss. *The kiss*, she exhaled, shaking off the nagging admission that her submission to him was no longer just about the money

He had apologized for the kiss, but she secretly wished he hadn't. It had stunned her—the way his wet tongue had invaded her mouth and lapped her own with a domineering urgency that wasn't easily refused. In an instant, his kiss tamed her rage and overwhelmed her defenses with an unexpected flood of sensuality and passion. *The expensive hand-woven fabric of his dress shirt.* She remembered the sensation of it beneath her fingertips as she clung to his strong biceps, willingly accepting his mouth over hers. The memory of his impassioned kiss still haunted her private fantasies, taunting her with a tingling yearning for more.

Clearly, it had all been for show—a juvenile competition of machismo between two egomaniacs. She was just the consolation prize, except for the fact that Sven's kiss made her feel like more than just a consolation prize. In those confusing, unexpected seconds of intimacy between them, a rush of heat and fire burned within her, ignited by the white hot strokes of his lusty tongue, arousing her with a fury that claimed her entire body and reminded her of how much she missed losing herself in the safety and security of a man's possessive embrace.

Ugh, she groaned.

Yes, his kiss was undeniably hot. *Oh. So. Very. Hot.* And yes, she was on the rebound after breaking up with Enzo. But five thousand Gs was worth more to her than giving in to her fleeting sensations of attraction. They barely knew each other, and technically, neither one of them could afford one night of indiscretion. He was her boss who needed a trusted chaperone, not the hassles and commitment of a real girlfriend. And she was only there for the money because she had her daughter and grandmother to support. If she gave in to his advances, she would end up being just another conquest under his belt.

Scrunching up a tissue between her fingers, she blotted her "Fuck Me Now" red lipstick into a more sensual "tease, but don't touch" hue. She had just dumped a cheating Ciao Bastard; she didn't need to trade that in for a surly, overpowering Dutch Master & Commander.

Sweeping up her hair into a sophisticated French twist, she reminded herself of why she was there—*five thousand dollars*. Five thousand dollars was the reason she had endured Sven's smarmy condescension during their interview. Five thousand dollars was the reason why she didn't bail after being mocked and fitted like a toy doll at Ebony's studio. Five thousand dollars was the reason why she was willing to dress up again like a high-class call girl and prepare for another night of charades.

She suddenly picked up her lipstick and reapplied it.

Five thousand dollars was more money than she could possibly afford to turn down and she knew exactly why he was paying her and what he needed from her. She wasn't there to have sex with him. She was there to support his attempts to appear as strong and invincible as he asserted himself to be—at least until the opening of The Spire at the end of the week.

And then, after that? After that, he would likely travel to Shanghai to deal with the Li Long melodrama and she would go back to her own life. Except this time, everything would be different because she'd have enough money to stop worrying constantly about how she was going to take care of

Luna and Nana. She had been afforded enough money to keep it all going for at least six more months. Sven's assignment to pretend to be his girlfriend had granted her at least six more months of financial security. And for that, she would be eternally grateful to him, even if he was a fucking asshole who made her wear high heels and nearly drowned her under the waterfall of Crown Tower.

A fucking asshole, she thought, zipping up her makeup bag. A fucking asshole who was also an insanely amazing kisser.

She sighed. Consumed by a fleeting moment of weakness, she indulged in the thought of what it would be like to be his real girlfriend. *Dreadful*, she muttered. Endless galas and banquets, uptight business dinners with annoyingly snotty guests, and ridiculous underwear ensembles like this one. She held up the new lingerie that Ebony had sent over for tonight's gown. Beneath the vanity's overhead lights, the strapless bra's ruby sequins and puffy ruffles glowed siren red. *Was it a freaking bra or a Moulin Rouge costume?*

She had twenty minutes to pump each breast—just enough time to drain the sting, but not enough time to reduce her cup size. Inhaling deeply, she wrapped the bra around her torso and cinched it, its bra cups barely supporting her heavy cleavage. She slipped on the matching scarlet panties, its shimmering satin backside trimmed with ruffles. *Moulin Rouge costume, definitely.* She eyed the silvery slinky gown hanging from the door hook. When she first saw it, she knew she was in trouble. Too many holes, not enough fabric. Now, she understood why. Tonight's gown was more about what could be seen, and less about what couldn't.

Five thousand dollars. It was just enough to make it all worth it, but barely.

She removed the dress from the hook and slipped it over her head. It poured over her shoulders like a flowing drink of mercury. *Lethal*. Its classic sleeveless bodice and floor-length hemline inspired a sigh of relief, but its halter-top neckline revealed the ruffled trim of her bra cups and the contour of her cleavage like a flirtatious tease. Then, she paused and frowned, slowly processing why she felt a drafty breeze washing cool air across her spine.

Twisting her head past her shoulder, she viewed her back in the mirror, spotting exactly what she had dreaded: an open back design, deliberately exposing the ruffles of her panties before closing together like a peep show curtain, just below her tailbone. And what was worse, it exposed her tattoo—a Japanese cherry blossom. *Ruffle panties and a conspicuous tatt*? *What the hell was Sven going to say*? She had no idea. But one thing suddenly felt certain: the universe was out to punish her—and cruelly.

She glanced at the clock and gathered up the heels—iridescent silver sandals, encrusted in rhinestones with an ankle zipper and five-inch stiletto—most certainly meant to keep her hemline from dragging across the floor, assuming she could even walk in them.

Rushing down the spiral staircase, she headed for Sven's bedroom. She had procrastinated in the shower longer than she expected and had taken extra time to pump and apply her makeup. Now she was certain he was impatiently waiting for her. She wound through the maze of obstacles in his penthouse—high-back chairs, pedestal tables, polished granite sculptures, even a free-standing cylindrical aquarium—all positioned in strategic points to help Sven navigate through the expansive loft. Without calling out to him, she hurried down the corridor leading into the master suite.

She abruptly stopped in her tracks the moment she saw him standing there—completely naked, fresh from his shower. She froze and held her breath, clutching her high heels against her chest, realizing her bare feet hadn't made a sound along the black marble floor. He didn't look up at her or even seem to notice her at all. *He's partially blind*, she reminded herself, like a bull in the corrida, unable to see the matador from a long distance, but spurred to charge by even the slightest wave of the flag.

She *had* thought about calling out to him. A simple, *Sven?*—would have been even more than enough to announce her entrance and give him fair warning. But she hadn't. Motionless, she stared at him with a vexing mixture of embarrassment and admiration. It wasn't like she was a curious virgin who hadn't seen plenty of naked men—and their cocks. But she certainly hadn't seen many men as perfectly sculpted as *that*...not even Enzo was built like a Roman warrior, someone who would and could kill with his own bare hands if he wanted to.

It had all been a façade, she realized. All of Sven's fancy European suits and metrosexual designer dress shirts hid the fierce lines of his aggressive build—muscular biceps, hard chiseled pecs, tapered waist—all culminating in a combative stance that silenced her sassiness into submission.

Protector. It was the first word that flashed through her mind before she dared to lower her gaze and take in the full contour of his masculinity. It was a voyeuristic indulgence that *should* have filled her with shame. But she wasn't ashamed; she was distracted by the slow pricking ache between her legs and the tingle in her breasts. Not only was she taking in the full view of his erection, firm and virile like an invitation, but she suddenly understood why he was primed and steady, and that reason was because of the portrait of her.

He had placed Enzo's portrait of her atop his La Brea black vertical dresser, and now he stood directly in front of it, studying the details of her expression with his unpatched eye. *Her expression of her arousal.* His naked body glistened with water droplets, his hair was slick and dark, and everything else about him signaled that he was lost in his own private spiral of voyeuristic thoughts.

Thoughts about her?

She quickly turned away and crept back down the corridor. Out of sight, she pressed herself against the mosaic tiled wall and cradled her shoes, listening for a sign that he had sensed her exit. When there was only silence, she deliberately exhaled to calm her racing heart before calling out into the air.

"Sven?" She touched her throat. The sound of her own voice, uncertain and meager, surprised her. It was supposed to be a warning shot, announcing her arrival, but it quivered with insecurity. She paused to slip on her heels while counting to ten before rounding the corner into his bedroom. This time, a plush white bath towel was draped around his waist as he stared at her with his usual punishing glare.

Her cheeks flushed and she perspired beneath her panties. She knew she was reading too much into his stern, callous gaze. *Clearly, he was struggling to see her from the distance.* She drew closer to him and watched his expression soften as he settled his unpatched eye upon her.

Their eyes locked and she stopped a short distance from him. Beads of water dripped down his chest and his towel barely clung to his waist.

"So there's good news and bad news..." She trailed off into uncomfortable silence, trying to ignore the fact that she had seen exactly what was under that towel.

His gaze snaked down her chin and dropped down her neckline, tracing the glinting sequined trim of her bra cups peeking out beneath the gown's plunging halter top.

"The good news is that you look stunning." He said it like an uncontrollable confession and pushed closer to her.

Her mind went blank as his firm, sleek pecs twitched involuntarily while his unwavering green gaze seized upon her lips.

She was suddenly self-conscious. *Too much "Fuck Me Now" red. Too damn much.*

"Yes, it's definitely an amazing gown," she stuttered, feeling her heart racing out of her chest. "So yeah...that's the good news." She paused and held her ground, attempting to regain her confidence under the weight of his scrutinizing gaze. "But the bad news is that Ebony forgot to send over its back."

Pivoting her waist, she glanced over her shoulder and displayed the gown's sensual opening to him—ruffled panties and all. It was a juvenile attempt to make a joke out of it. *Really, ruffled panties? Was she a piñata? Har har har...* Somehow, it felt better to openly mock it from the get-go rather than pretend it didn't exist.

But she lost her confidence when she only heard disapproving silence.

"I think Ebony knows exactly what she's doing," he finally said flatly and reached out to outline her cherry blossom tattoo with the edge of his fingernail. "She loves tattoos, but she knows that I despise them." His fingertip grazed her hip with a sensuality that shivered down her spine. "She's trying to prove a point because yours is quite... exceptional."

Inez shut her eyes with an inaudible sigh, savoring the way he said the word—*exceptional.* How long would she allow him to touch her before pulling away? She started to count…

"And I've never seen one with pink and white ink, and certainly, never one inked with such…delicacy."

"I got it the first time I visited Argentina with…" She stopped, completely uninterested in uttering Enzo's name as Sven's fingernail circled the full length of her cherry blossom.

The answer was ten, she thought, exhaling her shallow breath. She would allow him to touch her for ten seconds. Ten panty-dampening seconds before she rotated away and forced herself to face him.

The muscles along his jawline flinched, like a signal he wasn't ready for her to break their physical connection. His smooth chest, glistening with water droplets, edged closer to her. He adjusted his eyepatch with one hand while his wandering gaze drifted down onto her mouth as if he intended to kiss her. *Had he known she had seen him earlier? Had he, perhaps, even allowed it?*

She needed a distraction—or perhaps, an intervention.

"Did Ebony send ruffled panties for you to wear tonight, too?" she deadpanned.

It worked.

He broke into an uncharacteristic smile and nodded at the open garment bag lying on the bed. "Fortunately, no. Just a shirt, suit, and tie. Nothing nearly as worthy of viewing as your ruffles."

He gathered up the extra towel from the mattress and whipped it across his shoulder and hair. It cracked like a whip and she flinched as his muscles flexed. Steady and provocative, he squared his body towards her as he slipped on a pair of black briefs beneath his towel before tossing it away like it was a nuisance. She watched him staring at her, conspicuously bulging through his tight knit briefs without any hint of modesty.

Whatever his intentions, getting dressed wasn't one of them.

"Aren't we going to be late?" She deliberately asked, feeling less certain about her ability to avoid his advances than she had last night.

"Yes," he nodded. "But I'm the guest of honor. So I assume they'll wait for us."

He watched her, as if he was waiting for a signal that would let him know what she wanted from him. What did she want from him? Five thousand dollars? Or for him to pull her into his embrace again and kiss her like he had kissed her at the museum?

He edged closer, closing the gap between them. She had approximately five seconds to decide, or he was going to decide for her.

"Is there an agenda for tonight?" She intended to remind them both of their obligations.

He responded by reaching out and securing a wayward strand of hair behind her ear, as if for a moment they were a real couple.

"I need you to help me find a way to navigate the night so I can maintain my career despite almost certainly going blind." He sounded grim.

She closed her eyes, taking in both his words and his tender touch. "I was hoping you'd say something more like… have a few cocktails and dance the night away to *Journey* cover tunes."

He smirked. "Unfortunately, no. There likely won't be any opportunity for dancing tonight. And even less chance for fun."

She tried to contain her frown. "Really? Such a shame since we worked so hard at finding it today."

"Yes." He nodded, his bare chest gleaming with perfection.

"Not even some bad karaoke?"

"Extremely unlikely."

"I thought you were the guest of honor. Can't you request these things?"

She turned away to catch her breath. The tension between them was oppressive, and she simply wasn't strong enough to endure it. *Weak, weak woman.*

"Apparently, I can't even request a shirt from my tailor that I can button up myself."

He moved to the bed, taking off the starched shale grey shirt from its hanger. Passing his long arms through each sleeve, he let the cuffs dangle past his wrists before moving to her again.

She eyed the shirt, appreciative of the distraction. "It looks fairly normal to me. What's the problem this time?"

"The buttons," he replied, deeply annoyed. "They don't feel normal and I can't get them through the buttonholes."

Inez investigated the problem. "That's because they're not ordinary buttons, Sven. They're pearls."

He arched an eyebrow. "Really? Tahitian South Sea or Golden South Sea?"

"You ask that question like you seriously expect me to know the answer."

He straightened his posture, allowing her to slip each pearl button through the hole. "What color are they?"

"Black. Shining. Freaking gorgeous."

Satisfied, he nodded. "Tahitian South Sea pearls. And I suspect Ebony chose them to complement the sheen of your gown."

His words floated off his lips and down her neck as she worked down towards his waistline. "Less rare and precious than white or golden South Sea pearls, but naturally more exotic."

Bent forward, she offered him an unobstructed view of her cleavage, and they both knew it. "Exotic is overrated," she replied, concentrating on the final buttonhole. "Everyone prefers vanilla ice cream over peppermint swirl. Including you."

"I'm not sure about peppermint swirl. But I think today you convinced me to give chocolate a chance."

She rose and adjusted his straight point collar. "Is that why you were willing to fight my ex-boyfriend even though you're basically blind?"

He slowly lowered her hands from his collar and clasped them into his own. "I was reasonably sure that I would land the first punch."

"Reasonably sure?"

"Yes." He nodded with a sly smile. "After that, I assumed I'd have the advantage of a dirtier technique."

"Head lock?" she teased.

"Vengeful ex-girlfriend with vampire fingernails." He lifted up her hand to display her long, fake fingernails. "I'm fairly certain you would have found a way to come to my rescue."

He held her hands and gazed at her longer than necessary. *Helpless little kitten*. She needed an out.

"I don't think I would have rescued you if I knew a trophy was going to end up on display in your bedroom." She nodded at the portrait propped up on his dresser.

He eyed her, as if he recognized the bitterness in her voice. "It's intended as a compliment to you, not to him."

"It feels more like a punishment, Sven."

He angled his head like he had heard something unexpected in her answer. "You're genuinely upset that I refused your request to destroy it?"

"Yes," she reluctantly answered.

"Why?" he probed.

She glanced at the photo and bit on her acrylic fingernail. She studied her image, the way her head dropped back in ecstasy. Her eyes were shut, her mouth forming a perfect "O". She didn't even recognize herself.

"Because I hate that portrait. It's a total lie." She had betrayed more than she had intended. And he knew it.

"Inez?" he said, reading her uncharacteristic silence. "Is it because what he said is true?"

He meant about Enzo, she thought. What Enzo had said about her never being able to come.

"Really, does it even matter?"

"No," he offered, softening his voice, sensing the fragility within her own. "Except that it would be a shame, if it were true."

"Whatever, Sven," she shrugged, feigning indifference. "Men believe whatever they want to believe about the women they're sleeping with. It's all just a game to them." *Bitterness and cynicism*. It filled her like poison and it seeped out in her reply.

"But it's not a game for you, is it?" He pushed closer, his unpatched eye fixing on her, searching out the cure for her pain.

"No," she confessed, not understanding why she yearned to reveal herself to him—that she wasn't as badass and unbreakable as she pretended to be.

In a gesture of tenderness, he gently swiped his thumb across her trembling lower lip. She was struggling not to cry, not to release the swell of gut-wrenching heartache that she refused to feel. He tamed it with his perceptive silence and unyielding gaze.

She closed her eyes, willingly submitting herself to whatever happened next. But he did not take advantage of her moment of weakness. When his fingertips deliberately pulled away from her chin, she sighed—not with relief but with disappointment.

"Okay," he conceded. "You win. I will get rid of it. But not until tomorrow. I did pay two thousand dollars for it so I am entitled to enjoy it for at least one night."

She challenged him with a glare. "Define the word,'enjoy'?"

Attractive and commanding in his silver hand-spun shirt and tight black boxer briefs, he flashed her a smile. "I'd rather not."

She rolled her eyes. *Perv.*

"Okay, fine, whatever. One night. And then, after that, we'll break out the permanent black markers, right?"

He pulled up his suit pants and tucked the folds of his shirt neatly into the pleated beltless waistband as if he had done it a thousand times before. "And what? Deface it?" His voice rose in horror.

"Yeah, with a Groucho Marx moustache. And scissors. Definitely scissors."

He sighed, slipping on his silver-spun grey suit jacket. "Whatever you would like. You're the one wearing the ruffled panties tonight. You are in charge."

"I'm serious, Sven. You get one night with it. Then it's gone."

He edged towards her. "And I am serious as well. One night. I promise you."

The sound of his firm resolve disarmed her. It was hard to believe that she had just negotiated him out of something that had cost two thousand dollars.

"Okay, great. Deal." She held out her hand to shake on it.

"Deal," he said, grasping her hand and unexpectedly drawing her into his body. Her eyes fixed on his lips, like the moment he had kissed her in the gallery, and she gasped as his mouth bypassed her own and whispered against her ear.

"Now, I need a promise from you."

She closed her eyes, savoring the scent of his aftershave—crisp and cool like the Arctic. Her fingertips pressed against the strength of his chest underneath his sleek suit, perfectly tailored with its French seams and slim fit, as if she was relinquishing every last bit of herself to him. If he requested her to unclasp her gown's halter neck and peel down its straps, she was certain now would be the moment she would give into him. If he lowered his chin against her neck and kissed the hollow of her throat, she would sigh and relax into his embrace. If he nestled his lips between her breasts and feathered his hot whispering breath across their arcs, she would drop her head back and allow him every inch of her. If he stripped down her bra cups with his fearless hand and exposed her nipples to his suckling mouth, she would moan and willingly submit herself completely to him.

"I need you tonight, Inez," he confessed, the lilt of his accent, smooth and soothing, against her ear. "More than you realize."

Her defenses melted away as his nose touched against the tender part of her lobe. "Promise me you'll never leave my side."

"Of course," she whispered, feeling his hard chest flexing under her fingertips. She expected him to release her, but her answer didn't satisfy him.

"Promise me."

Drawing her even tighter against his body, she melded into him like his lover, her breasts against his pecs, his pelvis square against her own tingling aching need.

"Yes, Sven. I understand," she replied, turning her chin upwards to meet his lips. "I promise."

"Good." He nodded, peering past his eyepatch at her, like he had done so many times before. Stern. Rigid. Punishing.

"It's going to be a long, arduous night, Miss Sanchez. I am completely counting on it."

Chapter Fourteen

SVEN EXHALED—DEEPLY, DELIBERATELY—as the limousine coasted to the curb. He had been lost in thought the entire drive to Navy Pier, considering all the challenges he had yet to face that evening. Tonight's gala was one of the most prestigious architectural events of the year and he was the guest of honor. He would be receiving an award for designing one of the most daring and controversial structures in Chicago—The Spire. He would be expected to flawlessly navigate the ballroom of guests with wit, charm, and confidence. There would be many powerful men and women who expected him to speak about his work on The Spire and why it was one of the most masterful architectural achievements of the twenty-first century. They would inquire about his future plans for accepting more commissions, and of course, about his involvement in the Li Long Towers.

But no matter how many times Sven turned all the scenarios of glory and admiration about in his mind, they all seemed like an impossible charade. He was going blind, and there was no indication that he was getting any better—only worse. And what would he be able to accomplish without his eyesight?

Nothing.

It was always the same bleak reply, haunting him like a ghost hovering over his anxious soul. What would he be capable of without his eyesight?

Absolutely nothing.

Blindness would render him incapacitated and useless in a world where he had once reigned like a prince, and that looming prospect filled him with resentment and dread. There had been many sleepless nights—more than he cared to admit—that he had lain awake, endlessly pondering his uncertain future. Without his eyesight, it would be impossible for him to maintain his status as a world-renowned architect. Once it was publicly known that he was completely blind, The Spire would be not only his most celebrated commission, but it would also be his final one.

And to make matters worse, he was going to lose his equity ownership of it. As the majority shareholder, Eliot Watercross planned to force the sale of The Spire to Harvey Zale in exchange for the Li Long construction contracts. Without his eyesight, it would be impossible for Sven to participate in the design of the Li Long Towers. His brother and Watercross would use his name, his reputation, and his patented designs to develop the project without him. It would be a project stolen away from him by his ruthless business partner and his estranged brother, and Sven would be left with nothing except for the bitter injustice that everything would have been different if he had never been injured.

Never been injured, he repeated in his mind.

Sven touched his eyepatch and glanced up, feeling the limousine come to a complete stop. He waited in silence, barely casting his gaze to the opposite side of the seat where he could keenly sense her presence. She, too, had been silent the entire drive, as if she was intentionally avoiding conversation by diverting her attention out her own window.

Was she regretting her decision to accept the role as his girlfriend?

He certainly hadn't made it easy on her and he had already complicated their relationship by trying to seduce her last night. His focus dropped to her shimmering stiletto heels and quickly traveled up the smooth reflection of her bare legs, crossed at her knee and slanting to the side, while the high slit in her mercury dress exposed her curvy thigh.

Naturally, what man wouldn't try to seduce her?

He had consciously chosen not to make another advance this afternoon—not because they were expected at the gala—but because he wasn't certain she would have him. He had already put her in the awkward position of refusing him; he wasn't about to do it again. His pride still stung from her rejection and he knew her limits. She had expressed them very clearly. Although he wasn't sure why she needed the money, she wouldn't allow him to compromise the limits of their arrangement, and he respected her for it.

He respected her for it, he thought.

But it wasn't only his respect for her that intrigued him. It was also that edge of resentment in her voice, simmering just beneath her sassy comebacks and wry sarcasm. He recognized it because it was the same bitterness and animosity that threatened to ruin him.

She was a woman who had been betrayed by her boyfriend—the man she thought she loved. But there was more than just schoolgirl heartbreak fueling her cynical exterior. *What was it?*

He knew very little about her, other than she was orphaned at a young age and had been forced to attend a mediocre local university when she clearly was smart enough to attend a better one. But he was certain of one thing: her sarcasm wasn't a symbol of her strength; it was an armor of protection. Rather than willingly submit to the helplessness within her life—the injustice—she resorted to mocking it. He recognized her cynicism because it consumed her the same way his consumed him.

"You're staring the wrong way."

Her comment cut through his thoughts. He lifted his gaze from her fleshy thigh and settled onto her glare. *She had caught him.*

"Please don't tell me that's our next ride."

Inez leaned over him to peer out his window, the top of her breasts passing below his sightline while the fragrance in her hair relaxed the tension in his shoulders. *Honeysuckle and ginger?* He wasn't sure exactly, but it definitely promised a sweet aftertaste underneath all that spice.

"Yes, it is," he confirmed, focusing on the way her wrist was touching his outer thigh as it supported her weight. "The Modern Architecture Foundation has chartered a yacht for tonight."

He followed her gaze out the window, unable to make out the sleek black yacht he knew was docked there. She turned her face towards him. "You never said anything about a yacht."

"Well, of course. We're going to sail out from Navy Pier so we can see the cityscape, including a fully illuminated view of The Spire. Is there a problem?"

"I hate boats and I can't swim."

He noted the uncharacteristic vulnerability in her voice and his instinct told him not to make a joke out of something betrayed so earnestly. "It's a big boat, Inez. I doubt there's much chance you'll end up in the water."

"What if your ex-girlfriend succeeds in throwing me overboard?"

"I will promptly dive in and rescue you," he countered automatically. "Then, I'll offer to marry you in front of her."

He waited for her reaction, but his comeback silenced her—a rarity.

He had said it partly in jest and partly just to push the invisible boundaries between them. She stared directly at him. Her luscious red lips were directly in front of him, and if he wanted to, he could pull her into his lap and overwhelm her with a kiss. *The same way he had done at the art gallery.* The taste of her kiss still lingered in his mouth, and it had aroused him all evening. But what taunted him even more was the fact that she had kissed him back. He had bought her for four nights to pretend to be his girlfriend. She had made it very clear that she was only there for the money. And so he hadn't expected to feel her body—and tongue—submit to him so willingly. She was not the type of woman who easily surrendered herself, especially not to him. But she had kissed him back, and it flamed his forbidden desires.

"I think I prefer for you to just let me drown." She pulled back into her seat, widening the physical gap between them.

He laughed aloud. It was exactly the kind of response he expected from her. "You would prefer that, wouldn't you?" He contained his smile, but delight seeped out of his reply. "Well, no drowning until you've helped me tonight. Remember the promise you made me?"

"Never leave your side," she repeated with a sincerity that affirmed his trust in her.

"Yes. Good."

"Just make sure your ex-girlfriend doesn't get all up into my grill."

He peered at her. Her face was blurry, and he barely made out her dark, challenging eyes. "I'm not going to even ask you to clarify what that means."

The passenger side door whisked open and the driver extended his hand to Inez.

"It means I've got your back," she clarified. "Just make sure you've got mine."

She accepted James' hand and he pulled her from the car and out of sight. For the few brief seconds they were apart, Sven acutely felt her absence. *A restless void.* He smoothed down his slate gray silk tie and waited for his driver to open his own door.

What sort of a woman would agree to pretend to be his girlfriend for five thousand dollars a day? He wasn't sure, and her black searing eyes revealed nothing more than a warning: *don't assume he could guess.* He knew he couldn't guess; he only knew when he looked at her he no longer felt completely overwhelmed by helplessness and rage because he no longer felt completely alone.

The door flung open. He pushed himself out of the limousine and braced his hand against its polished black surface. The wind from the lakefront whipped across the lapels of his suit and rushed across his cheekbones like a slap.

"Back by eleven, James," he instructed his driver and started to move away from the curb. Then, he hesitated. *Which way was his destination?* He made out the white spiraling lights from the Grand Ferris Wheel, rotating above Navy Pier's boardwalk. But the dark, sloshing waters of the marina and black fiberglass of the yacht's hull blended together against the canvas of night, making everything else indistinguishable to him.

"You do realize you're following me, don't you?" Her voice rang out like a rescue bell.

He squinted directly ahead of him and seized on her petite silhouette. Despite her assertive tone, she shivered from the autumn chill in the air. Her black mink wrap barely offered protection from the wind invading her sultry gown.

"I wouldn't have it any other way." He sauntered forward, enveloping her body into his arms to shield her from the breeze. His palm covered the lower half of her exposed back and he noticed how she leaned into him and accepted his touch.

"Good. I just want to make sure we understand who's in charge tonight."

"You most definitely are," he conceded, heeling to her pace as she led them forward along the Navy Pier's boardwalk towards what he assumed was the docking ramp.

"Good evening, sir," a friendly voice greeted them from afar.

"Who is that?" Sven murmured under his breath. It was a moonless night and the distance was too great; he could barely make out the unfamiliar form shrouded by shadows.

"A hottie wearing an über tight sailor's uniform."

"You mean the captain of the yacht?" he clarified in a low, even tone. This time, he understood her slang.

"Yep. And his friend is even hotter."

Sven felt a swell of petty jealousy expand his chest. She had that juvenile effect on him.

"His first officer," Sven corrected her.

"Glad to have you aboard, sir." The captain greeted him. "We've been waiting for you."

"Handshake, six o'clock," Inez warned.

Sven nodded and extended his hand. "Thank you, gentlemen. My date is especially glad to see you both. Apparently she's quite fond of men in uniforms."

Juvenile and petty, Sven thought after he had said it. But she deserved it.

The first officer offered his hand to Inez as her escort. For a moment, Sven wondered if she would accept it, abandoning him—and her promise. But to his surprise and pleasure, she declined the offer and stayed by his side.

"I prefer to stay with the guest of honor," she said, overtly flirtatious. "I can't swim and Mr. van der Meer has promised to rescue me if I fall overboard."

She took possession of Sven's hand and guided him up the apex of the steep incline. "There's a gap of about two feet at the end of the ramp," she whispered.

"You mean between the ramp and the deck?" he whispered back.

"Yes."

"Good."

Without warning, he swiftly lifted her into his arms. "I offered to rescue her *and* to marry her," he bragged to the captain and the first officer as he swung her over the threshold and onto the yacht's deck—just for show.

She gripped the railing to steady her balance and peered down into the undulating waves.

When they were out of earshot, she turned towards him. "I'm pretty sure I'm the one who's supposed to be in charge." Her dark eyelashes fluttered with fury. Clearly, she was unnerved.

"You still are," he said, confidently stepping over the gap and boarding the ship's promenade deck. "I just happen to know more about yachts." He cupped her elbow and encouraged her towards the sound of live music drifting out from the belly of the vessel. "Shall we?"

He guided her deeper into the interior of the ship where they met a man dressed in a black maître d' uniform.

"This way, please," he said, ushering them towards the white sliding double doors leading into the ballroom. But as they moved past the maître d' and into the yacht's main foyer, Sven's confidence suddenly deserted him.

"Inez," he whispered, tugging her hand and pulling her back. "Something's wrong."

"Yeah, no kidding. Whoever decorated the ballroom clearly has a black velvet fetish," she replied, straining to catch a peek into the ballroom as the sliding doors pumped open for the catering waitstaff to dart in and out of it. "And the corridors of this yacht look like the villain's lair in a James Bond flick. Tinted windows, ebony wall paneling, and pinstripe blue neon lighting. I mean, really...is this a respectable gala or Dr. Evil's bachelor party?"

"No..." Sven stammered as his vision faded away into disorienting darkness. He surveyed his surroundings, attempting to capture a flare from a wall lamp or the glow of an overhead chandelier—any bit of light that would produce an image. But the yacht's dim lighting and dark paneling cloaked everything in darkness. For the first time since the aftermath of the accident when his eyes were bandaged for weeks, he was completely sightless.

Distress raced through his veins. "Inez, I cannot see anything. Not even your face." He reached out and cupped her cheek in his palm, struggling to focus on her lips and profile.

Abruptly, the sound of the revving engines and the spinning propellers caused the cabin to vibrate, and the deck rocked away from the dock.

As panic set in, he turned, then hesitated, uncertain which direction they had entered. "We need to get off this ship."

Stubbornly, Inez pulled back on his hand. "Whoa...no way," she protested. "No way are we leaving now. I just spent the entire car ride over here, psyching myself up to show my ruffled panty ass to all your fancy high-class friends, and now you want me to leave before I even get a glass of champagne?"

He raised his head higher, like he was treading water through invisible waves, fighting to capture a wisp of light. But everything around him had disappeared into a uniform veil of murky shadows.

"Inez—" He seized her chin, turning her face towards him, needing to ensure that she was looking at him and registering the severity of the situation. "I cannot see anything," he insisted, his voice wavering. "Nothing at all."

She lowered his hand and crowded him into a corner, away from the blaring music filtering from the ballroom and the foot traffic of the catering staff.

"It's a moonless night, Sven. Not even the vampires are finding the pretty girls tonight."

The live jazz music swelled to its climax before ending with the festive blare of trombones. She turned towards the direction of the applause.

"And just for the record…if I have to muster up the confidence to get on a yacht despite my ridiculous fear of water and wear ruffled panties tonight in front of that entire ballroom of people, you are going to have to find a way to muster up the confidence to get up on that stage and accept your freaking genius award." She paused, as if she wanted to make sure he was listening. "And maybe even sing some bad karaoke."

The edge in her voice kept him calm and focused. He slowly exhaled through his nostrils, quelling the adrenaline pounding through his chest.

"The Rolling Stones?"

"No way. Too easy," she replied. "More like Cyndi Lauper."

He exhaled again, realizing he was completely trapped. The sliding doors pumped open. He squinted in their direction, attempting to discern anything beyond them, but he could see nothing except obscuring shadows. He adjusted his eyepatch and cleared his throat, calculating the odds of navigating all the challenges that lay ahead of them. A hush invaded his soul. She was right. She had her own fears to conquer and she was willing to do it for him. He didn't want to fail her.

"How many people are in the ballroom?" he asked.

"Do you want me to lie or tell the truth?"

"The truth."

"The truth is…" she paused, wavering. "The truth is you're one of the most influential architects of the twenty-first century. How many people do you think are in there?"

He clenched his jaw. "More than I can possibly fool."

"People are easy to fool, Sven. The hard part is believing that we can do it."

She touched his cheek. He covered her hand with his own.

"How?" Dread dampened his tone. The odds were completely against them.

"With the help of loads of alcohol," she asserted, as if it had been the plan all along. "So how many drinks does it normally take to get you plastered?"

"To get me what?"

"*Plastered*," she insisted louder, like he simply didn't hear her. "I want to make sure we stop right before you get so staggering drunk that you won't be able to walk yourself back to the limousine."

"Inez, I have never been that drunk in my life."

He heard her cluck, like she was supremely disappointed or annoyed—or both.

"Oh…right. I forgot. You're *European*. You've probably never been wasted, just for the pure sake of being wasted, right? Okay, fine. I'll use my best judgment." She paused and pulled away, checking him out from head to toe. "Over six feet tall and a little more than two-hundred pounds, mostly muscle, but no dinner…okay, so probably six shots over the course of a few hours, maybe eight, if we're mixing up vodka with a few of your precious Belgium ales."

"You cannot possibly want to get me plastered tonight. I cannot think of a worse plan."

"It's the perfect plan, Sven. And it's the only way we're going to get through this reception. Excuse me?" she abruptly called out to someone.

"Yes, ma'am?" The waiter slowed his pace and doubled back towards them.

"I'll take three of those…thanks." She swooped up two shots from the waiter's tray while leaving the third one behind. "Sven…tip him, please."

Without a beat, he obeyed, reaching into his pocket, unfolding his handkerchief, and withdrawing a single hundred dollar bill between his fingers.

"Dang," the waiter drawled and accepted the bill. "Thank you very much, sir."

"He's the guest of honor, so there's more where that came from," Inez replied.

"For real? The guest of honor?" The waiter sounded young, eager, and easily impressed.

"Yep," Inez confirmed. "So please let your manager know that Mr. Sven van der Meer has arrived, and he would like the band to play 'So What' by Miles Davis to announce his entrance."

"No, Inez," Sven cut in. The last thing they needed was an obscene amount of attention drawn to them when they entered the room.

"Shhh," she silenced him, handing over the first shot and watching him down it. "You just focus on drinking. Nothing distracts people more than good music and there's nothing better than masterful jazz like Miles Davis. It's your night. You're the guest of honor. You deserve a grand entrance."

"Damn straight, girl," the waiter agreed, like they were on the same team. "Plus, if I may say so, Mr. van der Meer...that's one fierce eyepatch. Definitely worthy of a cool jazz serenade."

"Wait until you see him on the dance floor after he's had a few shots," Inez added, swapping out his empty glass for a fresh one.

The waiter snapped his fingers and pointed at Sven. "Dawg."

Sven threw back the second shot—premium Russian vodka. Oh, God… what horrible mistake had he made? Allowing Inez to be in charge?

"Inez—" Sven cautioned her and returned the empty shot onto the tray.

But she ignored him. "Okay, good. So that's the plan. What's your name, by the way?"

"Devin, ma'am."

"Good, Devin. Now, go tell your manager that Mr. van der Meer has arrived and make sure that the band plays his request. Got it?"

"You got it, Ms. van der Meer."

"Oh, and make sure you check back in with us every half an hour to refresh Mr. van der Meer's drink. I don't want to ever see his glass empty." Inez nudged Sven in the ribs. "Tip him again, honey…please."

Sven sighed and held up the bill between two fingers.

"Pheeeeeww," Devin whistled, accepting the second hundred dollar bill. "Endless rounds of primo Stoli and some Miles Davis. Coming right up."

Sven heard the waiter rush away, certain he had just wasted two hundred dollars.

"I could get used to this," Inez said proudly.

He savored the casual intimacy of her fingers against his chest, straightening his tie and smoothing his lapels. "What? Giving away my money? Getting me plastered? Or pretending to be Ms. Van der Meer?"

He waited, wondering if she would take the bait. She didn't, of course. Her silence confirmed she was all business tonight, and as much as he tried, he still couldn't make out the expression on her face.

"Okay, drink up." She handed over the third shot to him.

He grimaced like it was poison. "I much prefer Belgium ale."

"Sorry, cranky pants. Blind beggars can't be choosers." She coaxed the shot rim to his lips.

"Inez, getting me drunk isn't going to magically cure my blindness."

"No, but it's going to make you a helluva lot easier to manage. And trust me, you're going to be a lot more charming if you're drunk than if you stay sober with that rigid stick up your—"

He thrust forward and seized her entire body into his arms, covering her haughty, saucy mouth with his own like a punishment.

He was tired of her incessant talking and he wanted nothing more than to force her into silence. He kissed her like he intended to set her on fire before cooling her down with each wet, persistent stroke of his tongue. He had wanted to kiss her like that since this afternoon—kiss her without restraint and make her feel the same sexual yearnings that he had been forced to repress. She had been the one to assert the professional boundaries between them, and now, with every order that she gave him, he wanted nothing more than to smash them to pieces and assert his domination over her.

He exhaled into her throat, feeling her supple tongue entwining with his own—the same way they had kissed at the museum. His cock grew hard and hungry, and if they had been anywhere else, he wouldn't have given a fuck about his professional obligations. He would have pushed her up against the wall, forced up her dress, tore down those damn ruffled panties to tease her clit with his tongue until her thighs parted and her head dropped back in surrender—all just to prove that her ice queen persona was a bigger charade than their arrangement. He would have ravaged her wetness, relishing each of her panting gasps as he invaded her glistening slit until she moaned and groaned and dug those fake fingernails into his scalp. And he would have savored—and denied—every disingenuous plea for him to stop until he made her shake, quake, and heave with shuddering satisfaction.

Instead, he made sure to be the first one to pull away from their rapturous kiss. Downing the rest of his third shot, he winced as the sting peppered his throat. He couldn't make out her expression, but he could hear her accelerated breath, flustered and shallow. And, of course, he had gotten what he had wanted—her silence.

"So tell me, Miss Sanchez…if this was Dr. Evil's bachelor party, which sexy Bond girl would you be?" He couldn't help it. He suddenly felt invincible again.

"Whichever one gets to kick 007 in the balls," she shot back, wiping her lipstick off his mouth.

"Naturally." He nodded, licking her taste, still lingering on his lips, and feeling the effects of three drinks invigorating him. Apparently, she was right. He felt a lot more charming inebriated than sober—sightless or not.

Chapter Fifteen

INEZ CLOSED HER EYES AND TOUCHED her lips, unable to believe he had just kissed her—*again*—and unable to believe he had been the first one to pull away. When she opened her eyes, part of her wanted to slap that arrogant smile right off his smarmy Dutch face, but the other part of her wanted him to do it again, claiming not only her lips, mouth, and tongue, but her entire body, and relieving the aching tingle of wetness between her legs.

Bastard. She glared at him, knowing he couldn't see her rage. *All of this was a game to him.*

The mellowing sound of Miles Davis subdued her. She had come up with a brilliant plan to get them through the night, and no matter how much of a pain in the ass Sven intended to be, she had meant what she said: she wasn't going to let him skip out on attending one of the most prestigious events in his career just because he was sightless. She had been hired by him for *exactly* that reason, and she wouldn't fail in her job by letting him fail tonight. Plus, getting Sven through tonight meant scoring her another five thousand dollars. Sven kissing her was just a distraction. The arousal of his tongue swashbuckling her into submission was just an annoying diversion. He had tested her from the moment they first met, and he was testing her again.

Fuck him. She would not fail.

Feeling the heat from his kiss flushing her cheeks, she unfastened her mink wrap and drew it off her shoulders, abandoning it on a nearby lounge chair. She had a job to do and he had a gala to attend. There was nothing stopping them except the inconvenient fact that he was completely dependent now—more than ever. The only thing more inconvenient than that was the fact that the crotch band of her ruffled panties was damp—yet again.

Ugh. Bastard.

The smooth trumpet of Miles Davis' jazz signature piece crooned through the sliding doors. That was their cue. No more screwing around—literally.

"Give me your hand," she ordered him. "And don't move, talk, or speak unless I tell you to."

With a dreamy expression of amusement, he shifted his eye down onto her lips, as if he was enjoying the stern edge in her voice. "Yes, Mistress Inez."

She eyed him, uncertain he intended to obey. There was no time to find out; she had to get him into the ballroom before the tempo change. She nudged him towards the sliding double doors and held her breath, listening for the band's melodic climax. Right on cue, they stepped through the sliding doors. She held onto Sven's hand like they were jumping out of an airplane together. Just as she had hoped, the ballroom erupted with applause. Bright spotlights flashed over them as a booming female voice introduced them through the microphone.

"Ladies and gentlemen, the man of the hour has finally arrived, the recipient of this year's Modern Genius Award—Mr. Sven van der Meer."

Sven stood his ground, like he was used to receiving applause at every entrance. Inez, on the other hand, squinted past the blinding spotlights, struggling to make out the details of the crowded ballroom. With her hand shielding her eyes, she barely spotted the stage, the band, and the sea of shadowed faces peering back at them. Inexplicably, she bounced forward with an uncontrollable yip.

Sven had just goosed her.

She shot him a death glare. *Was he freaking crazy?* There was a spotlight and a thousand eyes on them and he was nipping her freaking ruffled ass!?

"I've wanted to do that all evening." He gazed at her, like it was the most natural explanation in the world. Sven—tipsy and disruptive—was clearly going to be a bigger challenge than she thought.

The applause slowly waned and the spotlight faded, and a heavyset woman rushed towards them. "Hellooooooo," she called out with a wave. "We've all been waiting for you."

Sven tilted his chin towards the sound of her voice, as if he was struggling to identify it.

"Woman in her fifties," Inez whispered. "Heavy set, red hair dyed like a strawberry lollipop."

"Amara Cartopolus." Sven confirmed. "I tried to lick her strawberry lollipop last year in the steward's cabin."

"You. Did. Not." Inez tried to suppress her horror—and failed.

Sven relaxed with a grin, as though he was reveling in the fact that he had made her pitch change by an entire octave. "It's true. I didn't. But that doesn't mean I'm not going to try to get someone else I know in there."

He twitched his eyebrow and reached out to goose her again. Just in time, she dodged his hand and glared back at him. *Oh friggin' hell. What monster had she just created?*

Sven laughed and swayed, momentarily off-balance before sauntering in the wrong direction. Inez cut in front of him and rotated him towards Amara.

"We're honored to have you here with us tonight. And just in time for the presentation of the award." Amara showered Sven with lavish kisses on both cheeks like he was her long-lost nephew.

"Lovely to see you, Amara. As always. This is my girlfriend, Inez Sanchez."

The hairs stood up on the back of her neck. *Girlfriend.* It wasn't the first time Sven had presented her as his girlfriend, but it was the first time she noticed how much she liked it.

Amara extended a bejeweled hand. "A pleasure...and don't worry. I'll only steal him away for five minutes for the acceptance speech and then he will be all yours again."

"Miss Sanchez knows I am more than happy to be all hers all night." Sven eyed Inez's exposed ruffled bra.

Inez rolled her eyes while Amara giggled and cooed. Apparently, Inez had miscalculated. Inebriated, manwhore Sven was *way* more of a threat than sober, stick-up-his-ass Sven. Then, like the worst timing in the world, Devin, the fresh-faced waiter, eagerly cruised up to Sven with a fresh vodka shot.

"Here you are, Mr. van der Meer," he said, offering the shot glass. "Just like I promised."

"Thank you." Sven accepted it and unexpectedly downed the entire thing. "Perfect for making that acceptance speech slur right out. Don't you think, Amara?"

Amara bustled behind Sven, encouraging him towards the direction of the stage. "I think you'll be charming no matter what you say."

Inez fretted, realizing the looming threat of their separation.

"Sven, I think you've forgotten something," Inez called after him, opening her purse and pretending to search for something, anything—just to stall. "Your glasses," she finally blurted out. "You *know* you can't read your acceptance speech without them."

He passed his empty shot glass off to her. "It's true. I can't see anything. I'm blind as a bat." He cackled with laughter, like he had just delivered the punchline to a hysterical joke.

Inez stared at his Mad Hatter glee. They were in trouble. Big trouble.

"Maybe it would be a good idea if I came up onto the stage with you to help you read it," Inez replied sternly. It was a desperate move.

"Not to worry, dear," Amara cut between them with her heavy bosom. "In my experience, the best acceptance speeches are always the impromptu ones."

Like a bad nightmare, Amara escorted Sven through the crowd and up the half flight of stairs to a black platform performance stage. Amara attempted to pass off the glass sculpture into Sven's hands, but he fumbled it, almost dropping it on to her foot. Barely able to stomach the consequences of her broken promise, Inez winced and looked away. She chewed on her fake fingernail for comfort until his petition echoed in her mind: *never leave my side.*

God, what had she done?

Spurred by guilt and desperation, she bolted into action and pushed through the crowd of tuxedos and sequined gowns before someone ensnared her hand, intentionally holding her back.

"That is quite possibly the most revealing dress I've seen all night."

She glanced down at the masculine hand encircling her wrist. Its owner sneered at her with bright teeth and malicious delight. "And the only thing better than a revealing dress is the irresistible woman revealed beneath it." He tilted down his gaze, pouring his breath down her plunging neckline.

Inez recognized him from yesterday's cocktail hour. *But what was his name again?* She scanned the lapel of his white tuxedo suit jacket, as if she expected to find a nametag. Then, like a curse, his full name floated across her lips: *Eliot Watercross.*

Mercenary and vengeful, his fierce green eyes settled upon her. "Inez Sanchez, right?"

She nodded and attempted to writhe away, but he pinned her against his own body.

"Miss Sanchez," he repeated with a hiss. *The hiss of a snake*, she thought. "You know…I never forget a name or a perfectly sculpted…hand."

He drew her arm to his lips and kissed the inside of her wrist. It was hard not to acknowledge how attractive he was—prominent cheekbones, tanned complexion, Hollywood smile—if he didn't reek of cognac and foie gras.

"And I never forget a face or a man with bad breath," she tossed back.

His smile spread wider as he processed her impenetrable glare. His eyes shifted towards the stage and onto Sven who stood in front of the crowd while holding the microphone with ease, looking dashing in his slate gray suit and slicked back hair. The overhead lights illuminated him like a mythic demigod.

"You know, your boyfriend is about to accept the Genius Award," Eliot replied, lowering his sharp profile to her cheek. "But he hasn't been very smart about agreeing to fully cooperate in our next business venture. Just a bit of advice, Inezzz Sanchezzz," he paused and buzzed his warning against her ear. "If you care about Sven, I would do everything in your power to convince him that working with me is much better than working against me. With or without my bad breath."

His strong hand constricted around her wrist like a python before finally releasing her.

Gag. Foulness filled her senses as he turned away, sauntering towards the caviar table and disappearing into the shadows.

Inez gazed back at Sven. Not even five minutes into the banquet and she had already broken her promise never to leave his side. And now, he was up there, alone on the stage, standing in front of dozens and dozens of guests, staring out into the crowd like a lone warrior fighting to maintain his balance—and his pride.

"Good evening…" he said carefully as the microphone amplified his Dutch accent. "Thank you everyone for allowing me the opportunity to accept this award. To aspire to build one of the tallest buildings in the world requires not only genius, but sheer stubborn…" Sven paused inexplicably and gazed out into the crowd. His black eyepatch and European accent afforded him an air of distinction and the ballroom hushed themselves into silence.

"Blindness," he finally pronounced into the microphone.

Inez shook off the physical sting of Eliot's warning and squeezed through the crowd to the foot of the stage.

"Blindness to the fact that an impossible feat is not impossible at all. It simply requires a large measure of bravado and an even larger quantity of…" he stopped again. "Straight premium Stoli."

The audience laughed. Like a foolish schoolboy, Sven grinned, his hidden dimples made prominent by the blazing stage lights. The panic in her chest receded. He seemed relaxed, confident, and in command of the crowd. He was acting as if the whole thing was a joke—on them.

Inez waved her hands, attempting to catch his attention. He stared down at her, as if the bright stage lights offered him the illumination he needed to form an image. *Perhaps he could see her now?*

"The Spire has been a much maligned project from its very inception," Sven said, addressing the crowd again. "For this reason, I am grateful to receive this award from the Modern Architecture Foundation. I would like to thank Amara Cartopolus, The City of Chicago, all its city officials and to all of you who have supported our efforts to bring it to fruition. But…" he paused and swayed. For a moment, Inez feared he was about to fall forward off the stage. "There is one person I would like to thank tonight above all others…and that is my fiancée."

Fiancée? Like all the other guests, Inez scanned the room, wondering who in the world he was talking about? Numbness paralyzed her body as the men and women in the crowd slowly cast their eyes on her. *He meant her.*

"I am grateful to her for affording me the opportunity to accept this award tonight," Sven continued, waffling briefly before pushing out his words. "And accept it without the blindness of ego that fueled my ambition to build The Spire, but rather a humility that now quiets the soul. Thank you, Mistress Inez. And thank you, all. Good night."

The crowd tittered and erupted with applause. The band swung into a new Miles Davis tune as gestures and words from the crowd encouraged Inez towards the stage's stairs. It was the perfect opportunity to rescue him.

She bounded up the steps and rushed to him. "So apparently it only takes four shots to become your fiancée?"

"Get me a fifth one and I'll marry you tonight."

He drew her body against him like he owned her. She attempted not to indulge in the intoxicating scent of his cologne or notice the way his hard chest pressed against her breasts.

"I think it's better if we just stay boyfriend and girlfriend." She pinned his wrists against his sides, trying to quash his game of grab-ass. "Can you see better now with the stage lights?"

"Yes, just barely. Which is fortunate since you broke your promise."

She frowned. "Sven…I am so sorry about that."

"Shhh." He covered her mouth with his palm. "Perhaps I'll let you make it up to me."

She lowered his hand, fearing his manwhore answer. "How?"

He nestled his lips against her ear. "By helping me find the bathrooms so I can take a piss." He handed her the fragile glass award, as if he wanted to relieve himself right there on the stage.

"Okay, that I can help you with," she answered and guided him down the stage steps.

The stage lights faded and the whole ballroom fell into subdued darkness, accentuating the twinkling Chicago cityscape through the yacht's panoramic windows. Caught off guard by the change, Sven stopped and hesitated.

Inez halted herself next to him. "Oh my God..."

"What?" he asked with concern.

"The view, Sven. It's stunning." She nodded towards the cityscape, steering them towards the ballroom's exterior windows. The yacht turned and churned through the crisp black waters, rotating its starboard side towards the majestic skyline. "You probably can't see it, but The Spire looks breathtaking from all the way out here on the lake. Really breathtaking, Sven."

He closed in on her from behind, dropping his chin over her shoulder. "Tell me about it."

She exhaled as his possessive arms wrapped around her waist. "Well, it's the tallest thing in the skyline, by far…but it's also the brightest. And it's radiating light, not like the Hancock Tower or the Sears Tower, which are just twinkling antennas and building silhouettes. The Spire is actually…sparkling. Like a mirrored disco ball, reflecting everything around it."

There was a long pause of silence as she took in the view and the way his breath rose and fell in steady intervals against the sensitive curve of her neck.

"Thank you," he finally whispered. "Thank you for tonight."

"You're welcome," she whispered back, relaxing her hand on his forearm, considering all the implications of allowing him to cradle her body against his own.

"I'm fairly certain we should be sharing that award since The Spire was a Van der Meer project." The voice called out from behind them. "But as usual, you're taking all the credit for everyone else's accomplishment."

Hans pushed towards Inez and swept the glass sculpture away from her. Sven raised his drowsy head as if he had been asleep and faced the sound of his brother's unmistakable voice.

"Yes, you run our business, Hans. But I am the architect. The Spire was my vision, my design."

"And I'm the one who got it approved and funded," Hans asserted. "And like all things between us, you didn't even bother to thank me."

"And like all things between us, you steal everything away from me because you assume it's your right to have it."

"Oh, boys." Inez slipped between them. "Can't we just kiss and make up?"

"No," Sven seethed. "Because there is no brotherly love between us."

"That is usually the outcome when you try to kill someone," Hans countered.

Sven lunged at him with the threat of violence, but Inez blocked his path. "I only regret not succeeding."

"Sven…no. Don't—" she insisted, barely holding him back. "Not here. Not tonight."

She tugged on the lapels of his suit coat, like she was attempting to control a wild stallion. His nostrils flared and his hot breath fumed against her chin. Whatever credentials she thought she had going into this job, horse whisperer was not one of them.

Fueled by rage and alcohol, he was aggressive and unpredictable, and she felt uncertain as to whether or not he would sweep her aside or heed her protests. Desperate, she forced him to look at her with a slap—a clean, crack against his hard cheek that shuddered him into submission.

"Did you just slap me?" With glossy, incredulous eyes, he stared at her and rubbed his cheek.

"What the hell is wrong with you?" she countered, dragging him away from Hans and into a secluded corner of the ballroom. The band's trumpets blared through the melodic jazz piece. Inez glanced around the room, hoping no one had noticed their altercation.

"Look at me." She redirected him by his chin. "What did he mean?"

"Whatever will justify his actions to make me Cain to his Abel."

"Very biblical, Sven. But newsflash: this is modern day America. Which means you don't just get to go around threatening to kill people for the fun of it. So please tell me this feud between you and Hans is about something more than just Celeste?"

As if she had finally said something that resonated in his heart, he looked deeply into her eyes before turning away, unwilling or unable to answer her.

"Well, I hardly think I'm worth fighting over, especially when you're already engaged to someone else." The spritely female voice cut into their moment of privacy and answered for him.

Ugh. Inez reluctantly turned towards Celeste's unpleasant clown smile.

"And *such* a precious moment tonight," Celeste drawled, waving her champagne flute through the air. "Dedicating your entire acceptance speech to someone you've only known for…how long?"

"You sound jealous, Celeste," Sven retorted, fixing his eyes on the slinky black velvet gown that clung to her curveless body. Her perfectly moussed French bob cut across her high cheekbones, accentuating their severity.

"Not jealous, Sven. Just…unimpressed." Her eyes smoldered beneath purple eye shadow while narrowing her gaze onto Inez like she was nothing more than a sock puppet. Celeste scanned her hand with a frigid glare. "I'm actually surprised you're engaged without an engagement ring."

"And I'm surprised that Sven just received the Genius Award and you haven't even congratulated him," Inez shot back.

"Sven knows I'm his biggest supporter." Celeste lowered her voice as if directly addressing Inez was beneath her. "I may not be the fiancée who receives his praise in his public speeches, but Sven knows I'm the one who supported him—and his work on The Spire—from the very beginning. Even when few people wanted to." Celeste unexpectedly pushed closer to him and reached out her thin fingers to stroke his cheek. "And even after the accident."

Sven flinched, deflecting her touch. "Your memory is flawed, Celeste. I was alone after the accident. You had already chosen to leave me in favor of my brother."

Celeste dropped her hand like he had shot her with a bullet. "It's a curious thing how our memories revise the past, Sven. The only thing I remember is choosing to move on from our relationship because you refused to commit to me."

"I committed to you for two years, Celeste."

"Because I was committed to supporting your work."

Like divorced parents, Inez watched them escalate their conversation into an uncomfortable rehashing of past wounds and blame.

"I think the only thing that matters now is that Sven enjoys his night," Inez interjected, slipping between them. "After all, he is officially a genius now."

"And as my reward, Inez promised to get me home early to give me a bath," Sven announced with a carefree grin.

Both women turned and stared at him. He hiccupped and drew Inez towards him, nestling his nose into her neckline. Inez held her ground, enduring Celeste's smoldering stink eye, while Sven's hot breath whispered over her bare shoulder. *It was all for show. Clearly, all for show.*

"Well, I can't imagine when you intend to get married," Celeste countered. "Especially since Sven is expected to participate in the Li Long project in Shanghai at the end of this week."

Sven raised his lips from Inez's neckline. "I have not decided whether or not I'm going to Shanghai. And I'm certainly not going without Inez."

Inez stared at him. They had never discussed their "arrangement" extending beyond that week, much less extending overseas. She replayed Eliot's warning to her. "What happens if you don't go to Shanghai, Sven?"

"He will miss out on the most prestigious commission of his career," Celeste answered for him. "The Li Long Towers will make The Spire look like a rough draft in comparison. All of Chicago knows about the van der Meer brothers because of The Spire, but the whole world will know about Sven if he designs the Li Long Towers."

"Not if Hans and Eliot Watercross take all the credit for my work," he replied.

Celeste laughed, the pitch in her voice rising with a nervous flutter. "They can only do that if you let them. It was your design of The Spire that was revolutionary, and no one else can design the Li Long Towers better than you. They need you, Sven. They know it. And you know it."

Just then, Devin zipped up to them and handed off another shot to Sven. "Another Stoli for you, Mr. van der Meer."

The bugles and snare drums closed the band's set with dramatic verve. The audience clapped and the chandeliers briefly flashed. Devin's manager flagged him from across the room.

"Okay, there's my cue to start making the rounds for clean-up and final drinks. Is there anything else I can bring you all?"

Sven downed his shot and tossed another hundred onto Devin's tray. "Just a final request to the band." He leaned in and whispered into Devin's ear and handed over an additional hundred dollar bill.

"You got it, Mr. V."

"And Devin—" Sven called after him. "Tell them I'll tip them a grand if they can find a singer to do justice to the song. I want to dance with my fiancée. The slower, the better."

"Us? Dancing?" Inez protested. "We can't. Not in front of all these people."

"No?" He frowned at her, wounded by her rejection.

"Sven is one of the best dancers I know," Celeste interjected, sipping her champagne and seizing the opportunity to ease the expression of disappointment on his face. She inched closer to smooth down Sven's shiny rose quartz tie. "It's a shame your fiancée doesn't appreciate it."

"Put on some Macarena, and maybe I'll be persuaded," Inez slung back.

Celeste turned on her heel and tossed a sidelong glance at Inez through her spider lashes. "Congratulations on your engagement. Hans and I have put our own wedding on hold until he returns from Shanghai. I suggest you consider doing the same—for Sven's sake." Celeste strode past Inez, bumping against her shoulder before catwalking like a model across the ballroom.

"Celeste is always such a bright ray of sunshine to be around, isn't she?" Inez mused.

"She's still angry at me for not marrying her." Sven swayed to one side. Clearly, the effects of his fifth shot were wearing on him.

Inez rushed to offer her support. "Well, I can't imagine *why* you didn't sweep her off her feet and carry her down the aisle when you had the chance. Especially since she acts like she's always plagued with wedgies that she can't pick or scratch."

Sven shrugged. "Maybe she was right. Maybe I was only committed to her because she was committed to supporting my work."

"Or maybe you just didn't love her the way that she loved you." It came out of her mouth before Inez had a chance to filter it.

"Perhaps. Or perhaps I was waiting…" he paused, careful not to mispronounce his words.

"Waiting for what?" She rushed forward, propping him up as he sagged slightly, placing his precarious balance into her care.

"For someone who better suited me to come along."

Sven let the sentiment dangle like a lure on a fishing line. Inez replayed the sensation of his lips against her own, considering what would happen if she tugged on his bait. Instead, she forced him to regain his own balance and pretended to ignore him.

"Well, regardless…none of that gives Celeste the right to run off and sleep with your brother."

"No. I didn't think so either," he agreed. "But in the end, the way that I handled it made everything worse than it had to be."

He touched his eyepatch. Inez stared at him, noticing how they were avoiding the elephant in the room. She shifted her attention across the ballroom and spotted Celeste standing next to Hans and Eliot Watercross near the champagne fountain.

"Sven…what happens if you don't go to Shanghai?"

"I'll probably be ruined," he answered. "But even worse…I'll be destined to act like Celeste for the rest of my life…plagued by wedgies that I can't pick."

Inez eyed him, containing her smile. "Do you even know what a wedgie is?"

"No," he confessed with a smirk. "But it sounds terrible."

He swayed again and she steadied him with her hand. He held it like a lifeline.

Shanghai. The Li Long Towers. His career, his reputation, and his future. They were all likely a part of the intoxicating fears that consumed his emotions while filling Inez with dread. How was Sven going to travel to

Shanghai and design the tallest buildings in the world without his eyesight? And what was going to happen if he expected her to go with him?

"I'm a fool to want you…"

The title line of the famous jazz ballad dampened the chatter of the crowd. The lights dimmed and the mournful melody silenced the ballroom.

"*I'm a fool to want you…*" the singer repeated, crooning the first verses of Sven's song request.

"Perfect," Sven said, drawing her towards the band.

"What, the dance? Now? In front of all these people?"

"Yes, especially since it sounds like the band has found a worthy singer." He lifted her arm into proper ballroom dancing position and snaked his other arm around her waist, settling his palm over the small of her back, guiding her body to follow his lead.

Breathy and seductive, the singer's words hushed the ballroom.

He drew them towards the direction of the piano's melancholy solo. The notes tinkled like the soothing sound of raindrops as Inez watched several couples join in around them for the dance.

"I'm a fool to hold you…such a fool to hold you," the singer crooned.

"You're a pretty good dancer for being blind," Inez said, reluctantly giving in to Sven's embrace, seeking to close the gap between their bodies.

"Plastered and blind," he said nonchalantly, maintaining the rhythmic sway of their simple foxtrot.

She kept her chin lowered and her eyes firmly planted on his tie. But her body felt the intimate curls of his breath, rising and falling along his firm chest as he effortlessly glided them across the ballroom.

"Well, not exactly plastered," she replied. "You are still standing, your underwear isn't exposed, and your tie isn't wrapped around your head."

"Ah, I see. So I guess that means I can still have another drink."

His hand dropped lower across her ruffled panties and stopped right above her tailbone.

"I know it's wrong. It must be wrong…but right or wrong, I can't get along…without you," sang the singer with morose heartache.

"I think another drink would probably be a bad idea," she replied, nudging his hand back up onto the small of her back.

"Then you should have a drink instead." His hand drifted lower again.

"That would be an equally bad idea." She coaxed it upwards.

He pulled her closer against his chest and unified their bodies with every flowing step. The masculine strength of his lead mixed with the tenderness of his touch melted her into his embrace. She dared not look up at him.

"Sven…what are you going to do about Shanghai?"

He stopped them, as if her question unnerved him. "Ask for you to come with me."

His reply filled her with angst. He frowned again, as if he seemed to sense it. Without warning, he released her from his ballroom hold, as if he wanted to free her completely before she answered him. But there was nothing uncertain about his insistence. "Come with me."

She peered at him, mentally preparing herself for the consequences of refusing him. "Sven…I can't."

"Can't or won't?"

"Sven, you don't understand."

"So help me to understand?" he urged her, drawing closer. "Whatever it is, whatever financial burden you're struggling with, let me help you. Let me pay for it."

"Not everything is so easily solved with the snap of your billionaire fingers, Sven."

"Isn't it?" he shot back.

"No—" she glared at him. "It isn't."

Their eyes locked until he softened the edge in his voice and pulled her back into his arms. "You can trust me," he whispered and touched her cheek, as if he had finally unearthed her most vulnerable weakness. She stared at him, wanting to believe him, until she reminded herself that every private moment between them was tainted by their public charade.

"Congratulations on your engagement."

The comment came from the couple dancing next to them. With a warm smile, the attractive woman with dark hair addressed Inez. "I don't think I've heard a more romantic dedication than that in a long time."

"Isabel is less impressed with genius and more impressed with romance," her dancing partner quipped with his British accent.

"I'm less impressed with *ego*," Isabel stressed, "and more impressed with public expressions of affection."

"Isabel is an incurable romantic. One of the best parts about her," her partner replied.

"And Phillip is an incurable cynic," Isabel said curtly. "One of the worst parts about him."

Phillip smirked and kissed her hand. Turning his attention to Sven, he said, "I'm not fond of modern architecture, but I am impressed with innovation, van der Meer. 'Tis a shame you're channeling it onto the wrong projects by partnering with the wrong people."

"If you mean the Li Long Towers, I haven't decided on anything," Sven replied.

"No?" Phillip angled his head to one side, the overhead lights reflecting off his dark hair and Roman profile. "Well, then…call me when you've decided. We're moving forward on the Old Main."

He shifted his assertive blue eyes onto Inez. "Congratulations again on your engagement." Phillip nodded cordially before taking Isabel's hand and leading her off the dance floor.

"What was that all about?" Inez asked Sven, tracking them as they moved off the ballroom.

"Phillip Spears. He's an adversary of Eliot Watercross."

"Really?" Inez glanced across the room at the burst of laughter coming from the small group of guests mingling at the bar. Eliot Watercross roared with elation like a man on a mission to be seen. "In that case, I like him already."

"Spears is attempting to restore the Old Main Post Office."

"The Old Main Post Office? I love that building." Inez blurted out.

"Yes, so does my mother. Her royal jewelry collection will be permanently showcased in its newly restored Beaux Arts lobby. But the rest of the building is a blight along the riverfront. Four thousand square feet of premium riverfront downtown property that should be flattened to make more space for newer, modern developments."

"Like another Spire?" she taunted him gently.

But he clenched his jaw and corrected her. "More like four of them. Which is the reason why no one has taken on the challenge of restoring it except Phillip Spears. It's going to cost him more than three hundred million dollars to redevelop that building, but it's going to take more than just cash and grand ambitions. He is going to need a good architect to turn a million square feet of dilapidated warehouse into something worth more than demolition."

"Sounds like a job for a genius."

"Or an incurable romantic."

"Or both."

"Yes," he conceded. "Likely both."

He gazed at her, as if something drastic had just changed between them. Slowly, he reached out and grazed his fingertips along the curve of her cheek. "For a moment, I thought I saw your face," he whispered, his unpatched eye scanning the details of her lips, hair, and eyes. "No...I think it was only in my mind's eye," he finally said with disappointment before pulling his hand away.

"I think you're pretty drunk, Sven."

He nodded. "Likely plastered."

She smiled. "I think it's time to get you home."

"Yes," he agreed. "I'm still waiting to take a piss...and for my bath."

Chapter Sixteen

BARELY CLEARING THE THRESHOLD with his cumbersome body, Sven stumbled through the entrance of his penthouse.

"Forty-nine bottles of beer on the wall, forty-nine bottles of beer, take one down, and pass it around...forty-nine bottles of beer on the wall." If he kept singing loudly enough, and if he continued to correctly count all the way up to fifty bottles, he would charm her. He would charm her with his singing and then she would agree to go to Shanghai with him. *She would be charmed enough not to say no.*

"Forty-nine bottles of beer on the wall, forty-nine bottles of beer, take one down, pass it around..." He paused to recover his breath before delving in again. "Forty-nine bottles of beer on the wall."

He would charm her.

"Lights, lights, lights!" he hollered out into the air. His penthouse lit up like a Christmas tree. He kicked off his shoes and laughed, then cackled, then felt the urge to weep. *Thank God, thank God. He could see.*

Not perfectly, of course. And many of the familiar objects in his house still retained their blurry contours in the distance, but no longer was he rendered helpless, trapped within the shadowy fog of murky disorientation. *Red, yellow, blue, green...* his eyes swept across the open living room; he spotted every color. *Thank God, he could see again.* Overwhelmed with relief, he untucked his dress shirt, unbuttoned his waistline, unzipped his fly and ceremoniously prepared to piss right there across the full length of his black marble floors until her voice shrieked out from behind him.

"No, no, no, no! God, no!"

He dropped his head back and grinned. *He loved it when she scolded him.*

"Don't even *think* about dropping your pants and urinating here. No, Sven. Not here. You've waited this long, so now you can wait five more seconds until we can get you into the bathroom."

"Yessss, Mistresssss Inezzzzz," he hissed.

She exhaled in a way that puzzled him. *She didn't sound charmed*? At least, not as charmed as he had hoped. And certainly not charmed enough to get her undressed and into his bed.

He winced as the full force of her fingernails dug into his wrists, towing him down the long corridor towards the master bedroom. *Perhaps he should sing again*? He needed to charm her. That was the plan.

"Forty-nine bottles of beer on the wall, forty-nine bottles of beer. Take one down, pass it around, forty-nine…"

She suddenly covered his mouth.

"Fifty," she insisted.

He peered at her beautiful blurry face. He could tell she was scowling at him with haughty displeasure. *No, she wasn't charmed—yet.* But if he could just get her dress off, he knew exactly how he could turn her frown upside down.

"Sven—" she protested, pushing away his tentacle-like hands and guiding him into the bathroom. "Focus on the task at hand. Not feeling up my ass."

"But I've been waiting all night," he whined.

"God, you are so ridiculously drunk. Do you think you're going to remember any of this?"

"No…" he snorted, pulling down his pants and sighing in relief as the warm release of piss flowed out of him. "God, that is the only thing I've wanted to do more than to suck your…"

"Shhh," she covered his mouth again. "Another word out of your mouth and I'm going to call your mother and have you repeat everything you say to me…to her."

He paused, processing her threat while shaking himself out. "You are a wicked woman."

"Yes, and if you don't take off your own pants and get into your own bed, I'll show you just how wicked I can be."

He slowly stepped out of his pants and fumbled to unfasten the pearl buttons of his shirt. "That sounds delicious."

"Flush," she ordered him.

He obeyed, resting his gaze on her defiant stance. She placed her hand on her curvy hip, accentuating the contours of her body—her sensual, seductive body. Her hair, her lips, her shoulders, her supple breasts. He wanted her so badly. He would do anything—anything she asked.

"Good. Now, turn around and make your way to the bed," she directed him.

He nodded, repeating the sharpness of her voice in his mind, imagining how he could soften it into a thousand sighs of submission. He had been that stern with her when they had first met and now she was returning the favor. Officially, he was her boss, but now it was she who controlled his fate.

How much money would it take to turn the tables back on her? *Ten thousand? Fifteen thousand? Twenty thousand? Fifty thousand dollars?*

Whatever the price, he would pay it tonight. Just one night to relieve the burning desire that consumed the very core of his being. One night for the cherished opportunity to be her lover. *If she would have him.*

He turned away from the urinal and the whole bathroom spun around him like a carousel ride. He stretched out his arms, seeking support from the doorway. Rushing to his aid, she slipped his arm over her own shoulders and guided him to the foot of the bed. *God, how he loved her scent.* The mysterious fragrance of spice and flowers overwhelmed him.

He wrapped his arms around her—certain he could bear his own weight, but not wanting to—and peered into her eyes.

"God, you're so beautiful."

"Whatever, Sven," she dismissed him. "You can barely see me, and only two days ago you told me I was average. And short."

"Two days ago I was a much bigger asshole than I am now."

"That's true," she conceded, peering back at him. "You were an asshole."

"Were? So I've redeemed myself?"

"I wouldn't exactly say…redeemed. But you certainly are more entertaining when you're drunk."

"And charming?"

"Uninhibited," she corrected him.

"Sexy?" He raised his head and slipped his hand around her ass. He loved feeling those fucking ruffles against his palms, imagining how her tattoo would taste along his tongue.

"Horny," she asserted, brushing off his advances.

He sighed with resignation and dropped the full weight of his head and chest against the plush mattress.

"Horny?" he repeated, puzzled. She always succeeded in puzzling him. "You mean like a goat?"

"Forget it."

She removed his socks and it made his cock twitch. He considered bleating like a goat. *Perhaps that would charm her?*

But she didn't give him the chance. Instead, she drew the sheet over his body, tucking him in while leaning across the bed with her heavy cleavage over him. He watched her as she carefully unfastened each pearl button along his dress shirt.

"You don't have to do that," he said.

"It's a silk weave. If you sleep in it all night, you'll ruin it."

He gazed at her, but she avoided eye contact. Every tug of her fingertips felt like a release. *Liberation.* When she unfastened the final button, she drew out his arms from both sleeves and carefully folded the shirt over the high-back side chair like it was a cherished possession.

The cool air pricked his bare chest. *He needed her warmth*. He held her gaze. She did not turn away. For a moment, he considered drawing her down into his arms, burying his head between her breasts, and nipping each dark luscious tit between his teeth until she softly moaned, granting her consent. He yearned to feel her mercilessly rake her fingernails along his shoulders, urging him for more.

More.

He wanted her to draw up the hem of her own dress and allow him to run his needy tongue along the crease of her red panty line, savoring the quiver in her thighs and the scent of her desire. *Her desire for him.*

Then he realized it. She was waiting, not for him to seduce her, but for her payment for tonight.

"You will find double the normal amount in the drawer of the night table next to the bed," he said.

He had anticipated this moment, plotting it carefully ever since their encounter last night. *Their encounter in which she had refused him.* She hadn't wanted to be turned into his whore and he respected her for it. But she also clearly needed the money, and whatever it was, whatever secret she was keeping, he wanted to help her. Now, he truly felt like a genius. She would be shocked to see ten thousand dollars. And she would be charmed by it.

"Double the normal amount?" she said, sinking onto the edge of the mattress.

"Yes."

"Why?"

It was such a simple, direct question. But it spun the ceiling fan faster and confused him.

"Because you need it. And I need you."

He lifted up from the pillow and wrapped his arms around her waist, burying his head into her lap. She did not protest. Instead, he only felt repetitive strokes of her fingernails through his hair. *He loved those fingernails*.

"Sven, our arrangement was for only five thousand a night. And that's all I'll take."

After an eternity of comfort and silence, she attempted to shift away from him.

Yes, he was completely drunk. And yes, completely unaccountable for his actions. And yes, it was a dangerous combination because he wanted her more than he had ever wanted any other woman. And the idea of being left alone—without her—was too much to bear. He peered up into her dark cherrywood eyes without letting her go. "What are you hiding behind that strength?"

She smiled down on him and touched his eyepatch. "Something I'm not certain you would understand."

"I think you should try to give me that chance."

But she did not give in to him. "It's almost midnight. I have to go now, Sven. But I'll come back early tomorrow to check on you."

He savored the way her fingernails ran through his hair one final time. Then, with a heavy sigh of acceptance, he uncoiled his possessive embrace. "Good night, my Mistress Inez."

"Good night, Sven," she said, rising and tucking him in. "Thanks for the dance."

"No, thank you," he whispered back, catching her hand at the last moment and drawing her into a tender kiss of gratitude before falling back against the pillow and succumbing to the heady weight of sleepy inebriation and infinite darkness that consumed him.

Chapter Seventeen

MY MISTRESS INEZ. His hot breath whispered down the sensitive nape of her neck as the flexing strength of his bare chest pushed against her body from behind her. She held her breath when he said the words like a petition. "Let me take care of you."

No— she exhaled, as if it was a punishment. She had been so guarded for so long, it was the only answer she would allow herself to express.

Let me take care of you, his voiced echoed while his hands wound around her torso, slowly enveloping her breasts into his palms.

She closed her eyes, opened her mouth, and released a moan as he massaged her into submission. Through her ruffled panties, she felt the insistence of his hard cock against her backside, awaiting her consent. *Would she allow him to dominate her*? Would she be able to let him conquer her with such a simple request—a request that promised to make things better and easier in her life and not harder or worse?

Let me take care of you, he whispered in her ear, stripping down her panties and pushing up her smooth shimmering gown. The cool air washed over the sensual dimples of her tailbone just above the soft contours of her bare cheeks. The teasing tip of his wet tongue circled over her cherry blossom tattoo before lapping the forbidden arcs of her backside.

He was determined to claim her.

She reached back to stroke his shaft, feeling the need to divert his attention away from seducing her. But he drew away her hands, affirming his quest to fulfill her—and only her. His hand slid over her thigh and cupped her pubic bone, teasing her clit before fingering her wetness. She dropped back her head with a submissive sigh and gushed for him. It was no longer possible to deny him. There was only the possibility that she would deny herself.

I know it's wrong. It must be wrong...

The haunting lyrics of the jazz ballad drifted through her mind as his lips feathered down the erogenous curve of her spine, drawing out every vulnerable emotion she had guarded every time he gazed at her. The possessive strength of his hands, grasping her hips. The heat of his pelvis against her backside. The firmness of his cock, pulsing against her cheeks with the full force of his desire. Everything about his domination reinforced the sentiment behind his plea. *He would take care of her—if she would only let him.*

She groaned, savoring the way his agile fingers slipped inside her. He confidently established a rhythm, building her up to an intolerable need before slowing his pace and teasing her more. She fell onto her hands and clenched the black silk sheets as he spread her knees wider across the bed. *She was surrendering herself completely to him.* His strong domineering body loomed behind her. She sensed what was to come, but she never would have anticipated how much she yearned for it. Then, she gasped as the full length of his cock penetrated her with one intimate thrust. He waited until she forced out her first exhale before rocking himself deeper and deeper into her. *He would not stop until he pleasured her completely.*

It was all too much too bear. She muted her scream with every vibrating wave of pleasure, but the climax never came…she had been close, so close so many times before, and yet, Enzo was right. She had never found a way to allow herself to come. Not with him, not with anyone.

Let me be the one to make you come. He said it like a sacred request.

She shook her head and whispered back. *I can't.*

You can, if you trust me.

She shook her head again and everything suddenly went black. *No, I'll never trust anyone enough.*

* * * *

Ping.

The ring of Inez's phone roused her from her sleep. She lifted her head from her pillow and glanced over to Luna's crib, where the sunlight from the window streamed across its empty mattress.

Nana.

Inez exhaled with exhaustion. She barely remembered crawling into bed last night before Luna sensed her presence and awoke, wanting to nurse. Inez remembered feeding her in bed, but almost nothing else. The entire night was already a distant memory, including her evening with Sven and her sexy wet dream. She glanced at the clock. 8:30 A.M. She paused and listened for Luna or her grandmother, feeling the prickling need to express milk. But the upstairs bedrooms were silent. They were likely downstairs, probably napping after breakfast, and neither one of them needed her now. Relieved, she fell back into bed.

Ping. Ping. Ping.

The urgency of her phone chimes forced her to sit up and retrieve it. She scanned the messages.

Te echo de menos

Perdona, mi amor

Necesito verte tan pronto

Inez flopped back against her pillow.

Ugh, Enzo.

She knew he would contact her—not to console her for using their private photographs in his public art exhibit—but because she recognized the flare of jealousy in Enzo's eyes after Sven had kissed her. And despite the fact that Enzo had slept around with half the single women in Argentina, Inez knew Enzo would never willingly stand by and let another man steal her away from him.

She stopped and considered the best response before resorting to the most honest one: *What do you want, E?*

She sent the text, despite already knowing the answer. What he always wanted: another chance.

He texted back: *To see you. And Luna.*

We're busy, she shot back.

He pinged her again. *You cannot avoid me forever. Luna deserves to see her papá.*

Ah, the guilty paternity play, she thought. He didn't use it often, but she had already grown used to it. She considered her day before typing back her response. *My grandmother and I are spending the morning with her, then I'm dropping her off at Sarah's later today before work.*

Good, I'll meet you there, he texted back.

Are you finally offering to babysit? It was a petty swipe at him, but she didn't care. He had been back for weeks, and there hadn't been a single day that he had offered to take care of their child.

I do not want to babysit, he zinged back. *I want to be a family.*

She rolled her eyes and considered turning off her phone. *We are not a family, Enzo*, she finally sent back.

You are her mother. I am her father. We are a family. Nothing can ever change that.

Inez was pretty certain that his whore-o-thon in Buenos Aires had irrevocably changed that.

Te echo de menos.

She stared at the words and considered their meaning: *I miss you.*

He often had said that phrase in Spanish to her—usually when they were in bed together, even when she was right there in front of him—as his way of expressing that she still wasn't close enough. Every time he said it, it stirred deep, visceral emotions inside her, reinforcing the simple fairy tale belief that she had found her one true love who loved her back with all his heart.

Now, she stared at those words, fighting their tempting promise of a happily ever after. Fairy tales were for naïve virgin maidens. She was an unwed, penniless mother whose heart had been turned into stone when her prince had slept around with the evil queen. There wasn't much upside in believing in fairy tales anymore.

How about the opera tonight?

The text appeared across her screen like a wayward dove passing through a bleak sky.

Sven, she thought, pretending not to feel anything when she re-read it.

I know you have your fitting with Ebony, but after that, we have the night off.

The night off? Inez texted back.

Yes. We're not committed to any public engagements except for tomorrow night for the opening of The Spire. So tonight is our night off.

Their night off. Flustered, Inez held her head, uncertain about the implications of spending her "night off" at the opera with Sven van der Meer. But Sven's text-to-speech responses were faster than her ability to reply to him.

Puccini's La Bohème. Private box seats at the Lyric Opera House, which is the antithesis of modern architecture. Nothing should please you more.

There was a pause before his next text pinged her phone.

Except attending with me. Of course.

A day ago, she would have rolled her eyes at his cockiness. Now, she just smiled.

Plus, you promised to come back and check on me today.

She sat up straighter and edged in her response: *You remember that?*

I remember a lot more than I probably should about last night.

She felt her pounding heart beating in her chest. *How much did he remember about last night? His dedication speech to her? His request to come with him to Shanghai? His emotional, inebriated kiss good-bye?* She reflected on all the intimate moments before opting to ignore all of them.

You're a fantastic singer, by the way, she answered.

She paused and waited, noting how the flow of his rapid replies had been interrupted. After a long pause of silence, he finally responded.

Just agree that you will accompany me to the opera tonight, and I promise not to drink, sing, or remove my pants.

Then, like an omen, Enzo's text pinged her. *You can hide from me now, but you cannot hide from me forever. I will meet you at Sarah's this afternoon. Tell your new dentist boyfriend that you are taking the night off. Te quiero, mi mujer.*

Inez stared down at his words: *I love you, my wife.*

Ugh, she hated him. She hated him so much for having the ability to do *that*—dangle the promise of a future together and succeed in making her want to believe in it.

She scrolled back and re-read Sven's request: *Just agree that you will accompany me...* She had failed to reply, and now, he pinged her again after several minutes of silence.

Okay, I can see that you're not going to commit yourself to the opera tonight. But does that mean you're going to break your promise, too?

Inez paused, the weight of the world heavy on her heart. *No, a promise is a promise,* she replied. *I'll be there at Ebony's for the fitting. But before that, I'll stop by and check in on you.*

He pinged back without a beat. *Good, I'll be taking a bath.*

Chapter Eighteen

IT HAD BEEN ALMOST A WEEK since Inez remembered being able to sit down at the kitchen table, eat her breakfast while nursing her baby, and not be in a rush to go anywhere.

"You're having man trouble, admit it," Nana said.

"Is it that obvious?"

"Yep, because you're silent. And when you're silent, it usually means one of two things: you're having money troubles or you're having man troubles."

"Or usually both."

Her grandmother smiled and shifted her useless cataract-ridden eyes up to the ceiling. "You said it. Not me."

"Enzo wants to see Luna," Inez finally confessed. "And me."

"Tell him he should have thought of that before he started sticking it every which way he could fit it."

"Nana—" Inez sighed, exasperated.

"What? It isn't true? Or a blind old bird like me isn't supposed to say it?"

"You've said it, like…fifty times."

"Well, I'm senile. What do you expect?"

"Nothing," Inez replied, resigning herself to the fact that it was true.

"Look, dear. Enzo knocked you up, left the country, and broke your heart. I'm gonna take the heartache and the hardship he caused you to my grave with me, just so I can promise to haunt the hell out of him."

"Okay, let's forget it's Enzo, for a moment. And instead, let's just refer to him as…Bachelor Number One."

"Bachelor Number One?" Nana sounded skeptical.

"C'mon, Nana. Play along. Like a game show…behind Door Number One is Bachelor Number One—sexy, attractive artist from Argentina."

"He sounds more like an unemployment candidate than a game show prize."

"Long-term relationship of two years," Inez continued. "My first true love—"

"You're young," Nana zinged back. "You know nothing about true love."

Inez overrode her, "The happiest I've ever been in my life."

"Hey, what about our road trip to The Badlands? Now, *that* was a rowdy good time."

"You mean the trip where you almost shot a tourist with a pellet gun, just so we could speed away and pretend we were Thelma and Louise?"

"You have never screamed and laughed so hard in your whole damn life, and you know it."

"Can I finish?" Inez insisted.

"Bachelor Number One." Nana feigned a long-drawn out snore.

"Father of my baby. Tells me he loves me. *And*...says he wants to be a family."

"Cock-sucking bastard," Nana cried out through cupped hands

"Nana!"

"Well, I'm just playing the part of a heckler in the audience. You forget that I was a nurse at a veteran's hospital for thirty-two years. I didn't last that long there using 'please' and 'thank you' when they had to shit in a pot, I can tell you that."

"Okay, forget it. Let's move on to Bachelor Number Two—"

"Bachelor Number Two, eh? I like him already."

"Handsome Dutch billionaire. Rigid, stern, asshole by day, but charming, unguarded playboy by night. Famous modern architect who's leaving this Saturday for Shanghai to design the tallest towers in the world."

"Hm..." Dubious, Nana chewed on her pancakes. "Sounds like nothing but more trouble."

Inez sighed in agreement. "Yeah, and that doesn't even include his bitchy ex-girlfriend with the crazy eyes who hates me because she thinks I'm sleeping with him, but really, it's all just a charade because he's actually paying me to pretend to be his new girlfriend."

"Ah, so that's what you've been up to this week. But you're not sleeping with him?"

"No, of course not. He's my boss."

"But do you wish you were sleeping with him?"

Inez answered with conviction. "No, Nana. It's just a job."

"Lying little slut!" Nana cried out again.

"Nana!"

"Well, I'm just calling it like I see it because if that were at all true, we wouldn't be playing this little game."

"Ugh." Inez buried her face in her hands. "So does that mean a veto for Bachelor Number Two then?"

Nana shrugged. "What's behind Door Number Three?"

"Endless nights of comfortable pajamas, homemade lasagna, and a marathon of watching weepy, melodramatic Meryl Streep movies with her foul-mouthed grandmother and her perfect princess baby daughter."

"Sounds like you got your answer."

"Yeah, I wish it was that simple."

"So do I." Nana nodded. "But I can tell you one thing for certain. Whichever door you choose, make sure the bachelor behind it realizes he's got you as a gift and not the other way around."

Chapter Nineteen

SVEN HELD UP HIS FOOT AND let the water from the bathtub's faucet drip onto it. *One, two, three, four*...he attempted to count his toes, struggling to discern the difference between each one. His vision was substantially worse. Last night, he had experienced both the terror of being rendered completely blind, and the exhilaration of reclaiming his sight, spurred by the radiant spotlights and the invincible inebriation that had consumed him. But this morning, weighed down by his hangover and exhaustion, everything was blurry and indecipherable again.

Like his memories of being with her.

He remembered everything about last night, but only in bits and pieces—hazy images of the ballroom interspersed with visceral sensations of being with Inez. The touch of her hand. The scent of her hair. The taste of her tongue. The warmth of her lips. The texture of her teasing ruffled panties. The sway of her lush body against his own. Through his trust in her and her trust in him, they had succeeded in buying him some time—another night to pretend that he was still an invincible genius. But now, it was the morning; she was gone and he no longer felt invincible.

Plink, plink, plink...

He raised his foot again and caught the droplets with his toes. *One, two, three, four*...

Even while squinting, he was still unable to make out the division between them. He submerged himself deeper into the whirlpool tub. Shanghai weighed heavy on his mind. She had promised to come this morning to check on him, but he needed a way to convince her to stay. *Stay in his life*. In less than two days, he had gone from a bitter, blind wretch to a faint shadow of his former self. There was a chance he might be able to keep his career from imploding by prolonging their charade. With her help, he might have a chance to travel to Shanghai and claim his position as lead architect on the Li Long

Towers. And in her care, perhaps his vision could be maintained, and perhaps, even slowly restored.

He shut his eyes and indulged in the steamy heat of the bath water against his skin. He had already ordered her a full wardrobe and luggage and he had put no limit on the budget. Their night at the opera together would be his opportunity to propose his plan—she would travel to Shanghai with him as his fiancée. He would pay her whatever she wanted, and she would stay with him in his hotel suite. And he would promise to take care of her there, the way she had taken care of him.

It was a daring proposal. He knew it. She was not a woman who could easily be bought or seduced, and she had made that crystal clear. Even after their first meeting, he had felt an unexpected intimacy between them—something that was not clear or certain, but rather something unspoken and undefinable. Yes, there was sexual tension, but it was more than physical attraction. It was an emotional connection. Despite being complete strangers, they understood each other, and it unified them in a way that underscored how painfully alone he was without her.

His phone vibrated against the hard, black tiles of the bathtub's ledge. He dried his fingers against the adjacent towel and answered the call.

"Yes?"

It was the doorman. "Sir, your girlfriend is here to see you."

Early, Sven thought, *a good sign*. "Perfect. Send her up, please."

He ended the call, tossed his phone onto the towel, and relaxed deeper into the steamy bath water. She would know how to enter the penthouse on her own. He had remembered singing aloud the combination for the front door keypad to her last night. It wasn't the only embarrassing thing he had done in front of her. He remembered pissing in the urinal and being unabashedly proud of it. He remembered stumbling into the bedroom, kicking off his pants and underwear, but needing help to unbutton his shirt. *Those damn pearl buttons*. He remembered allowing her to disrobe him, yearning for her every touch until the overwhelming haze of inebriation extinguished his arousal. He remembered how tenderly she coaxed him into bed, naked and impotent, before attempting to leave him. *He had refused to let her go*. He remembered catching her hand and indulging in a kiss—one spontaneous expression of his ultimate gratitude. Amongst all the foggy, vulnerable moments floating through his mind, it was the one memory he did not regret. In fact, it was the one memory that encouraged him to hope for more.

When he heard the creak of the bathroom door, he shut his eyes and dropped his head against the bathtub's rim. Grinning, he said, "You're early, which can only mean you do care about me."

"You know, I was afraid that I might be disturbing you, or that you wouldn't be alone. But I'm glad to hear you're happy to see me."

Disturbed by her unpleasant voice, he slowly opened his eyes, barely able to control his sagging smile. Celeste's blurry reflection ebbed across the water's surface.

"I don't think I've seen you look this relaxed since the night I first met you." She seated herself at the far edge of the bathtub, like a cat enjoying the sparkling glints in the water from the overhead lights bouncing off the tub's stainless steel basin.

He looked at her and suppressed his urge to shiver. "That was a long time ago." He paused, hoping his icy reply would convey that he was not pleased with her surprise visit.

"Well, apparently not long enough. Your doorman still thinks I'm your girlfriend."

"He has known me a long time. He knows I rarely only have one girlfriend."

He glared up at her. It was a comment intended to silence her.

"Ahhh, yes. You did go through an entertaining binge of ridiculously younger blondes after we broke up."

"You mean after you left me," Sven corrected her. "And those attractive, younger blondes were more than willing to entertain." He intentionally let the sexual innuendo hang between them. The fact was…Sven hadn't slept with any of them. They had all been paid escorts, one-night trials that eventually had served as precursors to his arrangement with Inez.

"Well, you certainly have had a dramatic change in your taste in women."

It was a comment intended to provoke him. It worked.

"You mean Inez," he said, realizing Celeste had come to draw blood. But not from him.

He rose up fully from the bathtub and let the water cascade off his naked body with a crash. He assumed she was staring at him, but he didn't care. He felt nothing. Not long ago, he had seduced her here—in his penthouse, within his bed, even upon occasion, in that bathtub—but he barely remembered any of it.

"She's definitely an interesting choice in a fiancée."

He peered into the mirror, unable to see her through the wafting steam.

"I always assumed you would marry someone more…sophisticated," she added. "Someone whose reputation and career would complement your professional achievements. Someone—"

"More like you?" he cut in.

"More your equal in every way."

Sven rotated slowly towards her, fully displaying every inch of his dripping body.

"I'm a wretched bastard, Celeste. I do not need my equal in every way. I need someone infinitely better."

Their eyes locked. Celeste released a nervous laugh. "So I suppose that means you've found your newest inspiration."

He pushed forward, reaching across her lithe figure to remove the towel from its hook. He shook off the water from his hair and turned away into the bedroom.

"You have come for a reason, Celeste. What is it?"

She followed him and withdrew a document from her alligator skin purse. For a moment, Sven thought he saw something flutter to the floor. But he lost sight of it as quickly as he had noticed it.

"I've come to deliver this." Celeste held out the document to him. "It's the partnership contract for the venture capital company that will be funding the Li Long Towers."

"Hans and Eliot are sending you as their emissary?"

"No, I volunteered to come. After all, we were friends once, Sven. More than friends. And I want to see you make the right choice."

She waved the document at him like a peace offering. He accepted it and pretended to flip through its pages, as if he was able to read them. But she confirmed what he already knew.

"It assigns you a majority stakeholder share in the new venture if you sign on to become the lead architect of the Li Long Towers."

"And if I don't?"

"I really don't see how you have a choice. Especially now that you have found your… inspiration." Celeste stroked her rabbit fur scarf and settled her gaze onto Enzo's seductive portrait of Inez, still propped up on Sven's dresser. "Eliot Watercross is planning to sell The Spire to Harvey Zale in exchange for the Li Long construction contracts. Once he does that, you'll become a diluted stakeholder in the new holding company—unless you agree to be the lead architect of the Li Long Towers."

"Inez is uncertain about coming with me to Shanghai and I cannot go without her."

Celeste gazed at him like she didn't understand him. "But you'll lose everything."

"True, I'll lose most of my money due to Watercross' Machiavellian equity dilution scheme. And I'll lose control over Van der Meer & Associates because Hans has no remorse about using the Van der Meer name without my participation in the deal. But I will not lose everything, Celeste. That's where you're wrong because I'll win the chance to gain back my happiness and a part of my soul."

"My, my," Celeste clucked, turning away from the portrait. "She truly has charmed you. Like a dangerous siren luring you into the rocks. Be careful, Sven. Don't mix business with pleasure. Your career, your reputation, your life's work…even your net worth. Do you really think it's wise to give that all up? And for what? For her?" Her voice quivered as if she feared the answer.

"I don't expect you to understand, Celeste."

"You're right. I don't. And I don't believe she would want to be the one holding you back from the peak of your career."

"The last thing Inez has done is hold me back."

"Then there's no reason why she shouldn't go with you to Shanghai. You're engaged now, after all. I was willing to do whatever I could to support your career, and I wasn't even your fiancée."

She sat down on the edge of the bed and crossed her legs in a way that made her tight skirt ride higher up her thighs.

"Tell Hans and Eliot they can make whatever plans they like—with or without me. If I choose to go to Shanghai, it will be on my own accord. Not as a pawn on their chessboard."

He tossed the contract beside her on the bed like a discarded surrender flag.

"What they're offering you is a continuation of your current partnership, Sven. The same partnership that helped ensure the construction of The Spire. Tomorrow is the opening night. Until then, consider all your options."

She rose from the bed and prowled towards him. Her blurred facial features came into sharper focus as she skated her sharp nails along his pecs. He could make out her thin, pink lips hovering near his face.

"Let me help you. Let me be the first person to make the announcement that you've signed on as lead architect of the Li Long Towers."

"The first person to make the announcement?" He eyed her, attempting to decipher her meaning. "So you're not here as a friend, but as a journalist looking for her next scoop?"

Celeste shrugged and touched his cheek. "It's the right decision for your career and you know it. I'm here to remind you of that fact—yes, as a friend, and as a fan, and perhaps even foolishly as someone who used to share your bed."

"Well, in that case…please don't let me interrupt your little moment."

Inez's sharp words stabbed like a knife into his chest. She was standing in the doorway of the bedroom, and although he had trouble seeing her face, her vicious sarcasm was enough to conjure her expression in his mind.

Celeste placed her hand on Sven's bare shoulder, letting it linger there until he moved away from her towards Inez.

"Sven and I were just discussing business." Celeste gathered up her purse and the contract.

"Good, because a threesome isn't really my style," Inez sniped.

Celeste laughed and tossed her bangs with a flick of her head.

Sven peered at Inez. She glared back at him.

"I only want what's best for Sven and his career," Celeste replied. "I hope you'll be able to say the same thing when it comes time to let him go to Shanghai." She circled the room and placed the contract on his dresser. "Good-bye, Sven. If you change your mind about tomorrow, let me know."

But Sven didn't respond. He simply gazed at Inez, waiting to speak until the diminishing click of Celeste's heels and the slamming of the front door signaled that she was gone.

"Well, I'm not sure why I'm even here. It seems you're feeling better already."

Inez's gaze dropped on to his nakedness. His jawline flinched, but he stood resolute. She had seen him naked last night, not hard with arousal like he was now—a consequence of her presence, not of Celeste's visit. But he knew she assumed the worst of him.

"She came unannounced. I was waiting for you."

Their eyes locked as she searched the truth beneath his even tone.

"What's that about?" She finally asked, nodding to the contract.

"Shanghai," he replied. He knew it was all that needed to be said because he was still waiting for her answer from last night.

"Well, maybe it would be better if Celeste goes with you. She seems to care more about your career than I do."

He angled his cheek as if she had just slapped him. *Bitterness.* He recognized it seething out of her. She bent forward, swept up something from the floor, and slapped it into his palm.

Perplexed, he studied its color and texture. *Black thong panties.* How or why she had found them, he had no idea, but he wasn't about to let her believe the worst of him.

"Inez, you're making assumptions—"

"No, I'm not making any assumptions because you're free to do whatever you want. We have an arrangement, and anything more than that is just—unpaid work. And I don't have that luxury of time."

"You will be paid for coming today, if that's what you're worried about."

She laughed, a mocking burst of condescension. "Good, because that's definitely the only reason why I'm here."

He stared at her, realizing their exchange had gone all wrong. He shook his head, unable to comprehend how things had turned so quickly against him. Seeking to redeem himself, he automatically moved to the safe, keyed in the code to open the door, and removed a stack of one hundred dollar bills.

Silently, he held it out to her.

She crossed her arms and held her ground in the doorway, as if she was deciding whether or not it was worth the effort to cross into his bedroom. Finally, she folded, pushed towards him and snapped the stack out of his hand. But in exchange, he snagged her by the wrist.

"Come with me to the opera tonight," he said, reeling her into his nakedness and his vulnerability. "Come back here after your fitting with Ebony. I want you to be here with me. I want us to have a pleasant evening—together."

He made the offer with tenderness in his voice, letting her read into his intentions.

“No, it’s not possible,” she replied coolly, enduring his grasp, but avoiding his gaze. “I’m not available. I’m meeting Enzo.” She deliberately accentuated the words, like she wanted nothing more than to wound him.

“I see…” He released her hand and backed away. She wasn’t the only one making assumptions that were wrong.

She fell silent. Painfully silent.

“Then perhaps it’s best that you go,” he directed her.

She abruptly turned to leave, then stopped and gazed back at her portrait on the dresser. “You promised me you would destroy it.”

It was as if she was determined to lance his heart with her dagger. His chest tightened with his own aching bitterness.

“And I plan to keep that promise.”

“Good,” she said. “I’ll be back here to meet you tomorrow night for the opening.”

“Don’t bother,” he replied flatly. “I will have one of my drivers pick you up and we’ll arrive separately.”

“Even better,” she punctuated.

He nodded and stood motionless until he was certain he heard her departure. Then, he exhaled and threw the panties across the room. Whatever she believed he was, whatever she believed he wanted from her, she was wrong. And whatever he had believed was between them, whatever connection he believed united them beyond their arrangement, he was wrong. She was using him. And he was using her. And with that realization, Sven swept his entire arm over the surface of his dresser, scattering her portrait and the depths of his rage across his bedroom. It was a certainty now—there was nothing that could save him from the looming threats of incapacitating darkness and despair. He was a man completely alone.

Chapter Twenty

INEZ STARED AT HERSELF IN THE three-way mirror, wearing the lilac gown with a slimming bodice, plunging neckline, and a floor-length train with slits up the right and the left thighs. "Please tell me this gown won't be exposing my underwear tomorrow night."

Ebony shifted behind her, tugging gently on the charmeuse and pinning together the final alterations. "That gown cost thirty thousand dollars," she mumbled past a pin between her teeth. "And it was flown in from Paris from one of my favorite couture dress shops in Montmartre. Even the panties were handmade."

"Yeah, I imagined all the little old French women sewing on the ruffles in the mezzanine of the Moulin Rouge."

Ebony smirked and removed the pin from her mouth. "What did Sven think?"

"He thought you were intentionally taunting him. He said you know that he hates tattoos."

"He does. And I was. But I also knew you'd look fabulous in it. Besides, it was the Modern Architecture Society gala. I wasn't going to send you there in some boring conservative Vera Wang knock off. And definitely not with your curves. Did he at least give you a compliment?"

Inez paused before answering, considering both kisses from Sven last night. They weren't from the stern, bitter man that she had assumed he was when they first met. They were kisses from a complex man with a constant undercurrent of heat and passion raging within him.

"I don't think he remembers much about last night," Inez finally said, forcing herself to dismiss everything that had happened between them.

Puzzled, Ebony frowned and wrapped her measuring tape around Inez's bustline. "You know, I don't get it. Your bustline changes size every time I see you. Like…an entire cup size bigger. Are you doing some sort of Suzanne Somers thigh-master for your boobs?"

"Nope. Something way higher maintenance."

Ebony narrowed her eyes, heavy with black eyeliner. "What could possibly be higher maintenance than a thigh-master for your boobs?"

"Breastfeeding."

"What?" Ebony dropped her measuring tape and stood back from the pedestal in disbelief. "You're a mommy? Does Sven know?"

Inez shrugged. "I think he just assumes I'm naturally a quad D."

"Of course he does." Ebony clucked. "Men."

"Men," Inez repeated, picking at her chipped fingernail polish and reflecting on her discovery of Sven—naked with a hard-on in front of Celeste—and her black thong panties.

"Wow, a mommy. I had no idea." Ebony's surprise faded into interest. "So what's your baby's name?"

"Luna. Sometimes, Lunita."

"Lunita—little moon. Aww, that's precious."

Inez nodded, fighting back a sudden wave of emotion. "She's the brightest light in my darkest skies. I never thought I would ever want kids, but then I got pregnant, and now there's no way I can think of my life without her."

"Well, I can tell you one thing," Ebony said with conviction. "I think Sven is starting to think he can't think of *his* life without you. He seems to be under the impression that you're traveling with him to Shanghai."

"What do you mean?" Inez asked, running her hands over the smooth fabric of her dress, taking in its soothing lavender sheen.

Ebony removed a pin from her mouth and darted it into the cushion around her wrist. "He called me yesterday and ordered an entire new wardrobe for you. He wants it finished by the beginning of next week and shipped out to Shanghai."

Incredulous, Inez stared at Ebony in the mirror. "That was probably before I turned him down this morning. He offered to take me to the opera tonight, but I told him I was planning on spending the night with my ex-boyfriend."

"Ouch." Ebony replied, sweeping out the hemline of Inez's gown and checking its length. "So you guys are still together?"

"Not really. Not anymore. Aargh, I don't know. It's all become ridiculous and complicated. And pretending to be Sven's girlfriend has made everything even more ridiculously complicated."

"Yeah, Sven is pretty complicated," Ebony conceded. "Especially after what happened with Celeste and his brother. It broke his heart, you know."

"Yeah, getting dumped by someone who sleeps with your brother is about as low as you can go," Inez confirmed.

"And losing his eyesight because of it just made everything worse for him."

Inez studied their reflections in the mirror and decided to take the leap. "What do you mean…losing his eyesight because of it?"

Ebony gazed back at Inez. "You don't know?"

Inez shook her head.

Heaving a deep sigh, Ebony propped the heel of her black leather boot onto the edge of the pedestal and fiddled with the final alterations along her waistline. "Well, I only know what Sven told me, which isn't much because…well, you know Sven. But apparently, they were all on his yacht together, the day after Sven had returned from a three-week trip to Shanghai. He had organized the getaway because he was preparing to propose to Celeste on the deck of the ship and he wanted Hans to be his best man. But instead, Celeste and Hans told him they had fallen in love while he was away and that they were engaged."

Inez's mouth dropped open. "Ugh…and I thought I was a cold-hearted bitch."

"Yeah, horrible, right? Anyway, I don't know exactly what happened, but Sven was furious, of course. There was some kind of a fight between Sven and Hans, and somehow Sven ended up overboard. He smashed his head against the hull and almost drowned. He was in the hospital for weeks and he permanently lost his vision in his left eye—the one with the patch. And if that wasn't bad enough…the headaches started and then his vision got worse in his right eye. That started about three months ago and he's been trying to hide it ever since."

"I had no idea," Inez replied.

"Yeah, it's been hard. Really hard on him. I mean, it's bad enough that he's losing his vision, especially since he's such a talented architect, but what's worse is how it's changed him. After the accident, he had a slow recovery, and it was like he was a different person—moody, bitter, and resentful. It was as if he hated everyone around him, but even worse, he hated being around himself. And it all seems like such a shame because I don't think he was even really in love with Celeste. I don't think I've ever seen Sven fall in love with anything except for his work. But losing his eyesight jeopardizes everything he's ever worked for. I'm not sure what's going to happen to him. I suppose I had a bit of hope yesterday when he called me and told me you were going to Shanghai with him because it was the first time in a long time that I almost heard the old Sven in his voice."

Inez closed her eyes. She knew what Ebony meant; she had met that Sven last night—charming, unguarded, and inebriated. But after their exchange this morning, it was clear that he was more Dr. Jekyll and Mr. Hyde than she could deal with—even for five thousand dollars per night.

"Well, unfortunately, this is just a job for me and it ends tomorrow night," Inez said. "After that, there's no more fancy gowns and no more galas. Faux Cinderella has to go back to being the unwed maiden with a baby to care for and no time or energy to be rescuing blind Princes or believing in happily ever afters."

"Well, I guess I'm just a hopeless romantic who believes every girl deserves a happily ever after. Or at least, a fabulous gown that makes her feel like a smokin' hot princess—even if it's only for one night."

They both fell silent and admired the lilac evening gown, flattering Inez's dark hair and olive complexion.

"You're very good at your job, Ebony."

"So are you, faux Cinderella. Or Sven wouldn't want you to travel with him to Shanghai."

"Maybe he's just enchanted with my quad D."

Ebony snorted through her nose ring. "Men."

Chapter Twenty-One

INEZ RAN UP THE DIM STAIRWELL with a hopeful heart. She planned to pick up Luna early from Sarah's care and meet Enzo for their first outing as a family—together.

A family. She could barely whisper the phrase in her mind. It felt like a shameful secret—her private longing to be a part of a family. *Yes, she had her grandmother*. And she owed everything to her grandmother for rescuing her from the dysfunctional foster care system after her parents died. But it took nearly five years of administrative paperwork, court hearings, and supervised social service visits to convince them that a legally blind seventy-year old woman could properly care for her granddaughter; and by that point, Inez had grown from an emotionally scarred child into a disillusioned, hardened teenager who had long since given up on the idea of being part of a traditional family. A mother and father, sisters and brothers are what everyone else had. She had her grandmother, and now, she had her own daughter.

And for Luna's sake, she wasn't ready to give up on the ideal of a traditional family. *Luna deserved better*; *she deserved a father*. Inez considered the possibility that she had been too quick to judge Enzo. He had been faithful to her for the time that they were together; she knew that much. And the same night he had taken the photographs hanging in the gallery at the museum, he had promised he would marry her. She had believed him because she loved him and she thought he had loved her.

She swallowed hard as she reached the third floor landing. There had only been one time when she had ever had sex without a condom—the night that they conceived Luna. It had been unplanned and unexpected, a moment of unbridled intimacy between them during their final night together before he left for Argentina. *The night he had promised to marry her—someday. And she believed him*. But in the end, the only thing an entire year of separation yielded was the birth of their child and the cruel lesson that her love was a gift that could be received, used, and returned—even without her consent.

Now, all those intimate nights making love in his studio loft seemed like a tragic love affair between two people who vaguely knew each other. *Except for the fact that she had loved him.* She had loved him, truly, deeply, and in a way that opened herself up to more pain from his betrayal than she could possibly endure because it not only shattered her heart, but also her dreams of a future together—together with Luna.

Was he really willing to start over and commit to her? Was she a fool for wanting to give him another chance? Heartache flared inside her, but the possibility of giving Luna something better than her own childhood seemed so much more important than punishing Enzo for screwing around, because she wouldn't just be punishing Enzo. She would be punishing Luna, too.

Was it too much to dare to wish for now, a father and a mother—together? For Inez, it had always been a splinter in her heart that she constantly sanded over with anger and resentment—anger and resentment at the world for depriving her of something as basic as a family. But for her innocent, unblemished baby, everything still seemed possible. It was this realization that spurred Inez up the final steps and through Sarah's unlocked apartment door. Yes, she was willing to swallow her own wounded pride if it meant giving Enzo another chance to prove that he meant what he had texted her—that he wanted to be with Luna and her, together as a family. But selfishly she was willing to offer him another chance because it meant holding onto the hope that those intimate nights in Enzo's loft weren't just a lost love affair between two strangers; they were moments shared between two people who had loved each other deeply enough to have a baby and who still could love each other that deeply again.

"Helloooooo?" Inez called out in a hushed voice, stopping herself in the living room and noting the unusual silence within the apartment. Only the broken blinds rattled like dry bones in the breeze wafting in through the open window. Inez crept along the hardwood floors of the hallway, knowing the most evil thing you could do to a babysitter and a baby was to wake them both up from naptime. She paused again, just outside Sarah's bedroom when she spotted Luna in the bathroom, strapped in her car seat, eyes open while sucking on her favorite giraffe.

But where was Sarah? Inez quickly unstrapped Luna and swooped her up into her arms. Her fresh baby scent and velvet skin soothed all her senses. "I missed you," she cooed, rubbing her cheek against Luna's dark, downy head of baby hair. She opened her mouth to call out for Sarah until she heard something from the bedroom that stopped her. It was a moan, too bass and guttural to be Sarah exhaling through difficult yoga poses. She carried Luna down the hallway and noted the bedroom door left ajar. She peered into it and everything turned to slow motion—Enzo's strong naked body over Sarah's bare lithe figure; the expression on Sarah's face, eyes shut, mouth slackened with ecstasy, enduring his primal thrusts; the churning of the ceiling fan that spun Inez's emotions into a visceral need to vomit.

Stirring in her arms, Luna spit out her pacifier and released an impatient whine. It was feeding time.

Sarah opened her topaz blue eyes and spotted Inez and Luna through the doorway. "Stop, stop, stop—" She scratched at Enzo's bare back while kicking him off her, as if there was some way she expected to cover up the fact that they were fucking each other.

Inez pushed open the door with one hand. "Oh please, don't stop because of us," Inez slung at them. "Your multiple orgasms are clearly more important than babysitting my infant."

"Inez," Enzo implored her, his hand stretching out to her like he expected her to join them. "Don't—"

"Don't what, Enzo? Call you both out for being assholes for leaving Luna alone in another room while you two hump each other like teenage rabbits?" Her fury shifted onto Sarah. "And you. I already knew Enzo was a manwhore. But I was under the illusion that you were my friend."

Sarah gathered the sheets around her naked body and flipped her long strawberry blonde hair over her shoulder. She shrugged and drew out a long-winded sigh, the way she did whenever she was smoking her Virginia Slims. "Well, it's not like you're still dating him."

Inez stared at her, unable to comprehend her complete lack of common decency.

"Wow, that's true, Sarah. Thanks for the reminder. I can't believe I even considered anything else except dumping him. Especially when he's more than willing to fuck anyone who will spread her legs and say please."

Sarah snorted, like she was both insulted and amused. They both knew she was always willing to spread her legs for whoever would take her.

Enzo jumped out of bed and confronted Inez, full frontal. "Sarah is right, Inez. You have not said that you wanted to come back to me. But now, I wonder if you are so angry because you are as jealous to see me with Sarah as I am when I see you with your new, fancy boyfriend."

Inez glared at him while Luna writhed in her arms. "The only thing I'm truly angry about is that I was so wrong about you, Enzo. So wrong about us." She fought to hold back tears. *She would not cry in front of him, damn it. She would not ugly cry.*

Still hard with arousal, he spread his palms open like he had nothing to hide. "Inez, *mi amor*…it is just sex. It is not love."

He kissed Luna on the head. Every fiber in Inez's body fought to keep from pulling her away from him. He was still Luna's father; nothing had changed except the foolish fantasy that he could offer Inez more than that.

"I'm not interested in being with a man who thinks sex and love are two separate things, Enzo."

He reached out and stroked her cheek. "Our kind of love made our child. Is that not all that matters?"

Inez saw her own reflection in his dark glossy eyes and it reminded her what she was capable of without depending on anyone. "The only thing that matters is that whoever I'm with makes me happy. And I've finally accepted, Enzo, that's not going to be you."

Enzo scoffed. "And is that what you are getting from your new, fancy boyfriend?"

She shifted her eyes to Sarah, and then thought about all the other nameless, faceless women he had slept with. "Well, I'm certainly not getting chlamydia."

It was a bitchy assault against them both, but she didn't care. Luna was hungry and fussing, and it was time to finally leave the disappointment and betrayal behind her. Turning out of the bedroom, she attempted to gather up Luna's car seat and head for the door.

"Inez—" He called after her, his voice stern and reprimanding. "We have a child together. You cannot deny that we will always be connected through her."

Exhausted and empty, Inez shot him a glare, her emotions spinning and repeating like a warped record. "Yeah, it's called child support, Enzo. Read up on it. You'll be getting a notice in the mail."

Chapter Twenty-Two

HAD HE LOST HER *or had he pushed her away?* Sven sank deeper into his black leather sofa and stared at the Monet painting. He had spent the morning counting and recounting the water lilies, certain every time he tried he lost one more lily in the process. It had been a bad morning with his visits from both Celeste and Inez, and now his eyesight was failing him again. He had one more day until the opening of The Spire, and then he would be forced to come to a decision about going to Shanghai. But all of that seemed impossible—even meaningless—without her help. But it was more than her help that he wanted, he thought, while his unpatched eye drifted over the blurry water lilies. It was also her companionship that he craved. She had come this morning to check in on him, exactly as she promised she would, but somehow, for some reason, his bitter and hardened heart had pushed her away the moment there was conflict between them. Yes, he had pushed her away.

He heard the familiar ring tone from his pocket. *His office.*

"Yes," he answered, irritated. He wanted the caller to know he was interrupting him.

"Are you alone or with your new girlfriend?" Hans fired at him in Dutch.

Sven paused, resisting the urge to fling an answer back at him. The only time they spoke Dutch was when they weren't alone and they didn't want to be understood by the people around them. Hans clearly intended to discuss something covertly.

"That depends…do you want to discuss business or my sex life?"

"Business, Sven." Hans sounded faintly amused. "I know you hold your sex life in high regard, but it is of little interest to me."

Ironic, Sven thought. Especially since he was now the one sleeping with Celeste.

"I do not think it's wise of you to be holding out on signing the Shanghai deal," Hans warned him.

"Is that why you sent Celeste here this morning? To convince me to sign as lead architect?"

"I thought that she would have more influence than me."

"Well, you were wrong," Sven sighed loudly and stretched out his legs. He was already growing bored with the conversation and he wanted Hans to know it. "Neither of you have any influence on me."

"Ahh, I see. Then, Celeste is right. The only one who influences you these days is the little girl."

Sven suddenly rose from the couch. The way he said *klein meisje* made it sound like Sven was fucking an under-aged teenager, and if Hans had been there—standing in front of him—Sven would have lunged at him with the same violence that inspired the accident on his yacht.

"You mean Inez," Sven stressed.

"Yes, the Mexican. Celeste says the only way you are going to Shanghai is if she goes with you. She says that you are in love, but I told her you've never been in love in your entire life."

"I am sure Celeste appreciates hearing that," Sven replied wryly. But Hans dismissed him.

"Are you really letting your cock determine whether or not you're going to sign on to the biggest deal of your career?"

"I thought my sex life was of little importance to you," Sven shot back. His patience was waning and his brother's crudeness reminded him of how different they were and everything he had hated about sharing the van der Meer name with him.

Hans laughed. "It's true, although the little girl certainly has put a spell on you. Watercross will not wait for you forever. After the opening tomorrow night, he's headed to Shanghai to meet with the Chinese officials about finalizing the construction permits for the Li Long Towers. I am planning on joining him. You should be there as well."

"And what will you do if I am not?"

It was a veiled threat and Hans understood it.

"Watercross is selling The Spire to Harvey Zale. He'll have the capital and the clout. I carry the van der Meer name. We will find a way to move forward without you, Sven. Can you say the same thing, brother?"

The line fell silent and for a brief moment, Sven simply didn't care. As if Hans feared he had lost Sven's cooperation completely, he softened his tone. "Watercross still needs an architect to design and build the towers, and there's still a new opportunity here to rebuild the van der Meer empire."

Rebuilding an empire, Sven thought. Two years ago, Sven had felt like an emperor, striving for professional acclaim through his most ambitious endeavor—his design and construction of The Spire. Now, as he sank back down into his leather sofa, he could barely count to ten water lilies on the Monet painting and his head ached with remorse while considering everything he had lost during his quest for greatness. He had become a shadow of the man he once was, and that man was someone he had no desire to become again. *Who was he now*? He dared not pose the question. He only knew that he felt financially and professionally trapped and going to Shanghai seemed like the only option for maintaining his shadow rather than endure the consequences of it disappearing completely.

"Bring the contract with you tomorrow night," Sven finally said, rubbing his forehead and surrendering himself to the undercurrent of pain that had plagued him.

He didn't wait for Hans' response. He simply hung up and tossed his phone to the other end of the sofa. His mind immediately focused on her. He was willing to pay her whatever she wanted to come with him. Double, even triple per night. *But would she be willing to accept him*? He doubted it. She thought the worst about him in every way and his actions towards her this morning reinforced all those beliefs. Still, a fleeting hope simmered beneath his stubborn pride and he quickly retrieved his phone.

"James?" he called into the receiver.

"Yes, sir?" his driver attentively answered.

"Did you already return Miss Sanchez to her home after her fitting at Ebony's?"

"Yes, sir. Of course."

Sven paused and hesitated before launching his next inquiry. "Was she accompanied by a man?"

"A man, sir?"

"Yes, like a boyfriend."

"No, sir. There wasn't anyone with her except for her baby."

A rush of confusion coursed through Sven's chest. "Her baby?" He rubbed his furrowing brow.

"Yes, sir. After Ebony's, she instructed me to return to the apartment building at Paulina. She told me not to wait for her because she was done for the day, so I idled the car at the curb for a few moments to check my phone messages. But then she came out again, saying that she had changed her mind, and asked if I would drive her and her baby to the mansion in Ravenswood Manor. So of course I drove them there."

"The same mansion you've taken her to the past two nights?"

"Yes, of course, sir."

Sven rubbed his jaw, painstakingly allowing every frame of interaction with Inez to flash through his mind. Then, he replayed them all again with one pivotal revision—*she was a young mother with a baby*.

"Please…" Sven finally said after a long pause of reflective silence. "Please meet me downstairs. I'd like you to drive me there as soon as possible."

* * * *

"Yes, sir. I'm certain this is it." It was the third time that James confirmed the address.

Sven peered out the car window at the rundown house. It had taken thirty minutes to drive from downtown to the Northside and across the river into Ravenswood Manor, and the thought of turning back without her no longer seemed like an option. He squinted harder. His vision was fading with every hour, but the bright afternoon sunlight allowed him to make out the familiar silhouette of the nineteenth-century brownstone and its aging white gables. He had redesigned and modernized so many of them during his first years as a junior architect that now it almost seemed like he was viewing an endangered species. Pushing open the rear door of the Rolls Royce, he exited on his own and guided himself up the stone stairs with the help of the rotting wooden banister.

He spotted the kaleidoscope of colors above the threshold of the front door. *Could it be an original Tiffany stained-glass window*? Raising up onto his toes to peer through it, he quickly realized it would be impossible for him to make out anything beyond its iridescent blue and green glass. He swept his hand along the door frame for a doorbell, but failed to find one. Instead, he zeroed in on the lion's head door knocker. *Original to the house*, he smirked, knowing the wear on its bronze patina couldn't be faked. He knocked twice using its nose ring, the solid walnut door shuddering with the tolling clank of the metal like an echo through a cavernous tomb.

His smile faded when a woman's sharp voice belted through the door. "If you bang on my door again, I'll call the police after I shoot you dead with my .45."

Sven raised his hands like he was under arrest. "I'm sorry..." he paused, waiting to be mortally wounded before backing away to the edge of the stairs. "I did not mean to be intrusive."

"That's what they all say," the woman's voice spat back like a slap. "Real polite like that, too."

Uncertain, Sven fell silent.

"Look, I'll do us both a favor and give it to you straight," the woman continued without opening the door. "I don't believe in God, so I don't need to be saved. I don't need any fancy makeup because I'm old and crusty. And I can't eat any of them Girl Scout cookies because of my blood sugar levels. So unless you're selling a frontal massage or a pack of Marlboro Golds, I ain't interested."

"I am not selling anything," Sven replied, surprised at the waver in his voice. "I am looking for someone. Miss Inez Sanchez. I was told she lives here, but I think I must be mistaken…"

He started to turn down the stairs when the sound of unbolting locks stopped him. He glanced back at the door and made out an image of a blurry old woman peering out the door.

"You don't sound like that cheating rat bastard boyfriend of hers, are you?"

Sven hesitated. He wasn't exactly sure how to answer that. "I hope not."

"Well…" The woman turned up her nose up into the air like she was sniffing him out. "You've got an accent, but it's not Argentine."

"No, I'm Dutch. My name is Sven. Sven van der Meer. Could you please tell Inez I'm here to see her?"

"Sven van der Meer? The famous architect?"

"Yes."

"The one who designed The Spire?"

"Yes."

"Oh, nuts." The woman sighed and suddenly closed the door.

Sven waited, perplexed by the fact that she seemed to know more than he did about the implications of his own name. He heard the unbolting of three heavy locks before the door swung fully open.

"So you're Bachelor Number Two."

Sven hesitated again. "I'm not sure. Is that a good thing?"

The old woman shrugged. "Can't say I've been rooting for you. I've got my bets placed on Eddie, the choral director at the church. But Inez is convinced he's batting for the other team."

Sven peered out at her, trying to make out her meaning. "You mean…he plays baseball?"

The woman huffed and rolled her eyes. "No, genius. Gay."

"Ah, I see."

"And still lives with his mother."

"Yes, well…that could get uncomfortable."

"Not when there's a baby to care for. All hands on deck, you know."

Sven fell silent. "You mean…Inez's baby?"

The old woman snorted like he was the dumbest man on the planet. "No, genius. Somebody *else's* baby that she found on the side of the road." Wearing only her flannel nightgown, she shuffled onto the porch in her slippers. "Yeah, of course, *her* baby—my great-granddaughter, Luna."

Luna, a baby girl, Sven thought. "Well, could you please tell her I'm here to see her?"

"Nope. She's out walking Luna in the stroller."

Sven's chest tightened with anticipation. "Please…could I wait for her then?"

"Depends," the old woman said, chewing on her thoughts. "How good are you at bingo?"

"I am the best there ever was." It was a lie. Sven had never played bingo in his life.

"You got cash?" The woman eyed him.

"Of course." He withdrew his handkerchief and flashed the bills at her.

The woman turned up her nose. "I'm legally blind, but I can smell the scent of fresh bills from a mile away."

"Hundred dollar bills. Mint condition."

"We're gonna get along."

"Better than Eddie, the choral director?" Sven asked in jest.

"Don't get ahead of yourself. I'm no sweet petunia that just got picked yesterday, and my granddaughter and great-granddaughter deserve the best."

"I'll bet you a hundred dollar game of bingo on it," he offered slyly.

The old woman seemed to consider the wager. "Well, c'mon then. Might as well take your money away from you while we're stuck here together."

She disappeared into the house, allowing Sven to pass inside the doorway and into the grand foyer. Immediately, its dim lighting crippled his sight. Everything fell into muddy shadows and he lost his bearings until the old woman's voice called to him from the other end of the hallway.

"Living room's in here. The house is drafty. I like to sit next to the fireplace."

He walked forward, touching the wall for guidance until he discovered a banister running along it. He gripped it like a security line and followed the scent of singed pine. It relaxed his senses and drew him into the bright, octagonal living room, its grand arching windows letting in the light through sheer curtains. He quickly adjusted his vision, expecting to see a room crowded with antiques and period piece furniture. Instead, he made out the image of a crib in the darkest corner of the room, a baby swing adjacent to it, and a changing table near the windows. He stepped forward, then stopped when he heard a squeaky toy below his feet. He retrieved it, a miniature rubber giraffe. The only things more abundant than baby items were towers of books, magazines, and newspapers, stacked like firewood against the far wall.

"C'mon, you can sit there…in Inez's chair."

She nodded to the wooden rocking chair across from her sofa recliner. He sat down and unexpectedly swept backwards with an eerie creak.

The old woman spread several cards across the coffee table like she was preparing for business. "Where's the pot?"

He flipped the hundred dollar bill into the center of the table. The woman picked up the bill and inhaled its crisp scent. Then, she retrieved a large magnifying glass from her knitting basket to inspect it. Satisfied with its authenticity, she dropped the bill onto the table.

"Ok, here are the rules: if you win, I get to keep your money. If I win, I get to keep your money."

"You drive a hard bargain."

"True. But you're in my house, waiting for my granddaughter, so those are the rules. Take them or leave them."

Shifting in the rocker, Sven pulled out his handkerchief and threw a second hundred dollar bill into the pot. The woman inspected it and whistled. "Now I know why you're Bachelor Number Two."

"I like to drive a harder bargain."

"Well, it won't get you out of being the game caller." She nudged the ball spinner across the table at him. "Give it a whirl and we're off to the races."

Sven obeyed, spun the cage with its handle, and withdrew a marked ball.

"May I?" he asked, holding out his hand for her magnifying glass.

She conceded and raised her nose into the air, as if she was sizing him up. "So you're far-sighted?"

"Partially blind," he corrected her and inspected the ball under the concave glass. "Fourteen…G"

"G-Fourteen," she corrected him. "Just as I suspected. You're not a bingo player."

"True." He smiled, recognizing Inez's bluntness. "You've found me out."

"Well, there's always a first time," the old woman sighed, reaching out for the magnifying glass and scanning her own card before placing a plastic dot over the G14. "So…Sven van der Meer, the famous architect is partially blind? I bet that's some horse and pony trick."

"Yes, it has been a trick," Sven agreed. "But your granddaughter has been helping me. Now I understand why she's been so good at it. She has had a lot of practice."

"Yep, since the first day she came to live with me after her parents died. Spin the cage," she directed him.

He paused, spun the handle, and retrieved the ball. She passed back the magnifying glass and he called out the number. "B-seven. So she lost both her parents at the same time?" he asked, not certain he had a right to know about Inez's past.

"Car accident. Black ice. Head on collision, killed her father instantly," Inez's grandmother confirmed. "Smashed his whole body against the steering wheel like an accordion. The other car's bumper clipped my daughter in the head. She lingered like a vegetable for a few weeks but didn't make it. Inez was in the car in the rear seat, but by the grace of God, she walked away without a scratch. Eight-years old. Tough as nails that little girl. Still tough as nails."

"Like her grandmother, perhaps," Sven added.

"Well, I can't take any credit for that," Inez's grandmother said, taking back the magnifying glass. "Childcare Services put her in foster care and I didn't get her turned over to me until she was almost thirteen. You lose a whole lot of innocence by the time you're thirteen and Inez was thirteen going on thirty by the time she came to live with me. And now she's got her own baby and her granny to care for, and I fear she's never gonna know what it's like to have fun and be young without a care in the world."

Sven accepted the shared magnifying glass and spun the cage. "I think there are many of us who have forgotten what it feels like to have fun and be young without a care in the world."

"Which is exactly why you two are playing bingo together—of course."

Sven and Inez's grandmother turned towards Inez's voice. Standing in the threshold between the living room and the doorway, she held her baby in her arms, but her accusatory glare fell upon Sven, challenging his intrusion into her private world.

Inez's grandmother shrugged. "Well, don't make it sound like it's a conspiracy against you…he came by here, looking for you, and he said he wanted to wait. Can't blame me for accepting his money to teach him how to play bingo."

"No, I don't blame you, Nana," she replied, sweeping up the two hundred dollar bills and stuffing them back into Sven's hand. "But I do blame him. Apparently, he's under the impression that everyone is for sale."

Sven crushed the bills into his fist, his hand burned by her rejection. Slowly, he rose from the rocker, cleared his throat, and avoided direct eye contact. The tension between them—*her against him*—lanced his heart without mercy. "I came here because I still have opera tickets tonight, and I would like you to accompany me."

Inez scoffed, as if it was not only insulting, but also inconceivable. "Well, I sort of lost my evening babysitter, and as you can see, I have obligations beyond just fancy nights of wearing gowns and high heels, pretending to be something I'm not."

He clenched his jaw and strained to hold her gaze. His sight was fading, and his conviction that he could steal her away with him was waning with every verbal strike she made against him. Her baby fussed in her arms, reminding him of the reality of her situation.

"Excuse me." She pushed past him towards the rocker. Settling into it, she unapologetically swept up her T-shirt and unclipped her bra. "Plus, I doubt I'd be able to do this very easily at the opera," she taunted him, openly nursing her baby.

Sven forced himself not to look away. She was testing him and he would not fail her challenge. He had been raised in a country where breastfeeding in public was routine; he had seen countless mothers nursing their babies and never thought twice about it. But admittedly, none of those women were women he had previously wanted—sexually. And now, he was surprised that the only desire that flared up within him was the urge to protect her.

"I have box seats, so we can do whatever you like, including bringing your daughter with us," he said, carefully, cautiously, without any other insinuations of obligation.

"To the opera?" Inez looked at him like he was crazy. "Clearly, you haven't spent much time around babies."

"No, but I'm willing to try."

"They cry—a lot." Inez swayed faster in her rocker.

Unaffected, he shrugged.

"They poop even more," she insisted.

He looked down at the tiny creature in her arms. *How much could she possibly poop*?

"They sleep—most of the time," Nana cut in, like she was watching a tennis match and she wanted to throw a beer can onto the courts, just for extra entertainment. "And crowded, noisy places will do just the trick. Unless it's Wagner. In which case, she might be scarred for life."

"Puccini," Sven replied. "*La Bohème*."

"You've got a winner," Nana said with a nod.

Inez glared at her traitorous grandmother. "I have nothing here to wear to the freaking opera," she asserted.

Obviously, she believed it was impossible, which made Sven even more determined. "Something for you to wear can easily be arranged," he replied and retrieved his phone.

"No—" she stopped him. "I'm not your little doll coming out of the cupboard tonight."

Sven lowered his phone. It was true, he was about to ring Ebony, but he swiftly ended the call.

"I have a dress…I think," she finally offered like a truce. "But I'm not wearing heels."

Their eyes locked.

"I don't even care if you wear sneakers. I just want you to come." He held her gaze. In that moment, he was committed to her—not to their arrangement—and he wanted her to know it. "What else do you need?"

Inez rocked with fury, then finally answered him. "A dress for Luna."

Sven exhaled with relief, certain he could meet that challenge. "Okay, good…these things can be arranged." He held up his phone again, waiting to see if she would protest. Instead, she added to the order.

"And probably a nicer diaper bag. Unless you think I can get away with Hello Kitty."

He followed her nod to the garish pink tote bag decorated with the famous cartoon emblem, lying on the floor near the entryway. He paused, wondering what else a mother might need to take care of her baby, but he suspected Ebony would have the answers. He started to make the call, but stopped when Inez interrupted him.

"This is seriously ridiculous." Her dark searing eyes fixed onto him. "Us—attempting to bring an almost four-month-old baby to the opera? You do realize this, right? Ridiculous."

"I don't think it's ridiculous in the slightest," he countered, flashing her a smile. "In fact, I'm certain it will be the best night at the opera I have had in a long, long time."

Chapter Twenty-Three

SVEN'S BLACK ROLLS ROYCE ROLLED up to the curb and stopped in front of the Lyric Opera House. Sweeping open the door, James extended his hand and assisted her out of the car. *It was all a surreal dream*, Inez thought, as taxis and limousines filed behind them. Women in fur coats and men in black suits mingled in front of the grand terracotta entryway. Inez glanced back into the rear seat, preparing to scoop up Luna into her arms until Sven suddenly appeared next to her.

Carrying Luna's entire car seat by its handle, he said, "I will do the heavy lifting if you guide the way."

"Deal." Inez noted his stylish masculine suit coat and tie, offset by the maternal black leather diaper bag slung over his shoulder.

He made it look so easy, she thought. She could barely lift Luna's forty pound car seat, much less carry it with Luna in it, plus her diaper bag. Now, Sven made it all look effortless, as if it was the most natural thing in the world, escorting his date in one hand while hoisting a baby's car seat in his other. Inez glanced down at Luna. She was chewing on her rubber, squeaky giraffe and kicking her socked feet past the hem of her frilly pink princess gown.

Inez accepted Sven's arm and guided them into the opulent grand lobby. Luna's brown eyes brightened, captivated by the sparkling chandelier lights and the murmuring sea of patrons.

"Look for the stairs to the mezzanine," Sven instructed her. "We will take them up to the box seats."

Inez nodded and led them through the crowd, scanning the faces of the ushers, certain they would soon be stopped by the opera police.

"Oh, look at *her*..." a woman exclaimed from behind her. Inez glanced back at a pair of older women in black sequined dresses. Expecting to weather the judgmental glare of Madame Nasty and her Nastier Twin Sister, she frowned at them until she realized they weren't noticing her simple black skirt or worn ballet flats. They were cooing at Luna with endearment.

"What a lovely family," one woman said to the other.

Drawing Inez's hand closer into his body, Sven smiled and nodded politely. *It wasn't that he just made it seem all too easy*, Inez thought, relaxing within the security of his arm. *It was the fact that he made her feel like she and Luna belonged there.*

"Stairs," she cautioned him.

"Yes, thank you."

Together, they followed the staircase up to the mezzanine where an usher in a black concierge uniform greeted them.

"Good evening, Mr. van der Meer. It's been a long time since we've seen you last. Welcome back to the Lyric." The usher extended his hand and Sven shook it warmly.

"Thank you, Andrew. It has been a while."

"And now, I understand why." The usher looked down at Luna and smiled. "Congratulations to you both."

Inez glanced over at Sven, but he did not correct the assumption that Luna was his own child.

"Thank you," Sven replied. "We are looking forward to an enjoyable evening."

"Nothing is more enjoyable or romantic than the arias of Puccini," the usher offered, spreading out his hands like it was a certainty. He guided them along a narrow corridor and past floor-length red velvet curtains into their private box seats furnished with two regal sitting chairs.

The chandelier lights flickered throughout the auditorium, signaling the imminent start of the performance. Inez leaned into the balcony, noting the gold gilt carvings etched into its wooden railing, and gazed down upon the people seated below them. Their chatter and laughter floated up through the air like gleeful bubbles and the arpeggios of the brass horns and strings from the orchestra pit rolled in waves through the auditorium's cathedral ceilings.

"I feel like a queen." She sat back in her seat against the plush velvet of the upholstered chair.

"Fitting." Sven nodded, as if he was enjoying the fact that she was enjoying herself.

The lights flickered again before slowly fading into darkness. Abruptly, the crowd broke into applause, welcoming the orchestra conductor onto the podium. Just as Inez had feared, Luna began to whimper and fuss. She quickly unclipped her car seat belt and swept her up into her arms. Searching for a way to keep her calm and quiet, Inez dug through the black leather diaper bag.

"She can't possibly be hungry. I just fed her."

Luna whined again, this time with enough conviction to project her reverberating cry over the balcony.

"Here, give her to me." Sven confidently reached out and drew Luna into his lap. Inez watched and waited, expecting Luna to writhe against him.

Then, as if on cue, the heavy velvet curtains swept open as the bright lights and lively music introduced the picturesque stage and two male opera singers.

Mesmerized by the booming voices of the tenors, Luna chewed on her rubber giraffe and settled into Sven's lap. He comforted her with a subtle sway, as if he had held a hundred babies before her. He didn't act like she was a *thing* he had to worry about; he simply treated her like an extension of himself. After a few minutes, he glanced over at Inez, sharing an intimate smile, taking pleasure in the rare moment of harmony. It had been the perfect plan and everything was under control. She smiled back at him and relaxed in her own seat. *Yes, it was a rare moment of harmony*, she thought, made rarer by the fact that she wasn't hiding who she really was or pretending to be someone she wasn't.

It only lasted a brief moment. She shifted in her chair, unnerved by the sensation of someone staring directly at her. She swept her eyes across the auditorium, searching out the source. *Eliot Watercross.* From the private box seats on the opposite side of the stage, he saluted her with a tilt of his head and a flash of his Hollywood grin while his fierce eyes fixed on her. She rubbed her wrist and winced, his constricting clasp still fresh in her memory from the last time they had met. She glanced at Sven who was unable to see beyond the private, insular world within their box seats. Then, she shot a glare back at Watercross, still watching them, delivering his subliminal warning—he was patiently waiting for Sven's cooperation. A sinking sickness consumed her from the inside out as she considered what would happen if Sven chose not to cooperate—or worse, if his failing eyesight made him unable to cooperate. *Watercross would ruin him.*

Instinctively, she reached out and enveloped Sven's hand in hers, unifying them. Sven peered down at her grasp, letting the soft curve of her hand meld into his own. She had held his hand many times over the past few days, physically steering him through lobbies and hallways, and socially escorting him to dinners and parties, but never had she felt such a sense of allegiance between them as she felt now.

When Inez shifted her focus again to the opposite side of the auditorium, the box seats were vacant and Watercross was gone. For a moment, she wondered if she had imagined it all until she saw his unmistakable shadow swaggering through the corridor running behind the box seat curtains. Sven noted the tension release from her hand.

"Are you enjoying yourself?"

"I am now," she said, nodding to Luna who had fallen fast asleep in Sven's lap.

"That's the power of Puccini," he replied.

"I guess that makes her a high society girl already."

"Yes, like her mother." He delicately shifted Luna's weight into the crook of his other arm.

"It won't last long, you know," Inez warned him. "In an hour, she'll wake up and want to be fed and I'll have to whip out my boob in front of the entire auditorium."

"Sounds wonderful," he quipped.

She flashed him a smile and looked down at Luna. "It's a long drive back to Ravenswood, so maybe we should make our escape at intermission?"

"Unless we take her home."

Home—Inez repeated the word in her mind. He let the invitation linger between them, like he had done so many times before. But this time was different. This time, he offered it and shifted his gaze away, fully preparing for her rejection.

Like she had done so many times before, she opened her mouth to refuse him until the music softened and the spotlight sharpened onto the lead tenor whose serenade to the gypsy flower girl soared through the auditorium and silenced Inez's soul.

"Okay," she finally replied with a nod. "Let's take her home."

Chapter Twenty-Four

SHE SAT IN THE LUMINOUS moonlight, nursing and rocking Luna to sleep within the solace of Sven's balcony suite, enclosed in glass and encircled by an exterior garden patio overlooking the vast starless night and the churning black waters of Lake Michigan. Somehow, someway, Sven had arranged a crib and rocking chair to be delivered to his penthouse. *He must have done it earlier that evening*, she thought, despite the fact that he had no assurance that Inez would agree to come home with him. Now, as she swayed back and forth with Luna nestled in her arms, she felt his silent presence in the adjacent master bedroom as he dimmed the lights to ensure her peace and comfort.

He did not want to disturb them. She reflected on his efforts to accommodate them since the moment he realized she was not just his sassy, opinionated temporary hire, but also a struggling single mother. *It had not been what she expected from him.* In the past several hours, he had surprised her at every turn, except perhaps for his offer to spend the night. And by finally accepting it, she had surprised herself.

Yet tonight was different than previous nights because he had offered her the balcony suite—her *own* room—to nurse and sleep with Luna without any hint that he desired more from her. He had offered it to her as a gesture of generosity and compassion rather than a complex extension of their business arrangement, and it made her feel safe and secure when there were so few times in her life that she had ever felt safe and secure.

She synchronized the rocking chair to the motion of the waves that curled across the surface of the lake, until she was certain Luna was fast asleep. After a few moments, she noticed a sudden shift in the light and peered out of the glass door leading into the garden patio. Barefoot and coatless, Sven was there, peering over the balcony railing with his head angled towards the sound of the ebbing and flowing crests. His dress shirt was untucked and his tie had been discarded, as if the open air and caressing breeze had lured him into abandoning all formalities. Rising from her seat, she cradled Luna, asleep and warm in her pink flannel onesie, and carefully transferred her into the solid wood crib, hand-carved and ornamental like a throne. *Clearly, he had spared no expense.*

She slid open the glass door and exited onto the patio. He turned as she approached him.

"Is she asleep?"

"For now."

He nodded and shifted his attention back to the hypnotic rhythm of the waves. She shivered and he revealed his suit coat in his hand.

"I thought you might be cold, but I did not want to intrude." His firm chest brushed behind her back as he draped his coat over her shoulders.

"Thank you," she whispered, noting the way his fingertips grazed her skin.

"You know, you had me fooled for a little while..." His voice trailed off as he fixed his vacant gaze on the black abyss beyond the balcony.

"Because I didn't tell you about her?"

"No." He dropped his head and drew his bare foot across the patio's smooth tiled surface. "Because you made it seem like tending to a baby would be much more difficult than I could manage." He flashed her a playful smile, clearly trying to get a rise out of her.

"Well, you made it seem *way* easier than it normally is," Inez replied defensively. "And really, you got off easy because you didn't have to change a poopy diaper on the floor of the men's bathroom."

"Yes, that sounds truly horrifying."

"Whatever, Sven. Let's wait and see if you still have that cocky smile when projectile baby spit-up is all over your three thousand dollar Armani suit."

"Unfathomable," he mused, leaning his back against the balcony railing.

"Okay, fine…you win," she conceded with a toss of her hair over her shoulder. "It was pretty easy tonight. Magically easy in comparison to so many other days that have not been so easy."

"I have no doubt there have been many days when it has not been so easy." He reached out and replaced a wayward strand of her hair behind her ear.

"But still so worth it," she whispered.

"I am certain of it."

Their gaze connected, and for a moment, she thought she saw his eyes focus on hers with clarity.

"Sven…I don't think I can go to Shanghai with you."

"I understand." There was no judgment in his voice. He made it sound like an obvious fact.

Her mind traveled back to the opera house and Eliot Watercross. "What's going to happen if you don't go?"

"I don't know," he replied, bouncing his weight against the balcony. "It is a strange feeling, really. When you are trapped, you have this inclination to fight your way out of it. Fight, fight, fight. That's why I hired you—to help me fight them to preserve my career and my reputation, the reputation of a man so consumed by anger and bitterness that he has forgotten why any of it matters in the first place."

"It matters because you're a talented architect who deserves the chance to achieve great things, and it's not fair that they're trying to take that from you."

"Yes, and I could try to keep fighting them if I wanted to. Or I could just accept that things have changed for me in a way that makes it impossible to fight them anymore."

"But you can't just give up either, Sven. You'll lose all your money."

He shrugged. "I will make more."

"They'll steal your designs and claim them as their own," she insisted.

"I will design something better."

"But it's not fair that they'll go to Shanghai and pretend that they deserve to build the Li Long Towers when that opportunity is rightfully yours."

"And they will all be miserable together," he said confidently. "But not me. I have been so consumed with the injustice of my loss—physical, personal, and professional..." He cleared his throat and adjusted his eyepatch. "But now I realize the true injustice is how much of myself I've truly lost along the way. And rather than feeling angry about everything I stand to lose, I feel somehow better about what I have to gain."

The intensity of his gaze arrested her. "What do you have to gain?"

"A reminder of who I was before all of this."

"I'm pretty sure I wouldn't like a happier Sven van der Meer," she teased.

"Because you've gotten so used to the moodier, disillusioned one?"

She nodded. "At least I'm certain the old, bitter Sven would keep taking Luna and me to tragic operas where the gypsy flower girl gets tuberculosis and dies at the end. The new, gleeful Sven might start taking us to *Sesame Street Live*, and I much prefer the tragic operas."

He smirked. "I am fairly certain the new, gleeful Sven would still be honored to take you and Luna to the opera."

"Well, if the new Sven is all sunshine and roses, then I guarantee he'll grow tired of the fact that I'm still as moody and disillusioned as the old Sven."

"No," he countered, drawing her hand into his own. "He would not have it any other way."

"How can he be so sure?" She breathlessly awaiting his answer.

He gazed at her, as if he heard her naming her deepest, most secret fear, and in response, he pressed her hand against his racing heart. "Because over the past few days, the old Sven has come to realize you are the main reason for his happiness now. And he has no intention of letting that go."

Their eyes locked, but this time—unlike the nights before—he would not allow her to pull away. Drawing her closer into his body, he nuzzled the interior of her wrist, letting the sensation of his kiss overwhelm her. She opened her mouth to protest—a weak, futile plea to release her before they crossed that invisible line of intimacy that prevented them going back from where they had come.

There was no going back.

She sighed as he grazed his lips against her cheek and exhaled his warm breath against it. She closed her eyes rather than refuse him. She no longer had the responsibility of getting home to her baby, nor the stubborn determination to maintain the formality of their arrangement. And as he laid a second kiss on the tender curve of her collarbone, she realized the real charade wasn't pretending to be his girlfriend; it was pretending to be a woman who wanted to remain alone and isolated in her own private struggles rather than allowing her mind and body to become vulnerable—and risk the pain and heartache of being hurt again.

He feathered her throat with his lips, closing the gap between them with the strength of his firm chest against her own. Sighing, she tilted her chin, allowing his mouth to drop lower down her neckline. She, too, had been fighting, and fighting, and fighting. She was exhausted by her own willful rage against the world, and she was tired of battling the chronic fear and disappointment within her own heart. But with every whispering kiss along the lobe of her ear and the pressure of his forearms crossing around her waist, he offered her nothing but peace.

A punishing gust of wind swept through the patio. She cowered against him and shivered. He wrapped his arms around her to protect her in his warm, steady embrace. Gazing up at him, she studied the way the moonlight softened the angular lines of his nose and cheekbones. Then, without knowing why, she reached out to trace the faded scar beneath his rigid eyepatch, pondering the severity of his injury and the burden it had placed on him. He flinched, only slightly, before relaxing into her touch.

"Ebony told me what happened on the yacht," she said carefully.

He shrugged it off, like he had so many times before. "It was an unfortunate accident for which I bear the blame."

"Is it true that you were planning to marry Celeste?"

His expression hardened and he exhaled forcefully. "At the time, yes," he confessed. "But now I realize it would have been a mistake because the basis of our relationship was using each other for mutual gain."

"Doesn't everyone do that in a relationship?" she asked somberly. "In one way or another?"

"I thought that, too," he conceded. "Until very recently, when I learned what it feels like to want to give up everything you have for someone you barely know."

He peered at her and fingered a loose tendril of her hair, letting her consider the sincerity in his voice. She raised her hands and passed them through his hair, searching for the elastic band of his eyepatch and liberating him from it.

As if the sudden exposure pained him, he lowered his gaze. She nudged up his chin. Reluctantly, he gave in and looked directly at her, granting her the rare privilege of viewing the beauty of his face in its entirety—his fair complexion, high cheekbones, boyish dimples, and sturdy green eyes, peering back at her with unwavering courage. There was a faint narrow scar that crossed his left cheek, just below his injured eye, lackluster like an unpolished emerald.

"Can you see me?" she asked.

He shook his head. "No, not the way you expect me to…" His voice trailed off, dark and solemn.

"I don't expect anything from you," she reassured him. "Most people live their whole lives as if they're blind, whether they can see or not."

"You could not have convinced me of that three days ago." He cupped her cheek. There was a heavy pause of silence between them as the moon passed behind a cloud, shadowing their faces. "But now, I am certain there are so many things I never saw until I met you."

Within the darkness, the intensity of their connection coursed through her body as he guided her lips to his own, transferring the intimacy of his confession through his reverent kiss. Their tongues entwined, gratifying each other's yearning. With every impassioned stroke, he signaled the sacredness of what she was offering and what he sought to claim—that tonight would be the night she would give herself over to him and he would attempt to fulfill her.

Without warning, he swept her up into his arms and carried her from the patio into the master bedroom. He left the sliding door ajar, an unspoken agreement that together they would listen for her sleeping child. But in that moment, there was nothing except the sound of the lakefront breeze shuddering against the panes of glass, mimicking her own shudder as he kissed her neck, throat, and lips with increasing urgency. She released a sigh of surrender as he set her down on the endless platform bed. Sliding his powerful body over her with the familiarity of a cherished lover, his hot breath buried into the sensual curve of her collarbone while his firm chest melded to her entire body. A needy gasp escaped her lips as his firm masculinity pressed against her, betraying how she flamed his desires.

Yes, she whispered, as his fingers pushed up the hem of her skirt and slipped between her inner thighs. *Yes*, she nodded, as they inched towards the soft cotton lining of her black knit tights, seeking to relieve the tingling ache beneath it. *Yes*, she exhaled, as he tore off her black velour sweater top and swept his tongue over the satin cups of her black bra. She arched her back and whimpered, allowing him to unclasp her bra and explore the fullness of her breasts with his hot mouth. Caressing his hair, she encouraged him with a breathy moan to tease her nipples and savor their sweetness. For longer than she could remember, her body had only one purpose—serving the maternal demands of her child. Now, with every erotic nip of her tits and seductive swirl of his tongue, he reminded her that she was not just a struggling single mother, but also a sexy woman who deserved to be pleasured and worshiped.

More… she moaned as he peeled her knit tights down to her ankles, whispering his nose across her exposed black panties, following her scent. He made it all feel so urgent, so necessary, his need to exhale his warm breath between her legs. As if he could bear it no more, he rose from his knees and pulled her down to the end of the bed, stripping her bare and admiring her nakedness against the midnight sheen of his satin sheets. She gazed up at him as he delicately traced the contours of her body with his fingers, absorbing the details he couldn't see through the sensuality of his touch.

"I want to be inside you," he finally whispered.

She nodded in consent, helping him unbutton his white shirt and shrug it off his broad shoulders. Backlit by moonlight, his smooth, sculpted chest loomed over her while he removed everything else, revealing the raw, primal strength of his own desire. She had seen him before, naked and fully aroused; but never this way, never with the intensity of his desire searing silence between them. He parted her knees with his hand, spreading her apart like the wings of a fragile butterfly. What previously had been nothing more than casual temptation had escalated into something beyond their control. Tonight wasn't just about their sexual fulfillment. It was an exploration of their own vulnerabilities and liberation.

The crackling of the foil wrapper confirmed he intended to protect her from repeating her past. *He didn't realize she was already protected.* He slipped the latex condom over the full length of his erection and squared his pelvis against her own. While seeking out her eyes and caressing her cheek, he made direct contact against her wetness. *Yes*, she heaved into him, savoring the sensation of his full cock—taut and sleek—pushing past the initial resistance and gliding through her. *God, how he filled her completely.* He pulled back, shifting higher before entering her again, striking her like a match and setting her aflame. Digging her nails into his forearms and clinging to the strength of his protective embrace, she opened her mouth without a sound as his steady, natural rhythm sparked the second and third tremors—low trembling quakes that radiated down, down, down between her legs before traveling back up her spine.

Drawing her hands over her head, he smothered her breasts with lustful kisses. "You're so wet and open," he exhaled in her ear, encouraging her to wrap her legs around his waist to allow him to drive deeper. She groaned and combed her fingers through his thick hair, leaning into the teasing way he thumbed her clit, glazing it with her slickness, priming her for even more.

"I want to be the one who makes you come."

His words hushed her soul. In the past, she had experienced false fits and starts of a climax, quivering up from deep inside her without ever progressing into something more. While lapping her tits with his tongue, he strummed her swollen clit and heightened her arousal with every deliberate thrust. She wrapped her hands around his neck and bit into his shoulder before crying out for relief. He silenced her with his mouth, a consuming kiss that matched his yearning to please her.

"I want to be the one," he whispered again, earnest in his desire to complete her.

She shuddered, inexplicably fighting the humming vibrations that always teased her towards orgasm without ever bringing her over the brink. Sensing her restraint, he enveloped her body and accelerated his pace, driving towards her release. She arched her back and gasped, *ohgod, ohgod, ohgod*, as the pressure mounted inside her core. But not even his masterful fingers or the powerful strength of his cock was enough to build her climax to match his own.

"I can't," she confessed, pushing him away, as if it was a dirty secret she was not only admitting to him, but also to herself. "I can't."

She had uttered those two words more times than she dared to count, filling her with shame more times than she cared to remember. With slow, panted breaths, he released her from the burden of satisfying his expectations and quelled his own climax. Cradling her cheek, he gazed into her eyes.

She felt him withdraw and sighed with regret, half-ashamed and half-overwhelmed by the honesty of their connection. She had never come with anyone—not even Enzo—because she had never fully entrusted her vulnerability into anyone's care. *For her, it was never just about the sex—it was about trust.*

He caressed her cheek and brushed away her tears of release. She tried to evade his eyes, but he coaxed her back with tender kisses.

As if he sensed the depth of her inhibitions, he sought out her reassurance. "Do you want this?"

She nodded, surrendering to him in silence.

He stared at her, refusing to look away while delivering an unspoken alternative—*bringing her to climax without her permission.*

Taking full control over her body, he rolled her onto her belly and smothered her back with his firm chest, settling his hard cock against her tailbone and snaking it down between her cheeks. She clenched the sheets and released a sigh of submission as the force of his possessive hands locked her wrists against the mattress.

Pinning his sharp chin into the sensitive curve of her shoulder, he exhaled his desires into her ear. "I want you to stain my sheets." His order was low and authoritative. *She wanted to please him. She wanted to gush for him.*

The smell of his sweat and the unforgiving edge in his voice excited her. He was the same man, but different— masterful, powerful, and domineering.

She gasped when his fingers slipped beneath her and cupped her pubic bone, teasing her with burning anticipation. He had given her a command; now, he intended to ensure that she followed through on it.

Yielding to her urge to obey him, she raised herself from the mattress, granting him access to the full length of her slit. With disciplined restraint, he fondled her with measured strokes, glazing his fingers with her arousal without ever fully entering her. She moaned, quivering from his slightest contact before he drew her hand down to her sex, initiating her own masturbatory touch.

"Deeper," he insisted, spreading her stance wider with his own knees and guiding her fingers with a depth and intensity that made her shudder.

Yes, yes, yes…the chanting of her breaths mirrored the pulsing pleasure he produced with his own simultaneous strokes. When he was certain she would not stop, he withdrew his fingers and kneaded her backside, loosening all her defenses and priming her for his forbidden touch.

A simple word flashed through her subconscious—*trust*.

The moment he circled her rosebud with her own wetness, she lowered her head and suppressed her groan with the sheets. She bowed deeper, her knees weakening, overwhelmed by the mastery of his seduction and her insatiable urge to be dominated by him.

"Beg me not to stop."

"Don't…stop." she barely exhaled, leaning into his cautious caresses as she continued her own rhythmic pace. "Please…don't…stop…" her voice dissolved away, melting into a visceral sigh of satisfaction.

"Never." He said it with a deep hush, signaling that he knew what she needed from him. "Not even if you scream."

Within the darkness, she only heard the anticipation of her own shallow exhale. Slowly, deliberately, he slipped his hard cock behind her, gripping her shoulder and bracing her in place like his sacred possession. *Could she trust him to fulfill her without breaking her?* She withheld her breath as he spread her knees wider, sending a naughty thrill of exhilaration up the full length of her slit. She ached and tingled for his domination. She knew what was coming, but she never could have anticipated how easily the hot tip of his hard cock would penetrate her in one stark thrust, deeper than she ever thought possible, as if he had unlocked a secret compartment of her sexuality for which only he owned the key.

She extended her fingers across the mattress and opened her mouth to scream, fighting the intensifying tremors that seized her sex and made her entire body tremble with pleasure.

Don't stop.

He drove into her again, fiercely, savagely, sparking an intoxicating sensation of heat and fire between her legs. *Faster, harder, deeper*… his masculinity dominated her like a tidal wave, sweeping her beneath the rushing acceleration of his conquest. She cried out with an intolerable need for a release.

"There you are," he whispered, strengthening his thrusts. "Now you are mine. And I'm not going to stop until you come."

He challenged her final resistance before shifting higher and breaching past it. A sensation of spontaneous gratification rolled through her pelvis, relinquishing every inhibition within her like a flashing burst of light. *A primal scream.* She heard it before she recognized it—the sound of her own seizing climax, surging in unison with his final ascent, followed by low, harmonious vibrations of ecstasy. *He had not given up on her—not before he united them.*

They simultaneously shuddered, trading kisses and breaths between each receding sigh. Whatever she had felt in the past, whatever seduction or arousal she thought she had experienced with other men, was nothing compared to the liberation Sven had granted her tonight.

Light-headed and drained, she fell forward. He guided her down into the bed, spooning her from behind with tenderness. She drew up her knees and settled into his protective embrace as the heavy darkness muted her afterglow, fading like a pulsating ember. They were no longer two strangers separated by the tension of their mutual attraction; they were two entwined lovers, who had exchanged the most intimate parts of themselves before retreating into the serenity of slumber.

Yes, she could trust—trust him in every way.

Chapter Twenty-Five

HE SUDDENLY OPENED his eyes. Whoosh, whoosh, whoosh… Perhaps it was the draft from the ceiling fan above him that first awoke him. Or perhaps it was the crisp night air that gusted in through the patio door, partially left ajar. Whatever it was, it most certainly was the absence of her warmth next to him that drew him up from the bed, but it was not her absence that startled him the most—it was the clarity of his sight within the darkness and his ability to confirm that she was gone.

He scanned the bedroom. Even within the shadows, he could make out the fine details of the furniture—his leather recliner, his end table, his dresser, even the number of rotations of the ceiling fan above him. *One, two, three, four…*he counted, certain he could spot the beginning and end of each whirling blade. Then, his gaze settled on something familiar, but different—something he thought he knew so well, and yet, he was barely able to recognize at all—the portrait of Inez, resting atop his dresser. *How many times had he stared at that photograph*? More times than seemed appropriate. Each time, he had squinted at it with curiosity, taking in the blurry expression of her face, letting his imagination fill in what his vision could not. Now, there was nothing left to his imagination. He covered his damaged eye with his palm; still, he could see it perfectly with his good eye, taking in the exceptional beauty of a woman he barely knew by sight. Her full lips, dark eyelashes, long black hair, exotic complexion. But it was her expression of arousal that surprised him the most. It was the same woman he had made love to last night, but he had never realized how much the sound of her sigh, the scent of her skin, the taste of her breasts, and the quivers of her body compensated for his inability to clearly see that exact expression on her face.

There had been so much more than that expression, he thought, savoring the sweet taste of her, flavoring his tongue, and the memory of the intimacy shared between them—an intimacy that had eluded him so many times with his previous partners. *She completed him*. And now, her absence pained him and his soul ached with emptiness. Slipping out through the patio door, his intuition drew him towards the balcony suite. It wasn't the return of his eyesight that filled his veins with adrenaline and guided him like a hunter in the darkness; it was his instinctive need to reclaim her. He yearned to be close to her—closer in every way possible.

He gazed up at the moon, its milky beams reflecting off the panes of the sliding glass door. *Luna*, he considered, realizing the reason for her absence while peering into the balcony suite. Even from the distance, he could clearly see her. Eyes closed and nursing her baby, she swayed back and forth in the rocking chair that he had bought for her yesterday. *It had cost him a thousand dollars. He would have spent a million*. The moonlight streamed in through the front bay windows, illuminating her with a glow. *Like an angel*.

Then, he frowned, reflecting on their last few nights together. It shamed him to realize how selfish and shallow he had been in his pursuit of her. She had struggled to maintain her commitment to Luna—even in the face of his lustful attempts to seduce her in which he unknowingly had pitted money and vice against her duty to her child. *Never again*, he vowed in silence, retreating to the master bedroom. *He was no longer the same man*. And like a sacred oath to her—and himself—he promised he would never allow her to struggle again.

Invigorated by the clarity of his sight, he strolled through his penthouse like a traveler finally returning home from a foreign land. Everything was clear to him, even within the darkness. He strode down the corridor towards his living room, seamlessly navigating through the expansive space without counting steps or reaching out for strategically-positioned furniture and sculptures. Edges and contours, once blurry and indistinct, were sharp and familiar. *He was home*.

Stopping in front of a closed door near the fireplace, he touched the handle, realizing that if it was locked, he wasn't certain he would know where he had left the key. *Not since the accident*, he thought and paused, considering the implications of clicking the door ajar and passing through it. His gaze followed the moonlight, streaming in through the skylight and cutting across the black marble floor. It ascended the sleek white wall, illuminating the glossy silver finish of the oversized black and white photograph of Chicago's skyline. *Taken during the construction of The Spire*, he remembered, admiring its exposed steel foundation, rising higher than any building around it. He had hung it on the wall like a prize—a symbol of his contribution to history, a reminder of how he had personally changed the cityscape for eternity.

Finally, after a long moment of deliberately avoiding it, he glanced down onto his drafting table. There, untouched and awaiting completion like it was only yesterday, rested his final designs for the Li Long Towers. He sank down into his swivel chair and stared at his drawings, studying the brilliance of their strength and simplicity, as if it had been designed by a complete stranger. He had forgotten how much he had loved it—his mastery of engineering and architecture, and specifically the challenge of designing the most ambitious building in the world and succeeding through sheer, stubborn defiance. *He had loved his work.*

"Your own personal studio?"

He turned to the familiar sound of her voice in the doorway, only this time, he spotted a woman who he hardly recognized. She was wearing his white silk dress shirt, buttoned up just below her breast bone, its lapels crossing at her thighs and its sleeves flipped back at the cuffs. Playing with a lock of her tussled black hair, she watched him—watching her—with her searing brown eyes.

"I didn't realize," she added slyly, "that the secret sauce of being a genius was sitting in front of your work in the middle of the night—completely naked."

He smirked, savoring her sarcastic smile and the wicked glint in her eye. She was right. He hadn't bothered to put on his clothes and her unexpected presence aroused him. *She was more beautiful than he had ever imagined.* He extended his hand, beckoning her. She pushed herself off the door frame to enter the studio and accepted his hand. He pulled her between his legs and nipped at her skin beneath the unbuttoned collar. She ran her sharp fingernails through his hair and down the back of his neck. *Her nails—the only artificial thing about her.* He sighed, savoring her tenderness, and relaxed his forehead between her breasts.

While whispering his breath along her breastbone, he slipped his hands beneath the tail of his dress shirt to feel the curves of her backside. *Bare.*

"Sitting in front of my work completely naked in the middle of the night is just bait. Catching beautiful wisps of inspiration is the genius part."

He coaxed her into his lap. She straddled him as he swiveled them around in a moment of simple happiness.

"How is Luna?"

"Well-fed, warm, and sleeping like a princess in a fairy tale."

"As she should be," he said, nodding his assurance. He stopped the chair and spun them in the opposite direction. "How is her mother?" he asked with playful grin, running his hands up the back of her thighs.

"Better now." She smiled, allowing him to feather kisses down her throat. "When I came back to bed, I saw that you were gone, I thought maybe…" She hesitated.

He pulled away and peered into her eyes. "Maybe what?"

"That maybe you had…changed your mind about last night."

"Never," he vowed, staring at her.

She met his gaze. Rarely did he allow anyone to see him without his eyepatch, fearful his ruined eye revealed a weaker man than he wanted to show the world. But she made him feel that he wanted to share every part of himself with her.

"Can you see me?" she slowly asked, as if she noted the difference.

"Yes." He nodded.

"How well?"

"Perfectly."

She fell silent, absorbing the significance of his answer. "But how?"

"I don't have any idea, really. I guess I just changed my mind last night, and decided I wanted to stop being a bitter blind asshole and start becoming someone who deserves to see how very lovely you really are."

She touched his cheek. "Not average?"

"Far, far from it."

"Yeah, you were an asshole."

"Yes, you'll have to let me seek forgiveness." He unfastened the top button of her dress shirt and brushed back the seam with his lips. He sought out her breasts, drifting his mouth over their sensuous curves.

She shivered with delight and allowed him to taste her tits. He wrapped his fingers around her backside and shifted her higher into his lap, tilting her soft nest of hair against his erection. She unexpectedly opened her eyes, studying the drawings on his drafting table.

"Those are your designs?"

He nodded. "I had forgotten how far I had gotten on designing the Li Long Towers."

He lowered his mouth, attempting to kiss her breasts again, but she pressed her hand against his chest, stopping him. "They're stunning, Sven."

"Yes, they probably could be one of the most influential, modern architectural projects in this decade."

"Probably?"

"Almost certainly," he whispered, completely uninterested in anything except the sensation of her warm pelvis melding against his own. "But I have not decided if I'm willing to leave to go build them."

"With those designs? You *have* to go build them."

"Not unless you come with me."

She looked at him in heavy silence. "And bring Luna?"

"Of course, I wouldn't have it any other way."

She didn't look convinced. "But someone has to care for my grandmother as well. I can't leave her alone."

"Then let's bring her along, too."

Inez scoffed, like he had truly gone mad. "My grandmother only leaves her house twice a week—once to go to Mass and the second time to play bingo in the church's basement. There's no way I could possibly uproot her to Shanghai. No. Way."

"Then I will hire a team of the best caretakers in Chicago to look after her while we are away. It would only be for a few months and we could fly back at least once to visit her. And..." he paused, choosing his next words carefully. "You know she wouldn't want you to stay behind because of her."

"No, she wouldn't," she replied with a defensive edge in her voice. "But maybe I would want to stay because of her."

He tightened his arms around her waist and held her gaze. "If I go...do you want to stay?"

She lowered her eyes and bowed her head, her thick black lashes quivering like he was inflicting pain on her. Finally, after a heartbreaking moment of silence, she stroked his cheek and lanced his heart with her answer. "Do they have opera in Shanghai?"

He exhaled, certain they had just sealed something precious between them. "I will make sure you have anything you want."

"French Martinis?"

"With imported Chambord, directly from France."

"Will you tow Luna and me around in a rickshaw?" she teased, tracing his earlobe with her finger.

"Anything," he promised, leaning into her caress. "Anything to have you there by my side."

He guided her lips to meet his own, entangling his tongue with hers and solidifying their allegiance through the heat of each stroke. He kissed her with every fiber of his being, communicating his commitment without words. *He wanted her in his life.* With his vision restored, he had to go to Shanghai to pursue his life's passion because it fueled the very core of his soul. But he also knew she was the one who had sparked the nascent ember inside him—the ember of a new man—and without her, he risked losing her guiding light.

She pitched herself higher in his lap, pressing against his erection. *God, how he loved the way she responded to every teasing nudge of his cock.* Slipping his hands around her bare ass, he lowered his head and exhaled his desire against her midriff. She edged herself upwards and guided his mouth lower between her legs. *God, how he loved her warm wetness and how easily she gushed for him.*

Fueled by her low, guttural moan, he lifted her into his arms and set her down against the stainless steel drafting table. She cried out with a gasp as its cool surface chilled her skin while he skated his breath down her belly, stopping at the seam of his dress shirt. He unfastened the final buttons and peeled back the folds, exposing her completely. His gaze settled on every detail of her nakedness—the maternal curves of her cleavage, the dark maroon areolas of breasts, the supple softness of her belly, the imperfect dimpling along her thighs, the nest of thick black hair between her legs. He christened every spot with an indulgent kiss before parting open her thighs and admiring her sex in the reflective sheen of the metallic table.

"We can't. Not now." It was a feeble protest and they both knew it.

"Then we won't," he teased, genuflecting on one knee and nipping playfully at her clit.

She rolled her hands over her head, exhaling her surrender. Wrapping his hands underneath her thighs, he touched his nose against her sacred scent. She was pink and slick, ready for the hungry strokes of his penetrating tongue. He waited as long as possible, heightening her anticipation as she glistened for him, before slipping his tongue down the full length of her slit, craving every bit of her desire. He wanted nothing more than to pleasure her like a goddess—*his goddess*—who had saved him from his own self-destruction.

He licked her again—a deep, impassioned lap. She arched her back and shuddered with a groan.

"Sven..." Breathless, she panted, as if she was fighting against her own inhibitions while hungering for more. He placed his hand over her belly to reassure her. *There was nothing he wanted more than to pleasure her.* Guiding her heel over his shoulder and tightening the crook of her knee around his neck, he aroused her with every lustful stroke.

There, there, there, he thought, as she wound her fingers around his head, nudging him in deeper and deeper with a silent gasp. *God, how he loved the sight of her, spread open on top of his drawings, submitting herself to him.* He braced her ass and forced her to accept every swirl of his tongue until she shuddered again, forcibly, uncontrollably, peaking with a moan before falling mute in disappointment.

"I need to feel you again..."

The urgency in her voice told him she would not be denied. He rose from his knees and smothered her with his chest, wrapping her legs around his waist and seeking out the slick heat of her slit with the wet tip of his shaft. Reuniting them as lovers, he pinned her arms above her head and nestled his nose against her ear.

"I want anything you want."

She closed her eyes and relaxed her wrists into his control. Like a forbidden wish, her request drifted out of the darkness. "I want to feel you. Just you. Bare."

She only needed to say it once. He settled the full weight of his body against her heavy breasts and squared himself against her wetness, thrusting deeply and completely inside her. She opened her eyes and released her breath. He cradled her head, steadying his cock until she exhaled—a release of quivering tension. Then, he drove into her again, arcing his cock upwards with a determined lunge. Her tremors rippled like a current between them. She gasped and dug her fingernails into his shoulder blades. He knew what she needed from him. He had discovered it last night while they were making love: she needed his unwavering commitment to unleash her from her own inhibitions—at all costs.

Pulling her up from the table, he sat back into the swivel chair and guided her back into his lap. He covered her groan with his mouth as the heat from their entangled tongues mimicked the rushing heat of his cock as he thrust himself fully inside her. The intimacy of his skin against hers fueled his primal desire to drive deeper, grinding his pelvis against her clit. *Wet, warm, open*—accepting of him in every way. She straightened up from his embrace, angling her clit into every lunge of his throbbing cock, seeking out her own attempts to stimulate herself against each persistent thrust. *There, there, there*...he heaved an uncontrollable moan. Her wetness glazed his bare skin, granting him the gift of driving deeper and deeper and deeper. *The gift of her sacred trust.*

He reached out to massage her heavy breasts, swaying in rhythm with his pace, before raising his lips and swirling his tongue around each tit. She threw back her head as he rocked harder and harder into her slickness, setting her free with an uncensored cry of gratification, signaling she was on the verge of her own climax. Accelerating his pace, he pumped and pumped and pumped until he thought he might break her, clenching his teeth and withholding his orgasm for the sake of her own.

Was he falling in love with her?

He had expressed the sentiment only a handful of times before in his life, but never during his own climax. *It had always made him feel too vulnerable.* But now, as he drew her face towards his own, and covered her heaving sigh with his kiss, he longed for every vulnerability that he could share with her and that she would share in return. She wrapped herself around him like her savior and screamed out until she was breathless with relief. Her whole body trembled in his embrace as he showered her neck, throat, and collarbone with a hundred kisses, silently making a hundred promises to make her come that way every time he made love to her because she had been his savior. They had saved each other.

Chapter Twenty-Six

HE OPENED HIS EYES WHEN her kiss whispered across his forehead. "I have to go, but I didn't want to leave without saying good-bye." He gazed up into her dark brown eyes. *Like a mythical nymphet.* Pushing up onto his elbow, he rubbed his face, groggy with slumber.

"Leaving so early?" He glanced at the wall clock.

She was fully dressed in her jeans and side slung T-shirt. Her long black hair was swept back into a casual ponytail and her lips were glossy and pink. He dropped his gaze onto Luna, strapped in her car seat and sucking on a pacifier.

"James is downstairs, waiting for me. He's going to drive me home."

"But why?" He reached out for her hand, challenging her. "We can buy anything you need. You know that."

"Sven..." she paused, willing him to understand he couldn't solve all her problems. "I haven't been home for an entire day. I have to check on my grandmother."

Surrendering her hand, he flopped down into the bed. *Dutiful to her core.* It was one of the many things he had grown to love about her. He propped himself up with an extra pillow as she lifted the diaper bag onto the bed and rummaged through it. Even as a single mother, wearing torn jeans and a simple T-shirt, she was still the sexiest woman with whom he had ever had the pleasure of sharing his bed and he wanted to keep her there with him—forever.

"Please say you're coming back soon."

"I'm pretty sure I don't have a choice," she mused, still searching for something in the diaper bag and failing to find it. She pulled out her phone, a baby blanket, a single diaper, two pairs of baby socks, a hand-held breast pump, and a plastic bottle filled with expressed milk.

"Tonight is the grand opening of The Spire. My final work night, right?"

"Yes, the grand opening," he repeated, as if he almost wished it wasn't the case.

"Although now that your vision is back to normal, I suppose that means I've become redundant," she teased, mocking his affected accent and their business arrangement.

He arched his brow. "Does that mean I get to fire you?"

"Maybe I'll just quit."

"Heartless, as expected."

She shrugged. "I make it a policy not to sleep with my bosses."

He lunged forward and swept her up into his arms. "Then I promise not to take your clothes off until after midnight."

He nestled his nose into her shoulder and kissed her neck. *God, how he loved her scent.* She cried out with laughter and sank down into his embrace. "You're assuming that I plan to be your sex slave every night."

"You say that as though you didn't enjoy it. Twice."

She gazed at him, withholding her smile. "I did enjoy it, but…" her voice trailed off.

He waited and held her tighter. "But what?"

"Sven…" she paused and circled her finger over the surface of his bare chest. "My life is really…complicated."

"I love complicated."

"But I have responsibilities. So, so, so many of them."

He touched her cheek, encouraging her to make eye contact. "We will share them."

She looked deeply into his eyes, as if she might allow herself to believe him—but only for a moment. "Sven…things were said and discussed last night that I'm not certain I can commit to."

"You mean Shanghai?"

She nodded. "I don't even have a babysitter for tonight, much less know how I could possibly entertain the idea of moving to another continent for three months."

He sliced his hand through the air to silence her. "Don't end it before it's even started." His voice was stern. He wanted her to look up at him.

But she avoided his gaze and fiddled with the sheets. With a whine, Luna stirred in the car seat and spit out her pacifier. Inez started to pull away, but he held her in his arms.

"Last night wasn't just about the sex. You know that, don't you?"

She nodded again and shrugged. He had seen that shrug before…*it doesn't matter*, she was telling herself, emotionally withdrawing from him before he had a chance to disappoint her.

"Inez," he insisted, lifting her chin. "And it's no longer about our arrangement."

"That's a shame," she quipped. "Because you were paying me really well."

"And I will still pay you for tonight, but not to be my sex slave."

"Too bad," she shot back. "I thought I was pretty good at being your sex slave."

He flashed her a smile. "You were excellent. But in the future, I want you to be more…so much more."

He led her lips to his own and kissed her in a way that he had failed to do this morning—warm, tender, and without any expectation other than the chance to convince her of his commitment to her.

Luna fussed again. Inez sighed and pushed him away. Reluctantly, he let her go.

"I've lost her favorite chew toy. That damn giraffe, I have no idea what happened to it. And if I don't find it, she'll cry the whole way home."

Without permission, Sven reached over the edge of the bed, unclasped Luna's belt, and drew her into his arms. "So go and find it. I will babysit."

Skeptical, Inez eyed him and mentally counted down 3-2-1 blast off for Luna's tantrum from being in his arms.

"She has stranger anxiety."

"You have the anxiety," he corrected her. "Babies love faces."

He donned the most ridiculous smile and tickled Luna's chin. "Your mommy does not trust me," he said gently. "But you trust me because we went to the opera together and you know that I will take good care of you."

Inez hesitated before turning away and returning to the balcony suite.

"Not there," he called out to her. "Try the master bathroom."

She doubled back and rounded the corner of the bathroom. "Found it!" she shouted in victory, her voice echoing off the tiled floor.

"See?" He smoothed his hand over the child's soft black hair, contemplating her dark eyelashes and cherub cheeks; her resemblance to Inez was disarming. He touched his nose against her forehead. She smelled like a mixture of baby powder and Inez's floral shampoo. Outlining the fuchsia heart on her flannel pink onesie, he lowered his voice, soothing. "And I promise to take care of your mother, too."

He kissed her forehead—the same way Inez had awoken him—and placed her back in the car seat. Luna fussed again until Inez rushed out of the bathroom and consoled her with the toy.

"I have to go now," she said, hurrying to gather up all her things. "James is waiting for me downstairs."

Sven snagged her hand again and pulled her towards him. "He's paid to wait. Let him wait."

He nudged her for a kiss. She did not give in easily—not at first. But he refused to let her go. Yearning for her companionship, he kissed her lips and waited until she kissed him back.

"Promise me you're going to spend the night here again—after the gala," he insisted.

"Sven, right now, I'm worried I don't even have a babysitter who can stay with Luna in the evening while we're there. My grandmother is great, but she's blind and ailing, and she can't watch Luna the whole day and night—although she'd never admit to it."

"I will take care of that," he said with certainty, wanting to prove he could solve all her problems. She eyed him again; this time, she almost seemed to believe him.

"Just promise me," he urged her with another kiss. "Promise you'll stay here tonight again."

"I promise," she whispered, touching his cheek before slipping away from him. She clutched the handle of Luna's car seat into both hands and disappeared from the bedroom without looking back.

Mistress Inez, he mused, *too proud to need anything but her own independence.* He flopped back against his pillows, pained by her absence before he even heard the front door click shut behind her. Gazing at the ceiling fan, he counted the rotations of the whirling blades. *She was right. He didn't need her—not any more.* But that made him want her in his life, now more than ever.

Ping, ping, ping.

He rose up from the bed, searching out the unfamiliar chimes of a phone message. Buried beneath the folds of the sheets, he discovered Inez's cell phone, forgotten in the wake of seeking out Luna's giraffe. He peered down at its screen. It was the first time he could remember being able to read a phone message without a magnifying glass.

ENZO, he read the name aloud and touched the screen to read the text.

I am here at your house but your grandmother tells me you and Luna are not here. You cannot avoid me forever.

A burning flame of jealousy flared inside Sven's chest. *If you are angry about what happened yesterday, it is because you still have feelings for me.*

Her phone pinged again.

And if you still have feelings for me, then I will not give up on us. Te quiero, mi amor.

Sven read the words over and over again until he realized the constriction in his heart had transferred to his clenched fist. Visceral memories overwhelmed him.

In a sudden flashback, Sven relived the last time he had vied for a woman's heart. He remembered the sensation of bobbing up and down while standing on the starboard deck of his sailboat and staring down his brother who had just confessed to stealing away Celeste. Hans had been right. He hadn't loved Celeste and he didn't deserve to marry her. But the betrayal of both his girlfriend and his brother enraged him. In a primal quest for revenge, he charged against Hans' chest, knocking him against the steering console and bloodying his nose with a direct punch. They scuffled, wrestling like schoolboys, before Sven struck him again—a cracking punch to the ribs. The windy night rocked the ship. Sven wrestled his brother like a mortal enemy until they were halted by the sound of Celeste's scream as they knocked her overboard into the churning waves. Hans threw the lifesaver to her while Sven drove into the black abyss after her.

The only thing he remembered was the scorching strike to his eye socket, crashing against the hull of the ship and bursting into light like a nova star, before his hands and legs turned limp as he was smothered beneath the waves.

He touched his injured eye, overwhelmed by the memory. *Smothered beneath the waves.* Now, just like then, he held his breath, fighting against the same sense of helplessness—being dragged down, down, down as the black waves suffocated him. It was happening all over again. He imagined himself back on the deck of that yacht, his emotions coursing through his chest like shards of glass scraping against his heart. *Yes, he would do it all over again*, he silently vowed. Because this time, he wasn't enraged by the possibility of losing the woman he thought he loved. This time, it was a certainty—*he knew that he loved her.*

Giving in to the same vengeful impulse that had ruined his life for the past year, he lifted up Inez's phone and texted back.

I am staying at 767 Washington Ave. Penthouse suite 1500. I will be here until three o'clock. Do not be late.

Chapter Twenty-Seven

SVEN LAY IN WAIT IN HIS dimly lit study, lounging in his chair as his eyes fixated on the video screen of the security camera. While sipping his Holland gin from his tumbler, he studied Enzo approaching the front door of his penthouse.

The doorman had called up minutes ago. Sven had given him permission to send up Enzo through the private elevator, and now, he watched him search for the door buzzer before giving up and pounding on the door. "Inez?"

The front door clicked ajar and Enzo passed through it.

Swiping the screen and switching cameras, Sven tracked Enzo's cavalier gait as he glided along the black marble floors through the living room.

"Inez?" Enzo called out again, meandering towards the exterior walls of glass, offering the panoramic view from the skyline. Met only with silence, Enzo doubled back through the living room along the ornamental mosaic wall and swaggered down the long corridor leading into the master bedroom, as if he expected to find her there, naked and in bed, awaiting his arrival.

"Inez?"

Enzo checked the bathroom before exiting onto the patio and surveying the balcony suite through the panels of glass. Then, he sauntered back into the master suite and stopped in his tracks, realizing he had missed a crucial detail during his first pass through the bedroom—a wall safe.

Like a hunter tracking his prey, Sven downed his drink.

"Open the safe," he whispered to Enzo's image on his video screen.

As if he heard the command, Enzo rubbed his chin, edged towards the safe, and peeled open the door that Sven had conveniently left unlocked.

Like a criminal, Enzo glanced around him, weighing his chances of being caught, before pulling out the massive stack of cash and fanning through the endless bills with his thumb.

"You are lucky that's intended for you," Sven called out to him, leaning against the doorjamb. "Otherwise, it would be considered robbery."

Enzo tossed the stack onto the bed. "Ah, a trick from the fancy dentist boyfriend. I should have guessed." He spread out his hands as if to show he had nothing to hide and circled the room. "Where is Inez?"

"She is not here. This is a meeting between you and me."

Enzo peered through his black eyelashes. "Really? Does Inez know this?"

Sven challenged him with a stern glare. "You are here because I have an offer to make."

"What kind of an offer?"

"A financial offer."

Enzo whistled. "So her new boyfriend is already pulling strings behind her back. I guess he is not as honest and perfect as she thinks." He nodded at the portrait of Inez resting on the dresser. "But he thinks he can buy whatever he wants, including her." Flashing him a cocky smile, he said, "Inez must still be in love with me."

Sven felt the rage rising within his chest. He pushed off the doorway's edge and prowled towards him. "Fifty thousand dollars—in cash—if you leave the country and never contact Inez again."

Enzo's gleeful smile faded. "That is a lot of money," he acknowledged, swallowing hard and staring down Sven.

"It is yours." Sven picked up the stack of cash from the bed and tossed it at Enzo's chest. "All fifty thousand of it. Just agree to never contact her again."

"But we have a daughter together. She expects to see me. Or at least, for me to see Luna."

Sven shrugged, cruel and unforgiving. "Luna will be fine without you. I am certain of it."

Enzo eyed Sven's determined stance, preventing his exit, and passed the stack of bills beneath his nose, inhaling their scent of authenticity. "And if I accept…this offer? What's to stop me from coming back into her life a year from now? Or two?"

"I don't think that would be wise." Sven said in measured words, slowly and distinctly. "I have a video of you entering my penthouse, going to my bedroom and my safe, and withdrawing fifty thousand dollars in cash. That video could easily fall into the hands of the police, and it would not look very good for you."

Enzo held up his hands like he had been caught. "Ah, I see…I've been trapped. Okay, fine…you win. I am not interested in trouble."

Backing away from Sven, he flung the stack back onto the bed and circled around him towards the door.

"I think you should reconsider…" Sven cautioned him, scooping up the bribe and holding it out to him like it was his final offer. "Fifty thousand dollars—and the only thing you have to do is disappear."

Accepting the stack, Enzo flipped through its bills again. "And what if she comes looking for me?" he asked, as if he had found a loophole in their ironclad deal. "Then, there is nothing you can do to stop her."

"She will not come looking for you—that I can promise you."

Enzo cast him a sidelong glance. "How?"

"Because I plan to love Inez and Luna more than you ever could."

Enzo held his hands over his heart, feigning devastation. "That is very poetic. But that doesn't change the fact that Inez and I will always share a bond that is stronger than love."

"Really?" Sven scoffed, unimpressed. "And tell me, what is that?"

"Our child," Enzo said firmly, his black eyes challenging him.

Sven shook his head and nodded to the bounty in Enzo's hands. "No, I don't think so. Not if you accept that and walk out the door."

They stared at each other in silence, waiting for the other to capitulate. But in the end, Sven knew there was no contest because he knew his own strength and his opponent's weakness—there was only one man in the room who truly wanted to be with Inez for the rest of his life, and it wasn't the man who had fathered her child. And there was only one man in her life who was willing to love her the way she deserved to be loved; and Sven was determined to make sure of it.

"I came from nothing, and I can go back to nothing," Enzo finally said, like a warning shot before an attack. "But now, I will not have to worry about it again."

He pocketed the cash and passed by Sven, intentionally bumping against his shoulder before disappearing down the corridor. Sven held his ground without glancing back.

It was done, he thought.

He had succeeded in removing his rival from their lives, but perhaps at a cost far greater than a simple monetary exchange. He gazed at Inez's portrait on his dresser, knowing she had gifted him her ultimate trust. The pleasure of his victory dissolved like melting ice through his heart. *Had he just bought her salvation or his own damnation*?

Chapter Twenty-Eight

"OH MY GOODNESS…ISN'T SHE the most precious thing you have ever seen?" Sven's mother swept up Luna into her arms and pressed her lips against Luna's perfectly shaped little head. "And look at this black hair and this tiny little nose, and these charming little feet!"

Sven flashed a smile at Inez. She had been skeptical that Sven's mother, Madame van der Meer—grand matriarch of one of Chicago's most prestigious families—would have any interest in babysitting Luna for three hours in Sven's penthouse while she and Sven attended the opening night gala of The Spire. Apparently, Inez had been wrong.

"Oh, dear me," Madame van der Meer exclaimed, swaying Luna back and forth in her arms like she was her own kin. "Look at the way she's grasping my finger with her precious little hands. And look at that little yawn. Like an adorable *katje*."

Inez peered at Sven, noting the flush in his cheeks. "Kitten," he translated for Inez.

He cleared his throat, almost like an apology for his mother's effusive affection. Inez controlled her urge to tease him. It was a side of Sven she had never seen—embarrassment. It was as if he was a twelve-year-old schoolboy who barely knew how to act around his mother in front of his playground girlfriend. The only difference was the fact that he was dressed in a black designer suit, awaiting to embark on the most important night of his career, and his mother was busy fussing and cooing over his girlfriend's baby.

"Mother—" Sven interjected, interrupting Madame van der Meer as she nestled kisses into Luna's belly. "Inez has left you the bottles and milk in the refrigerator. But you are not to heat it up. You must leave it on the counter for a little time before giving it to the baby."

Madame van der Meer shooed her son away with a dismissive wave. "How many children have I raised, Sven? Hmm?"

He sighed and rolled his eyes up at something imaginary in the air. He answered in Dutch, a reflexive response after being scolded by his mother.

"Yes, this is right," she answered back in English. "Two. Two *boys*, no less…so I am well aware of how to care for an infant—especially one as easy and lovely as this baby girl. And I certainly don't need any instructions on how to care for her unless it comes directly from the mother."

Sven held up his hands and backed away. "I will say no more."

"Good." His mother nodded firmly. Inez suddenly saw the source of Sven's authoritative demeanor. Her indistinct accent gave her an aura of sophistication while her striking green eyes and peacock face confirmed the origins of Sven's well-defined facial features and rugged beauty.

"Now, tell me, my dear," Madame van der Meer asked, lowering her eyes and voice towards Inez with deference. "What should I know about your daughter, so that I may put your mind at ease while you are away from her?"

"Just that she loves being held, she hates being in her crib, and if she cries, it's usually because she's looking for this…"

Inez passed off the rubber giraffe to Madame van der Meer, who tested its squeak with a delighted laugh. "Oh my, you *do* love that, don't you?" Sven's mother squeaked the toy more times than her son could apparently bear.

"Mother—" Sven finally insisted. "We're going to be late to a very important *work* function. You must let Inez say goodbye to her child now."

She turned away from her son with a shrug; she clearly didn't give a damn. "I am certain your fancy gala can wait." Turning to Inez, she said, "Sven and his brother, Hans, think that the only thing in life that is important is work. But as women, we *know* the exact opposite is true. Happiness. Happiness is the only thing that matters in life, and nothing would make me happier than to have my own boys grant me the gift of *kleinkinderen*."

Impatient and uncomfortable, Sven circled the kitchen island and cleared his throat again. "Grandchildren," he reluctantly translated.

"Yeah, I got that one that time," Inez replied, stifling a smile.

Earlier that evening, she had confided in Sven that she was insecure about meeting his mother. She had doubts that Madame van der Meer would be impressed with her status as a young single mother. Sven had shrugged it off, just like his mother shrugged him off now. He had divulged to her that not even his own mother and father had been married. The customs in the Netherlands were less conventional about nuptials and more interested in offspring. For Inez, it seemed impossible to imagine Madame van der Meer as anything other than a traditional socialite. Now, she realized that her assumptions had been wrong. Madame van der Meer may have been an heiress and philanthropist, but it was clear that in her own private moments Augustina van der Meer was like so many other women who simply loved children.

Inez studied Madame van der Meer's black beaded sweater top and passed over a baby towel to her. "And here…you'll definitely need this."

"For bathtime?" Sven asked earnestly.

Tsk. Sven's mother clucked like a hen, clearly annoyed at her son's ignorance.

"No," Inez replied. "For burping time, spitting up time, or just plain drooling time."

Madame van der Meer exhaled dramatically with a lamenting sigh. "How is it possible that men can build entire skyscrapers, but know so *little* about babies?" She tossed the towel over her shoulder and raised Luna up over it.

Sven tapped his foot and extended his wrist, glancing at his glimmering watch.

"Inez—" he petitioned for their rescue.

Inez caught a glimpse of her reflection in the stainless steel countertop of the kitchen island, certain her gown, hair and makeup were as ready as they ever would be. She moved towards Luna and gave her a gentle good-bye kiss on her head.

Sven instructed his mother. "We will be home before it gets too late, but if you grow tired, the balcony suite is made up and ready for you. A rocking chair and Luna's crib are also there."

She shooed him away again. "I'm just glad you have a date tonight. I hate it when you and Hans try to drag me to all of your company functions."

"We do it to keep you entertained, Mother."

"Then, give me more kittens." Taking the bottle into her hand, she started away from them and towards the balcony suite before quickly turning around and addressing Inez with a formal nod.

"You're wearing Prince Alexander's heirloom tonight, I see?"

Inez touched the emerald and diamond choker around her neck. Despite the crisp platinum setting draped against her skin, she had forgotten she was wearing it. "Yes, I hope you don't mind."

"No, not at all. It looks lovely on you." Madame van der Meer tilted back her head and peered down along her long, aquiline nose at the priceless treasure around Inez's neck. "And I hope you get to keep it. That way, perhaps I will have the pleasure of babysitting for you again." Shifting her hawkish eyes to Sven, she cautioned him in a maternal tone. "In the meantime, however, I will pray that my son does not ruin the chance of that for both of us."

Chapter Twenty-Nine

THE MOMENT INEZ STEPPED INTO the glass-paneled elevators, she knew she was trapped. The transparent doors closed and the cylindrical cab rushed upwards along the metallic exterior walls of The Spire, launching them like a rocket ship into the air. *Twenty, thirty, forty, fifty stories*...she backed away from the thin panels of glass and shut her eyes, halting her vertigo as the earth spiraled away from her. *Sixty, seventy, eighty, ninety stories through the evening sky.* After sixty sickening seconds, the elevator slowed its ascension and fluttered to a stop within the black abyss of the starry night sky—one-hundred floors above ground level.

Loneliness. The odd, unexpected emotion seeped into her heart as she swept her eyes across the adjacent skyscrapers, studying their diminutive antennas twinkling below her. There was nothing else around them but constellations, and nothing else competed for her attention except the unnerving gusts of wind, rattling the glass panes, and the gentle touch of Sven's hand, enveloping her own.

"Are you ready?"

She nodded, observing how his black designer tuxedo, crisp and elegant, mirrored the evening skyline surrounding them. He looked strong and intimidating with his hair slicked back, accentuating his sloping forehead and high cheekbones while his rigid black eyepatch hid his only hint of weakness. *No, there was no weakness in him*, she corrected her own thoughts. He was the man who had designed this fearless feat of structural brilliance, and it was not the work of a weak man. It was the work of a genius.

Behind them, a set of silver-toned doors chimed open, inviting them to step out of the elevator and into the unparalleled thrill of being at the top of the world. He took her by the hand and led her with confidence through a stunning atrium lobby, its curling, metallic walls shimmering like mirrors.

"Please tell me you planned that?" she said, her eyes rising to the unobstructed view of the full moon, reigning over them with celestial perfection.

He smiled at her and kissed the curve of her hand. "The only thing more beautiful than the moon is its dependability."

His gaze dropped to the flashing glint of her emerald choker necklace and the satin of her evening dress, its lilac sheen made scintillatingly white in the wake of the lunar glow.

Following the pulsing rhythm of the live band, he guided them through the grandiose, spherical entryway and into the elliptical ballroom. The vaulted glass and steel ceiling threw a shadowy pattern of endless hexagons onto the white glossy floors, drawing the guests into its seductive web. Within its oval shape, the ballroom had no traditional walls or windows, only curved panels of glass offering a breathtaking vista of the sleeping city to the west and the endless evening horizon of Lake Michigan to the east. If Inez thought she had experienced every part of Chicago, she was now proven wrong. She had never experienced the city—*her city*—this way, like an angel marveling at its beauty from the heavens.

Sven halted them every few steps, exchanging handshakes and accepting the murmurs of praise from men in black tuxedos and women in sequin and lace evening gowns. He confidently made his own way through the crowd, distinguishing each face through the iridescent glow of the chandeliers. *He no longer needed her*. It was a strange, fleeting thought that whispered through her mind when he turned his back on her to greet an older man with a long mustache and his wife.

"Such lovely things shouldn't be abandoned." The owner of the voice pushed his chin over her shoulder, allowing her to catch a whiff of his breath—garlic liver pâté.

"I've hardly been abandoned," she replied coolly, feeling the imposing build of his chest crowding into her personal space before she turned to face his menacing eyes and the flashing smile that matched the pearly sheen of his white tuxedo coat.

"Well, you certainly aren't being...well-taken care of." Eliot Watercross paused and shifted his eyes to the half-circle of guests huddled around Sven.

As a waiter rushed by them with a tray of champagne flutes, Eliot retrieved two glasses and handed one to her.

"I'm an independent girl, Mr. Watercross. I like to take care of myself." She returned the flute to the tray of another passing waiter and ordered herself a drink. "A French Martini, please. Extra Chambord."

Eliot eyed her disposal of his drink. "I can see that, and I admire it. But—" he countered, edging uncomfortably closer to her and murmuring his whisper against her ear. "The only time I ever believe a woman who proclaims her independence is when she's angry about being left alone and I'm there to fill the void." He slowly pulled away, but not before passing his nose over the scent of her hair. "Did you enjoy the opera?"

Inez glared at him, remembering exactly the one thing she didn't enjoy about it. *Seeing him.*

"The flower girl dies at the end," she managed to say, impatiently throwing a glance at Sven. *Still showboating*, she thought, trying hard not to dwell on the fact that he hadn't even noticed she was no longer by his side.

"The girl never fares well in a Puccini opera," Eliot commented, throwing back all the champagne in his flute. "I much prefer the female lead in Bizet's *Carmen* and her…fiery disposition."

She challenged him with her glare. "I'm pretty sure she dies, too."

"True," he said with a playful snap of his teeth. "A stab wound from her jealous lover. Such a shame." His insincerity oozed from his playboy smile.

"Heartbreaking," she seethed with sarcasm.

"I suppose the moral of the story is…don't be too tempting."

"Or have too many lovers."

"And certainly not jealous ones."

He reached out and slid his long finger down the contour of her bare arm. "You know, I received a phone call earlier today from Hans, saying that Sven has decided to move forward with us on the Li Long Towers. He said he thought you would be traveling there with him."

Inez bristled from his touch and avoided his gaze. Like divine intervention, a waiter appeared with her martini. She slurped it down, savoring its syrupy sweetness as it relaxed the tension in her shoulders. She even reconsidered her decision to kick Eliot Watercross in the balls if he touched her again.

"Sven will be very busy when he's in Shanghai. It's a big job and there's not a lot of time for...recreation."

"I thought your only concern was whether or not Sven designs your towers, not how he spends his personal time while he's there," she shot back, betraying irritation in her voice.

He threw his head back with a grating laughter. "Oh, I don't care how Sven spends his personal time. Only that he's not torn between entertaining you while he's working for me."

Inez crossed her arms, quelling her urge to shiver, and suddenly feeling nauseous at the prospect of being at the mercy of more than one rich and powerful man while in Shanghai.

"I'm fairly certain she'll be well-entertained," Sven replied, cutting in from behind them and sweeping Inez away from Eliot. He locked eyes with Watercross and clasped her hand. "I apologize for being detained. I can see that it would not be wise to let it happen again."

His arm stiffly encircled her waist like a band of steel. She winced. It wasn't his typical tender embrace, but rather an assertion of his possessive authority over her.

"Probably not." Eliot smiled slyly, goading him. "It's never a good idea to keep a woman waiting. Is it, Miss Sanchez? Especially not one who can obviously take care of herself. But I was still happy to make her aware of all her…alternatives."

He handed off his empty flute to Sven while deliberately shifting his focus directly onto Inez. "I'll be on the lookout for those tickets for Bizet's *Carmen* in Shanghai. Maybe we'll plan a night to attend it—together." His tiger eyes lifted to the upper libation balcony. "In the meantime, it looks like I'm being summoned by Harvey Zale. We're finalizing the terms of the sale of The Spire over a thousand-dollar bottle of premier Trinidad Rum. Sven…you and your lovely companion should join us to celebrate after the public dedication, especially since we're going to be spending so much time together in Shanghai."

He sauntered away through the buzzing crowd towards the live band.

Inez turned to Sven, attempting to shake off the discomfort of Eliot's advances. "You've already told him we're planning on going to Shanghai?"

"Well, yes…I phoned Hans this morning to let him know that I was interested in moving forward on my designs of the Li Long Towers, and that we've decided to travel…together."

"But have we decided, Sven?"

"Haven't we?" he said impatiently.

He met her eyes, but there was an edge in his voice and a distance in his demeanor that reminded her of old moody Sven. His vision had been restored for less than a day, and already everything seemed different between them. A fleeting whisper of fear flickered through her mind—*he no longer needed her.*

Hans mounted a translucent circular platform and the crowd erupted with unrestrained applause as he ascended above them. A sharp spotlight reflected off his flaxen hair and indigo blue tuxedo and he calmed the gasps of surprise and delight with a reassuring hand.

"We all know why we are here tonight." His distinct Dutch accent reverberated through his headset microphone like an echo through a canyon.

"Premium Beluga caviar!" a voice playfully heckled him.

The crowd tittered with amusement, but Inez frowned and swept her eyes around the overcrowded ballroom, studying the men and women in formal attire. It felt more like a Northwestern homecoming dance or a wedding bankrolled by the father of the richest girl on campus rather than a prestigious gala for one of the most influential architectural achievements in Chicago.

Pretending to welcome the interruption, Hans winked and nodded in the direction of the jokester. "We are here because we believe the City of Chicago deserves a building that is unlike anything the world has never seen. Tonight, we celebrate that achievement. Our achievement at Van der Meer & Associates. And the achievement of our faithful investors of Watercross Capital. And my own brother's achievement through his ingenious structural design of the tallest building in the country. Ladies and Gentlemen, I would like to present my dear brother, the genius *and* the asshole of the family, Sven van der Meer…"

Inez knew that Sven would have to leave her again. He had warned her on the car ride there that he would be placed in the spotlight for the public dedication, expected to deliver a speech to his guests. He released her hand, and for a brief moment, she hoped to receive a good-bye kiss on the cheek or a promise that he would return to her as soon as possible.

But instead, he abruptly turned away and mounted a second translucent pedestal, elevating him like a god amongst men. As he confidently addressed the crowd, she fought an uneasy sickness seeping down her throat. His classic black tuxedo, gelled hair, and freshly shaved jawline gave him an air of distinction, but his cocky grin and inappropriate jokes transformed him into a stranger.

The old Sven. He was becoming one of them again.

"Doesn't Sven look so handsome and happy, standing up there, presenting his life's work." Celeste grasped Inez's forearm with her bony fingers like they were sisters. "I've heard you finally persuaded Sven to go to Shanghai to work on the Li Long Towers. I didn't believe it at first, considering how much you seem to despise The Spire. But then again, there seems to be many things about you that I'm inclined not to believe." She tightened her grip and settled her chilling blue eyes onto Inez's emerald necklace.

"You know, I had a very interesting chat this afternoon with someone you know well. He's an artist-in-residence at the Art Institute. *The Tribune* sent me there to cover his current exhibit. And wouldn't you know," Celeste continued with singsong glee. "To my surprise, I found out we have more in common than our love of art."

"Was it your love of infidelity?"

Celeste's head flung backwards with laughter. "Well, we certainly discussed the curious intersections of our love lives…perhaps more than you would have preferred."

Inez pursed her lips and stared straight into Celeste's gaunt, powdered face. Whatever Enzo had said about her, whatever details he had shared about their relationship, she refused to be intimidated.

"Of course, he was very surprised to hear that I believed you were some sort of curator at the museum. He seemed quite insistent that you've never worked there, much less had a job that wasn't more than just a glorified secretary. But what I found *most* interesting was how forthcoming he was with the source of his…inspirations." Celeste rolled her single strand pearl necklace back and forth along her swan neck. "In fact, I'm fairly certain he even mentioned that you two share a baby."

Inez glared at Celeste and downed the remainder of her martini, spurring her protective maternal instincts and freeing the last bit of restraint she had in her.

"Her name is Luna. And I'm pretty damn certain she's none of your business."

"Perhaps," Celeste replied, her matte pink lips popping open again without a second thought. "But it isn't *my* fault when my interview subjects choose to tell me these things…off the record, of course. Especially the fact that Sven just paid him fifty thousand dollars—in cash—to disappear from your lives."

The lights faded around her and the ballroom erupted in distracting applause. The band started up a new tune, warped and off-tempo. Inez replayed the bewildering, garbled words spewing out of Celeste's clown mouth. *Fifty thousand dollars…to disappear from your lives.*

Wringing it back and forth like a noose, Celeste tugged on her pearl necklace and continued, "Well, the whole notion made me laugh, really. I mean…you're going to Shanghai together and a jealous ex-boyfriend with parental rights could really complicate an international trip. And only fifty thousand dollars, I mean…really? Such a trivial amount. I would *at least* expect Sven to bribe him with an amount more than his annual dry cleaning bill."

Had she drunk her martini too fast? Had the bartender put too much vodka in it? The ballroom started to spin and Inez reached out for something, anything, and snagged the pinky finger of Celeste's hand.

"What is wrong with her?"

Inez registered Sven's stern voice from behind her. He secured her in his embrace, holding her steady, but she brushed him off. *His touch sickened her.*

"Your fiancée and I are just chatting about our ex-boyfriends," Celeste mused, touching the black satin lapels of Sven's tuxedo.

"Inez?" he grabbed her hand. She attempted to push away from him and escape through the dense crowd of bodies.

"Inez—" He drew her towards him, his physical strength forcing her cooperation. "What's wrong?"

"Is it true, Sven?" she insisted, peering into his steady green gaze. "Fifty thousand dollars?"

Sven slowly surrendered his hold over her, but it was the change in his expression that confirmed her biggest fear. Celeste wasn't a lying bitch; Inez was the one who had been the naïve fool.

Hans appeared next to Celeste, just in time for the fireworks. "Sven…" he said impatiently. "Eliot and Harvey Zale are waiting for us."

"Let them wait," he commanded, his gaze never straying from hers. "Inez—" he pronounced her name like a warning. "Don't—"

"Don't?" she mocked him, her temper spinning out of control. "Don't what?"

"Don't—" he repeated, locking her in place with his punishing eyes. "Don't overreact."

She had seen that glare from him before—the moment he had challenged Enzo in the museum; the moment he had threatened his brother after receiving the "Genius Award", and now, the moment he challenged her to obey him. *No, she would not obey him. In fact, she was sick of obeying him.* She wasn't his girlfriend anymore—real or otherwise. And she suddenly regretted every moment she had submitted herself to him as a lover.

"Don't worry, Sven. I won't 'overreact'. I'd much rather just say good-bye."

She turned away, seeking relief from his callous glare and the pompous, superficial world that surrounded her. *His world, not hers.*

"No—" he insisted again, catching her by the hand and pulling her into his chest. Swimming with uncertainty, his eyes darted back and forth to meet her own.

"Don't do this." There was heartache in his whisper. She heard it and relished it.

"Do what…quit our *arrangement*?" Her bitterness spreading into a sadistic grin, seeking to hurt him as much as possible. "Well, then…I guess the good news is that you hired me for four nights, but you'll only have to pay me for three."

He braced her in his arms, enduring the heat from her rage as his mouth hovered over her lips and his gaze searched out something in her own. Then, he kissed her, long wistful strokes of repentance. *But it didn't matter. Nothing mattered. Especially not him,* she vowed, refusing to respond with forgiveness. Sensing her rigidity, he relinquished his reign over her and stepped away as if she was a stranger. *Two strangers pretending to be something they were not.*

"And by the way, in case it wasn't clear…" Her voice trailed off as she slipped her hands under her hair and unclasped the emerald necklace. "Luna and I aren't for sale. We never will be."

She deposited the heavy choker into his hand, letting the sharp angular clasp dig into his palm. Turning away from him, she prepared herself to feel the oppressive snare of his hand, detaining her in the prison of his arms. *A final futile effort to entrap her.* But like so many things about him, she was wrong. He did not chase after her or physically attempt to force her to stay. He simply let her escape, alone, through the crowd and disappear out of his life.

Yes, it had all been a shameful mistake. She had knowingly crossed the lines between their professional arrangement and their personal lives. She had lowered her guard and willingly shared the most important and intimate parts of her life. She had handed over her trust like a gift, and that was perhaps the biggest mistake of them all because not only were her pride and her dignity shattered into a thousand little pieces, but also her embittered stone heart.

Chapter Thirty

WHAT HAD HE DONE? The moment he felt her hand slip away from his own before she raced away from him, fading like a bittersweet memory within the crowd, he knew he had made the biggest mistake of his life. He darted forward, attempting to chase after her, but abruptly stopped when a strong hand gripped his upper arm and restrained him.

"You're a wanted man," Eliot Watercross said. "Harvey Zale is waiting for us in the balcony to celebrate with drinks. We're all expecting to finalize the exchange."

Sven nodded in assurance. "Yes, the sale of The Spire for the contracts to build the Li Long Towers." He had heard it a million times before, but even now, with his sight restored, it felt like an insurmountable challenge without her. "I'll be there as soon as possible." He forced a smile, persuading Eliot to relinquish his clasp on Sven's shoulder. "But first, I must attempt to find something that I fear I might have lost."

By the time he had crossed through the atrium and reached the elevators, she had already disappeared down them. He called James in desperation, but there was no answer. *She had gotten to him first...*

Sixty seconds to descend to the street. Three minutes to return to the condo building by car. Five minutes to change and gather all her things, including Luna.

Counting every second of the eight minutes he had calculated it would take her to disappear from his life forever, he ran—not walked—back to his penthouse from the Spire. All twenty-five blocks, stopping only once to attempt to hail a cab. *Downtown Chicago on a Saturday night.* Failure was a certainty.

When he finally arrived in the lobby and rode the elevator up to the sixty-sixth floor, he bolted through the front door, but it was too late. *He was too late.*

"Inez!" he shouted, rushing from room to room, desperately searching for something precious he knew he had lost and could never replace. "Inez!" He called out again—a final exhausted plea, but his soul ached in despair, knowing the truth. He had made a terrible, horrible mistake because he had been a terrible, horrible man. He was not Sven van der Meer, the invincible ingenious architect who deserved veneration from the masses. He was nothing more than a cruel egotistical bastard, blinded by ambition, who sought his own selfish gain at every turn. He knew she had always suspected it. But now she was certainly convinced of it.

A sharp pain seized his flank. Winded and hopeless, he dropped into a chair at the kitchen table, panting in anguish at the loss of a future that—only hours ago—had seemed lavish with endless possibilities.

"She left the car seat." His mother addressed him in Dutch from where she sat on the living room sofa. "She said it was too heavy and she didn't need it. She was going to take the train." After a long period of grim silence, she added, "she was very upset, Sven."

"Yes," he replied, nodding and covering his face with his hands.

"Can it be reconciled?"

"I very much doubt it," he answered, discouraging his mother's futile quest for hope.

"A shame," she finally pronounced, her lips frowning in disappointment as she looked away. "She seemed like such a nice girl. Different than all the others."

"Yes," he conceded, shifting his weight in his seat from the discomfort of the chunky emerald choker in his pocket. He withdrew it and tossed it onto the table like a distasteful memento.

She had been different. And she had made him different.

Chapter Thirty-One

TWO MONTHS LATER

INEZ SAT AT THE KITCHEN TABLE next to Luna, who was strapped into a high-chair, inspecting each bit of pancake before picking it up with awkward fingers and pushing it into her mouth. Breakfast time took an hour and required a bath afterwards. Inez was used to it. There had been so many "firsts" recently, it had been easy to lose track. Luna's first meals with them at the kitchen table. Her first solid foods. Her first pancakes. For the past two months, Inez had spent every day with Luna, watching her helpless four-month-old baby evolve into an attentive little six-month-old infant with bright eyes and an easy smile. *Curious about everything around her*, Inez reflected, *even something as simple as pancakes.*

Those were the small, magical moments that carried her through the long days and nights of the same daily routine. Inez loved being at home with her daughter, but she never could have anticipated how lonely she would feel without the stress of money and the constant need for babysitters occupying her mind.

"You're doing it again," Nana noted from across the table. "Drifting off into LaLa Land."

Inez had paused too long while reading aloud from the newspaper about the new tourist attraction at Navy Pier. It had become a common habit these last few weeks, and her grandmother rarely let her off the hook.

"You're thinking about Bachelor Number Two again, aren't you?"

"No."

"Yes, you are. Just like yesterday. And the day before…when you stopped reading cold that article about the true cost of the Millennium Park fountains."

Nana lifted her ruined, glacial eyes up into the air and sighed, "Svenka, the Swedish architect."

"Dutch."

"Yeah, whatever." Nana leaned back in her seat and exhaled again. "Mr. Metrosexual Moneypants."

Inez ignored the mockery in her grandmother's voice. "Do you even know what metrosexual means?"

"I sure do. You read me the 'Entertainment' section. But that's not the point. The point is that you can't even get through articles about The Art Institute or the Modern Architecture Society without drifting off into your pity party."

"Boy, I didn't realize I was such a joy to be around."

"Well, you haven't been. You've been a real pain in the ass," Nana shot back. "And just T-M-I, picking all the depressing articles to read first from the 'World News' section of the paper usually isn't a sign of jubilation."

"*F-Y-I,*" Inez stressed, correcting her. "And it's a big world, Nana. There are a lot of depressing stories out there."

"And what about all those weepy, melodramatic Meryl Streep movies I hear you sniveling at late at night?"

"Telling me not to cry when Meryl Streep cries is like elbowing me in the nose and telling me not to sneeze."

"And what about listening to all those melancholy Barry Manilow records," Nana goaded her, covering her heart and crooning the first chorus of "Weekend in New England" just to prove her point. "*When will our eyes meet?/When can I touch yooooou?/when will this strong yearning...eeeeeend. And when will I hold yoooooou again*?"

"Those are *your* melancholy Barry Manilow records, Nana!"

"Well, I play 'em because you're bumming me out these days, and at least Barry knows how to make me feel better."

Nana crossed her arms with a defiant *humph*. They both fell silent. Inez shut her eyes and rubbed her head. She had forgotten how nice it was to get out the house every day and away from the one person in the world who knew her better than she knew herself.

"Well, at least you have a date tonight," Nana finally offered. "That should cheer you up."

Inez pretended to enjoy the idea until she remembered the details. Her grandmother had set her up with Eddie, the choral director from the church.

"Apparently, he can play all of Bon Jovi's greatest hits on the organ," Nana informed her, trying to make him sound more macho and less effeminate.

"I think I would prefer Sasha, the janitor. And so would Eddie."

Nana paused, considering it. "Well, he says he's got tickets to some fancy show he thought you might like. What was it again?"

"Jesus Christ Superstar, the musical."

"See...there you go. A man who loves musicals is a sure bet."

Inez didn't challenge her. She had lost her appetite for challenging anything in her life. These days, she simply accepted whatever came her way—whether she wanted it or not. She was tired of fighting because it never affected the outcome anyway. It never made a difference. It was always the same—a monumental disappointment.

"Alright, enough already of this sulking..." Nana proclaimed in annoyance. "Tell me...if he showed up here today at the doorstep. What would you do?"

"Who? Eddie, the choral director?"

"No, the metrosexual blind billionaire."

"I'd tell him to go to hell."

"Okay. Then what?"

"I'd slam the door in his face."

"Yep. Then what?"

"I'd probably cry and eat the entire carton of chocolate ice cream and surf the TV for some more weepy, melodramatic Meryl Streep movies."

"Yep. See? That's my point. You're in love with him."

"Nana, I hardly think so. I only knew him for what? Like four days?"

"I knew your grandfather for four hours, and that was enough to feel the pinch in my heart," Nana confessed. Then, after a reflective beat, she added, "and in my pants."

Inez covered her ears and stood up from the table, "*Ohmygod*, Nana... really? Can we just stop talking about it?" Her hands trembled as she unhooked the tray from Luna's high chair. "I've moved on. He's moved on. It was no big deal, just another mistake in my love life. One of many. But I've promised myself to make it my absolute last."

Like a weepy, melodramatic Meryl Streep movie, the front doorbell rang. Inez and Nana both glanced down the hallway toward the front door.

"Ding dong," Nana mimicked the foreboding toll of the doorbell reverberating through the house's foundation.

With Luna in her arms, Inez scurried to the living room window and peered out through the sheer curtains. All she could make out was a tall dark figure.

"Someone's at the door," she whispered back to Nana.

"Duh," Nana scoffed. "It's not the neighborhood ghost playing ding door ditch."

"*You* answer it," Inez insisted.

"Yeah, whatever," Nana mumbled under her breath as she pushed back her chair and rose from her seat, scuffling down the corridor toward the foyer. "Totally not in love with him."

With her heart racing in anticipation, Inez paused and waited. She glanced down at herself—her favorite flannel pajama set, shapeless and stained with puréed baby food. Luna toyed with a long curl of her hair, which

Inez realized she hadn't washed in days. And she was fairly certain she had forgotten to brush her teeth last night—possibly even all of yesterday.

She heard Nana pull the door open as the bell rang a second time.

"Okay, okay, enough already," she protested. "I'm blind, not deaf."

"Sorry about that ma'am," an unfamiliar voice replied. "A delivery for a Miss Inez Sanchez?"

Inez closed her eyes and cradled Luna to her chest, sighing with a mixture of relief and inexplicable regret. *What exactly had she expected*? Without knowing the answer, she crept down the corridor and peeked into the foyer for a better look.

"A delivery?" Nana repeated, almost disappointed. "Is it a metrosexual hiding in an oversized stripper cake?"

The delivery man floundered, uncertain about how to reply. "No, ma'am. Just this..."

He hoisted up the large flat package, wrapped in ordinary brown delivery paper.

"Here, I'll sign for it," Inez interjected, quickly completing the task before grabbing the package from the delivery man and placing it onto the floor.

"So…what is it?" Nana asked, closing the door.

"Something I requested a while ago," she whispered, tearing away the paper and already knowing the answer—the intimate portrait of her arousal that Sven had bought from Enzo. She settled her eyes on the note, written in perfect penmanship on the simple white paper.

When I returned from Shanghai, I realized this no longer belonged to me. Our agreement was for me to destroy it, but I have failed in keeping that promise. I promise not to fail you again. ~Sven.

"What? Like an electric foot massage machine?" Nana insisted, peering over Inez's shoulder as if she thought she might be able to see after years of blindness.

"No, just something..." Inez's voice trailed off as she paused, biting her lip to hide the emotion in her voice. "Just something frivolous and impulsive that I can't afford to indulge in. I'll probably just return it. Or maybe throw it away. It doesn't suit me anymore."

Consumed by the bitter memories, Inez abandoned the canvas against the hall tree and turned away with Luna toward the kitchen.

"Well, that sounds like a shame," Nana called after her. "We could certainly use a few good vibrations around here. Even if they're just mechanical ones!"

Chapter Thirty-Two

"MERRILY WE ROLL ALONG, *roll along, roll along...merrily we roll along...o'er the deep blue sea*." Inside the gymnasium, Inez sat on the colorful parachute with Luna in her lap. All the other mothers and nannies lined its perimeter, each one singing and swaying with their babies to the nursery rhyme songs led by Debbie, the overly-enthusiastic leader of circle time.

Debbie's own baby, Abby, was a chubby, blonde eight-month old with chick fluff hair and sterling blue eyes, who was an exact image of her mother, just miniature.

"Okay, ladies, one more time…let's make it a good one!"

Debbie led the group in another hearty chorus of "Merrily We Roll Along" like it was the first time any of them had ever sung it before. The truth was, Inez and Luna had been there every afternoon that week. *Where else could you take a baby during the frigid month of December in Chicago? Certainly not the park.* It was something she hadn't considered when she had dreamt of all the time she was going to spend with Luna. Being a single mom without a job was a lot more monotonous than she had expected, but at least she wasn't struggling to find work. She had enough money to support Nana and Luna through Christmas, which meant she didn't need a job until after that. And she was thankful for it—even if it meant singing the same nursery rhymes over and over almost every day of the week.

"Okay, Ladies…everybody up on your feet for 'The Hokey Pokey!' " Debbie cried out, followed by a tweet of her plastic whistle.

All the women rose enthusiastically from the surface of the parachute.

"Hurray, 'The Hokey Pokey,' " Inez cheered, feigning excitement. It would be the umpteenth time she had put her right foot in and taken her right foot out.

She looked down at Luna, who had just started sitting on her own, balancing her weight on her cushy diaper. She rocked forward, then backwards, gauging whether or not she could launch herself into a full-on crawl. At the final moment, she sat back and lifted her hands to her mother. *No, not today. But soon...*Inez thought. *Soon...*

Succumbing to a sudden and sincere desire to perform "The Hokey Pokey" dance, Inez lifted Luna into her arms and sang along. No matter how cynical she was feeling about her life and all the challenges she had endured along the way, she only had to look at Luna and know it was all worth it.

She watched Debbie bounce her daughter's chubby baby hands in and out of the circle like a toy doll in her arms. Abby flapped her hands like a baby bird, ready to take flight.

"Well, hello there," Debbie suddenly called out across the gym with a gleeful shake of her left foot. "The workout room is down the hall to the left."

"Thank you, but I'm actually looking for someone..." the male voice trailed off when he met Inez's eyes.

"Well, in that case. Join right in." Debbie waved him forward.

All the women glanced at the doorway, noting the interruption as the tall, attractive man with golden hair strode along an invisible line directly towards Inez and Luna, as if he belonged there.

He absolutely did not belong there, Inez fumed, shooting Sven her best death stare to halt him in his tracks. It worked. He gazed at her. She glared back at him. *What was he doing there*? He belonged in a skyscraper in Shanghai with all of his asshole friends, not there—in a baby gym witnessing her performance of the "Hokey Pokey."

"We're just finishing up the Hokey Pokey and then we'll move right into 'The Wheels on the Bus.' "

"That sounds...invigorating." He braved Inez's obvious anger with his charming smile and endearing dimples. His eyepatch was gone and the intensity of his gaze made her perspire beneath her sweatshirt. *God, how she hated him.* And she especially *hated* the way the sunlight streaming in from the windows reflected off the symmetrical angles of his freshly-shaven face. *He looked happy and relaxed*, she thought, in his spandex athletic shirt and matching grey jogging pants. *Bastard.*

All the women shifted around the parachute to make room directly next to Inez. Sven nodded in appreciation and squeezed himself between Inez and an elated nanny balancing twins on each hip.

Losing all her mojo to hokey pokey, Inez turned her back on Sven. *How dare he show up there and pretend like it was no big deal*? She shifted Luna's weight to her opposite side and considered all her options. She could just walk out and abandon him there, but he would probably follow her. *And she couldn't escape him by going home.* Obviously, he had already started there and received instructions from Nana about where to find her.

Debbie abruptly blew her plastic whistle. "Okay, gang! Now, it's time for my favorite! Pick up an edge of the parachute and everyone walk toward your left!" She tweeted her whistle again before starting up an overzealous rendition of "The Wheels on the Bus." The whole group rotated the parachute in a circle.

"It requires coordinated pantomime," Inez muttered to Sven under her breath. "I think it might be above your skill level."

He smirked, as if he enjoyed her sarcasm. "I think I can manage pantomime. I'm fairly good with my hands."

"Is he your husband?" the nanny next to Inez asked while smiling at Sven who flaunted his ability to mimic a car horn.

"No," Inez seethed.

"Oh," the nanny replied, uncertain. "The father of your baby?"

"No."

"No?" The nanny arched her brow. "Your boyfriend?"

"Ex-boyfriend."

"Ohhh." The nanny frowned and nodded empathetically.

"And ex-boss," Inez added, glaring over at him.

The nanny gasped before whispering the gossip to the woman next to her, who relayed it to the mother next to her, until it traveled around the entire parachute like a game of *Telephone.* The women hushed themselves and watched Sven following Inez and Luna around in the circle.

"Luna's much bigger than I remember," Sven finally said, an obvious attempt to make idle small talk.

"Things change. Babies grow."

"And what about their mothers?"

"They end up at the baby gym being harassed by selfish, egotistical billionaires."

He nodded, enduring her spiteful words. "That's true. Billionaires are often selfish and egotistical. Perhaps they would benefit by hanging out more at baby gyms."

Inez stopped and stared at him, resenting his invasion in her personal world, and the way he treated it like mere entertainment. *Yes, she resented him*, especially every time he sang aloud the chorus of "The Wheels on the Bus" like a baby gym rock star. *Because it was all just a game to him.*

"Look, are you here for something—specific?" she demanded, attempting to control her anger. *Epic fail.*

Enthralled, the women on each side of Inez slowed their pace. Debbie slowed her gleeful tempo, noting their conflict from the corner of her eye.

"Yes," he answered, attempting to carry the tune while lifting his arms and hands, up and down, mimicking the people on the bus going up and down. "I realized how much I missed you and Luna while I was away in Shanghai."

"Aww," a nanny sighed from across the parachute, then quickly covered her mouth.

The other mothers and nannies quickly hushed her, anticipating Inez's reaction. Even Debbie fell silent as she joined the other women in watching the unfolding drama.

"Well, you're about two months too late, Sven."

He peered into her eyes. "Am I?"

"Yes."

"Why?" he challenged her.

"Because I've moved on…we've moved on."

"Really? With who? Eddie, the choral director?" His green eyes twinkled and a sly smile of victory spread across his face.

Inez glared at his playful expression. *She hated him.* And she wanted him to know it. "So, apparently bribing my ex-boyfriend out of our lives wasn't enough? You also had to turn my grandmother into a traitor, too?"

"Okay, grab an edge of the parachute, ladies!" Debbie cried out, diverting everyone's attention from the brewing storm. "It's time to go under!" Her loud voice ricocheted off the linoleum floors of the gym, encouraging the women to sweep the parachute into the air and duck beneath it, forming an inflated dome.

"Not exactly," Sven countered, taking advantage of the moment of privacy around them. "I did not have to bribe her. She told me willingly where you and Luna were. And she also told me about your date with Eddie, so she's more of a matchmaker than a traitor."

"Well, that's true," Inez confirmed, seizing the opportunity to make him jealous without knowing why she wanted to. "She's the one who set us up. He plays the church organ and he's taking me to a musical tonight."

"Hmm," he mused, not nearly as jealous as she would have liked. "I suppose that means I have competition. Except I'm fairly certain your grandmother said something about you still being in love with me." He flashed her a cocky smile.

Asshole.

Seeking to escape from him, Inez ducked under the parachute with Luna and sat down.

"Okay, now…let's practice saying the colors of the rainbow in English and Spanish to our little ones," Debbie instructed everyone. "Ready? Red, *rojo*…green, *verde*…blue, *azul*…"

Uncertain about the nylon shell above her, Luna fussed in Inez's arms. Sven appeared next to them and drew Luna into his own lap. Bouncing her on his knees, he held out her hands like she was flying and provoked her toothless grin.

"It looks like she still remembers me."

"Doubtful," Inez snarked back, except it almost seemed true. Luna sat quietly in Sven's lap, toying with the laces of his new tennis shoes. *Fluorescent white.* Inez skeptically checked their soles for wear and tear. There was none. *Faker.*

"You know, it's a shame you've moved on with Eddie, the choral director." Sven raised Luna to the concave ceiling of the domed parachute, allowing her to touch the flexing fabric. "Especially since I just bought you this."

Lowering Luna back into his lap, he pulled something out of his pocket and slipped it onto Inez's finger before she had a chance to refuse it.

"Are you seriously trying to woo me back with a two-dollar Hello Kitty ring?"

"One dollar. And you don't like Hello Kitty, anymore?"

Inez stared at his earnestness.

"Inez…I'm in a gym with a dozen women and babies beneath a rainbow-colored parachute. I do not know what I'm doing. The only thing I know is that I'm not leaving here without you and Luna."

She peered into his face, fancifully patterned with kaleidoscope colors. The conviction behind his eyes silenced her soul. She glanced around the interior of the parachute. Debbie and all the mothers and nannies were staring back at them.

"Okay, enough of the parachute," Debbie abruptly declared, signaling the end of the eavesdropping. "Bubble time!"

The parachute drew off of Inez and Sven, interrupting their intimacy. Debbie's farewell song boomed off the rafters as she sang goodbye to all the babies by name.

"You never should never have paid off Enzo to disappear from our lives," Inez suddenly said, lifting Luna from Sven's lap, rising to her feet, and attempting to move to the far corner of the gymnasium.

"Yes, that's true," he agreed, snagging her hand, halting her in place. "It was a selfish and egotistical billionaire move, which is why I contacted him last week and called off the arrangement."

"That doesn't change anything."

"Maybe not," he said, gazing deeply into her eyes. "Unless it's true what your grandmother said."

"My grandmother is senile."

"Really? She seems wonderfully lucid to me." He embraced her hand, testing her response.

Inez closed her eyes, evading his gaze, trying desperately to ignore how the heat from his hand transferred through her own. *The same hand with the ridiculously cute Hello Kitty ring.*

"She lives in a fantasy world and so do you, Sven. You're a hot shot billionaire architect and I'm…just a single mom who can never be who you need me to be. I hate wearing heels. I've never had a job that pays more than minimum wage in all my life. And I can't travel with you anywhere—not ever—but especially not to Shanghai."

"Well, that's something we have in common because it didn't work out for me very well in Shanghai."

Inez blinked twice as she tried to understand the significance of his words and the defeated expression on his face. "What do you mean?"

"I did not cooperate with Watercross and my brother in their plans to construct the Li Long Towers. Instead, I sold my designs to Harvey Zale for a trifle of what they are worth. And now, I'm likely ruined because Harvey Zale will be the one who builds the Li Long Towers, not Watercross and Van der Meer & Associates. And there will be consequences for that. But I don't care. I don't care at all because while I was in Shanghai, the only thing that consumed me was the realization that I was missing something essential in my life."

"Deodorant?" she deadpanned. He did smell like sweat and aftershave and unbridled masculinity. And it would almost be irritating, if it wasn't so unbelievably intoxicating.

He held her gaze. "No, you," he whispered, cupping her cheek and leading her lips to meet his own.

He pulled her into his arms, with Luna between them, and kissed her with heartbreaking sadness, tenderness, and relief, conveying to her the transformation within his soul—whatever decisions he had made, whatever pain he had caused her, it had all been a terrible mistake for which he would gladly seek her forgiveness. *If she would only grant him a second chance.*

Breathless, Inez pushed against his chest and tore away from his kiss.

"You do realize that if I accept this ring, it only means I'm giving you a chance to grovel your way back into our lives?"

He folded his forehead against her own and stroked her hair. "It would be my pleasure to grovel for as many days as it takes."

"Weeks," she corrected him. "Probably months."

"Well, then…in the meantime, let's consider it your prize for being right…all my friends were assholes, including me. And I regretted every day I was there because I wasn't here…with you and Luna."

"Is that why you look so relaxed now in your jogging suit?" She tugged on his tight spandex shirt.

"Maybe. Or maybe I just enjoy singing 'The Wheels on the Bus'."

He drew her in for another kiss, long and sweet, promising her something that she had never felt before from him—unconditional love.

She glanced upwards. A sea of bubbles drifted down upon them—transparent globes, swirling with iridescence. Sven caught one in the palm of his hand and guided it toward Luna's nose. *Pop*! With a grin as wide as her face, she swatted her hands and bounced in her mother's arms while her joyful eyes tracked the curious floating spheres.

The buzz of Sven's cell phone in his pocket threatened their moment of serenity. He ignored it. Instead, he sat down on the blue gymnasium mats and watched the bubbles wobble through the air toward him.

"Don't you want to answer that?" Inez pressed him as his phone continued to ring.

"Nope," he answered, crossing his feet at his ankles and waggling his new sneakers like a child

"Nope?" Inez echoed, eyeing him. "That doesn't sound like the Sven I know."

"It's the new, unemployed Sven."

"Ahh, right. Ruined and aimless. Except you do have an authentic Monet painting hanging in your living room, so you aren't exactly penniless."

"No, but that painting belongs to my mother. It wouldn't be right to expect to live off my mother's wealth."

"True," Inez agreed. "At least, not unless you give her kittens."

He flashed her a smile and reached out to draw her and Luna into his lap.

"Does that mean you are offering to help me with that?"

But before she could answer, his phone buzzed again. Shifting her weight off his legs, she encouraged him to check his phone. "C'mon, maybe it's important."

"Nothing could possibly be more important than this." He nestled her and Luna deeper into his lap.

His phone vibrated beneath her as a text message arrived. "Sounds like someone really wants you to think otherwise." She slipped her hand into his pocket, withdrew his phone, and tapped the screen, investigating his messages. "One voice mail. One text. Both from a…Phillip Spears?"

Sven shifted his chin over her shoulder and peered at the screen. Clearly, she had piqued his interest.

"Who's Phillip Spears?"

"Watercross' main competition. You met him at the Modern Architecture Society banquet."

"Ahh, right. See…? Ruined or not, you're still a very important architect. And I doubt a life of baby gym—day in and day out—is going to suit you very well."

"It suits me just fine," he insisted, his eyes scanning the text. "Although he is offering me a curious proposition. He's heard of my resignation from the Li Long Towers."

"Wow, news travels fast."

"And he wants me to be the principal architect on his project—the redevelopment of the Old Main Post Office."

"Does that mean you're officially employed again?"

"I don't know. He wants to have a meeting with me tomorrow. He's offering me ten percent equity ownership of the project."

"Hmm…how much is the project worth?"

"Three hundred and fifty million dollars."

Inez let out an incredulous laugh. "Lose your entire billionaire soul in one deal. Gain it back in another deal. Sounds like the old Sven van der Meer."

"As long as it's the one you're still in love with." He took Luna from her hands and snuggled them both in his arms.

Inez ran her fingernails through his hair and considered all her options. "Well, that depends on if I still have to pretend to be your fake fiancée or not."

"I'd rather you just pretend to be my real one." He nudged her for a kiss. Daring to trust him, she closed her eyes, responding to the urgency and passion of his tongue entwining with her own. He pulled her carefully into his embrace, keeping her from drifting away like all the twinkling, floating bubbles, fragile in their journey through the unpredictable future.

"And you do realize," she added, tearing herself away to catch her breath, "that you've also committed yourself to baby gym every day to prevent yourself from turning back into a selfish and egotistical billionaire."

He nodded before kissing her again. "Good. I wouldn't have it any other way."

Chapter Thirty-Three

SIX MONTHS LATER

HIS HANDS… IT WAS THE ONE thing she never could resist giving into whenever he wanted to make love to her—the way his strong hands embraced her body and traced all its curves like an act of worship, arousing the sensual core of her femininity and igniting her desire to be touched in every intimate way.

A year ago, she could barely stand the thought of having to act like his pretend girlfriend. Now, the way his hands massaged her breasts, cupping them with the perfect balance of strength and tenderness while offering them up to his lips for sensual nips of adoration, conveyed only one message—he wanted nothing more than to pleasure her because she was his muse. It was all so different than those dark, bitter days a year ago, before she had met him and she was a struggling single mother who had forgotten what it felt to truly love and be loved.

She lifted her chin and cracked a playful smile. It was a familiar signal that she wanted him to continue feathering his hot breath down her neck as his mouth grazed the surface of her skin to the tips of her tits. He complied. He always complied, but first he made sure to tease her, drawing her entire body against his own and melding his cock against her pelvis, preparing her for the slow burn of making love to her, deeply, passionately, as if he intended not only to ravish her body, but also honor the essence of her soul.

He truly loved her.

And it always started with his hands. *His hands…* they never failed to remind her of his desire to be closer to her, even within the cramped space of her tiny bed at Nana's house with Luna's crib flanking one side and her messy desk wedged against the other. She always awoke to the caressing sensation of his fingers, toying with strands of her hair or nestling themselves between the warmest part of her thighs. It was hard not to smile while nudging him away. She never would've guessed—from the very first time they had met in his office for her job interview—that he was a man who liked to cuddle.

"I'm not going away until you kiss me," he liked to tease.

"You have bad breath," she would always say, and roll over completely away from him. It was a lie, but she knew he liked it when she played hard to get. Still.

"Then, I'll just focus it somewhere better than your mouth."

She smiled as his head ducked beneath the covers and warmed her inner thighs, seeking to pleasure her into submission. It worked. It always worked. She lifted her arms above her head and heaved an exhale of surrender, especially the moment he forced the heat from his lips against the cotton crotch of her panties. *Off.* It was always the same irresistible tug from his hands, coaxing her to lift up her hips and assist his quest to strip away all barriers.

It would be the first of many times he would try to make love to her today. But early morning was his favorite.

Wider. His hands spread apart her knees, but she always resisted until the first stroke of his tongue discovered the wet, dewy truth, as her body betrayed how difficult it was to play hard to get with him. As usual, her laugh gave her away, a signal that his foreplay had successfully produced the tingling ache for more. Running her hands through his fair hair and encouraging him to hold her closer, she sighed heavily in relief that they had come this far. *So far.* She could trust him—completely. And she loved the satisfaction and freedom that unconditional trust always brought her.

But this day was different. This day, her bedroom door suddenly burst open. It was both startling and completely expected.

"Ugh, Nana," Inez groaned, pushing away Sven's seductive advances and pulling the sheet above any exposed skin.

"What?" Nana snapped, as if she was annoyed that Inez was annoyed. "Your fornication can wait. My issue is a childcare emergency." Nana reached her hand into Luna's crib, searching for the missing item. "And besides, I'm blind. So it's not like I'm gonna go peeking at his schlong."

Sven raised his head from beneath the covers. "My what?"

"I worked as a nurse at a veteran's hospital for thirty-two years. I saw some of the biggest shlongs to fill my wet dreams for a lifetime, so I don't need to refresh my memory."

She held up the pacifier in triumph and shuffled out the bedroom, slamming the door behind her.

"Schlong?" Sven repeated, his Dutch accent making it sound like a formal name for the male organ.

Inez groaned again and flopped back against the pillows. "This is why you always propose that we sleep at your penthouse."

"No, not at all. I love this tiny bed. I love sleeping next to Luna's crib. But most of all, I love your Nana scolding us like teenagers every morning when I get your panties around your ankles. And I think she loves it, too."

"We can't keep on like this..."

"We absolutely can. It's been working for the past six months. There's no reason why it cannot work for six years more."

"Six years? I can't even think about what I want for breakfast much less what life will be like six years from now."

Sven looked at her curiously. "No?"

"No," she replied. "And we can't possibly all live here together much longer, but Nana will never leave this house."

"No, she won't," Sven conceded, tracing his finger along the slope of her shoulder. "And I wouldn't expect her to...she's comfortable with her routine here. And so am I."

"Even though she's determined to let us know every time she hears us having sex?"

"I consider it a challenge now," he whispered, slipping his body over hers and kissing the arch of her neck down to her breasts. "To have my schlong sneak into you as quietly as possible."

Inez cried out with playful laughter as he pushed his cock against her wetness. He covered her mouth to silence her. "That is not particularly quiet."

"We cannot go on like this, Sven," she muttered through his palm.

"I'm fairly certain we can," he replied, showering her with long, indulgent kisses and coaxing her with every tender nudge of his bare cock.

She lifted her chin, exhaling in satisfaction, as his first thrust took away every worry she had about anything in her life.

"You make it seem all so easy... she tossed back with another sigh of gratification, as her wetness enveloped the full length of his longing for her. "That's what I love about you."

He pressed his lips against her ear. "It is all so easy, so long as we're together."

"Like a little family." Hearing her own confession surprised her, but in the heat and intimacy of the moment, it felt as natural as having him inside her.

"Which is why we should add onto it," he whispered, low with desire.

She gasped, breathless, as he increased his pace and filled her completely. Yearning to unite them, he kissed her with the familiarity of a soulmate, entwining their tongues like their bodies, persuading her to allow her heart to melt away into his protective embrace.

When he finally released her, she breached for air and uttered a sassy afterthought. "Well, Billions...you're a genius architect. I'm sure there's a way you can just draft up plans to add an addition onto the house."

He suddenly slowed his rhythm without withdrawing and curiously peered into her eyes. "No, I mean...add onto our little family."

She gazed back at him, searching for the meaning behind his words. But it was obvious and inescapable. Before she could respond, he kissed her again while angling upwards, and rowed against her most sacred spot, knowing exactly how to trigger a rush of pleasure and harmony all over her body—and her soul.

An addition onto their little family?

As the intensity of her own climax overwhelmed her mind and senses, she couldn't imagine what that would possibly look like. But as he surged inside her, warming her core with the unspoken promise of forever, she could guess what it might feel like...*unconditional love.*

* * * *

"Nana, your homemade pancakes with maple syrup are always delicious."

Sven licked the buttery syrup from his fingers before adjusting Luna in his lap to feed her the tiny morsels. She clapped her hands and tested her new word of the week. "Cake, cake."

"Nice try, Svenka. But flattery doesn't fly in this house. I still know what you and my granddaughter were doing upstairs before breakfast because these rafters creak like hell when you're doing it."

He glanced slyly over at Inez. "We were making plans for an addition."

"To - the - house," Inez clarified, considering kicking him under the table.

"Really? An addition?" Nana shuffled to a chair at the Formica table next to Sven and Luna. "Will it include a pool?" Then, after a moment of serious consideration, she added, "And a pool boy?"

"Nana!" Inez considered kicking her under the table. "A pool boy!?"

"What!? You're the ones proposing an addition. I'm just adding to the wish list. And besides, why should you two be the only ones who get to hanky panky around here?"

Inez covered her face and mouthed O-M-G to Sven, who held her hand to calm her. "It can include anything you want, Nana. You have quite a large lot at the rear of the house. We'll have plenty of space if we trim down the garden."

"Garden?" Nana huffed. "There's that flattery again. I like to refer to it as weed city. And trim away. Maybe if we do hire a pool boy, he can be in charge of the ongoing trimming. And he can start on my bikini line."

Sven smiled at Inez and handed Luna her sippy cup. It was just another morning at her grandmother's house.

"Oh, and while you're at it, add an accent to the list," Nana asserted.

"An accent?" Inez replied, seriously annoyed with the conversation. "What is this? Drive-through BoyToyland?"

"Hey…you've got a metrosexual billionaire with an accent, so why can't I have a pool boy with one."

"We can certainly try," Sven replied, attempting to keep the peace.

"And make it French or Mediterranean," Nana directed him. "But not Scandinavian. No offense, Svenka, but your accent doesn't do it for me."

Inez just about freaked. "He's Dutch, Nana. Not Swedish."

Nana raised her palm with her best "talk-to-the-hand" gesture. "I'll even settle for South American. Especially, if he's got a really good set of—"

Sven came to the rescue. "We are also making plans for a vacation."

Surprised, both Nana and Inez simultaneously repeated him. "A vacation?"

"Yes, a vacation," he confirmed, as if it was the most natural proposition in the world.

"What? Like shipping me off on a fancy cruise or something?" Nana turned her glacial eyes to the ceiling, as if she was considering the possibilities of tripling the number of pool boys in her future.

"No, we'll all go together," Sven clarified.

"Go on a vacation with Nana?" Inez looked over at her grandmother, who grinned wide like she was in on the joke.

"Yes, and it will be lovely." He fed Luna the last bit of pancake before lowering her to the floor where she could play with her toys. "I will arrange everything."

"I think you're having post-orgasmic hallucinations," Inez shot back, no longer caring about maintaining the privacy of their sex life. "We cannot possibly go on a vacation—together—much less now. We don't have time. You have the opening of the Old Main Post Office in a week, and I've got my internship at the Art Institute to finish or they will never promote me beyond cataloging obscure, dusty basement artifacts."

Sven took up his coffee mug and relaxed against the back of his chair. "I thought you were enjoying cataloging all their obscure, dusty artifacts like those Victorian death lockets."

"Mourning brooches," she corrected him.

"With real hair from dead people," Nana added, just to remind them that she hadn't dozed off.

"Loved ones," Inez overrode her.

"Who are still dead," Nana insisted. "Like that woman who kept the heart of her dead husband…what's his name again?"

"Percy Shelly. One of the most famous poets in Western Literature, by the way."

"With a nutjob for a wife. Who the hell keeps a heart in her desk as a keepsake?"

"The author of *Frankenstein*," Sven added. Inez shot him a glare.

Nana nodded, like he had confirmed her point. "Nutjob. So please tell me that's not one of the items that's sooooo important to catalog that you can't be bothered to go on a vacation planned by your billionaire boyfriend."

Inez resolutely looked at Sven. "We are not going on a vacation—together."

"Too late. I've already bought the tickets." He sipped his coffee and slipped several airfare tickets out from beneath his placemat.

Inez scanned their destination. "Paris?"

"For a few nights. And then…onto Giverny."

Monet's studio and gardens, Inez imagined. All her annoyance melted away as she gazed into his soft green eyes, confirming one thing—*they could make time and it would be perfect.*

"Are there pool boys in Giverny?" Nana interjected.

"No, Nana…just ponds and lily pads and Monet paintings." Inez reached out to touch Sven's cheek. "And I love it."

"Hmm. I think I like the idea of being shipped off on a cruise better."

"That's afterwards, Nana." Sven embraced Inez's hand into his own. "We'll sail wherever you like—for the honeymoon. But first, I would like for you to be with us in Giverny where I intend to marry your granddaughter."

He lifted Luna from the floor as she clutched her favorite teddy bear and retrieved an opal and diamond engagement ring strung from a red ribbon around its neck. He untied the knot of the ribbon to release the ring, and held it up to Inez. "Will you marry me, Miss Sanchez?"

She stared at him, then the ring, hearing the words without comprehending them. "Marry you?"

He nodded. "Yes, because there's nothing I want more for our family—and our plans for an addition—than for you to agree to becoming my wife in Giverny."

Everything fell into slow motion, and yet sped through her mind at the speed of light—their first interview and their arrangement for her to become his pretend girlfriend; their confrontation with Enzo at the Art Institute where Sven first kissed her and set aflame her soul for wanting more; and their night together at the opera with Luna, and their subsequent relationship that had grown from a whirlwind affair spanning four days into a year-long courtship of mutual affection and respect in which he had become more than just her lover or boyfriend—he had become her faithful partner and trusted best friend, and even a dutiful parent to Luna, as if she was his own. But now, as he lowered himself on one knee and offered her the engagement ring, it was as if he was offering even more than all of that. *Even more.* Because he was offering her the promise of maintaining that commitment to her as her husband—everlasting.

A searing pain abruptly nipped her side. It was Nana, violently pinching her.

"Ouch!" Inez cried out. "What the heck is that for?"

"Because you're taking too damn long to say yes," Nana scolded her. "And if you don't agree to marry him, then I sure as hell will."

Nana swiped the ring from Sven's hand and deposited it into Inez's palm.

She gazed at it, daring to believe in the fairy tale and its happily ever after that she had once scorned as trite and fanciful, an unobtainable myth believed by everyone else in the world—except her.

"Will you marry me, Inez?" he repeated, low and steady, as if he didn't want to rush her, but also couldn't bear the thought of not having her in his life—forever.

Rising from her seat, she slipped into his lap and cupped his cheek, kissing him as if she couldn't bear the thought of what her life would have been like without him.

"Yes."

Nana let out a long, nauseating snore. "Oh, brother. More hanky panky." Bending down and lifting Luna into her arms, she announced loudly, "C'mon, munchkin. Better rescue you now before they start going at it on top of the table."

"Don't worry, Nana," Sven called after her. "I promise I'll draft up plans for an addition."

"Really?" Inez eyed him, seeking clarification. "An addition to the house?"

"Most definitely." Sven nodded, dropping his chin down between her breasts and kissing her as if he intended to steal away her heart. "How else will we have room for all of our kittens?"

She laughed and ran her fingernails through his flaxen hair. "All of them? We're having more than one?"

With one swift motion, he whisked Inez into his strong embrace, preparing to take her back upstairs to repeat everything that had confirmed their love only hours ago, but this time, as his real fiancée. "We're certainly going to have fun trying…"

THE END

Exes

Aria Hawthorne

Exes – Book Summary

When Chicago real estate tycoon Harvey Zale pings a "friend of a friend" with a flirtatious text, he never expects to start an addictive sexting affair with a complete stranger. He's a billionaire who can get any woman he wants, but he can't have her—his mysterious, sultry Contessa, who inspires his nightly confessions and soothes more than just his conscience from the consequences of his own shallow ambitions.

He's determined to build the tallest towers in the world and he needs to sell his Chicago riverfront property to finance it. But when Alma Castillo, the Lara Croft of antique hunters, shows up on his land, claiming the existence of a priceless Tiffany stained-glass window and doing everything in her power to muck up his deal, he knows he's got more than a stray cat to collar and tame. She's not only on a mission to save long-lost antiques; she's also on a personal crusade to hate his guts.

He would know. She served him divorce papers a year ago, just to prove it.

And he'd care a helluva lot more if his ex-wife's sassy tongue and wicked intelligence didn't turn him on every time she called him "a**hole" and if she didn't look so damn cute in those baggy overalls, disguising her affinity for being naughty as much as being nice.

Perhaps even as naughty as his Contessa, who unlike Alma, doesn't know anything about his real identity or flawed, billionaire reputation, which flames his desires to escalate their fantasy relationship into the reality of one scorching night of mindblowing...

If he could only get his mind off his ex-wife—the only woman he's ever truly loved. God, woman...if she would just let him pleasure her scornful frown and turn it oh, oh, oooohhhh so upside down, maybe he could convince her to marry him again.

But no one ever said it was easy being a greedy opportunistic billionaire bastard, especially one who happens to know there's nothing better than make-up sex with an ex…

Chapter One

GAZING AIMLESSLY OUT THE WINDOW of his riverfront home, Harvey Zale slouched deeper into his leather recliner. The twilight sun washed swaths of solar orange across the mirrored panels of Chicago's endless skyscrapers. *Skyscrapers that he had helped to build.* He couldn't remember their names—only their current worth on his balance sheet, which had become the sole measure of his life. *A damn financial piece of paper. His life summed up in numbers.* He sloshed the whiskey in his tumbler, but failed to take another sip. He had already drunk two full glasses and was starting to feel the effects—the unforgiving judgment of his inner demons. *Demons that threatened to destroy him.*

His cell phone rang. He sat up straighter in his seat with hope. *Was it her?*

Then the unpleasant ring tone dampened his spirits. He withdrew his phone from his pocket and answered the call in silence.

"It's done Harvey," the man on the other end confirmed. "He's sold them to you."

Harvey felt nothing but dread. "How much did you have to pay?"

"Less than we even expected. Van der Meer wanted anyone other than Watercross to have his designs for the Li Long Towers. Even if it meant selling them to you at a discount."

"Gee, thanks," Harvey muttered, taking a long swig from his tumbler and feeling the sting of the premium whiskey in the back of his throat.

"Well…you know the old saying: good men live through history; great men make it. Congrats, Harv. You're going to build the tallest buildings in the world."

Harvey stretched out his long legs and peered down at his well-worn cowboy boots. *The tallest buildings in the world*, repeated in his mind, wondering what the man who owned the rights to build the tallest buildings in the world would say to the man who wanted to jump from their pinnacles.

Six months ago, the news that he had secured Sven van der Meer's designs to construct the Li Long Towers would have been the only thing he wanted to hear. Now, he only heard the disconcerting echo of hollowness in his chest, like a coin dropping through a wishing well that had long since run dry.

The man cut off the call without saying good-bye. Exactly how Harvey liked it. No formalities. No bullshit. Just business. It was always "just business" to Harvey Zale. Cold, calculated financial transactions. And the whole world knew it.

Ping.

He glanced down at his phone before dropping his head back with relief. The whole world knew what a callous egocentric bastard he was—except for her.

Are you alone?

Harvey read her alluring text. He had hoped to hear from her tonight and the fulfillment of that wish fueled his unguarded emotions.

Yes, he replied. *And I've been waiting for you for three days. That's the longest you've ever been away.*

Awaiting her reply, his heart beat like a sledgehammer inside his chest. The spontaneity and unpredictability of their mysterious affair intoxicated him almost into insanity. The possibility that she could disappear tomorrow and never be heard from again excited him, but it also made him uncomfortably vulnerable. He reached over and pulled the short gold chain on the banker's lamp next to him, settling into the darkness.

You could have texted me, she answered. *If you needed something...*

He imagined her saying it with a playful smile, perhaps while running her fingernails through his hair. She was always playful this time of night and it comforted him when so few things in his life did.

Maybe I prefer to wait until you're ready...and willing.

His phone fell silent. He stretched out his legs and counted...three, two, one. He had initiated the first innuendo—a sly signal that he wanted what she was able to offer. *He always wanted it,* he thought, ever since that first reply to his text zipped across his screen—initiating their sexting affair. Now, he sipped from his tumbler, patiently awaiting her reply.

I'm definitely ready and willing, she finally answered. *I just shaved everything and the whole time I thought about you.*

He closed his eyes and dropped his head back with a sigh, sinking deeper into his recliner. *God, how he loved it when she teased him like that—right from the start.*

Shower or bathtub? he prodded her.

Tub, she answered without a beat. *With only the light from my lavender candle guiding my way.*

Harvey unbuckled his belt and withdrew it from the loops like a whip. *And now?*

Still damp with a white towel around my body, but open in the front. Relaxed and lying on my bed...wondering what you're doing tonight.

He had just gotten the news that he could build the tallest buildings in the world, and the only thing he wanted was to imagine himself in the bathtub with her.

I was thinking about my life and work and how none of it mattered...unless I heard from you.

You always flatter me like that, but I don't believe you. Men love their work more than their own wives and children.

He read her reply, almost able to hear her mocking laughter.

I have neither, he shot back. He wanted to make clear that this was not an extra-marital fling for him. He may have been an opportunistic asshole in his professional life, but he wasn't a philandering scumbag in his personal life. *And I have more work and money than I'll ever need or want.*

He paused, concerned he may have crossed a line. *Perhaps he had been too confrontational?* He didn't want to be harsh with her. He was tired of being brisk and aggressive in his daily business routine, and in the isolation of darkness, the only thing he wanted was to be free—free from all the empty trappings of his beleaguered life.

No discussion about work, she suddenly pinged back. *Rule number one, remember?*

He remembered. It was one of the many things he loved about their exchanges. She didn't know he was Harvey Zale, billionaire real estate tycoon and the most reviled man in his industry. He could be anything he wanted to be with her—including himself.

I love it when you lay down those rules, he texted her. *Remind me of what happens when I break one of them.*

His screen went dark. For a moment, he thought she had abandoned him.

A serious rule? Like not discussing the details of our personal lives? Or a less offensive one, like not unzipping your pants?

Harvey smirked and proceeded to unzip his pants.

Definitely the less serious one, he thumbed back, releasing a sigh while holding back his desire to propose the punishment. *Cat and mouse.* He had to lure her in.

Okay...no discussing work or our personal lives, he continued. Fair enough. *Then how about you tell me something you've never told anyone before.*

Something I've never told anyone? she replied. *You mean, like a secret?*

Yeah, definitely.

Oh my…you're drinking again tonight, aren't you?

He downed his whiskey and eyed the bottle on the counter of the entertainment bar. *Just getting started*, he answered her. *Go on…I want to hear it.*

You mean something other than the way I fantasize about you being in the tub with me?

This time, he hesitated. She was testing him, seeing if he could be distracted enough by sex not to pursue his original question. It was tempting. *Very tempting.* But Harvey wanted something more tonight, and he wanted her to know it.

How about what keeps you awake at night?

I'm telling you that I'm fantasizing about you being in the bathtub with me, and you're feeling philosophical?

I'm always philosophical, he countered. *And I'm pretty sure you like it.*

Well…confessing my secrets to you hardly seems fair. I much prefer you to think I'm a perfect sinless sex goddess.

It's not fair, he nudged her. *But neither is making me sit here alone, in the dark, half-drunk with my pants half-unzipped, wondering why your phone call is the only thing I look forward to during the day and the only thing I want to experience at night.*

There was a long pause. It made Harvey consider whether or not he had admitted too much. *Fuck it, he didn't care.*

And you and I both know damn well that no one is perfect, he shot back. *If you were a perfect sinless sex goddess, I wouldn't be interested in you. Trust me. I'm no saint either. Perfect and sinless is boring, and boring is far worse than flawed. So, c'mon now…the truth…what keeps you awake at night?*

The text thread suddenly went silent. After a moment longer than seemed comfortable, she messaged him her answer:

Regret.

It was a simple response—almost like a dismissive shrug—that made him rub his chin. He needed to tread carefully. But she made it easy on him.

Are you surprised by that answer?

No, he reassured her. *I just think that's a tough one. I rarely regret anything. Probably because I'm such a heartless asshole.*

You weren't heartless the other night.

He stroked his jaw again, reflecting on exactly how he hadn't been heartless the other night. *Yes, it was true.* He'd been seductively charming, at least enough to convince her to remove her panties and describe herself to him—in graphic detail. And it had been the crossroads of their seemingly casual, flirtatious sexting affair—the tipping point that officially stoked the flame of his desire and spurred his hunger to explore the mysterious connection between them.

*Then that means you can trust me...*he texted back, reeling her in. If she had actually been there, he would have drawn her into his lap and kissed her neck before slipping his hand between her thighs and gently stroking her into submission. *So tell me...I'm listening. What's something you regret?*

He almost thought he heard her heave a heavy sigh. He wanted nothing more than to make her exhale like that in surrender—over and over again.

Oh... sometimes it seems like everything, she finally responded. *Sometimes I replay the scenes in my life and think about how I could have been a little bolder and a little less fearful. I think about how I should have taken more risks and shouldn't have been so cautious. I think about how I could have spoken up more for myself and not worried so much about what everyone would think of me if I did.*

Harvey kicked off his cowboy boots—a gift from his ex-wife—and shifted his weight in his chair. He loved these moments, these intimate confessions in the dark that made him feel inexplicably alive.

I just feel like I spend all my time hiding from my own life and myself, she added, like an afterthought.

It was an ironic confession. She was, after all, sexting with a complete stranger and avoiding names and personal details while doing it.

I think we're all hiding behind something, he cautiously typed back. *Even us tough guys who pretend we're not.*

*Maybe...*she paused, as if she was weighing her thoughts. *But you sound like someone who doesn't care about what people think of you.*

I don't, he shot back before revising that statement in his head. He cared about what she thought of him, but he wasn't ready to say that. *But being perceived as a fearless bastard isn't as glamorous as you'd think.*

You make it sound like you're someone very important...

He was important—important enough to know that fame and fortune was a zero-sum game, the one cancelling out the other, ending in a soulless existence.

I think you're being too hard on yourself, he finally replied, intentionally evading her observation. *You seem to be able to express yourself just fine.*

Yes, with you, I say exactly what I feel. There's never any regret. It's always effortless.

Well, then...you'll just have to spend more time talking with me. Problem solved.

If she had really been sitting there on his lap, he would have brushed her hair behind her shoulder and nudged her for a lustful kiss. Instead, their connection dissipated into the digital netherworld. Harvey's screen faded to black and he wondered how to proceed—if at all. Then her next text guided him out of the abyss.

Okay, your turn, she urged him with a ping. *What keeps you awake at night, tough guy?*

He stared at her text. She was sassy. He liked sassy.

Yes, it was his turn, he thought, mulling over his response. He knew exactly what she wanted from him, but could he deliver the same intimacy and honesty that she had granted him?

Well…probably realizing I've wasted my entire life chasing power and money and influence when none of it matters to anyone—least of all to me.

There was a long pause before she answered. *So you're wealthy, but unfulfilled.*

In one single text, she ferreted out the core of what he'd been hiding from the world for years. *Very wealthy, but completely, hopelessly lost*, he finally replied, struggling with his decision not to lie.

She responded with a smiley face poking himself in the eye. It was almost comical, as if she was mocking him and the ridiculous paradox of having loads of money and daring to complain about it.

He resisted the strange urge to reciprocate with an emoticon—an irreverent animated one like a smiley, bonking her emoticon with a hammer. Normally he wouldn't be caught dead using emoticons. He was Harvey-fucking-Zale, after all. *But that was her effect on him.*

Hmmmm. That's too bad, she added to her emoticon. *I don't generally like very wealthy men because you're right...they are usually heartless assholes.*

Harvey laughed aloud. *Good*, he replied. *At least we've gotten that out in the open.*

Yes, we wouldn't want to be unclear about that.

Harvey imagined her sarcastic smile spreading across her beautiful face. Even if she wasn't beautiful, it didn't matter to him. The only thing that mattered was that she understood him. At this point in his life, Harvey couldn't think of a single person who truly understood him.

Why not just donate it all? You know, write one big check to a children's hospital or something?

Yeah, I've thought about that, he admitted. *But I'm cynical enough to know that they'd probably just squander it. And what money isn't squandered will be laundered by someone at the top equally as ruthless and corrupt as me.*

Oh my…so you're a complete jerk then, too?

The worst of the worst, he stressed.

That explains a lot because I tend to date a lot of jerks.

Well, okay then…one more thing to get out in the open from the start: no dating this jerk.

Deal—because I much prefer our current arrangement.

Sexting without regrets? He teased her.

Definitely without regrets, she confirmed. *And...*

Harvey's phone abruptly fell silent. He watched and waited, then exhaled in exhilaration when she completed her text.

...without limitations. So tell me...how far down are your pants unzipped?

He'd been stroking himself the whole time, but he wasn't going to confess it.

Tell me first about how wet you are...now, after your bath. And whether or not you'll let me onto the bed to help keep you that way.

There was hardly a beat before she answered him. *I would prefer that you kneel...*

Harvey relaxed and smiled. He knew exactly where she wanted him to take it and he was more than willing to oblige. He texted her back with sly calculation. He knew she liked it when he took it slow—descriptive and sensual, occasionally dirty but never disrespectful. Within moments, he was at the foot of the bed, slipping his hands beneath her bare luscious ass and running his lips over the tender curve of her waist. As in their past sessions, he took full control, parting her knees, spreading her thighs, and dismissing her insincere protests that maybe they should stop before they took it too far.

Too far? Unlike revealing the details of their personal lives, there were never any lines drawn or rules made regarding their sexting affair; there was only an understanding of what they had done thus far and what they hadn't. If she had texted him to stop, he would have. But she never did, and tonight was no different. Instead, she told him that there was a draft in the room and she needed to feel his hot breath between her legs. He told her to prepare herself because she was going to feel a lot more than just his hot breath.

Yes, she was definitely granting him a gift—the gift of pleasuring her fully and completely in a way that he hadn't before. He wanted to honor that gift; he wanted to make her quiver and moan and come without accepting anything from her in return. He would climax on his own, just by imagining her on the bed, exposed and butterflied open, offering her glistening sweetness to him while she writhed and groaned from the invading intimacy of his every lustful stroke. But it was rare for him to find a woman who made him want to please her more than himself. *That was her effect on him.* It wasn't just about the sex for him. It was about their mysterious bond and the trust that seemed to be growing between them.

It was an intimacy that had been absent in his life. A trust and understanding, that even he—Harvey-fucking-Zale—needed in his life. And right now, she was the only one capable of fulfilling it.

Chapter Two

"I cannot believe you did that!" Alma shrieked.

"What's the big deal?" Alma's younger sister, Conchita, dismissively waved her hand from the other side of the diner booth. "You're freaking out like I just borrowed a pair of your favorite shoes without asking and stretched them out with my monstrous size ten feet."

"Borrowing my shoes without asking is totally forgivable," Alma replied.

Conchita fluttered her fake eyelashes. She wasn't so certain.

"But—" Alma insisted "—posting my profile onto VenusDatesMars.com without my permission? That's an unforgivable invasion of my privacy."

"How can it be a bad thing when you're being courted by a stud like this?" Conchita flashed her phone's screen at Alma who scanned the image of a bare chested man in tighty-whities, sprawled across a red velvet bed.

Alma read aloud his profile name in horror.

"KardashianButtLover82? Ohmygod, Conchita. What have you done?" Pulling her turtleneck sweater up past her nose, Alma shrank lower into the booth.

"I've found you a man." Conchita purred with interest, flicking her long black hair over her low-cut cotton candy pink mohair sweater. "And one who loves big butts is definitely top of my list." Her long fake fingernails, studded with gold beads, swiped the screen through all the details. "Oh là là. Look at this close-up. Come here now, ButtLover, and help me scratch my kitty itch. Meow."

"*Ugh*!" Alma groaned and covered her ears. "Forget borrowing my favorite pair of shoes. It's like borrowing my *only* lingerie set and returning it—unwashed."

Her sister grimaced. Alma frowned. Then, they both simultaneously shivered, realizing that…no, nothing could possibly be *that* bad.

Conchita reprimanded her with a *tsk.* "Don't even joke about that. Lingerie is sacred. Silly fake social media profiles are frivolous entertainment. And besides, you already have a profile on VenusDatesMars, so it's not like I'm guilty of identity theft. I just wanted to…you know, spice you up a little bit. And trust me, Alma…the results are pretty darn panty melting. Prrrrr..."

Conchita rolled her Rs and licked her frosted pink lips while shamelessly ogling KardashianButtLover82's profile. "Come on, you're a fine arts antique expert. Appraise this masterpiece of a man." She flashed her phone again at Alma.

Alma adjusted her red-framed glasses and skeptically eyed the photograph. "How do you know those photographs are even real? I mean…look at that? Is it even possible to have that many abdominal ribs?"

Conchita twirled a strand of her hair. "Those aren't ribs, they're abs. It's called a washboard stomach for a reason. And if you're really lucky, he'll let you soap them up and rub your dirty laundry up and down them."

Conchita shimmied in faux ecstasy as she imagined Suds Washboard standing there in front of her.

Then their waiter appeared.

"Can I get you ladies something to drink?" He flipped back a fresh page of his order pad.

Conchita sighed and fanned herself with her phone, quickly diverting her attention off its screen and onto the hunky waiter. "Definitely something cold and icy." She smiled brightly and batted her distracting fake eyelashes. "A chocolate milkshake, please. Extra chocolatey."

Alma knew that look. She had seen her sister display it a thousand times and get exactly what she wanted every single time.

"With whipped cream?" The waiter asked.

Conchita cracked her gum. "What do you think?"

Alma rolled her eyes. From the waiter's angle, she was fairly certain he could see down Conchita's low-cut V-neck sweater—exactly how her sister liked to play it. Unfortunately, the waiter was clearly a student—easily college-aged, probably undergraduate. Cute with his blonde hair and athletic build, but way too young for her shamelessly flirtatious sister.

"Milkshake. Extra chocolate. Extra whipped cream—on the house," he said, flashing Conchita a sparkling smile. She smiled back, propping her elbows onto the table and squeezing together her cleavage while simultaneously trimming her waistline. Alma watched them undress each other with their eyes. Meanwhile, she tightened her turtleneck around her own neck, gagging as she strangled herself with a conspicuous cough.

"And you?" The waiter finally said, turning away from Conchita with a faint exhale as if she had just given him a hand job.

Alma was used to it, but that didn't mean it didn't still bother her. Feeling insecure and undesirable, she took off her glasses and glanced through all the items on the menu.

The waiter turned his attention back to Conchita. Over the rim of her menu, Alma barely made out the blurry images of her sister and the waiter easily trading smiles and small talk. A hot surge of blood rushed up through Alma's cheeks. She wasn't jealous that her sister was hitting on their waiter. That was just Conchita—her younger, sexier, spunkier sibling who could get away with anything and routinely did. There was no stopping her. But that didn't mean Alma wasn't frustrated at herself for wishing—in even the smallest of ways—that it could be her.

"I'll just have the same thing," Alma awkwardly answered, realizing she was helplessly blind without her glasses and equally ridiculous for caring what an underage boy-band-wannabe student waiter thought about her appearance.

When the waiter finally left, Conchita rotated her phone's screen back to Alma who replaced her glasses and tried to visualize KardashianButtLover82 as a date. She failed. "You do realize it's supposed to be me going on these dates and not you?"

Conchita sighed through her nose ring. "Yes…painfully aware of it, actually. I do love Mario and our sex life is amazing, but I had no idea creating an online dating profile for you was going to bring home so much hot succulent bacon."

Only Conchita could so flippantly reveal how amazing her sex life was with Mario—her boyfriend of only two weeks—as if she was commenting on the weather or the color of Alma's new eyeshadow shade. TMI was not in her sister's lexicon.

"Look at this one…" Conchita rotated the screen to Alma again.

Alma narrowed her glare onto his profile name. "RomeroLuvsItSlow?"

"Sizzle, sizzle," Conchita sighed again.

"So why are ButtLover and SlowPoke Romero even responding to my profile anyway?" Alma lifted her phone from her purse and scanned through the profile she had created for herself on VenusandMars.com. "0" responses glared back at her.

"Because I lied." Conchita shrugged. "Duh."

"You lied?" Alma echoed, frowning in disappointment, as if for a moment she thought her sister had the power to unlock some secret social media trap door of fun and frivolity that had always been hidden from her.

Conchita passed her phone over to Alma who swiped through its screen until she arrived on her sister's fabricated personal description of her. "Flight attendant who would love to climb beyond cruising altitude with just the right co-pilot. Loves hot tubs, back rubs, and naughty trips to the cockpit." She stopped reading aloud. "Are you seriously kidding me?"

Conchita shrugged again. "I thought about including, 'bonus frequent flyer miles for smoothly taking off and landing—every time.' But then I decided it was just easier to select the number of times you enjoy having sex as twice a day."

Alma covered her face with her hands, controlling her deep, visceral urge to scream. "Please tell me you did not do that."

"What? Is that too conservative?"

Alma suddenly felt the need to retch. "If that's what it takes these days to get a response from a man, I'm going to join a convent."

Conchita squinted through her spider eyelashes as if she was imagining Alma in a Catholic nun's habit. "That's actually a brilliant idea. I bet you'd get loads of requests from all sorts of guys thinking you were a virgin looking for your first true fu—."

Alma held up her hand. "Stop, please. Thank you for trying to help me, but no thank you. I love you, Conchita. But some days, I have no idea how we are even sisters."

"Oh, *whatevah*," Conchita drawled like she had heard it all before and it was equally nauseating. "Don't give me that crap because you're right—I *am* your sister! So I know all your dirty secrets that you'd probably love to forget about, including the time you fucked Mateo Jones in the woods during half time at your junior prom."

Horrified, Alma corrected. "Third. Base. Only!"

"And what about that time you dirty-talked Xavier Costello into his first orgasm. Remember? We still had landlines back then, and I eavesdropped on the entire conversation from the phone in Mama's bedroom."

Alma gave her sister the evil eye. "I always knew there was someone else on the phone."

Conchita tittered with delight. "How do you think I learned so much about sex by the time I was thirteen? I learned it from watching you!" she dramatically cried out, reciting the infamous line from the public service announcement.

"That was high school," Alma replied, crossing her arms, pleading no contest. "Who isn't boy crazy in high school? I'm in my thirties now. Things are harder and men are—"

"The same little boys with bigger penises?" Conchita interjected, swiping through her screen. "The point is…don't try to play me like I'm one of your uppity University of Chicago friends or one of your fancy antique clients. Yes, I *am* your sex-crazed sister who also happens to know you. The real you. And underneath those baggy worn-out overalls and 'Oh-dear-I-could-never-do-that' façade is a sex goddess waiting to be unleashed on the right man with enough stamina and *cojones* to handle it. So yes…God and Mama forgive me because I do, in fact, think you deserve to be boinked twice a day like a virgin nun by AngelisyourDevil45."

Conchita flashed her phone at Alma, revealing the photo of a handsome Latino man wearing a cowboy hat, jeans, and chaps, straddling a mechanical bull.

Deferring to her sister's points, Alma fell silent. It was all true—well, at least, *partially*—she just didn't feel like admitting it. Instead, she adjusted her glasses and twirled her ponytail. "I'm not like you, Conchita. I can't date that kind of man and you know it."

Sighing in resignation, Conchita laid her phone onto the table. She did know it, but they had finally arrived to the heart of the problem.

"Then what kind of a man can you date, Alma?"

"Someone who's willing to take the time to get to know me before I have to ride him like a mechanical bull."

"But that's the whole point of dating. It's not death-do-us-part. It's just supposed to be casual and fun. You *are* supposed to ride him like a mechanical bull before you have a chance to find out how bad his feet smell or before he figures out how bitchy you can be before your morning coffee."

Ugh, Alma sighed. It was going to be harder than she thought…this dating thing.

"Look, nobody wants the truth when they're first dating," Conchita continued. "They want the fantasy. The roses, the courtship, the romance, the sexy times. These big ideals of yours—truth, honor, true love, soulful intimacy—sure…those things are great, but they're the kind of things you want in a marriage, not in a first date fling."

"I just got out of a marriage, Conchita. I'm definitely not interested in getting into another one." Alma tried to sound convincing, but both she and her sister heard the waver in her voice. Somehow, she thought if she said it aloud, it would ring true.

But the truth was Alma had never engaged in anything frivolous, and they both knew it. Everything in her life was a conscious choice—a result of careful planning and thoughtful deliberation. Even her recently failed marriage had started as a relationship in college, which she naively expected to last her entire life because she had fallen in love with someone who had come to know her better than she had ever known herself.

"I guess I just like to pretend that there's still a chance to meet someone the old-fashioned way."

"Which means what?" Conchita pushed back.

"Oh, come on, you know," Alma replied, exasperated. "We meet by chance in the park. He's playing Frisbee. I'm walking my dog."

"You don't have a dog, Alma."

"Okay, then…I'm just going for a long walk, just to think."

"That, I'll buy."

"Okay, good. Now, we see each other, and there's a connection, you know? But I can't explain it, except that it's just something…special."

"In the park?" Conchita raised a manicured eyebrow. "And you're feeling woozy and seeing stars because you think he's 'the one' and it's not because he had bad aim and hit you in the head with his Frisbee or something?"

"It doesn't have to be the park. It could be anywhere. On the bus, or in the grocery store while both of us are picking out our produce."

"Oooh, okay…is he squeezing the mangos a little harder than he should?"

"Come on, Conchita. Work with me here. I just mean…is it so wrong to want to meet someone based on that spark or soulful connection that only he and I feel and crave and understand?"

"It's not wrong at all," Conchita conceded. "I just think we're talking about the same thing by two different names. You're calling it romance. And I'm calling it romgasm." She slurped up the last bit of her chocolate milkshake to emphasize how good it felt to indulge in something supremely gluttonous.

In contrast, Alma glanced down at her barely touched milkshake, realizing she had lost her appetite. Acknowledging they had exhausted every angle of the conversation, her sister changed the topic to their routine family gossip.

"So what's happening today at the shop with Papi?"

"Nothing much. He's re-organizing the basement and I'm spending most of the day restoring an antique Louis Comfort Tiffany stained-glass window."

Conchita flopped her head forward and snored. "Zzzzzzzzzz…"

Alma rolled her eyes, ignoring her. She knew it wasn't worth discussing the details of her job with Conchita, who never understood why anyone would pay good money for something preowned and made by dead people.

"Really, how do you expect to find a date working in that tiny little shop with Papi?" Conchita said, returning to the original topic like a dog with a bone.

"I guess maybe I don't expect ever to fall in love again."

"Exactly…which is why you need someone like me helping you out."

Abruptly, Alma's phone pinged with a message. She peered down to read it.

I can't stop thinking about last night…

Alma's cheeks flushed. She pulled away the sweater from her neck, seeking cool air to soothe her burning skin.

"Because you know if I don't get involved in your love life," Conchita continued, "you're going to end up a brittle sexless old maid with only a bunch of dusty antique vibrators to help keep you company at night."

And I can't stop thinking about you until I know when I'll have a chance to do it to you again...

Slowly tuning out her sister, Alma crossed her legs, quelling the tingle rising up between them. It was her one dirty secret that she hadn't confessed to anyone—not even Conchita. She *was* actually engaged in a sexual relationship, just not a conventional one, or one with a man who she even knew at all. But that was the irony of her secret. No one would have believed her if she told them she was sexting with a complete stranger. In fact, she almost couldn't believe it herself until he texted her, just like that, suddenly expecting her to resume the role of his forbidden mistress.

It had been that way from the beginning, since the very first time he pinged her phone, stating that he was a friend of a friend who heard she might be interested in getting together for a drink. Alma hadn't a clue who he was or which friend he was talking about, which is perhaps the reason she pretended to be someone else. *Someone sexier. Someone sassier. Someone infinitely more interesting.* And that's how it all started...her anonymous affair with him. No names. No real-life details. Just deep intimate confessions and incessant dirty talk without the promise of it leading to anything more than superficial entertainment and the occasional sexting romgasm.

"Alma?!" Her sister sharply snapped at her from across the table. "I asked if you've got a ten-dollar bill for a tip?"

"Ten dollars?" Alma repeated, distracted by the third ping on her cell phone.

If you expect to silence me with your silence, it won't work...

Alma waffled, torn between his texts and her sister's intention to leave an outlandish tip.

"The check is only five dollars."

"I know...but I'm leaving my phone number," her sister replied, scratching the numbers onto the bill. *That was so Conchita*, she thought, engaged in casual sex with one boyfriend while always keeping open the full range of possibilities.

He relentlessly pinged her again. *I'll simply interrupt your normal daytime life with every dirty thought I've had about lowering my mouth between...*

Alma dropped her phone into her lap and blushed uncontrollably. His texts glowed back at her like both a warning and an invitation. What she was doing was crazy and risqué and completely out of her comfort zone, but it also felt amazing to throw aside every instinct of caution and prudence that had marked her life, and instead, pretend to be someone fearless and uninhibited—someone she rarely allowed herself to be.

He had that effect on her. She had let him take them farther last night than ever before. He'd texted her the details of his fantasy—spreading her across her bed, legs dangling off the side, knees butterflied open, pleasuring her with a patience and persistence that changed the dynamics of her teasing sexual innuendos into masterful acts of submission and domination.

She had assumed the role of his submissive last night, yielding to his unrestrained advances to finger her without mercy while tasting every drop of her desire for more and more and more…*God, how she had so wanted more…* More of his stern commands to release every inhibition holding her back. More of his dirty determination to gain her trust and cooperation so that she would text him—in graphic detail—how wet he was making her with every inching advance of his fingertips inside her. More of his persuasive assurances that he wasn't going to stop until her thighs quivered from the prick of the stubble along his jawline as the heat of his warm tongue tested her sweetness and the vibrations of his hot breath hummed her into a state of unchartered ecstasy. Alma was the furthest thing from a whore…but with him, she was finally able to let go and invent the woman she had always longed to be.

While Conchita distracted herself with freshening up her lip gloss in her compact mirror, Alma finally took the opportunity to text him back. *I suppose that means you expect to hear from me again tonight?*

No, because I'm certain I can't wait until tonight...

He wanted her now. She could almost feel his intentions through her phone.

She needed a way to keep him appeased. *What if I promise to make the wait worth it?*

She imagined his needy sigh trailing after his next text. *Tell me more…*

"Hey, what the hell is wrong with you?" Conchita said. "You're completely ignoring me. I asked if you wanted me to walk back with you to Papi's shop, so he could scold me instead of you for being away this long."

"No, I'm fine. It will be fine."

Conchita eyed the awkward way Alma was cradling her phone against her chest. "Who the hell are you texting, anyway?"

"No one," Alma replied. Anxious to ditch the diner before she lost his attention, she swept up her purse and heavy coat, pecked her sister on the cheek, and scurried away toward the diner's front door. "See you later. I'll call you after ButtLover and I meet up and exchange baking recipes."

"Whatevah, you snarky little bitch," Conchita called back. "Just promise me if you decide to respond to ButtLover or AngelDevilMan that you'll forward me all their naughty selfies."

Safely out of the diner and striding down Wacker Avenue toward her father's antique shop, Alma shivered as a gust of Chicago wind pelted her back. It was already April, but still the Chicago River had chunks of floating ice. Her heart beat wildly and her body was aflame with yearning for the pleasure he promised behind every word of his texts.

You're making me wait for your response—again. And I'm not a man who's used to waiting. I'm a man who's used to getting exactly what I want when I want it.

Alma felt her alter ego taking over her personality. She wasn't sure why he was the one who inspired her sassy, sultry side; she simply knew she loved embracing it.

Well, revise your expectations, sport. It wouldn't be any fun if I was always available whenever you wanted me.

She sent her tart reply, invigorated by her own ability to both tease and defy him. As she scurried along the broad sidewalk, her rapid pace eased the anxiety of waiting for his response. When the vibration buzzed in her hands, she looked down at the message.

I don't want fun. I want to control every part of your body and make you so wet that you'll beg for me to slide myself into you.

A flush of heat rose up between her legs, kindling her need for a release, the same way it did last night when he brought her to the brink. But despite all their sexually explicit exchanges, they hadn't yet crossed over into the fantasy of full-on intimate intercourse.

She hurried under the elevated tracks as the Brown Line train screeched across its rails, like a banshee warning her that she was no longer a schoolgirl getting to third base behind the bleachers during halftime of a football game. She was a thirty-year-old woman—recently divorced and perhaps a bit too desperate for validation that she was still a sexy and desirable woman—and now, for better or worse, she was trapped in this addictive web of secrecy and fantasy, seeking out affirmation of her sexual self-worth from a complete stranger.

When she finally glanced down, he'd already sent another text.

Plan on answering my phone call at midnight.

A phone call? As always, he was pushing the boundaries of their affair and asserting his control over her. Quivering with anticipation, she silently acknowledged the dangerous consequences of his proposition—extending their sexting affair into the unguarded reality of conversation. But that was exactly what excited her about him: his demanding way of tempting her to explore everything she had to offer him.

Alma could see the antique shop just ahead of her. She stopped in her tracks, yearning to respond with something, anything to ensure that he would keep his promise.

Midnight is a long time to wait. Be prompt or don't bother to call at all.

Alma closed her eyes, unable to believe how natural it was for her to conjure up a bold, vixen voice—much less actually use it.

Without missing a beat, he zipped back his reply.

Don't disappear until you tell me where I can send you something special for tonight...

She repeated his request in her mind. *Something special?*

...name any location and I'll have my driver deliver it there.

With her mind in a whirl, she halted along Wacker Avenue. There was no way she was dumb enough to give out the number of her condo building or the address of her father's workshop, but the notion of a physical gift from him intrigued her. *What could he possibly want to give her?*

*Think, think, think...*She had to come up with an answer quickly, a place she knew well, a place where she could easily visit after work, a place where a public package could be left anytime—without being noticed—and in turn, where she could pick it up without being noticed. And maybe even somewhere symbolic—a place that would say something about her.

She thought about her favorite book aisles in the Harold Washington Library or the secluded antique rooms in the basement of the Art Institute. But then, the grand image of an even better possibility floated through her mind.

The Tiffany Ballroom in the Cultural Center, she texted him with finality. *In the corner on the eastern windowsills. There's no public event tonight, and no one will notice it there. I'll pick it up before the building closes at six o'clock.*

Good. It will be there for you and I expect you to be wearing it when I call tonight.

Alma shut off her phone and cradled it against her heart.

Who was he and how did they come this far? She had no idea, but the only thing that mattered was that she yearned for every fantasy he promised her.

Chapter Three

Arriving at her father's antique shop, Alma thrust her entire body against the wooden front door, stuck by the spring frost. The old-fashioned shopkeeper's bell jingled above her head. *Bright, airy, and ringing with anticipation,* she thought. In fact, she was so distracted by her own glee that she caught herself singing along to the Bach concerto filtering out from her father's vintage radio. As she hung up her scarf and coat and returned to her workbench, she hummed the famous refrain, reminding herself of how much she preferred Bach to Mozart.

Settling back into her work, Alma studied the kaleidoscope of colors through the magnified lens of her jewelry appraiser's loupe. She delicately propped the windowsill onto her lap and meticulously cleaned the far right corner of the pane, revealing the silky opalescence of the stained glass hiding beneath years of soot and abandonment. Even though decades of dirt had dimmed the radiance of the window, she could still spot the signature artistry of the man behind its creation: Louis Comfort Tiffany. She pushed up the loupe from her eyes and redirected her headlamp onto the rejuvenated section of glass—luminescent hues of shimmering turquoise, lavender, and pink sparkled back at her, a mesmerizing scene of wild flowers ensconced within evergreen dappling. When she finished restoring the entire stained-glass window, she would reveal a captivating paradise—an Elysian forest or a mythical river of life—illuminated from behind by natural sunlight, seducing the viewer into believing that the promise and hope of a better world resided within its beauty.

She was so absorbed in her work, she barely registered the sound of the bell. In the background, she heard her father ascend the basement steps and greet the visitor. After a few minutes of casual conversation, he called out to her.

"Alma, please come here. Your expertise is needed."

She cringed. She knew her father had scheduled an appraisal appointment for that afternoon, but she had hoped she could work on her restoration project without being bothered. Although her father was the shop owner and an antique expert when it came to eighteenth-century European furniture and paintings, she was the expert on twentieth century jewelry and glassworks.

"Alma, please…we're waiting," her father repeated.

Fat chance, she could hear Conchita say, whenever it came to the possibility of their strict Argentinian father relaxing his expectations for his eldest daughter. Conchita got a pass because she was the younger, more foolish child, but never Alma, who had always assumed the role of the more dutiful, sensible offspring, especially since the death of their mother more than a decade ago.

Reluctantly sliding off her stool, she carefully covered the windowsill and laid it across her work table.

Alma gazed at her father and the guest through the magnification of her bug-eyed appraisals loupe.

"Alma, please—" her father murmured, shielding his eyes from the spotlight of her bulky headlamp.

"Oops, sorry," she replied, fumbling to turn off the light. "I was just working on the restoration of a Tiffany."

Her head lamp awkwardly tilted to the side, its headband pulling her lopsided pony tail into further dishevelment.

"Madame van der Meer, this is my daughter, Alma," her father said, formally introducing them. "Madame van der Meer's son is getting married, and she's brought us a few family heirlooms to appraise before giving them to his bride as a wedding gift."

Her father's tone was rigid and formal. He sternly peered at his daughter, conveying how important this particular client was to their business. Alma internally sighed. *Every client was important.* It was the reason why he'd been in the antiques appraisal business for forty years, since arriving from Buenos Aires as a young man. Everyone knew Enrique Castillo in Chicago. And everyone trusted him.

She shifted her gaze to Madame van der Meer, an elderly woman with a beaked nose and aristocratic profile. She wore a full length black sable fur coat and held her chin above the impressive mink collar like royalty. If Alma hadn't been dressed in her denim overalls and heavy leather restoration gloves, she probably would have given in to her urge to curtsy.

Mechanically, Alma held out her leather glove to Madame van der Meer who shook it without fear of staining her thin, wispy hand with dust. But her father glared at his daughter's oversight. "Alma, please—"

When she realized her error, she promptly removed her gloves and curtsied in apology. Even in overalls, there was just no way around a curtsy at this point.

"Louis Comfort Tiffany is one of my favorite nineteenth century artisans," Madame van der Meer confirmed. "Are you restoring one of his Favrile lamp shades?"

"No, a windowsill. A teenager found it in the basement of her grandmother's house after her death and tried to sell it on eBay for fifteen dollars."

"Good heavens, no." Madame van der Meer gasped as if she had just seen a horrible car accident.

"Yes, that's how I felt," Alma agreed, comforted by the fact that Madame van der Meer shared the same horror that an authentic Tiffany stained-glass window had almost been sold for so little. "The family just thought it was an old dirty stained-glass windowpane from the grandmother's church. But I tracked down the parents and convinced them to let me restore it, so that it could properly be sold at auction and pay for the daughter's entire college tuition."

Madame exhaled in relief. "Well, then…it sounds like you're the perfect woman to appraise my jewelry."

Alma gazed at Madame van der Meer, taking in her subtle European accent and the fact that perhaps she wasn't just another rich client looking for reassurance that the value of her family heirlooms still made her wealthy.

"My son is getting married," Madame van der Meer continued, "and I'm seeking guidance on just the sort of wedding gift to give to his fiancée."

Alma felt the blood rise into her cheeks. Considering her own failed marriage, she hardly felt qualified to help pick out wedding jewelry.

"No, please—" Alma insisted. "I guarantee you I'm the absolute last person on earth who should be doling out wedding advice of any kind."

But Alma's father swiftly moved out from behind the counter. "Yes, of course, Madame van der Meer. We would be happy to assist you in any way possible."

Overriding his daughter with an attentive smile, he unsnapped the band of the crushed velvet jewelry roll and spread it across the lightbox on top of the glass countertop.

"I'm quite enchanted by my son's fiancée," Madame van der Meer explained. "She's very much unlike all his past girlfriends. She's a spirited girl who is rather unimpressed by his wealth and status in the world. Exactly what my son needs to keep him in line. I would like to give her a piece of jewelry for the wedding. However, I fear she may not accept it unless it's just right."

Alma gasped, taking in the rarity of what lay before her. "Is that an authentic Milan van Stein wristwatch?"

With a wry smile, Madame van der Meer peered at Alma's father. "You're exactly right, Enrique. Your daughter does know her jewelry makers."

"Yes, of course." Alma nodded, almost overcome with the feeling of such an exquisite piece of jewelry in the palm of her hand. "He was a jeweler who owned a prestigious shop in Amsterdam called 'The Diamond House' because he was known to design with only the finest cut diamonds in all of Europe. He made intricate rings, necklaces, and bracelets for the Dutch elite. But what is less well-known is the fact that he was also an incredibly skilled horologist."

Alma's father shot her a glare. "Horologist? *Qué es estó*, Alma?" he questioned her in his native tongue, something he only did in front of clients when he didn't want to reveal his own limited knowledge.

"A watchmaker," she clarified in English while repositioning the loupe over her eyes and investigating the detailed artistry of the feminine cocktail wristwatch. "I mean, I've read all about Milan van Stein's masterfully crafted watches, but I've never actually seen a real one."

Under the magnification of the loupe, Alma scanned the piece's art deco design, perfectly accentuated by endless baguette and round cut diamonds set within hand-engraved white gold filigree on a shimmering platinum band. She studied its distinct hexagonal-shaped dial and mother-of-pearl face, decorated with petite rubies studding each hour marker. Its winding stem was augmented with a brilliant sapphire—a signature van Stein touch. Alma held the wristwatch up to her ear and closed her eyes; its movement was flawlessly silent.

"Milan and his wife were very much in love, you know," Madame van der Meer said. "He designed each wristwatch specifically for her every year as a gift for their wedding anniversary."

"Lovely," Alma whispered, as if for a moment she wished she could trade places with Milan's wife. Then, she drew her loupe up onto her forehead and questioned Madame van der Meer with bewilderment. "But I don't understand…finding an authentic Milan van Stein watch is incredibly rare. It's true that he only made a handful of them, but they were all believed to have been seized from his jewelry shop by the Nazis after they invaded Amsterdam. Over the decades, only a few have been recovered. How did you get this one?"

"I received it from Milan van Stein's widow herself—Miriam van Stein."

Madame van der Meer paused to allow the significance of her answer to be absorbed by Alma. "You see...I was born and raised in Amsterdam where my father was a well-known art dealer, and Milan and my father were very good friends. And very smart men. They both realized that Hitler posed a grave threat to not just our country, but all of Europe. For this reason, when I was just a little girl, my father arranged for my mother and me to leave for America, along with as many works of priceless art and jewelry from his shop as we could carry. Milan convinced his wife to travel with us. During our trip, she smuggled all twelve of her wristwatches out of Amsterdam. Years later, she passed them onto me. She said she always considered me the daughter she never had."

Alma stared at Madame van der Meer, barely able to formulate her thoughts into words. "Then they are truly priceless pieces of history and artistry, and I can't even begin to place a value on it…something likely north of—"

"No, please—" Madame van der Meer's fragile hand rested onto Alma's arm to silence her, as if a declaration of its monetary value would sully the work itself. "I simply would prefer to have the assurance that it is the right gift to give to my future daughter-in-law. She's not your average woman, impressed by royal jewels and wealth. But I hope if I tell her the story of Milan and his wife, and ask her to care for it on my behalf, perhaps she will accept it."

Alma peered down at the watch one last time, considering all the years of love and adoration its maker had symbolized with its beauty. "I'm sure she will be honored to receive it from you. It's a very generous gesture."

Madame nodded in appreciation. "Thank you for your time. I shall call you next week to arrange an appointment to appraise the rest of the watch collection. I would like to see them passed onto a private collector or museum curator who will do something more with them than I have."

"It would be our pleasure," Alma's father insisted, pushing past Alma to the shop door and opening it for Madame van der Meer.

Madame van der Meer took up the jewelry roll and deposited it in her black, hand-beaded clutch before bidding Alma and her father farewell with a nod of her aquiline profile. This time, Alma resisted the urge to curtsy—but just barely.

As she watched Madame van der Meer pass out of her father's shop, Alma marveled at the realization that she likely was one of only a handful of antiques experts who had actually seen an authentic Milan van Stein wristwatch.

"Please let's encourage her to keep them," Alma petitioned her father. While most antique dealers would push to publicly catalogue the entire collection in preparation for selling them at auction, Alma felt the need to protect their existence like a secret.

Enrique Castillo raised his eyebrow at the urgency in his daughter's voice. "Within the local community, Madame van der Meer is a great patron of the arts. She has donated the majority of her Impressionist paintings to the Art Institute and her Royal Jewelry collection is the main tourist attraction within the lobby of the Old Main Post Office. If she chooses to make the collection available to the public—either for sale or for donation—we should be prepared to assist her with the appraisal."

The thought of Milan's watches—private gifts to his wife—being sold at a public auction broke her heart.

Enrique Castillo reached out and cupped his daughter's chin, reading the distinct frown on her face. "You're a romantic at heart, Alma, and it is admirable. But the reality is that nothing remains hidden forever. Even our deepest fears or our most intimate secrets must always be eventually confronted or confessed. Sooner or later, everything concealed in the darkness comes into the light. And for beautiful, priceless works of art, there has never been an exception."

He nodded over to her rescued Tiffany windowsill, knowing that it proved his point.

"There is one exception," she muttered, turning away from him.

Her father smirked and placed his hands on his hips, just above his meticulously polished black leather belt. "Ah, claro que sí…your favorite art history legend—the whereabouts of Tiffany's *Eternal Love*."

"It still hasn't been found," Alma sassed back.

"Well, there's a perfectly valid explanation for that," he mused, as if he was enjoying her childish belief in a myth. "Because it does not exist." His sharp Argentinian accent punctuated his skepticism.

Like a silent act of defiance, Alma replaced her leather gloves over her hands and the bulky magnification loupe over her eyes and returned to her work. She knew Louis Comfort Tiffany's history better than her father, and perhaps even better than any other antiques expert or art historian in Chicago, but still, she knew her father was right about one thing—there was no verified historical documentation of the existence of Tiffany's most mythical stained-glass window. There was only her own hopeless romantic desire that it was out there, somewhere, still awaiting discovery.

The startling ring of the vintage rotary phone ended their discussion. Enrique answered it while Alma replayed their conversation in her mind. It wasn't until he hung up and addressed her again that she knew someone important had called.

"Well, it looks like you might be right after all," he teased, lifting his wool jacket and fedora from the nearby ornamental coat rack, as if he was preparing to depart the shop. "That was Jacques Blanc, calling for you."

Alma rolled her eyes. "A*nnnnnnd*?" she drawled, feigning ignorance. She knew full well it was the fifth time Jacques had called her, and he still couldn't get the hint that she was avoiding him.

"This time, he says he has found something that will interest you."

Completely uninterested, Alma lowered her loupe and set about cleaning dirt from the corner of her windowsill. "Like what?"

"The site of a few unclaimed Tiffany treasures."

Chapter Four

Accelerating the throttle, Harvey Zale navigated his new speedboat like a racecar toward the narrow fork separating the North and South Branches of the Chicago River, as if he fully intended to crash into it. He gripped the steering wheel and endured the vibrations from the revving engine, barely clearing the curving wake of choppy, frothy waters churning behind him. That was how he liked to make his mark on the world and today was no different.

Along the way, he had raced past at least five of his downtown properties. None of them were remarkable contributions to Chicago's architectural history, nor were they memorable works of modern engineering like Miranda Towers or The Spire. But all of them were towering high-rises offering commercial space—fully leased and in the black. It was a simple mercenary business that made him a rich man without any obligations to the world other than his own goals to turn a bigger profit than his competition every time he bought and sold a property.

He cruised past all the historic riverfront warehouse buildings that had since been converted into luxury condominiums with added balconies and manicured riverwalks. If he had owned those warehouses, he would have torn down all of them and modernized the area with skyscrapers, maximizing the profitability of every square foot. Sure, he would have been hated by the local community for standardizing the riverfront into a row of gaudy mirrored properties, severely lacking in historic charm or architectural merit. But then again, he was already hated by the local community for routinely bringing his brand of profitability to Chicago's downtown—the bottom line above all else.

Harvey reduced his speed and guided the boat's hull up to the dock of his riverfront home, a mid-century modern haven with a series of Weese-inspired glass triangles, each rising higher than the next one in an eclectic series of sharp peaks and flaring angles. During the day, it looked like a surreal crystal garden, floating between industrial plants and converted warehouse condos. At night, it was a nautical prism of transparency and solitude, completely translucent to anyone who dared to view its interior. It was still one of the best kept secrets, the fact that he routinely slept at his riverfront house. Almost everyone he knew assumed he resided at the top of the world in a lavish penthouse at the pinnacles of one of his downtown skyscrapers.

Those who assumed they knew him were often wrong.

And every time he hopped over the stainless-steel rails of his speedboat to moor it, the rough sensation of the braided rope against his palms invigorated him—*living on the edge of the water was like living on the edge of life*. He wouldn't have it any other way.

His phone rang.

Swaggering along the glinting metallic slats of the pier, he fished out his phone from the jacket of his black leather coat, which protected him from the vicious March wind. He had just come from a business deal where he'd finalized the terms of the contract that would allow him to construct the tallest buildings in the world—the Li Long Towers in Shanghai. He was waiting to hear from his real estate lawyer that everything was moving forward with the sale of the property that would ensure he could finance it. He'd already bought and flipped plenty of buildings for twice what he bought them for, but the sale of his riverfront parcel—an irregular swath of overgrown prairie land along the river's North Branch bought nearly two decades ago—promised to turn him a fortune. Back then, nobody wanted to build on the polluted river behind the city, except for opportunistic men like Harvey Zale who took pride in owning a piece of Chicago's blighted history—and the dirtier, the better.

He answered the call. "Tell me the good news, darlin'."

"Well, I'm glad to hear that you're in a good mood," the woman's gravelly voice teased through his phone, "because I don't think you're going to feel like celebrating after what I have to tell you."

Harvey stopped outside the gate of his house and frowned.

"They've stopped the demolition over at the prairie," she continued. "Jacques is there now."

"We're closing in a week, Nicolette…" Harvey paused, feeling his blood pressure rise. "The parcel needs to be cleared before then."

"Yes, Harvey, dear…I know. But word has gotten out that you're tearing down an old historic train depot without a permit and The City of Chicago intends to stop you."

"The City? Or Jacques Blanc?"

"What do you think?" she replied, her voice growing huskier after a long indulgent drag.

"Here's what I think," he answered. "One hour. I'll be at the property in one hour, and if I have to, I'll gladly be the one who operates the bulldozer, especially if Jacques attempts to stand in my way."

It wasn't a veiled threat. Harvey had paid his way through college by joining the union and working weekends on the demolition crew for developers who were re-gentrifying the South Side. In that moment, he had every intention of plowing down Jacques Blanc.

"Harvey, dear," Nicolette said, attempting to rein him in. "I don't like our little French friend—and his preservation crusade—any more than you do. But Harvey...there's a lot of money at stake here and we can't afford for you to go off the rails, making this personal."

"Don't worry, Nicolette. It's not personal," Harvey fumed. "It's war."

Chapter Five

When Harvey arrived outside the run-down train depot, his only emotion was fury. The bulldozer was completely idle and the main wooden structure was still fully intact. He expected to see an army of picketers surrounding the perimeter of the building, cursing his name and waving protest signs with slogans like CAPITALIST PIG and CHOOSE PRESERVATION, NOT PROFIT."

But as he trudged over the wrought iron railroad tracks, sunken into the ground and hidden by weeds, he noted only silence as the wind rustled the overgrown prairie grass. *An eerie disquiet*, he thought, like a cemetery without headstones, only unmarked abandoned graves.

"Somebody better have a really good reason for not following orders," he announced from outside the train depot, knowing his booming voice would carry through the cracked panes of the ornamental stained-glass windows that decorated the exterior of the building. Why anyone would bother to spruce up an industrial train depot with colorful stained glass and imported teakwood shutters was beyond his comprehension, but he certainly didn't have any qualms about destroying the whole damn thing now.

"A reason *très excellent*!" The French accent called back like a bad punchline.

"Tray ex-sell-ont," Harvey exaggerated with a grumble, repeating the effusive French phrase with disgust.

Wading through a maze of ivy that camouflaged the front entrance, he emerged through the heavy wooden doors with grass in his hair and flecks of bark in his mouth.

"Bonjour, Harvey. So glad that you could finally make it." Jacques' pearly smile flashed like a camera bulb, putting Harvey on edge, making him want to punch the man who spoke like he should be serving him a fine steak, not thwarting the hundred million dollar sale of his property.

"Boner, Jacques," Harvey repeated back, intentionally butchering Jacques' chipper French accent with his less elegant, Chicago-inspired one. "I got the call that you and your entourage were trespassing on private property and I couldn't resist the opportunity to throw you off my land with my very own two hands."

Jacques gleefully turned to Harvey and squared off in front of him. "That won't be necessary," Jacques retorted, slapping the official summons into Harvey's hands. "I'm entitled to be here on behalf of the City of Chicago. You are in violation of Section A398, which states that you must have a permit to demolish this structure."

Harvey peered down at the summons. Then, he glared at Jacques' silk patterned neck scarf and matching pocket square tucked neatly beneath the lapels of his double-breasted cocoa brown twill coat. He sniffed the air, expecting to catch a whiff of women's perfume mixed with...manure. That was always his experience when interacting with Jacques—*odeur de toillete.*

"It's private property, Frenchy. Pr-iiii-vaaaaaate," Harvey stressed. "Do you need a direct translation of private? It means: none of your business. Kinda like all those naked selfies you send to your mother every night is none of my business. Revolting, for sure. But none of my business."

Rodrigo, Harvey's silent hulking foreman, snorted out his laughter. He'd been standing in the corner with his sledgehammer since Harvey's arrival, just waiting for his boss to give the order. Harvey smirked, appreciating the audience.

A satisfied smile crossed Jacques' face, as if he enjoyed the insult because it gave him the chance to prove he had the upper hand.

"It is my business, Monsieur Zale, because we believe that it is a historic building, one of the last historic train depots along the North Branch line. And just because you are planning to destroy it and sell the parcel to someone else does not mean the rest of the world should permit you to do it."

Harvey shifted his gaze to Rodrigo, who wrung the handle of the sledgehammer with his massive hands. He and his crew had already plowed a gaping hole through the exterior brick wall on the south end of the train depot, and were impatiently waiting to finish the job. Harvey knew Rodrigo had four kids and a wife who expected him to be home by five-thirty sharp every night for a home-cooked dinner. It was five minutes to five; the clock was ticking. They could easily smash down the rest of the wall in ten minutes flat the moment that Harvey nodded his command.

Instead, Harvey drew the last straw of grass out of his hair and inserted it between his teeth, chewing on it like a cowboy. "I'm surprised you're even bothering to pay attention to what I'm doing these days, Jack." Crumpling the summons into a little ball, he dumped it back into Jacques' palm. "It's kinda flattering to know you're my stalker."

"I do not need to be your stalker, Harvey." Jacques smoothed out the summons and flattened it out like a victory flag. "You have made such an infamous reputation for yourself that it is easy to assume that every time you are selling a property, you are also most likely to be destroying something valuable in the process. The girls at City Hall keep me well-informed. Let's just say that I take care of them and they take care of me."

Jacques swept his gaze across the train depot's duplex interior before tacking the summons through an exposed nail, just above the narrow staircase leading up to the balcony.

"You mean you send them your naked selfies, too?" Harvey quipped. "And they actually like it?"

Rodrigo snorted again. Harvey chewed on the wad of the grass and spit a ball of it dangerously close to Jacques' Italian leather shoes. The clock was ticking, but Harvey knew his crew didn't expect him to surrender—especially not to a Frenchman wearing a neck scarf.

"They were the same girls who issued me the summons," Jacques countered, stepping forward to challenge him. "You would be surprised how much flowers, chocolates, and fine wine wins over a woman's heart. That's how I was able to woo your ex-wife. Let's just say she was a bit starved for some...romantic attention." He casually circled away, scanning the open rafters like he was inspecting his new home.

Harvey locked eyes with Jacques. It had been all business until that moment—when Jacques clearly intended to make it personal in order to fucking piss him off. And it worked.

"Yeah, romantic has never been my strong suit. I usually just focus on making a woman come—more than once. That usually does the trick." Harvey kept his gun metal blue eyes fixed on Jacques. Extending out his hand to Rodrigo, he said, "Give me the keys to the bulldozer."

"Don't—" Jacques held up his hand like a traffic cop and thrust himself forward, awkwardly sliding on the white marble floor, glazed with years of undisturbed dust. "Don't be a showman, Harvey."

"Show-off," Harvey corrected him, irked by his French accent. "And trust me, if I wanted to be a show-off, I would pull your underwear band out of your khakis and up to your nipples, and send a selfie back to the girls at City Hall. Instead, I'm going to play nice and take care of the demolition myself."

Harvey stripped off his black leather jacket like a streetfighter preparing for a brawl. It was almost five-thirty, and Jacques' interference was not only infringing on Rodrigo's curfew, but he was also threatening to disrupt Harvey's own evening plans. Supremely annoyed, he removed his cuff links and rolled up the sleeves of his white dress shirt; he'd expected to finalize a closing today, not perform the demolition himself—literally. At least he was wearing decent shoes for the job: his well-worn cowboy boots.

"Ignoring my official summons is the same as breaking the law," Jacques insisted.

"That summons only prevents me from hiring contractors to perform the demolition without a permit," countered Harvey, striding toward the rear exit door where he knew he'd find the idle bulldozer stationed on the south side of the parcel. "As the owner, it doesn't prevent me from doing the work my damn self. So, it's a good thing I grew up on the South Side of Chicago, where I've been driving bulldozers since I was eighteen, rather than hanging out in Paris, engorging myself on escargot. Because yeah...you're right. I am a showman. And plowing down my own property with a three-ton machine is going to make a much better Facebook Live stream for those girls at City Hall than naked selfies of you sucking snails out of their shells. Even if it is less romantic."

Jacques stomped his foot like a petulant child. "You will regret this, Monsieur Zale. I will be sure of it."

"Oh, I've done an entire lifetime of things that I regret, Monsieur Jackass. And it hasn't stopped me from being an asshole yet."

"I'll definitely agree with that."

Harvey stopped cold and turned toward the familiar female voice. The woman fixed her black, smoldering eyes on Harvey, her judgmental gaze sending a shot of unexpected adrenaline through his heart.

"*Mon chèri*!" Jacques emphasized dramatically as he attempted to draw the woman into his body to greet her with a double-cheeked Parisian kiss. "So glad you received my call."

"Well...when you said that someone was preparing to destroy a historic structure— possibly with Tiffany stained-glass windows—I should have immediately guessed who it was."

Harvey tracked her movements through the weeds and vines of the front entrance and across the depot's main interior lobby. Despite the filthy floors, soot-stained walls and rotting wooden benches, she was clearly in her element. He scanned her appearance—rebellious red-framed glasses, youthful ponytail, denim overalls, oversized construction boots, heavy leather gloves, and a miniature black backpack. *The Lara Croft of antique hunters*, he thought, mocking her in his mind because she was too cute for her own good. Whatever she had come there to do, Harvey guessed she wouldn't stop until she was successful. *Which meant, he was fucked.*

"Hello there, Miss Castillo," he purred, smoothly greeting her as if it might just matter to her.

It didn't.

"Hello, Monsieur Asshole," she tossed back.

He muted his smile, fighting how her sassy insult amused him. It had been a long time since they had seen each other, and if there was one person in the world who could get away with addressing him as "Monsieur Asshole," it was Alma Castillo.

"Well…now that Miss Castillo is here, the party can officially begin." Harvey bowed like the ringleader of a circus. "You're just in time for the grand finale."

"Which includes what?" Alma challenged him.

Cupping his hands to his mouth, he announced, "Personally flattening this entire building with my 'dozer!"

She scoffed as if she knew better than to ever take anything he said at face value. "You can't possibly be serious about destroying this building?"

"It's private property, Miss Castillo," he shot back. "Both you and Jackass are trespassing. But I'll be kind and give you five minutes to get off my property. Otherwise, I'll have Rodrigo shout out a warning—as a courtesy—three seconds before I cut through that wall with my tank, just so you don't have to witness Frenchy shitting in his pants."

"*Tsk*—" Disgusted, Alma clucked and turned away from him as if he was the most vulgar man she had ever met. He probably was, and he knew she hated it when he flaunted his unrefined, blue-collar upbringing. But even though he'd become a successful real estate billionaire, it hadn't happened because he talked pretty all the time and wore Gucci.

"You're a man-child, Harvey," Alma flung back. "So I certainly can believe that you equate your big, fancy machines to your penis prowess. But I also know that you're the last person who's going to bulldoze anything with authentic Tiffany stained-glass windows."

"Really?" he said slyly, chewing on his blade of grass, wondering if she was actually contemplating his penis size. "And why it that, Miss Castillo?"

"Because if they really *are* Tiffany windows—and some of his earliest ones, which are the rarest kind—they could each be worth up to a million dollars. And if they're sold together as a set from the same location, they could fetch even more at auction."

Harvey's eyes darted around the train depot, quickly counting all the stained-glass windows.

"That's only ten million dollars. Maybe fifteen million at the most."

"Rodrigo—" Alma called out to the foreman. "How much is Harvey paying you these days? A million dollars an hour?"

Rodrigo huffed like *that* was the biggest joke of the day.

"Exactly my point," Alma snarked, turning to directly confront Harvey. "He could be…if he wanted to take the time to properly remove all these windows. Or he could just bulldoze the whole damn structure and keep paying you twenty dollars an hour."

Harvey eyed her, noting the way her girlish ponytail and denim overalls made her look ten years younger than she actually was, and how her glossy, red-framed glasses confirmed she was smarter than he was. With her fancy Ivy League education and art history expertise, he knew she was intellectually his superior in almost every way. And truth be told, he secretly liked it—when it wasn't inconveniencing him.

"Maybe you haven't heard, Miss Castillo, but I have a closing at the end of the week for this land, and they're expecting it to be free and clear. And I will lose way more than fifteen million dollars if the sale doesn't go through."

"Yeah, you'll also lose a part of your humanity."

He looked at her, sidelong. *His humanity*? She was still the only woman in his entire life who cared more about the status of his soul than the size of his bank account, and it irked him more than he expected.

"How do you even know those are authentic Tiffany windows, anyway?" Harvey questioned her, surveying the lightless panels of stained glass, which looked like they had been glazed with hardened maple syrup. "You and I both know that they're more likely just worthless amateur copies. Everybody thinks every stained-glass window is a priceless Tiffany until they find out it's just a ten dollar junkyard imposter."

"True," Alma conceded. "Which is why I need another day—and ideally the morning light—to properly evaluate them." She walked up to Rodrigo and removed the sledgehammer from his hands. Rodrigo frowned and glanced over at Harvey as if he had just lost his favorite toy.

"Another day?" Harvey scoffed, amused by her proposition. "You actually expect me to delay the demolition—and potentially endanger my closing—just to appease you and my lacking sense of humanity? That would make me less of an asshole than you thought."

"Or a bigger one who sees the opportunity to make an extra fifteen million dollars—just by granting me one more day to know for sure."

He pushed closer into her personal space and suddenly caught the familiar scent of her perfume, faintly floral and intoxicating.

"Which one do you think I am, Miss Castillo? The bigger one or the lesser one?"

She held up her hand and touched his chest, her fingertips subtly driving him back. He edged forward, even closer, just because he knew he could get away with it.

"The bigger one, Monsieur Asshole," she smarted off, like she couldn't help herself. "After all, you do have a reputation to maintain."

He lowered his chin to meet her gaze. "You're still wearing the perfume that I bought you for your birthday." Through the lens of her intellectually superior glasses, he stared into her steady eyes. Her dark bewitching eyes always enchanted him, even when they glared, expecting him to act like the biggest asshole in the room.

"It was a ridiculously huge bottle," she whispered, allowing his nose and lips to graze her cheek. "Another statement of your manhood."

"Lucky for me," he countered softly, closing his eyes and inhaling her sweetness, reminding him of those years when there wasn't so much animosity between them. "My manhood still appreciates it." Then he exhaled in disappointment as she handed back the sledgehammer and pulled away.

"Well, it seems that we are in stalemate," Jacques interjected, conspicuously drawing his hand around Alma's body to steer her toward him. She yielded to Jacques' touch, making Harvey's blood boil with envy. Suddenly, he was no longer interested in enhancing his humanity, especially not if she was going to play dirty by sleeping with his archenemy.

"The only thing stale about this situation is my patience to entertain it," he warned Jacques with a growl. "So I'll tell you exactly how this is gonna go…I'm gonna smile and shake your hand and promise to honor your summons. You will go merrily on your way, and probably even invite Miss Castillo back to your apartment for a candlelight dinner to celebrate your mutual victory. And when you return in the morning, the depot will be flattened like a house of cards, and Rodrigo and I will greet you with some hot coffee and a box of tissues, just in case you feel like you need to blow your snotty sense of entitlement on something other than my sleeve. Now get the fuck off my property."

Alma glared at him, her wounded eyes and pouting scowl drawing battle lines between them.

Just then, the heavy wooden doors of the train depot groaned open. Alma's father pushed through the entanglement of vegetation and emerged into the lobby, brushing himself clean of thistles and ivy. "Really, Harvey…can't you afford a gardener? Or even a lawn mower?"

Enrique Castillo suddenly stopped and eyed the sledgehammer in Harvey's hand. "Well, looks like I made it here just in time."

"No, Papi. You're too late," Alma answered, directing her next words at Harvey with disdain. "As usual, bad boy billionaire Harvey Zale is choosing his own engorged net worth over anything else that might have value in life. He's determined to bulldoze the building by tomorrow and he's throwing us off the property."

"Well, really…do we expect anything less from Mr. Zale?" Enrique mused, approaching Harvey and offering him a cordial handshake. "It wouldn't be a Harvey Zale property if there wasn't some kind of a melodrama."

"I'm glad to see someone at least understands how I like to do business, Enrique," Harvey confirmed, accepting his handshake. Enrique Castillo may have been Alma's father, but at least he was also a businessman. He was also a loyal White Sox fan, which sealed their unspoken bond beyond his status as an ex-son-in-law. "Your daughter and Jackass over there want me to delay my hundred-million-dollar closing, just so they can preserve an old train depot with a dozen Tiffany window knock-offs that should have been demolished a century ago."

Enrique's eyes lifted to the rafters of the cathedral ceiling before following the natural arc of support beams down to the perimeter of the foundation.

"Well, I hate to break this to you, Harvey…but this structure is anything but a train depot. Whoever told you that is either a liar or an idiot."

Harvey shot an accusatory glance over at Jacques. *He'd put his money on both.*

Suddenly, the room fell silent as everyone stopped and turned their attention to Harvey.

"What?" He questioned them all with an awkward smile. "Don't tell me my fly is open."

Slowly approaching him, Alma held up her hand to shield his face from the flickering ray of twilight descending from the upper balcony.

"What is that?" she asked slowly, noting how the rainbow of colors illuminated the palm of her hand. Both she and Harvey turned and gazed up to its source.

Through the punctured roof and patches of missing brick, a tangled web of elm branches had long since invaded the building and woven a dense stronghold across the entire upper balcony. Water-stained trusses and a crumbling chimney seem like a foregone conclusion that nothing but nature had benefited from decades of neglect and structural decay. But in an instant, the flickering ray of kaleidoscope light held the promise of something unknown—even magical—behind all that foliage.

Before Harvey could stop her, Alma rushed up the spiral iron staircase leading to the balcony. Submitting to his instinct to protect her, he braced its wobbling base from below until she safely reached the top.

"Damn it," he cursed aloud as he squeezed himself up the narrow steps. Whatever she thought she had seen, whatever visceral impulse that ray of light inspired in her, he knew she wasn't going to leave his property until she investigated it.

When he reached the final step into the balcony, a sticky cobweb ensnared his face.

"Ick, ack, yuck!" He shivered and swatted away the ghostly remnants of silk. He really, really, *really* hated spiders, possibly even more than he hated snotty preservationist Frenchmen.

"Alma?" He called out to her again, but this time the edge in his voice melted away into uncertainty. Like a mysterious secret garden, the invading branches of the crown of the tree completely obscured his view of anything beyond him except the perplexing reflection of colors seeping through the intermittent spaces between the limbs and oak leaves.

"I'm here." Her response hinted at her location, just beyond the natural barricade of branches. Harvey found a small opening in the foliage and forced himself through it.

"Really, Alma... I suggest next time you trespass onto somebody's property, you make sure it doesn't belong to someone who's willing to tie you up, sling you over his shoulder, and carry you away, kicking and screaming—"

He stopped in his tracks, frozen by the prismatic shades of green, pink, turquoise, and white light cascading down upon him.

"What the hell is that?" His voice betrayed the shock and awe of being dwarfed by the twelve-foot stained-glass window positioned in the rear exterior wall of the balcony.

"You're not going to believe me if I tell you," Alma uttered, her eyes fixed on the intricate panels of opalescent glass and its portrayal of a mother and child, embracing each other in an enchanting field of lavender lilacs while basking in the orange rays of a twilight sun.

"Another priceless Tiffany?" Harvey replied, trying hard not to mock her.

"Not just another Tiffany," she answered slowly, as if she was in a trance. "Something so much more..." But her voice trailed off as she suddenly backtracked and attempted to push past him.

"So much more?" He ensnared her hand and interrogated her. "More what?"

"I'm not even sure..." she stammered, peering down at his grasp and submitting to it. "But I'm certain you aren't going to understand even if I try to explain it."

He drew her closer, the urge to prove her wrong swelling inside him. "There was a time when you told me everything and I understood you. So try me." He lowered his voice and strengthened his grip, keeping her profile—and body—squarely in line with his own.

"That was a long time ago...when I was young and foolish. And you..." she paused, as if she was weighing whether or not anything she said to him mattered.

"What?" He encouraged her with a gentle nudge of her arm.

"You smelled better," she deadpanned.

Harvey cracked a smile, realizing how much he missed her sassy unforgiving tongue.

"Well, I definitely was a better man when you were my wife. There's no question about that."

Their eyes locked, as if his admission echoed a sentiment that they both knew was true.

"Not only do I think that window was made by Louis Comfort Tiffany, Harvey, but I think that window is Tiffany's legendary, long-lost masterpiece, the *Eternal Love*."

The gravity of her confession glinted in her eyes.

"That sounds extremely good for you and terrible for me."

"It could be very good for everyone. If I'm right, that window may be one of the most important works of Tiffany's entire career—he would have made it around the time of the 1893 Chicago World's Fair, making it one of his very first experimentations with Favrile glass. But more importantly, it's claimed that he made it as a sacred memorial for his first wife."

"First wives are a sacred thing," Harvey confirmed, looking deeper into her eyes than he knew he should.

"You can't destroy this property, Harvey. You can't." She turned to the stained-glass window and grimaced, obviously pained by the threat of its destruction.

"And what if you are right?" He challenged her. "This train depot—or whatever the hell it is—is sitting on a thirty-acre riverfront parcel that I intend to sell for a hundred million dollars. I need the money to fund an even bigger deal in Shanghai, and instead, you expect me to hold up the entire deal on account of some…treasure hunt?"

"At least," she pleaded, "not before you give me a chance to find out if I'm right."

"That's what I'm afraid of, Alma. You're always right." He glanced back at the window and hesitated. "And what if I don't let you? I am Monsieur Asshole, after all."

"Then you will have to tie me up and drag me away from here because I won't let you destroy this building until I know for sure."

On cue, Jacques' nasal voice echoed through the rafters. "Is everything alright up there, *mon chéri*?"

Alma locked eyes with Harvey. "Plus, I'll claim sanctuary and Jacques will turn it into a media spectacle. You'll get more bad press than it's worth."

"It might be worth it," he answered, noting the way she winced at the sound of Jacques' use of her pet name. "If it means I get to tie you up."

He said it partly in jest and partly because her spitfire and stubbornness still turned him on. Mulling over the way her glasses made her look so much more prudish than he knew she was in bed, he reached out and removed them from her face and cleaned the dust from their thin lenses against the fabric of his shirt.

"If I'm right, Harvey," she replied, peering up at him with shiny, earnest eyes, "and that window is what I think it is, it could be worth tens of millions of dollars. One single window."

"I offered you a lot more than that when we separated, and you refused it." He studied her face—the same schoolgirl idealism and glossy pink lips. He hadn't seen her in over a year and she had barely aged.

"I never cared about your money and you know it."

"Yes. You made that very clear when you divorced me," he added, brushing the cobweb out of her bangs.

"Twenty-four hours, Harvey," she offered, as if she was the one in charge of the negotiation. "That's all I'm asking for. Otherwise..." her voice trailed off with uncertainty.

"Otherwise what?" He encouraged her with a smirk. It was hard to take any threat from her seriously.

"Otherwise…" The words lingered on the tip of her tongue. "I'll never forgive you," she finally whispered.

She held out her hand for the return of her glasses. He didn't comply. She had never cared about his money and he never cared about making it while he was with her—until he did. And when that day had come, he knew it would be what ultimately drove them apart.

"Uck-hem."

They shifted their attention to the sound of someone clearing his throat, announcing his entrance. Harvey expected to see Jacques and fought the sudden reflex to punch his lights out for interrupting the one private moment of intimacy with his ex-wife that he had been granted in over a year. But instead, his anger retreated when he turned and saw Alma's father. *How long had he been standing there*? Harvey didn't know. But at least his former father-in-law had enough decency and respect not to interfere in personal matters that were not his own.

"You drive a tough bargain, Miss Castillo," Harvey said, stressing her maiden name in acknowledgment that times were different and the past couldn't be repeated or changed—and neither could the heartbreak.

He placed her glasses back on her face, taking a moment to remember the way she looked without them, in case he never saw her again. In that moment, impulse and nostalgia had taken over his cold, rational mercenary mind. But he knew he had it in him to go back on his word, especially once he arrived home and called his real estate lawyer to relay the details of their agreement—and its domino chain of adverse implications for him.

"I'll give you one day," he announced, backing away and asserting his all-business persona through the edge in his tone. "One day to entertain your little treasure hunt. But after that, be prepared to call the police,

Enrique. Because at the very least, I intend to make good on one Machiavellian scheme—and that's tying up your daughter."

Chapter Six

Alma repressed her urge to vomit. She didn't know which gut-wrenching emotion to feel first—unfathomable elation that she might have just discovered over a dozen new stained-glass windows designed by Louis Comfort Tiffany, or that she found it on the property of her capitalist pig ex-husband who had promised nothing more than its destruction unless she could prove their monetary worth to him—and prove it within twenty-four hours.

He hadn't always been a capitalist pig, she thought. *That was part of the problem*. There was a time, long ago, when they were college students and young lovers—both sharing the same goals and dreams. He'd always wanted to buy properties and renovate them. She had always wanted to preserve their historic treasures. But years passed and ambitions changed, and so had the mutual love and admiration that had once bonded them. Now, ironically, when she saw him again, she only recognized the thin veneer of the man she once knew, and not even that fragile connection seemed worthy of preserving.

"That was quite a speech about the *Eternal Love*."

Alma looked up at her father like she was a teenager who had just been caught sneaking back into the house. Their drive back to the antique shop had been a silent one. Now, he eyed her as she rushed to gather up her belongings and head out the door.

"I didn't realize you were there, spying on us."

"Spying is a strong word," her father answered, circling behind the shop's counter. Sitting on his favorite wooden stool, he kicked off his shoes and stretched out his legs, as if the drama of the day was too much for arthritic ankles and knees. "And I didn't announce myself because I didn't want to interrupt whatever you two needed to say to each other."

"Nothing," Alma countered, feeling the weight of the lie on her tongue. "The only thing that needed to be said was whatever it would take to get him to agree not to destroy the building."

"But Alma," her father said, lowering his chin and peering over his spectacles at her with censure. "You and I both know that stained-glass window in the balcony is not a lost treasure."

Alma shrugged. It was true. She had bluffed. It was a remarkable stained-glass window that definitely had all the hallmarks of an early masterpiece. If not a Tiffany, then perhaps one of his collaborators like de Forest or even maybe one of his chief competitors, like John La Farge. But without closer examination in the proper light, she couldn't be sure of anything. And without some sort of understanding of what that building was and why it had even been built there in the first place, there wasn't any reason to believe it was Tiffany's *Eternal Love*.

The real truth: she had needed some way to stall Monsieur Asshole, and tricking him into believing he had a priceless artistic masterpiece on the property he intended to destroy was the only way to buy herself some time. Obviously, her ex-husband had forgotten how many times he'd forced her to play poker when they first had started dating in college, and how well he'd taught her how to bluff him out of his royal flush with only her pair of eights.

But there was always one person in the world she couldn't fool and that person was her father.

"He trusts you, Alma," her father continued. "You should not betray that trust."

"He's a selfish billionaire who's willing to destroy priceless art for monetary gain," she tossed back, completely annoyed that her father was hinting at her own dishonesty without acknowledging the fact that Harvey Zale had become the epitome of greed. "Why are you taking his side, Papi?"

"Because he was my son-in-law before he was a billionaire, and he treated you well for as long as you would let him."

"So you're still angry at me for divorcing him?"

"No," her father replied. "Not angry, but concerned."

"About what? The fact that you might lose him as your weekly baseball game buddy?"

"Alma—" Enrique spread open his hands like he had nothing to hide. "My friendship with Harvey is not on trial here."

"Well, neither should my actions to stop him from destroying a collection of beautiful stained-glass windows just to make one more billionaire buck."

"It is true that it would be more than a shame to lose those windows," her father agreed. "But it is Harvey's property and so he has the right to do whatever he wants with them, and right now, he has agreed to delay their destruction by granting you an opportunity to inspect them tomorrow. What more can you ask from him, *mi amor*?"

Alma fell silent. She knew the answer, but she didn't want to confess it. She wanted the old Harvey—the Harvey who would have relished the idea of joining her in the quest to discover rare pieces of hidden art inside a forgotten, abandoned building and who would have seized the opportunity to rescue them at all costs. But that Harvey was a myth now; almost as fictional as the myth of the *Eternal Love*. She hadn't seen or recognized that Harvey in so long that it almost made her feel as though he'd never existed and her entire marriage had been nothing more than a sham.

"Harvey is not a bad man," her father quietly offered. "I think you are too hard on him sometimes."

"Maybe you're being too easy on him," she replied. "Don't you see how much he's changed?"

Her father absorbed her question with pensive silence. "The only thing I know, Alma, is that when you were married to Harvey, you were happy—until you weren't. And now, you are worse than unhappy. You are lost."

Alma gazed at her father, feeling a frown settle upon her face. Everything he said was true, but that didn't mean she had to admit it. Instead, she lifted her backpack and turned on her heel without another word.

"I assume you are done for the day?" he asked, noting the time on the wall clock.

The bell chimed above her head as she threw open the front door and stopped in its threshold. "Yes, it's getting late and I have a date tonight. I'm trying to move on from my ex-husband who I don't recognize anymore as the man who I loved and married. It would be nice if you could be a little more understanding."

"Divorce is not a punishment, Alma. It is a painful conclusion."

"Trust me, Papi. No one feels the end of our marriage more painfully than me."

* * * *

She had a date tonight. The words rang in her head, partly because it was a bold-faced lie and partly because she wanted to believe it to be true.

It wasn't exactly a date, but it wasn't an innocent platonic relationship either. *So what exactly was it then*?

Diversion, she thought, reflecting on her conversation with her father. A simple distraction to alleviate the pain of choosing to separate from Harvey.

Everyone acted as if it had been an easy decision for her, and in many ways, that hurt her even more. It had never been an easy decision and she hadn't chosen to divorce Harvey as a punishment. She had chosen it because he had chosen his real estate deals and his fancy skyscrapers over their marriage. Her father and sister wanted to pretend that things hadn't been that bad between them, but they weren't the ones who had been promised more time together—dinners to make up for miss ones and getaways to forgive all the weekends he chose to work over spending time with her. And even the luxury gifts that he bought her as consolation were always bittersweet because the only thing she ever really wanted from Harvey was less discussion about his growing real estate empire and more discussion about their future together—as a family.

And now, here she was a year later, seeking out an escape from the one part of her life that pained her the most. *But was it more than just an escape*? She didn't know...exactly. And she wasn't sure she was willing to find out. Despite the fact she had caught herself attaching more significance to her texting "encounters" with a total stranger than she likely should, she wasn't confident that she was willing to accept his mysterious invitation to take their "relationship" to another level—a *personal* level. What had started as a teasing midnight exchange with subtle sexual undertones had developed into an addictive flirtatious sexting affair. But by asking her to propose a place where he could delivery something "special" to her, he had breached the fantasy of their purely digital connection and slipped himself into the reality of her everyday life.

If she chose to follow his instructions, it could mean the difference between pursuing their connection in a more meaningful way rather than simply keeping it an entertaining sexual diversion of cat and mouse. As she hurried along the winding riverfront sidewalks of Wacker Drive towards the Cultural Center, she actually wondered if that's all it was to her—a desperate quest for diversion—or was she really starting to have feelings for a man she barely knew at all?

She glanced down at her phone. Five minutes to six o'clock. She paused to catch her breath outside the Cultural Center's arched bronze-framed doors of the Washington Street entrance. She knew every security guard there and she knew she would be allowed to stay inside the building past its closing. She simply had to make the choice to enter. *What would she find there—or not find there*? The endless possibilities swam through her head, but her fear filled her chest with anxiety. What if she had put too much stock in her schoolgirl sexting infatuation with a perfect stranger, and he failed her—or her expectations of him? What if tonight affirmed nothing more than the cold, hard truth: the illusion of pretending to be someone else was easier than accepting the reality of who she really was, and the fact that she was in an insecure, fragile emotional place in her life.

"Good evening, Miss Castillo," the security guard said, pulling open the door as a courtesy and encouraging her through it. "You're right on time with five minutes to spare."

Alma hesitated before forcing herself to pass into the building's vaulted lobby, its walls of Carrara marble inlaid with sparkling green and cerulean mosaic glass tiles.

"Good evening, Reggie." She nodded with a smile. She knew he had just started working there three weeks earlier, fresh out of high school, but his silver security badge and formal navy blue uniform made him look older than she would guess.

"You meeting someone here this evening?" he asked, allowing the door to shut behind them. His question halted her as she started to climb the grand staircase.

"Maybe?" she replied. "Has anyone stopped by and asked you for directions today? Directions to the Tiffany ballroom?"

"Oh, you know how it is," Reggie answered. "Lots and lots of folks. All tourists." He returned to his swivel chair and reclined into it with a heavy sigh. "And a man…" he finally added.

"A man?" Alma repeated, slowly losing her confidence and backing down the staircase.

"Yes, ma'am," Reggie confirmed. "A man. Came by about five minutes ago. He told me he was heading up to the ballroom to meet his next wife."

Alma glanced upwards without a reply, as if the echo of her voice against the hallway's white marble vaulted ceiling would announce her to whoever might be waiting for her beyond the grand staircase.

"Did he look normal…or crazy?" she whispered to Reggie.

"Ah, shoot…don't know about crazy, ma'am," Reggie answered, as if he was pondering the possibility. "But he was tall with a big smile like a movie star. And he had a package in his hand. Something done up real pretty with a white bow."

Like a movie star? Alma clung to the thought. That couldn't be a bad thing, right?

But just because he was potentially attractive didn't mean he still couldn't be a psychopath. In fact, all signs pointed to it. He was, after all, sexting with *her*—and she was acting like a phony femme fatal. *But why did something so wrong feel so right?*

She quickly removed her glasses and withdrew the rubber band around her ponytail. *Just in case he was still up there.* But there was nothing she could do about her overalls except brush the dust off their worn fabric. *It was definitely wrong to expect him to look like a Hollywood star while she looked like Dora the Explorer.*

After a moment of hesitation, she forced herself to ascend to the top of the landing and into the center of the Tiffany ballroom—one of her favorite places in the city. The soft illumination pouring through the grand ceiling dome fashioned with Tiffany's signature Favrile glass seduced her deeper into the oval ballroom. Like a scene from a movie, she almost expected a tall, handsome man to be waiting for her. With a rose in his hand, he would flash her a warm smile, letting her know she had made the right choice. But to her disappointment, no one greeted her. There was only the dull drone of Michigan Avenue traffic seeping through the sweeping two-story windows overlooking Millennium Park.

In the corner of sills of the eastern windows...her own instructions to him percolated in her mind. Drawing forward, she replaced her glasses and scanned the sills, immediately spotting what she had missed all along—a powder blue gift box with a conspicuous white bow.

Alma took a deep breath. It was not difficult to recognize the significance of the jewelry box—Tiffany & Co. Her mysterious suitor seemed to be making an effort to connect the location that she proposed—the Tiffany ballroom—with something that he thought she would enjoy, and it unnerved her until she undid the bow, removed the lid, and waded beneath the waves of white tissue paper.

The distracting flare of prismatic light reflected off the lens of Alma's glasses and she quickly closed the lid of the jewelry box. *No, that wasn't what she thought it was...it couldn't have been.*

Suddenly, her phone vibrated within her backpack. She dug through it and retrieved her phone.

Did you get it? His text pinged with expectation.

Her palms started to sweat as she peeled back the folds of the tissue paper again and withdrew the opulent triple-strand diamond choker necklace with a stunning five-carat emerald pendant as its centerpiece.

Clearly, he was exactly what he said he was—a man of wealth and importance—and he intended to prove it.

Yes. It was the only thing she could manage to text back. Her hands were shaking.

After a long pause, he texted her back. *But you don't like it...*

There was nothing at all that she didn't like about it. It was both stunning and completely baffling.

I'm trying to figure out how you got it, she replied. *It's the kind of thing that only comes up at auction once every few years.*

Every decade, he corrected her. *Glad to see you appreciate fine jewelry. You're a smart girl.*

SMART ENOUGH TO KNOW IT COSTS OVER A MILLION DOLLARS, she wanted to scream back, but she contained herself. It was a one-of-a-kind vintage Tiffany piece, and simply by the cut, carat size, and quality of the emerald, she knew it was a rare nineteenth-century gemstone, likely one of the original treasures that Charles Lewis Tiffany, Louis Comfort's father, brought back from his trips to Europe and Russia where he had become the imperial jeweler to royal families. It was the most beautiful piece of jewelry she had ever held in her hands, and the last thing she wanted to convey was that she wasn't grateful—even if he was a psychopathic mafia criminal.

Okay...you caught me, he shot back after enduring her silence. *It was a purchase that I made over a year ago. But circumstances changed, and well...* There was a pause, like he was holding back something before suddenly reversing his decision. *Let's just say...I've felt the void of not having the right woman in my life who would appreciate receiving it from me—until now.*

Alma stared down at the choker's magnificent glints of fire and ice that caught every angle of light within the ballroom. The weight of its authenticity and the significance of his confession made her realize she was no longer playing a flirtatious game of sexting. What had been a relationship born exclusively within the realm of fantasy had just shifted into something deeper—it was no longer just about an escape.

I don't know what to say, she finally answered back. *Except thank you.*

Don't say anything...until tonight. He answered with authority. *Then I expect to hear every detail about how you look wearing it. And nothing else.*

Chapter Seven

Sexy…sultry…naughty…super naughty…just down right slutty. Alma drifted across the window display of a high-end lingerie boutique at the Merchandise Mart, perusing its merchandise of seductive lingerie and torturing herself about whether or not she had the guts to go inside and make a purchase.

White satin chemises…black corsets trimmed with lace…pink chiffon babydoll nighties...siren red garter belts and matching G-strings. Black leather chastity belts.

Sure, they all looked appealing on perfectly sculpted plastic mannequins. But it was hard to imagine herself in any of them, much less standing in front of a man and keeping a straight face.

There was, however, one option beyond the window display, near the rear of the shop, that caught her eye. It was a sophisticated lavender bra and panty set, embellished with petite white and pink rose buds and embroidered with floral lace. With its soft palette of pastels, it was as enchanting as an impressionist painting while still offering a hint of the risqué with its peekaboo promise to conceal almost nothing beneath the sheer veil of lilac tulle.

Alma convinced herself that its authentic beauty drew her through the boutique's main entrance and into the quaint surroundings of the lingerie shop—where only a few other women were browsing the tables of French-cut thongs laid out like colorful candies. Rows and rows of silk hangers lined the walls—all with provocative satin pushup bras and bustiers, arrayed in every shade of red, pink, green, turquoise, and ivory.

God, what was she even doing there?

The only time she had ever worn lingerie in her life was when she was married, and that already felt like a life lived by another woman. It no longer was her—*now*—and certainly not when she was the one buying it for herself.

Or perhaps…buying it for his benefit.

Passing by the drawers of pantyhose near the rear of the store, she sought out the lavender bra and panty set and lifted the hanger to inspect its padded bra and satin straps. She was so used to wearing sports bras, buried beneath her overalls and heavy sweaters that she barely could remember what it felt like to wear something uniquely feminine and seductive.

"Twice in one day—it must be fate."

She closed her eyes, too horrified to look ahead of her in the mirror and confirm the identity of the male voice directly behind her.

"I assume that's for Jacques?"

His accusation infuriated her. She spun around to challenge his smug chiseled face and the glinting blue eyes. Her emotions changed from tingling embarrassment to red hot retaliation.

"It's none of your business, Harvey."

He flashed her a smile, as if he detected the flush in her cheeks and savored it. "I'll take that as a yes. That's definitely your color," he noted, peering down at the bra and panty clenched in her hands. "But I doubt Jackass knows anything about getting a woman in or out of one of those…so you might have to draw him a diagram."

"Unlike you, right?"

His smile widened, like a schoolboy cherishing the negative attention. "Well, I'm certainly not an amateur. But neither are you, if I remember correctly."

He held her gaze. Until this afternoon, she had forgotten how attractive he looked when he hadn't bothered to shave in the morning or when the right angle of light fell on his tanned skin. He was coatless, as if the bitter wind didn't faze him, and the long sleeves of his denim-blue shirt were rolled up past his elbows. During the frigid spring months of Chicago, only men who worked outside had sun-kissed skin, and that was Harvey—golden, fearless, and looking for trouble anywhere he could get it.

"Okay, so you've guessed what I'm doing here," Alma said, fueling his false assumption about her relationship with Jacques, just to test if he was truly jealous. "So tell me then…what are you doing here?"

"What do you think I'm doing here?" he shot back.

Ugh, that was so typical Harvey. Never give a straight answer, especially if it allowed you to conjure up the worst case scenario about him.

"Enlighten me," she sassed back.

"A true gentlemen doesn't kiss and tell, sweetheart. So, let's just say…I'm here for the same reasons you are. But I'm actually more surprised to see you here than you probably are to see me."

"Well, I'm a new woman now. I buy my own lingerie."

"That's a shame. Jacques isn't doing his job then." He pushed his lips closer to her ear, and whispered his words down her neck. "Part of the fun is imagining what she'll look like in every single sultry piece. At least, that's what I used to do when I came here to buy it for you."

Alma tried to avoid getting lost in the nostalgia of the past, but his masculine scent of pine and musk brought it all back. She tried equally hard to push from her mind that she was actually in a lingerie shop with her ex-husband—who was buying sexy outfits for someone new in his life.

"You're forgetting the stockings," Harvey suddenly said, turning his attention onto a collection of long silk hosiery.

"No, I haven't," Alma replied, trying to hide the bra and panty set beneath crossed arms. "I just haven't decided on the right color."

"White—if you want to keep it...clean," he instructed her. "Black—if you want to make sure he's straight." He lifted a pair of slinky black stockings, trimmed with deep purple lace at thigh level. "I always liked seeing you in something a bit more..." his voice trailed off as his eyes roamed the store for an example of his point.

"Whorish?" she offered, finishing the thought for him.

He smirked and locked eyes through her lenses, seizing the attention of the real woman hiding behind them. "I'm pretty sure you enjoyed it, too."

"I can't remember," she lied, breaking eye contact. "But I'm sure your newest conquest will enjoy whatever item you choose. Here...let me help." She drifted over to a black and white ruffled ensemble that looked suspiciously like a naughty French maid's uniform with its triple D nipple circles cut out.

She fingered through the selection before passing over a nylon gold bodysuit with matching gold-studded leather collar. He accepted it, but his attention stayed squarely on her, as if he couldn't get enough of her sassy comebacks and undertone of disdain.

"Tell me something, Miss Castillo. After you divorced and banished me from your life, what did you do with all those whorish outfits that I forced upon you?

"Why? Do you want them back so you can re-gift them?"

She held up another option—a black spandex bodystocking with single slit over the crotch.

Amused, he relaxed his weight against a rack of garter belts. "Maybe I just want to know if it was as easy to get rid of them as it was to get rid of me."

Unexpectedly, she noticed that his wedding band was gone. *Of course, it was gone.* They were no longer married. But it was the very first time that Alma had actually registered that it was gone. When they were married, Harvey had been so stubborn about wanting to wear it, even though he knew men on his construction sites who had lost fingers after their rings were caught on heavy machinery. Still, Harvey refused to take it off. Now, he stood there, casually staring at her, waiting for her reply. But she could barely remember the question.

"I donated them to my local church." She stared straight at him, bluffing again.

Without warning, he edged closer and lifted her chin to meet her eyes. For a moment, she feared he would kiss her until she realized it was simply a vague whisper of hope imprinted in her heart.

"I'm sure the nuns were most grateful," he whispered, passing his lips over hers before letting her go and sauntering towards the door.

The store clerk noticed his imminent departure and called out to him. "Is there something I can help you find, sir?"

Harvey stopped in his tracks and glanced back at her with his easy, Hollywood smile.

"I'll come back another day when it isn't so crowded."

Then his blue eyes seized onto Alma. His jawline flinched, as if he was holding himself back from leaving the store without saying another word.

"And just for the record, Alma…you were never just a conquest. You were my wife and the love of my life. So no matter what you choose to believe about me now, I won't let you believe anything less than that."

He turned and passed out the door, disappearing from sight. After a moment of silence, the store clerk glanced at Alma for clarification.

"He's a Leo," Alma offered, pretending to ignore the impact of his unexpected confession. "They're all melodramatic like that."

"Ohhhhhh," The store clerk groaned and grinned with relief. "I totally get it. I was in a relationship with a Leo once, too. It's true. But he was also the best kisser I've ever dated, probably because he was so freaking sensitive. Totally get the melodrama." She quickly turned back to her inventory list. "Let me know if I can help you find anything."

The store clerk's words echoed in her mind while the memory of Harvey's expression arrested her—*you were my wife and the love of my life.*

Was she being too hard on him? *Was she still bitter and angry about everything that had happened between them*? He talked a good game now, but when it really mattered—when things were distant and troubled between them—she only remembered the sound of silence.

Did it really take a divorce and a year apart for him to realize that marriage wasn't like one of his demolition projects? Something abandoned and neglected over time before being patched up and sold away to the highest bidder?

The real Harvey Zale—the one she had married—was as passionate about art and architecture as much as she was, and together they had indulged their dreams of finding and preserving all the historical treasures within a city they both loved as much as each other.

Alma shut her eyes and dismissed the past and everything painful within it. It had already been an emotional day, and there was nothing to be gained by dwelling on the darkest and most depressing parts of her life. Harvey Zale had made his billions dismissing the romantic ideals of preservation in favor of capitalistic greed at whatever cost. And regardless of his spontaneous declaration tonight, there was nothing in his actions or words that proved otherwise. Their relationship had simply become another one of his properties—neglected and in need of preservation. But the truth was: it was easier to destroy it with a wrecking ball than maintain it over time with an inextinguishable flame of eternal love.

"I'll take this one," Alma suddenly announced, replacing the lavender bra and panty set in favor of a black leather bustier with a chrome zipper running up its middle and squeezing everything together into a perfectly sculpted, heart-shaped fantasy of deliciousness. Then she selected a pair of sleek black garter stockings to match the black zippered G-string thong.

Harvey had been completely wrong in his assumptions about her and Jacques, but if there was one thing that he was right about, it was the stockings. She wasn't looking for anything clean tonight. In fact, she was determined to prove to herself that she was capable of indulging in the exact opposite with a man other than Harvey Zale.

Chapter Eight

There was nothing she had been looking forward to more all day than returning home, taking off all her clothes, crawling into her bed, and waiting for his call.

His phone call.

Tonight would be different than all the others. It would be a significant evolution in their flirtatious sexting affair. It would be the very first time she would actually be hearing his voice, saying all those naughty, provocative exchanges rather than reading his texts and imagining the man behind every sly, cocky comeback and confident sexual directive. She never thought it would develop into anything meaningful, much less breach the sacred barrier of her real life as Alma Castillo. But he was attempting to ensnare the mythical seductress that he inspired within her—an infinitely more invincible and alluring woman, a playful, teasing temptress who attracted his attention and enjoyed the challenge of remaining just beyond his reach.

Ironically, he had become more than just an entertaining diversion. He had become her ultimate escape. Without him, she was only a recently divorced antiques expert working in her father's antique appraisal business who faced the reality of a failed marriage and the fear of another broken heart. Today she had been unfortunately reminded of how badly she had suffered from that broken heart. She never expected to run into Harvey, much less end up on his property and at his mercy, attempting to convince him not to be the premiere asshole she knew he'd become. She thought that enough time had passed. It *had* been almost a year since she filed the divorce papers. But if time heals old wounds, then the clock between them had stopped. The pain and resentment of their separation was still as fresh as the day she realized her husband was no longer the man she had married.

But when he agreed to halt the bulldozer and grant her a chance to inspect the windows in the morning, there had been a brief moment of truce from all the heartache and a glimmer of the way things used to be between them. *Was he doing it for his own monetary gain, or had she successfully stirred up the integrity of the old Harvey who she had once known and deeply loved?*

And yet, her secret hope that he had done it to prove to her that he was still that same man quickly faded when she ran into him at the lingerie shop—his favorite place to buy her gifts when they were married. Clearly, he wasn't there shopping for her. He was there shopping for someone else, and perhaps that realization bothered her more than even his capitalist greed.

He had moved on from their marriage.

And she?

Publicly, she acted like she had. But privately, she knew she hadn't.

She moved through the inky darkness of her condominium without turning on the lights. It had been the only thing she requested in their divorce settlement—ownership of their full-floor vintage penthouse within a seven-story, Burnham-inspired greystone overlooking the South Branch of the Chicago River. She had gladly signed away her marital rights to all his other commercial properties that he had acquired during the last years of their marriage and all the billions of dollars in wealth he had made from them. She didn't want any of it, except the vintage penthouse they bought together when they were both struggling college graduates, striving to rescue and renovate architectural gems along the riverfront that otherwise would have been auctioned off and demolished by opportunistic real estate developers like Harvey Zale.

Now, it almost seemed painfully ironic that her home was a nostalgic memento of a time when things had been different between them. *When he had been a different man.* She remembered every inch of its restoration: sawing, sanding, gutting, drywalling, painting and decorating. *Side by side, they had done it together.* She remembered meticulously researching every renovation option and his insistence that he could create whatever she could imagine for the space. And despite the cathedral ceiling in the loft-style living room overlooking the Chicago River or the embellished silver and pearl chandelier in her dining room from an Adler & Sullivan building they couldn't save, her favorite room in the penthouse was still her bedroom, a whitewashed haven with arching bay windows and ornate vine and blossom terracotta moldings, twisting up the walls like a protective garden. French double doors sealed off her sanctuary from the outside world and the steady glow from the enormous stone and marble fireplace burned with such warmth and intensity that it made her question all the merits of living in the modern world.

On a few special nights, the gleaming oak floors reflected the shining rays of stark moonlight through the only source of color within the room—the circular Tiffany stained-glass window, *Woman on the Crescent Moon*, that he had bought for her at an auction. With its portrayal of a fairy-like woman balancing in the curve of the crescent moon, her scarlet gown undulating with the midnight breeze of cobalt blue, it represented the epitome of everything she loved about Tiffany's work—mythical, sensual, romantic. How many times had she stared at it after they had made love, drifting to sleep in his arms, listening to the steady pace of his heartbeat, appreciating the fact that she had married someone who loved her so completely?

She had lied about giving away all the lingerie he had bought her. She hadn't gotten rid of any of it. Moving to her dresser, she pulled open the bottom drawer and surveyed its contents. The reality was: she had kept every piece, and she still remembered every intimate occasion they shared together while she was wearing each one. And it was true what he had said about her—she did enjoy all the sultry outfits he had bought her because he'd been the only man who she had ever trusted enough to inspire her naughty side, not to mention the only man who had ever made her come.

Perhaps all that would change tonight.

She lifted the lid off the powder blue gift box and flipped open the velvet jewelry case. Even in the dim moonlight, the round-cut diamonds still scintillated with brilliance. His final text instructed her to wear the diamond choker necklace…*and nothing else.* But after meeting Harvey in the lingerie store, she realized she wanted—no, *needed*—to prove that she could be someone other than the woman he assumed he still knew.

Lifting the boutique's shopping bag out of her purse, she set it atop her vanity and slid out the black leather bustier, matching zippered thong, and black garter stockings from the silk pouch. Tonight she vowed not be that same woman. She had a chance to rebel against every limitation she had ever placed on herself, and she intended to indulge in every minute of it.

And it was all because of him.

Her mystery suitor had been the one who afforded her the opportunity to disappear from the confines of her everyday persona and reappear in a way that no one in her real life—not even her ex-husband—would recognize. *Her mystery suitor had been the one who had liberated her.* And it was this liberation that made her yearn to exceed his every expectation for their exchange tonight.

Slowly, a cloud passed over the full moon, extinguishing the brilliant light passing through the Tiffany window.

Empowered by the darkness, she undressed and slipped into her black leather bustier and zippered thong. Freeing the rubber band from her hair, she let her long dark hair flow over her bare shoulders while admiring the reflection of a shadowy enchantress in the vanity's oval mirror. Somewhere, out there in the world, was a stranger who had just gifted her a million dollar necklace without any assurances that he would ever hear from her again. Instead, she could barely resist the magnetism of their connection because he seemed more familiar than any other man she had known in her real life.

With surreal urgency, her phone rang. She wanted to make him wait before answering it until she realized she was only torturing herself.

"Yes—" she whispered, attempting not to betray the quiver in her voice.

"I've been waiting so long for this moment," he said with dark intentions.

She closed her eyes, soothed by his deep, masculine voice.

There was a long pause of silence before she gathered the courage to reply.

"So what do you think?" she said, subduing her voice to match the persona she planned to adopt for tonight.

"Your voice is the loveliest thing I've heard all day."

His compliment infused her with a sexy confidence. She had always imagined his voice in her mind. But now, in a moment of weakness, she caught herself projecting Harvey's face onto it. *She had just seen him. Clearly, he still affected her.*

"You must have had a really bad day," she responded, feeling the sudden urge to assume whatever role he expected her to play."

"Not anymore…" he exhaled, sipping from his unknown drink.

"I suppose that means you expect me to say something…seductive."

"Nope." He paused and took another sip from his tumbler as the ice clicked against the side of the glass. "I don't generally expect anything from lovely things, other than the pleasure of enjoying them."

She couldn't believe it. Her mind was really playing an emotional game with her heart. *He sounded just like Harvey.* And he had that same way about him, as if everything he said was really a subtle sign that he was interested in getting to know her more—if she would only let him. And although she could tell he had been drinking—perhaps too much—it didn't make him sound sloppy or incoherent. It made him sound honest and vulnerable, as if he'd been waiting for months, possibly years, for her to call and rescue him.

"Tell me you're wearing it," he urged her. "It was originally made for an Italian Contessa. You've only told me that you have dark hair and dark eyes, so I thought it would be fitting."

Attempting to still her trembling hands, she focused on the distinctive edge in his voice—a richer, huskier tone, tinged with an inebriated lilt that playfully courted her. *Yes, only a bit like Harvey now*, she thought, and more like someone she knew she shouldn't trust—and it excited her.

"Yes, I'm wearing it. And yes, it's lovely. No, *gorgeous*," she stressed, carefully lowering her voice to mimic the dark sensuality within his own. "But you know that I can't keep it. It's important to me that you believe me when I say that I'm not interested in your wealth. Which is why I plan to return it to you tomorrow."

"Cruel woman," he shot back. The ice cubes jangled louder as he downed his drink. "That's like returning my heart."

Whenever she read his teasing texts, she was always emboldened to tease him back. But now, hearing the vulnerability in his voice gave her pause; she expected to embody the role of an icy femme fatale—seductress, temptress, the symbol of his ultimate fantasy. And yet, the trace of humility within his reply inspired the more genuine, tender side of her femininity.

"Perhaps you were too quick to give it away," she softly replied.

"I've never had a problem giving it away, just with finding the right woman."

"And how can you be so sure I'm the right woman?"

"Because you haven't hung up on me yet." The spontaneity of his laughter relaxed her, and the blend of his dry wit and his Chicago-native frankness convinced her there was nothing phony about him. "And because you don't seem to mind that I'm a soulless bastard who wants to buy you expensive jewelry."

"You definitely don't sound soulless," she countered, adding a hint of jest in her voice. "But I don't want this—whatever *this* is—to be about expensive gifts."

"It's not. It's about gaining your trust."

His resoluteness disarmed her. She glanced at herself in the mirror and traced the outline of the diamond choker necklace with her fingertips, feeling its heavy platinum setting pressed against her flesh.

"Well, it certainly proves that you've got money."

He laughed again. "Or that I'm a criminal."

"Or perhaps a little bit of both," she teased back.

"Yes, likely both," he mused with an unguarded exhale. She took pleasure in their easy connection and their mutually playful bond. "Or maybe I'm just a fraud," he finally added.

"Or maybe this is the real you, and you're a fraud to everyone else."

Her comment silenced him. After a moment, he responded in a low, slightly menacing tone.

"So tell me, Contessa…what if you found out what I was really like during the day? That the truth was…in the real world, I was a corrupt, unscrupulous business tycoon who everyone hated, loathed, and despised."

"I wouldn't believe it."

He pressed the point. "What if I told you that I did horrible things like close orphanages and animal shelters?"

She withheld her smile. "I'd call you a terrible liar. We've talked about children and puppies, and you like both."

"Okay," he conceded, knowing she had caught him. "Maybe it's worse than that. What if I told you I'm just a worthless, miserable bastard who has lost all the joy in his life?"

She heard the weariness of pain beneath his wry tone, like a tiny crack within a slab of impenetrable concrete that would only get worse over time.

"Then I'd just ask you to stay on the phone with me all night and tell me more because that doesn't make you a worthless, miserable bastard. It just makes you human."

He fell silent again. This time, her resoluteness seemed to disarm him.

"Well…" he cleared his throat and lowered his tone almost an octave, signaling he was preparing to reveal his darkest secrets. "You know, I learned a valuable lesson about a year ago—things you love can easily go away and there's no guarantee you'll ever get them back. So what's the point of trying to be the good guy when the miserable greedy one gets you the same outcome either way?"

She was surprised to hear the tenor of isolation within his voice—and the fact that he trusted her enough to express it—and it made her tread carefully.

"I think it's more important not to focus on the outcome, but the fact we have a choice to contribute to life in good ways or bad ways, and that choice matters."

"Yeah, I used to think that it mattered," he replied, almost mournful. "But now I know that nothing matters because you'll lose it all in the end, anyway. One way or another, life will come knocking on your door and take something away. And at the end of the day, I'd rather be a filthy rich son-of-a-bitch than a struggling one with the same amount of heartbreak."

"I don't believe you believe that," she said, feeling the need to challenge him. "I may not know your name or your age or what you do exactly for a living—"

"Mass produce plastic vampire teeth that pollute landfills," he interjected.

"But I *know*," she overrode him, "that you're sophisticated enough to realize that money won't ultimately make you happy."

"No, it's true. It will ultimately destroy me. But in the meantime, it's absolutely worth the cost of my soul because I've been waiting all day to imagine you wearing that million dollar diamond choker necklace—and nothing else."

And that was how he always did it. As if it was the most natural transition in the world, he transformed their soulful late-night confessions into a primal game of seduction. And it was exactly the reason why she was always lured in by him.

"You know, I have my own confession to make…" she paused, listening to the rise and fall of his breath. "I'm not exactly naked."

"That sounds both unfortunate and intriguing."

"Well…I decided since it was our first time talking on the phone, it might be a good idea to wear something special for the occasion."

She let the innuendo hang in the air. It made her feel sexy and powerful, and the certainty that he would follow her lead excited her. He may have been the one who initiated the game, but she was the one who was in charge of how they would play it.

"Something special that needs to be removed? Or something that needs to be kissed?"

She smiled. She loved the way he escalated their foreplay.

"That depends on your preference." Relaxing onto the edge of her bed, she crossed her long legs, accentuating her black garter stocking. "I'm looking at myself right now in the French heirloom full-length mirror, and the arcs of my breasts are the only things exposed in this black leather bustier."

Almost as if he was there, next to her in the bed, he exhaled through the phone into her ear—an unconscious release. Not only had she raised the stakes, but she had granted him permission to raise them as well.

"If I were there, you know I wouldn't settle for just the arcs."

"I'm not certain there's anything you could do about it. It's cinched up with satin cords that have to be cut off."

"If I were there, I'd much prefer to cinch it tighter and tighter until you beg me to pull down the cups and nip your tits between my teeth to relieve the ache."

She closed her eyes and inhaled, indulging in the constricting sensation of the bustier around her torso and the arousing fantasy of being bound and pleasured by him.

"And what would you do to relieve the ache between my legs?"

She waited and listened, desperate to hear the strength and conviction behind his threats.

"I'd suck you off, harder and harder, then spread you wide at the knees and force you to show me every glistening moment of yourself in heat in that full-length mirror."

"That's assuming I'm fully exposed below my waist."

She savored his sudden silence. She knew he hadn't expected that.

"If you're not, I intend to do something about that." His husky restraint turned guttural and provocative.

She lowered her voice, intending to draw him in, as if she were revealing a dirty secret. "I'm wearing a black leather thong with a chrome zipper crotch. You'll have to be good with your hands."

"Who said anything about my hands?"

A shot of adrenaline rushed up Alma's legs and tingled her inner core. She never could anticipate what he would propose next, but she knew it would always be something naughtier than she would ever propose to him.

"Are you looking at yourself in the mirror?" he asked, foreshadowing his intentions.

She shifted her backside to the edge of the mattress and shifted her weight off of it.

"Yes."

"Spread nice and wide…"

She slowly spread her knees as wide as possible, yearning to please him.

"Yes—" She sighed in submission.

"Good. Because I'm kneeling before you now, running my hot breath up those luscious black stockings before stripping them down to your ankles and letting them dangle there like an invitation. Then I'm going to taste every inch of salt along your bare skin, creating one solid wet line, starting from the tip of your ankle bone, up your calf, and around to the back of your inner thigh before burying my nose in your scent."

She closed her eyes and imagined every action he had described to her.

Releasing a quivering breath, she encouraged him for more. "Then?"

"Then I'm going to lick that metallic chrome zip with my tongue before pulling it down with my teeth."

"And if I try to push you away?" she whispered.

"I'll brace your wrists and invade you like the whore I know you're dying to be with me."

Dropping her head back, she lowered her hand over her own crotch, unable to contain the need to imagine what he might do next.

"Do you want to hear me unzip it?"

There was a long pause, as if she had surprised him that her lingerie wasn't an elaborate lie.

"Yes—" he sighed, releasing his own yearning to believe it was all real.

She lowered the phone between her legs and buzzed down the zip, slowly exposing the most vulnerable part of herself to him.

"Are you pleasuring yourself?"

"Yes," she confessed, breathy and unguarded. "Just for you." She had already began fondling herself, unable to contain the fantasy that he was there, stroking her into ecstasy.

"Good," he answered, "Because I'm going to think about that image while I'm licking your clit and loving every drop of your sweetness."

She groaned as she pushed her fingers deeper inside herself. The thought of him between her legs, mouth hovering over her glistening slit, his hot tongue massaging her clit while she stimulated herself in front of him was more than she could bear.

"I'm so wet for you," she whispered into the phone, placing her full vulnerability into his care.

"And you taste amazing," he whispered back, heightening the taboo exchange between them. "Now, tell me…how deep can you go?"

"As deeply as you want me to go…"

"Trust me," he said, slyly. "It's not going to be deep enough."

She wondered what he meant until his next command explained everything.

"Draw it out of your drawer for me."

Shifting her gaze from the mirror to the nightstand, she released a moan of surrender. *She knew exactly what he meant.* She had teased him about it during one of their many casual sexting exchanges. But the truth was…it had been something she had never experimented with until after her breakup with Harvey. He had been the only man who could ever make her come, and after their marriage fell apart and they separated, she was forced to use a vibrator to initiate her own orgasms. Its existence had been such a shameful secret until her sexting affair with him had turned it into an empowering extension of her naughty persona. *How many of her secrets had she confessed to him*? She couldn't remember all of them. She only knew that it seemed impossible to hide anything anymore, including her desperate yearning to obey him.

"Do you have it in your hand?" he finally asked when the creaking hinges of the opening drawer betrayed her.

"Yes," she responded with a nod, slipping it out of its black satin pouch and trying to remember the last time she used it. *Far too long.*

"Good girl," he replied, pausing to savor the image. "Now, turn it on its lowest setting and let me hear you wet its tip with your tongue."

God, how he had mastered her. In less than five minutes, he had turned the tables and turned her own wicked attempt to tease him back on her. She obeyed his command and flicked on her vibrator, immediately feeling its titillating pulsations in the palm of her hand.

Hearing its low hum through her receiver, he whispered, "Lick it, then drop it down against your clit where I'm waiting for it."

She released an unfettered sigh and fell back against the mattress, spreading her legs and imagining him in her bedroom with her, kneeling before her, taking over in every way. The vibrations coursed through her pelvis as the fantasy of his presence heightened her arousal beyond her control. With her breathing accelerating, she fought to soften every pant, but there was no hiding her increasing desire to stimulate herself deeper and deeper.

"I want you to tell me how much you'd love to feel my cock inside you," he coaxed her.

"God, I'd love to feel…" but she could barely find the breath to finish the sentence.

"Push it deeper and switch it on stronger," he instructed her in that dangerous tone that she had come to love. "And tell me how much you wish it was my hard dick, sliding back and forth against your slickness."

Yessss...she wanted him to know that he was bringing her to the brink. *But would she be able to allow herself to fully let go*?

"Don't stop until..." Her voice faded away as she gave into her need to penetrate herself deeper and deeper, certain the swelling ache of repressed arousal would break her in half.

"Until I make you come," he stated, as if it had been his plan all along. "No, don't worry, my naughty Contessa...I'm not going to stop thrusting my cock into you until I hear you scream for mercy and beg for me to flip you over and force my way into you from behind. Can you take it?"

"I can't—" she answered, but her scant breath and the accelerating rhythm of her hand signaled that she was lying to him—and to herself.

"I think you can and you will. You're going to roll yourself over onto your belly and raise your ass in the air and imagine all the forbidden ways I plan to dominate you."

"How?" she asked, hearing her own voice quiver, already knowing the answer as she moved onto her hands and knees.

"I'm going to wrap my hands around those pretty smooth cheeks of yours and slide the wet head of my cock against your pretty pink pussy."

She sighed, breathy and inviting, while guiding the vibrator exactly where she knew he was describing. A shuddering ripple of pleasure undulated throughout her entire core. Involuntarily, she cried out.

"Good girl," he assuaged her. "Now, imagine that's how it's going to feel when I press my chest against your back and rock my entire cock into you."

Alma sighed and imagined it. *God, how she imagined it.* Bracing her weight onto her knees and lowering her head against the mattress, she allowed all the blood to rush into her cheeks with a tingling haze. Then, yielding to his order, she watched herself in the mirror as she shifted the vibrator behind her, penetrating her most tender spot. The change in position sent a shocking thrill of stimulation through her entire body. This time, she opened her mouth to scream, seeking to release the building pressure inside her, but nothing came out except a guttural groan for more.

"Deeper," he said firmly. "I don't want you to stop until I hear you come."

The vibrations pulsed through her, reverberating throughout her belly and backside, bobbing her back and forth towards the tantalizing waves of climax without fully sweeping her into their shores. *Could she endure them without pulling away*? Like a dismissive reflex, she shook her head. She did not want to disappoint him, but she couldn't do it alone.

"I can't…" she finally confessed.

"Yes, you can," he commanded her with militant certainty. "And you will because I'm not getting off this line until I hear you shriek."

She groaned with an exhale, knowing that she was at his mercy.

"Louder," he insisted.

"Yes," she moaned louder as the ebbing and flowing undercurrent of arousal increased in frequency.

"Fast and deep, fast and deep," he commanded her, tight and controlled.

"Yes, yes, yes…" She throttled her pace, enduring the sting of friction from the speed before she fully opened and seized with a shuddering ache, signaling the start of her first orgasm in over a year.

"Now, bear down and imagine my throbbing cock exploding its warm cum inside you."

Whatever expectations Alma had before their phone call, whatever she thought she knew about herself or their arrangement, was suddenly transformed in an instant when her body abandoned all its inhibitions and surrendered itself to a fluttering soprano scream—a scream of liberation that had eluded her in every other relationship with every other man.

Except one.

Now, that had all changed. Sighing in relief, she concentrated on how her entire body relaxed against the mattress and resonated with low, harmonious hums of satisfaction.

Cradling the phone to her ear, she listened to his own panting breaths withering into lulls, comforted by the fact that he had released himself only after he had released her.

After a long pause between them, he finally broke their smoldering connection of silence.

"Do you want more?"

"Yes…" she sinfully said, admitting what her body craved, despite her pride being too ashamed to confess it.

"Good," he said, rough and raspy. "Because I want you to know that the next time we do this, it's going to be in-person and it's going to be more than once."

Click.

Chapter Nine

The next morning, when Alma arrived to the train depot on Harvey's riverfront parcel, she caught herself humming.

Yes, literally humming.

It wasn't a specific song or recognizable tune, just a whimsical melody that signaled she wasn't worried about any of the challenges that lay ahead of her that day. And she certainly wasn't fazed by the one contentious person who posed the biggest challenge, despite the fact that she knew he would be there.

But her carefree humming quickly trailed off when she approached the front entrance of the dilapidated building and realized that the overgrowth of weeds and prairie grass had been cleared into a tidy, storybook pathway, luring her into his treacherous lair. She passed through the heavy wooden entrance, strangely free and clear of all the wild vegetation that had entangled it yesterday, and moved into the center of the lobby, noting the unobstructed swath of rainbow light shining over her.

"Good morning, sweetheart." Harvey's familiar booming voice rained down over the balcony. "You're just in time."

"For what?" she called back, squinting upwards and catching a glimpse of his bare chest, backlit against the patterned stained-glass window. The kaleidoscope of colors glinted off his pecs and tapered waist, making it obvious that he was shirtless.

"For the grand finale."

"Oh brother," she muttered to herself, half-expecting to witness his jeans and underwear being tossed over the balcony's railing. Despite being separated for more than a year, Alma was reminded of how the contours of his lean, naked body were not easily forgotten. *Seriously annoying*.

Then she remembered another annoying thing about him—he never wore underwear.

Replacing his safety goggles and adjusting his gloves, he revved the chainsaw twice before slicing it back and forth across the final tree branch.

"Aren't you coming up to have a better look?" he hollered at her.

"I think I prefer the view down here."

After several minutes of Texas Chainsaw massacre of helpless vegetation, Harvey finally stopped his destruction and descended the spiral staircase.

Alma wasn't prepared for his entrance and she caught herself—staring. Bare. Buff. Hulking. Sweat-glazed. And those were just impressions of his exposed, muscular chest that seemed to greet her before anything else. His denim jeans and the cowboy boots said "hello" next, even before he flashed her his typical "get-me-if-you-can" smile—all mood, attitude, and…sex. Intentionally brushing past her to retrieve the soda can on the side bench, she felt like she was in a commercial for men's low-rise jeans in which the leading man dusted off his backside with his leather gloves before offering her a taste from his own frosted and phallic Coca Cola bottle. Removing a glove with his teeth, he ran his hand through his dark slick hair, rebelliously sending it ten different directions of switchblade.

He always did the same thing whenever he exited the shower, she remembered, trying hard not to remember all the times she had seen him flick off his towel and rub it across his muscular body. He deliberately advanced his looming height into her personal space, reminding her of what it was like to smell his raw masculinity.

"You need a shower," she stated, attempting to remind him.

"I was waiting until you arrived," he quipped.

"I'm surprised you even waited to destroy the building. I half-expected you to go back on your word."

His pectoral muscle involuntarily flinched. "I considered it. But I wanted an excuse to have another conversation with you that didn't start with you screaming at me. Besides, my dearest ex…you might think the worst of me, but I made a promise and despite all my faults, I'm still a man of my word. Which is more than I can say about you."

"Which means what?" She crossed her arms and studied his devilish smile.

"You know…" he eyed her, taking a swig from his soda bottle. "Little Miss Bluffette."

She flopped down her backpack and adjusted her glasses. "How did you know?"

"Because your eyebrow twitches whenever you're bluffing, and you were twitching all over the place yesterday. Unless, of course, it was just because you were happy to see me."

She rolled her eyes—excessively.

"I'm pretty sure you believed me long enough to realize one thing—"

"That I'm still attracted to women who are smarter than me?"

"That feeling is going to go away fast when I tell you I still think these could be valuable Tiffany windows hidden for some reason in this run-down train depot."

"Well, your father doesn't even believe that's what it is. And he's smarter than both you and me combined."

"Is that why you're still involved in a bromance with him, despite being my ex?"

"Baseball fandom transcends divorce. It's man code."

"Well, you and your man code will be happy to know he's more on your side than on mine. He thinks it's your right to do whatever you want with this building because it's your own private property."

"Your father is an honorable man. But he's not the antique glass expert of the family. So that leaves me to rely on the opinion of my ex-wife. And in that situation, the man code states that I'm nothing short of being royally fucked."

"This man code of yours sounds pretty dismal."

"It's never failed me before."

"Maybe that's your problem. You don't know when you're failing it or when it's failing you."

He shrugged nonchalantly. "So let's test it. How about dinner with me tonight?"

She squared off and crossed her arms, daring him. "Not a chance."

"See?" he countered. "Exactly as I expected."

"Failure?"

"Man code 154: never expect your ex to cooperate with you unless you give her a very good reason."

"Like…?" she prodded him.

"Like…giving you more time to convince me that I should give you what you want—over dinner."

Alma narrowed her eyes, searching out his own agenda. "Just dinner? That sounds too…"

"Easy?" he offered.

"Innocent," she corrected him. "Especially for you."

"What's not innocent about McDonalds drive-thru?"

"Oh, I see. You're willing to splurge."

"I just know how much you hate those fancy five-star, five course restaurants. Especially the ones that I own."

"Yes, especially since I've heard you're serving a cocktail that's named after me."

"Rumors can be ugly things unless you consider the source."

"My sister. She said you drank five 'ballbusters' in her presence."

"Hmm," he paused before giving in like a guilty schoolboy. "It seems your sister is a reliable informant. I did almost go with 'nutcrusher' instead," he admitted, as if it was an acceptable alternative. "But ballbuster just rolls right off the tongue."

"How about a name that had nothing to do with the destruction of your anatomy?"

"Ex-wives don't get that privilege. Sorry."

"But we get McDonalds drive-thru?"

"Man code!" he rejoiced through cupped hands. "In fact, I'm pretty sure it's a mandatory event a year after a divorce."

"You mean like a divorce anniversary?" She was unconvinced.

"Exactly. A divorcary. We can even skip dinner and go straight to your favorite—dessert. Two apple pies and one sundae. Two spoons."

"I'm not sure if that sounds fun or depressing."

"Neither. Just for old times' sake," he answered, catching her hand and holding it as long as she would allow him, as if his genuine need to reclaim their past outweighed the present conflict between them. "It's been a long time and I know you clean up well."

Reaching out, he removed her glasses and wiped the lenses with his pocket handkerchief before sliding them back over the bridge of her nose. *Brazen bastard*, she thought, turning away from his smug smile. It was an intentional gesture of both intimacy and defiance. He had once known everything about her, and just because the law said they were no longer man and wife didn't change that fact.

"You clean up well, too," she tossed back, pushing forward and swiping away a cobweb from his broad shoulder.

He closed his eyes and dissolved into a shiver. "Please tell me you're bluffing again."

"No, I just suddenly remembered how much you hate spiders," she said, muting her smile while brushing him clean.

"Hate," he punctuated.

She nodded and circled around him, checking for their presence. He was such a fearless, confident man in every other way—except for his aversion to spiders. His pecs twitched again as her nails grazed the curve of his waistline.

When she circled back to face him, he unexpectedly ensnared her into his arms, pulling her against his hard, firm body.

"It's just dinner. And all you need to say is yes."

"Not true, Harvey. According to your man code, you're supposed to give me a good reason. And part of me fears that you're not going to be happy for long when I tell you what I want."

"I know what you want. You want me to save your precious window." He glanced up at the fully illuminated stained-glass window, casting raindrops of pink, lavender, turquoise, and emerald down upon them.

"But what about the other dozen smaller stained-glass windows along the perimeter of the main floor?"

"Are they Tiffany?" he pressed her.

She hedged. "Well…it's a possibility. They're probably not priceless, but still important and highly valuable."

Their eyes locked. *Highly valuable.* He seemed to chew on her words, carefully considering her meaning. If nothing else, she knew he would care about their monetary worth, and she suddenly resented him for it.

"I actually believed you that time," he finally said, studying her face. "But unfortunately, time isn't on my side, and salvaging historical artifacts isn't in my wheelhouse anymore."

"So that means you intend to bulldoze them without even considering rescuing them?"

"Rescuing all the windows?" He swept his eyes around the lobby. "Maybe. But rescuing the whole property? Not a chance. I've got a hundred million dollars riding on the sale of this parcel and demolition of this building is part of the deal. I am a businessman, after all, Alma. Not the fairy godfather of architectural antiques."

She glared at him like she wanted to sear a laser hole through his forehead. "Yes, I know. You made that very clear on the day you gave the greenlight to demolish the old Stock Exchange Building."

His jawline flinched, like he had just been slapped. He stood his ground and narrowed his eyes in response. "Is that what all this is really about?"

"It's a very similar situation, don't you think, Harvey?" she flung back.

"No, not at all, Alma." He pushed towards her. "A man died in that building. The floor collapsed beneath him."

"While trying to save the last few historical ornamentations designed by Adler and Sullivan before you destroyed them."

"He was trespassing inside a building that was condemned as a public safety hazard. Everyone in the city knew it, including you."

She scoffed. "I did and I tried to do something about it because I was married to the property owner—the man who could have renovated it, or at least helped stabilize the site. Instead, you exploited the tragedy of Richard's death as a reason to expedite the building's destruction. Then you sold the property for millions of dollars and never looked back. And you'll do the same thing with this property because that's all you care about now. Because that's all that's in your 'wheelhouse'."

Disgusted by her own memories of the past, she turned away from him, but he grabbed her by the wrist. "You're wrong. I look back every day. Every day. Trust me."

He searched her eyes for someone who used to be there.

"I don't trust you, Harvey," she replied, challenging his unwavering blue gaze. "Not anymore."

A subtle change crossed his face, as if she had punched him in the gut and he was fighting hard to pretend she hadn't injured him.

Intimately familiar. The phrase echoed through her mind as he glared at her. Yes, they had once been intimately familiar with each other, which ultimately meant they knew how to hurt each other worse than anyone else.

Stern and controlled, the tenor of his voice revealed how quickly the dynamic had changed between them. "Well, Miss Castillo, you can trust this: I'm not about to let anyone else trespass on my property, especially not scavenging for anything in the name of preservation. So thank you for your time. But now, it's time to get off my property."

"Now *that's* a plan that I finally can get behind..."

The sharp female voice rang out against the plaster walls like a dissonant bell. Alma turned around and spotted a tall woman wearing flashy chandelier earrings and jangling bracelets strutting through the front entrance in her five-inch platform heels. Her full-length leopard print coat swept by Alma like a queen's coronation robe. The woman tossed her long black hair over her shoulders and peered at Harvey through distracting fake eyelashes.

"Oh God, Harvey," she cried out with orgasmic glee, taking in Harvey's exposed muscles, still glazed with sweat. "I love it when you've got your shirt off and your cowboy boots on because it usually means you're going to get down and dirty. And nobody does dirty better than Harvey Zale." The woman grinned and flicked her black eyelashes at him, just to be certain he caught her meaning.

Pretending to gather up her things, Alma glanced away. But she felt her cheeks flush hot and red. In her torn denim overalls, sneakers, and mousy ponytail, it was hard for Alma not to feel inferior around a woman who physically towered over her like an Amazonian goddess. Plus, Alma was already on the defensive. She was the scorned ex-wife. This woman was clearly someone on Harvey's side—and quite possibly, someone who shared Harvey's bed.

Harvey retrieved his white undershirt and slipped it on with one suave stroke. Then, he replaced his wallet in his back pocket and his gold watch on his wrist, its crystal face glinting in the morning sunlight.

"I'm surprised to see you here, Nicolette," he said, wiping his face and neck with the edge of his undershirt. "It takes a lot for you to get up by ten in the morning, even if it means seeing me."

Nicolette threw her head backwards and laughed aloud like he had just tickled her in the naughtiest of ways.

Alma shot him a glance. Only five minutes ago, he had been flirting with her like a lost lover. *And now*? Now, he seemed as cold and callous as a stranger in a bar, cruising for a one-night stand with the prettiest woman in the room.

"I heard through the grapevine about your temporary insanity," Nicolette replied. "Stalling the destruction of this property in order to entertain some kind of a request for charity? But it looks like the grapevines are all gone and you've come to your senses."

"It's not charity," Alma spat out, unable to contain herself. "It's a legitimate request for historical preservation of this site."

Nicolette glanced at her, pretending it was the first time she had noticed someone other than Harvey in the room. "And you are?" she sang out, looking down at Alma from the bridge of her surgically-enhanced rhinoplasty nose.

"His temporary insanity," she fired back.

"Well..." Nicolette mused. "I can see there's no reason here to worry that it will be permanent."

Harvey stepped in front of Alma, interjecting an introduction, but only because he sensed that Alma might punch her. "This is Nicolette Mead. My commercial real estate lawyer."

"Real estate lawyer—by day," Nicolette scolded him. "But by night, I'm usually the only woman able to keep up with Harvey at the bar and on the dance floor."

"That reminds me," Harvey said, pulling out his phone and checking his calendar. "We've got the Anderson Gala this Sunday."

"Oh, darling, I don't need the reminder!" Nicolette cried out with her crystalline voice. "I've already picked out my gown and ordered you a matching tie."

Darling? A matching tie? Alma had to suppress the gag swelling up from her throat. That used to be *her* job, attending high-class functions with Harvey when he began acquiring upscale commercial buildings in favor of run-down properties with historical value. She was even planning on attending the same gala—just not with him this year. But now, as she stared at Nicolette—with her glinting jewelry and elaborate hair extensions—she accepted the fact that she had been officially replaced by a woman who perhaps would be better suited for Harvey than she had ever been.

Like a whisper of relief, her phone hummed inside the deep pockets of her overalls.

Tell me where we're meeting tonight...

Alma sighed. *Her mystery suitor*. It was a welcomed distraction from Harvey's moody game-playing. She rushed into a far corner of the train depot to ensure her privacy.

But when she re-read his text again, she reeled from the implications of his proposition. *A real-life physical encounter?*

She caught Harvey's gaze, tracking her from the opposite side of the depot's lobby as he scrolled through his own phone, impatiently expecting her to return to the battlefield. *Ugh, the battlefield*. The last thing she felt like engaging in was a war with an ex-lover, especially a man who seemed intent on punishing her for initiating their separation.

Like an escape, she slipped into the sassy persona that he had come to expect from her and she pinged him back. *You can't even wait twenty-four hours before you need more of me?*

I definitely need more, he replied without a beat. *I made you a promise last night, and there's one thing I hope you've learned about me by now—I never break my promises.*

Alma's hands trembled. *More than once*. That was his promise to her last night at the end of their phone call—to meet her in-person and make her come more than once. She glanced up, staring straight ahead at the only other man who had ever given her that pleasure. Harvey was ignoring her, consumed by his own phone messages—and his own life that had moved on without her.

Since you're the one making all the promises, you name the place, she texted back, feeling him out. If he offered some suburban address in a dingy apartment, she knew it was time to bail.

Then, before he had the chance to reply, she gave herself an out. *And I'll warn you now...proposing to meet is setting yourself up for a dangerous challenge. If you don't impress me within the first seconds of hello, then you risk making it good-bye forever.*

She paused, watching her screen shadow over when he failed to answer back.

After an eternity, he zinged his final message: *The Peoria. Bar lounge on the 66th floor. 8pm tonight. And don't worry, Contessa. The only danger is that I'll succeed in making you want to stay until the morning.*

Alma had about ten seconds to indulge in the fantasy of waking up with him the next morning before Harvey slipped his own phone in his rear jeans pocket and squared off against her.

Back to the battlefield, she thought.

"Well, I can certainly see why you'd want to demolish this building," Nicolette declared with a shiver. "It feels like a tomb in here with all this cold, white marble and dark windows."

With the sun rising from the east, only the grand gothic-shaped window in the balcony was fully illuminated. The remaining windows were dark and unimpressive, their normally resplendent glass appearing dreary and opaque without direct sunlight.

"Yeah, and I'm not in the business of preserving tombs," Harvey said dryly, gathering up his shirt and slinging it over his shoulder. "I'll have my crew spend the rest of the day removing as many of these windows as they can before sunset, but then after that, it's over," he warned Alma. "There's no reason to keep fighting me over an old train depot that offers nothing but the false promise of something more."

The false promise of something more...the words rang in her head as she studied his cold, confrontational gaze. Years ago, he had been willing to stand by her to search out priceless artifacts abandoned by a superficial world that no longer valued them. Now, she was still holding onto the glimmer of hope that he wasn't really a part of that world, but instead, a part of her world that aimed to protect precious things that had long since been forgotten. But she was wrong and he was right. She was still clinging onto the false promise of something more; the false promise that perhaps he could still change back into the same man she once knew; the false promise that he could still change back into the same man she had once loved.

"And as Harvey's lawyer," Nicolette squawked like his pet parrot, "I'll do whatever it takes to ensure that no one prevents him from selling it whenever and however he chooses." Alma heard her, but pretended that she didn't.

"I'll go call the buyers now, Harvey, and let them know that everything is moving forward as planned." Nicolette withdrew her phone from her bubblegum pink designer handbag and flicked her fake eyelashes around the room with a condescending sneer. "One hundred million dollars is a lot of money—much more money than anything on this property could possibly be worth."

When Amazon Woman was safely out of earshot, Alma gave in to Harvey.

"Fine. Whatever you salvage can be sent to my father's antique shop. He'll send you the paperwork about representing them at auction and make sure the compensation will be worth your time and effort. But you're right. The rest of the fighting isn't worth it...not anymore."

They held each other's gaze. It had been a year of heartache and misplaced blame. And yet, cutting into scars from the past seemed more painful than moving forward into the future, bleeding and alone.

She stared at him, staring back at her, noticing the light in his eyes soften from anger into a strange mixture of bewilderment. She had simply spoken the truth—nothing more, nothing less. She hadn't intended to wound him—

ever. It was simply the result of two people who knew each other's strengths, but only focused on each other's weaknesses.

When his eyes settled uncomfortably onto her chest, she glanced down and noted the shadowy silhouette of a keyhole, patterned against the bib of her overalls.

Harvey pushed forward, inspecting the mysterious shape. "Tell me something," he said, low and cautious. "How is it that you—and your witchy ways—always seem to make magical things like that happen?" With the tip of his finger, he traced the keyhole silhouette over the denim of her overalls, just to be certain it was real. The sensation of his touch between her breasts made her want to slap him, if it hadn't already made her yearn for more.

"I don't know," Alma whispered, lowering her chin to inspect the curious illusion herself. "But this witch doesn't feel like being burned at the stake anymore by billionaire Harvey Zale, so it's probably better not to find out."

With his firm knuckles, he nudged her aside, allowing the silhouette to drop onto the white marble floor and cast a shadow onto a square panel of stone directly in front of them.

Turning his attention above them, he shielded his eyes from the direct ray of sunlight passing through the lantern in the mother's hand of the stained-glass window in the balcony.

"Yeah, I'm pretty certain it would be better, too," Harvey agreed, taking in the source of the enigmatic symbol. "But the problem is...you never manage to bring out the reserved side in me."

Without warning, he took up the sledgehammer from a side bench into his hands and slammed it right into the shadow of the keyhole, obliterating the marble beneath it with one violent stroke.

Alma covered her ears as a choking cloud of dust wafted through the air, obscuring the pile of rubble left behind in its wake. Harvey moved forward and picked through it, discarding shards of stone like a man intent on proving himself wrong. *He wasn't wrong*, Alma thought, the moment he lifted a metallic tin box from beneath the shattered floor and presented it to her. *He rarely was wrong*. It was still the one thing she loved and hated about him.

"You do the honors, Miss Castillo. It's your treasure hunt."

Their eyes locked again. This time, his adventurous blue eyes filled her with a familiar sensation—allegiance.

She peeled open the creaking lid of the dusty tin box and said, "Unfortunately, it probably opens something on this property." Like an omen, she displayed the antique skeleton key in the palm of her hand. "I doubt you'll be interested in playing Indiana Jones much longer if it means delaying your closing."

"Oh, I dunno. Does the gig comes with a cool Fedora hat?"

"Unlikely. It wouldn't exactly match the cowboy boots." Her eyes drifted down to his favorite footwear, remembering the exact moment she had picked them out for him during their honeymoon in Vegas. *Black ostrich leather.* Somehow the wild, daring spirit of a cowboy fit the South Side Chicago boy she had loved.

"Well, then…I guess I'll just have to settle for the whip." His smile twinkled at her. In that moment, they were newlyweds again.

Passing her thumb over the handle of the key, Alma curiously noted the inscription. Squinting hard at the tiny cursive engraving, she read aloud from it. "*In my darkest hour, the only peace I doth keep is—*" But she struggled to make out the final phrase.

Harvey took the key away from her to inspect it himself. "*—the promise of our eternal love*," he said, finishing the sentence before breaking into unexpected laughter. He glanced up at the stained-glass window in the balcony, then back down at the keyhole silhouette that had almost disappeared with the change of light. Then, he ran his hand through his hair and muted his bemused smile, as if he was trying to determine why the universe had bestowed this hoax upon him.

"Harvey—" Alma pleaded for something she could only articulate with her eyes.

He held up his hand to silence her. "That key could open any door in the city. Hundreds of thousands of doors. And you know it."

"Yes, I know," she answered, acknowledging the improbability of finding its match.

"It could take years," he insisted. "Or more likely…never."

"I know," she nodded, closing her eyes in surrender, preparing to endure the sting of his rejection—again.

Sighing with frustration, he lifted the tin canister and wiped its lid clean before handing it off to Alma. "There's another inscription etched into the tin of the canister's lid."

Alma furrowed her brow, wondering how she had missed it. "What does it say?"

"Give the lady what she wants," he read aloud.

For a moment, she thought he was joking. But the foreboding tone in his voice told her otherwise. Perplexed, Alma gazed down at it. "That's the Marshall Fields' slogan."

"Yep," Harvey replied, like he didn't need convincing.

"Harvey…" Alma chose her words carefully. "Field was a huge benefactor of Tiffany's glass artwork at the Chicago Exposition in 1893. It's one of the reasons why the Field's building has two Tiffany mosaic glass ceiling domes."

“Give the lady what she wants,” Harvey repeated dryly, as if he couldn’t believe the irony of the situation. Slipping on his blue denim shirt and buttoning it up over his undershirt, he peered at her, sidelong. “Looks like it’s going to be my slogan now.”

A flash of adrenaline coursed through Alma’s heart as her false promise of something more just became true.

Just then, Nicolette clopped back into the building like a Clydesdale and announced her victory. “Everything is taken care of…” Her high-pitched voice resonated into the rafters, disturbing a pair of mourning doves.

Gathering up his worn canvas messenger bag and slinging it sideways across his chest, he turned to Nicolette, commanding her attention. “Good. Because we’re delaying the closing.”

“What?” Nicolette choked on her own disbelief. “But Harvey, that’s impossible. We *have* to close—”

“And we will,” he said cavalierly. “But for now, tell the buyers that my ex-wife has just laid claim to the property. So we’ll need another day to clear the title.”

Nicolette glanced at Alma, then back at Harvey. With her bracelets rattling like her voice, she sputtered out her exasperation. “No, Harvey, no. We absolutely cannot!”

“Sure, we can, darlin’. Happens all the time,” he stressed with a smirk. “Being divorced is a real bitch.”

Chapter Ten

G*ive the lady what she wants…* It was the first thing that flashed through Harvey's mind when they entered the grand foyer of the iconic Marshall Field's building.

*Makeup, purses, gloves, jewelry, lingerie, stockings…*he surveyed all the luxurious women's goods that lined the aisles and counters of the historical department store. His gaze drifted upwards to the vaulted ceiling, suspended five stories above them and decorated with an intricate mosaic of sparkling iridescent glass. *Yep, Marshall Field knew what women wanted and he created a sanctuary for them to shop for it.*

Too bad for Harvey, his woman didn't want to shop for blue eyeshadow or a leather handbag. His woman wanted priceless Louis Comfort Tiffany art.

Lucky fucking him.

He contemplated the absurdity of his situation as he followed his ex-wife through the modern department store, as if she knew exactly where she intended to find a nineteenth-century mythical treasure.

"Okay, Mr. Tiffany," Harvey hollered up at the vaulted dome. "Just tell us where you've hidden your hundred million dollar window and we'll be on our merry way."

Oblivious to the mosaic masterpiece that arched above their heads, casual shoppers bustled around him, browsing through the merchandise that lined the glass countertops.

Yes, he was mocking her. And he was mocking them. He was mocking the entire situation because it was ridiculous. But that's what she always inspired in him—insanity.

Turning a cold shoulder on him, she peered up at the dome, as if she could actually decipher a hidden message encrypted within the millions of pieces of shimmering mosaic glass.

Those damn overalls, he thought, noting the sewn holes on the back pockets of her overalls. *And she considered herself low-maintenance, despite dragging him here to chase century-old myths*. He scoffed. The noise made Alma glance back at him.

"Heartburn." He feigned chest pain.

"Because you're worrying about losing your one hundred-million-dollar deal?" she asked, almost as if she actually cared about thwarting one of the biggest real estate deals of his career.

"No, I just ate too many onions with that hotdog."

"Yeah, I saw that. I even thought about warning you. You had a stomach ulcer even when we were married."

"You mean *because* we were married?"

"You can blame me all you want, but I'm not the one who scarfed down an entire pile of onion rings and cheese fries."

"I'll only blame you if you make me kiss you with bad breath. That's never pleasant for anyone."

He wanted to see just how far he could push it. *Not very far*.

"You won't have to worry about that."

Her certainty invigorated him.

"No?" He exhaled into his cupped hands and took a whiff, just to be as juvenile as possible. "It's pretty bad."

But, of course, she ignored him and kept walking through the aisles of the department store.

"Anyway…let's wait and see, Miss Castillo. You're auto-programmed to doubt me, but I've got a knack for proving you wrong. So let's just admit there's a chance you'll end up changing your mind when my key fits into your keyhole."

He held up the key and brushed past her to assume the lead.

"When?" she repeated, calling him out on his arrogance. "I'm pretty sure you told me it could take years…or never. Sounds like spending time with me is turning you into an optimist."

"Optimistic that you're actually enjoying it," he wise-cracked.

"Enjoying is an overstatement. Tolerating is closer to the truth."

"Negative attention is better than no attention." Harvey passed by a rack of furry snow bunny earmuffs and slipped a pair over his head like oversized headphones. "That's part of my game plan. The more time you spend with me, the more ways you'll likely behave in ways you know you shouldn't." He flashed her a flirtatious smile.

"Like kissing a man with onion breath wearing earmuffs?"

He suddenly stopped, letting her bump into him—intentionally—and grinned. "Exactly."

He enjoyed the way she gripped his bicep as she faltered, attempting to regain her balance. *Still clumsy as ever*, he thought, as she peered up at him with a frown, expecting an explanation. He considered kissing her. *Would that be a good enough explanation*?

"Did you forget to put one foot in front of the other?"

He took the liberty to adjust her crooked glasses. "I forgot you're the one who knows where the hell we're supposed to be going."

Realizing he was right, she traded places with him, leading the charge with a brisker pace, leaving him behind in her wake. She was proving she didn't need him—her favorite thing to do these days—which was exactly why he couldn't resist attempting to lure her back to him.

"Is there something I can help you with?" The sweet voice came from the young sales clerk at the jewelry counter.

Harvey turned towards her. "Yes, my ex-wife—the one who's ignoring me." Then, he decided to get creative. "She and I are looking for something to exchange when we renew our wedding vows."

"Aww…that's such a lovely sentiment," the young woman replied. "I can certainly help you find something for that. Do you have anything in mind?"

The sales clerk's warm smile put him at ease. "Well, Maribel," he said, noting her nametag. "Something not too conventional or flashy. My wife isn't exactly the modern gold and glitz type. And not something that fits on her hands. She lost the first engagement ring during her pottery class. It's still buried inside the lopsided vase sitting on the windowsill in our house."

Surprised, Maribel opened her gorgeous brown eyes even wider. "You mean you didn't try to break it open to recover the ring?"

Harvey smiled. He had heard that suggestion before. "It was the first vase she ever threw on a potting wheel. She was pretty excited about that. You can destroy and replace a ring, but you can't destroy and replace memories."

"Okay, then." Maribel nodded in agreement. "So no rings and no modern gold and glitz. Any other considerations?"

Harvey leaned into the glass counter, studying Maribel's innocent gaze that made him want to confess everything. "Just that she hates me and we're actually divorced. But if you help me pick the right piece of jewelry, maybe there's a chance I can win her back."

Maribel glanced over at Alma and smiled like she had heard it all before. "Well, she looks like a rather sensible woman."

"That's her talent. *Looking* sensible."

"And women generally *are*," Maribel countered, eyeing the furry women's earmuffs over his head. "It's the men in our lives who might make us behave otherwise."

"Fair enough," Harvey said, removing the earmuffs and noting how mature she seemed for her age.

Glancing through the jewelry counter, Maribel sighed and considered the challenge. "So you think just the right piece of jewelry will really do the trick?"

"No, probably not," he conceded. "But it's a lot more sensible than what she really wants, which is trying to figure out which keyhole in this building fits with this key." He held up the key like a nuisance, resisting the urge to toss it into the nearby trashcan.

"Oh, that's easy!" Maribel exclaimed. "I know that key. It looks exactly like my key."

Turning away from him, she unlocked a white drawer under the register and pulled out a formidable ring of keys. Finding the match, she paired them together and presented her discovery to Harvey. "See? It's the key to the old freight elevator that leads to the basement."

Maribel pointed to a private corridor in the far corner of the grand lobby.

Harvey stood up straighter when he realized she was right—the two skeleton keys were an exact match. "What's in the basement?"

"Well, there's the public pedway as well as the candy department," Maribel replied. "But the old freight elevator leads to a private section where there's a bathroom that all the girls on the floor like to use because it's the prettiest one in the building."

"Any chance there's a stained-glass window in it?"

Maribel paused in thought. "Why, yes. Actually, there is."

Harvey's skeptical smile faded away. "Thank you, Maribel. I'm pretty certain you just saved my marriage."

Maribel narrowed her eyes at him and teased, "I thought you were divorced."

"Only on paper," he countered with a wink, taking up her sales card and stuffing it into his back pocket. "And when I get her to say 'yes' again, I promise to call you for that jewelry recommendation."

"No rings. No modern gold or glitz. I'll remember." Maribel nodded as Harvey backed away with a salute and returned to Alma's side.

"Found it," he declared, snatching the straps of her overalls and dragging her into the far corner of the lobby.

"What?" she insisted, attempting to free herself from his clasp.

"Your precious *Eternal Love*."

Alma halted near the perfume section and crossed her arms. "Oh, really? You found it?"

"Yep."

"Where?" she challenged him.

"In the woman's bathroom in the basement," Harvey announced, like it was the most obvious place in the world to hide a priceless Tiffany stained-glass window.

"In the woman's bathroom?" Alma repeated, just to verify he heard his own insanity.

"Yep."

Alma rolled her eyes and dismissively settled her attention on the perfume bottles—anything other than his grand revelation, just to signal what little faith she had in it. Spritzing perfume onto her wrist, she tested its scent and rubbed it across her neckline. "Frankly, I expected more from you, Mr. Jones."

"Call me, Indy," he replied. Guiding her towards him, he kissed her mercilessly on the lips. She resisted him at first. *Of course, she would*...until his tongue melted into her lush mouth, reminding her what it was like to do more than just tolerate him.

When she closed her eyes, surrendering her body into his embrace, he lost himself in the memories of making love to her. Pressing his chest against her breasts and drawing her hips to his own, he overpowered her with every arousing stroke of his desire, conveying everything he had missed in the year they had been apart, until he forced himself to pull away from her, just to prove to her that she still needed him.

Passing his nose along the hollow of her throat, he whispered. "And my perfume is still better than that."

"True," she whispered back, attempting to recover her balance—and purpose in life.

"C'mon," he said, controlling his desire to win her back with another impulsive deep-throated kiss. "Let's finish what we've started."

He led them through a private door, marked STAFF ONLY, but she tugged back on his hand.

"Harvey...I'm not going to have sex with you in the basement of Marshall Field's."

"Who said anything about the basement?" he tossed back, advancing towards the heavy pair of iron elevator doors, barring the entrance like a fortress, at the end of the corridor.

"Or an elevator—" she insisted.

"Give me fifteen seconds to change your mind..."

Like magic, the doors slowly rolled open. Harvey took it as a sign to ignore her.

Sweeping her up into his arms, he carried her into the elevator cab and eyed the keyhole just below the interior call button. Taking the key from her and thrusting it into the hole, he braced Alma's body against the wall as it shuddered into motion. His mouth hovered over her lips, feeling her hot, accelerating breath feathering his chin. *Just give in, woman.* Peering deeply into her eyes, he was waiting for a sign—just one damn little sign that she wanted him—*needed* him—the same way he throbbed and ached for her. But her taunting gaze only dared him to try to convince her. Slowly, they descended downwards with a cavernous groan of steel. That was their relationship—a furious, incessant, uncompromising tug of war, equal in every way. *Which made him want her in every way.*

When the elevator chimed and its doors slid open, he heard the overzealous squeal ricochet off the walls of the metal cab before he saw its source.

"Oh. My. God. You're humping in the elevator!?"

Harvey turned towards the gum-cracking voice behind them.

"Oh my God, it is really you!" Conchita exclaimed.

"And you're in the secret 'staff only' basement of the Field's building because...?" Harvey questioned her, hoping Alma's sister was a figment of his imagination.

"She works here," Alma clarified, looking more annoyed than ever, slipping out of his arms and into the long white-washed corridor leading to an unknown destination. The voices of shoppers above them murmured through the vents and galvanized pendant lampshades marked their path like fireflies. Just ahead were a set of French doors with an inviting interior glow, brightening their panes of beveled lead glass.

"In the candy department," Conchita added, chewing hard on her bubble gum and unabashedly adjusting her push-up bra. "I'm down here, like...five times a day. Depending on how good the free coffee is on the sixth floor." Turning to Alma, she gushed, "My God, my God! Is this really happening? Have you guys finally made up?"

"Made up or made out?" Harvey quipped.

"Either!" Conchita clapped with a bounce, like she would take whatever she could get.

"Neither," Alma stressed. "We're just here to use the bathroom."

"Together," he said, insinuating as much as he could.

Alma rolled her eyes while Conchita giggled. That's how it always had been between them. Conchita loved him like a loyal dog. Alma made him work for it like a heartless cat.

"So you're here...together...using the bathroom, eh?" Conchita rubbed elbows with Harvey like she got the man code.

Harvey's eyes tracked Alma as she pushed through the French doors and into the women's bathroom. "Your sister is also in the process of ruining my one hundred-million-dollar real estate deal unless we find her priceless Tiffany stained-glass window hiding in this basement. But that's just my ulterior motive to get her to talk to me."

Conchita reached out and wiped the lip gloss off his upper lip. "Looks like you guys were doing more than just talking."

"I came. I swooned. I conquered. And..." Harvey's voice trailed off like a drum roll. "Your sister still hates me."

"Ballbuster," Conchita said with a smack of her gum.

He suddenly remembered that the name of the drink had been suggested by her, not him. And now, he remembered why he went along with it—because it was true.

Harvey followed his ex-sister-in-law into the women's bathroom. "Yeah, and unless I find this Tiffany window, I don't think I've got a chance in hell of getting Alma back." His gaze flicked up to a small, unimpressive rectangular window, patterned with geometric shapes of stained glass. "And unfortunately, something tells me...that ain't it."

"I hate to break it to you, but there's nothing 'priceless' hiding inside this bathroom except for my secret stash of Twizzlers and tampons."

"There's not a Tiffany window in here," Alma repeated Harvey's assessment as she studied all the bathroom walls, patterned with iridescent snowflakes. "But I think this might actually be original Tiffany snow crystal wallpaper." She pushed closer to the wallpaper, holding herself back from touching it directly. Even underneath the bathroom's modest lighting, gilded silver and gold geometric shapes glinted like icicles against a power blue background, mimicking the spiral of snowflakes floating down to earth during a sunny winter morning.

"I just thought it was vintage Martha Stewart," Conchita replied. "You know, before she went to jail and got all into cooking with Snoop Dog."

"Wallpaper was a huge fad in the 1890s," Alma corrected her. "Every major designer in America was creating their own signature patterns, including Tiffany. But I'm not sure...I've never seen real examples of it. Only black and white pictures. It's incredibly rare. Most examples have been lost to fire or demolition, or maybe even plastered over during renovations. But this wallpaper actually looks original to the building, like no one's bothered to touch it for over a hundred years."

"You do realize your brain is like a little Wikipedia page," Conchita said.

"More like one of those fast-talking QVC saleswomen," Harvey chimed in. "With their Ritalin-addicted crazy eyes."

Alma turned to face him, just to be sure he saw the glare in her eyes. "You think I'm bluffing again?"

"I think you believe what you want to believe when it's convenient for you to believe it."

"When you love something, you follow it to its bitter end," she muttered like a secret code. "I know you've never understood that concept, Harvey."

"Oh, I understand it. Believe me. Especially when it fights so hard against you that you realize the ending isn't just bitter—it's dead."

His macho instinct to fight got the best of him, but the moment he spoke the words, he wanted to shove them back down his own throat and choke himself to death.

Exhaling with a frustrated sigh, he moved away from her and dropped his head like a man who had just realized he'd won the lottery before accidentally flushing the golden ticket down the toilet. One minute, he had her in his arms, kissing her like she was still his wife; the next minute, he was her ex and every dumb-stupid-idiotic thing he said just reinforced it.

Secretly, he caught a glimpse of her expression in the decorative wall mirror—that same mixture of disappointment and disapproval that had become so familiar whenever he failed to meet her expectations. *Fuck.*

"Oh dear Lord, all this talk of bitter, dead ends is giving me a yeast infection!" Conchita complained. "Now, you both are just acting like a miserable old married couple."

"Except we're not married anymore," Harvey corrected her.

"And Harvey prefers divas now," Alma added.

"And you know what they say about old, crabby couples?" he countered with one final jab. "They're so damn crabby because they're usually the only ones willing to listen to the other's bullsh…"

But he failed to finish the punchline when something in the mirror distracted him from its delivery. "Gu-i-d-ing…an-ge-l?" Harvey sounded out the strange pattern of letters that he was making out in the reflection of the mirror. "Does guiding angel mean anything to you?"

Alma nodded slowly, noting the expression on his face, as if he had just seen a ghost.

"Okay, you win, Miss Castillo. Because our boy Tiffany is sending you a message."

He pointed out the letters, hidden within the snow crystal wallpaper in the reflection, but appearing backwards in plain sight.

"Guiding angel," Alma read aloud, verifying the encrypted phrase in the mirror's reflection. "He must mean his stained-glass window, *Guiding Angel*. It's an example of one of the many memorial windows that his studio made for his first clients, but I don't think they know who commissioned it or why. It's on display in the Stained Glass Gallery at Navy Pier."

"Navy Pier?" Harvey heaved a sigh of exasperation. "This guy really had no sense of geographic economy."

"Well, Harvey…if this is truly a treasure hunt, Tiffany would have set it up without knowing where his pieces would end up a hundred years later. You're lucky I didn't say Paris or London."

"No, you're lucky because there's no way I'm going to Europe. And at this point, Navy Pier is a stretch."

"What's the matter, Harvey? Got a hot date tonight?" Conchita quipped.

"Several," he declared.

"That makes two of us," Alma unexpectedly added.

Both Harvey and Conchita stared at her. Then, Harvey remembered Alma in the lingerie shop—and those white virgin stockings.

"Ohmygod!" Conchita braced her sister's forearm. "With RomeroLuvsItSlow?"

Alma held her tongue and challenged his envious gaze.

"You give up your plans tonight and I'll give up mine," he suddenly offered.

Was he serious about giving up his plans tonight to meet up with his mysterious Contessa? He didn't know. But he did know that he needed to test how serious Alma was about meeting RomeroLuvsItSlow.

"We could plan to go tomorrow morning instead," Alma suggested as a compromise.

Jealousy tightened his chest. *Clearly she was serious.*

"No," he fired back. "My real estate deal can't wait that long."

She narrowed her eyes at him, as if she knew he was intentionally pressuring her to choose—her date tonight with Romero or the opportunity to continue chasing long-lost Tiffany art with Monsieur Asshole. Unfortunately, he miscalculated, failing to remember one of the most important characteristics about his ex-wife: she was not a woman who would allow herself to be cornered by anyone, especially not by her billionaire ex-husband.

"Fine then," she surrendered in an even tone. "Go ahead with your harem of women tonight and your building demolition tomorrow. Just leave me the skeleton key, and I'll go to Navy Pier on my own. Like you said, salvaging precious artifacts isn't in your wheelhouse anymore, so there's no reason to waste any more of your valuable time. Besides, you're probably right. It's probably just a dead end, anyway."

Ballbuster.

He shouldn't have felt the sting as deep as he did. After all, they were his own cruel words, boomeranged back at him. She held out her hand, waiting for him to drop the key into it. *Her final gesture of independence*. She didn't care anymore what he did because she no longer needed him, and perhaps that was the true source of the sting—her apathy wounded him more than her anger and disapproval.

For a moment, he thought about arguing to keep the key. It had been found on his property, after all. He had the right to keep it without turning it over to anyone—not even her. But if he kept it, he would be doing it for the wrong reasons. *Petty, selfish, juvenile reasons.* And sadly, he would be keeping it as a means for keeping her in his life—just a little bit longer. But clearly there was nothing in the world she wanted less than to continue to associate with him.

With the gentlest touch he could muster, he placed the key in her palm, closed it into a fist, and sealed it with his kiss. It would be the last time he would kiss her and he intended to remember it. *Wildberry hand lotion.* Her skin still tasted the same.

"Enjoy the treasure hunt, Miss Castillo," he said, holding her gaze, wanting to be clear there was no mockery or condescension in his voice. "I hope you find something that will make you happy."

He didn't wait for her response, nor did he say anything more—not even to Conchita. He simply pushed out the French double doors of the bathroom and walked down the lonely corridor where he rode the elevator back up to street level. Later, when he recounted the moment in his mind, he was unable to tell himself what expression she had on her face.

Probably relief.

After dodging several taxis to cross State Street and aimlessly meandering along Michigan Avenue, he ended up on the grand granite steps of the Cultural Center.

Realizing there was still an hour before its doors closed at dusk, he pulled out his phone and quickly sent the text.

I'm leaving you a gift at our regular spot. I expect you to wear it for me tonight.

Circling the corner of Washington Avenue, he waited an eternity for her response. She always made him wait. Finally, the vibration buzzed against his palm.

You're a very demanding man. What makes you think I'm even in the area?

He re-read her text. *God, he loved that moment.* The moment she sassed back. Invigorated, his chest expanded like he was inhaling fire. It was true. He was a demanding man, and he liked it when she put him in his place.

Because we're meeting tonight at the Peoria, and I doubt you would agree to that unless you're a downtown girl.

Harvey paced up and down the street while waiting for her response. After an eternity, she finally quenched his desire.

Maybe I'll end up being someone different than who you expect...

He paused and pondered her point. *What did he expect?* Nothing, actually. Nothing, other than to continue their affair because he needed to escape from everyone, including himself.

The only thing I expect is for you to be wearing my gift.

I doubt you'll be able to top your first one, she pinged back.

True again. He'd originally bought that gift—a rare antique diamond choker—for Alma for their fifth wedding anniversary, two weeks before she served him divorce papers. It was a one-of-a-kind vintage piece that cost him more than his speedboat, and it felt like a sick form of therapy to finally give it away to another woman. She was right; there was no topping it. But that didn't mean he couldn't relish the challenge of buying something specifically for her.

Probably not, he replied. *But this time, I'll actually have the chance to feel it against my own lips.*

He loved pushing the physical boundaries of their affair. She probably never thought he would take it this far, and neither did he. Their phone call had been the first successful breech. Tonight would be the next. *Yes, he wouldn't be able to top his gift to her.* But he would be able to top the way he planned to seduce her. And if nothing else, he was still a man who kept his promise.

He gazed at his phone, remaining silent. It always did whenever he promised to cross the invisible line she set for him. Pulling the business card out from his back pocket, he dialed the number and retraced his steps back to State Street.

"Hello there, Maribel…This is Harvey Zale. I was just at your jewelry counter about an hour ago, looking for something to impress my ex-wife. Yes, well…let's just say, I've given it some thought and I'd like to swing by again to pick up something that caught my eye."

Chapter Eleven

Because we're meeting tonight at the Peoria, and I doubt you would agree to that unless you're a downtown girl.

Alma's face flushed in anticipation, first reacting to the implications of his text, and then as a symptom of her insecurities. *Would she actually have the courage to meet him tonight?*

Maybe I'll end up being someone different than who you expect...

After she sent her response, she regretted it. It betrayed her deepest fear, but she couldn't help it. Playing the role of a sassy, sex goddess behind the shield of her phone was much easier than the prospect of meeting him—face-to-face—and fulfilling his fantasy of that persona.

"Who are you texting like a teenager?" Conchita eyed her sister's reflection through the bathroom mirror while applying frosted lip gloss. "And why didn't you tell me you had a hot date tonight?"

"Because I'm not certain I'm actually going to go through with it." Alma held her phone like a rosary, praying for his next response to guide her decision.

The only thing I expect is for you to be wearing my gift.

Her heart fluttered in wonderment. What else could he possibly want to give her?

She texted back her response. *I doubt you'll be able to top your first one.* She was playing hard to impress, because she knew he liked it. But secretly, she couldn't wait to walk—no sprint—over to the Cultural Center.

"Well, looks to me like you've got a fish on the line who's tugging at your G-string." Conchita smacked her lips with a pop and gathered up her purse.

Probably not, he shot back. *But this time, I'll actually have the chance to feel it against my own lips.*

Alma stuffed her phone into her overalls pocket, trying to rein in her shameful desire to read his text over and over and *over* again.

"So what the heck was all that anyway?" Conchita asked, exiting the women's bathroom. "You and Harvey? And all that weirdness about the key? It's not like it's the only one out there…"

Conchita presented her version of the key to Alma before leading her through the corridor to a small side door with a matching keyhole. "Had I known you and Harvey needed to have couple's therapy in the ladies' lounge of my workplace, I would have just given you the damn key myself."

Alma stared down at the key and frowned, noting its similarities to her own key. Conchita was right. If the key was unique to the building, it seemed less likely that their discovery of the bathroom—and the hidden message within the Tiffany snow crystal wall paper—was significant in any way.

"It was the farthest thing from couple's therapy." Alma sighed. "And as usual, it's all my fault. I started something foolish this morning and we ended up here. But now, it just feels like a horrible ending to a bad dream."

"Like the one where you're naked and you're being flogged in the dark with pelts of seaweed? Or maybe wet straw?" Conchita opened the side door and guided them through a maze of corridors that ultimately ended into the candy department in the basement of the Field's Building.

"More like the one where all your teeth fall out, so you go to your dentist and he pulls down his surgical mask and you realize it's your ex-husband."

"Hmm. I've never had that one." Pondering it, Conchita tapped her fingernails on the exterior glass of the candy counter. "Maybe it's because I want to have sex with my dentist."

Pulling out a fresh box of chocolate-covered cherries, Conchita offered the box to Alma.

"No, thanks."

"Well, you had me in cardiac arrest when those elevator doors rolled open and he was mowing you down like a fertile patch of grass."

Alma propped her elbows onto the counter and held her head, trying hard not to relive the sensuality of his tongue and the arousal of his intoxicating kisses. "It was a total train wreck. Like a bad accident that just overwhelms you in slow motion until you suddenly feel the whiplash."

"You're telling me! I almost gave myself whiplash from the double-take. You two had me thinking you had actually gotten back together. And did you see the way you destroyed Harvey the moment you picked your date with Romero over him?" Conchita popped two cherries into her mouth. "Baaaaaaaall-BUSTER!"

"Oh, thanks for that, too, by the way," Alma snarked. "I heard it was your idea to name the cocktail after me."

"Well, it was fun going through all our options. It was either that or...SchlongLover. But Harvey and I agreed that was more me." Conchita popped two more cherries into her mouth, filling it with pink gooey goodness. "Anyway, you do realize that was the night you served Harvey with divorce papers? He was so distraught that he called me to come over to his bar and explain to him all the ways he had failed you in your marriage."

Alma tried hard not to allow her sister to guilt her into regretting their separation. "Well, I'm certain he's over it now. He's too busy managing his own sexcapades with women twice my height and bra cup size. And in one of the more incredibly awkward moments of my life, I caught him in a lingerie shop yesterday. And not the tasteful section in the front, either."

Conchita's mouth gaped open. "In the slutty section at the back?"

Alma nodded.

"Well, hello...? What do you expect?" Conchita slapped the lid over the chocolate-covered cherries and placed them back into the display. "Have you seen that man's ass in Levi jeans? It's not like he has any trouble getting laid. It's probably his version of couple's therapy. If I were him, I'd be fucking every six-foot triple-D woman I could get my cock into. Duh."

"Thanks for that pep talk. It does wonders for my five-foot five, 36B bra cup ego." Alma watched her sister devour two chocolate cream truffles from a silver platter near the register. "Don't you think you've had enough candy?"

Conchita sighed, knowing it was true, but she still couldn't resist the temptation. "So why were you in a lingerie shop, anyway?"

Alma hesitated, realizing she had let more slip than she had intended. Then, after a quick back and forth in her mind, she dropped her guard and took the plunge. "In case I decide to go through with my date tonight."

Conchita gazed at her sister, reaching out for an ornamental swirl sucker and unwrapping it. "Wow, really? That serious already? You just springboarded right over coffee at a café and a lunchtime matinee to fuck-me-now-because-I'm-a-horny-divorcée?"

"Basically. I've always been terrible with normal relationships. Just look at my track record. I almost had sex with my ex today in a freaking freight elevator."

"Yeah, no kidding," Conchita agreed, licking her lollipop. "He's a billionaire who can afford any hotel penthouse suite in the city and you almost let him go down on you in a dingy department store basement."

Alma gazed at her sister, on the verge of confessing everything about her sexting affair with her mysterious suitor and her intentions to meet up with him tonight. But then she realized if she confessed her secret, she would never go through with it.

"Well, at least have *one*," Conchita insisted, pulling the box of chocolate-covered cherries out of the display case again and flipping off the lid. "Chocolate is the third most effective aphrodisiac in the world, and it sounds like it might be just what you need tonight."

"Thanks, by the way," Alma said, finally surrendering and indulging in two cherries. "For naming me Ballbuster rather than SchlongLover."

"No problem," Conchita replied, eyeing the last cherry before consuming it herself. "That's what sisters are for."

* * * *

Alma greeted Reggie, the security guard, on her way through the grand ornamental lobby of the Cultural Center.

"Mr. Hollywood just came by again," he announced as she rushed up the white marble stairs leading to the Tiffany ballroom.

Alma slowed her pace. "Mr. Hollywood?" She played dumb, despite the fact that she knew exactly what he meant—the tall man with the movie star smile.

"Yes, Miss Castillo," Reggie nodded. "He whistled all the way up the stairs like he owned the place. He said I should tell the first woman who passed through these doors that he was waiting for her. I told him we'd be closing in thirty minutes. Told him I didn't think we'd be having more visitors. But here you are."

"Is he still up there?" Alma asked, doubling back down the stairs, almost terrified to know the answer.

"Could be." Reggie nodded, shifting his eyes upwards and noting the silence. "I didn't see him again after that."

Unable to face the prospect of meeting him prematurely—without fresh makeup or even a decent pair of panties—Alma lost all her confidence and retreated to the entryway, gauging whether or not to run out the door, away from every doubt that had plagued her about tonight.

"Did he say anything else?"

"Nope. Just kept on whistling."

Whistling? Was that the sign of a sane, happy man or a crazy unstable serial killer?

Alma wasn't certain—there was a fifty-fifty chance it could go either way. Gazing up the white marble banister, inlaid with ornate Tiffany glass, she regained her confidence. This was her building. Her haven and sanctuary. And there was no reason to turn away from it, fearing she couldn't fulfill the fantasies of a man who barely knew her.

Especially not a man who whistled.

Alma took a deep breath and started back up the stairs. The Tiffany ballroom was quiet and she was thankful for it. No whistling meant there was a chance he wasn't there, waiting for her, which meant she still had time to decide whether or not she planned to meet him tonight.

The moment she ascended the staircase, she spotted the gift box resting on the sill of the arching cathedral window. Sensing nothing but the golden rays of twilight glinting through the panes of glass, she crossed the ballroom and picked up the box. It was satin white with a silver bow decorating its lid as well as a matching note card attached to it. She flipped over the card and read the inscription, formally typed in stern uppercase letters: THE LESS YOU WEAR, THE BETTER IT WILL LOOK.

She studied the box again and quickly pulled off its lid. After digging through the plumes of crimson tissue paper, she withdrew the treasure beneath it—a ruby and diamond anklet. Three strands of petite cut diamonds encircled the anklet while tear-drop rubies delicately hung down from its base like sizzling sparks of flashing fire. It was sexy and flirty and spontaneous, everything she felt whenever she engaged with him. She had feared his gift would be a piece of perverse lingerie that matched his fantasy for the night, or some kind of ring that would inadvertently advertise his awkward desire for a deeper commitment. But the anklet was the perfect gift, a subtle message reaffirming his uncanny ability to know exactly the woman she wanted to be whenever she was with him. It was more than perfect; it was empowering, and it was that feeling of confidence that attracted her—time and time again—into his dark, unpredictable maze of seduction.

Chapter Twelve

Butterflies still churned in his stomach whenever Harvey rode the elevator up to the top floor of any of his skyscrapers. But this time was different because it was his newest acquisition, The Peoria, a garish symbol of wealth and power and elitism that only he could love.

Its design was a deliberate modernization of the quintessential Chrysler Building in New York City, quickly turning it into an object of scorn and controversy before they even broke ground. With its contemporary flare and distinct ornamental crown of superiority, it reigned over all of Chicago's adjacent heavy-load buildings in the Loop, most of which were built fifty years earlier without the industrial benefit of steel and glass that bolstered The Peoria's towering height fifty stories above them.

Soaring strength. No matter where he stood along Michigan Avenue in downtown Chicago, he could always see it, rising up from the skyline like a newcomer who refused to be ignored.

When Harvey had been given the chance to buy The Peoria from his competitor, Phillip Spears, he jumped at it, paying a rare premium to secure the privilege of calling it his own. Previous to that purchase, he'd only been known in the real estate community for flipping low-end "scrap" projects. Vulture plays—run-down warehouses, condemned residential buildings, shuttered factories, polluted parcels along Chicago's riverfront. In contrast, The Peoria offered over seventy stories of luxury commercial office space with an unobstructed view of Lake Michigan. Its tenants included some of the most prestigious international companies and their leases were set in stone for the next twenty years. The Peoria cost a fortune to purchase because it generated more cash flow than a small country, and he'd leveraged almost every single asset on his balance sheet to close the deal, but he had no regrets. Harvey Zale had finally arrived, and he wanted all of Chicago to know it.

It was fitting that he was meeting her here, in his newest conquest at the top of the world, he thought, as the elevator halted with a chime and he stepped out of the cab with the air of a man who knew his net worth trumped everyone's in the room. While the majority of The Peoria was commercial office space, its top five floors were designed as luxury living suites for business executives and their guests, offering a panoramic view of the lakefront skyline rivaled only by The Spire and The Hancock Tower. And at its apex was Harvey's favorite achievement: ownership of one of the most exclusive bar lounges in the city—The Vault, a secluded getaway salon that promised an experience of privacy and exclusivity, where all secrets revealed over five-hundred dollar bottles of Cognac and contraband Cuban cigars would be locked away from viewing by the ordinary world.

He had proposed meeting her there to impress her. *Of course*. Like a teenager who wanted to show off his flashy red convertible. He felt like a teenager. Cocky. Arrogant. Invincible. Deep down, he knew he wasn't. He knew his flaws and what he could and couldn't change about his lifestyle and his reputation. But on the outside, she offered him an escape—the chance to start with a clean slate and prove he was a man of character and strength rather than simply a greedy opportunist who disregarded the needs of others in favor of his own.

He had tried to prove that today to his ex-wife—and failed. Now, his Contessa offered him a rare second chance.

He approached the bar and sat on the high-back white leather chair.

"The usual tonight, Mr. Zale?" the bartender asked.

"No, Andy. Tonight, I'll need something stronger. Let's break out one of the premium, limited edition vodkas," he replied.

"You got it, sir." The bartender nodded, slapping his white towel over his shoulder.

Harvey reflected on his request after the bartender disappeared behind the bar's salt water aquarium backsplash to fulfill it. *It was a bad habit, drinking hard liquor whenever he was nervous*. But if he was really honest with himself, he almost sadistically enjoyed the uncomfortable sensation of being uncertain about tonight. He liked the challenge of facing the unknown and testing his ability to master it. And he loved rolling the dice and placing all his bets on the outcome of finally meeting her. Weeks and weeks of sexting exchanges had fueled his desire for more; there was no going back to where they'd started. And as a gambling man, he knew the odds were against him—the probability of failing hard seemed inevitable. But he also had learned long ago that his best wager and biggest win would always be to bet on himself.

The bartender zipped back to the bar and presented him with a hand-designed bottle of vodka, decadently lined with green Swarovski crystals.

"The color of money," Harvey noted. "Perfect."

The bartender opened the bottle and poured him a shot. Accepting it, he heard the chime of the elevator and swiveled towards it. *Announcing her entrance*, he thought, noting how his heart pounded through his silk shirt. He had made an effort to dress up tonight. His darkest grey Italian suit paired with his glacial blue business shirt, unbuttoned at its spread collar—no tie.

He had thought long and hard about his cuff links. He wanted something that made a statement as well as something that could easily be removed—if needed. He had settled on one of his favorites—navy blue lapis gemstones intricately crafted in an octagonal 14K white gold base with a whale flip-back enclosure. The perfect amount of bling for a man who struggled to leave his jeans and cowboy boots at home.

So when she stepped out of the elevator cab, he almost spit out his vodka. At first, he wasn't certain it was her. *It couldn't be*, he thought, as she strutted along the lounge's illuminated floor in her low-cut pink blouse and tight leather skirt. But her distinct gait in those high-gloss black stiletto heels and back-seamed sheer black stockings made every head in the room turn towards her. The coincidence was too preposterous. Alma Castillo had her date tonight in his building at his bar lounge. He felt the need to mutter the famous Bogart line from *Casablanca*, but he held his tongue when her eyes fixed on him like she was seeing a ghost.

She quickly glanced away, pretending not to see him—at first. That was his strategy, too. But when she stood in the middle of the lounge, conspicuously waiting for someone to claim her—and he failed to do so—her pride eventually kicked in and she sauntered directly towards him.

"I should have known you'd be here," she said dryly, taking a seat at the bar, deliberately keeping one vacant chair between them.

"Really?" he mused, pouring himself a second shot and watching how cool she played off the bizarre situation. "Why's that?"

"Because my sister has a big mouth, and I'm certain she told you that I was meeting my date here tonight." Placing her beaded clutch on the bar and dropping her guard, she pulled out a compact and freshened her lipstick as she had done a thousand times during their marriage. "And I know nothing would give you more pleasure than introducing yourself to him as my ex-husband."

Before he had a chance to retort by citing the irony of how she was sexing herself up in front of him for the benefit of another man, she crossed her legs with a jangle. He lowered his gaze, first onto the lace garter band of her black stockings, peeking out from the high-slit of her leather skirt, then onto its back-seam drawing a seductive line along her calf down to her ankle—and the lavish ruby and diamond anklet encircling it.

For a brief moment, he almost didn't recognize it, as if he was looking at a curious counterfeit, mesmerizing him with its similarities. Later, when he replayed the memory in his mind, he remembered every frame of it in slow motion—the sensuality of her sheer stockings, the plump curve of her calf, the tear-drop ruby pendants dangling from the diamond-encrusted anklet. Then, he recalled deliberately altering the expression on his face, morphing his mouth from a cocky smirk to a serious gaze of contemplation as the realization sank into his consciousness: *she was his Contessa.*

There could possibly be one and only one reaction:

Fuck.

Then, he had a second, equally exasperating thought:

Conchita.

The perpetrator of the hoax flashed through his mind. She had recently handed off the phone number of a "friend" who, according to Conchita, was looking for something fun and casual—no names, no strings attached. He didn't expect to ever call her. But in a moment of weakness, after the divorce had been finalized and the realization that he was no longer married to the love of his life burned deeply into his heart, he dialed it and she answered.

Why hadn't they uncovered each other's identity sooner? As Alma glanced at her wristwatch, anxiously waiting for another man to walk into the lounge and whisk her away from him, it seemed almost too impossible to believe. But she had changed her phone number after their divorce and he no longer had it. And his phone call with Contessa was unrecognizable as Alma. Contessa was a dark, sultry vixen, deeply seductive and forbidden—a completely different persona that her voice mirrored in every way, as if she had intentionally pretended to be someone else.

And after he purchased The Peoria, Harvey had changed his number, wanting a new business phone dedicated only to his building tenants and commercial contacts. Alma obviously didn't realize he owned the building, and she certainly didn't realize that she was ultimately waiting for him.

"You look nervous," he finally said, clearing his throat and mentally discarding the script he had written and re-written in his mind for this exact moment. "I assume this is a first date?"

She shot him a glare. *Even if she did look nervous*, she silently warned him, *she didn't need him pointing it out.* "I don't think you should make any assumptions, Harvey."

"Okay, second date," he teased, dismissing her warning. She had left her glasses at home, allowing her dark penetrating eyes to fire imaginary bullets directly into his forehead. He hid his smile and secretly wondered how many bullets he could get her to fire.

"Actually, we've known each other for a while," she declared, glancing over at the elevator cab, hoping for her immediate rescue. "We've talked and texted each other for weeks."

Harvey grinned. He couldn't help it. The way that she claimed to know "him" while not knowing he was sitting directly in front of her was both endearing and perversely entertaining.

"Sexting…I mean, texting each other for weeks," he repeated. "Sounds like a very serious relationship."

Sensing he was laughing at her, she straightened her posture, inadvertently enhancing how the neckline of her sheer pink blouse cut between the valley of her breasts. Harvey wasn't sure, but he guessed she might be braless. Physically affected by the image of her—naked and at his mercy—his amusement quickly faded as he succumbed to his desires and adjusted his strategy.

"Okay, my fault. Let's try this again." He removed his suit coat and swung it across the back of his chair. Then, he unfastened his lapis-studded cuff links and tossed them into the empty cigar tray on the bar. He hated business attire and its pretense of formality, and he wanted nothing more than to abandon their charade of fancy-pants phoniness.

"As usual, I'm being a jerk by putting you on the defensive when you shouldn't be. You look amazing, Alma. Really stunning. Your hair, your makeup, that blouse and skirt and legs…absolutely dynamite."

She glared at him sideways, noting how he casually rolled up his cuffs past his wrists. When she seemed certain he was genuinely complimenting her, she uncrossed her legs again and relaxed her shoulders with an audible sigh.

"You don't look too bad, either," she offered as a truce, her gaze falling onto his cuff links. "Those were always my favorite."

"I know," he said, remembering the exact moment he had chosen them for tonight. "C'mon, let me buy you a drink." He nodded to the bartender to gain his attention.

"No—" she protested, "I can't drink on an empty stomach. You know how much alcohol affects me. I'll turn into a giddy impulsive schoolgirl." Shifting in her chair, she attempted to adjust her leather skirt, as if she knew she was exposing more of her garter than she intended. Harvey pretended not to notice, hoping she would drop her guard and reveal even more.

"Yep, I know. But I like it when you're a giddy impulsive school girl. And you know I'll always try." He shot her a sly smile. "Besides, I'm pretty sure you're going to need something to get you through tonight. Andy, can you please bring a Lemon Drop for Miss Castillo."

"Right away, Mr. Zale."

Alma arched her eyebrow. "They know you by name here? Impressive. You must bring all your dates here."

He waffled. "I'm sort of friends with the owner."

"I see..." She clearly sensed he was holding back more than he should because she still knew him better than anyone.

He deliberately changed the subject. "So, do you think he knows you're allergic to shellfish?"

"Who?"

"Romero."

"I'm sure there will be other things to eat." She reached out for the appetizer menu and scanned through it.

"Saw shark soup?" Harvey offered.

Alma scrunched up her face and shook her head.

"Yeah, I expected a veto on that one."

"But you got the drink right." She unexpectedly laughed with relief as the bartender placed the glinting syrupy martini in front of her.

"I've had plenty of years of practice," he answered, studying the way something so simple made her so happy. "You know...you're really easy on the eyes when you smile."

She flashed him a sassy "whatever" smirk over the rim of her martini. It was a corny comment, but he didn't care. Cradling his cheek in his palm, he absorbed the relaxing effects of two vodka shots while she playfully licked the sugar-encrusted rim with her agile tongue. When she did things like that, she *was* easy on the eyes—and every other part of his body.

"How about the white truffle duck soufflé?" he proposed.

"Yum, that sounds delicious." She shifted her attention back onto the menu. "Where is that?"

"Second to last choice."

"Dear God!" she cried out, spotting its price. "One-hundred and thirty dollars?!"

Harvey waved away her horror. "Don't worry. We'll put it on Romero's tab."

He took the menu from her hands before she had the chance to flip it over and spot "Ballbuster" under the selection of cocktails. "You know, your date is going to be a lucky man tonight—if he actually has the balls to show up." He glanced at his wristwatch. "So how late is he?"

"Eleven minutes," she replied.

"Hmm, that's a tough one." He rubbed his freshly shaven chin pretending to be in serious contemplation. "He could have a valid reason. Or he could just be an asshole."

She ignored him, opting instead to down the first half of her cocktail in an effort to shore up her waning confidence.

"But then again," he continued, "I probably would get cold feet, too, if I spotted a drop-dead gorgeous woman like yourself waiting at the bar for a rough-around-the-edges joker like me."

"We were married, Harvey. You spotted me all the time and you never got cold feet."

"*Touché*. But I usually spotted you in morning, wearing bunny slippers and flannel pajamas." He waved to the bartender to replace her cocktail. "That's a little bit different than a leather skirt and garter stockings." He raked his eyes over her wardrobe, indulging in its full effect. "But I still got you out of those pajamas whenever I wanted."

Just like when they were sexting each other, he was testing her, pushing the boundaries, just to see if she would push back or let him tiptoe across them. She didn't push back, but she didn't encourage him either.

"I wore high heels on plenty of occasions while we were married."

"And you hated every minute of it," he said, noting that half her foot was slipped out of her heel.

"True," she admitted. "Neither one of us were very comfortable at all those real estate hoity-toity networking galas."

"Or your fancy-schmancy antique auctions," he lobbed back. "Which is why I always dragged us to the local taquería afterwards."

"To get me drunk on margarita mix," Alma replied, sipping from the second martini served to her by the bartender, and savoring the relaxing effect.

Harvey leaned in, closing the distance between them. "No, it was always to fatten you up on pork carnitas."

"With extra sour cream," they both added in unison like an absurd comic routine.

"I never complained," she said, crossing her legs and inadvertently showing off the anklet that he'd bought for some other nameless, faceless woman. Now, it seemed impossible to imagine it on anyone else other than her. "It's not like I'm a very high-maintenance girl, Harvey."

He muted his smile. A low-maintenance girl with stratospheric expectations.

"No," he conceded. "And it still is one of your best attributes."

"Well, if my date does ever show up, please don't tell me you're going to hang around to hassle him."

"I considered it." He reached into his pocket and checked the time on his phone.

"Where's your own date, anyway? I expected you to show up with an entire entourage of women."

On cue, a strikingly beautiful Persian woman stepped out of the elevator. Harvey knew her well. She was a foreign diplomat at the Iranian Embassy and a regular guest of the CEO of a major airline company who was a current resident within The Peoria's luxury suites. Harvey enjoyed having drinks with them. The CEO routinely offered to teach Harvey how to fly his private jet and she spoke six languages, all of which peppered her English with various accents.

"That's my cue," he announced, standing up from his chair and sliding his arms back through his suit coat. "Hey, Andy...can you please make sure that anything Miss Castillo eats or drinks goes on my tab." He winked at her. "Just in case Romero forgets to bring his wallet."

Alma frowned as he prepared to leave. He quickly sent a flurry of text messages, and her purse vibrated across the surface of the bar. But she failed to notice.

"Don't forget your cuff links..." Scooping them into her palm, she moved forward to refasten them for him. Closing his eyes, he turned into her body, indulging in the scent of her perfume and the way her long dark hair whispered against his arm.

"Thank you," he said softly, fixing his eyes on her own.

"You're welcome," she whispered, as if she wanted to say something more, but chose silence over vulnerability.

After a moment, he forced himself to pull away and cross over to the other end of the lounge. Like a masterful showman, he extravagantly greeted the exotic woman with kisses on both cheeks. She held out her bejeweled hands to embrace him like a lover. *It was a scene everyone in the bar would notice, including her*, he thought, feeling both ingenious and devious.

And after fifteen minutes of wining and dining with the Iranian diplomat in a private booth in the VIP section of the lounge, the only regret still lingering in Harvey's heart was the fact that he had chosen the low road over high road—as he had so many times before. He could spin it a thousand different ways, ensuring the final judgement was always in his favor, but still, there was a nagging pang of doubt plaguing his own sense of peace. *She always expected more from him and he always failed to deliver*. It was the reason why she had ultimately divorced him, and it was the reason why she was willing to accept the advances of a stranger who seemed to offer her something he never had—dependability. In fact, the only thing consistent in their relationship was the fact that Harvey routinely disappointed her, choosing his own selfish needs over her own. *It had been his fatal flaw*, he reflected, especially the moment he finally glanced over to the end of the bar and processed the reality that Alma was gone.

Chapter Thirteen

It wouldn't have been so bad if he didn't flaunt it, Alma thought, as Harvey greeted his date at the far end of the lounge. *Another Amazon princess.*

Trying to numb her sense of inferiority, Alma slurped down the second martini the bartender had placed in front of her. She had been naïve to let Harvey flirt with her while he was simply killing time, waiting for his real date. But that was Harvey's special talent—making Alma feel both eternally irresistible and utterly foolish. *Bastard.*

She glanced up at the clock. *Sixteen minutes late.* Then, she realized she had failed to check her messages.

Renewed with hope, she rummaged through her purse and sighed with relief when she discovered his text:

Sorry I'm late. I'm definitely an asshole who doesn't deserve you for making you wait…but if you accept my apology, I promise to make it up to you in the Turkish Suite.

The Turkish Suite? Alma's hands trembled. She hadn't expected to accelerate things so quickly, or at least, not until she had a chance to meet him in a public place, face-to-face. She expected to be reassured—even masterfully seduced—by his charming conversation and natural swagger. Perhaps then she would allow herself to accept his offer to extend their night together in a more intimate setting. But that fantasy abruptly turned into dread which spiraled into a queasy sickness. *God, how could she be so naïve*? *Naïve and foolish.*

She knew how. It was the same reason she had allowed Harvey to shower her with attention, despite knowing nothing good would come of it. It made her feel like someone different. Someone she used to be, and someone she yearned to become again—a sexy, attractive, supremely desirable woman.

Before she had a chance to decide whether or not she would respond to his text or simply gather up her purse to leave, severing their relationship through silence, a ridiculously handsome man in a waiter's tuxedo approached her with a silver tray balanced on his hand.

"Good evening, Miss Contessa…I am here to deliver you this. It is his sincerest wish that you accept it."

Realizing he was simply the messenger, Alma stared down at the shiny black keycard.

"For the Turkish Suite?" she asked.

"Yes, one of our finest," the waiter replied. "Simply take the elevator up to the seventy-seventh floor. It's a private penthouse suite. He'll be there waiting for you."

With his boyish charm and deferential gaze, it was hard not to trust him—or whoever was sending him. She took the keycard into her hands and nodded her thanks. Glancing in Harvey's direction, she noted his familiar boisterous laughter, ricocheting off the frosted glass table tops. She looked away, unable to see exactly where he placed his hand on the exotic woman's shoulder. She only knew another man had just arrived to their table, and she no longer wanted to wait around like the most awkward wallflower, languishing in the corner.

Clutching her calling card in her hand, she strode towards the elevator. She had just received an invitation from the most enigmatic man in the room. Now, she just had to prepare herself for the consequences of accepting it.

* * * *

Alma gazed at herself in the polished brass walls of the elevator doors.

Was she ready for this?

She wasn't sure. But her reflection whispered back that she was dressed as though she had hoped for it all along—free flowing hair, suggestive sheer blouse, tight leather skirt, garter stockings, and stilettos that she endured, even though she hated every minute wearing them.

It had all been for him. She had spent the whole day trying on different combinations of dresses and shoes before finally settling on the one that would best reveal her ruby and diamond anklet. Wearing a braless low-cut blouse and a leather skirt insinuated that she was the same seductive woman he'd come to know through the phone, but calling out his gift and complementing it with garter stockings and her only pair of high heels signaled she was prepared to pursue something more. He'd promised her more, and she intended to give him the chance to make good on his promise.

Maybe running into Harvey had spurred her into action over indecision. Yes, it was true that he was more used to seeing her in bunny slippers and flannel pajamas than dressed up like a high-class hooker. And it was also true that she had played the role of his dutiful wife, rarely stepping out of her comfort zone; she didn't need the reminder. But over the past few weeks, her life had changed. *She had changed.* Without anyone realizing it, she had cultivated a bad girl persona through a sexting affair that enabled her to escape the entrapments of her daily life. If she were truly honest with herself, she would admit she had only one expectation for tonight—the expectation of her ultimate liberation.

Confident in her decision to meet him in the private suite, she reached out to press the call button for the seventy-seventh floor until she realized it didn't exist. Flustered, she checked again, scanning the numbers to ensure she simply hadn't missed it. She hadn't. The call buttons ended on seventy-six.

She was flooded with doubts until she remembered what she was clutching in her hand—*the keycard.*

Glancing above all the call buttons, she spotted the keycard slot and exhaled a prayer. Inserting the card into the slot, the elevator cab hummed to a start and slowly ascended.

It was the longest elevator ride of her life. Counting every floor in numerical sequence until she arrived to number seventy-six, she held her breath, waiting and watching as the cab continued beyond its mysterious, unmarked destination for what seemed like an eternity before finally floating to a silent stop. *Trapped like a bird in a golden cage, suspended at the top of the world*, she thought, before the doors rolled open and released her into a candlelit garden paradise.

Garden of Eden—at midnight. It was the only thought that fluttered through her mind as she exited the elevator, lured into the decadence by the serpentine pathway pebbled with polished jade stones and the sound of percolating water from unseen fountains. Golden oil lanterns flickered against the Mediterranean tiled walls while delicate glowing orbs hung from miniature lemon trees. Guided by crystal lights illuminating her way, she wound through the maze of flowering shrubs and ornate trellises ensnared in moonflower vines until everything opened into an airy glass atrium, its domed ceiling revealing the starry night beyond it. And beneath the atrium, brilliant beams of moonlight streamed down upon the opulent octagonal sauna, a white marble sanctuary accented by Arabian archways and pillars inlaid with enameled mosaic tile. She halted in front of the oval-shaped bathing pool encircled by golden tealights and decorated with floating pink lotus flowers—one of her favorites.

Had she told him?

She couldn't remember, and it didn't seem to matter the moment his voice echoed against the hard surface of the marble.

"You're one ballsy woman—meeting a stranger in a strange place."

Addressing her from the white marble throne on the opposite side of the room, she immediately noted how his face was conveniently ensconced in shadows, except for the profile of his chiseled chin and the hint of his strong shaven jawline. But the rest of his body—and its masculine, athletic physique—was hard to ignore. Clad in a black silk shirt and matching pajama pants, he sat casually to one side with his leg propped on his opposite knee, holding his tumbler like a man used to getting his way—both physically and professionally. Later, when she would attempt to recount every detail that had made her trust him, she curiously remembered his feet—bare and perfectly manicured.

"Ballsy," she repeated, detecting a hint of mockery in his tone. "I usually consider that a good thing. And normally, so do you."

"Yes, I definitely do," he agreed, his voice deeper and sterner than usual. He swirled the ice cubes in his tumbler before lifting it into the shadows for a sip. "Which is why I'm trying to determine whether or not I should reward you or punish you."

It was the only time she thought of Harvey. The playfulness in his voice, the luring tease of his threat. She had just seen him, flirted with him, and even reconsidered all the reasons why she had separated from him. And he was also the last man she had slept with—over a year ago. She would be lying to herself if she didn't acknowledge her burning desire to change that fact. Her ex-husband had already moved on from her. And now, Alma was equally determined to do the same.

"Neither," she sassed back. "Because we're not really strangers, are we?" Placing her hand on her hip, she pitched her leg forward through the high-slit of her skirt, accentuating the sparkle of her anklet and insinuating every dirty text that had come before it. "If we were, I'm not certain you would have invited me here. And I'm not certain I would have accepted."

Strangely, he fell silent, as if he was searching for the hidden meaning within her tease.

"No, definitely not," he finally said, like the answer to a riddle. "So I guess it's a good thing for me that a stranger as bewitching as you is also the only woman that I want to make climax."

And as simple as that, he turned the tables on her, challenging her own ballsiness. She attempted to formulate a witty comeback, but it was useless. She was there for one thing—and they both knew it. He had named her deepest darkest desire, and in doing so, he asserted who would dominate who—and how.

Setting his drink aside, he exhaled and loosened the knot along the waist band of his pajama pants.

"Take your clothes off, pussycat. It's time for your bath."

Without warning, the hanging Moroccan lanterns dimmed above him, allowing his figure to fall completely into darkness.

"Start with your blouse," he said evenly.

The red glass torchlights along the walls intensified their illumination. *Like the devil's lair*, she thought, as she slowly put her fingers on the first button, knowing she was braless and vulnerable to his voyeurism once she removed it.

When it slipped away from her body and onto the white marble floor, she only heard the faint sound of his arousal, mirroring her own. Even in total darkness, she recognized it, the whisper of his desire and the betrayal of his weakness in her presence—his inability to contain his need to pleasure himself.

"Now your skirt and stockings."

His tone turned brisk and husky; she heard his uneven breathing between every stroke.

Following his command, she buzzed the zipper down the curve of her hip until the heavy leather dropped down past her ankles, revealing her black leather G-string through her sheer garter stockings.

"Don't – rush," he warned her.

Rotating a quarter turn, she slid her fingers down the side of her leg, bending forward to unfasten the clasp on her heels. *It was all for show*. She could have easily slipped out of them without granting him a full view of her backside, perfectly cut in half by her taut black leather G-string. But it was one of her best features and she was empowered to use it. He had confessed many times during their sexcapades about all the ways he had fantasized about her ass—dirty, naughty, taboo ways that she flagrantly dared him to make good on now. It was her only source of power—seducing him beyond the brink of self-control—and the vixen inside her was determined to challenge his domination until he could endure no more.

After stepping out of each heel, she slowly prepared to peel off her stockings.

She searched out his face, obscured within the darkness, but sensed his hungry gaze rolling over every inch of her body.

"Slower," he whispered, directing the pace of how she slid the waistband down over her G-string.

A tingling pang seized her sex. *Damp and in heat, exactly how he liked her*, she thought, desperate for his touch.

Flinging her stockings away from her, she confidently adjusted her stance, knowing she held his unseen gaze. *Her final rebellion*. Like a sultan indulging in his favorite harem girl, he had turned her into his possession. But ultimately, she knew she had the power to test his endurance, simply by standing before him in nothing but the G-string, awaiting the moment he would cave and request her to strip bare, exposing herself completely to him.

"Bath time—" he said with unexpected resolve. His hand relaxed within the shadows, and he cleared his throat as if he was attempting to regain control over his shallow breath.

Her gaze scanned across the oval-shaped hot tub, bubbling and glistening like gold before her.

"There's another gift for you in the oyster tray. I want you to put them on."

Alma glanced over to the edge of the tub where the iridescent shell of a splayed oyster shimmered beneath the dimmest glints of light.

Kneeling beside the edge of the bath, she lifted the pair of chandelier earrings from the shell. They flashed fire and ice, their ruby and diamond stones matching the sparkling beauty of her anklet. But as she lifted one to her ear lobe, preparing to slip it on, she quickly realized it lacked a traditional earring post.

"Lower," he said with a seductive tease.

Alma studied them again, inspecting their contracting clasp. *Nipple rings.*

"I want you to adorn those beautiful tits." His intimidating voice lowered as he drew closer to her. Squinting into the shadows, she spotted his silhouette rounding the perimeter of the room, stalking her with silent footsteps.

"Do you trust me?" Low and steady, his voice was directly behind her now.

She didn't answer immediately. Her mind was in a whirl.

"If not, Contessa…we will stop now." His dangerous voice encroached upon her; she shivered from the surprise and anticipation. Sweeping her long hair to one side, he traced his fingertip over the tender curve of her neckline. "We can stop whenever you wish."

Closing her eyes, she absorbed the fear and excitement of being touched by him for the very first time.

Did she trust him? She wanted to—more than ever. *But should she trust him*? Any sane woman would have said she was irresponsible for allowing herself to come this far. But she was no longer a sane woman; she was a submissive in the presence of her master. And now, the only thing she trusted was the throbbing ache between her legs and the way she grew wetter and wetter with every teasing stroke of his finger along the band of her G-string.

"Yes, I trust you," she finally confess, almost breathless.

"Good girl," he said in his familiar way, dissolving her inhibitions.

Without warning, everything went black before she realized what was happening—*a blindfold.*

"Trust," he repeated into her ear.

As the heat from his breath calmed her anxious heart, she shut her eyes beneath the blindfold and gave in to his game. For a brief moment, she expected him to bind her hands and whisk her away to his sex cave. *Whips, handcuffs, deviant sex toys…*nothing seemed unthinkable now. Instead, the unexpected intimacy of his bare chest against her back made her gasp until the erotic touch of his masculine hands, enveloping her breasts, massaged her into submission.

Trust, she repeated in her mind as he pressed her body against his hard, firm pecs, seeking full control with his embrace. *Yes, yes, yes…trust.*

Whatever fears or doubts she had about tonight—the anonymity, the secrecy, the blindfold—all melted into arousal with every intimate caress. Phone sex and sexting seemed like juvenile games compared with the raw sensuality of being pleasured by him now.

"Such a good girl," he whispered as the jangle of the chandelier ring crossed beneath her chin.

Her nipples grew hard in anticipation. *Would she cry out the moment he placed it over them*? She grit her teeth and braced herself for the initial nip. But it never came. Instead, she heaved an exhale of satisfaction when the sensation of his mouth suckling her entire areola overwhelmed every sense. His hot tongue flicked her left nipple, priming it—erect and ready. When he finally fastened the first ringlet, she forced out a breathy moan as the cold, stark clasp tightened with an erotic squeeze.

"Shhhh," he soothed her, securing the second ringlet in place, balancing out the pricking tension between them. "Now, you look like a queen."

She sighed, yielding to his domination, relishing how the nipple jewelry made her feel cherished like an idol. The alternating waves of pressure and pleasure on her tits spiraled down her inner core, sparking a slow burn of yearning at the base of her slit. *He knew exactly what she needed…all too well.* He was making her slick and needy with his foreplay until she surrendered every part of herself to him, craving even more.

Reading her cue, he snaked his fingers down the supple curve of her ass, fingering the leather band of her G-string. *Would he slip beneath it*?

She dared not move or breathe.

Nudging his lips against her cheek, he directed her in a low, foreboding tone. "Down on your knees."

Her heartbeat raced as she obeyed him, listening to his footsteps circle around her.

"Tell me how much you love being my naughty vixen."

"I love it," she whispered, knowing it wouldn't be enough.

"Convince me," he insisted, sweeping up the locks of her hair into his firm grip and running the wet tip of his dick between her breasts.

"I love being naughty with you in every way," she confessed, leading him up to her lips, wanting nothing more than to taste drops of his own desire. But he only allowed her a single lick of his sheathed cock, a brief sampling, just to conjure an image of its full length and strength.

"Yes," he exhaled, suppressing his own yearning to allow her to fully take him into her mouth. "That's good. Because you're going to prove it."

Dropping onto his own knees behind her, he grasped her hair and pulled her head back, forcing her to widen her stance. His warm pelvis cushioned her ass while his hard cock pressed against the small of her back, slowly lowering itself along her crease, nestling its head against her rosebud. When he was certain he had secured her submission, his fingers slipped down the front of her G-string, fondling her swollen clit and testing her wetness, as if he wanted proof of how much she had enjoyed the taste of his cock. But it wasn't until she felt the titillating sting over her clit—initiating her raw, guttural moan—that she realized what he had done.

His confession confirmed it. "A bejeweled clit clip for my naughty vixen," he betrayed, as the hard gemstones of the ringlet pricked against the sensitive folds of her labia, intensifying the gratification of his thumb strumming over it. "Now my queen, let's see how pretty you are."

Guiding her forward onto her hands and knees, he withdrew her G-string down past her thighs, fully exposing her slit to his domination. She knew she was glistening and slackened, desperate for his touch. *But would it please him*?

The moment the tip of his lush tongue made contact with the clit ringlet, she quivered and heaved her release. She was losing all control and she no longer cared about the consequences. She only wanted to open herself wider and wider, submitting to the teasing pressure of his tongue licking her labia before finally slipping beyond it.

Bearing down, she shifted deeper into his penetrating strokes, unleashing a ripple of undulating waves deep within her core. *Yes, yes, yes*…she chanted in her mind, pleading for him not to stop. With every flick of his thumb, her clit ached against the constriction of the ringlet, building up a series of frenzied contractions as the rhythmic pace of his tongue accelerated against her most sacred spot. Before she could control herself, she released an undignified climactic cry.

Could she come for him now? Without anything more than this?

"There you are," he reassured her, fully exploring her sex while she panted for relief. "Now, just a little something extra to make you mine." Withdrawing his tongue, he slipped completely behind her.

What more could she endure? *How far would he go to bring her beyond the brink*? Slowly, seductively, he massaged the curve of her backside, savoring the smooth contour of her cheeks. She fully expected to feel the forbidden lick of his tongue, shuddering her into ecstasy. It had been so long since she had been seduced without boundaries or limitations, and she wanted nothing more than to entrust her secret lock to his masterful key. But it wasn't an illicit act of his tongue that ultimately made her tremble and groan. It was the unexpected invasion of warm oil seeping into every erogenous crevice of body.

Flowing, slippery, and intrusive in every way.

Its scent—a disarming blend of honey and spice—overwhelmed her as she bowed her head against her hands, overwhelmed by the arousal of his next forbidden act.

God, oh God…

When he flicked on its lowest setting and delivered its first crescendoing vibrations directly against her, she melted into the reverberations of sexual fulfillment.

"You made me imagine how you looked, using one last night," he said. "Now, I want to see it for myself."

Oh, God…yes, yes, yes…

Whatever doubts she had about her ability to orgasm were completely erased now. He had taken her dirty shameful secret, and turned it into an empowering one that would climax her into oblivion. She backed herself against the cushy rim of its massaging head and heaved out her exhilaration. On her hands and knees, doggie-style, with her G-string slung down around her thighs while her chandelier nipple ringlets dangled off her tits, she wanted him to make her scream like his whore. He responded by placing his sturdy palm on her tailbone to tame her while admiring the view of his domination—oiled and glinting, awaiting his ultimate conquest. He fondled her ass with titillating intimacy, soothing her irregular breaths into murmuring purrs, priming her for what they both knew she wanted most—her first virgin thrusts.

Steady and determined, he coaxed her to arch her back and rub her clit against its thick, palpitating tip. It was so much more masculine and sophisticated than the vibrator she used on herself, and for a moment, she thought she might prematurely climax when he invaded her wetness and arced upwards against her G-spot, sparking a surge of spasms inside her. But he would not let her come—not yet—not until he guided it deeper, deeper than she ever thought possible, and synchronized its mechanical thrum with the rhythmic motions of his penetrations.

Oh…de-e-a-a-r-r…G-G-G-o-d-d. So very deep.

She gasped. He held her—tight, forcing her to endure it. So many times she had simply given up when she reached a safe plateau, reducing the speed on her own vibrator and simmering into a dependable, dignified orgasm rather than going full-throttle into a wild shrieking banshee release. But there was nothing dignified about the way he oiled her from behind, letting the warm honey-scented syrup cascade down her ass and between her legs, or the way his deviant tongue slid between her slit, stealing a taste of her riches. And there was nothing dependable about the way he gripped her bare ass from behind and replaced the cold, mechanical vibrator with the primal warmth of his cock. A rush of adrenaline shot through her sex. *He intended on climaxing inside her.*

With one uncompromising lunge, he heaved fully inside her, securing her stance to accept his unyielding thrust. She cried out with a fluttering string of notes before tremoring with uncontrollable shudders.

"There you are—" he exhaled, pinning her in place and coaxing her acceptance of the full-length of his cock. "Tell me how much you love it deep."

A guttural groan escaped her as the thick trunk of his shaft breached the last barrier of resistance. *Deeper than she ever thought possible.* His cock grinded against her clit clip as he rocked back and forth inside her. *God, how he conquered her with every merciless inch.*

With quivering knees, she lowered her head, attempting not to faint. He hadn't asked for permission and she hadn't granted it, and yet, it was the only thing she wanted in the world—his fingers digging into her flesh, his thighs slapping against her backside, his cock striking against her G-spot, over and over while driving towards its ascent, seamlessly bringing her to the brink with his unforgiving pace, and then…soaring her beyond.

Beyond.

Seized with the pulsating rush of pleasure, she tremored with a velocity that set free the loudest, most frenetic scream she had ever produced in her life, climaxing into a soprano pitch that harmonized chords of rapture throughout her entire body. Nothing about tonight had conformed to her expectations, and yet, everything about tonight exceeded them. He had kept his promise, making her come not two separate times, but in endless, multiplying succession—one orgasm after another after another—like a raging tsunami swirling and whirling over open waters before crashing against the depths of her quaking inner core.

After he withdrew his cock and rolled away the condom, brimming with his own cum, he lifted her into his arms and submerged them both into the steaming, frothy hot tub of bubbling water. The consoling blend of his compassion and strength relaxed her into his care. Spreading her arms across the smooth edge of the bath's tiled ledge, he encouraged her to support her own languishing weight. Later, when she reflected on the surreal reality of everything that had happened, she barely could remember the moment his nimble fingertips liberated her nipples and clit from its constraining jewelry, or the way he removed her blindfold, trusting her to maintain their unspoken agreement of his anonymity. But like a secret guarded within the privacy of her mind, she vowed never to forget the massaging sensation of the streaming jets, deliberately positioned against her breasts and sex, lulling her into a state of eternal bliss—and the tenderness of his kisses, feathering her cheek, earlobes, and neckline, until she fell fast asleep.

Chapter Fourteen

"You are in soooooooo much trouble."

Harvey fished out a peppermint candy from the porcelain bowl and lobbed it at Conchita, who was organizing gingerbread men along a decorative display tray.

"Well, hello to you, too." She glanced down at the mint, wedged between the crease of her cleavage, accentuated by her padded fuchsia pushup bra. "It's not every day I get pelted with peppermints by a hot man in tight jeans. *Prrrrrrr…*"

Conchita tossed the peppermint back and Harvey caught it with his mouth. "Bullseye!" she cried out with a boisterous bob up and down.

"Okay, babe. Enough fun and games. I'm here about something serious that's all your fault."

"Really? You make it sound like I'm actually productive and useful." Conchita lifted a gingerbread man and bit off his leg. Harvey noticed that half of the men on the tray were missing limbs.

"You're very productive when it comes to meddling in other people's business. Useful is another question."

"Is this about me finding you and Alma in the elevator together, almost having sex? Because that was all your doing. I was just trying to have a pee break."

"No, it's about setting us up."

Conchita fell unusually quiet and fluttered her fake eyelashes. "What do you mean?"

"You know exactly what I mean," he asserted. "Giving me the telephone number of your 'friend' who just got a divorce and wasn't looking for anything serious? Just some sexy texts?"

"Ohhhhhhhhh, right," Conchita feigned a cloudy memory. "So whatever happened with that?"

"We met last night."

"Oh, my effing God!" Conchita cried out, covering her own scream with her glittering acrylic fingertips. "You're RomeroLuvsItSlow?"

"In a word, yes…except there was nothing about last night that was slow."

"You mean you guys...actually…?"

Harvey answered with a visual. Taking the icing pouch from Conchita, he squirted out two D-cup flowers on the gingerbread man's chest before stealing away a gingerbread man with phallic chocolate chip genitals and sandwiching it over the feminine one. "All because of you."

Conchita looked down at the fornicating gingerbread. "Well, what the hell are you complaining about?" She clapped her hands and spun around in celebration. "This! Is! Awesome!!!! You two have been miserable wrecks since the day you split up and I've been miserable having to mediate your misery. So now you both have finally figured out that you belong together, which can only mean one thing—I'm going to get to be an auntie!"

Crushing her misplaced cheer, he overrode her. "Except she doesn't know it was me."

Conchita halted in mid-twirl and scrunched her plump face into a frown. "What do you mean she doesn't know it was you?"

"She. Doesn't. Know. It. Was. Me," he punctuated, pointing out their respective roles in his gingerbread diagram. "She was blindfolded the entire time."

"Oh come on," Conchita squawked, as if she was used to him pulling her leg. "The entire time?"

Harvey squirted a band of icing across the face of the feminine one, and adjusted the gingerbread man behind her.

Gazing down at his artwork, she considered the possibility that he was not pulling her leg. "Wow…really, Harvey? Kinky."

"Dumb. Stupid. And completely selfish."

"Oh, I dunno know." Conchita shrugged, taking up the icing pouch and decorating more of her gingerbread men with blindfolds. "Sounds like it was what you both wanted. And maybe a little something extra." Swiping icing tongues onto their mouths, she repositioned the male's head at the base of the female's legs.

"She's never going to forgive me."

"She's probably going to come back for more, Romero."

"Even if she does, I can't let this happen again. And I can't tell her the truth. So what am I supposed to do now?"

"Honestly, I'm still in shock that you two didn't find out you were the ones sexting each other this entire time. I mean...how does that happen in this day and age? Don't people sext photos of their genitals anymore? Or am I showing my age?"

"Really, Conchita. I'm in trouble here and so are you. When Alma finds out that you're the one who encouraged the swapping of our phone numbers, she's going to want to flambé the both of us."

"Hmm, that's true," she acknowledged, unwrapping a long swirled lollipop and pensively sucking on it. "But then again, I'm not the one who had sex with her as Romero."

"Ughhhh." Harvey bowed his head and heaved out his desperation. "I am so screwed."

"Well, figuratively, probably not again…unless you fess up and hope she sees the positive side to all of this."

"What's the positive side?"

"Give me a few minutes and maybe I'll come up with something."

"Ughhhh," he groaned again, flopping his forehead into the peppermint basket, wallowing in self-pity.

"For God's sake, Harvey," Conchita exclaimed in exasperation. "How can you be one of the richest, sexiest men alive and still be so clueless about the secrets of a woman's heart? What about the make-up sex? That's positive, right?"

"I'm pretty sure we're never getting back together so I doubt there's any chance of us having make-up sex. Alma hates my greedy selfish billionaire guts."

"That's exactly my point. Sex with your ex is never about getting back together. It's about releasing all the animosity and bitterness you've been carrying around since breaking up and channeling it into hot, unbridled make-up sex. It's like a mutual truce to stop hating each other's guts and start moving forward with your lives. Plus, there are soooooo many added benefits of having sex with your ex. No awkward discussions about latex allergies. No judgement about cellulite. And no weird surprises like anal fingering by someone who doesn't realize it's not cool on a first date. All that matters is the chance to fuck each other's brains out, and then afterwards, maybe she'll remember how good everything was when you were together and when you used to love her like your best friend. Or in your case, your best friend with kinky benefits."

"Not a best friend," he corrected her solemnly. "A soul mate."

Conchita handed over her sucker to him like a consolation prize.

He took a bite and pondered his predicament with a crunch. "She's still the only woman who knows me better than I know myself and there's nothing about being separated from her that feels right. So I don't want just make-up sex or kinky blindfold sex. I want her back in my bed, every day, for the rest of my life."

"Then just give her whatever she wants, Harvey, and watch her fall in love with you all over again."

"I'm not certain I can do that."

"Sounds to me like you figured it out last night." She lifted a gingerbread man and nipped off his chocolate chip.

"In a fantasy world," Harvey stressed, gnawing the sucker to the stick and tossing it into the trashcan. "An illusion constructed to escape from reality because in the real world, I'm not the kind of man that Alma wants anymore. And maybe I'm not even the kind of man she deserves."

"Because you've become a self-centered, self-serving capitalist pig billionaire?"

"Well, yeah...basically."

"Well, la dee dah, boo-fucking-hoo!" Conchita threw up her hands and returned all the gingerbread men on her tray. "Really, Harvey. What good is all that money if you can't have the one thing you want most in your life?"

Harvey stared at her face, noting the uncanny resemblance to Alma, searing her words into his heart.

"Just give her want she wants and move onto the make-up sex, so then after that, you can move onto the relationship sex, and the wedding sex, and the honeymoon sex, and the babies, which will give me what I want, which is to be a favorite auntie someday before I'm old and crusty and suffering from diabetes."

Conchita stuffed her mouth with the gingerbread men that they had decorated with bras and blindfolds before replacing the tray back in the display.

Slipping his handkerchief out of his pocket, he fished out a fifty-dollar bill and tossed it on the counter. "You're still not off the hook, you know that, right?" he said, taking the largest box of chocolates under his arm.

"Yeah, well...you can't blame me for trying. She's your soulmate."

"You're right." He nodded and snatched a swirled lollipop from the elaborate sucker display. "I definitely can't blame you."

Chapter Fifteen

I can't get you off my mind.

The text pinged her phone like a magical chime answering her most sacred wish. The whole afternoon, she had waited calmly, patiently, for his communication. Earlier that morning, when she was roused from her deep sleep by the first rays of dawn streaming across her plush hotel bed, everything still seemed like a dream. Expecting to feel his masculine body lying next to her, she rubbed her eyes and stretched out her hands and feet. She didn't remember being carried onto the bed, but she did remember the security of his smooth chest spooning against her the entire night. It was this absence of warmth that startled her awake, raising her from the cocoon of the billowy white bed, searching out the silence within the suite before flopping back in disappointment when she realized he was gone.

Completely gone.

Covering her face with her pillow, she whimpered in her shame.

A one night stand. Of course, it was. How could she be so naïve?

It wasn't until she flipped the pillow off her head and looked down onto the bed that she noticed the white box, resting atop the adjacent pillow. She quickly opened it and fingered through everything she had worn last night—the ruby anklet, the chandelier nipple rings, the diamond clit clip, and the gold satin blindfold. Touching it to her lips, she felt the slow rise of her heartbeat as she spotted the handwritten note scrolled across a cocktail napkin beneath the mementos of their fantasy night.

The Palmer House Lobby. Tonight. This time...without the blindfold.

She hurriedly dressed, tucking the velvet jewelry box into her purse, and left the penthouse suite the same way she had entered it—through the elevator. With only a few hours to return to her own condo, shower, and change into her regular clothes, she barely had a chance to process the implications of meeting him again. She only considered how the harsh daylight revealed her life as a bland, ordinary routine, convincing her that everything extraordinary she remembered about last night couldn't possibly have happened at all. But it had happened, and every time she doubted it, she removed the napkin—hidden like a lover's locket in the front pocket of her overalls—and silently indulged in its existence. She repeated this ritual over and over until his message finally pinged her phone that afternoon.

I can't get you off my mind.

Finally, she thought, strangling her phone. *Thank freaking God.* She had waited for hours to hear from him, quelling her desperate urge to ping him first. He hadn't disappointed her.

The shop bell rang, announcing the entrance of a visitor, but she ignored it. Her attention remained fixed on those seven simple words—*I can't get you off my mind*—confirming his need for her.

"Alma!" Her father's muffled voice hollered up to her from the basement. "I think we have a visitor…"

"Knock, knock," Harvey quipped, lurking directly over her shoulder, waiting politely outside an imaginary door.

She rose from her workbench, supremely annoyed by his interruption and deposited her phone back into her pocket.

"I've come bearing gifts." He presented her a blooming bouquet of pink Gerber daisies and a ginormous box of chocolates. "Dark chocolate truffles. Your favorite."

"Why?" Completely skeptical of his motivations, she scrutinized his gifts through the lenses of her glasses.

"Because I want to make up for last night." He wagged the box and flowers, coaxing her to accept them.

"Why?" she repeated, crossing her arms and arching her eyebrow, just to make sure he knew she wasn't buying it.

"Because it was rude of me to leave you at the bar by yourself. I should have at least stayed and met your date."

She snorted out her cynicism. "You mean so you could have embarrassed me in front of him for your own entertainment?"

"Well…" Harvey sighed, like he couldn't quite admit she was totally wrong. "I would have at least told him to mind his manners and have you home before midnight."

"Harvey!" Enrique called out as he plodded up the wooden staircase. "*Qué tal, mi hijo*? What are you doing here?" He held out his hand in greeting.

"Visiting your daughter," Harvey answered, as if it was the most natural thing in the world.

"Well, that is a very pleasant surprise." Enrique surveyed the bouquet of flowers and the box of chocolates and narrowed his glare, silently ordering her to be gracious. But she stood her ground and refused.

"Yeah, well…she had a big date last night and I was just checking in to see how everything went."

"Really, Alma? I did not know that..." Her father's voice trailed off as he took the gifts from Harvey and set them on the counter. "But it was very nice of Harvey to stop by."

Alma shot Harvey a death glare. He smirked, absorbing her fiery gaze like a demon who enjoyed it.

"Nicer than her date who was twenty minutes late," Harvey added. "Good thing I was there to keep her company or it would have been really uncomfortable."

Cracking open the box of chocolates, he extended it to Alma, tempting her to take one. "But something tells me he made it up to you." When she refused to take one, he flagrantly popped a truffle in his mouth and munched on it with a smirk.

Instead, she glared at him, wondering what game he expected her to play.

"It was nicer than our first date," she finally shot back, seeking to turn the tables back on him. "When you made me ride the Ferris wheel at Navy Pier to take my mind off my swelling face after feeding me deep fried shrimp, and I ended up vomiting all over the people below us."

"Ahhh..." Harvey sighed, like he loved that memory. "At least I helped figure out you're allergic to shellfish. I'll admit hanging out in the ER on a first date isn't as classy as rendezvousing at some swanky bar at the top of the world, but it sure tests how much you like a girl."

There was no mockery in his voice—only genuine nostalgia. Their eyes locked and it briefly drew her in. She noted his freshly ironed blue shirt that accentuated the color of his eyes. An image of him, shirtless and gleefully humming near the ironing board, flashed through her mind. She hated ironing and he hated wrinkles, and more than once during their marriage, she came home to find all of her laundry—including her underwear, bras, and socks—had been freshly ironed, folded, and put away in her dresser, still warm to the touch.

"Think you'll see him again?" he prodded.

Alma's father huffed from the opposite side of the shop where he was polishing silverware, pretending not to eavesdrop.

"I don't know, Harvey. Are you actually jealous?" she countered, irritated that he was forcing her to have a conversation about her love life in front of her father. Her irritation simmered into a scowl across her face.

Lifting a ridiculously oversize lollipop out of his rear pocket, he unwrapped it, then sucked on it with the innocence of a school boy. "Not jealous. Just wondering if maybe we should double date?"

Conchita, she thought, suddenly recognizing the origin of the sucker and the box of chocolates. *Of course.* He'd talked to Conchita, which meant nothing but trouble.

"Why? Are all your Amazon women nothing more than giant eye candy, but incredibly boring conversationalists?"

"Worse than boring," he confirmed with a long drawn out lick. "They actually agree with me most of the time. It's like medieval torture. I much prefer our conversations, which are akin to having my shins kicked—repeatedly. Painful and merciless, but never ever boring. Especially the ones that end with you convincing me that I'm a greedy soulless jerk."

He *was* a greedy soulless jerk, but she didn't have the time or energy to care anymore about whether or not he intended to change.

"I'm your ex, Harvey, which means I'm just supposed to pretend to be civil to you."

"Ugh, that sounds like misery," he whined. "Because that kind of civility, coming from you, is gonna drive me insane."

He brazenly pulled out his phone and checked his messages.

Her back pocket chimed.

"Gonna get that?" Harvey nodded down to the ping in her pants. "Sounds like a booty call to me."

He stared at her, eyes twinkling, daring her to check it in front of him. She crossed her arms and challenged him back. Jealous or not, he had no right to waltz in there and make a play-by-play commentary of her dating life.

"You do realize that if you don't check it, you might miss your opportunity for some hotline bling tonight on account of me."

Alma held his gaze, pretending there was absolutely no merit to anything he said, despite secretly wanting nothing more than to check her messages and loudly recite whatever steamy, inappropriate text was waiting there for her.

"Okay, don't worry…" Harvey finally said, giving in first. "I'll be right over here, inviting your dad to a Sox game. Enrique? What are you doing this Friday? I've got nosebleed seats right behind the batter's cage. Your favorite."

When he had meandered a safe distance away from her, she slipped out her phone and quickly swiped open her messages.

Making me wait for your response will only give me plenty of time to imagine all the dirty ways I plan to punish you for it.

She sighed. It was his standard flirtatious threat, and now she knew he had the power and prowess to make good on it.

Sorry…I'm in the middle of helping a customer.

That sounds kinky, he shot back without a beat. Unless it's another man, in which case, I'm insanely jealous.

Alma glanced up at Harvey, who was reviewing batting averages of various players on his phone with her father.

If I were a cruel woman, I would let you believe you had competition.

Well, I know from last night that you're far from cruel, and in fact, I verified that you're much sweeter than you pretend to be.

Alma closed her eyes and let his sexual innuendo pervade every part of her body.

So no competition, huh?

She glanced back at Harvey—in his tight jeans and cowboy boots, licking his oversized lollipop, bantering back and forth with her father like they were best friends. She coolly texted back, as if she were trying to convince herself of its truth.

None.

"Ouch!" Harvey suddenly roared.

Startled, Alma shot him a glare.

"Looks like the home team needs to bring their A game," he cried out through cupped hands.

Tuning Harvey out, she scanned her phone for his reply: *Good, then there's no reason to punish you. See you tonight at the Palmer House.*

"Enrique," Harvey brashly announced. "I forgot to mention something. I plan to remove eleven stained-glass windows from my property at the riverfront parcel before the train depot is demolished later today. And I intend to hire you and your daughter to represent them at auction."

Stunned, Enrique glanced over at Alma, then back at Harvey. "Yes, of course, Harvey. Whatever you would like…"

"But there's only one problem," Harvey said. "There's a missing window that will require the services of an expert because I think it could be a very rare, very valuable Tiffany."

"What missing window?" Alma stood up from her workbench.

"Well, I wish I knew exactly," Harvey replied. "That's what I expect you to help me find."

Was he mocking her? Her interest drooped into a frown. He meant renewing their pursuit of the *Eternal Love*. She had given up on yesterday's possibility that they had found something worth searching for, and now, the last thing she wanted was to renew false hope. "No, Harvey. You were right yesterday. I was wrong. It all was just a waste of time."

"A waste of time?" Harvey crowed. "Dumber words have never been spoken, especially by such a greedy soulless jerk." He flashed her a self-deprecating smile. "So c'mon…let's just consider today a new day with a fresh start, and since I'm a gambling man, I'm willing to pay the only person in the city who knows enough about stained-glass windows to help me figure out where to find the next clue in the treasure hunt. Enrique…does fifty thousand dollars for a couple hours of Alma's time sound like a decent hourly rate?"

Speechless, Enrique's mouth fell open.

In contrast, Alma snorted, unable to contain herself. "Wow, Harvey. The civility between us really is driving you insane."

"Completely bonkers," he agreed, as if her snarky comebacks invigorated him. "Better up it to one hundred thousand."

Alma's father made a sound like he was having a heart attack.

"No, Harvey," she protested, recognizing the serious edge beneath his offer. "It was something that I never should have started, and now I regret it."

"Regret it?" He angled his chin, like he heard something uncomfortably familiar. Why?"

"Because it's not a fearless quest. It's a foolish fantasy. And I'm tired of being a hopeless romantic."

"Ahhh, I see…well, it's a good thing that's one of the things I still love about you."

She stared at him, letting the dramatic phrase play back in her mind, listening for the flippant sarcasm in his tone, conveying he meant the exact opposite of what he said. But it never came. He only gazed at her with a disarming resolve that tested her own.

"Then you should also know that I can't be bought," she said softly.

"That's true," he conceded. "And I also expect you to be completely uncooperative. Another thing that I find strangely charming about you. So, let's make a deal. You're a world-renowned Tiffany expert. I think I have a Tiffany window that needs to be found. I want to pay you to be my consultant for the next two hours. But you refuse to accept payment for your services. So don't accept my money, but still come with me, and we'll just consider it…" He paused before taking the leap. "A date."

"A what?" Alma grimaced like he was offering her a lick of his contorted, discolored lollipop.

"A date," Harvey repeated, as if it was the most natural suggestion in the world.

Cold silence fell between them until Enrique whistled a famous tune to a death march.

Harvey eyed him. "Gee…thanks for that vote of confidence."

Alma's father shook his head like he was about to witness a man being shot by a firing squad. "Call me about the twelve windows, Harvey, and I'll be more than willing to help you. The rest of this conversation…" Enrique's voice ominously faded away as he disappeared into the rear workshop "…is a young man's game of risk. And I am an old ailing man."

When they were left alone, Alma gazed at Harvey and his blue and yellow sucker-stained lips.

"I am not going on a date with you."

"Okay, fine. Then come with me as a Tiffany expert and I'll send your father the check."

"No you won't. You'll send bags of cash to our doorstep, just to irk me."

"Probably. But only because you refused my truce."

She heaved in exasperation. "We're divorced, Harvey. Divorced couples don't date."

"When have we ever done anything like a normal couple? Or even like two remotely normal people? Well, okay…one extremely handsome quasi-normal man, and one slightly quirkier woman with a crucifixion fetish." He cocked his head and looked down at her restoration work of a small ecclesiastical stained-glass window of Jesus nailed to the cross. "By the way, I'm pretty sure if you leave him like that, he's not going to get any worse while you're away with me." Leaning into her workspace, he flipped the cleaning rag over Jesus' missing loincloth, and nodded with certainty that his improvement had truly fixed everything.

But that was so Harvey. Simply buy a bouquet of flowers and a box of chocolates and assume everything had been magically fixed.

"I don't want to come with you," she finally uttered, stating the pure unemotional truth.

The look on his face slowly absorbed the fact that she was serious, but in typical billionaire-Harvey-Zale-fashion, he persisted anyway. "You're telling me there's not a single thing I can possibly do to make you want to come with me? Wax my chest hair? Trim my nose hairs? Brush my teeth—*and* floss? How about this… I promise that whatever we find together, I'll let you be the one to claim it in the name of preservation?"

"The billionaire-real-estate-tycoon-Harvey-Zale that I know wouldn't do that," she countered.

"The Brazilian-waxed, nasal-trimmed, minty fresh Harvey Zale promises that he will…and if you know one thing about me, it's that I never break my promises."

But she still resisted, hesitating about whether or not to admit her reason.

"C'mon," he pressed her. "We'll take my speedboat to Navy Pier. It's only a few hours and it might even be fun—"

She shook her head, interrupting him. "Harvey…I have a date tonight at The Palmer House and I want enough time to go home and get ready. I don't want to go with you to Navy Pier now. I'm sorry."

He held her gaze and slowly chewed on her words. "The Palmer House, huh?"

She fully expected him to finally get it and give up whatever weird, jealous agenda he was pursuing by pursuing her. But the only thing she could expect from him was the unexpected. "He must really know you well. That's one of your favorite buildings. Looks like I better splurge on cotton candy *and* caramel corn on our date."

He locked eyes with her again. He wasn't going to give up and he wanted her to know it.

"Just for the record," she replied, "you're the one who likes that bright carcinogen blue cotton candy, not me." She couldn't help it. He always assumed he was buying it for her, and she secretly hated it.

"Yeah, that's what you always say before you end up eating half of it. So, does that mean you're coming with me to finish what we've started or not?"

Extending his hand, his cocky smile dared her to take it, enticing her to believe in something she knew would ultimately only lead to disappointment. But the mischievous glint in his eyes and the way his mouth was stained blue like he had just eaten a Smurf made the whole thing seem juvenile and ridiculous.

"Okay, fine. Fine! But only for two hours *and* only because I know you'll never leave me alone unless I say yes. But not because I want you to pay me any money, and not because this is in any way, shape, or form—a date."

"A date?" he repeated, echoing her sentiment that it was the most absurd suggestion in the whole wide world. "Of course it's not a date. We're divorced. Duh."

Chapter Sixteen

NOW THAT HE HAD HER THERE, what the hell did he intend to do with her?

His insistence on resuming their hunt for Tiffany's *Eternal Love* was a complete ruse. He didn't believe there was any long lost window, and even if there was, he certainly didn't expect to find anything there that would illuminate where it was or how to find it. It was all just an elaborate excuse to spend time with her. And she bought it…

Well, sort of, he thought, following as she led the charge down the interior corridors of Navy Pier on their way to the stained glass gallery. It was a given that Alma wouldn't accept his offer to pay for her time, but her refusal to label their time together as a "date" bruised his ego more than he wanted to admit. And despite surrendering her ultimate trust to a complete "stranger" during last night's blindfolded sexcapade, Harvey found it more than ironic that she barely trusted him to keep his promise to return her to the shop before sundown.

She knew better than to fully trust him. Even throughout their marriage, she always challenged his motivations. Spare change into the Salvation Army bucket? He really just hated the jangle of loose change in his pants, and she always called him out on it. Free coffee and donuts to every cop in the vicinity of one of his buildings? She knew he did it just so he wouldn't get a ticket for parking his Ferrari in the fire lane. In fact, every time her judgmental brown eyes peered at him with skepticism rather than affection, it roused his latent conscience and ignited his need to be a better man. *Yes, he had his flaws*, but there was at least one redeeming value hidden within his opportunistic heart: he was a man of his word and when he made a promise he always kept it. *Always.*

Now…*getting* him to make a promise wasn't always easy and as far as he could remember, he was the kind of man who passed through life, rarely feeling obligated to make promises to anyone. *Until he met her.*

It had been the biggest promise of his life—his decision to marry her. So when he uttered those vows—*his promise to love, honor, and cherish her—forever*—he did so with every intention of fulfilling them. And although he may have failed her in other ways by surrendering his youthful pursuit of civic justice in favor of big money and corporate greed, he never faltered in wanting to be the man to share the simple, happy pleasures in life with her—feeding her donuts in bed; licking the crumbs off her legs; serenading her with sappy renditions of love songs in his open convertible; catching fireflies in his bare hands because he knew she loved their enchanting glow; making love on a blanket in the dark while stargazing in the park…

And if he was honest with himself, returning to the Tiffany stained glass gallery at Navy Pier was hard to bear. *The place where he had proposed to her.* He hadn't said it and she hadn't acknowledged it. Neither of them needed the reminder and it wasn't exactly a coincidence that yesterday's pursuit ended with her decision not to come there with him. But it was on his mind with every step that drew them closer to the gallery.

His sentimental side would have drowned itself in a downward spiral of melancholy and nostalgia if it hadn't been for the interruption of his phone, vibrating in his back pocket.

I'm trying to decide between the red or the white panties for tonight…

He ran his hand through his hair and re-read the message. Just down the corridor, a few steps ahead of him, Alma strolled along in her baggy overalls, red-framed glasses, and mousy ponytail, simultaneously drafting steamy texts to Romero.

Red has an open cage-style, ribbon ass, locked with a lace bow. White is a crotchless thong with a peekaboo ruffled skirt.

Harvey's eyes almost rolled back into his head. Did his ex-wife really just text him about her crotchless white panties?

From afar, she looked like she was casually checking her phone, barely aware of anything around her. But as he scanned her texts, trying to keep his swelling cock from impairing his judgment, he intended to make sure she didn't get away with it.

That's an obvious choice. No panties.

He eyed Alma as she paced in an aimless circle.

You're really going to pass up the opportunity of seeing me in one or the other?

Harvey rubbed his face, trying to maintain his composure.

I can't wait that long. Send me a picture. Now. I dare you.

It was a dirty, devious request, but she deserved it for tempting him to keep up the ruse of their affair, right there in front of her.

That might take extra time to prepare… she replied, neither denying nor committing to it.

Damn straight you little whore, he thought as his eyes raked over the hidden curves of her body, chewing on all the lascivious ways he could seduce her without having to reveal it was him. *God, he was such an amoral son-of-a-bitch.* And yet, he couldn't help it because he wanted her back in his life and back in his bed.

Dirty and devious, he thought. But he wanted to push her to the edge where he was standing, just to see if she would jump with him. He watched her reading his text and wondered if she would flounder in front of him or excuse herself to the bathroom and prove she actually had more balls than he did.

Let's just keep you guessing on what I plan to wear tonight…and whether or not your tongue will enjoy it.

Harvey groaned and fell to his knees, just to prevent himself from rushing at her like a madman, pinning her to the ground, and forcing his hot wet tongue into her saucy little mouth until she realized he had been the one to make her come last night—and he could be the one to make it happen again and again.

After a minute of wallowing in his sexual frustration, she finally looked up from her phone. "What's wrong with you, anyway? Sugar rush?"

Sugar rush? He narrowed his eyes, tracking her approach like a tiger ready to pounce, imagining all the ways he could make her feel her own damn sugar rush.

"Sort of," he muttered.

"Well, probably best to lay off Big Blue for a while." She plucked off the top tuft of his cotton candy, taunting him with the way she curled the soft tendrils of fluffy confection around her finger before sucking it off.

"Keep picking at my cotton candy like that, I'll make you eat the whole thing."

Stealing away a second tuft, she flashed him a sassy smile and strutted away towards the gallery entrance.

She had better run away, Harvey thought, estimating how many bags of cotton candy it would take to wrap a soft nest of sweetness around her naked body clad in only white crotchless panties. The stark silence outside the gallery's entryway confirmed they were the only people in the vicinity. Most tourists never walked all the way to the end of the interior pier, and most locals never went there at all.

Slipping through the glass doors, she disappeared into the shadows of the dim gallery, bathed in the muted glow of stained glass. He watched her petite figure pass from darkness into a mystical swath of colorful opalescent light before drifting back into darkness again. *Like a nymph returning home*, he reflected, as she stopped in front of her favorite Tiffany motif—a landscape scene of wild passion flowers, their bursts of turquoise and emerald green foliage intricately replicated with mottled and confetti glass.

The same spot where he'd proposed.

He pulled back the glass doors and followed her into the shadows.

"Still your favorite one?" he asked quietly.

"I never get tired of looking at it," she uttered, almost to herself.

"Well, I think it's safe to say you might be the only one." He swept his finger along the dusty edges of the window, wondering if they were the only visitors to the gallery in days, maybe even weeks.

"Most people aren't interested in stained glass unless it's Aunt Bee's thirty dollar hand-me-down that looks a lot like the thirty-thousand dollar Tiffany dragonfly lampshade on that antiques TV show."

"Really?" Harvey mused. "How could they possibly not be interested in learning more about this guy?" Standing in front of the cathedral window, he mimicked the depiction of the archangel Michael holding up a sword, preparing for battle.

"Because people want something they can hang up on their bathroom wall, not something with historical and artistic significance."

"Yeah, it would be pretty hard to take a piss in front of a righteous archangel threatening to maim me where it counts."

She stole back his cotton candy and finished its last fluffy tuft. "I think most men would probably clean the toilet seat better if a righteous archangel was threatening to maim them if they didn't."

"Hey," Harvey cawed, seriously offended. "I always cleaned our toilets. And our showers. And I did all our laundry. You may have hated all the buildings that I bought and all the money that I made, but I should at least get a gold star for domesticity."

"I bought you an apron and oven mitts for your birthday, didn't I?"

"And I wore them every time I cooked us dinner. *And* cleaned the dishes."

"*I* cleaned the dishes," Alma corrected him. "You just re-cleaned them."

"Because the dishwasher doesn't work unless you put them in there—cleaned first."

"That's what the dishwashers are for, Harvey."

"That's just what those dish soap commercials want you to believe."

"Okay, fine, you win." She threw up her hands, sensing his need for validation. "You were the perfect housewife, Harvey."

"Thank you very much. The defense rests his case."

She had stopped paying attention to him, stolen away by the haunting beauty of the various stained-glass windows within the gallery. He could be as witty and charming as he wanted to be, but ultimately, it was nearly impossible to compete for her attention if there were antiques in the room.

He stuffed his hands in his pocket and circled in front of the mysterious window in a secluded corner of the gallery. "So what do you think our boy Louis is trying to tell us by sending us on this wild goose chase?" he called out, noting how the window's title matched the inscription in the wallpaper—*The Guiding Angel.*

"I don't know…" She moved towards him, scanning the window like a mother who had seen her child a thousand times, but every fresh glimpse still offered a new experience of enchantment. "But I know that finding a collection of stained-glass windows, fully intact and without significant damage in the middle of Chicago is like finding a bag of diamonds in the middle of an abandoned field. How could you not wonder where they came from or how they got there?"

"Because I would only want to know how much they were worth, and if there could be more?" Harvey slyly insinuated.

"If you cared about whether or not there could be more, then you probably shouldn't bulldoze the best clue we have to finding whatever else might be out there."

"Easier said than done, Miss Castillo. I can't exactly sit on a piece of property that's under contract for over a hundred million dollars, especially since the proceeds from the sale will roll right into my next project, which is the kind of opportunity that comes along only once in a lifetime."

She placed her hands on her hips and challenged him. "Oh really? What's that?"

He squared his stance against her own, confident in his ability to impress her with his answer. "I'm going to build the tallest towers in the world."

She exuded the longest nasal wheeze in the history of mankind. "Ohhhhhh...*brother*."

He frowned. "I get a gold star for cleaning dishes, but building the tallest towers in the world gets me sinus congestion?"

"What do they look like?" she asked, more like an interrogation than a question.

"What do you mean what do they look like?" he repeated, feeling the need to stall his answer. "I only have preliminary designs. They haven't been fully—"

"They look like two big penises jutting into the sky, don't they?"

Harvey placed his hands on his hips, just to mirror her conviction, and pondered her suggestion. "Well, not *exactly* like penises."

She rolled her eyes and cleared more sinus congestion.

"Alma," Harvey stressed, spreading open his hands, seeking only an ounce of sympathy. "Asking a man to pick moral righteousness over penile prowess is like asking a dog not to scratch at his own mange-infested neck."

"So in this scenario, you're saying I have to buy you one of those dog cones, just to keep you from selling the riverfront parcel?"

"It probably would help."

"Harvey...if you need to publicly wear a cone of shame, just to get you to do the right thing, then I don't think anyone can help you. Not even me."

"C'mon...don't be like that," he implored, grabbing her hand, testing her acceptance of his touch. He didn't come here to fight with her and he wanted her to know it. "What really are the chances that all those windows in my train depot are authentic Tiffany's, huh?"

She heaved a long drawn-out sigh and tugged back against his grasp. "I don't know…would it matter to you either way?"

He reinforced his hold over her hand and nodded. "Yes, because it would matter to you."

His conviction unnerved her. Her hand trembled within his own.

"I would need more time to study them in order to answer that. Tiffany wasn't the only person working with opalescent glass at that time, and they could have been made by any number of craftsmen working with him. So, it's hard to know right now if they really were designed and produced by Tiffany, and if not…then you're probably right. The building itself might not be worth saving at all." She forced herself away from him, as if she needed to maintain their physical separation in order to justify her emotional one. "Which would mean it's impossible to know if the *Eternal Love* is something that really exists or if it's just a sad, desperate wish."

Alma's voice trailed off as she stopped in front of a luminous stained-glass window depicting an angel embracing two cherubic angels.

"But there were letters about it, right?" Harvey said, encouraging her in a way that surprised himself.

She nodded. "There are letters, written by Tiffany's sister-in-law after the unexpected death of his first wife. He was so heartbroken that he literally dropped off their young children at his sister-in-law's house and disappeared for almost a year. I guess it's a romantic fantasy to believe that he spent that year pouring his heartache and grief into a memorial window—a masterful expression of his exquisite genius—inspired by his eternal love for her."

"Or maybe he just drank himself silly for that entire year," Harvey interjected. "I know that's what I did when I lost my wife."

She crossed her arms, confronting him. "Except your wife didn't die."

"Yeah, she chose to leave. Way worse."

"Well, even you felt the need to commemorate it, didn't you, Mr. Ballbuster?"

"Just consider it my masterpiece of exquisite genius." Harvey smarted back, like a teenager reveling in the amusement of his own bad behavior.

"I'm sure you make good use of it, Harvey. In fact, I bet you order those ballbuster drinks for all your dates."

"Only as a test, just to see if they can handle it." He caught her by the hand as she attempted to drift away from him. "They can't, of course."

She avoided meeting his gaze, but the gentle touch of her free hand against his chest convinced him that she yearned for a time when they were lovers, not enemies.

"Tell me, Miss Castillo," he said in a hushed voice, his lips only an inch away from her own. "If I had been a little less of a jerk the last few months of our marriage, would you have reconsidered divorcing me?"

She shut her eyes as if his question truly pained her. "Are you actually admitting to the fact that you were a jerk?"

Lifting her chin to meet his gaze, he searched out any sign of forgiveness. "I've admitted to being worse." Then, glancing back at the archangel, he said, "And now that I'm under threat of being maimed by a supernatural force, I suppose it's easier to admit the fact that I know I'm not the easiest guy to love, honor and cherish—forever."

"I don't think there was anything you could have done. You and I had grown so far apart in every way that we seemed like strangers."

She tried to pull away from him, but he was stronger and more determined to keep her in his arms. "And how does it feel right now, stranger?"

"It feels like you need to go your way and I need to go mine."

"But what happens if we start going the same way again?" he offered.

"Harvey—" she said his name in a way that foreshadowed her rejection. "Thank you for agreeing to salvage the windows in your train depot. But it doesn't change the fact that—"

"That…it's still not enough," he said, completing her thought.

She bowed her head like a plea for him to stop. "This…distance between us isn't about the windows or your buildings or your money."

"No? What then?" He searched her eyes, trying to kindle that same spark of passion that she carried for her long-lost window.

"It's about everything between us being so much harder now than it used to be."

"Then let's try to make it feel easier again, Alma. Let's try."

"Harvey—" She shook her head, struck by the irony that he was now the hopeless romantic. "You're…" She hesitated before peering down at his pants. "Vibrating."

"I thought you generally like that," he replied, unflinching.

She cracked a reluctant smile, and for a moment, they were united. But the persistent buzz of his phone quickly disrupted the mood, spurring her to seek an escape from his embrace.

He relented, letting her go. *This time.* But he recognized regret in her voice, a longing for the way things used to be between them, and it filled him with more than just sexual desire. It filled him with hope.

He didn't bother to pull out his phone or check the message. Instead, he doubled back to the mysterious window of the angel enveloping a woman within its opalescent wings, protecting her. He stared at the window, waiting for something unusual or strange to jump out at him. Instead, he only had one thought—*serenity*.

His gaze lowered along the curve of the angel's wings, its mythical feathers layered like waves of pearl, lavender, teal and celestial blue until he reached the base of the window and spotted a series of numbers etched into the surface of the lead frame.

"Alma?" He said her name quietly, uncertain he wanted to show her what he had discovered. Then, realizing he couldn't withhold it, he repeated her name, the second time, with more conviction. "Alma? Do these numbers mean anything to you?"

She drifted over to the window as he swiped his fingers along the frame, removing mounds of dust partially obscuring them. "Like some type of auction house inscription to tag and track the window?"

She leaned in and read off the series of numbers. "No, it's nothing that I recognize."

He closed his eyes, like she had just shot him in the back. "That's what I was afraid of."

She curiously looked at him. "Why? What's wrong?"

"Because I recognize those numbers." He heard the edge within his own voice harden like steel. "That's a surveyor's legal description for a parcel of land—the plat survey system. Every piece of property in every county in every state has its own unique numerical description based on the subdivision of land into lots and blocks."

"And you recognize those numbers?" Alma said distrustfully, as if she knew better than to believe him.

"Yeah," he replied solemnly, turning away from the window. "Because I've seen it a hundred times in the past week. That's the legal description for my riverfront parcel. It's listed on every document pertaining to the sale."

He tried to control his urge to punch his fist through one of those damn windows.

"So we've been sent all this way, just to be sent back to the beginning?" Alma insisted. "But that doesn't make any sense."

"It does if there's something about my property that's more important than we realize..."

Their eyes locked. *What had he just said? What did it even mean?* He wasn't sure and neither was she. Silence fell between them as they both stared at the window, attempting to piece together the significance of the numeric clue below it.

Harvey's phone buzzed twice. This time, he pulled it from his pocket, grateful for the distraction, until he read and re-read the flurry of texts awaiting him. He shook his head, grinning at the perverse irony of their content before contorting his mouth into an imbalanced smile and unleashing a troubled laugh.

Alma chased after him down the gallery towards the exit. "What, Harvey? What is it?"

"Un-fucking-believable. That's what," he said without slowing his pace.

She grabbed his arm to stop him. "Harvey?"

He pulled away from her, avoiding confrontation, silently weighing whether or not to keep the truth from her. When he glanced back at her, she was frowning, not in disapproval, but in sorrow of her own inability to read his mind. When they were man and wife, he had been unable to keep secrets from her. He realized he didn't want that to change. "It's a text from my real estate lawyer."

She smiled at him like she was winding up a snarky aside until he clarified it was all business. "They've stopped the removal of all the windows."

All traces of her signature smartassiness fell off her face. "What do you mean?"

"Jackass Jacques. That's what. He's just served me a cease and desist notice for the demolition of the train depot. The city has granted him a forty-eight hour stay, preventing me from doing anything with the property until he has a chance to hire a third party expert to review the building and determine its historical significance." He suddenly burst into unsettling laughter. *It was just too damn precious.*

She stared at him, struggling to put the pieces together. "Who could he possibly intend to hire?"

Harvey's gaze locked onto hers. If there was one time in his whole life that he wished he didn't want her back, it was now. "You."

Chapter Seventeen

JACQUES' FLAMBOYANT GREETING rang out throughout the store, mimicking the high-pitched bell announcing his entrance into the shop. "*Bonjour, mon chéri*! I have some news *magnifique* to tell you! I have saved the train depot from Monsieur Money Monster, Harvey Zale."

Jacques slapped the official city documents onto the counter in front of Enrique.

Alma winced at the "magnificent" news. Only two days ago, she was prepared to help Jacques in any way possible to prevent Harvey from bulldozing his property. Now, she was less certain and more conflicted about the decision to pit herself directly against him. Harvey had already agreed to remove the windows and allow her father's auction business to represent them. That concession would have allowed her the opportunity to determine if they had any value in the first place. It was a respectable compromise in the face of so much tension and conflict between them, and their time together today at Navy Pier reminded her of how nice it was not to harbor an undercurrent of resentment against him. In fact, it was better than nice. *It was liberating*.

Enrique glanced at his daughter. She recognized the shock on her father's face. It had been her expression, just hours earlier, when she received the news from Harvey.

"We have permission to inspect the property tomorrow at 8 a.m.," Jacques shrilled with glee. "Then you will turn in your written evaluation to the city's Historical Preservation Department."

"What kind of written evaluation are you seeking?" Enrique questioned him, scanning the cease and desist notice on the counter.

"That is your job to tell me, no?" Jacques said, angling his delicate profile towards Alma with a triumphant smile.

Enrique read the summons. "I am not sure that the building on that parcel is a train depot, which is what you have stated here, nor am I certain that the building has significant historical value at all."

"*C'est impossible*!" Jacques squawked. "Your daughter has confirmed the windows are significant. Is that not true, *mon chéri*?" He slung his long cashmere scarf over one shoulder and twirled his body to face Alma, hiding out in her corner workspace.

"I haven't had a chance to confirm anything," she said, resenting being turned into a pawn in his game. "Harvey was going to remove them and send them here for evaluation before you stopped him."

"Well, no need to wait. The permission is granted. You will see them tomorrow in their natural space and light."

Expecting praise for his achievement, he leaned over her workspace and sought out his reward. "Shall I take you out for dinner tonight to celebrate our victory?" He thickened his French accent, just in case it would help persuade her.

Alma internally rolled her eyes. Jacques had been pursuing her since she had divorced Harvey, and although she had moments of admiring his love of architecture and his natural flair for confrontation against property owners, she couldn't get past the way he called her *mon chéri* like she was his pet poodle.

"I can't tonight, Jacques. I already have plans."

He curled up his thin lips in disapproval. "I see… well, I hope you have not already forgotten about your agreement to accompanying me to the Anderson Gala tomorrow night."

A little part of her withered and died inside. *Ugh, she had totally forgotten.*

"Meet you at the gala," she corrected him, attempting to diplomatically weasel out of the egregious mistake of agreeing to it in the first place. "But I may not have time if I'm working on your summons tomorrow. It certainly should be my main priority."

"*Tsk*," he clucked at her, as if she had just gnawed on his pant leg. "You will have the whole morning and afternoon, and there is no one who knows antique glass in the city better than you. You are an expert *très superbe*. And once the word spreads about what we have done with Monsieur Money Monster's property, everyone will know how well we are working together." He let the innuendo float off his lips like an invisible bubble over her workspace. She wanted to reach out with her finger to pop it.

Opening the store's front door for his departure, he sang out in harmony with its chiming bell. "*Au revoir, mon chéri*!"

Alma cringed, waiting for the door's thud to stamp his sprite voice out of her mind.

"Harvey is not going to be happy about this," Enrique finally said, as a long moment of silence passed between them.

"He already knows." She listlessly gazed out the window across the river, remembering the look on his face the day she told him she wanted a divorce. It was the same expression she had seen a few short hours ago. "His real estate lawyer texted him about it while we were at Navy Pier together."

Enrique whistled ominously. "And how did he take it?"

"Like I was a traitor, of course. He was already planning to remove the windows, so I think he felt betrayed."

"No, I'm sure he does not blame you."

"How can he not? I still don't think he should destroy the train depot and he knows it."

"Because you believe there is still something valuable there?"

"Something more than just the windows?"

She nodded. "If I say no, then I'm lying because I don't want to be the one responsible for ruining Harvey's business deal. But if I say, yes, then I'm choosing to believe in something that may not exist anymore, and Harvey might be the one who suffers for it."

"But you do realize, *mi amor*...if you refuse Jacques' request to submit your written expert assessment to the city, then he will just find someone else," he warned her.

"There is no one else, Papi,"she replied, breathless, as if the weight of being trapped was crushing her. "No one better than us, and you and I both know it."

"Yes, that is true." Her father sighed as if it pained him, too. "Then I suppose Harvey will either be very fortunate or very unfortunate to have us."

Chapter Eighteen

HER PHONE HAD BEEN SILENT since this afternoon. It was a momentary observation followed by a fleeting whisper of insecurity as she studied her appearance in the mirror and applied the finishing touches of her makeup.

It wasn't like him to remain so silent.

She glanced down again at her phone, its screen dark and idle.

She considered pinging him with something…suggestive. But it was different now. *A sexy text no longer seemed enough.* Last night, he had tempted her to breach the barrier of their relationship in the most intimate of ways, surrendering herself completely to him for the sake of carnal pleasure—his and her own. It had been an exploration of the mysterious and undefinable fantasy they had built between them, and forcing her to stay blindfolded was exactly what she needed to go through with it. *And she loved that he knew it.* She had not met him—*officially*. But she had felt him, every masculine part of his body, and it was enough to quench her aching thirst while promising to satiate her with more...*even more tonight.*

Was it all just about the sex? Yes, initially…it had been. She enjoyed their sexual banter and appreciated the easy way he obliged her need to hide behind her temptress persona. But now, there was no more hiding behind her texts or even her own voice. He had lured her beyond all that, disposing of everything she had used as concealment, exposing her—bare and vulnerable—to his domineering lead. Last night had sealed her bond to the mysterious man she didn't even know by name, and the sacred intimacy shared between them proved there was nothing worth hiding anymore. There was only the necessity of one final revelation—meeting face-to-face.

Brushing the final strokes of powder across her cheeks, she puckered her lips, tossed her dark strands of hair over her shoulders, and leaned over the sink to see how much cleavage her slinky indigo cocktail dress actually revealed. *Too much*, she thought, considering how its dramatic V-plunge neckline mirrored its thigh-high slit skirt. Then she considered the last time she wore that dress—*New Year's Eve with Harvey*. It had been a gift—one of many new designer dresses packed within an overnight bag for their impromptu visit to Paris. Despite the fact that she always preferred casual and comfortable over formal and fancy, Harvey had learned early on in their relationship that if he did it just right, she would go along with anything he planned. Like a gemcutter seeking out her most brilliant facets hidden beneath the security of her rougher surfaces, it had become his special talent—discovering all the complex layers of her femininity. It was one of the many reasons she had fallen so hard for him; he was the only man bold enough to explore every sparkle of her diamond, and the only man daring enough to love every unexpected inclusion that he uncovered.

When she finally took off her glasses and squinted into the mirror, she released a tense sigh, comforted that she now looked almost nothing like herself. *She strove to be completely unrecognizable.* She wanted to separate herself from everything that defined Alma Castillo and escape into the new world that he had created with her: a sanctuary where they were united on their own terms without any personal background or baggage. It was a welcome distraction from her real life in which marriage, divorce, and heartbreak had marred her entire existence for the past year. And with Jacques' plan to stall Harvey's demolition of the train depot based on her own official evaluation of it tomorrow, there was no end to the stress and conflict that plagued her life—no reprieve but the charade of new persona evoked by his presence.

*It was all a charade…*Lost in thought, she gazed out the window of her taxi, watching the lights and sounds of downtown Chicago streaking by below her. Reliving every word and touch she had experienced with him last night, she closed her eyes, preparing her mind and body for the possibility that it could all come to an end. *Perhaps even tonight.* She didn't want it to end, but she also knew the chance of everything staying the same was against them. Meeting him tonight would likely destroy every illusion she had been willing to believe about him, and yet, she was still willing to take the risk. Perhaps it would prove to be more than just a masquerade, or perhaps it would simply initiate the beginning of the end.

As she paid the fare and stepped out of the taxi in front of the Palmer House Hotel, the merciless Chicago wind whipped through the slit of her dress and punished her bare legs. She clenched the lapels of her faux fox fur coat and accepted the guiding hand of the bellman who escorted her through the bedazzling art nouveau entrance, embellished with lavish ornamental peacocks, hand-wrought in bronze by Louis Comfort Tiffany. She absorbed the surreal reality of being there. It was one of her favorite historic hotels in Chicago and she never grew tired of descending its regal white marble staircase, flanked by two winged angles—two of Tiffany's largest bronze statues in his collection—and entering into its world-famous lobby, illuminated by lustrous Tiffany candelabras, gilded in twenty-four-karat gold, and topped with a decadent ceiling of Grecian frescos.

It always made her feel like a queen, she thought as she strode across the polished granite floors towards the gleaming nineteenth century mahogany bar. She inconspicuously glanced around her. No one was in the lobby except the attentive bartender.

"What can I get for you this evening, miss?"

Slipping onto the plush maroon velvet bar stools, she considered ordering one of her favorite cocktails, just to take the edge off. But then she thought better of it.

"Just a glass of Riesling, please."

"I apologize…but our available white wines by the glass are Chardonnay, Sauvigon Blanc or Pinot Grigio."

"Then just a glass of Chardonnay, thank you."

He nodded and turned away to fulfill her order. Setting her clutch on the bar, she slowly removed her coat and glanced into the backsplash mirror to catch the reflection of anyone in the room who might be watching her. Her heart sank a little in her chest when she saw no one. *He would likely make her wait again.* She avoided the temptation of opening her purse and checking her phone. She had just checked it before exiting the cab; he had been silent since this afternoon and it was killing her.

Trying to maintain her composure, she decided to patiently wait, feigning poise and confidence, for at least three more minutes. *One hundred and eighty seconds.* She started counting, certain she would never make it to the end of her goal without caving in to peek at her phone, but at least she had invented a distraction to keep her there for the longest three minutes of her life.

One hundred and eleven, one hundred and twelve, one hundred and thirteen…

The bartender arrived with her wine glass and set it in front of her. Against her better judgment, she reached into her purse again and scanned her messages. *Nothing.* Her eyes darted across the mirror, searching for any face that might be looking back at her until she suddenly recognized the distinguished man at the top of the white marble staircase.

"Unbelievable," she uttered, lifting her clutch to obscure her face and downing a gulp of her Chardonnay.

Casually shoving one hand in his pocket, he flashed her his Hollywood smile, knowing he could do anything he wanted, whenever he wanted to, and get away with it. He was dressed in one of his finest suits—a sharkskin grey wool suit with a tailored fit that accentuated his athletic build and innate swagger—and his gelled hair and freshly shaven jawline reminded her how naturally handsome he looked after a shower. And his pale pink shirt and chocolate brown tie gave him a modern flair in a room filled with dark hues and gilded antiques. *Pink*, she thought, noting how well it complimented his strong cheekbones and rugged face. He was the only man she knew who was masculine enough to get away with wearing pink.

But he wasn't there to impress her; he was there to punish her, *clearly*. She slouched in her chair and rotated her shoulder away from the direction of his approach. Whatever form of mockery or shame he intended to bestow upon her, she was determined to keep her cool and assert her disinterest in engaging with him.

Without warning, his firm hand pressed against the small of her back before he whispered in her ear. "You have no idea how hard it is to be divorced from the most stunning woman in the room."

She closed her eyes and silently sighed, trying not to notice how much she still enjoyed his touch. But his presence was a complication, which was exactly what he enjoyed being in her life—*an unpredictable complication*.

Sliding atop of the bar stool beside her, he fixed his gaze on her reflection in the mirror. "I always loved that dress on you."

She pretended not to hear him, irked by the fact that he was doing it again—crashing her date.

He ignored the fact that she was ignoring him. "He's late again, isn't he?" he noted, glancing down at his gleaming wristwatch.

She crossed her legs away from him. If she was being watched, she wanted to send a message that she needed to be rescued. "Please, Harvey…don't embarrass me." She sat straighter in her seat and invented some reason to dig through her purse. She found her lipstick and quickly applied another coat.

"Embarrass you? How could I possibly do that?"

"I could think of a thousand different ways," she retorted, slapping shut her compact and returning it into her clutch. "Especially since I'm here to meet someone else and you're here…coincidentally?"

Her comment stopped him cold. He smiled like he had been caught in the act of scheming and leaned over the bar with his hands folded in penance.

"Definitely not a coincidence," he said slowly, fidgeting with his cuff links. They were silver inlaid with mother of pearl, an antique pair that she had bought him for the first closing that he had decided to attend in a suit rather than jeans.

"Then why are you here?" she confronted him.

Again, he fell silent, as if he wasn't prepared for her adult challenge to his juvenile games. "Because you're here, all dolled up in one of my favorite dresses that I bought you, waiting for another man to enjoy it."

"So you're jealous?" she said, hardly believing it.

He smirked. "Maybe."

"Why?"

His blue eyes sparkled behind his long eyelashes. "Because he's my competition."

Alma heaved out her frustration and turned even farther away from him. *Petty and impulsive.* It wasn't about her; it was about never losing at all costs.

"Please, Harvey…go away. This isn't college where the popular frat boy sleeps with the studious virgin girl to win the group bet."

"I'm pretty sure I impressed you with our mutual disdain for rich, entitled frat boys. And you didn't sleep with me until I worked every morning on the Bell Tower renovation and dropped two hundred dollars on Puccini tickets at the Opera House."

"I wanted to be certain you weren't just interested in getting down my pants."

"I was very interested in getting down your pants. Best two hundred dollars I ever spent, even though you still didn't sleep with me afterwards." He reclined his elbow against the edge of the bar and popped a handful of almonds into his mouth.

She eyed the distinct way he chewed food. "Sometimes, I think it's the only reason you keep bothering to pursue me. I've never given into you without a challenge."

He rested his cheek against his knuckles and gazed at her with amusement. "It's true. I've never liked quickies, and I definitely preferred to take my time whenever I was with you."

He popped another handful of almonds into his mouth like he was commenting on the size of the room or the live music filtering in from the adjacent ballroom rather than the most sensual, intimate moments of their lives. She took up her clutch, realizing she needed to escape from him if she wanted to avoid the contradictory emotions that he produced within her heart.

"Let me buy you a drink," he suddenly offered, watching her rise from her stool.

"I think it would be best if you didn't."

"C'mon," he protested. "You're in one of your favorite hotels, surrounded by Tiffany treasures. How can you not feel like having a drink with your ex-husband?"

"Because you're my ex-husband."

"Technicality."

She anxiously glanced around the room. "And because I'm waiting for another man who shouldn't know I have an ex-husband."

"You mean you haven't told him about us?" Harvey feigned injury.

"I know, Harvey. Shocking you aren't the first topic of conversation with every new man that I manage to meet."

"You're the first thing I mention to every woman that I meet," he asserted.

Her gaze lingered on his own, just to see if there was any hint of jest in his voice. There wasn't. He seemed sincere in every way.

"C'mon," he grasped her hand and coaxed her back towards the bar. "He's only..." Harvey flicked out his wristwatch from his cuff and examined it. "Fifteen minutes late. Let me buy you one drink."

"I already have one," she replied curtly. She hated the fact that he was here, but she hated it even more that she was being stood up.

"But you don't look like you're enjoying it very much." Harvey swigged from her wine glass and nearly coughed it back up. "And clearly that's half the problem. That's Chardonnay. You hate Chardonnay."

Her eyes flicked up to an attractive man at the top of the white marble staircase. He was tall and commanding, dashing in his espresso brown suit and burgundy tie. "Please, Harvey…please just go away."

"Not until I order you something you will actually drink," he insisted, raising his hand to flag the bartender. "Hello there…could I please have two glasses of sparkling Riesling, preferably from Austria."

"Harvey, they don't have it." She returned to her seat at the bar, tracking the man's steady gait down the staircase. Her heart raced in her chest as the mysterious man approached the mahogany bar and greeted her with a smile until she realized he was acknowledging the bartender and not her.

God, how could she be such a fool? Slouching in her seat, she rubbed her temples and impatiently scanned her phone. Silence.

"How about that drink?" Harvey said, pulling a hundred-dollar bill from his wallet and flicking it across the bar, catching the bartender's eye.

"Riesling from Austria, sir. I'll do my best to find it," the bartender confirmed, sweeping up the bill and disappearing from sight.

Harvey smiled at her with a wink and downed her Chardonnay. "Your date is twenty minutes late. We should at least enjoy ourselves in the meantime with two glasses of your favorite wine."

"You don't drink Riesling, Harvey."

"That's true, which is why both glasses are for you."

"I can't do that without dinner, and you know it."

"I do," he confirmed with a nod. "So let's wait and see if Señor Romero shows up to sweep you away from me." Harvey angled his gaze down to her ruby and diamond anklet. "I'm surprised that Mr. Perfect didn't suggest to meet you in the Red Lacquer room, decorated with those Tiffany garnet-draped chandeliers."

"It doesn't really matter if he doesn't show up at all," Alma replied, settling into the shameful reality that she was being ghosted.

Harvey seemed to notice the change in her demeanor. "Well, if it would make you feel any better," he offered as a consolation, "we could sneak up to the Red Lacquer room and gaze at the antiques for a while. I know the building engineer. I give him season tickets to Sox games to make sure he personally polishes your Tiffany chandeliers."

Barely registering his offer, Alma checked her phone again and heaved her resignation. Obviously she had been the biggest fool to believe he would come tonight. Perhaps she had been a fool all along.

The bartender returned with two wine glasses and a silver ice bucket. Displaying the label before uncorking the bottle, he poured out a sample before receiving the signal to fill both glasses.

"Now, this is exactly what you need to feel better." Harvey passed the sparkling golden treat to her. She quickly consumed half of it and sighed, indulging in its fruity scent and sweet finish.

After a minute of deliberate silence, Harvey glanced at his wristwatch again. "So besides being grossly unpunctual, what's so amazing about what this guy has to offer you than...say...what I offered you?"

Alma downed the rest of her wine, needing every drop to truthfully answer him. "An escape from you."

He gazed at her, sidelong. "You do realize that makes the challenge of getting back together with you extremely difficult."

"I'm pretty sure I've never been an easy conquest."

"That's definitely true," he agreed. "Okay, what else?"

"The freedom to be anyone I want to be."

"I'm pretty sure if you had wanted to pretend you were a French maid or a flight attendant, I would've gone along with it."

Tsk, Alma clucked and turned away from him. But his boisterous laughter forced her to shoot him a glare.

"C'mon, don't be like that...I'm only kidding and you know it. How else am I supposed to stomach the idea of you falling for another man?"

She eyed his sincerity, surrendering to the relaxing effects of the full glass of wine. "I don't really know him that well. And he really doesn't know me that well. But we still have...*had* a connection. And I liked that."

"Ahhh, I see...the mystery, intrigue, danger," he quipped. "It's the same reason why Batman is so sexy. Except for the tights. And the cape. And the pointy plastic bat ears. Okay, maybe it's just his car."

"No, Harvey...it's the fantasy," she stressed, like it was so very obvious. Taking his wine glass into her hand, she sipped from it like it was her own. "The fantasy of being flawless in someone else's eyes. He doesn't know that I snore when I'm really tired. Or that I can't see farther than your face without my glasses or contacts. Or that I really hate wearing heels and fancy clothes. He only knows what I've told him or shown him, and that woman is someone different than the woman you married."

"I doubt she's that different," he replied, watching her down half his wine. "In fact, I bet she's actually very similar to the sassy, sexy, wickedly smart woman that I married, which is exactly the reason why I married her in the first place."

Alma stared at him, looking for a way to sum up everything that was wrong about their relationship. "Except with him, Harvey…there is no baggage."

"What?" he crowed, almost falling out of his chair. "No baggage? That's impossible. Every relationship ends up with baggage."

"It was too new for baggage," she reflected sadly. "And besides, I wouldn't have minded trying some new baggage.

"Like what kind of new baggage? That ubiquitous black carry-on crap that gets easily confused with everyone else's baggage?"

Alma looked up into the air, as if she was seeking out the answer there. "Just something…different."

"Different?" he repeated, almost offended. "You mean you don't enjoy how our baggage only locks if you sit on it, and the wheels always spin in the opposite direction that you want them to go?"

"Harvey—" she slowly leaned over to cover his mouth with her hand. The effects of the wine and his verbal swordplay were wearing her down…too…damn…much. "Just. Something. Less. Difficult."

"Well…for the record, I loved our baggage," he muttered through her palm. "Our baggage was the best part about our relationship. It's like that teal hard shell baggage from the sixties. Vintage. Irreplaceable. And completely worn-down and used up like an old bone by its owners."

Exasperated, she dropped her hand from his mouth. "Harvey, I don't want old bones. I want something…fresh."

"Fresh, huh?" Harvey glanced down at his wristwatch. "Well, he's definitely refreshingly late, which in some cultures is considered rude and unreliable."

"Less reliable than you are?"

"I'm here, aren't I?"

"And why is that again?" She squinted at him. She was having a hard time focusing on his face, and an even harder time remembering what had been said.

"Because I want you to reconsider your love of our old baggage."

He reached out for her hand and enveloped it in his own. Relaxed by its security and warmth, she swayed to one side. Even when she tried to avoid it, he always reminded her that their physical and emotional bond still existed even in the absence of their legal one.

*Which made everything about this so difficult…*she thought.

"That's easy for you to say now, but what happens tomorrow morning, when I have to show up at your property to conduct Jacques' evaluation of your building that will ultimately thwart your business deal?"

"Tomorrow is tomorrow," he said, shrugging off her concern. "Tonight is fine wine and satisfying conversation with my ex-wife who's dressed like a goddess." Lifting up her hand, he kissed the interior of her wrist, sending an unexpected quiver of arousal throughout her entire body. "Somebody needs to take advantage of it."

"That makes you an opportunist, Harvey." She peered at him without pulling away her hand.

"Surprise, surprise," he joked. "But it isn't always a bad thing. Especially not when the only woman in the world I've ever wanted is waiting for another man to whisk her away, and I get to fill in for him instead."

His earnest expression of contentment blurred in and out of focus, reminding her of what it was like when they weren't arguing about his money or his greedy ambitions.

"But don't you see, Harvey? There's still so much dividing us."

He shook his head, as if she couldn't be more wrong. "There's nothing dividing us, Alma. There's only two people who loved each other—not that long ago—and lost their way."

Without knowing why, she reached out and touched his cheek. "You were always a very attentive lover, but you weren't always a very reliable husband."

He leaned in to her touch. "I never cheated on you and I liked doing your laundry. Some things in a relationship are more important than others." He took her by the hand and guided her out of her seat. "Like the fact we have access to the top-floor honeymoon suite and its private pool, hot tub, and sauna."

She closed her eyes, afraid of the consequences of following his lead. "We're going to regret this in the morning," she warned him.

He brushed her hair over her shoulder and gazed into her eyes. "I won't have a single regret."

"You will when you lose your hundred-million-dollar deal because of me."

For a moment, there was a familiar unspoken connection between them, then he drew her against him and whispered in her ear. "And there could also be a zombie apocalypse. Either way, I won't blame you."

She raised her chin, encouraging the tender way his lips grazed against her cheek. "If there was a zombie apocalypse tomorrow, I think I would prefer to be with someone who reliably did my laundry."

Dropping his mouth lower and lower down her neckline, he replied, "Clean socks and underwear are way more important during a zombie apocalypse than being with someone different and less difficult who doesn't even know your favorite color or middle name."

"Your favorite color is pink," she exhaled. "And your middle name is Reginald."

"It's my favorite color because it's your favorite color," he asserted, feathering the tender hollow of her collarbone with his breath. "And you know I hate my middle name, so no need to go blabbing it to everyone you know."

"I won't." She whispered her sigh of surrender before allowing Harvey to support her weight. "Okay, I give in. Let's go swimming before the zombies get us."

Chapter Nineteen

IF THERE WAS ONE THING that Harvey would never forget about their ride in the private elevator up to the luxury penthouse suite, it was the taste of her—the sweet finish of Riesling mixed with the sensation of her luscious tongue, entwining with his own.

How many times had he imagined this moment since their separation? Every morning in the shower. Every afternoon when he ordered carryout for two and saved the leftovers. Every time he was alone in their bed—without her. The heartbreak and sadness had calcified into sharp barbs of anger and resentment, armor that he used to protect his pride and reinforce his reputation as a self-serving son-of-a-bitch. But his desire to maintain that image melted away with every penetrating kiss—each one deeper and deeper than the next until she fully surrender herself into his arms, as if she was accepting him back into her heart.

Why had she punished him in the first place? He didn't care. None of it mattered. The only thing that mattered now was that she accepted his advances as he braced her body against the mirrored walls and coaxed her knee upwards against his hip. His hand followed the sensual bare curve of her leg, slipping beneath the high slit of her dress and revealing a peek of her white satin panty line in the reflection.

White crotchless panties. It took everything in his power not to go down on her right then and there.

"We should wait until we've made it into the room…" her voice trailed off as she glanced up into the corner of the elevator at the security cameras.

He ran his mouth along her shoulder and wrapped his hands around the curves of her ass. "We've been divorced a year, Alma. I cannot possibly wait another second...especially if I know that you're wearing white panties."

"Virgin white," she teased into his ear.

He closed his eyes and buried his groan between her breasts. "And you expect me to wait?"

She laughed. "You always made me wait whenever we had sex."

"Wait until I pleasured every part of you." Peeling back the folds of the cowl neckline, he exposed the lace contour of her white satin pushup bra. "Just to prove there wasn't a damn virginal thing about you. And it's going to be the same tonight."

Tracing the arcs of her cleavage with his lips, he imprinted her flesh with ravenous nips and bites. She reluctantly sighed louder. "But what if I change my mind?"

"I promise to change it back," he asserted, heightening her arousal with every flick of his tongue. Her whole body melted into his arms as she pressed her fingertips against his scalp, encouraging his exploration of her nipples beneath her bra cups.

"That sounds like a recipe for regret in the morning," she managed to breathe out the words, enduring his long, drawn out suckling of each tit.

The elevator chimed as the cab halted its ascent.

Harvey stopped his foreplay and raised his head to meet her eyes. "Then tell me to stop."

He challenged her with a smirk. She challenged him with her silence, waiting an eternity before threatening him with her own crafty smile.

"If you stop now, I'll never forgive you, especially since you told me it was the honeymoon suite with a private indoor pool, sauna, and a hot tub."

That was all he needed to hear…

The moment the elevator doors rolled open, he swooped her into his arms and carried her over the threshold like his newly anointed bride.

He wanted to christen every part of her…as if it was their first night as man and wife.

Kissing her with passion and desire, he swept her through the luxury penthouse, its polished stone floor imprinted with dark angular shadows from its modern décor. Pushing through the French double doors, they entered the master bedroom suite, its plush circular bed floating atop a round marble platform offering sanctuary and serenity like a full moon in the darkness.

"A circular bed?" she noted, coming up for air after a series of intoxicating kisses. "Is that the hottest trend in honeymoon suites these days?"

She glanced around the room, taking in the crystal chandeliers and golden-threaded accent pillows and tapestries.

"No idea." Lowering her onto the mattress, he slipped off her heels and lavished her bare calves with sensual kisses, slowly working his way up her leg. "I only care that it's comfortable enough to make you come more than once."

"I'm pretty sure your feet are going to hang off the side," she remarked, as if she didn't hear him—or worse, pretended not to care. Instead, she scanned the circumference of the bed, attempting to size up its dimensions. "You have pretty big feet."

He paused his make out session with the back of her knee. "I'm not sure if that's an insult or a compliment."

She shrugged and propped a pillow behind her head. "Just an observation." Her gaze fell onto his dress shoes, which he kicked off like burdensome weights. "Kind of freakishly large."

"Like so many other parts of my body," he shot back, removing his suit coat to assert his height and athletic build before undoing his own belt and pulling it through the loops.

She feigned a sigh of disinterest and rolled over onto her belly, exposing the zipper of her dress. "I don't know. I can't really remember. You'll have to remind me."

He gladly took her cue and spooned his body against her own, pressing his pelvis against her backside while buzzing down her zipper. She exhaled deeply as his fingers slipped off the straps of her dress from each shoulder. The loose tendrils of her hair parted over the nape of her neck, offering him an unblemished canvas of skin to decorate with seductive nips. He could have unclasped her virginal white bra, but deliberately chose to wait. *Yes, he did always make her wait as long as possible—especially when she made fun of his feet.*

Pulling the zipper over the final arc of her ass, he stopped it just below her tailbone, exposing her white panties—and their naughty peekaboo cage-style thong.

"What have we here?" he said with a tease.

"A surprise…" she singsonged back.

"Such a devilish surprise from a woman in angelic panties."

He tugged upwards on the thong with his teeth. She clenched the edges of the pillow, anticipating more. He definitely intended to deliver more, especially if there was another surprise awaiting him.

"You were right. I'm not so angelic," she replied, inching off her dress with his assistance and turning onto her back to reveal the full, sultry view of her glossy white bra cups and matching crotchless panties.

Harvey closed his eyes, just to keep himself from ravaging her. "Definitely not angelic."

"Nope!" She laughed, flirtation mixed with inebriation. "Aaaaaand…" she announced, mimicking a drum roll before slowly parting her knees to command his attention between her legs.

He covered his face like he dared not dream. "Waxed?"

She crossed her legs, obscuring his view of the peep show. "Wouldn't you like to know?"

Yep, he absolutely would, filthy little wench.

Without another word, he pinned her beneath him with the strength of his body, and dominated her mouth with the urgency of his tongue. She pushed her hands against his pecs, gasping between kisses as he cupped her sex and invaded the secret opening of her crotchless panties with his fingers.

He released an incredulous moan of bliss when he pierced her wetness and glazed the bare surface of her labia with it. "You never waxed while we were married."

"Consider it a benefit of not being married," she whispered into his ear, arcing her back with a moan as he strummed her deeper and deeper.

"That means we can't get back together afterwards."

"I'm fairly certain we won't be getting back together," she replied dreamily, fumbling to unfasten the buttons on his dress shirt.

He heaved out his arousal, absorbing the warmth of her gushing nectar, intent on tasting it. "You mean this isn't make-up sex?" He skated his lips down past her belly and dipped his chin between her thighs

"Make-up sex?" she echoed, shuddering as he exhaled his hot breath between the transparent white gauze, barely covering her crotch. "No, not unless we're making up?"

Puzzled, he slowly rose up from his descent. "You're telling me that we're not getting back together after this?"

"I don't think so. I mean…I dunno." She seemed confused and overwhelmed by his question. "It depends on a lot of things, Harvey."

"Really? A lot of things?" he repeated, certain that wouldn't be true if he got her to climax with just his tongue. He prepared to flick her clit, but she quickly sat up before he had the chance.

"Yes, Harvey. A lot of things," she insisted with a hiccup. "Because right now, there's still all these feelings…" But she paused to consider her feelings when he pulled up from the bed to remove his pants and briefs.

"Alma, I don't have feelings right now. I have an erection."

He did have an erection. And it was magnificent. "But doesn't it bother you that I did all this" —she waved her hand across her crotchless panties, insinuating everything beneath it— "expecting to meet someone else?"

Of course it would have…he wanted to declare. It would have driven him insane with jealousy, if she had actually been sleeping with someone else. But the fact that she thought she was sleeping with someone else, and instead, was on the edge of choosing to sleep with him, more than made up for it.

"Honestly, Alma—" he paused, considering the fact that she deserved to know the truth. "The only thing that matters to me is that you want to be with me—here and now."

Climbing onto the bed, he wanted nothing more than to smother his naked cock between her warm, supple thighs.

"Tonight, yes," she agreed and stroked his shaft with a slow, arousing rhythm that only she performed better than he. "But tomorrow is likely a different story."

"Then let's not call it make-up sex," he offered, wanting to say anything to shut her up, so she would just relax and feel as good as she was making him feel now. "Let's call it something else."

"Nostalgic sex?" she suggested.

"Nostalgic sex?" His voice ticked up an octave as she licked the top of his shaft with her tongue.

Alma nodded, certain of it. "Like an '80s nostalgia band. You know, the kind that still performs their greatest hits despite being together for thirty years."

She licked him again, this time with a longer stroke, almost like a challenge. He rolled onto his back, disarmed by the lush sensation of her tongue washing over his cock before clenching his jaw, refusing to be distracted from making his point.

"So you're telling me that having sex right now would bring you the same amount of pleasure as hearing Bon Jovi performing 'Living on a Prayer'?" Wrapping his hands around her head, he guided her up to meet him face-to-face. "Nostalgic sex sounds more like something you'll forget immediately after we do it."

She unclasped her bra and flung it across the room. "I just don't want to put any pressure on it, Harvey."

Harvey gazed at her, then at her bare chest. If nothing else, she was a complicated woman made up of bewildering contradictions.

"Okay, but if we settle on nostalgic sex, I'm pretty sure I'm still supposed to make you come." Dropping his mouth between her breasts, he consumed them as if they were the last delights on earth.

"More than once," she corrected him, sighing with a smile. "In case I forget it the first time."

"Deal," he whispered back, stripping down her panties and exposing her beautiful sleek pussy. "But I promise you one thing. You're not going to forget it."

With an impassioned kiss, he braced her wrists against the mattress and thrust his pulsating cock between her thighs, priming her for the moment he intended to shock and awe her prim and proper expectations of nostalgic sex.

* * * *

What was it about him that kept her coming back for more and more?

She gasped and arched her tailbone into the mattress.

Thisssssssss, she hissed with shallow breath as he dug his chin against her flesh and swirled his tongue into her waxed slit.

"God, I could eat you up like this all day…" He lowered his mouth again and invaded her wetness with long, merciless strokes.

Raising her hands over her head, she released her exhale and spread her legs wider. Things were always so easy between them. She never felt inhibited with him. He knew exactly what she liked and how she liked it, which made it possible to lose herself in the rhythmic rowing of his desire. He hummed his lips against her clit while flicking it with urgency. She shuddered as the vibrations resonated throughout her sex, rising and falling like peaks and troughs of blissfulness. It was all so different from her sexual encounter the other night, where she had allowed herself to be conquered by an unknown stranger—a dark erotic fantasy, never to be shared or repeated.

With Harvey, she only felt closure. He didn't hate her; she didn't hate him. And everything she had been trying to escape—all those months of heartbreak and resentment—melted away with every exhilarating lap of his tongue.

She ran her fingers through his hair, nudging him deeper and deeper.

"Yes, there…please," she moaned, knowing he loved it when she begged him for more.

He obliged, rolling his tongue through her glistening slit, as if he craved every drop of her arousal.

God, yes, yes, yes... She butterflied her knees against the mattress, letting him relish her.

What was it about him that kept her coming back for more and more? The question resurfaced like a delayed echo through her inebriated mind.

Because he knew her better than anyone else in the world, she admitted silently, gushing beyond her control. *And it set her free...*

Delving deeper than ever before, he penetrated her to the brink. Another torrent of quakes undulated throughout her pelvis, promising to catapult her over the edge—if she was willing to allow it.

But she couldn't allow it.

Not now.

Not without him.

"Harvey… I don't want to come yet," she petitioned him, breathless. He always selflessly gave her the time and attention she needed to reach her orgasm first, but tonight, she wanted even more…

"Shhhh—" He pushed away her attempts to stop him. "Just shut up and enjoy it."

"Harvey—" her voice fluttered upwards, mimicking the sensation of his tongue. "I don't want to come without you."

He heaved out a sigh, a mixture of annoyance and aching torture. "Alma, licking your bare slick pussy is going to do the trick for me. I promise."

"Harvey—" she insisted, lifting up onto her elbows and shoving her heel against his forehead before he could resume his conquest. "It's been over a year since we've been together. I *need* to feel you. I want to feel you—inside me."

He locked eyes with her and prowled like a tiger onto the bed, fulfilling her request with his hard, naked body and forcing the heat of his cock between her legs.

"Are you absolutely sure about that? Because I'm going to fuck you harder than I ever have in the past. You do realize this?"

He nipped at her tits and fondled her tingling slit with his fingers.

"I'm counting on it," she confided in his ear, angling her pelvis into every nimble stroke. There was a reason why he always brought her to climax when so many others had tried and failed before him.

It was because he never quit.

He increased his rhythmic pace, stirring awake the most sensitive nerves inside her.

God, yes… she bit into his shoulder, aching for relief. Reading her mind, he replaced his fingers with the tip of his hot cock, nesting it against her own slick heat.

"But what about the condom?" she reluctantly uttered.

"Isn't that a benefit of having sex with your ex?" he replied, wrapping her legs around his waist.

"But I've slept with someone else," she suddenly confessed, feeling the whispers of sobriety tugging on her conscience.

"I know and I don't care," he asserted. "Because I'm sure he got the condom."

She paused, pondering his complete lack of envy. "Yes, he did…but…what about all your other harem girls?"

Pulling back from her body, he looked down at her. "Alma, I'm both flattered and annoyed that you think I've slept with half the women in Chicago—"

"But it isn't true?"

"No," he declared, straddling her into his lap and supporting her ass with his strong, workman hands. "Believe it or not, it's hard to meet other women when I'm still in love with my ex-wife."

She stared deeply into his clear, earnest eyes, wishing they didn't have to face each other as adversaries in the morning. "But how can you still be in love with me when I'm such a ballbuster?" She ran her fingers through his switchblade hair, layered on top, trimmed close on the sides.

"Easy. You're the only woman I know who can chatter this much during foreplay and my dick is addicted to it."

She broke into easy laughter. He grinned and nudged her for a kiss, a gentle breathy expression of reverence that quickly escalated into deep, endless exchanges of their entwining tongues. They had been friends as much as lovers, and tonight's reunion recaptured that—his corny jokes and flirtatious banter, her inebriated trust and acceptance of whatever he proposed, their familiar camaraderie and unspoken connection—they were all characteristics of the man who had once been her closest ally, her best friend, and her soul mate, and they were all traits she had missed whenever she summoned the strength to reflect on the consequences of her choice to divorce him.

He swept his desire throughout her mouth until he could no longer wait to reclaim her. Securing her in his lap and kneading the cheeks of her ass, he ground his pelvis against her clit, grooming her for the moment he would drive past all the boundaries she had placed between them. Bearing down on her knees, readying her stance, she hugged his chest and endured a series of shudders seizing her gushing slit, unlocked by his cock gliding against its slickness. Then, suddenly, she lifted her chin and parted her mouth, overwhelmed by the sheer masculinity of his first intimate thrust. A slow burn of pleasure diffused throughout her sex as he slid his bare warmth deeply inside her, radiating heat through her body. There had been so many nights when she had yearned for this moment—the raw, primal intensity of making love—boundless and unprotected—knowing it had only ever been something she had experienced with one man, and that man had been the only man she had loved with all her heart.

"God, you're so tight around my dick," he said with a hush, fully aware that she loved dirty talk as much as she loved the way he lingered inside her while she quivered in his arms. "Like my little virgin bride. I can't believe you've forced me to go an entire year without your warm wet juicy pussy."

She couldn't believe it either.

Shifting her higher into his lap, he fondled her rosebud with forbidden caresses. She lowered her forehead against his shoulder, disarmed by the masterful way he inspired her desire to be his whore.

"There you are," he whispered, slowly withdrawing his cock as she slackened with arousal, relinquishing all her defenses. "Open and ready for me."

She was so very open and ready…

He embraced her like his sacred possession, guiding her down onto the mattress and pinning her knees against his torso before driving into her with a determination to prove they were one. Tightening his clasp and jolting her upwards, over and over, until she crescendoed into an uncontrollable shriek as the full length and strength of his relentless cock dominated her completely. He soothed her cry with his kiss, deepening each lunge with a pace that she had come to depend on for her own climax.

God, how she loved the way he set her free...

The first spasm of ecstasy rose up from her pelvis and reverberated through her body, mimicking the pulsations of his throbbing cock pumping harder, faster, deeper…

Oh, so very deep, deep, deep...

She spasmed and screamed, scratching against his muscular arms and biting into his neck, but he had no intention of letting her go. Instead, he held her tighter and pressed his lips against her ear.

"Tell me how many naughty ways you want me to pleasure you tonight..."

"So very many," she said, almost like a plea.

He didn't wait for the end of her trembling quakes before he rolled her onto her belly and pushed her onto her hands and knees, forcing her to accept the taboo stimulation of his tongue, invading her without restraint.

"Good. Because I want your beautiful curvy ass and your luscious bare pussy kept high in the air until I make you scream out my name."

Forcing her into submission, he extended her arms out longer and spread her knees wider before steadying her hips with his assertive grip. She released an inaudible moan as he slipped the tip of his shaft beneath her, glazing himself with the rewards of his conquest.

She twitched through her tingling ache, rising up from a secret cavern of gratification.

"Please…I need you inside me," she dared to confess, bowing her head down onto the bed.

"Not until I pleasure you from behind and release every drop of myself inside you."

He worshiped her smooth, chaste backside and teased her tautness. Her thighs quivered, barely able to support her own weight as he unleashed every sacred stroke.

God, how she loved the way he owned her, mastering her into obedience and taming her instincts to challenge him at every turn.

She no longer wanted to fight him. She only wanted to give into her desperate yearning to be dominated by him…*just…like…this…*

With one powerful lunge, he breached past the initial folds of friction and drove his hard hot cock upwards, striking the chords of her most sacred spot. She panted out an orgasmic cry, an incomprehensible series of syllables, mirroring the thunderclaps of ecstasy that contracted her sex with every accelerating thrust. He was ravaging her, savaging her, raiding all her defenses while simultaneously commanding her trust until she could no longer feel what it was like to be separated from him—only what it was like to be united with him until eternity.

God, yes, yes, yes…

She released a frenetic cry, fueling his acceleration and heightening them towards their mutual ascent. At the very last fragile moment, he returned her into his impassioned embrace, kissing her with fury, challenging her every conviction that they would not be a couple again in the morning. Sliding inside her for his final series of thrusts, he pumped and pumped and pumped until she gyrated with soaring, breathless convulsions that initiated his own climax and oozed his warmth and tenderness deep inside her, reminding her of what it felt like to be completely vulnerable, but still protected—and what it felt like to be unconditionally loved by a man she had attempted to cut out of her life.

Chapter Twenty

SHE AWOKE TO THE FAINT sound of splashing water in the distance and the sensation of heat warming her naked body.

Morning.

The rays of sunlight streamed through the French doors that separated the master bedroom. Alma opened the doors and followed the seductive sunlight passing through a soaring art deco glass atrium and reflecting geometric patterns across the aqua waters of the palatial swimming pool. But it wasn't the imported marble pillars surrounding the oval-shaped room or the stone dragon fountain recirculating water through its six heads and tongues that caught her attention. It was the sight of Harvey's powerful, muscular body torpedoing beneath the surface of the heated pool, coming up for air only when he reached its opposite end.

Steam wafted off his smooth bare chest. Slicking back his hair, he prepared to submerge himself for another lap when he detected her presence.

"Well, good morning there, sunshine…" His jovial voice ricocheted off the enameled ceramic tiles. "Nice to see you smiling and well-rested. But you're overdressed."

He nodded to the white velveteen robe that she had found in the master bathroom in contrast to his tan, naked body undulating beneath the water.

"I'm not certain I'm prepared to swim," she called back. "That was supposed to be part of last night's agenda."

"Last night's agenda took a fabulous detour." Stretching his long sculpted arms across the edge of the pool, he let his feet float to the surface.

She knelt down and dipped her fingers into the water to test the temperature.

"Heated," he noted. "But if you prefer something *really* scorching, the hot tub is right over there." He smiled mischievously at the raised Jacuzzi, bubbling with a low inviting murmur. "But you'll have to leave your robe behind."

The underwater lights glinted off his blue eyes as he watched and waited, daring her to strip down in front of him.

"For now, I think it might be a better idea if I just kept it on." She gazed upwards at the grand gilt bronze wall clock. "It is getting late and I'm a working girl with a very important commission this morning."

"Work, work, work, work—" He drifted across the pool with a casual backstroke. "Why on earth would you want to work when you could just play hooky with me instead?"

"Harvey," she said, sitting down along the tiled ledge of the pool. "You know I can't do that."

"Sure you can," he retorted, gliding over towards her. "Who's going to miss us?"

"My father. And Jacques. And likely your beast witch of a real estate lawyer."

"Beast witch, huh?" He unexpectedly reached out to snag her hand. He was so much taller and stronger, and without much difficulty, he drew her into the pool and settled his lips against the hollow of her neck. "Well…she's actually my date to the Anderson gala tonight, but I'd much rather take you."

"Exactly my point," she said, her voice rising in pitch as the water saturated her skin through her robe. "I'm supposed to be going with Jacques. And if we don't stop now, it's going to create a huge conflict of interest."

Unwrapping her like a candy bar, he pulled off the robe and enveloped her into his arms. The sultry temperature of the water and the sleek, firm surface of his chest soothed her senses.

"There's already a huge conflict of interest. My dick wants you and you're not cooperating."

He consumed her with lusty kisses, swordfighting her tongue with long swirling strokes, until she finally kissed him back. After an endless session of passion and desire, he bobbed their weightless bodies deeper into the water.

"Don't you want to make sure that neither one of us does something that we regret?"

"No, the complete opposite," he replied, rocking his swelling cock against her sex. "I'm an opportunistic egocentric billionaire. My entire net worth is built on actions that I regret. It's what we billionaires do best."

"No, you billionaires excel at world domination. The rest of us are just left to regret it."

He carried her to the main pool entrance, a broad white marble staircase in the shallow end of the pool. "I'm pretty sure you don't regret my domination last night." Spreading her body across the steps, he smothered her with his chest before slipping his fingers between her legs and alleviating every reason she should regret last night.

"Harvey…" she moaned and fluttered her eyes. "We can't do this again. We can't—"

"Too late. Regrettable actions are already in full progress."

"Harvey—" she insisted again, this time, wedging his chin between her fingers, just to be sure he understood her. "I'm not on the pill."

He stopped sucking her nipples and blinked.

"I'm sorry. I should have told you last night."

Rolling off her into the shallow water, he sighed like he was pretending to care about their dilemma. "You told me a lot of things last night. You made fun of my feet. You tried to convince me that we weren't having make-up sex. I had a hard time shutting you up, kinda like now." He brushed back her hair and whispered kisses along her shoulder, pressing the tip of his persistent erection against her clit.

"But that was last night, and now, it's the morning….and we should really try to be more responsible."

"Or we could just try to be as irresponsible as possible, so we can have lots and lots babies and let your sister babysit them. Then you won't be able to refuse me when I offer to marry you again."

He rotated her into his arms and gazed intensely into her eyes.

Did he just offer to marry her again? Alma asked herself.

Everything fell into slow motion, including the ring tone of Harvey's phone on the lounge chair, lighting up with "Welcome to the Jungle" by Guns N' Roses.

Alma shook herself free from his embrace and nodded at the distraction.

"It's my beast witch of a real estate lawyer." He frowned, acknowledging that it had ruined the intimate moment between them. "She usually sends texts, but calls when there's really bad news."

"Then you better answer it."

He stared at her. She stared at him. The distinctive screech of Axl Rose's voice foretold their doom.

"I'll let it go to voice mail," he finally said. Their playful banter cooled as he exited the pool and wrapped a towel around his waist.

An awkward pang of jealousy surged in her heart. Harvey had changed his phone number after their divorce, and it suddenly seemed unfair that his real estate lawyer had access to it all this time, but Alma officially didn't.

Pressing the phone against his ear, he waited and listened to the message while his expression turned grim.

Without saying a word, he tossed his phone back onto the lounge chair and paced away from her.

Alma remained in the pool, eyeing his intentional distance. "No wonder you'd prefer to take me to tonight's gala instead of her," she said, attempting to lighten the mood. "If a mere voice mail from her has this effect on you, I can't imagine what it's like when you both are in the same room."

"My buyers for the riverfront parcel are pulling out of the deal unless we close tomorrow morning," he relayed, devoid of emotion. "And we can't close tomorrow unless Jacques retracts his cease and desist summons for historical preservation of the train depot with the City."

Alma shut her eyes, as if she almost expected it. Her biggest fear had been realized, and now, the only uncertainty was Harvey's reaction. "And he'll be using my evaluation to bolster his case."

"Yep," he said, attempting to dampen his annoyance—and failing. "Just like you said he would."

"Harvey—" she said slowly, noting the way he refused to make eye contact. "If Jacques doesn't hire me and my father to perform the evaluation, he'll just find someone else who will. You know that, right?"

"Yep. One of the *many, many, many* dozens of other stained-glass antique experts in Chicago." His sarcasm wounded her.

"I still might be able to help you," she offered, hearing her own voice crack.

"Help me how, Alma?

She hesitated, sensing he was angry at the world, which included her. "Even if my father and I determine that the building has historical value, we could propose alternative options that might give you some leeway—"

He scoffed. She had seen that look before during their marital fights. His pride was at stake and he didn't appreciate her pity. "Look, Alma...I appreciate your concern, but this issue comes down to two things: my private property and my public reputation. And I'll be damned if I let anyone stop me from doing exactly what I want. Especially not somebody who eats French croissants."

He tore off his towel and rubbed his head dry. It was hard to take him seriously when his dark hair was pointing in every direction, like he'd just been electrocuted. And yet, she knew better than to directly debate his Libertarian sense of entitlement.

"Harvey...I like eating French croissants," she replied, opting to remind him that he needed less enemies and more allies.

"Yeah," he said, watching her exit the pool. "And I like eating your French croissant, so I'll give you a pass."

He handed her a towel and gazed at her. She accepted it and gazed at him. He wasn't fighting against her. He was fighting against the world who had no right—in his eyes—to meddle in his business affairs.

"So what will you do?"

"If I have to..." he started to say before pausing, weighing the consequences of all his options. "I'll destroy the building and let Jackass Jacques and the City of Chicago sue me."

She closed her eyes in pain. "Please, Harvey...don't say that." When she opened them again, she hoped against all hope that she wouldn't recognize the ruthless businessman she had divorced.

"I'll still try to save you the windows, Alma," he interjected, softening his tone, "but not if Jacques pushes me against the clock and I have to bulldoze the damn thing myself in the dead of night to get my deal closed."

She stared into his cold, hard eyes. "You would do that, wouldn't you?" But it wasn't really a question because she already knew the answer.

"Yes, I would," he finally confirmed. "I absolutely would."

Their eyes locked and she gazed at him, feeling her emotions change from disappointment to heartbreak.

But you promised... Her silent judgment of him turned into sickening disappointment, knowing it didn't matter to him. In an instant, they had turned from passionate reunited lovers to bitter exes with irreconcilable differences.

*Of course they had...*she thought as he broke eye contact and brushed past her towards the master bedroom, seeking his clothes and an end to their stalemate glares. *It had always been this way. And it would always be this way.*

Had she been a fool to believe that he could change?

She definitely felt foolish, standing alone by the pool with sodden hair and shivering breath, protected only by a flimsy hotel towel and her utter lack of surprise, especially the moment she heard the door of the honeymoon suite slam shut behind him.

Chapter Twenty-One

WHEN HARVEY ARRIVED at the train depot, he fully intended to make good on his threat to Alma. The bulldozer was still parked outside from earlier that week. He still had the keys. He simply had lost the conviction to do something about it—until now.

It wasn't her fault, she was just a pawn, he thought, trudging through the overgrowth of prairie grass towards the front entrance. But that didn't mean he was going to roll over and let that righteous, twerpy Frenchman ruin the closing of his one hundred-million-dollar deal. He had been willing to compromise—for her sake. He had been willing to organize the removal and the delivery of the stained-glass windows to Enrique's auction warehouse—and into her care. *And that would have been enough*, Harvey fumed, shoving open the heavy walnut door with a creaking groan. *Enough for her and enough for him*. And instead of standing there, in the middle of a glorified shanty with fancy windows, he would have been back at the Palmer House's honeymoon suite, making love to his ex-wife in the hot tub, strategizing how and where he planned to propose to her again.

And she would have accepted, he nodded before shaking his head in disgust. If it hadn't been for motherfucking French fuckwad Jackass Jacques.

He shouted a frustrated series of indecipherable expletives that quivered the rotting rafters. Pigeons scampered. Flaking ceiling plaster drizzled onto his head.

"Thank you for that welcome, Harvey."

Brushing the pebbles of debris out of his hair, he turned and spotted Alma's father in the doorway. "You shouldn't be surprised, Enrique. You've known me long enough to know that I'm not the type to roll out the red carpet and serve you tea and crumpets."

"And definitely not croissants," Alma uttered sarcastically, emerging from behind her father.

"Yeah, especially not when you're working for the enemy," Harvey shot back.

Enrique considered Harvey's abrasive tone and the way Alma brushed past him without acknowledging him. He sighed, realizing there would be no quick truce. "Which is why I brought your favorite drink instead. Black, no sugar. Pinch of salt." Enrique passed the take-away coffee cup to Harvey. He accepted it.

That was Enrique. A gracious gentleman to his core.

Savoring the extra hint of salt, Harvey sipped it while stealing a glance over at Alma. *It tasted like her skin*, he thought, reminding himself of last night, whether she cared to acknowledge it or not. She was the only person in the world who knew he liked salt in his coffee. *Clearly, she told her father*. It seemed like a meager consolation in the wake of her refusal to look at him. But he'd take it. Everything about her was business as usual—baggy overalls, glossy red-framed glasses, ponytail as well as her silent determination to despise him.

"Where is your French fry of a leader, anyway?" Harvey sniped. "I expected him to be here, gloating in his beret and women's panties."

"Oh, he wanted to come," Enrique confirmed, removing two hard hats with headlamps from his duffle bag and handing one off to Alma. "He called us this morning, telling us he planned to meet us here, asking us how long we intended to stay. But Alma cut him off. She threatened not to participate if he was going to be present during our visit."

"Why? Does a man who likes to wear women's underwear creep you out?" Harvey lobbed his question at Alma, attempting to force her into the conversation.

"Not as much as men who pride themselves on wearing no underwear." Flicking on the headlamp of her hard hat, she directed it onto Harvey's crotch. He peered down at the spotlight. She knew him well. He always went commando in jeans.

"Neither one of us works well under pressure," Enrique clarified, stepping between them and redirecting Alma's light onto the floor. "And the circumstances surrounding this particular evaluation are already rather…unusual."

"You mean, the fact that I could claim conflict of interest since I used to be married to your daughter and she still hates me? Or are you referring to the fact that the property is obviously a worthless old train depot that I should have flattened three days ago, but instead, I got played like a man-doll?" Harvey kicked up his glare to the window in the balcony, remembering the reason he had stalled the demolition in the first place.

"Only because you were acting like a man-child," Alma huffed under her breath.

"Better than a man-whore, which you originally assumed. So I'll take that as a compliment."

"You could still claim conflict of interest," Enrique offered. "But it would only drag out the process more. And right now, it sounds like you need to clear your title as fast as possible, which I'm pretty certain I can accomplish for you in five minutes."

"If you can clear my title in five minutes, Enrique, then forget marrying your daughter again. I'll marry you instead."

Alma scorned him with her familiar laser-beam glare. Enrique saw their exchange and interjected his opinion. "Jacques Blanc has specifically requested an official evaluation from me regarding the building's historical significance as one of the original train depots along the North Western Line. But the good news is that I don't think I will be able to support Jacques' request for preservation based on the historical significance of the structure as a train depot because I do not believe this building is actually a train depot at all."

"Papi?" Alma cried out, as if he had just defected and joined the enemy. "How can you be so sure so quickly?"

"Because Chicago's first railway lines were constructed in the 1830s and all the depots along it were built not long after." Enrique lifted his gaze to the ornamental ironwork of the balcony's railing. "And most of them burned to the ground like the rest of the city during the Great Chicago Fire of 1871. This building is constructed of brick, which was used exclusively after the fire, and employs a curious neo-classical architectural style, which clearly dates its construction sometime in the 1880s, maybe into the 1890s. And it was clearly constructed for some other purpose. A train depot was meant to shelter passengers until the steam engines arrived, often hours and hours behind schedule, but there are no signs of built-in benches and no fireplaces to warm passengers."

Enrique studied the sweeping arched ceiling and prominent upper loft. Where there had once been a rainbow of color shining through the balcony's stained-glass window, there was now only flat dull light, seeping in like a cloudy haze from the rainy spring morning. "No, this building was obviously made for a reason more sacred, like a chapel or private memorial. But not as a train depot during the height of America's Industrial Revolution."

He removed his reading glasses and a copy of the official "Cease and Desist" notice from his pocket. "Jacques' summons specifically states that my evaluation should determine whether or not the structure located on your property is a historical remnant of the Chicago & North Western

Railway. And I can say without a doubt…" he paused, flipping over the proposal and scribbling two sentences. He held out the paper to Harvey like a victory flag. "This building is not," he punctuated with his definitive signature.

"So are you telling me you just called bullshit on Jacques' preservation proposal?" Harvey stared at him, unable to fathom that simple technicality would shield him from Jacques' political encroachment.

"I am simply doing my job, Harvey," Enrique said, like a well-trained diplomat. "I'll leave the bullshit to you."

He turned and headed for the door, stopping only when Alma called after him.

"But what about the windows, Papi? It's obvious that the windows have historical value."

"Oh, I'm not saying the building doesn't have historical significance," Enrique unexpectedly agreed. "And yes, the windows are clearly something of merit. But I am not the expert in antique glass. You are, *mi amor*. But we were not summoned by Jacques' notice to render our opinion on the windows unless that opinion bolstered his theory that this building is a piece of railway history. And you know as well as I do that they do not." Enrique glanced at his watch. "That took four minutes and thirty-five seconds. And although I have no interest in marrying you, Harvey, I will accept an offer to buy me lunch."

"Lunch, dinner, a brand-new sports car…whatever you want, El Che."

"Just lunch, Harvey. This is Chicago, after all. You are my former son-in-law and a brand-new sports car would look like a bribe. And regarding lunch…I will need to accept a rain check because I believe you and my daughter may need more time here—alone. So, I will go now to drop off my written expert opinion to City Hall this afternoon. You will have a clear title by five o'clock. In the meantime, I expect that you will give Alma a ride home in that fancy speedboat of yours, won't you?"

"Vroom, vroom," Harvey answered.

"Good." Enrique nodded, turning to leave.

"Papi—" Alma chased after him. "Is there really nothing more that can be done?" she whispered urgently.

Enrique shrugged and replied in a tone that made it clear he wanted to be heard. "It is Harvey's private property. He is entitled to do anything he wants to it. Losing the windows would be regrettable, I agree. But only he can decide if it would be more or less regrettable than losing his deal. Perhaps you can help him with that decision, but not me."

Noting the sound of pattering rain, he slipped on his coat and placed his hard hat into his duffle bag. Then he kissed his daughter on the forehead and promptly departed, leaving Harvey alone with Alma to fend for himself.

"Your father is an extremely efficient man. I always liked that about him."

"You're gloating."

"Me? Gloating? I wouldn't know how to gloat, even if I tried." He stared at her, his smile beaming brighter.

"Congratulations. You win. You're getting exactly what you wanted."

"I want you not to hate me."

"I don't hate you, Harvey. I just hate everything you do."

"Yeah, for some reason that's not very comforting."

She turned away from him and headed for the front door.

"Where are you going?"

"Home."

"I'm supposed to take you there, remember?"

"I prefer to walk."

"In a thunderstorm?" He grabbed her hand, but she shook it off.

"Yes, absolutely. I prefer to take my chances on getting struck by lightning over having to spend another minute with you."

Now, she was being almost as melodramatic as he could be.

"Come on…don't do this." He reached out to her again, but her eyes warned him that she would bite off his hand like a dog if he dared to try.

"Are you going to destroy this building? Yes or no?"

He hedged. "Alma, everything is not always black and white."

Ignoring him, she crowded into his space like a boxer waiting for an opening to throw the first punch. "Yes or no, Harvey?"

He looked into her searing brown eyes, realizing he couldn't lie to her anymore about anything. "Yeah, probably yes," he reluctantly confirmed. "Because if I don't destroy it now, Jacques will just come back to me tomorrow with another preservation summons, claiming this building is a shrine or a mausoleum or private chapel of Chicago's most beloved vaudeville entertainer, *Foie Gras Ménage à Trois*."

Alma narrowed her eyes at him, silently condemning him to man-childhood. He distinctly heard her unspoken words.

"Good luck on building the tallest towers in the world, Harvey. If you succeed, they will serve as proof that your ambition for money and fame are exactly the reasons why we're no longer married."

Her words struck him like a slap as she turned to leave, fully prepared to abandon him forever.

"Then tell me why I should save the building?" he called after her.

She stopped in her tracks, keeping her back towards him.

"Tell me the windows are valuable Louis Comfort Tiffany masterpieces. Give me a reason—a concrete reason—to at least consider ruining my net worth over them."

"I can't confirm that Harvey," she said slowly. "These windows don't have signatures. Many of Tiffany's earliest windows weren't signed and it would take weeks of research and documentation for me to confirm that with professional authority."

"Then tell me they're some of the rarest examples of stained glass that you've seen in all your years evaluating antiques."

Alma stared at Harvey through the grey muted light of the rainy day. She flicked the headlamp back on and studied the nearest windows in the bright beam. "They're lovely examples of nineteenth-century opalescent stained glass. But the ones on the ground floor are small and secular, and their flower motifs and color palette aren't particularly rare or original. And even the balcony window, the most impressive of the collection, is most likely the work of one of Tiffany's studio artisans or craftsmen, or a competitor who admired his work and skillfully replicated it."

"So it's far-fetched to think they're true original Tiffany masterpieces," he replied, seeking out support for his case, but he didn't get the confirmation he wanted. Instead, she shifted her helmet's light onto the shattered marble floor where they had discovered the metallic box and skeleton key inside it.

"What about the key hidden in the floor?" she retorted. "And the message in the Tiffany wall paper at the Field's building? And the survey description in the frame of Tiffany's *Guiding Angel*, leading us back here?"

Harvey shrugged. "What about them, Alma? You tell me."

They hopelessly locked eyes, their impasse as frequent and familiar to Harvey as his inability to make things right between them. Lightning flashed outside. Alma flinched as the crack of thunder followed, rattling the building's crumbling foundation. *It was all very gothic and tragic and menacing*, Harvey reflected. *Fitting, since Jane Eyre was one of her favorite novels.*

Silence smothered their bitter deadlock until an awkward sound beneath their feet became too difficult to ignore.

Alma was the first to break into an uncomfortable smile. "So...what's that noise?"

"You mean the noise that sounds like a ghost taking a very long piss?"

She shut her eyes and relaxed into tempered laughter as the singular stream of water continued to pour down a clanking drain pipe. "I'm afraid to even consider that option."

"Yeah, that's definitely not Casper the Friendly Ghost." Harvey paused, listening hard to the gradual crescendo of urination. "It sounds like it's coming from the basement."

"Basement? What basement?"

"The basement that's below us. It's the only way a building like this could still be standing after a hundred years...with a foundation dug and poured beneath the frost line."

“So what’s in the basement?” she asked.

Harvey glanced at her, knowing exactly what she was thinking, and wanting nothing to do with it. “Not a long-lost, hundred-million-dollar Tiffany stained-glass window, I’m certain of that.”

Like a dismissive reply, she retrieved the sledgehammer from the corner and handed it to him. “Two or three more strikes through the floor, and I’ll be able to shine my headlamp into the hole, just to see what’s down there.”

“Two or three more strikes?” He gawked at her. “You say that like I’m the almighty Thor, and wielding my hammer is easier than living among mortals and stringing together a coherent sentence.”

Alma crossed her arms, challenging him. “The comparison is not that far off.”

Harvey hiked the hammer over his shoulder and glared at her. *Some piece of work.*

“Yeah, thanks, but no thanks. Two days ago, I was trying to impress you. But now, we’ve already had sex and you still detest me, so I don’t see how sledging through a solid marble floor, and crippling myself like Quasimodo, is going to win me any brownie points.”

She paused to consider his ability to earn brownie points. “Well…I always had a soft spot for Quasimodo. It’s one of the reasons why *The Hunchback of Notre Dame* is one of my favorite novels.”

“Yeah, so is *Frankenstein*,” he quipped. “But every man has his limits.”

“I’ll give you a massage afterwards,” she said, clearly annoyed that he was being as uncooperative as a two-year old.

He considered her offer—carefully. “Where?”

“On – your – back,” she answered emphatically.

Disappointed, Harvey dropped the sledgehammer from his shoulder and handed it back to her. “I’d just rather use the stairs.”

Chapter Twenty-Two

ALMA COUGHED THROUGH the plume of dust that overwhelmed them after Harvey battered through the old iron padlock on the pine door with the sledgehammer. Stairs?! Why didn't he tell her there were freaking stairs? And a freaking basement?

Flicking on her headlamp, she shone it down the stairwell, illuminating a series of modest, descending planks leading into the underbelly of the building. The cold, dank air reeked of mildew and rotting leaves. Feeling like she was submerging herself underwater, she pinched her nose and held her breath, taking the first step down the staircase.

Harvey yanked her back by the straps of her overalls. "You must really think I'm an asshole if you believe I'm letting you go down there ahead of me."

Holding her like a cat by the scruff, he deposited her behind him and blocked her attempts to resume the lead.

"Really, Harvey? After all these years, you still think I can't handle myself?"

"Oh, I definitely know you can," he said, assessing the stability of the century-old staircase. "And every time you told me about trespassing into some abandoned shell of a building for lost antiques, my heart almost stopped. Which is why I'm absolutely not letting you do it now."

Shining her headlamp ahead of him, she caught a glimpse of the basement. "I've been through dingy crawl spaces and creepy attics that were way worse than this. And it's not exactly trespassing if I'm with the owner of the property."

"Exactly. So let's leave the unfortunate event of getting crushed by a loose support beam to me."

She heaved a sigh, just to ensure he heard her excessive eye roll. But secretly, deep down, she appreciated his attempt to protect her

"Well, there certainly isn't anything to find down here," he called back, sweeping his flashlight across the dirty wooden floors and crumbling stone foundation. Soggy bundles of old newspapers and cords of rotten firewood littered the space along with pine benches and wooden tables buried beneath piles of grey soot and rubble.

"There's your fireplace," Alma joked, nodding over to the cast iron stove toppled onto its side like a useless heap of junk.

"Yeah, not doing much good warming anyone down here." He turned to the right, spotting something else that was pot metal black and overturned in the corner.

With her spotlight, Alma trailed the intonation in his voice. "What is it?"

"I'm not sure…" Ducking underneath a dislodged rotting ceiling beam, Harvey waded through mounds of unidentifiable debris to the opposite end of the basement.

Alma followed closely behind him. "Harvey…I hate to be the one to break this to you, but you probably shouldn't be charging ahead like that."

"Oh? Why's that?"

She reached out to brush off something crawling on his shoulder blade. "Because there are definitely going be to spiders down here."

Freezing in his tracks, Harvey held up his hands and shivered in revulsion. "Just tell me you still have that key, so we can get out of here."

"What key?"

"The skeleton key," he punctuated.

"Ohhhhh-hhhh," she acknowledged, patting down her overalls, realizing it was likely in one of her pockets. "Voila!" she exclaimed, whipping it out of the bib's pocket and handing it to him.

"Good. Now, just keep your light shining on me, and if you see anything else crawling up my back, slap me like I'm your greedy, egocentric, opportunistic ex-husband."

"No problem," she smarted back.

Crouching onto his knees, he hoisted the black metal strongbox upright onto its feet.

"Is that a safe?" she inquired.

"Yep," he confirmed.

"And you really think our key is going to fit it?" Her heart raced as she pondered all the possibilities.

Slipping the key into the keyhole, Harvey grinned like a bank robber when it clicked to the right. "Yep."

The moment its rusty door screeched open, Alma rushed forward, squirreling in front of him to obtain an unobscured view of the safe's interior.

He stepped back, allowing her the honors of the big reveal. "Stacks of cash, bags of diamonds, bars of gold. I'll be content with one out of three."

But when Alma didn't respond, he glanced over her shoulder and released an obscene noise of disgust. "Tell me that's not the only thing in there." He bent down and swiped his hand through the safe, confirming there was nothing else inside the strongbox. "I braved spiders for that? A photograph?"

She gazed at the photograph. "Harvey…this is big. Really big," she whispered.

"Not bigger than diamonds or gold, Alma."

"Yes…maybe—" Her voice choked up, almost unable to speak. "It's a photograph of the *Eternal Love*."

Giving her the benefit of the doubt, he peered over her shoulder and examined the photograph again. "Alma…all I see is a black and white picture of two men, shaking hands in some old-fashioned room that is one velvet curtain and crystal ball away from resembling the place where we got hitched in Las Vegas."

Alma looked up from the photograph and frowned. "There was a crystal ball?"

"I'm not surprised you don't remember. You were so tipsy that you giggled all the way through our vows. But I clearly remember the fortune-telling Elvis pronouncing us man and wife."

"Harvey—" she said, adamantly shoving the photograph into his face. "Look closer at the reflection in the mirror directly behind the two men."

Harvey squinted harder. "Maybe a woman. Maybe a child. Maybe it's a stained-glass window or maybe it's just a painting. Alma…you're really reaching here."

"Now, look directly at the two men. Look at them, Harvey. One is Louis Comfort Tiffany and the other is Marshall Field."

"Or," Harvey countered, "just two men with white beards who bear uncanny resemblances to Santa Claus."

She ignored him. "This is incredible. I have to figure out where this photograph was taken." She started towards the staircase until he snagged her by the elbow, restraining her.

"You're not going anywhere without me, remember? Your father specifically assigned me the role of your chauffeur."

"Then chauffeur me to the Chicago Historical Society so I can verify the authenticity of this photograph."

"No, Alma. I'm done." He resolutely stepped back, releasing his hold on her. "I've got a deal to close by tomorrow, and I can't keep going on like this."

"But Harvey…if it's true that this photograph really shows Tiffany and Marshall Field together in a room with one of his windows in the background—possibly *the* window we've been searching for—then it would only prove that this building is significant in some way to Tiffany."

"This building?" Harvey questioned her, spreading his hands out to emphasize the filthy remains of whatever "this" used to be. "Do you really think if this building was something important to one of the most esteemed designers of the twentieth century, it would've been left like this?"

Alma nodded, as if he had just made her point for her. "Tiffany died a broken, penniless man. His company went bankrupt and looters ransacked his studios and destroyed many of his works in order to steal valuable bronze and copper parts. So yes, this building could be nothing at all, or maybe it's an example of what happens when people value bars of gold and bags of diamonds more than preserving history for future generations."

"Well…when you put it that way, you make it seem like I'm a monumental asshole."

"So don't be an asshole then," Alma challenged him.

"Are you still going to the gala tonight with Jacques? Or will you consider going with me instead," he challenged her back.

"Are you trying to make me a deal?"

"No, I just want to know where I stand."

"I can't separate who you are from the things you do, Harvey."

"But this is business. You have to recognize that."

"It wasn't always business for you. Not always. There was a time when we would have worked together to save this building, or at least you would've supported me in my quest to discover its secrets before the world decided they weren't worthy of being discovered. Now, you're on the other side, battling against me, and there's no way for me not to take it personally."

Without warning, Axl Rose screamed out "Welcome to the Jungle" from Harvey's phone. He fixed his steely blue eyes on her, recognizing it as an unspoken test, before finally breaking away and answering the call.

"What the hell is going on down there?" his beast witch real estate lawyer shrieked.

Alma could hear every word of Nicolette's banshee voice, matching the pitch of Axl Rose's screech. "I just got the phone call from City Hall. That was the fastest clearance of title I've ever seen. How in hell did you do that, Harvey?"

He shifted his phone against his jawline. "Well, let's just say I got some help from an old friend."

"She better not be prettier than me!" Beast Witch cried out.

"Certainly not as skillful at making me money, darlin'," he replied.

Man-child, Alma seethed, turning away from him.

Beast Witch peeled into excessive grating laughter. "Well, save some of your celebrating for tonight. What time are you picking me up?"

The gala, Alma thought, suddenly remembering they were going together.

Harvey paused, glancing over at Alma.

Was he waiting for her to change her mind? Was this her last chance to move beyond their differences and reconcile everything that had separated them?

When he was only greeted with silence, he deliberately turned his back on her. "Eight o'clock," he answered into the phone, like the verdict in the trial of their relationship. "And don't forget to bring me that matching tie."

He ended the call and pushed past Alma towards the staircase.

"So that's it? You're destroying the building, selling the property, and celebrating your victory?"

The defiance in her voice halted him in his tracks. "You can't expect me to be the same man that you married. People have to be allowed to grow and change and move on. So, that's what I'm doing, Alma. I'm moving on."

"I never expected you to stay the same," she shot back. "But I never expected you to change for the worse."

Mean, vicious, spiteful, and exactly what she had wanted to say directly to his face ever since the divorce, but never had the opportunity. She was the one who served the divorce papers, the one who ruined their chance for a happily ever after, the one who walked away from working on their marriage because she didn't want to patch up something that was infinitely wrong and broken. Even so, she had never been willing to drive the final knife into his heart by spewing out the deepest venom of hatred inside her—the burning resentful truth that she no longer had the ability to love him because she no longer respected him.

He clenched his teeth, his muscles along his jawline twitching like he was controlling the urge to rage against her.

Go ahead, Harvey, she glowered at him. *Go ahead and rage,* she dared him.

Instead, he swiftly strode towards her, encircling her forearm in his uncompromising grip and drew her body against his own. She gasped as the strength in his hand and the firmness of his chest forced her into submission. As he stared at her in infinite silence, the heat of his breath hovered over her lips. He waited, his hard blue eyes watching for the moment when she might betray a hint of desire and vulnerability within his arms. But she betrayed nothing except resignation—it was the end of their relationship, their friendship, and their reunion. And it had been the end for a very long time.

"I may be a worse man than when you first married me," he said in a hush, deliberately pronouncing each word as if it was the last thing he ever intended to confess to her. "But I'm definitely still a man of my word, so no matter how much you hate me and all the things that I do, I want you to know that I've meant every single word that I've said to you in the past two days, and nothing you do or say to me will ever change that." Releasing his grip and the threat of his kiss, he broke eye contact.

She rubbed her arm and fought back tears, silently cursing him. *No, he didn't deserve to see her cry. He absolutely did not.* And he sure as hell didn't deserve the satisfaction of knowing how much she wanted to cry over everything lost between them.

She got her wish. Without glancing back, he charged up the staircase without her. "Be on my speedboat in five minutes at the river dock. I told your father I'd take you home."

Chapter Twenty-Three

HARVEY WAS REMINDED of the reason he loved his speedboat—there wasn't any chance for conversation. Zipping across the surface of the river, full-throttle, he only experienced the wind whipping in his ears and the violent churn of the frothy wake behind him.

He had dropped her off at the edge of the riverfront boardwalk near her condo building, and watched from the pier until the light flicked on in the top-floor penthouse unit—the one they had bought and renovated together. The glow illuminated the circular stained-glass window of a fairy-like woman sitting on a crescent moon, signaling like a beacon that she was safely inside.

Safely inside— and away from him, he thought, revving the boat's engine and motoring through the glistening waters, reflecting the rays of twilight. It was a sentiment that echoed in his mind all the way home to his own riverfront home. He repeated it over and over as he cast off the docking lines and pivoted the boat into the pier, and by the time he finally trudged up the wooden staircase to his entrance, he had accepted it like a man accustomed to coming home to a silent house.

Soulless silence.

Kicking off his shoes and untucking his shirt, he grabbed a tumbler and a bottle of his favorite brandy and sank down into his leather empire armchair. It would have been now—in these vulnerable moments of heartache and loneliness—that he would have taken comfort in the distraction that his nameless, faceless mysterious Contessa had provided him.

"Nameless, faceless no more," he called out, toasting his glass into the air with a sad, indignant chuckle, as if their situation was too ironic to be true.

Vzzzzz.

His phone vibrated in his pocket. Pulling it out, he scanned the text, then shut his eyes as if he couldn't bear it.

I never expected only one night.

He rubbed his forehead and sloshed his drink around in its glass. *Was she really still pursuing it? Even after being stood up?*

Of course she was. A greedy, deceitful scumbag like him wouldn't be allowed to get off that easy by disappearing into thin air without a good-bye or an explanation.

He stroked his chin, considering his options. But as always, she forced his hand.

And I certainly never expected to be left waiting the other night, especially since I made the effort to wax myself bare for you.

He dropped his head and exhaled a long wistful sigh. How cruel the universe was to corrupt the one thing that had given him a tiny measure of solace all these lonely nights.

I'm sorry I left you waiting alone, he texted back. *You must think I'm a detestable bastard.*

Oh, I definitely know you're a bastard, she immediately sassed back, reminding him of why he'd been drawn to her from the very beginning. *And I didn't wait alone for long…*

He paused, recognizing the voyeuristic window she had just drawn open. He knew it would be wrong—so very wrong—to look through it. But still, he couldn't help it.

No? he casually answered, luring her in. *And why was that?*

Because I met an old acquaintance. You'll be happy to know he bought me a few drinks and kept me entertained.

Sounds like he made it easy for you to forget about me.

He was supposed to be jealous, no doubt. *Was that the only reason she was texting?* He wondered. *To prove she had moved on?*

But after a brief silence, she finally answered in a cryptic way that unnerved him. *It was easy…until it wasn't.*

He stroked the smooth leather of the chair and stared through the bay window at the view of downtown Chicago. Not long ago, he would gaze out into the city, wondering who she was and where she lived. Now, he knew exactly who she was and where she lived—and it tortured him.

He circled his thumb over the screen of his phone, uncertain how to respond. In that moment, he considered revealing everything. He knew he should have already revealed everything. But she beat him to it and revealed something unexpected.

I'm coming out of a long relationship and perhaps I assigned more importance to our arrangement than I should have to help me get through it.

And just like that, she told him everything.

Our arrangement is very important to me. It's been the only uncomplicated thing in my life—until very recently.

Then, as if she needed to confirm her biggest fear, she sent out her next text:

Are you married?

He paused, feeling the need to come clean. *I used to be.*

Girlfriends?

He had to smile. Even in her fantasy world, he was a player with an entourage of women.

None.

Before she could propose other possible excuses and complications, he saved her from having to imagine them.

You'll just have to trust me. If I could have been there with you, in the way that you wanted me to be, I would have done it. Everything else is just excuses.

He could have left it at that, but his final words echoed in his mind—*everything else is just excuses.*

He could have steered the conversation away from his failure to meet her and rekindled their affair. He could have asked her what she was wearing—or what she wasn't wearing—and expressed his need to fondle her waxed slit before slipping his bare cock between her legs, seeking out her warmth and wetness—one last time. He could have sat back and waited, slowly regaining her trust in order to extend the charade, perhaps even for one more night. *Just one more night.* But ultimately, he knew she deserved more from him.

I need to see you again, he finally replied.

When?

Tonight.

It's not possible. I have an important function I have to attend.

Never did he feel like such a conniving deceitful bastard than he did in that moment.

Then tell me where...and I'll meet you.

She made him wait, clearly weighing the risks of answering the question over choosing never to see him again. He sat up from his chair and paced the living room. He wasn't sure of his own intentions. He only knew he needed redemption.

It's a gala at the Field Museum. It starts at eight o'clock. But I'm not certain they'll let you in without an invitation.

Don't worry, he confidently shot back. *I have connections. I'll take care of it. Just be sure to wear your antique diamond choker. I want the pleasure of seeing you wear it.*

Chapter Twenty-Four

BREATHTAKING...When Alma arrived at the top of staircase of the Field Museum, she was reminded of how much she loved Chicago and all its glory. The museum's Pantheon-inspired grand hallway transported her back in time and she briefly forgot who she was and all the turmoil in her life. Her gaze traced the repeating curves of the archways and vertical lines of the Roman pillars sweeping upwards to the vaulted ceiling, patterned with a checkerboard skylight. Its three hundred-year-old limestone floor embedded with fossils gleamed like modern-day polished granite. Sue, the world's best, most preserved Tyrannosaurus Rex specimen greeted her with an enigmatic smile—*sweeter than the Mona Lisa*, she thought, marveling at its twelve inch, dagger-like teeth and massive head the length of a grown man.

One of the museum's countless historical treasures, Alma thought, savoring how the seventy million-year-old dinosaur fossil perfectly blended into the sumptuous ballroom décor. Dramatic white chiffon drapes cut across the grand hall from floor to ceiling, illuminated by the diffused glow of floor lights. Pristine white tablecloths covered dozens of round tables crowned with majestic floral centerpieces in blown glass vases. Women in evening gowns and men in tuxedos milled around the main attraction—the auctioneer's podium and viewing pedestal beneath a billowing white canopy where dozens of privately-collected fine art pieces were scheduled to be auctioned off to the highest bidders.

Alma scanned the crowd, looking for familiar faces within the infinite elegance of the grand hall. Aldermen, city officials, wealthy patrons, and even a few of her father's clients stood out among the sea of champagne flutes and inebriated laughter. But no one conspicuously stared back at her.

He would make her wait again, she thought, descending the ornamental wrought iron staircase beneath the soaring, half-dome belvedere to the main floor. *This time, she had come emotionally and mentally prepared to wait for him.*

Lifting her chin and sweeping off her faux rabbit fur shawl, she nodded in appreciation to the attendant who exchanged it for a ticket at the foot of the staircase. Alma had taken a painstaking amount of time in deciding what to wear tonight. She knew it had to be a worthy companion to his stunning antique diamond necklace, but as someone who routinely wore the same pair of overalls every day, she fretted for hours before finally settling on the one precious piece of clothing she had stashed away in the back of her closet—a floor-length mother of pearl silk charmeuse gown that radiated with opalescence under the chandelier lights. Its formal sheath bodice created a clinging silhouette all the way down its fluid, minimalist train while its hidden high slit evoked sophistication with every step. Decorative crystals embellished the one shoulder strap, calling attention to its plunging cowl back design—the only vintage flair of the dress—upstaged by a heavy, emerald-cut diamond choker that framed her neckline.

Without warning, the firm touch of a man's hand pressed against the small of her back.

"They finally valeted the car. Let us hope the auction goes smoother than the parking."

Alma exhaled, relieved to see her father by her side. His familiar touch guided her towards the center of the grand hall to the auctioneer's podium. Despite his confident stride and impeccable black tuxedo, Enrique tugged on his bow tie, compulsively attempting to loosen the noose of the starched collar. Alma recognized the displeasure on his face, knowing how her father hated the high-maintenance game of dressing up as much as she did. But attending luxury galas and auctions hosted by their roster of wealthy clients was just part of their business, and no one was more gracious and courteous in an uncomfortable tailored suit than Enrique Castillo.

A familiar face rushed up to them.

"Where have you guys been? I've been here since four o'clock and I've been waiting hours for you to show up."

Surprised, Alma scanned her sister's catering uniform and serving tray. "You're working as part of the staff tonight?" She reached out for a flute of champagne.

"Papi pulled some strings and got me the job."

Their father eyed her. "Are you being good, Conchita?"

"Of course, Papi!" she cried out, flicking back her long black hair and adjusting her red lace bra beneath her white blouse. "I haven't even had the urge to spit in anyone's drink yet. Not even once."

Alma almost spit out her own drink. Enrique, on the other hand, ignored his youngest daughter.

"Alma, please stay with your sister. I see a few of our clients on the other side of the hall. I will go and greet them. Come over when you can."

He lifted a flute from Conchita's tray and sauntered across the grand hallway like a man who had been to a thousand galas before this one.

"He expects you to babysit me," Conchita said, lifting one of the flutes and downing it.

"I can't imagine why."

"Yeah, probably because you've been doing it my whole life." She swigged from a second flute. "Who's he talking to over there, anyway?"

Her eyes followed Conchita's gaze over to the chocolate fondue fountain. "One of our clients, Madame van der Meer. We appraised her collection of rare antique watches and she's auctioning off a few of them tonight."

"So I'm interrupting your work as usual."

Alma nodded, admiring her father as he worked the room. "Yes, probably. He's so much better than me at being the social butterfly. I much prefer standing in the corner like a wallflower at these functions unless someone needs me to talk about the differences in appraisal values of jewelry from the Victorian, Edwardian, or Art Deco eras. "

Conchita flopped her head forward and loudly snored.

"Yeah, I know how much my art history expertise impresses you."

"About as much as your sex life impresses me," Conchita snarked. "Although you never dress up like that unless you're trying to get laid." She paused, as if she suddenly expected to be clued in. "And I do believe there's been some movement on that front, right?" Popping a miniature puffed crab cake into her mouth, she crudely thrust her finger back and forth into her hand shaped like an "O."

Alma stared at her sister, wondering how often Harvey and Conchita traded the details of their relationship. *Wasn't naming her Ballbuster enough*?

"There's nothing to relay about Harvey and me, if that's what you mean."

"That's exactly what I mean," Conchita insisted, stopping one of her catering colleagues and swapping out her champagne flutes for his hors d'oeuvre tray. "I expected you both to show up here together tonight."

Alma defensively crossed her arms. "Whatever Harvey told you *may* have happened," she insisted, "it wasn't without a lot of alcohol and regret. Trust me."

"I'm pretty sure the only sex worth remembering involves a lot of alcohol and regret." Conchita gauged her sister's empty champagne flute before making the leap. "So you're not mad at me?"

"Mad at you? For what?"

"For hoping that you two would get back together—even if it was just for one night of fuck-your-heart-and-brains-out-sex-with-your-ex. It was getting old watching you both pretend to hate each other."

"Oh, we're definitely not back together. And I definitely still hate him."

"Okay, sure. Which is why you're wearing your wedding gown to a public event where you know you'll run into him."

Alma marveled at her sister. God, how Conchita had a freakish photographic memory when it came to everything related to shopping and clothes.

"It was supposed to be my wedding gown," Alma corrected her. "Except Harvey and I eloped and I never had the chance to wear it. I only wore it tonight because it was the only thing I had that could be paired with the necklace."

Conchita's gum fell out of her mouth and onto her serving tray. "Holy whoredom, Alma! Did Harvey give you that? Dang…if I got one of those every time I had sex with my ex, I sure as hell wouldn't be dumping him—again. How can you be so heartless and cruel?"

"Me? I'm the one being cruel?" Alma protested. "I'm not the one acting like a megalomaniac billionaire titan who completely disregards anything without obvious monetary value."

"Ugh!" Conchita plugged her fake fingernails into her eardrums. "My ears burn when you talk like a public service announcement. Yes, I know. I get it. I get it! You hate how Harvey's become a filthy rich stud muffin. But most wives would just live with it because he's still a stud muffin—an attentive, faithful, loyal stud muffin. Hell, most wives would freaking love every minute of it, and if they didn't, they would just get revenge by maxing out his credit cards, not divorcing him."

"Well, I don't want to be a wife who stays in her marriage for the *bling*," Alma sassed back. "And I certainly can't keep waiting around for Harvey to change back into the man that I married, so I'm doing the only thing that I can—"

"Treating your ex-husband like he's the fast food equivalent of sex on the side?" Conchita interjected. "Or wearing your wedding dress like that creepy Charles Dicken's character, Miss Havisham?"

Alma deliberately ignored her. "I am trying to put it all behind me and move forward." She swept her gaze through the crowd, hoping to catch a stranger's eye. "Which is why I'm waiting to meet someone else here tonight."

"Reeeeeeeeeally?" Conchita's perfectly penned eyebrow arched upwards. "Someone other than Harvey? That would mean you're sleeping with two men at the same time, and now you've suddenly impressed me. Maybe I'm the one who needs to start babysitting you."

"*Bonsoir, mon chéri*!" Jacques' shrill greeting cut through the murmur of the crowd as he scampered up to the women.

Frowning, Conchita glared at his egg-shell satin tuxedo and pink neck scarf. "Okay, suddenly no longer impressed," she announced to Alma before sweeping her serving tray in the other direction and abandoning her sister to endure Jacques' barrage of double-cheeked kisses.

"*Mon chéri*, you look like…" He paused and scanned the contours of her fitted gown longer than he should. "Glittering starlight. A snow queen. A ray of moon beam."

Alma forced herself to accept his fawning. "Thank you. But I had no idea you were wearing white, too."

"*Très chanceux*! What a coincidence *parfait*! Together, we look like royalty."

Alma was thinking more like characters from Disney on Ice.

"Let us come out of the corner. There are so many people waiting to see us." He attempted to place his thin, cold hand on her exposed back to draw her away from the corner and into the crowd, but she consciously escaped his touch. She knew she would have to spend time by Jacques' side tonight, but she had no idea how truly annoying it would be.

"I'm here mainly to support the auction," she replied, reminding him she was there on her own merit and not as his official date. "There were several pieces that I appraised and I want to be on-hand in case there are any questions from our clients or the bidders."

"Even more reason to mingle together," Jacques said, drawing her hand into his own.

"Well, not exactly," Alma answered, slipping away from him—again. "My father is a thousand times better at working the room than me. I just tend to drink too much champagne and trip over things."

On cue, she stumbled over the flowing hem of her silk gown while backing away from him. Seeking a distraction, she spotted the oversized black and white photographs hanging on the wall.

"The 1893 World's Columbian Exposition held in Chicago," she noted, diverting his attention from her and onto one of the most important events in the city's history.

Jacques stroked his scarf and eyed the photographs of men in top hats and women in long, bustled skirts who curiously surveyed African oddities like Egyptian sarcophagi and big game animals preserved through the strange new science of taxidermy.

"*La Belle Époque* of the development of Chicago." Jacques sighed, as if it was the city's best and only era worth remembering.

"Three years to prepare and millions of dollars to construct dozens and dozens of new buildings," Alma added. "All designed by the most influential names in architecture to showcase the world's greatest achievements in arts, science, and culture."

Jacques turned away from the photographs and fiddled with his pink neck scarf. "And now…what has been left to show for it? Only one building still stands today."

"Most of the buildings were meant to be temporary, Jacques. Constructed quickly to amaze and enchant visitors who came all over the globe to drink newly-invented carbonated soda, experience the magic of electric lights at night, and ride the world's first Ferris wheel."

"Yes," Jacques mused. "The Great White City. And now, all we have is archived photographs and our imaginations. *C'est une grande pitié*."

"We have museums like this one," Alma offered, feeling the strange need to counter Jacques' cynicism. "Founded by Marshall Field after the Exposition to display all the natural curiosities from across the world. It's still the only place you can see an extinct passenger pigeon or a dodo bird."

"Perhaps stuffed birds do not invigorate me like the preservation of art and architecture, which is why I am so disappointed by your father's evaluation of the train depot this morning. I intended to submit another proposal for preservation tomorrow to City Hall, but I have received word that Monsieur Money Monster has already destroyed the building."

"Destroyed the building?" Alma repeated. "Are you sure?"

"Yes, it is what I have heard."

"Even the windows?"

"*Oui, bien sûr*," he confirmed. "I have heard everything is gone. It seems that nothing more can be done."

Alma closed her eyes, as if Jacques had just punched her in the gut. In the background, the auctioneer's voice boomed through the microphone.

"Sold for six hundred and twenty-five thousand dollars!"

Gasps of astonishment and delight rippled through the crowd before applause erupted like a thunderclap, echoing off the Plaster-of-Paris walls and ricocheting across the vaulted ceiling.

"Your father looks pleased," Jacques commented. "It must be one of your clients."

As if she were in a surreal dream, Alma gazed around the room and caught her father's eye.

"It must be Madame van der Meer's antique wristwatches. She wanted to sell four of the rarest within her collection to a private collector or philanthropic institution that would put them on public display."

Alma scanned the floor, seeking out the auction paddle of the highest bidder. "They are rare and highly desirable artifacts from World War II, so we started with a reserve of two-hundred thousand dollars, anticipating only a major museum or arts foundation would be willing to shell out that kind of money."

"Instead, it looks like it is a private collector who prefers to remain anonymous." Jacques noted the auctioneer's assistant, delivering the crimson velvet palette laced with four bejeweled watches to the successful buyer. He dashed up the staircase, disappearing into one of the curtained balcony suites.

Moments later, the assistant retraced his steps down the stairs and marched directly towards them.

"Miss Castillo," he called out confidently, as if he was certain he had found the right woman.

"Yes?" Alma answered.

"This is for you." The assistant presented the velvet palette, lined with one of Madame van der Meer's diamond-studded wristwatches. "The buyer would like you to accept his gift." The assistant removed the antique timepiece from the palette and passed it over to her. Alma stared down at the rows and rows of petite baguette cut diamonds, scintillating back at her.

"Please, you must have made some mistake," she said, fumbling to replace the watch on the palette.

But the assistant returned it to her along with a business card. "No, definitely not, Miss Castillo. The buyer was very specific in his request. Enjoy."

She glanced down at the message scrawled in ink across the back of the card: *Hall of Gems. Eight o'clock sharp. By the way, you look ravishing...*

Her gaze shot up to the balcony. *He was watching her.*

She flipped over the card, spotting the emblem for the Peoria Hotel—in case she needed the reminder. She didn't. Her whole body remembered every intimate, seducing touch from that night.

"That is most irregular," Jacques said, a hint of jealousy dampening his grandiose French accent. "As its appraiser, you must reconsider accepting it."

"I have no intention of accepting it," she snapped. "And I certainly don't need anyone reminding me of the ethics of my job. Excuse me."

Realizing the Hall of Gems was on the second floor, she scurried up the staircase, pausing only to admire the sweeping aerial view of the grand hall when she reached the top step. When she was certain she had escaped Jacques, she headed for the entrance of the Hall of Gems and slipped inside it.

Dark, quiet, and empty, she noted, feeling her heart rate exploding as she crept deeper into the secluded gallery. During normal business hours, she knew the Hall of Gems was a bright, airy room crowded with patrons looking to catch a glimpse of the 5890-carat Chalmers topaz, a brilliant cut oval gemstone weighing over two and a half pounds, almost the size of Alma's palm. Its unblemished translucence flashed cosmic blue as it spun on a circular pedestal beneath the showcase's spotlight. The only other light in the room was the automatic illumination within each display case, triggered by movement along the glass panes.

"One of the largest topaz gems in the world," the masculine voice called out from the entrance.

She shut her eyes and deliberately withheld her gasp. When his footsteps closed in on her, she whirled around to face him. His chiseled profile passed out of the shadows and into the light of the nearby tanzanite display case.

"Ugh, Harvey! Could you stop doing that?"

"Doing what? Following you into a dark, private corner of a museum, just to whisper, boo?"

"Yes, exactly." She anxiously glanced behind him, realizing the last person in the world she wanted to deal with at that moment was Harvey.

"Because you were expecting someone else?"

She turned away, avoiding his question. But he pressed the point.

"Isn't it kinda strange that whenever you're looking to meet Romero, you keep running into me instead?"

"Strange isn't the right word," she answered, noting his formal tuxedo. He was one of the few men she knew who could pull off wearing a contemporary silver-grey shirt with a traditional black tie.

"Stalker-ish?" he asked.

"Warm, getting warmer," she replied.

He swept his eyes over her diamond choker and curve-hugging silk gown, sensing her discomfort. "You look nervous."

"I'm not nervous."

"Antsy?"

"No."

"Apprehensive?"

She crossed her arms and glared at him.

"Annoyed?"

"Not until this conversation."

He laughed aloud. "So let me ask you something...do you think there's a reason Lois Lane never questioned why Clark Kent looked so much like Superman? I mean, can a pair of glasses really fool a woman that much?"

"Denial goes a long way."

"Denial? Or just hot sex with a man who doesn't have an obvious first name?"

Closing her eyes, she drew in a deep breath to compose herself. *She needed to get rid of him.* "Can we please discuss your comic book fetish later? I would prefer to be alone right now."

"Really? Alone? Or just not around me?"

"Please, Harvey—" she insisted, hoping he would just take the not-so-subtle hint and leave the gallery.

Instead, he looked into the jewelry case, studying the stunning pendant necklace, its lustrous aqua-violet gemstone in a square white gold setting, inlaid with endless petite diamonds. "What if I promised only to talk about gemstones in a highbrow, intellectual manner? Like the fact that tanzanite is a thousand times rarer than diamonds, and still, nobody ever says, 'Honey, can you please buy me a big honking tanzanite ring for my birthday?'"

Ugh, he was seriously not going to take the hint. She glanced down at the time: *five minutes to eight.* Perhaps if she indulged him for one minute, she could persuade him to go away.

"I definitely wouldn't consider the use of 'honking' in any conversation as highbrow."

A smile flashed across his chiseled face. "Good point. I forget how many times your highbrow has had to lower itself to my lowbrow over the years."

She shrugged, a subtle affirmation. "Highbrow would be the fact that tanzanite is a thousand times rarer than diamonds because it's only found in one place on earth."

"The flagship Tiffany & Co. store on Fifth Avenue in New York City?"

"Near Mount Kilimanjaro in Tanzania," she corrected him.

"See…that's exactly what I mean. You have to trek up a treacherous volcanic mountain just to find it. Now that screams love."

She crossed her arms and expelled an intentional sigh of exasperation. "Harvey, I'm not here to banter with you about gemstones."

"No? That's a shame. I thought you might want to talk antiques. It is, after all, an antiques auction and it looks like you might have gotten something more than just a nice commission from that winning bid."

He eyed the diamond wristwatch in her palm until she shifted it behind her back.

"It's very lovely," he said. "Almost a perfect match to that diamond choker necklace. Someone must know your tastes well." His voice lifted to the Tiffany stained glass masterpiece window, *Mermaid*, at the far end of the gallery. "A little too well…"

Alma curiously stared at him. "You sound jealous?"

"Would that really shock you, Alma?"

The sudden sincerity in his voice arrested her. "Yes, it absolutely would. Especially since I assumed by your words and actions this morning that you really couldn't care less about me anymore."

His jawline flinched. "I'm just surprised you're willing to give this guy another chance despite the fact that he stood you up the last time. It kinds makes me wonder if you think you're in love with him."

She narrowed her eyes at him. "And why would you care?"

He held her defensive gaze. "Because you're up here, waiting to meet him."

His comment enraged her. *Was it any of his damn business*?

"Shouldn't you be downstairs, Harvey? Schmoozing with all your city hall buddies, making sure they grant you the title clearance you need to sell your riverfront parcel tomorrow, especially now that you've demolished the building and all its windows?"

"Is that what you've heard?"

She confirmed it with silence.

"Well, in that case, I'm also sure that Jacques told you I built a pagan altar with the gold from the sale of the land and sacrificed virgins who refused to sleep with me."

"I didn't believe the virgin part," she replied. "Although it was tempting."

"Tempting to believe the worst about me? Kinda like that other myth that the only thing that matters to me is money."

"Isn't it?"

"It didn't used to be, Alma. You know that."

"And now, Harvey?" she challenged.

Challenging her in return, he stepped forward, locking eyes and crowding her against the display case. "And now, I have to wonder…if you didn't know anything about me—if you didn't know I was a greedy unscrupulous billionaire who willingly sold his soul to make an exorbitant profit with every business deal—could you still fall in love with me the way you fell in love with me years ago?"

She searched his unflinching eyes, his clear blue gaze reflecting her own truth. "The only reason I hate your money is because you're the one who makes it the most important thing about you."

"What if it didn't matter to me as much as you think," he offered, slowly reeling her in by her hand until he secured her bodice against his stylish tuxedo, forcing her breath to rise and fall in sync with his own. "And what if, despite the fact that you despise everything that I've done to make money, you still find yourself drawn back to me again and again?"

"Harvey…" she paused and bowed her head, truly pained by the familiar scent of his cologne—*the same one she had bought him for Christmas every year*. "Please…you can't keep doing this, telling me you want me back, but then not acknowledging any of the reasons why we separated in the first place."

"I do acknowledge them, Alma. I just don't accept them. Especially not when you let me make love to you like you did the other night."

"Please don't make this about the other night. I was alone and vulnerable, and I had too much to drink, and…"

"And what, Alma?"

"And…it was a mistake." She looked up to meet his eyes, ensuring that he would not only understand her, but that he would also believe her.

"A mistake?"

"Yes, a mistake," she repeated quietly. "And you know it was, too."

He released his hold on her and backed away. "No, I really don't," he replied, the edge in his voice cutting between them. "I would never cast aside a night that we spent together like that as nothing more than a casual mistake."

"It was a mistake because it complicated things that didn't need to be made more complicated."

"No?" He glanced at her sidelong, mocking her rationale. "And what about the complicated night before that?"

Alma felt the blood drop out of her cheeks. "What night before that?"

"You really don't know?" he fished. "Or maybe you're a little bit too much like Lois Lane, and just a little too good at fooling yourself."

Her eyes darted back and forth over his enigmatic expression, decoding the message hiding there.

"You?" She could barely pronounce the single word through her lips, unable to believe it was true.

He flashed her a roguish smile, as if he'd been caught in the middle of a jewelry heist. "When I bought The Peoria Hotel, I knew owning an upscale business lounge like The Vault would come in handy. But I never expected to enjoy something like the Turkish Suite—until you came along that night."

She darted forward, striking that arrogant, cocky, billionaires-can-do-anything-they-want smirk right off his face. *S-M-A-C-K*!

After absorbing the sting of her slap, he realigned his jaw. "Please tell me you did that because there's a spider on my cheek."

"No, Harvey. I did that because you're a lying son-of-a-bitch who deserves far worse than that."

She attempted to strike him again, but he seized her hand and forcefully drew her towards him. She fought to escape his grip, but he was stronger and more determined to settle the score.

"Are you really that angry at me?" he asked, his voice simmering with emotion beneath its low, steady tone. "Or are you angry at yourself for falling in love with me again?"

"I have SO not fallen in love with you again."

"Are you absolutely sure about that, Contessa?"

He braced her tighter—tighter than he ever had before—and waited for her to surrender to the almost forgotten sensation of their bodies melding into one.

"Yes, I'm certain because you lied to me."

"No, I didn't lie," he flung back, wanting to believe it. "I didn't know we'd been texting each other until the night at The Vault when we were having drinks at the bar. And then, once I realized it was you, everything just spiraled out of control and—" his breath lingered over her lips, seeking out a fleeting moment when she might be convinced not to hate him into oblivion, "—and into one of the best nights of my life."

"Exactly. So instead of telling me the truth, you fucked me."

His mouth twisted into an awkward schoolboy smile. "Fucked is a strong word, Alma. Although you did climax twice, and I don't remember you complaining much about it at the time."

"Ugggggghhhh!" she grunted in disgust. Shoving herself away from him, she slipped off her heel and chucked it at his big! fat! inflated! billionaire! head!

He successfully ducked.

"Asshole!" She flicked off her other heel, winding up her next pitch.

"Alma—" He warned her, taking cover behind a display case showcasing a ninety-carat ruby and diamond necklace. "Stop and think about how impaling my forehead with your heel isn't going to change the fact that you clearly still have feelings for me."

"Feelings for you?" she raged. "You mean, feelings like misguided infatuation? No, I don't, Harvey. I had those feelings for another man who wasn't supposed to be you!"

She launched her other heel, but overshot his head, missing him and the gleaming perfection of his slick, sculpted hair.

"Which is why I gave you the fantasy that you wanted. Doesn't that count for something?"

Alma freaked. "I wanted someone else, Harvey! *Someone else*. That's not called a fantasy. That's called moving on!"

"Well, maybe I wasn't ready to let you move on. I'm still not ready."

Throwing her hands up into the air, she paced barefoot across the hardwood floors. "Are you actually listening to yourself? You, you, you, *y-o-u*… Well, newsflash, Monsieur Asshole. The nights we spent together? Our sex-lationship? They weren't all just about you. The whole success and failure of our marriage? It was never just about you and what you want. And it was never just about your money or your properties or your business deals or even about the demolition of the train depot and its windows. It was never all just about you. It's about respect, Harvey. Respect and dignity and integrity and trust. Trust, Harvey. *T-r-u-s-t*!"

Harvey blinked, noting the rabid spittle flying out of her mouth. "I didn't think you'd take it this badly."

"UGH!" she shrieked.

He tracked her erratic movements around the display case containing a pearl bigger than the size of his frown.

"Okay, message received. I screwed up—again. But you can't blame me for wanting you back."

"Wanting me back? How about *earning* me back?"

He blinked again, this time, the truth of her words sunk in his expressive face. "I never planned for any of this to happen."

She stared at him. He stared at her. It was their typical, gut-wrenching deadlock.

"So what happens now?"

"This..." she whispered. Unclasping the diamond choker from her neck, she slapped it into his hands along with the antique wristwatch that he had bought for her.

Then she gathered up her shoes, determined to leave him—and everything she hated about their relationship—behind her. But he stepped in front of her, refusing to accept the bitter finality of their split.

"So that's it? I'm supposed to just skulk back into the shadows and let you...move on?"

"I had already moved on, Harvey. The moment I filed for divorce. The only difference now is...I have even more regrets."

She attempted to push past him again, but he thrust his arm across the doorway, blocking her path.

"Well, I don't have any regrets, Alma," he stressed, his chin lowering to meet her gaze, ensuring that his words rang true. "And I'm not sorry about the fact that you thought you had moved on with some other man when really...you just proved how easy and natural everything can be between us when we're not trying to tear each other's hearts apart. So no. I'm not sorry about that at all. I'm not sorry one bit."

He locked his eyes on hers, searching for the woman he had loved, honored, and cherished so many years ago. But when she coldly, silently rejected him, he shifted away from her defiant glare and withdrew his arm, allowing her to abandon him—forever.

She hurried down the staircase, cradling her shoes in her arms, desperately trying hard not to cry. *No, she would not cry—damn it.*

As she rounded the corner and passed into the main floor of the grand hall, she wiped her eyes and focused on the one visceral feeling coursing through her body—*she needed to escape.* Squinting beyond the flaring lights swirling floral patterns of green and purple across the white walls, she scanned the unfamiliar faces within the crowd near the auctioneer's podium. She searched out the distinct black hair and moustache of her father. He was nowhere in sight. She fretted and searched again. She needed to let her father know she was taking a taxi home, and then it would be safe to breakdown. But it was in that moment that she halted in her tracks, unexpectedly spotting something on the center stage beneath the halo of spotlights, something so hauntingly beautiful that it drew gasps from the audience and captivated them into collective silence.

Alma dug her fingernails into her wrist. *It wasn't a dream.* It was the stunning stained-glass window from the balcony of Harvey's rundown building.

"Here we have a rare, exquisitely preserved example of opalescent stained glass with a mother and child in a field of lilacs, circa 1890s, in excellent condition," the auctioneer said, introducing the window. "It is part of a collection of eleven stained-glass windows, all from the same riverfront building slated for sale. All the works within this lot are unsigned and unattributed, but skillfully exhibit the trademark design of influential American glassmakers of the time such as Louis Comfort Tiffany and John La Farge. For this reason, we shall start the bidding at one million dollars."

One million dollars? A flurry of panic raided Alma's soul. That was a bargain for an entire lot of late nineteenth-century opalescent stained-glass windows. If they were authentic works of Tiffany or La Farge, each window could easily fetch a million dollars or more, and everyone in that room was savvy enough to know it. A million dollars for the whole collection was just a tease. Every major museum director at the gala could afford to take a million dollar risk that an eleven window lot of stained-glass windows would turn into a ten million dollar Tiffany or La Farge jackpot. But few museum directors could compete with the flurry of bids from individual collectors and fortune hunters who drove the price up to three million dollars within a matter of minutes.

"I never thought it would work, but Harvey was certain they'd take the bait."

The woman's sultry voice snaked over Alma's bare neck and shoulders, sending shivers down her spine. She glanced behind her, knowing exactly who she would find there—Harvey's beast witch real estate lawyer. *What was her name again? Nicotine?* The stale scent of cigarettes wafted from her breath. *Nicolette.*

In the background, the auctioneer called out the bids in rapid-fire succession. Bidding paddles bobbed up and down. "Three and a quarter million. Yes, there, number 48. Do I have three and a half million? Yes, there, number 12. Do I have three and three quarters million? Yes, there…I have three and three quarter million. Do I have four million dollars?"

Alma incredulously glanced up at the stained-glass window, meticulously cleaned and illuminated in its full glory. "I don't understand. I heard he had demolished it. Everything."

"That's what was *supposed* to have happened," Nicolette laughed, flipping back her shiny black locks over her bare shoulders. The long strand of golden South Sea pearls jiggled down through the center of her green velvet evening gown, the sweetheart bodice boosting her cleavage like two perfect cantaloupes ready to be plucked off the vine. "I told him to just bulldoze the whole thing and be done with it. But apparently, he said he got it from your expert authority that the windows might be valuable."

Nicolette glared down at Alma. She was a least a foot taller, maybe even two feet with her chunky heeled pumps, especially with Alma completely on the defense without any footwear. "Harvey was certain collectors would recognize their worth if we included them in the auction. He said it would raise the value of the riverfront parcel because word would spread through the real estate community about the auction—"

"But I thought that was exactly what he didn't want," Alma interjected. "It just gives Jacques another reason to attempt to pass a preservation summons through City Hall."

"Not if the windows are gone, sold off to someone else," Nicolette replied, as if she was revealing a trade secret. "He's using tonight's auction not only to profit from the sale of the windows, but to also market the property. We're collecting back up offers in case our current buyer attempts to renegotiate the price or wants to back out of the deal completely."

Both women fell silent when a voice rose from the crowd.

"Five million dollars," the salt and pepper-haired bidder definitively announced.

The auctioneer acknowledged his bid with a nod. "I have five million dollars. Do I have five and a quarter million?"

Nicolette eyed the man, her black penciled eyebrow arching into a perfect curve. "That's the owner of the Centennial building along South Wacker. He tried to put in an offer on the riverfront parcel in the first round, but he dropped out when the price soared above eighty million. Maybe now he'll be more willing to cough up the cash if he thinks there's more art treasures to be found." She released a dramatic sigh through her red lava lipstick. "I should have known better. Harvey is always right about how to make the most amount of money from the worst parcels of real estate. That man has the biggest knack for flipping garbage into gold. It might even be the sexiest things about him. Well, almost the sexiest…if you know what I mean."

Alma gazed at Nicolette's sophisticated curves and flawless cinnamon complexion, wondering if it could possibly be true that she had already slept with him.

At that moment, Harvey descended the staircase. Nicolette rudely abandoned Alma and rushed up to him with a delirious smile. Greeting him with a kiss, she smeared her glossy territorial mark across his sculpted cheek. He was self-assured and stylish in his fitted modern tuxedo and she was buxom and exotic in her green ivy gown. Their presence together attracted conspicuous glances from the crowd.

They were the perfect couple, Alma thought, as the clap of the auctioneer's gavel rang out across the grand hall. *They deserved each other*.

"Sold to paddle 187 for nine and half million dollars," the auctioneer finally pronounced, calling out the successful bid. Applause erupted throughout the grand hall.

Alma pushed through the crowd and rushed towards her father. Spotting the bidder holding paddle 187, she cried out frantically. "It's a private collector, Papi. Not a museum director or representative of a public arts foundation."

"Yes, Alma. I think you are right."

Her lips trembled as she controlled her urge to weep. "But he'll decorate his mansion or office building with them, and no one will ever see those windows again. How can we let that happen?"

"Alma, it is done. There is nothing we can do."

The fatalism of her father's words rung in her ears. She covered her face with her hands, overwhelmed by the helplessness and meaninglessness of everything in her life. What good was her expertise of nineteenth-century fine arts if it simply helped rich, mercenary men purchase art to display like trophies for their own private enjoyment? What good were all her attempts to salvage the wreckage of historical buildings when property owners like Harvey Zale could sell them off for pure monetary gain?

Gala guests swarmed to Harvey and Nicolette like they were celebrities. Several men in tuxedos slapped Harvey's shoulder and offered their handshakes and congratulations. Nicolette reacted to their jokes with giddy, animated laughter. They were the beautiful, rich, powerful patrons of the auction and their elite circle of jovial banter and air of untouchable prominence fueled her despondency. But it was also the possessive way that Harvey wrapped his hand around Nicolette's voluptuous hip, drawing her to his side, that ultimately made Alma want to flee.

What good had come from all those years she had been together with Harvey if none of it mattered to him now? How had he changed so completely from the man she had once admired and loved to the man she now loathe and despised? Alma murmured her good-bye to her father and turned to leave before he had a chance to respond. She hurried up the staircase, forgetting to retrieve her coat, and exited into a relentless blast of wind that constricted her gown around her body like a choking hand.

"A taxi, please," she uttered to the parking attendant who blew his whistle, signaling over the first available cab.

What good had come from taking a risk all these weeks, involving herself with a stranger with whom she was convinced she had a deep, mysterious connection, only to find out that it had all been a complete lie?

"Nothing," she whispered, as if saying the word finally made the pain real—real enough to acknowledge that it had all been a wasteful dream. "Nothing," she repeated through bitter tears, extinguishing any desire to ever dream again.

Chapter Twenty-Five

HARVEY SHOVED THE loaded hot dog into his mouth, savoring the juicy, greasy, gluttonous pleasure. Stretching out his legs, he relaxed against the hard plastic of the ballpark seats. This was the only thing he needed in life—junk food and baseball.

A concessions vendor jogged up and down the concrete center staircase, hollering out Slurpee flavors. "Wild cherry, blue raspberry, mango pineapple! Icy, cold, fresh!"

Harvey held up his hand and signaled for two before passing a five-dollar bill to the stranger next to him. The bill rippled through the hands of the fans in the row until it made its way down to the vendor who exchanged it for two bright neon frozen drinks. Harvey smiled, admiring the synchronization of everyone in his row passing the two drinks back to him.

Sure, he could easily afford box seats behind home base or swanky private clubhouse seats. But it had been their tradition for years, hanging out at the game together in the outfield with the other die-hard, blue-collar White Sox fans who never made you feel alone, even when their boys lost a home game.

"Are you feeling better yet?" Enrique asked, eyeing Harvey as he sucked down half the red slushy before coming up for air.

"The world is no longer spinning like I'm on the inside of a washing machine," he replied. "But I still feel like a teamster steamrolled over my head."

Enrique nodded like it was a certainty. "You were very inebriated last night."

"Yeah…and unfortunately, I still remember most of it." Resigning himself to the full effect of the sugar rush, brain freeze, Harvey slouched into his seat, watching the pitcher's windup and trying hard not to think of all the ways he had been an asshole last night.

"Thanks for giving me a ride home, Enrique. And sorry about spewing vomit all over your front seat."

"Don't worry. I'll have it cleaned and send you the bill," Enrique quipped.

"Just pick out a new car and I'll buy it for you."

"Really, it's okay, Harvey. I like my old car just fine." Enrique slapped Harvey on the shoulder—a gesture to let the point go. "Besides, it's just a car. Better than what happened to your lawyer's shoes."

"I did try to aim low to avoid her gown," Harvey added as a consolation.

"I don't think she appreciated the effort."

"Yeah, probably not." Harvey focused on how the first baseman fumble the ball. "It's not like I can offer to buy her new feet."

With the roar of the crowd, both men suddenly jumped from their seats and cursed as the fumble turned into a double for the rival team.

"No, money can't always solve everything," Enrique answered, shaking his head at the defeat. "And sometimes, it just makes things worse."

"Yeah, like ruining a marriage."

"I don't think Alma is upset with you about your money, Harvey."

"I know. She's upset that I care more about making it than she does."

"Yes, that's probably closer to the truth."

"And she's back to hating my guts for selling off those windows."

"That was a surprise to us both."

"But it worked like a charm," Harvey replied. "We got three backup offers this morning on the sale of the property and all of them for more money than the original offer. It forced the buyer to agree to move forward." Harvey glanced down at his wristwatch. "We close in five hours. And then I can move onto my Shanghai project."

Enrique nodded. "Then you have done what you have needed to do. Alma will recover. There are many other priceless works of art in attics and basements yet to be discovered."

Harvey remembered their hunt for the *Eternal Love* and the mysterious photograph they found together in the basement of the train depot.

"She will move on with her life and you will move on with yours," Enrique continued. "And you both will learn that all this time fighting each other wasn't worth the year that you spent on it."

Harvey watched as Enrique tossed caramel corn into his mouth, as if he hadn't just proselytized like a wise old sage, and wondered if the unexpected loss of his wife was the source of his cool, calm advice.

"So how did you do it, Enrique?" Harvey asked. "Stay married to the same woman for twenty-five years?"

Enrique shrugged. "I loved making her happy."

"It was that easy, huh?"

"Yes," Enrique replied, crunching each kernel. "Women aren't as complicated as they pretend to be, Harvey. The problem is that men are too simple to understand that they really only need one thing from us..." he paused to take a calculated sip from his blue Slurpee.

"Chocolate?" Harvey finally guessed.

"No."

"Diamonds?"

"No."

"Casanova biogenetically crossed with the Terminator?"

Enrique snorted, as if he finally understood why Harvey had so many marital problems. "Dependability," he stressed, slowly rising from his seat to track the course of a long fly ball. A group of old timers stood up as well until the left fielder casually caught the ball. In unison, they all exhaled a sigh of relief.

Enrique nodded in approval and returned to his seat. "After we give them dependability, everything else falls into place."

Harvey peered down at Enrique's hand. Even a decade after his wife's death, he still wore his wedding band. With a wistful sigh, Harvey flipped his baseball cap backwards and slurped down the rest of his wild berry slushy, wishing everything about love and marriage came that easily to him.

"You know, Enrique…you should start your own talk show and air it on Facebook Live. People could call in and ask you to appraise both their antiques and their relationships."

Enrique almost spewed blue Slurpee through his nostrils. "Thank you, but no thank you. I have two daughters and a billionaire ex-son-in-law. That is enough drama for me."

Chapter Twenty-Six

ALMA PICKED AT HER steaming chicken pot pie, realizing she no longer had the appetite to eat it.

"How about this one?" Conchita flashed Alma her phone while stuffing her face with a bite from her Cobb salad. "He looks cute. Nerdy, but cute. He even wears the same kind of glasses as you."

Alma barely lifted her eyes to view the image.

"CosmoScientistGetsHisGrooveOn," Conchita read aloud. "*Oooooo-hhhhhh*...he sounds fun. Like somebody who would be the first one to jump out on the dance floor at a wedding."

"Dusting off his disco moves," Alma replied, stabbing the pot pie with her fork.

"Or maybe," Conchita cooed, attempting to elicit interest, "his sophisticated ballroom dancing moves."

"More likely his awkward Michael Jackson dance impressions."

Conchita ignored her. "CosmoScientist," she repeated, digging deeper into her salad. "So...he probably likes nerdy, but intellectual things like space and stars and planets and—"

"UFOs," Alma interjected.

"Well...a moonwalking UFO scientist really wouldn't be *all* that bad, right? I mean, maybe you could make-out with him in a planetarium."

"I think I prefer not to make out with anyone anymore."

A half-eaten tomato literally dropped out of Conchita's mouth. "Oh dear Lord, my ears are burning. Please tell me you did not just say that."

Alma stabbed her pot pie again and left the fork, upright and immersed, in its center. "I am completely serious. I'm giving up men, sex, and all the dramatic garbage that comes along with it."

Conchita calmly inhaled and spread both her hands on the surface of the linoleum table.

"Look, Alma…I know I screwed up. Big, big, *BIG* time, okay? And I get that you're still mad at me for giving your phone number to Harvey, and I know I should have never stuck my big fat foot into your relationship, expecting that you and Harvey would just meet, make-up, and get on with having babies for the sake of my own selfish desire to babysit them. And I know I've sworn to make it up to you through a thousand years of servitude—"

"Two thousand years," Alma corrected her.

"But—" Conchita raised her voice. "You cannot give up on men and sex, just because of what happened."

"Why?" Alma crossed her arms, challenging her.

"Because no one intended to hurt you. Least of all…Harvey."

"Exactly my point. Look what happens when the man isn't even *trying* to be a selfish egotistical bastard. He just naturally is one."

Ouch, Conchita mouthed, as if she finally understood just how pissed off Alma was at her ex-husband. "Look, I know Harvey has his flaws, and you two were together a long, long, *long* time, and a lot of love and trust has been lost, but that does *not* mean you should just give up on ever finding the right man again."

"I don't need to find the right man, Conchita," Alma insisted. "He needs to find me. And right now, I'm more interested in hiding out in my boring, sexless bed with my boring antique trade magazines, stuffing my face with ice cream and wearing flannel animal pajamas, than I am in being found by anyone with a big fat dick promising to make me come."

Conchita squinted through her fake eyelashes and pursed her pouty pink lips. "Really? Flannel animal pajamas?"

Alma shrugged. "I haven't officially bought a pair yet, but I've been considering it."

"Wow. I really have come too late to your pity party, haven't I?"

Alma stared at her sister and nodded. "Sometimes a girl just needs to be left alone to wallow in her own self-pity. Especially when no one intended to hurt her, but still, a whole lot of hurt is the only thing she's left with."

"Ugghhh," Conchita heaved a nauseated sigh. "That makes me feel soooooooo guilty, but okay…I'll accept it. But only if you promise me one thing."

"Not to pick farm animals over the mythical creatures?"

Conchita nodded. "Anything, but a pig or a goat. That just seems wrong on so many levels."

"I was thinking about the unicorn ones."

Her sister exhaled in relief. "Quirky, but acceptable."

"Don't worry. I'll probably just stick with wearing the same thing I've worn for the past decade."

"That old, ratty, boy band T-shirt from that concert where I lost my virginity?"

"No," Alma answered, drawing out her fork and finally taking a bite of her meal. "Harvey's worn-out pinstripe flannel pajamas. Even though I hate his guts."

"Ugh," Conchita slumped her head forward like she had just suffered a stroke. "That's the saddest, most messed up thing I've heard all year."

"Yep," Alma said, realizing her chicken pot pie had already turned cold. "It's called a pity party for a reason."

* * * *

True to her word, Alma ordered a pizza that night, put on her worn-out pinstripe flannel pajamas, and flipped on the gas fireplace before cozying up in her bed with a steamy romance novel that she had started long before she became entangled with her sexting affair.

Who needed the real thing, anyway, she thought, huddling under the covers, when she could have a smarter, sexier version of a billionaire on demand?

It already felt like the best decision she had made all year. She was moving on. The warm crackling glow of the fireplace mellowed her inhibitions. The fresh gallon of double chocolate ice cream was thawing on the counter. And Beethoven's grim, dramatic second movement of his Symphony No. 7 filled the isolating silence.

Composed in honor of soldiers wounded and defeated in a battle against Napoleon. The music selection was a deliberate choice to match her mood. Even in the face of despair and destruction, these men—who had lost so much—still had to find a way to carry on. *And so would she...*

Then her doorbell rang.

She glanced at her clock. The pizza delivery man took less than ten minutes. Clearly even the universe supported her plan of obtaining serenity through junk food tonight.

After slipping out of bed and scrounging through her purse for a generous tip, she rushed to the door and opened it without even peering through her peephole.

"That was the fastest pizza service I've ever..." her voice trailed off in disappointment when the man in front of her offered her a plain white box instead of a hot zesty pizza.

"Delivery, ma'am."

"From who?"

"Card is on top of the box. Just need your signature for receipt."

He handed over the clipboard and she scribbled out her name before passing off the ten-dollar bill.

"Wow. Thank you very much, miss." He pocketed the tip and headed towards the elevators. "Have a great night."

Alma gazed down at the plain white box and lifted the lid. Sifting beneath the tissue paper, she retrieved a black velvet pouch. Based on its weight and chucky contour, she immediately guessed what was inside it, but the message on the white calling card confirmed it: *I can't take it back because it's rightfully yours. ~HZ*

Alma closed her eyes, vowing not to look at it. She had loved the antique choker so much the first time she had received it that it would be unbearable to have to look at it now, reinforcing the fact that it had really been from him all along.

Instead, she searched for her phone and impulsively sent him a text: *gifting me a million-dollar necklace isn't going to change anything.*

She waited, half-expecting to receive a message that he had changed his phone number again. But if he did receive her text, she knew he would either respond immediately or leave her hanging the whole night without clarification or closure.

When her phone buzzed in her hand, her heart leapt with fury, as if nothing had changed and he was still the same mysterious man who was courting her.

I know. It's the end of us, Alma. I get it.

Alma re-read his text, hearing an uncharacteristic surrender beneath his succinct reply.

So why are you sending it back?

After a long uncomfortable moment of silence, he finally answered, as if he no longer had anything to hide. *Because I bought it for you as a gift for our fifth wedding anniversary, right before you ended our marriage.*

Ugh. She bit her lip, hard, and shook her head. *So you tried to give it away to another woman you were sexting? Looks like that didn't work out too well either, did it?*

Her response was beyond snarky and rude, but that's exactly what he deserved from her—merciless punishment.

Depends on how you look at it, he replied. *Yeah, I tried to give it away. But in the end, it still found its way to you.*

Whatever she texted back was going to make her sound like a bitter, ungrateful bitch, so she simply fell silent, giving him the last word.

Just consider it my final love letter or swear it off as a miserable curse. Save it, donate it, sell it or even just dump it in your trashcan. It's yours, not mine, so you're right...nothing is ever going to change that fact.

When her phone went dark, she returned to bed with the velvet pouch in her hands and her heart harder and heavier than stone. If he had sent it back to make her cry, break her down, and convince her take him back, it would have been better than what he had accomplished, which was make her realize that he had completely given up on their reconciliation.

For once in a very long time, he'd finally given her exactly what she wanted—and ironically, it was the one thing that made her cry. *It wouldn't all hurt so much if their relationship had been all bad*, she confessed to herself while slipping under the covers, her only safe haven in the world. At least that way, she could look back on the past ten years of her life and know with certainty that it had all been an unfortunate mistake.

But it hadn't been all bad; it had simply been too hard. Untying the satin ribbons and opening the throat of the pouch, Alma dumped the antique choker necklace into her hands. The five-carat emerald pendant flashed like an amulet until its facets clouded from the heat of her palm. On the back of its filigree bezel setting, she spotted an inscription engraved across its smooth platinum: *It was fun while it lasted…*

Yes, it was fun, she nodded, finally allowing herself to dissolve into tears. *But it was also heartbreaking.*

Chapter Twenty-Seven

ONE MONTH LATER

LMA SAT IN THE ELEVATED train and peered out the window as it snaked along the "L" tracks, encircling the skyscrapers in Chicago's downtown loop. It was her favorite part of her morning commute.

The sunlight reflected off the glass windows of the high-rises and the urgency of spring turned the sky into a stunning shade of cobalt blue. The train stalled and lurched, making its usual stops along the Brown Line, before picking up speed and screeching its wheels along the century-old steel as its third rail flashed like festive sparklers. She enjoyed looking at the exteriors of all the historical building, studying the flourishes of design and architecture from a nose-length perspective. Every glazed terra-cotta ornamentation, every brick of load-bearing masonry, every decorative stone corbel, every copper molding crowning a windowsill offered a story to tell from its era—a story overshadowed by the glamorous height and might of the adjacent, modern-day skyscrapers unless someone bothered to pay attention to it.

Alma loved leaning her forehead against the windowpane, attempting to imagine all those stories until she inevitably passed by a series of cookie-cutter commercial buildings that disrupted her romantic daydreaming.

"Like that one," she uttered, pulling away from the window as the train slithered to a stop beside the steel structure, void of any architectural significance other than size. *How many rentable square feet could be crammed into forty stories of vertical air space*? Alma answered her own cynical thought. *Enough to be worth millions upon millions of dollars every year.*

She suddenly felt nauseous.

The train shuddered again before rocking back into a slow start. Maybe it was the uneven sway of the train cars or her decision to skip breakfast that caused the queasiness to inch up to the surface of her throat before retreating down it like an intolerable burn. Maybe it was the realization that she was likely viewing one of *his* buildings, shifting her ride from a relaxing journey into a somber reminder of things that could have been. She had successfully avoided thinking about him all week—until now, when she cradled her stomach and rose from her seat, seeking to exit the train the moment the doors opened, despite the fact it wasn't even her stop.

Her escape was accidentally blocked by a young mother attempting to pull the rear wheels of a stroller over the landing gap and into the train. Bending forward, Alma lifted the front plastic wheel and nudged the stroller forward to safety. The mother smiled in appreciation, but only the image of the baby's sleeping face lingered with Alma as she darted into the corner of the station, wafting with the stench of urine and garbage, and unleashed her own putrid addition to the mix.

Chapter Twenty-Eight

"ALMA, YOUR EXPERTISE IS REQUESTED."

She closed her eyes, wishing she could just be left alone for one more minute. She had made it to her father's shop—after vomiting up her entire stomach—and successfully settled herself onto her workbench stool without the uncontrollable urge to repeat the performance.

And most mornings, her father was too busy with his own work to give her more than a simple greeting when she arrived. But this morning was different. This morning, she had barely removed her coat when the shopkeeper's bell rang and an older gentleman passed through the front door.

A client appointment, she remembered, knowing her father relied on her opinion for most appraisals. Rising to her feet, she steadied herself and made her way over to the front counter. Her father peered at her over his spectacles, sensing she was struggling to compose herself. *Three, four, five*…she counted every step until the waves of nausea subsided, allowing her to note the curious glass box in front of the elderly man whose grey trench coat looked a size too big over his curved posture and drooping shoulders.

"Alma…Mr. Harrington is here to receive our opinion on an heirloom. I met him at the Fields Museum gala. He's a friend of Madame van der Meer."

"It's a René Lalique original glass jewelry box," she said in disbelief, knowing exactly what she was staring at without having to search out the signature of its maker. "Where did you find this one, Mr. Harrington?"

"It belonged to my wife," the gentleman said, running his hand over the rectangular top of the turquoise opalescent glass, as if it contained her ashes. "She received it from her mother who bought it with one of her first checks as a salesclerk at—"

"Marshall Field's," Alma said, finishing his sentence.

"Then you know?" Impressed, the man raised an eyebrow on his distinguished face.

"Marshall Field was known to purchase luxury goods from Europe as a way to distinguish his department store from all the others. I'm familiar with his relationship with American glassmakers like Tiffany, so it makes sense that he would have been interested in European glassmakers as well."

"Field was a very progressive businessman. He was one of the first men to realize you would sell more to women if you hired women as salesclerks. And my wife's mother was one of the first ones to be hired by Field's."

"Well, it's a wonderful piece," Alma replied, touching the frosted glass bas relief of charming nymphs molded onto the lid. "Lalique was one of the great art nouveau artists whose glass and jewelry flourished in popularity around the beginning of the twentieth century. He worked in Paris, but only with glass until his death in 1945. Then his son took over his studio and converted everything to crystal. During Lalique's lifetime, he was more known for his opalescent glass perfume bottles and even his light fixtures and chandeliers. He made less than a hundred glass jewelry boxes. They're extremely rare and only a few have ever come up for auction."

"Oh, I definitely don't intend to sell it," Mr. Harrington cried out. "I would much prefer to donate it to a museum that would have it."

"Based on my daughter's assessment," Enrique assured him, "I'm certain there is no shortage of museums that would be happy to receive it into their collections."

Mr. Harrington nodded. "My wife would have been very happy to hear that. She loved art museums."

Alma recognized the quiver of nostalgic heartbreak in his voice. "It sounds like your wife had excellent taste."

"Yes, she married me, surprisingly. That was my first clue that I should hang onto her. And I did—for over forty years."

Alma smiled. "Is that the secret to a good marriage, Mr. Harrington? Hanging onto someone you love and never letting them go?"

"Oh, dear me, no," he huffed. "That is the secret to insanity. The secret to a good marriage is hanging onto her while trying your damndest to be a loyal, decent husband, and then stepping back on occasion and waiting for your wife to forgive you when you inevitably do and say the stupidest things of your life."

Alma glanced over at her father who shrugged in agreement.

"Please," her father said, inviting the gentleman into the rear room of the shop. "Let us take pictures of the box so that Alma may draw up a formal appraisal."

Enrique ushered him into the rear room. The timing couldn't be more perfect. The horrible sickly green goblin seeped up from the pit of her stomach without warning. She didn't even make it to the bathroom. Instead, she grabbed the wastebasket and gagged into it.

Returning for his spectacles left behind on the counter, Enrique paused to survey Alma, cradling the wastebasket with her glasses slanted off her face.

"*Todo está bien, mi amor*?" he asked as a look of concern furrowed his brow.

"Yes, just something I ate, I think." She was lying; her father sensed it.

"Perhaps you should take the day off?"

"Yes, Papi. Thank you. I think I will."

Chapter Twenty-Nine

ALMA SWEPT IN FRONT of her sister and face-planted her forehead onto the display of frosted marshmallow Rice Krispy treats, neatly arranged like bars of chewy gold across the counter.

"Well, hello to you, too," Conchita muttered, pushing the more fragile caramel-topped cream puffs and delicate chocolate eclairs to the side. "I can see you're having a difficult morning. Cinnamon bun?"

Alma didn't respond. She simply whimpered and held up something long and plastic in her hand.

"Ugh…? Is that what I think it is?"

Alma whimpered again—a faint, but discernible, yes.

"Oh - my - God." Conchita covered her gasp. "One line or two? One line or two?!" Grabbing the plastic stick out of Alma's hands, she stared down at the results. "Holy freaking crap—two lines. Two, two, two!!!! This is my dream come true!" She clapped her hands and jumped up and down like she had just won the baby lottery.

Alma lifted her head and glared at her. Conchita's glee over something that was specifically her fault was truly irritating.

Conchita ignored her sister's stink eye and buzzed with joy. "This is so a-m-a-zzzzzing. So what did Harvey say? What – did – he - say!"

"I haven't told him." The look on Alma's face said everything.

"Oh." Conchita stopped bouncing. "But you're gonna tell him, right?"

Alma flopped her forehead again onto the Rice Krispy barricade with an indistinguishable answer.

"Alma…you have GOT to tell him," Conchita asserted.

"How does this even happen?" Alma whined. "I mean…we were married for years and

nothing *ever* happened. Then the one time we have sex like teenagers…boom."

"You get knocked-up like a virgin on her prom night!" Conchita sang out.

"You're enjoying the fact this is me and not you."

"Hell, yes. Because given the number of shameless one-night stands I've had this year, this is totally something that should be happening to me and not you. But thank God, thank freaking GOD, it's you. Two lines. It's you!!!!"

"Ugh. What am I going to do?"

"Well, duh? You're going to tell your billionaire baby daddy that he boinked you up, that's what. Hopefully after that, everything will end up like something out of one of my smutty romance novels."

"Can't I just disappear into a convent where nuns will take care of me and the baby in secrecy?" Alma offered.

"You seriously read too many Victorian novels. Besides, Papi would find out from me and spill the beans to Harvey. Especially if he and Harvey are still going to those Sox games every other week. You know how neither one of us can keep a secret."

"Gee, thanks, family."

"Just sayin'."

"Well, I actually have no idea if he's even in town. The last time I heard from him, it was over a month ago, when he sent me something that I tried to give back to him. He told me it was mine forever and that he couldn't keep it."

"A vibrator?"

"A necklace," Alma stressed. "A ridiculously expensive one-of-a-kind antique Tiffany necklace for our fifth wedding anniversary."

"Awww..." Conchita melted into a sigh. "And you tried to give it back? You heartless bitch."

"I don't even know if I still have his number or if he changed it again. For all I know, he could be in China, working on his buildings in Shanghai."

"Well, you have to tell him." Conchita lifted a stick of vanilla ice rock candy and gnawed on it.

"Via text? And say what? Please come home. We have a 'situation'?"

"Yes, and then you say...P.S. please bring Oriental massage oils and a whole suitcase filled with expensive jade jewelry because I'm having your love child." Conchita suddenly rummaged through her purse for her phone.

"What are you doing?" Alma asked.

"I'm doing what you should be doing," her sister replied, punching out the message. "Texting your Preggonator."

"Dear God. Don't do that!" Alma tried to grab the phone, but Conchita successfully pressed send. Holding up her screen, she read aloud, "*Hi Hot*

Stuff...are you in town? Very important. Smiley face emoji hitting himself with a sledgehammer."

"A sledgehammer?"

Conchita shrugged. "Yeah, it's sort of my fav right now. You'd be surprised how hitting yourself with a sledgehammer gets people's attention." Conchita's phone suddenly pinged in her hands. "See...?" she cooed, indulging in her success before reading aloud his message. "*Yes, but leaving in two days. Would prefer not to change plans. Are u in trouble?*"

Alma's stomach dropped like she was on an emotional rollercoaster. "He's leaving in two days? Am I really supposed to dump this news on him before he leaves?"

Conchita gazed at her as if she understood her predicament.

"Well, let's just see what he's up to..." Conchita cued up her next text and read it to Alma before hitting send. "*No trouble. Just wondering if you will be keeping this same number?* *Smiley face with question mark eyes*."

Immediately, her phone buzzed in her hands like an annoyed wasp. Conchita read his response. "*Love you, C., but don't be playing matchmaker again. I'm tied up right now and don't need any more relationship complications.* Ouch—" Conchita waved her hand with the imagined sting of his slap.

"He's moved on," Alma said somberly. "It was the one thing that I wanted from him, and now he's finally done it."

Sensing her sister might be right, Conchita pondered her next text before replying, "*Okey-dokey, Smokey Pokey. Have a nice trip. Talk to ya later.* *Smiley emoji in Hawaiian shorts and holding sun umbrella*." She tossed her phone onto the counter. "Well, okay. Maybe you are screwed if he leaves before you have a chance to tell him. That just means you'll have to find a way to tell him tonight."

"Tonight!" Alma freaked. "I just found out...sixteen minutes ago. I can't tell Harvey tonight."

"Alma, it is his baby, after all. Even if you guys don't officially get back together, he still deserves to know."

"And I will tell him." Alma waffled. "Just not tonight."

"When then? Via text? After he's gone because you pushed him away and made him think it was completely over between the two of you?"

Alma locked eyes with her sister. "Isn't it completely over between us?"

"I don't know, Alma...but even if you're never going to be a couple again, don't go messing up this new chapter before it's even started."

Alma covered her glasses and bowed her head, certain she could deal with anything but this... *Not this.*

"Hey listen—" Conchita reached over the counter and squeezed her hand. "I know you don't feel like it, but this is going to be the most amazing gift of your life."

Alma grimaced. "I feel like I want to vomit."

Conchita handed her a stick of rock candy. "Ginger-flavored. It will help with the morning sickness and I've got you covered with an unlimited supply. Just make sure I'm consulted when it comes time to pick out baby names."

"Harvey is going to want Harvey Jr."

"And you're going to want some ridiculous literary Gothic name like Rochester or Esméralda."

Alma sucked on the ginger rock candy, easing her sickness. "Those are both really good suggestions."

Conchita rolled her eyes. "Yeah, exactly my point. This poor baby is already going to need me to come to the rescue."

Chapter Thirty

WHEN THE DOORBELL RANG, Harvey considered loading his hunting rifle and shooting the bastard trespassing on his private riverfront dock and up four flights of stairs to his front door at the crack of dawn.

"A dead man," he cursed, rolling out of bed and stumbling through the dark hallway. He was hungover and dazed. He hadn't slept three straight hours since everything fell apart a month ago, and he had been dealing with the insomnia in the only way he knew how—by drinking himself into oblivion every night.

He decided against his rifle as he trudged into the foyer, barely bothering to peer out of the glass prisms of the Weese-inspired triangular windows before swinging the front door open.

He just did it. And then he wished he hadn't.

Alma stood there, staring at him. He hadn't bothered to get dressed because he had intended to holler at the ding-door-ditching teenager and use his shameless nakedness to frighten him away.

But he didn't scare away anyone, much less impress her. She barely noted his absence of clothes like it was as normal as her unannounced visit before sunrise.

"You look terrible," she confirmed, pushing past him into the foyer, as if she still lived there.

"Thanks," he said, tracking her entrance in a daze. "I smell even worse."

Was he dreaming? Was he still drunk from downing half the bottle of Cognac?

She removed her coat and hat, and hung them up on the stainless steel folk art sculpture that she had bought at an estate sale before they were married.

As if she still lived there… For a brief moment, it seemed as though it could be true. She still had keys. Her clothes were still hanging in the master bedroom closet. Her pink towels were still folded on the shelves in the master bathroom. And her bottles of shampoo, body lotions, and decorative jars filled with bubble bath beads were still arranged on the bathroom countertop. He never threw out any of her things. He just drifted around them like a ghost haunting her possessions until she came back to claim them. Except she never came back—until now.

Why was she here? Quickly, the most obvious reason resonated in his inebriated mind—*to shout at him, clearly*.

Yanking open the foyer's closet door, he fumbled through its contents until he found his beanie cap with ear flaps. It had a pom-pom on the top and a rabbit fur lining, exactly what he needed to do the trick.

She eyed his curious choice of head gear. "Are you planning on going…skiing?"

"No, I'm getting prepared."

"For a blizzard…in the buff?"

"No, for your arrival." He pulled the cap snuggly over his ears. "Okay…now, I'm ready."

He crossed his arms and winced, waiting for her to let him have it. He couldn't specifically recall what he had done wrong lately, but he knew the list of his faults was endless and his penance was lacking.

"You've been drinking."

"Only a modest amount." He hiccupped. "In my modest state."

They both looked down at his naked body.

"Would you like me to wait here while you get dressed?" There was irritation in her voice.

Lifting up his foot, he removed his sock and hung it on his swelling cock, aroused by her observation of its immodesty.

Between the beanie on his head and the sock on his cock, his sobering consciousness knew he looked ridiculous. But at least she wasn't yelling at him.

"I used to have pajamas," he stated, like it was a serious concern. "But I have no idea what happened to them."

She frowned, as if his answer unexpectedly annoyed her. "I took them."

"Oh." He frowned back, pondering the most confusing revelation of his life. "You refused to accept my fifty-million-dollar divorce settlement, but you took my fifteen-dollar pair of flannel pajamas?"

"You never bought more?"

"I'm a man, Alma. I'm useless when it comes to practical, common sense things like buying pajamas."

"Or underwear," she noted.

He leaned against the wall, fighting off a yawn. It didn't work. "Are we going to have a long intellectual discussion about pajamas and underwear in the hallway? Or would you like to come inside?" Breaking into another yawn, he shuffled down the corridor without waiting to see if she would follow him. He was too tired and his head pounded like the heavy wheels of a freight train, trying to roll over which misdeed had brought her there to scold him.

She glanced around the living room, taking in everything familiar. "You haven't redecorated?"

"Nope." He flopped onto the couch and watched as she anxiously bit her fingernails. It strangely relaxed him. All the blood rushed out of his throbbing head and into his sock puppet cock, simply because it was aware that she was in the room. "Not unless you count my collection from Italy." He nodded to the obscene tower of empty pizza boxes, winding upwards like a spiral staircase, just barely grazing the industrial steel rafters supporting the soaring glass atrium. "I'm shooting for a world's record. I figure it's easier than attempting to be domestic again. Apparently, I'm only good at being domestic when I have a mate to impress. If it wasn't for the cleaning lady, I'd be buried under a pile of my own plastic forks and dirty gym shorts."

His confessions of squalor were clearly more than she could take. Without warning, she turned and ran into the bathroom. Seconds later, he heard the sound of violent vomiting and subsequent groans.

Hmm, he pondered. Either the thought of his dirty gym shorts had that effect on her or she had been drinking even more than he had.

Harvey waited and waited and waited. "Everything okay in there?" he finally called out.

"No."

Hmm, he pondered again. *Well, at least she'd still have her pink bath towels.*

After an awkward length of silence, he tried again. "How about now?"

"I just need a minute, Harvey…please," she requested softly.

Pulling himself up from the couch, he plodded into the kitchen and flipped open the refrigerator door. "How about something to eat like…" he dithered, uncertain about what he had to offer. "Like some beef jerky and…a packet of ketchup?"

Then he heard her—all the way from the bathroom—puking out her guts.

Okay, definitely not an appetizing combination.

Moving back into the living room, he said, "Or maybe I should call for a pizza?" Whenever she was hungover, he remembered she liked to eat anchovy pizza.

She answered with the flush of the toilet.

Harvey paused and listened. *Rinsing and gargling*, he thought, as she took her time. Apparently, she felt like she was home. He missed her being home.

When she finally emerged from the bathroom, she looked sexier than when she had entered it. She had removed her glasses. Her hair was tossed out of its ponytail and her cheeks were flushed from bending forward and hurling into the toilet bowl. Taking out a candy stick from the pocket of her overalls, she sucked on it. Harvey felt himself grow shamelessly harder. Mr. Sock Puppet approved.

"It's five o'clock in the morning, Harvey," she said, acting as if nothing had happened. "Aren't you going to ask me why I'm here?"

"Why are you here?" he mechanically repeated, having absolutely no idea until his original theory popped back in his brain—*to yell at him.*

"Because…" she started to say, then stopped sucking on her candy stick to collect her thoughts. "I heard you were leaving town in two days and I wanted to say something important to you."

Oh, brother...here we go. He exhaled in resignation and pulled his hat snuggly over his eyes as if he was about to be slayed by a firing squad. "Okay, shoot."

"It would be better if you looked at me, Harvey."

He peeked open one eye. "Only if you promise not to throw anything at me."

"I definitely promise not to throw anything at you."

"Or break anything that's mine and not yours. Your collection of antique opera glasses is fair game, but my baseball card collection and flat-panel TV are off-limits."

She wheezed out her sigh. "Yes, fine. I promise."

Harvey nudged up his beanie and peered out at her. "Okay, good. Shoot."

She took in a deep breath and blurted out, "Harvey, I'm…" She stopped again when she spotted a curious light emanating from the master bedroom in the loft above them. "I'm…"

Her voice trailed off as she squinted at the first rays of dawn shining through the glass atrium that flickered mysterious prisms of color on the geometric tiled floor of the living room. "Harvey…what is that?"

"Something that cost me twice as much as what I sold it for," he replied casually, plopping onto the leather sofa again and stretching himself far across it like a rubber band.

Alma peered beyond the loft's balcony, realizing exactly what was stored there. "You bought it back?"

He nodded.

"But why?"

He shrugged. "Because I changed my mind."

"About what?"

"About selling it."

"You mean you didn't sell it?"

"Oh no, I sold it." He swung one bare foot off the edge of the sofa, wondering why he felt the need to confess everything to her. "But then I bought it back. I bought everything back."

"But why?" she asked again, unable to make sense of it all.

"Because you were right. I was being a greedy asshole and I didn't feel like being a greedy asshole anymore."

She stared at him, as if he was turning green and growing horns. Or maybe it was just because his sock puppet was raised again.

"Why didn't you tell me?"

He crossed his hands and rested them over his bare chest. "Because you hate my guts, remember? And I figured...it was too late. I've always been too late when it comes to us. Too stupid and too late." He smirked, hiding the pain, and wagged his foot again. It was finally something he was comfortable admitting. Some people used professional therapy to gain enlightenment. He preferred booze and sleepless contemplation.

"So you're not going to Shanghai in two days?"

"Shanghai in two days?" he repeated.

"Yes." She nodded, glancing down at his sock puppet. "To build your penis towers."

"Ah...no. I've decided my penis prowess is just fine."

"But my sister said you were leaving in two days," she pressed him.

"Yeah, motoring off downstream for a while. I figured no one would miss me and it would get me out of the house, which I really haven't done in weeks, and it isn't doing me any favors these days."

She eyed his tower of pizza boxes. "That's true. It's definitely not."

"So..." He thumped his own chest like a melon, waiting for the big announcement. "What's the big important thing you've come to tell me?"

"I don't think I can tell you anymore."

"Really?" He furrowed his brow. "That's confusing."

"Somehow when I knew you were a greedy asshole, it seemed easier. I was just going to count to three, blurt it out, and leave. But now..."

"Now?" he encouraged her with an overzealous inflection in his voice.

"Now, you've just gone and complicated everything."

Harvey rubbed his forehead, like she was speaking a different language. "I guess I could go back to being a greedy asshole if you'd prefer?"

"It certainly would be a lot more dependable."

"So you would prefer me to be a more dependable asshole." He said it like a statement, not a question, just to make sure he was catching all of this.

"Yes, exactly. I think so," she nodded, lowering her quivering lip. "This on-again, off-again asshole routine is far worse than just counting on the fact that you're going to be an asshole." She turned away from him and bolted towards the door, but he caught her arm, yearning to fix whatever was upsetting her.

"Okay, so fine. I promise to be an asshole. Just don't leave. Not yet." He scrutinized her eyes, focusing on that same sad expression he knew he had the ability to correct, if she would only let him. "You came for a reason, so stay until you've said whatever you need to say to me. I can handle it."

She shook her head.

"C'mon. The last time I saw you, you threw shoes at my head—twice. So now, we'll make a pact." He looked around the room for something to raise the stakes. *Her ceramic vase from sculpture class.* It was the perfect bargain. He lifted it from the fireplace mantel and deposited it into her hands. "Okay, here. Take this..."

"You kept this?"

"Of course. I love that lopsided, semi-deformed, overbaked ceramic vase. And that doesn't even take into consideration the fact that it still has your engagement ring buried somewhere inside it."

She tested its weight and its awkward shape in her palms. "And what am I supposed to do with it?"

"I give you permission to chuck it at me if you feel I deserve it. But I promise you...this time, I'm ready and steady and feeling completely certain about my ability to—"

"I'm pregnant," she whispered.

Harvey blinked, dumbfounded. *She didn't even count to three.*

"And...it's mine?"

He studied the complex expression that spread across her face, conveying one thing with certainty: *he needed to work harder on his stupid filter—much, much harder.*

Without a word, she slapped the ceramic vase into his hand and headed for the door.

"Ugh," he groaned, chasing after her. "Alma, don't. Don't—"

She jerked open the door, but he slammed it shut. She flinched, as if she felt threatened.

He closed his eyes, cursing at himself. "Don't—" he said, calmly.

"Don't what?" she challenged him. "Don't leave regretting that I came?"

"Don't leave. Period," he urged her. "And don't regret it. Any of it."

He gazed into her eyes, desperate to touch her cheek. But her smoldering black eyes warned him that she would likely slap him if he tried.

"I only came here to prove that you were right," she answered in a cold even tone. "You're too late when it comes to fixing things between us. And I don't even need to throw anything at you this time to make it obvious."

She tried to open the door again, but he braced it shut with the force of his forearm.

"Well, it looks like I get nine more months to figure out how to fix it."

"I don't want you to fix it anymore. I just want you to leave it alone—untouched and unbroken."

"Easier said than done. I'm a man-child, remember? I don't learn my lesson until I hold something in my hands, toss it up for fun and then drop it, shattering it into a thousand pieces."

He dramatically dropped the ceramic vase, breaking it apart into irregular shards of clay across the tiled floor.

She covered her ears and rolled her eyes. "Was that really necessary?"

"Yep." He bent forward, picking through the debris. "Because now I've got this." He popped up from the floor and presented her with a dusty ring. "And the last thing I'm going to let you do is let you leave here, knowing you're going to be the mother of my child, without offering you a reason to stay."

She wiped the grime off the raised stone, revealing the iridescent opal, glimmering with pastel shades in its pearly white surface. She hesitated for what felt like an eternity before handing the ring back to him. "I'll probably just lose it again." It was her way of rejecting him—again.

Ballbuster.

"Then I promise to be the one who fishes it out of the baby's diapers," he wise-cracked, deciding he wasn't going to be busted so easily.

"I'm not certain a baby and a ring change anything, Harvey."

"They absolutely don't change anything," he agreed. "Because you're still the only woman I want in my bed every night and I'm still the only man you love to hate."

Edging closer, he felt a wisp of her hair grazing his collarbone and smelled the ginger on her breath.

"I don't hate you, Harvey. I just hate how hard it is to count on you and what you're going to do next."

"Well, then…I guess that means you're really going to hate this—" He cupped her cheek and kissed her, knowing she wasn't just the same woman he had loved and failed for years. She was now a completely different woman—the mother of his child—who he vowed never to fail again. When she sighed and surrendered herself to the flowing strokes of his tongue, he enveloped her in his arms and kissed her harder and deeper than ever before until there was zero ambiguity about how much he wanted to be back in her life.

When he finally allowed it, she pulled away, brushing her cheeks dry. "You're right, Harvey. I do hate you."

"See?" he said with a cocky smile. "I'm more dependable than you think."

Drawing her back into his arms, he kissed her with long, full strokes of his tongue and sought out the clasps of the bib on her overalls. *Those damn overalls.* Unfastening them as if he was freeing her from chains, he tore them down past her thighs, determined to strip her bare of the routine of animosity that marked their professional lives. *Fuck their professional lives*, he thought, fingering the soft cotton crotch of her exposed pink panties, indulging in her sigh of acceptance, before sweeping his hand to the tender curve of her belly below her T-shirt. She was pregnant with his baby and the only thing he wanted to prove more than his loyalty to her was his desire to impregnate her again, and again, and again…

Sweeping her into his arms, he carried her up the stairs into his bedroom, determined to take total control of her body, and make up for the year they had lost and all the ways he had disappointed her.

But he suddenly stopped and floundered in the darkness when he realized the most important piece of furniture in his bedroom was missing. She noticed it, too.

"Harvey? Where's our bed?"

He exhaled, regretting the distraction. "I got rid of it."

"You got rid of it?" She slowly slid herself out of his arms and circled the room, searching for the plush billowy mattress, certain he must be joking. "But why on earth would you do that?"

"Because it drove me crazy, sleeping in it without you."

"And you replaced it with…this?" She gestured to the rigid piece of furniture in the middle of the room.

"It's a bamboo acupuncture platform bed. Custom made in Japan."

"It looks like a medieval torture device."

"It cost me ten thousand dollars. It's supposed to help with insomnia."

"Does it work?"

"Not at all." He grabbed her hand and whisked her back into his arms. "Why do you think I was up almost every night, sexting with you instead?"

"So, what are we going to do now?" she asked, as if she couldn't think of any other alternatives. But Harvey could. If nothing else, he was completely dependable on that front.

As if he was rescuing them from the prospect of a sexless reunion, he rushed her into the next best place where he knew he could fuck her brains out—the bathroom.

Shoving open the door with his bare foot, he hauled her into the master bathroom suite, its whirlpool tub dominating the center of the sanctuary like a throne.

Flicking on the faucet, the water spewed out like a jolt of adrenaline, mirroring his surging desire to skip the bath and make love to her against the heated floor, spreading her open against the glossy glass tiles and filling her to the brim with his aching need.

But she was pregnant now. The mother of his child. *Un-fucking-believable...How did that even happen?*

He remembered every single detail of how it happened. And except the part where he had been a selfish greedy billionaire asshole, he wanted to repeat it all over again.

She nibbled on his earlobe in that familiar way that made him hard and impatient. But when the water rose past the jets of the tub, he stripped off her T-shirt and tongued her luscious mouth before dunking them both inside it.

Warm, wet, soothing...just like being inside her. The jets blazed on, churning the water into a gourmet soup of imminent sex. Not too hot, not too cold. *Just right*, he thought, like everything about that moment until his cock sock puppet floated up to the frothy surface.

She lifted it from the water. "It wasn't a very good look for you."

"It got you naked in the tub with me, didn't it?"

"*Half*-naked," she corrected him. "Which isn't a very good batting average."

He submerged his hand in the water and fished for the elastic band of her panties before depantsing her like a pro.

"Homerun," he called out like an umpire, slapping the sodden pink trophy over his shoulder and lifting her bare ass into his lap to claim his real prize.

She narrowed her dark eyes, as if she wanted to slug him in the face. He laughed. *God, he loved how sexy she looked—with wet eyelashes and matted wet hair—completely infuriated with him.* Winding her arms around his neck and her legs around his waist, he nudged her for a conciliatory kiss. It was a little too late for hate. Next time, she would have to work harder at not letting him get her *half*-naked...much less letting him rub his cock against her slit. He backed her ass against the pulsing jets, knowing it would slacken her pouty frown into a reluctant inaudible moan for more...

He would give her more. He would give her everything he had to offer her for the rest of his life, if she would only say yes.

He drew his lips down her throat, recognizing the nostalgic flavor of bubblegum soap on her skin. It spurred him to reach over the tub's ledge and stretch himself to the counter, grabbing a handful of her pearly pink soap beads from its dish.

She watched as he scattered them across the surface of the simmering water like a chef adding spices to his sex stew.

"You've never used those before...have you?" she said.

"Nope, but clearly you still do," he answered, flicking the last one into the water before nipping at her hard budding tits. "And the taste of it is making me want to eat up every pink part of you." He enveloped each plump, buoyant breast into his hand and guided them to his mouth, sucking on each areola, attempting to gratify his insatiable thirst for every bit of her sweetness.

She sighed, stroking his wet hair and letting her nails softly scrape against the nape of his neck. "I think when we were married, I was the only one who ever used this bathtub."

He skated his mouth up her throat. "I think we've safely established that I was an idiot when we were married."

She lifted her chin, relinquishing herself to his caressing lips. "Which is the reason you don't know that you're only supposed to use one or two bath beads at a time. You just dumped in a month's supply." She nodded to the foamy layer of pink bubbles rising over their shoulders, threatening to smother them beneath a sudsy bubblegum-scented blob.

He grinned. "I'm certain this can only be a good thing." Ensnaring her in his arms, he scooped up a handful of bubbles and lathered her shoulders and lower back—slippery and smooth—to ensure his chest could ride against them the moment he thrust past the barrier of friction he loved to conquer whenever they had underwater sex.

She clutched the stainless steel hand rail and exhaled as he fingered her, using her breathy moan to guide the depth of his teasing strokes. *There*, he exhaled, cradling her in his lap, earning every inch inside her without the aid of her natural lubrication. *Oh, so very raw and tight*. When she spread herself wider, freeing all her inhibitions, he replaced his fingers with the tip of his dick, controlling his instinct to dominate her. Slowly, deliberately, he broke through her initial resistance and murmured his dirtiest desires to explore every sacred part of her. The rhythmic whirl of the sudsy water and the sight of her supple, naked body at his mercy intensified his swelling arousal. He pressed his forehead against her shoulder blades, barely able to contain his climax as her lushness enveloped him like a familiar lover. Her groan increased in pitch as he sought to build and rebuild her to her own summit. *Every persistent grind. Every strum of her clit. Every grip of her curvy ass*. God, how he loved ravishing her from behind, but he loved looking into her eyes even more, especially the moment she surrendered herself completely to him with the love and trust that he needed to bring her beyond the brink.

At the last possible moment, he lifted them out of the water. He loved surprising her with his strength, supporting her fully in his arms and steadying her backside against the midnight blue tiled wall. Thrusting upwards into her core, he threatened to break her in half if she didn't unleash an indecent scream. He accelerated into a savage pace—harder, faster, deeper than anything he could achieve while lying down, making love to her in their old plushy bed. Her shaky voice soared higher, an admission of ultimate gratification, as she pressed her palms against the lacquered tiles that reflected all those damn luscious curves. He relished the view of her perky tits and bare pussy, dripping in sensuous pink spume, seeping into every indecent crevice and lubricating his ascent towards something unchartered between them. He could feel every part of her psyche, shaking and quaking like a torrent, as if she was relinquishing every fear about their relationship to the rushing, aching, pulsating climax, fueled by unconditional trust. He could hear himself panting and huffing like a deep closing stallion breaking out at an unsustainable pace. But it wasn't just about the sex or the climax for him. It was about her acceptance of his flaws and all the stupid selfish mistakes he had made in the past, and her willingness to give him another chance—a second chance to finally make things right between them.

I promise, he mouthed into her ear, embracing her as his sacred lover, and driving her to the final heights of her fulfillment where he followed with his own, releasing every drop of his promise inside her. But one climax wasn't enough. It was never enough for him, and as he slid them back down into the sloshing waters, he fingered her intimately, extending her pleasure, until she quivered and trembled and moaned against his chest and she finally shuddered with a succession of harmonious heaves that convinced him he had achieved exactly what she had deserved.

God, how he would promise to love and cherish her forever again—if she would only let him.

As her back rested against his chest, he spooned her like her protector, vowing never to let go. As the pink frothy waters scented his relaxation and the rising and falling of her respiration regulated his own, he tilted his head against the tub's rounded edge, and made another resolute pledge that he knew he could fulfill—*if that didn't count as make-up sex, then watch out, woman*...because he swore he'd keep trying until it finally did the trick.

Chapter Thirty-One

IT HAD BEEN A LONG, long time since she had been in their house. *Too long*, she thought, turning her head towards Harvey, awakened by his subtle snore of slumber while he cradled her in his arms. She smiled and relaxed her head against his chest. Even his whistling snore she had missed—more than a little.

It had been hard for her to be away and even harder to force herself to stay away. Home had always been more than a physical location to her—more than just a house in the city. It was the place she had shared her life with the man she loved, the place where they had shared all the simplest, happiest moments—together.

The rim of the inflatable mattress jiggled with every drawn-out exhale of Harvey's wheezes. She realized she had even missed the inflatable mattress where she had slept—more often than not—in the last weeks of their marriage. Maybe it was the familiar scent of the sheets that brought back all the nostalgic memories or maybe it was the way Harvey made love to her again with such tenderness after their bath that filled her with nothing but fondness for everything around her. *Yes, it was good to be home.* Home was wherever she could sleep in his arms, roused awake by his distinct snore. *Yes, this was home.*

For the next twenty minutes, she gazed at the mystical stained-glass window Harvey had rescued from the balcony of the old train depot. It stood upright, bolstered by an intricately engineered wooden frame that he had clearly constructed himself, and was strategically positioned near the railing of the duplex master bedroom, where the unfiltered rays of morning sun poured in through the glass ceiling and illuminated the image. The mother and child glowed like iridescent angels while the lilacs shimmered in a rippling sea of lavender. Both times Alma had been in the building, she had felt pressure to evaluate the window under scant, inferior light. Now, as she lay awake in his arms, feeling his warm breath against her cheek, she took the time to gaze at the details of the window's artistry—the distinct shades of purple, ivory, and green melded within the opalescent glass as well as the balanced composition of each leadline. She had never been certain about the artist's identity, but now, as she surveyed the piece again under ample light, she was convinced it had been constructed by someone as masterful as Louis Comfort Tiffany.

"Are you thinking about how nice it is to wake up next to a fifteen-million-dollar piece of art? Or is that just me?"

His teasing voice suggested he had been awake longer than she thought.

"You caught me," she replied, rolling over and stroking the soft stubble along his prominent jawline. "And then I couldn't help but wonder..." but her words faded as she considered whether or not the discussion was worth disrupting the serenity of the moment.

"Wondering what?" he encouraged, shifting on top of her and nestling every firm muscle of his body into every soft crevice of hers. "Why we didn't make love on this cushy thing before?" He jiggled the inflatable mattress, letting the curve of her pelvis conveniently bob up and down against his erection. He lowered his mouth between her breasts and feathered her skin with his lips. "If I had known how much you enjoyed bouncy sex, I would have installed inflatable pads all over the house."

"Like an insane asylum," she sassed, running her fingers through his hair, layered on top, faded on each side.

"When have we ever pretended to be sane?" He nipped at the tip of her chin before settling his mouth over hers for a lustful kiss. She indulged in it until the stunning beauty of the stained-glass window swirled carnival patterns across his face. Harvey pulled away and held up his hand like he was catching droplets of rainbow rain. "Especially when the mother of my unborn child gets more aroused by staring at my stained-glass window than staring at my—"

She placed her hand over his mouth. He didn't need to say it, even though there might have been a hint of truth to it.

"I like all your body parts just fine," she said, trying to keep the peace. "But it's hard not to admire the window without thinking about what it might be trying to tell us."

Her gaze turned downwards as a shifting ray of sunlight cast the familiar silhouette of the keyhole onto Harvey's washboard stomach.

"Shhhh...I think it's trying to say—" He stopped, pretending to listen to the secret message coming from the shadow. Squeezing together the skin around his belly button like a puppet, he murmured, "Ma-rrrrrr-yyyy meeeeee."

"I never said no," she offered as her answer. "And a proposal from your belly button makes it very tempting."

"Thennnn saaaaay yeeeeees," his belly button encouraged her.

But she hesitated again. She wasn't ready to commit to it again—at least, not yet.

Diverting the subject away from marriage, she traced the keyhole symbol on his stomach and pondered its significance. "So, what do you think it is about that photograph that would make someone put it in a vault and hide the key?"

He lifted her chin to meet his eyes. "If I figure it out, will you agree to marry me?"

"I doubt you want to make that wager. It doesn't seem very likely we'll ever figure it out."

"*Tsk,*" he clucked and unexpectedly slipped out of the bed. "Now you're starting to sound like a boring cynical realist billionaire. And for the sake of our baby, we can't have two parents who don't believe in dreams and treasure hunts and fairy dust and happily ever afters," he asserted, waving his hand like a magician, intending to make her wish come true. Then, disappearing into the master bedroom closet, he came back with his favorite pair of worn-out jeans.

Alma sat up from the mattress. "What are you doing?"

"We're going to go back to your place to get the photograph and figure out what it all means, so I can get you to say yes to marrying me." He disappeared again, then returned, pulling a black T-shirt over his bare chest.

"Well, that's very valiant of you, but you don't need to go anyway because I think I have it here with me."

Harvey eyed her naked body. "That would be some sexy trick."

"No, I mean…in my overalls."

"I knew there was a reason why I loved those overalls. Efficiency." He nudged her for a kiss before charging down the staircase.

"Got them!" he announced after a brief search before racing back up to the bedroom and digging in the bib's pocket to retrieve the photograph and the skeleton key. After smoothing the photograph against his thigh, he held it up and inspected it, as if he actually knew what they should be looking for. "So, you really think these two men with Santa Claus beards could be Louis Comfort Tiffany and Marshall Field?"

She nodded. "I've seen pictures of them both and it's not completely unreasonable."

"And you think they're looking at something important in front of them, reflected in the mirror?" He squinted harder. "Some kind of painting or tapestry?"

"Or stained-glass window." She eagerly nodded, peering over his shoulder as he sank down on the edge of the mattress.

"But I can't tell exactly what," she confirmed. "I've tried looking at it a hundred times under my loupe, but I can't make out anything more than the faint reflection of a woman's face. And I haven't been able to figure out the meaning of the inscription on the back either."

"What inscription on the back?" He flipped over the photograph.

Alma recited it aloud, knowing it by heart. "It says, *1892 – In eternal gratitude to M.F. Conway III.*"

"M.F. Conway, the Third?" Harvey snorted. "Boy, that guy sounds like a barrel of laughs. Let me guess…he's another fan of Santa Claus beards."

"I have no idea. I'm not familiar with that name. I've never heard it in all my research of Chicago's history. And yet, it seems like he was someone important enough to thank and then hide away the photograph under lock and key."

"On my riverfront property," he added. "With all your unsigned Tiffany windows."

Her tone soured. "I just don't know what it all could possibly mean."

Sensing her surrender, Harvey changed their approach. "Okay, let's step back and remember all the clues: the tin box with the inscription, the skeleton key, the Tiffany wallpaper…what do they all have in common?"

"Marshall Field," she answered quietly.

"Okay, good. And where do all the clues lead us, even Tiffany's stained-glass window of the Guiding Angel at Navy Pier?"

"Back to your riverfront parcel."

"And what did we find at my riverfront property?"

"Maybe almost a dozen Tiffany windows," she answered, following his game. "And this photograph, locked up in a vault with a skeleton key."

"So, let's forget the reflection in the mirror for a minute, and let's look at the rest of the room in the photograph. What do we see?"

Alma took the photograph into her own hands. "Two men with white beards shaking hands in a late-nineteenth century parlor room. And, specifically, a parlor room within a wealthy residence because there's a rosewood piano for entertaining, a mahogany fireplace mantel, a Victorian settee, a walnut sideboard, a grandfather clock and lighted chandeliers."

"You mean chandeliers that look like they should be in Count Dracula's mansion?" Harvey wisecracked.

Alma gazed at the chandeliers, then slowly constricted her hand around his wrist. "Oh my God, Harvey. "In eternal gratitude to M.F…"

"Are you suddenly remembering that M.F. Conway, the Third, was some kind of famous antique collector?"

"Yes," she answered, certain all the blood was draining out of her face. "Because M.F. is Marshall Field. That's Marshall Field's parlor room, in his private residence at 1905 S. Prairie Avenue."

He arched a skeptical eyebrow. "How can you be so sure?"

"Because of those…"

"The Count Dracula chandeliers?"

Alma nodded. "Exactly. Because this photograph is dated 1892 and electricity on a broad scale didn't exist in Chicago until years after the 1893 World's Fair, when one hundred thousand incandescent street lamps were unveiled as a grand novelty. It's the reason why Chicago was dubbed the 'The White City'—because it was the first time patrons ever saw an entire city illuminated at night. Before 1893, there were only a handful of private residences in Chicago featuring electric lights and—"

"Oh golly gee, let me guess," Harvey interrupted. "Marshall Field's mansion was one of them."

"Yes, one of the first." She nodded with certainty. "M. F. must stand for Marshall Field."

"God, woman…why do you have to be so wickedly smart? It makes my cock hard just thinking about your IQ." He drew her into his lap and licked each tit until she pushed him away.

"Okay," he relented, attempting to refocus onto the photograph. "So, let's assume that you're Marshall Field—the richest man in Chicago at the end of the nineteenth century—and you're an early investor in Tiffany's glass studio, and you want to help protect one of his most beloved stained-glass windows created as a private memorial to his dead wife. Your own private mansion would be just as good as any place. So, we'll just have to go visit the parlor room of Marshall Field's mansion and see if there's another clue there somewhere. But only after I make love to you again." He sprawled her body across the inflatable mattress and unzipped his jeans.

"No, we can't, Harvey," she said, propping herself up onto her elbows.

"We absolutely can. You're already naked and it will take me less than five seconds to depants."

"No, I mean we can't go to The Field's mansion. It was torn down in the '50s by building developers."

"Ugh," he sighed, rolling off of her. "Damn greedy real estate billionaires."

"Yes, it is a shame." She nodded. "The George Pullman House, The Palmer Potter Castle, the Cyrus McCormick mansion, the Marshall Field House—they were all some of the richest, most influential figures in Chicago's history and none of their residences were saved. So that means the photograph is just another dead end."

The moment Alma said the words aloud, they reminded her of the last time they had come to a dead end. Pulling away from Harvey, she slipped off the mattress and went into his closet, searching for a fresh T-shirt she knew was neatly arranged in his third dresser drawer.

"It can't be a complete dead end yet," he called after her. "We still don't know who Mr. Conway, the Third is?"

"I don't think it matters," she called back, pulling the oversized white undershirt over her body, remembering how all his shirts fit like dresses. "If Tiffany's *Eternal Love* was being kept in Marshall Field's mansion, it was likely destroyed when it was torn down. Which makes it pretty much a complete dead end."

"Unless it was moved somewhere else before that?" Harvey proposed.

Alma emerged from the closet and leaned against the doorway. "Doubtful."

"Unless there are other buildings in the city that fit this key?" He stared at the key, pondering all the possibilities and re-reading the inscription. "*In eternal gratitude to M.F. Conway III.*" Then a devilish smirk spread across his face. "Guess what?"

"What?"

"I think you're going to have to say yes to marrying me again."

Skeptical, Alma crossed her arms. "And why's that?"

"Because I have a hunch that Conway, the Third, isn't a person after all." He withheld the punchline, just to taunt her.

"And why's that?" she repeated, coaxing him to spill it.

"Because it's a place—a place with a Beaux Arts exterior that was on the verge of being torn down and sold when you and I were first exploring all the historical skyscrapers in Chicago."

"The Burnham Center," Alma slowly replied, making the connection.

"Formerly known as the Conway Building." Harvey grinned.

"Oh my…" At a loss for words, Alma fell silent. She joined Harvey on the air mattress to inspect the key. "And it was built with money from Marshall Field's estate, right after his death."

"Which is why Conway, the Third is really Conway 111…" Harvey paused, as if it was the set-up to a rhetorical game show question. "It's 111 West Washington Ave."

The tingling magic of believing in fairy tales and romantic happily ever afters suddenly seeped back into Alma's heart. "Do you really think…?" she whispered, needing his validation to help make the leap.

He drew her closer and kissed her deeply, sensually, and enduringly, as if they had just been pronounced as man and wife. "M.F. Conway, the Third. He's going to help fund our extravagant honeymoon."

Chapter Thirty-Two

WHATEVER HAPPENED, HE was going to get her back...That was the only thought driving him through the revolving doors of the Burnham Center. Even in the middle of the afternoon, its dramatic two-story, white marble lobby was starkly empty, a serene tomb that had protected secrets for decades. *Until now*, Harvey vowed, determined to unearth its last precious secret.

"So should we just take the stairs up to the first floor and ransack it inch by inch, or should we ride the elevator all the way to the twenty-second floor and start at the top?"

She frowned at his suggestion. "They're all private offices, Harvey. We can't just barge in like tourists looking to snapchat the best view of Chicago's skyline."

"Sure, we can. It's called bravado."

Alma looked at him like he had lost his mind. But he was dead serious. He would spend the entire day there, investigating every closet of every office if it meant finding something else that might lead them towards another clue and closer to their wedding.

"Well, you can conserve your bravado because I don't think we're going to find anything." There was a doom and gloom in her voice that he recognized and it haunted him.

"C'mon now. Don't get all Debbie Downer on me. We've come this far. We've got a photograph and a skeleton key and M.F. Conway, 111. Now, we just need to find the window."

"I doubt there's any chance of that," she replied, circling the lobby as her eyes lifted to its coffered ceiling.

"Why the heck not?" he asked, infusing as much bravado into his tone as he could muster. "We've got the smartest sexiest antique hunter in the city and her valiant billionaire boy toy who's willing to bribe every front desk receptionist with a few Benjamins and barge into a few corner offices if that's what it takes." Pulling out his wallet, he whipped out a handful of hundred dollar bills, just to prove he was willing and able to serve his woman and her cause.

But, like always, Alma was significantly unimpressed by his money. "Boy toy?"

Harvey spread out his hands. "W.I.T—Whatever. It. Takes."

"Well, unfortunately, even my valiant billionaire boy toy and all his Benjamins can't undo modernization."

Harvey followed her gaze up to the ceiling, recognizing the modern-day materials of renovation. "You mean some greedy opportunistic billionaire bastard has already screwed things up for us?"

Alma nodded her head. "This building was Daniel Burnham's final skyscraper before he died. Burnham is known for his lofty glass atria like the ones in the Rookery Building and the Field's Building. Burnham's designs are all about light and space reaching up into the air as far as possible. But this atrium has clearly been closed up and sealed. And if the atrium has been modernized without regard for Burnham's original Beaux-Arts design, then there's not much hope that anything else of historical or artistic merit has been saved within the building—"

"Well, she's certainly got that right."

They both turned towards the security guard, sitting in an isolated chair in the corner of the lobby. "Even the billionaire bastard part," he confirmed.

Harvey studied the old man in the shabby uniform as he slowly rose from his seat and hobbled over to them.

"Originally, there was an open lightwell in the center of the building, but the group who owned the building in the '60s extended the floors across it to expand their leasable square footage. Broke my heart a bit, I can say that much."

"You worked here in the '60s?" Skepticism created an uptick in Harvey's question. He didn't mean to be rude, but he didn't want to be taken for a fool either.

The old man huffed. "And the '50s and the '40s. I've been working in this building longer than you've existed on the planet, son. So don't be getting snotty with me."

Harvey stood up straighter, realizing he had just been bitch-slapped by an octogenarian. "Yes, sir."

Alma approached the guard. "You remember what it was like then? Before they made the renovations?"

"Oh sure. I've worked here almost every day for the past seventy years. Started as a young boy working as an elevator attendant back when they had those sorts of jobs." He nodded over to the gleaming golden elevator doors. "And just kept moving my way around every time she gets sold. New owners just never think to fire me."

"Yet," Harvey added.

Alma shot him a glare—was he really catfighting with a man three times his own age?

Harvey stuffed his hands in his pockets and moseyed away. *Yes, yes…he was. Because he was a man-child, after all.*

"So then you might know something more about this…" Alma held up the skeleton key.

The old man squinted his cloudy blue eyes onto it. "Oh sure…but first you've got to tell me what you're doing here. It's my job, you know. Security and all." He tugged on the iron-on security badge of his shirt.

"We're looking for a place to get re-married." Harvey interjected from across the lobby.

"You mean you've already married him once?" the guard asked Alma, as if Harvey wasn't standing ten feet away.

Alma smiled and nodded.

"And how'd it go the first time?" he prodded.

She gazed over at Harvey. He pantomimed ten stars.

"About as well as you'd expect," she finally replied.

The guard huffed again. "Bet he screwed it up and now he's itching for a second chance."

"Itching for more than that," Harvey answered through cupped hands, just to make sure the security guard could hear him—hearing aids and all. "But she still hasn't said yes."

"Smart girl," the guard muttered, inspecting the key in the light before passing it back to Alma. "Yep. Haven't needed it in years, but that's the old elevator key that let us into the top floor penthouse where Mr. Graham had his private office."

"Ernest Graham?" Alma incredulously asked. "Daniel Burnham's business partner?"

The security guard nodded. "The same. He liked the view from up there until he ran into trouble with Burnham's sons and moved his whole outfit into the Railway Exchange Building."

"You mean, The Santa Fe Building," Harvey corrected him.

"Yeah, but that's not what old-timers like me call it," the security guard snapped back. "Building owners come and go, names change, but the true pulse of a building beats within the heart of the person who first built it."

Harvey shot a glance at Alma. *Now, who was the one who was entertaining crazy?*

"So the only thing you know is that the key fits the elevators," Harvey pressed him.

"Used to," the security guard abruptly set him straight. "Until they changed that, too."

"Is there any part of this building that hasn't been changed since the time you first started working here?" Alma asked, the last bit of hope faltering in her voice.

"Nope. It's all been changed. The only thing left is me."

"Aren't we lucky," Harvey snarked before Alma grabbed his arm and led him away.

"Thanks so much for your time," she said to the security guard. "It looks like we'll just have to rethink getting married after all."

She pushed Harvey towards the revolving doors, but he pushed back on her.

"Wait, that's it?" He settled his weight on his heels, stopping her cold. "We can't just give up now." He couldn't help but think how far they had come and how easily she was willing to accept defeat. "You're the mother of my child and the love of my life, and I'm not letting this end with you as my ex."

Taking her by the hand, he reversed their direction, dragging her back to the security guard.

"So, here's the deal, Mr. Security Guard…we've got a key and a photograph and a hunch that this building is important somehow, but we don't know why, and I really need my ex-wife to agree to remarry me. So, isn't there anything else you can tell us about it?"

"You mean in terms of where to get married?" The security guard furrowed his brushy eyebrows.

"I just mean…" Harvey faltered, realizing he was reaching for something that was as elusive as his own belief in it. Alma squeezed his hand, giving him permission to give up the way she had.

"Okay, yeah. Sure. Suggestions for where to get married." Harvey sighed, taking anything he could get.

"Are you really sure he's the one?" the guard asked Alma, just to spite Harvey.

She turned and gazed into Harvey's eyes. "Well, if he's not the one, he's definitely the one who's going to drive me crazy trying to prove it."

"Yeah, that's the sense I get, too." The guard nodded. "Melodrama."

Harvey spread out his hands. "I am standing right here, you know."

The security guard shrugged like he couldn't care less. "Well…if you want big and fancy and *melodramatic*, your best bet is to go over to the Rookery. At least that's still got an original Burnham lobby and you could probably jump down with a parachute from the balcony and make a memorable entrance."

"Because breaking every bone in my body would be the epitome of melodrama," Harvey noted with sarcasm.

"It *would* be memorable," Alma teased.

"You're saying no to remarrying me in Paris, London, or Rome, but yes to a full-on body cast?"

"I promise to nurse you back to health." Lifting up his hand, she pecked his knuckles with a kiss.

Gee thanks, he snuffed, envisioning the scene and considering the fact that the only part of his body he cared about didn't have a bone.

"Otherwise…" the guard paused, almost long enough for Harvey to nod off to sleep. "If you don't mind something smaller and more informal, there's always the little chapel just down the street with the pretty stained-glass window."

Say what? That was enough to jolt Harvey awake.

"What little chapel with the stained-glass window?" Alma insisted, sliding her hand into Harvey's for support.

"The one they moved from Mr. Graham's office when they renovated his penthouse office into an entire floor of cubicles. A real damn shame, but at least they had the decency to move it. It was Mr. Graham's favorite."

"And did it have a name?" Alma insisted. "The window?"

"I'm sure it did, but I don't remember it. But Mr. Graham liked to call it his lady. She had a really lovely face that would glow every time it was sunny in the mornings."

Harvey looked down at Alma's hand. It was trembling.

"Please…" she treaded carefully. "Can you tell us where we might find it?"

"Well…" the guard paused, giving Harvey the geriatric stink eye. "I'm happy to tell you anything, but not your friend. For him, it'll cost one of those Benjamins."

Harvey rolled his eyes. *Ahhh, of course*. He knew there had to be a catch. It was all a fanciful lie to bilk them out of money. The scheming old-timer bastard had them from hello. "Yeah, because I'm a lot less gullible and trusting than my wife." Harvey removed the hundred-dollar bill from his wallet and lifted it up between two fingers.

"Ex-wife," the guard corrected him. "And if I were her, I'd be giving it some second thoughts myself." Swiping away the hundred-dollar bill from Harvey, the guard passed it over to Alma.

"There used to be a charity box inside the chapel, just past the doorway on the right. I haven't been back to that hospital since my wife passed on, but if it's still there, maybe you can make a donation for me."

"I'd be happy to," Alma replied, accepting the honor. "So, the chapel is inside a hospital?"

The security guard nodded. "Lutheran General. Right off of—"

"—Lake Shore," Alma finished his sentence.

"The same. You know it?"

But Alma didn't answer. Instead, she abruptly ended the conversation. "Thank you so much for your time. You've been most generous with it."

She turned away and headed toward the revolving doors, forcing Harvey to rush after her.

"Hey, hey, hey…slow down there." He caught her arm. "Don't go believing in everything he said before we check it out for ourselves."

"No, I don't believe it," she answered flatly. "And I'm not going to bother checking it out either."

"Really?" Harvey peered at her, stumped by the cold glare in her eyes. "That's supposed to be my line. Your line is supposed to involve begging me to come with you and bribes of sexual favors."

She folded up the hundred-dollar bill and returned it to Harvey. "Let's just go home." She started for the exit, but he blocked her, confused by the abrupt change in her mood.

"C'mon. You're making this too easy, which wouldn't be like you. Normally, you're a complete pain in the ass and I love you for it." He stopped her again, knowing better than to accept her surrender. Gazing into her eyes, he searched out a clue, but she only offered him an expression that she rarely showed—distress.

"I'm not going back to that hospital."

"Back?" he asked.

She fell silent, as if she had told him enough.

"Because you've been there before?"

She looked down at the floor. He knew immediately it was one of the few subjects that they never discussed.

"Your mother," he offered, suddenly realizing exactly why.

"I can't go back there," she whispered like a mantra. "Not even for this."

He could've said a thousand things, but none of them would have been as right as drawing her into his arms and hugging the hurt out of her. "I'll go with you. We'll do it together."

He felt her shake her head. "I don't want to. I'd rather just never know."

"Fair enough. But you told me you would consider marrying me again if we find this damn stained-glass window, and if it means I have to go there without you and take a selfie all by myself next to your hundred-million-dollar Tiffany stained-glass window, I still expect you to respond with a yes."

She covered her face with her hands. "Please promise me you'll take the selfie with your clothes on."

"No way…Not unless you come with me and keep me dignified."

She attempted to pull away from him. But he knew he couldn't give up. "We've come so far. Your mother would've never wanted you to quit now, just because of her."

Alma considered his point. "My mother was a very principled, uncompromising woman. She would have hated you, you know."

He shrugged in agreement. "At first. Then she would have loved me."

"Oh really? And why's that?"

"Because I'm the man who knocked up her daughter with her first grandchild."

"Out of wedlock," Alma stressed. "She would have killed you."

"True. Until she saw how crazy in love I was with you."

"Or just crazy..."

"I would have helped her in the kitchen," he insisted, drawing her into his embrace.

"Wearing one of her aprons?"

"The floweriest one."

"Yes, she would have loved that." Alma relented, accepting his kiss. "And you would have charmed her with your Spanglish."

"Tomates, lechuga, ensalada, la cucaracha," Harvey replied in his most pronounced gringo accent. "See? We can't let her down. Not now. Señora Castillo is expecting great things from us."

Chapter Thirty-Three

UGH, THE SMELL. It was the first thing that hit her the moment they passed through the sliding glass doors of the hospital's front entrance.

Alma immediately backtracked, but Harvey caught her.

"We can do this," he whispered. "Together."

Unable to speak, unable to breathe, she shook her head. She wasn't so sure. She had never told him what had happened there, and just because he was there with her now, wasn't a guarantee that she could emotionally endure it.

She mechanically turned down the hallway towards the intensive care unit—the same direction she had turned every day for an entire month. *An entire month.* She had spent an entire month clinging onto every smile from the nurses, every reassurance from the doctors, every whisper of hope invented by her father about her mother who clung to life while the ventilator did the breathing for her.

Until it didn't.

Alma closed her eyes and stopped in the middle of the hallway, scented with a mixture of bleach and bodily fluids. *She never got used to the smell.* Just like she never got used to the idea that her mother had needed to be there in the first place—or the fact that she never made it out.

It wasn't supposed to end that way. Her mother was a strong, healthy, radiant woman who caught a bad cold that forced her to rest in bed. One minute, Alma got a call from her father that her mother was wheezing uncontrollably and could barely breathe, the next minute, she heard they were rushing to the hospital where she was admitted to the ICU.

And after a long-drawn out month, she never made it out.

It had been over ten years ago, and still everything in that hospital hallway looked the same—the linoleum floors and the frames of chintzy art hanging on the white-washed walls. Alma and her father stayed there every day for twelve hours a day. Conchita tried to visit, but usually left after a few hours, unable to bear it. Watching her mother, sedated in bed, face covered with an oxygen mask, feet bound in puffy boots, losing weight every day, proved too much for her to handle. It was too much for Alma, too, even though she pretended it wasn't until the day her mother's heart unexpectedly stopped. It had been the only time that afternoon her father had left the room to eat. Alma remained with her to keep watch. The machine's alarms rang out. The nurse called code, and a cavalcade of nurses and doctors swept to her mother's bedside. *It wasn't like the way they portrayed it on TV,* Alma remembered thinking. It wasn't loud, frenzied, and dramatic. It was all very eerie and silent as everyone surrounded her mother's bed and studied the monitor displaying her vital signs while two male nurses pumped her chest. *Four times they shocked her with the defibrillator…at least four…maybe more.* Then when it was clear it had come to an irreversible end, they simply stopped, all before her father even had a chance to return to the room.

It had been ten years and still she couldn't talk about it: the moment she saw her mother's life slip away without even a last chance to say good-bye.

And now, she was back there in that hospital, when she didn't have to be, and she absolutely couldn't stand it.

"I can't." She dodged Harvey and headed back for the entrance.

She made it all the way through the sliding glass doors before he caught up with her again. She covered her face with her hands, trying to hide her tears. He had seen her cry many times before. But this was different. This was private, sacred pain that couldn't be shared or discussed.

To his credit, he didn't say anything—not at first. He simply enveloped her hand in his own, and waited until she stopped sobbing. Then he offered an alternative.

"If you turn the other way down the hall, there's a gift shop."

She dried her runny nose on her sleeve. "A gift shop?"

He nodded and used her confusion to his advantage. "With cotton candy."

She considered the oddity of selling cotton candy in a hospital, but then realized even children needed to be coerced into entering the building.

Leading them back through the entrance, he pointed out their destination, away from the ICU.

"You know…have I ever told you the reason why I love buying cotton candy so much?"

She shook her head. She just always thought it was because he knew she liked it, too.

"Because when I was a kid, we never got to eat candy unless we stole it. Whenever my dad sent us to the corner store to buy him a pack of Marlboros, my brother and I used to have to shoplift it."

They entered the gift shop and Harvey headed straight for the rack with miniature Mylar balloons, stuffed animals, and bags of pink and blue cotton candy.

"Now, I love the feeling of being able to buy it whenever I want." He took out a hundred-dollar bill from his wallet. "Blue or pink?" he asked her.

"Pink," she answered.

He smiled and moved to the register. "Dumb question. I should have guessed."

"I didn't know…" Alma started to say, reaching out for a travel-sized pack of tissues next to the postcards. "About you having to steal it as a kid."

Harvey shrugged and waited for the sales clerk to ring up the purchase. "I never liked the taste of cigarettes, but the taste of sugar definitely took the edge off of the everyday struggle."

Alma accepted the bag of cotton candy. She had known about Harvey's childhood—the fact that his father was an alcoholic and his mother had divorced him. But he never talked about it and he acted as if it never bothered him. But now, she knew that he understood. Even though some pain couldn't be shared, it didn't mean it wasn't acknowledged.

"Will that be all for you?" the sales clerk asked.

Harvey paused as something at the other end of the shop caught his eye. "And one of those Minnie Mouse headbands."

When the clerk retrieved it and handed it to Harvey, he placed it on Alma's head like a crown.

"There," he said, proudly inspecting his purchases. "Cotton candy and Minnie Mouse. What else does a girl need to get her through a tough time?"

"Chocolate," the sales clerk chimed in.

Harvey glanced at Alma, checking to see if it was true.

"I ate a ton of dark chocolate after our divorce," she admitted. "Conchita used to bring it over at the end of every work week."

"Oh, me too," the sales clerk sympathized. "Sometimes it was the only thing I ate for dinner. Besides three glasses of wine."

Alma bobbed her head in agreement. Harvey had his man code. Women had their divorcée code.

Harvey swiped a handful of Ring Pops from the candy basket and tossed them onto the counter. "Okay, then. We'll add five dark chocolate Ring Pops. One for each finger."

The clerk rung up the register. "That will be $8.65. Would you like a bag?"

"Wait—" Alma interjected. "Can we add one more thing?"

The sales clerk nodded. "Of course."

"That headband, please."

"The one with the red plastic horns?"

"Yep." Alma accepted the headband from the clerk and slipped it onto Harvey's head.

"What? The halo didn't speak to you?" he quipped.

"Nope," she said, turning him towards the wall mirror. "What do you think?"

"I think I also need a pair of sunglasses." He removed a pair with chrome-tinted lens from the nearby rack and added them to their bounty.

"Twenty-five forty-two," the sales clerk said, finalizing the total and sweeping everything into a small plastic bag.

Harvey traded the hundred-dollar bill for the bag then dumped all the change into the tip jar. "And just for the record," he said to the sales clerk, "no man is worth the stomach ache of eating only chocolate for dinner. Next time, at least order carry-out."

He stuffed an extra hundred into the fishbowl before strutting his devil horns and obnoxious sunglasses in front of the women. "Now, what do *you* think?"

"I think we have a better chance now of getting stopped by security," Alma quipped.

"Good," he said, offering her the crook of his arm. "That's exactly how I like to roll."

Chapter Thirty-Four

THEY STOOD OUTSIDE the door of the hospital chapel, waiting…Harvey wasn't sure for what, but he knew better than to rush her.

"What if we go in there and we find it?" she finally said.

"Easy," he replied. "We suddenly become millions of dollars richer and you have to agree to marry me again. I'm way more concerned about what happens if we don't."

"So am I." Alma held up her hand and pressed it against the surface of the door, as if she was sensing whether or not to push through it or walk away forever.

"You know…there's no shame in believing in fairy tales," Harvey offered, knowing she was the type of girl who put too much stock in trying and failing rather than the joy of trying at all. "Even if there's no hidden Tiffany window on the other side of this door, the journey still took us pretty damn far." He lifted her hand into his own and feathered his lips against her inner wrist.

She eyed his kiss. "A surprise out-of-wedlock pregnancy and a ruined hundred-million-dollar business deal? That's not exactly your traditional fairy tale."

"Traditional is boring and overrated. I much prefer our version of happily ever after—a baby conceived during mad crazy make-up sex and a chance to prove my penile prowess through sleepless nights of bottle feedings and changing dirty diapers."

"We'll see about that." Skeptical, she crossed her arms. "I've seen you with only three hours of sleep, and it usually ends with you dozing off on the toilet and me struggling with whether or not to leave you there."

"Which is why you're the only woman in the world who I want to marry. No one else has ever had to consider such a dilemma."

"So, are we really going to do this?"

"You mean shatter our little storybook fairy tale?" He stared at the door, wondering if it was worth it to pass over its threshold. "I dunno…but I'm pretty certain as long as we're together, we'll find another one to believe in."

She smiled at him. "Promise?"

"Promise," he replied, resolute in every way.

Armed with the assurance of his support, she took a deep breath and nodded at the door. He complied, pushing it open and allowing her to enter first.

Untouched.

It was the first word that came to his mind as he followed her into the dim room resembling his grandmother's bedroom from the fifties. He half-expected votive candles and heavy wall tapestries depicting each religion's version of life ever after, but there was none of that. It was distinctly spare and non-denominational with a few chairs arranged around the perimeter and a few bas-relief wooden carvings—symbols of some of the world's most popular faiths—hanging on the taupe walls. And, of course, there was also a stained-glass window. But Harvey didn't need to be an expert to know that it was contemporary in its design and amateur in its execution—a triple-paneled folding window with frosted opaque glass illuminated by floor lights and dominated by swirls of robin's egg blue and canary yellow. Safe, secular, and absolutely the opposite of everything they had hoped would fulfill their quest.

Alma surveyed the window. Even though he had known her a long time, he had only seen that fragile expression of disillusionment on her face twice in his life. Once—now, as she absorbed the disappointing finality of their journey, and the other time when he had consciously broken his promise to salvage the windows from his riverfront parcel the morning after they had made love in the Palmer House honeymoon suite.

He drifted up behind her and encircled her waist.

"Not exactly what we were expecting, huh?" he said, leaning his chin over her shoulder.

"Nope," she whispered, allowing him to tighten his embrace, a mutual sign that it would somehow still be all okay. "I don't know why I kept believing…" Her voice trailed off, as if the disappointment and embarrassment was too much to bear.

"Listen…if you never dream, not even a little, then you'll never seek out anything worth finding."

She shot him a glare. "Did you read that in a fortune cookie?"

"Nope. Learned it from my wife."

"Ex-wife," she wise-cracked. "We didn't find it."

"A man can still dream."

Her mouth spread into that enigmatic smile, the one that hinted she was warming up to anything he might propose—and getting warmer.

Then, with a curious look of wonderment, her eyes shifted from his face to something above his forehead.

"It's the devil horns. Admit it. You can't agree to remarry a man who flagrantly wears devil horns, right?"

But she didn't answer. Instead, she reached out into the air, attempting to touch something mysteriously floating through it. When he glanced up, there was nothing to see, except dancing glints of color reflecting off her palm. They both turned to follow the source of the light—an unexpected ray clearing the top of the amateur stained-glass window.

"Harvey? Why is my hand green and purple and red when there's no green, purple, or red in that window?"

She was right. It was either the strangest of optical illusions, or there was something peculiar and unexpected behind the amateur stained-glass window.

"Because you—and your witchy ways—always seem to make magical things like that happen."

He craned his head above the window, seeking out the source of the colored light. When he couldn't get a good look, he tested its side panels, forcibly folding back its right flap and producing a tiny sliver of space.

Alma peeked into it.

"Do you see anything?" Harvey asked.

"Yes," she confirmed. "It looks like there's something back there, but I need a better look."

"Well…here's your chance to investigate it now, because in six months, you're not going to be able to fit back there."

Alma raised her arms, held her breath and flattened her chest as far as she could in order to squeeze her petite figure through the opening.

Harvey peered into the crevice, but he could barely make out the silhouette of something built into the exterior wall. He waited another minute, whistling a ragtime tune to keep himself company, before calling over the top of the amateur window as if he was checking on her from outside a dressing room.

"Everything okay in there?"

"You're not going to believe me if I tell you," she finally answered.

He smiled. "Probably not. But you can try me."

Without warning, his phone buzzed in his pocket. He retrieved it and saw the text from CONTESSA. *Fitting*, he thought, as he gazed down at the image on its screen, slowly absorbing the significance of what she had sent him. Something more stunning in its mastery and artistry than he could remember seeing in all his life.

"That's it, isn't it?" He surveyed the picture of the stained-glass window, portraying a glowing unearthly woman in a flowing scarlet cloak within a midnight garden illuminated by shimmering pale blue waves of moonlight. It shone with the scintillating brilliance of rubies, emeralds, diamonds, amethysts and aquamarines, and for a moment, Harvey wondered if Tiffany had actually melded bits of priceless gemstones within the opalescent glass.

I can't speak, she texted back.

He smiled again. Contessa, his hopelessly romantic.

You know, we don't have to leave anytime soon, he texted back, knowing the picture likely couldn't compare to the overwhelming experience of finally standing in front of it. *You can just stay there...drooling for a while.*

He heard a burst of laughter through her silent tears. It had been an emotional day. *Hell, an emotional year.* And it was finally coming to an end.

Harvey glanced up at the ceiling. The flickering pattern of colored light ebbed and flowed across it like rippling waves until it slowly faded away.

The light just changed.

Just saw that.

That's probably why no one knows what it is. She sent him another text with a picture. This time, he could barely make out an image within the window, tinted almost black.

Pretty hard to discover a priceless Tiffany stained-glass window when it's hidden in the dark—unless you're the smartest glass antiques expert in Chicago.

I don't think we should tell anyone about it.

He re-read her text, no surprised she would want to guard the secret.

Fair enough, he replied. *We can just pretend we never found it. On one condition...*

What's that? she buzzed back.

He lifted a chocolate Ring Pop out of the bag, unwrapped it, and shoved it through the narrow opening. *You say yes.*

Chapter Thirty-Five

SIX MONTHS LATER

HARVEY SAT ACROSS FROM Alma in their usual old-fashioned booth in one of her favorite confectionaries on Chicago's West Side, and watched as she devoured her weekly treat—banana split ice cream sundae.

They had visited there every week since the end of her first trimester. He ordered one ice cream sundae for her and a chocolate malt for himself. She had cravings and only the ice cream parlor's signature hot chocolate sauce and extra whipped cream did the trick.

But for that visit, they were there for more than just the ice cream. They had an agenda. Their baby's due date was looming and they still needed to agree on baby names.

"Okay, I'm going to start with boys' names because I'm pretty certain we're having a boy."

"Oh really?" Alma said, stuffing her mouth with the maraschino cherry and a spoonful of whipped cream, officially starting her indulgence of the sugary temple of gluttonous bliss. "How can you be so sure?" She drew her agile tongue across the spoon, lapping up every last bit of cream off of it.

Harvey made a mental note: *buy more whipped cream.* They still made love every week, even when she pretended she didn't want to, because he knew that it relieved more than swollen feet and achy joints. *Especially when it involved whipped cream.*

"Because you're big and buxom and beautiful, and I'm certain it's all because you're carrying my tank of a son."

"I think the only reason you think it's a boy is because you want to name him Harvey Jr."

"Not true. I know you're not thrilled with that option, so I've been hard at work coming up with alternatives."

Harvey took out a sheet of paper from his pocket, unfolded it, and cleared his throat. Confidently, he delivered the first name on his list. "Ivan."

She scoffed. "As in…The Terrible?"

"Well, that's *your* association with it," he insisted.

"And six centuries of history."

"So, is that a veto?"

"Veto," she muttered through a solid barrier of ice cream, just to make sure he understood her. Harvey thought having the baby discussion over ice cream would soften Alma's resolve to hate every one of his picks. Clearly, he was wrong.

He cleared his throat again and leapt. "Boris."

She looked at him like he had sworn at her. "You really expect me to name our child Boris?"

"Now, don't shoot it down yet before you give it a fair shot. It's short, memorable, and it fits the profile of a chubby baby. Even an ugly one."

Alma dropped the spoon out of her mouth. "You're expecting us to have an ugly baby?"

He fell silent, realizing he'd just shoveled himself into Stupidsville—again. It was likely the reason she hadn't officially agreed to remarry him.

"I'm simply covering all our options."

"Veto," she punctuated, striking out that option.

He nodded. He deserved that one. "Okay, how about this one—Anton."

"As in Chekhov? That's a bit too literary—even for me. Plus, I'm not a fan of *Three Sisters*."

Harvey scrambled to find a replacement on his list. "Okay, here then…Baryshnikov."

She eyed him, sensing something questionable about his list. "You do realize Baryshnikov is a famous Russian ballet dancer, right?"

"Hmm," he chewed on the revelation. "I didn't. But he seemed like a pretty famous dude and his name was hard to spell, so I went with it."

Her black eyes narrowed on him. "You intentionally googled the most famous Russian names in history so that Harvey Jr. would seem like a great option in comparison."

Honestly, he thought she would have caught on even quicker than that. "I'll only admit to googling names and maybe including a few that I couldn't pronounce."

Alma sighed and pushed away her empty ice cream sundae dish. "You really want Harvey Jr. that much? And what happens if it's a girl?"

"Easy." Harvey nudged the tray of extra chocolate sauce in front of her. "Harvette."

She snorted with scorn. "I am so not marrying a man who wants to name our daughter Harvette. And I'm pretty sure every woman on the planet would back me up on that."

She drove her spoon into the extra chocolate sauce and swirled it around her tongue, just to take the edge off. It was a good thing, too. Otherwise, Harvey was pretty certain she might threaten to divorce him again before they even had a chance to remarry.

"You know, we could just get rid of fifty percent of this baby name conflict by finding out the sex of the baby in advance."

Alma looked at him like he had just climbed up onto the table and stomped on her sundae.

Stupidsville.

"You know what?" Harvey said, attempting to redeem himself. "Let's forget I ever said it. I love endlessly bantering about baby names with you. So, c'mon...let's see what's on your list."

Accepting the challenge, Alma set down her spoon with a firm clank. She dug through her purse and pulled out her own list, scrawled onto a miniature napkin. Their eyes locked, like two competitors battling for the World's Best Baby Name Championship.

"Dickens," she finally pronounced.

"V-e-t-o," he flung back in faux slow motion.

"What, just like that? You can't veto a name without even considering it."

"Hmmmmmmm," he pondered, feigning consideration. "Nope. Still veto."

She refused to surrender. "Charles Dickens is one of the greatest novelists of all time."

"Sorry. My kid is not having Dick anywhere in his name—period. It's man code."

She heaved another sigh of disgust. This one, distinctly familiar. She *hated* his man code and she wanted to make sure he knew it. He did, but he also knew he was saving their child from years of adolescent locker room mockery, and that was completely worth it.

"Fine..." she acquiesced, scanning the rest of her list and settling on a second place contender. "Jameson."

"Nice, but too alcoholic. Veto."

"Copperfield."

"As in the magician?"

"*David* Copperfield," she stressed.

"As in the magician?" he repeated.

Exasperated, she rolled her eyes and jumped down to the very end of her list.

"Heathcliff," she said resolutely.

Harvey snorted through his malt straw. "You gave me flack for Boris, but you seriously expect me to greenlight, Heathcliff? Veto."

She refolded the napkin and glared at him. "This is why I haven't married you."

"Because I won't let you name our child, Heathcliff?"

"Yes."

Harvey knew it was her hormones talking and not his impassioned, emotional, pregnant lover. But he also knew there was some truth in it.

"Well, what happens if it's a girl?" he said, flipping her question back onto her

"Then I thought we could consider…"

"Harvette?" he interjected slyly because she was too cute in her maternity overalls flecked with stray chocolate sauce not to tease her.

"Naming her after my mother," she replied quietly, hesitant about whether or not to propose it.

He propped his elbow on the table and rested his chin against his hand. "Well then…we better hope it's a girl. Or Harvey Heathcliff Zale-Castillo is going to have a hell of a time in school."

"Castillo-Zale," she corrected him with a reluctant smile, knowing they had finally arrived on a truce. "And it will build character."

Warm, getting warmer, he thought. "So, does this mean you're going to marry me?"

"I'm still considering it." It had become her standard reply.

"It's the ring, isn't it? Be honest." She was still wearing the chocolate Ring Pop that she gnawed on throughout the day, forcing him to replace it every morning with a fresh one.

"It has nothing to do with the ring, Harvey, and everything to do with what comes after it."

"A baby, lots of amazing sex, and more babies. What else is there to worry about?"

"Oh, you know…the usual."

Her eyes drifted up to the fancy stained glass chandelier lamp shade that hung above them.

"You're still certain they're real Tiffanys, huh?"

Ever since they had started coming there, it had been the same discussion.

She nodded. "Yep."

"Which makes them worth about how much?"

"One hundred thousand dollars each at auction…possibly more."

Harvey darted his eyes around the room, counting at least four of them. Then he shifted his glance to the old frail woman sitting behind the antique brass cash register.

“That’s a lot of sundaes. I bet Margie wouldn’t mind retiring to someplace warm and cozy with a nest egg like that.”

“So, you think I should tell her?”

Harvey noted the marble soda fountain and miniature jukeboxes that had given the ice cream parlor its authentic charm for the past fifty years. “I think Margie probably likes serving you sundaes more than she likes the idea of retirement.” Swiveling back to Alma, he reached out and swiped a taste of chocolate sauce from her almost-empty tray.

“I’d like to think that you’re right.”

Taking out his usual hundred-dollar bill from his wallet, he tossed it on the check and flashed her a smile. “I’m always right, which is why convincing you to remarry me is going to be one of the smartest decisions of my life.” Leaning across the table and pecking her on her sugar-glazed lips, he said, “C’mon on, let’s get out of here, you big, beautiful, buxom mother of my nameless child. I’ve got something special I want to show you.”

Chapter Thirty-Six

"I REALLY DON'T SEE HOW getting us arrested for breaking and entering is going to convince me to remarry you."

Alma scuffed her boots along the polished linoleum floor as Harvey led her by the hand through the iconic atrium of the Marshall Field's department store. It was dark and empty, and despite her protests, he had managed to get them through the main revolving doors afterhours without triggering an alarm. He claimed he had scored security clearance through his connections with the owner, but she knew better than to trust Harvey's real estate "connections," especially when they potentially resulted in criminal charges of trespassing.

She trailed behind him, dangling like a kite, as he charged past the perfume counters and women's accessories on a mission to prove her wrong. Apparently, he thought jail was just as good a place to deliver their baby as anywhere else. He also thought Harvette was going to fly.

When they arrived at the luggage department, he suddenly stopped and spread out his arms like she should be obviously thrilled, enamored, and enchanted with his achievements.

"We're here."

"In the luggage department?" She noted the elaborate displays of matching leather suitcases and miniature carry-ons. "Are we going on a trip?"

"Not until the little one comes. But in the meantime, I thought we'd attempt to get rid of our old baggage and start fresh."

"But I thought you loved all our old baggage," she said, trying to emphasize the fact that their discussion had been a metaphor. She crossed her arms, attempting to sound more perplexed than annoyed at the possibility that he had dragged her there afterhours, just to discuss buying new luggage.

"I do. Did. But not if it's getting in the way of us moving forward. So I figured maybe it's just better to purge our old baggage and start over. You know, a fresh start with new baby baggage."

He rolled away a massive cardboard sales display, depicting a carefree couple in bathing suits, holding hands and running towards their picturesque beach getaway, and revealed the unexpected surprise behind it—a complete ensemble of newborn furniture and equipment, including a brand-new snow white bassinet, full-sized mahogany crib, free-standing baby swing, baby dresser topped with a changing table, rainforest-themed baby bouncer and a hot pink baby carrier.

Astonished, Alma pinched herself, just to make sure she wasn't hallucinating from her sugar rush. "Wow, Harvey….that's a whole lot of new baby baggage."

"I know...see?" He swiped up the hot pink baby carrier and slipped it over his shoulders like a backpack. "How can we not be ready to start a new life together with all this brand spanking new baggage?"

She peered at his broad shoulders and long arms, entangled in the straps of the carrier, and reached out to slip it off him before he accidentally tore it apart. Swapping it from his back to his chest and adjusting the position snuggly across his pecs, she revealed the proper way to wear an infant carrier. "Newborns are pretty small. It's going to take some time before you get to give piggyback rides."

"Can't wait," he said, pulling her into his arms.

"You do realize it's not about our old baggage?"

"What? The reason why you still haven't agreed to marry me?"

She nodded.

"Yep." He nodded back. "And I've got that covered, too." He led her into the adjacent mattress department. "Which is why we're also getting this…"

He presented her with a king-sized, pillow-top, two-layered memory foam mattress. Crawling on it, he immediately made an imprint into its billowy surface. "It's hypoallergenic, sleep-number adjustable, and heated," he recited, like he had become best friends with the salesman. "And it does this…" Reaching over the side, he pressed a sequence of numbers on its flat-panel control, raising the mattress' header and footer into the air.

"Is that comfortable?" Alma asked, trying not to sound ungrateful.

"Bliss," he exhaled, his body scrunched up like he was resting in the folds of an accordion.

She eyed the mattress' conspicuous price tag. "I'd like to think there's a simpler, less expensive way of getting me to marry you again."

He keyed in a new number into the control panel and flattened the mattress again before drawing her onto it.

"Back rubs?"

She smiled as she rolled on her side and nestled against his chest. "Warm."

"Foot rubs?"

"Warmer."

"Butt rubs?"

His hand curved over her backside. She laughed and pretended to shrug him off, but as with everything about him, she secretly enjoyed it.

"Ah, I know," he said. After a few robotic beeps, the bed slowly hummed like an engine until it mellowed into a constant vibration.

"Wow." Alma sighed in relaxation, feeling his warm body enveloping her own. "That might actually do the trick."

"And if not, maybe this will." He snaked his hand through the loop of her arm and displayed a small red velvet box. "The other one was a bit scuffed up from years of being entombed in clay. The jeweler didn't think he could rescue it, so I picked out this…"

She gazed at the box. "Harvey, you didn't have to."

"Yes, I did," he replied, slipping off the plastic band of the half-eaten Ring Pop from her finger. "It's not as easy to replace my stash of chocolate Ring Pops as you might think."

"I enjoy the Ring Pops." It was true. They satiated her anxious cravings and amused her in a way that reminded her not to take it all too seriously. *Just like Harvey.* Now, as she gazed down at the velvet box, she knew that they couldn't avoid serious forever, no matter how much they pretended to. They had a baby on the way and whatever baggage they had in the past, Harvey was right: they had to purge everything and start fresh.

"Are you afraid I'll disappoint you?" he asked, noting her reluctance to open it.

"No," she whispered. "I'm afraid we'll disappoint each other."

"That's pretty impossible unless you stop having sex with me," he quipped. "And even then, I won't be disappointed. I'll just be horny."

He nudged himself up against her tailbone, just to prove his point. She reluctantly smiled. Everything was so easy and uncomplicated in his world—even when it wasn't.

She sat up from the mattress without opening the box. The vibrations were making her nauseous. "Don't you think it would be wiser not to change anything until after we have the baby? You know, wait to make sure everything goes well afterwards?"

She touched the tip of his chin. She wasn't rejecting him. She was rejecting her fear of changing what had been the best months of her life.

"When you love something, you follow it to its bitter end, Alma. Which means I'm all in, no matter what happens afterwards."

"Breast pumps, and midnight bottle feedings, and bitchy hormones?"

"Yes, yes, and double yes," he stressed, cradling her cheek. "I want it all because I love it all, Alma. Because it's all part of you."

"There are going to be a lot of sleepless nights," she insisted. "And they're not going to be easily cured by an eight-thousand-dollar mattress."

"Well, when the baby turns us into sleep-deprived zombies, we'll come here and do exactly what we're doing now. Relax—"

He guided her down onto the mattress, positioning their heads at the foot of the bed and directing her attention up to the ceiling.

"Lights," he called up into the air and waited.

Like little attentive gnomes, the sensors responded to his command and clicked on a ring of beaded lights around the perimeter of the ceiling, illuminating the shimmering iridescence of the Tiffany mosaic glass tiles.

"Wow," she heaved a sigh, overwhelmed by the serene beauty of the moment. "You don't get this kind of view when you're here during the day, when it's filled with department store music and busy shoppers.

"Nope," he agreed, taking her hand into his own and holding it as if they could stay there forever.

She squeezed it. "I don't want a bitter end, Harvey. I want us to be happy."

"Which is exactly why you should marry me because I'm not going to promise you a mythical happily ever after. I'm going to promise to try my best to be dependable and to make it all okay. Even when it's not and I can't—every torturous sleepless night and every exhausting, hectic, unbelievably unpredictable but incredibly awe-inspiring day. But it will all be okay as long as we're together because I love you. And I will always love you. In fact, it's probably the most dependable thing about me."

She gazed into his earnest blue eyes, wanting to believe it would all be enough. "Has your building owner friend really agreed to let us come here at night, whenever we want, and hang out on all these mattresses with our crying newborn?"

"Yep. And he even thinks we should check out the lingerie section."

She narrowed her eyes at him. "*You're* the building owner?"

His blue eyes glinted at her. "Suuuuuuurrrrrrrrprise," he singsonged.

"But how?"

"You know, it's the darnedest thing," he replied. "When one deal closes, another one opens."

"And your riverfront parcel?"

"Sold off to a British real estate developer named Phillip Spears, who I used to despise, until he promised in writing to preserve the building and the stained-glass windows, and let you visit whenever you wanted."

"I don't know what to say…" She grew quiet, unable to comprehend how he had accomplished all of it—just for her.

He flopped his forehead between her heavy breasts and groaned in agony, "For the love of God, woman. Just – say – yes."

He flipped open the velvet box, revealing the stunning cushion cut five-carat tanzanite surrounded by diamonds in a gleaming white gold filigree setting. She recognized its art nouveau design—Louis Comfort Tiffany.

She contemplated everything they had been through together—as both exes and lovers—in the past few weeks, months, and years before answering him with a playful smile. "Warm, getting warmer."

He groaned and swept her into his arms, passionately kissing her, just to prove he meant every word he had said. "Just wait until I get all your clothes off and change your answer to scorching, white hot."

THE END

Priceless

Aria Hawthorne

Priceless - Book Summary

Contemporary Erotic Romance - Suitable for mature readers; 18+ years only - Full-length, stand-alone novel with HEA.

On the night before Valentine's Day, everything changes when jewelry store clerk, Maribel Martinez, assists the building owner, Miles Braxton-Worth, with a luxury purchase. Was it just her imagination, or did he feel their mysterious connection, too? Will Maribel be willing to relinquish her mind, body, and soul to the enigmatic billionaire for the chance to be the woman--special enough in his eyes--to receive his priceless gift? Will he accept her love for free, or will she be the one to pay the price?

Billionaire real estate tycoon Miles Braxton-Worth has carefully watched Maribel Martinez work in the department store of his downtown property for years without ever approaching her--until now. It's the night before Valentine's Day, and Miles decides to pursue the only woman in the world who has the power to save him from himself, and he's bought her the most expensive necklace in the jewelry case--just to prove it. But will she accept him? Or will his attempts to buy her love cost him something even more priceless?

Chapter One

GILLIAN. His gold-plated smartphone vibrated in his hand as the name flashed across its screen. Miles swallowed—hard. He was in the elevator. It was almost 8:45 p.m. on a Friday evening in downtown Chicago. There was no good reason to take the call. And yet, he wasn't the kind of man who avoided people. They avoided him. And he certainly wasn't about to hide from Gillian.

Miles punched the elevator's emergency STOP button. The cab ground to a halt and its piercing alarm rang out with warning. He flipped open the emergency call box, lifted up the phone receiver, and peered up into the security cameras.

"Kill the alarm, Kent," he ordered. It was his elevator, after all—his building. He could do whatever the hell he wanted.

"Yes, sir," Kent confirmed through the receiver.

The alarm faded into stale silence, seeping out of the elevator cab like escaping oxygen.

In the privacy of the elevator, Miles could finally take a moment to just *think*. He watched his smartphone buzz with urgency, then he glanced at his reflection in the shimmering elevator doors—he was tired, annoyed, and generally disinterested in taking on another fight, but his thirst for domination persuaded him to take the call.

"I'm not signing the deal," he answered, preparing for battle.

"Well, Happy Valentine's Day to you, too," the sly feminine voice said.

"Tell your tenant to find another landlord. I'm not signing *that* deal."

"Oh, trust me, Brax. I've tried," Gillian pouted. "But there's a short supply of prestigious downtown properties with curb appeal, and you own half of them."

It was a back-handed compliment, and they both knew it. There *was* a short supply of prestigious downtown properties, and Miles Braxton-Worth *did* own most of them. Gillian was forced to stroke his ego, and he was forced to work with her if he wanted to lease out his buildings with high-end commercial retailers.

"Twenty-year lease, thirty-five percent expense share of the common elements, and a fifteen percent annualized rent escalation," he countered with corporate ruthlessness.

"Brax..." Gillian lowered her voice in deference. "Fifteen percent rent escalation is a little much, don't you think?"

"No," he punched back. "And besides, it's better for you and your broker's commission, and you know it."

Gillian laughed. It pealed out like a golden bell, which was fitting because Gillian *loved* gold. Miles had bought her more gold jewelry than he cared to admit, and now she was spoiled and used to getting want she wanted.

"You know, Brax...these deals were a lot easier and a lot more fun when we were sharing a bed. Let's go have a drink and hammer out the details. It is Friday night, after all."

Miles pulled the phone away from his ear. Getting Gillian out of his bed was the best business decision he had made all year, but he fought the urge to say it. He pounded on the emergency STOP button. The elevator cab lurched downwards. Having a drink with Gillian to finalize the terms of a business deal they had been negotiating all day was the *last* thing he felt like doing, but he also knew that she was going to make it hard for him—very hard—to get what he wanted. He had to play this just right.

"C'mon on, just one drink. I know we can come to a consensus. Besides, what else are you doing for Valentine's Day?"

"Valentine's Day is tomorrow, Gillian," he corrected her. Miles hated her imprecision, but hated being boxed into a corner by her even more. Day in and day out, he coordinated with property management companies, lawyers, real estate brokers, potential tenants, accountants, business partners and investors; it had all slowly become a tedious routine, a tourniquet that squeezed out every other passion in his life. He was sick of hammering out escalations, lease terms, commissions, and contingencies. It filled him with scorn. It had become all about maintaining, maintaining, maintaining everything—including his wealth.

His stern expression in the elevator doors stared back at him. Looking up at the descending numbers, he rubbed his forehead and counted down...four, three, two—*ping*, ground level. The mirrored doors glided open, revealing the Grand Lobby of the department store. There, he spotted her. *Maribel.* Yesterday, he had noticed her in the lingerie section. Tonight, she was back at the jewelry counter. He had enjoyed seeing her last night in the lingerie department, wearing a tight cigarette skirt, stiletto heels, and fishnet stockings. It was an image that he had a hard time putting out of his mind.

He glanced at his watch. It was 8:50 p.m. The department store closed at nine. He suddenly felt inclined to make a purchase.

"I have to finish some shopping tonight," he said, hinting he was in a rush.

"Really…? How romantic of you," Gillian sassed back with honey and spice. "Try not to spend too much money on me. Although it does always help to sweeten the deal."

Miles listened, but didn't reply. There had been so much wheeling and dealing in his day that he craved an interaction with someone who would remind him that there was more to life than just business negotiations. His eyes fixed on the jewelry counter; he knew the only way he was going to save his sanity tonight was by getting there before nine.

"I'll be at home, Brax, drinking wine and taking a long bath in case you change your mind and feel the need to close a thirty-five million dollar deal—tonight," Gillian dangled the offer. "Because, you know…making us wait until the morning for your formal counteroffer may work against you. Remember, my clients could always sign a lease instead with Harvey Zale. Just making you aware—as a friend—because I know how much you like to have the upper hand." Gillian ended the call.

Miles savored the silence, as if the weight of a headstone had been removed from his chest. Sure, it was true. He could simply accept the deal and move on. But he didn't like giving up more than he should, especially not to Gillian. Still considering his plan, he swept his gaze back across the department store. *Yes, it just might save him.*

Lost in thought, he gazed out the grand revolving doors at the commercial skyscraper across the street. It was Harvey Zale's building—his competition. Then, he surveyed the iconic Tiffany glass-dome ceiling of the Field's building—*his* building—and thought about calling back Gillian to finalize the thirty-five million dollar lease deal that he had stonewalled all day until he peered across the Grand Lobby at the jewelry counter. *No, this was a better plan*, he thought. And certainly one with the potential to initiate something in his life other than just more negotiations.

Chapter Two

MARIBEL MARTINEZ STOOD behind the jewelry counter and wondered what it would be like to be courted and wooed on Valentine's Day. She watched a young couple in the perfume section as they flirted and snuggled each other while testing the pink fragrance bottles at the Valentine's Day display.

The young man sprayed the mist behind the young woman's ear, and then pulled her close to nibble at her neck. She laughed and shrugged playfully every time he nestled his chin over her shoulder and whispered into her ear. The young woman was dressed in designer jeans and a fashionable winter coat. Maribel recognized the coat. It was one of the most expensive items in the women's apparel section. *Had he bought it for her?* She had eyed it for herself, but despite working as a sales clerk at the department store for the past ten years, she knew she still couldn't afford most of the items in the store. She noticed the young man's blue uniform jacket, white shirt, and tie. *He was a trader on the floor of the Chicago Board of Trade*? Maribel had helped many customers who worked in the exchange pit. They would come into the department store during their breaks and purchase luxury jewelry like solitaire diamond pendants and natural pearl necklaces for their girlfriends and wives. She watched as the young man glanced over at the jewelry counter, pulling the young woman towards it. But the girl shook her head and enveloped his hand with her own. She simply enjoyed his flirtatious attention and didn't want it to stop. Maribel understood the sentiment. Love—true love—was the most priceless gift he could give her.

"Oh, gag me with a chain saw…"

Maribel turned and saw Crystal, leaning over the counter and sneering at the couple.

"Oh, Crystal…don't be so cynical." Maribel sighed and moved behind her register. "They look like they're in love."

"Exactly, which is why I hate them. Happy freaking Valentine's Day." Crystal smacked her gum and swung around to meet Maribel on the other side of the register. Both women eyed the couple from afar.

"Oh, please tell me you are *not* moving into my lingerie section," Crystal cried out.

"Shhh—" Maribel hushed her.

Crystal lowered her voice and tracked the couple with a glare. "It is quitting time, Romeo and Juliet. I'm in no mood to be working overtime tonight."

Maribel glanced up at the wall clock. It was fifteen minutes to nine. She was in no hurry to be anywhere. It was Friday night and Valentine's Day weekend, but she planned to spend it the same way she spent every weekend—in bed with a book at home and alone.

"Nice footwear," Crystal said, noticing Maribel's bedroom slippers, crowned with a ladybug emblem and trimmed with red and black lace.

"Thomas had me help Sharon yesterday in the lingerie section. You were off and it got busy because of all the Valentine's Day discounts. But I'm not like you…" Maribel paused and gazed down at Crystal's cherry red stilettos. "Six hours in heels make my poor cramped feet cry for mercy. That's why I love hiding behind the jewelry counter."

"It's true." Crystal peered down at her flashy red shoes, admiring them with affection. "My feet definitely *are* my best asset."

Crystal's dark eyes returned to the young couple who were circling the red velvet gift table decorated with pink, red, and black lace panties tagged with heart-shaped messages like BE MINE and FOREVER YOURS.

"Even if I could fit into one of those black lace thongs," Crystal pondered aloud, cracking her gum, "I certainly wouldn't want it stuck up my ass—much less stuck up there for anyone else to pick it out."

"Shhhhh…" Maribel hushed her again, but they both giggled because they knew it was true. "You never know, Crystal. You might be persuaded to wear a black lace thong by the right man," she teased.

"There is no man on earth who could possibly persuade me to wear XL thongs. Trust me, Maribel. No. Man," Crystal punctuated it with certainty. Then, her confidence waned as she gazed far across the Grand Lobby. "Correction… no man, except for maybe him."

Maribel followed Crystal's eyes, and both women watched as Miles Braxton-Worth exited the elevators.

"Hubba hubba alert," Crystal announced, nodding in his direction. "Now there's a man who could pick at my ass any day."

Both women stared at Miles, dressed in a dark European suit and designer Italian dress shoes. The girls were used to seeing the tall, handsome, and ridiculously wealthy building owner exit the elevators into the Grand

Lobby at the end of each work day. His offices were on the top floor, but he rarely shopped in the department store. *We're too trashy and cheap for someone rich and beautiful like him*, Crystal loved to snipe. But unexpectedly, he stopped, turned, and strode towards them—not cutting through the cosmetics section or turning down the middle aisle into the leather accessories—but coming directly towards the jewelry counter.

"Bite me, he's coming this way," Crystal warned and wheeled around to the opposite side of Maribel's counter.

Crystal was right. He *was* coming right towards them. Maribel shooed Crystal back towards the lingerie section.

"Maybe he's planning on making some last minute V-day gift purchases for his favorite vajayjay," Crystal hissed at Maribel.

Maribel quickly smoothed down her black pencil skirt and adjusted her long dark hair. She had never had the pleasure of assisting him with a purchase. Now, as Miles Braxton-Worth approached her counter, the only thing that filled her mind was the fact that he was the most elegant man she had ever seen.

"Hello, Maribel."

She felt herself flush. She thought she had forgotten to put on her nametag this morning. She touched the collar of her blouse and confirmed its absence. *Maribel.* She replayed the way he had said it with smooth refinement. He made it sound like the name of a queen.

"I'm looking to find the right gift for someone. Would you be able to assist me?"

"Of course." Maribel nodded and forced a smile. She automatically moved towards the mid-end jewelry case—a routine sales strategy to determine whether or not a shopper was a serious buyer or merely a casual browser. But Miles Braxton-Worth was no casual browser; he was a real estate tycoon. She hesitated. His attractive face and confident blue eyes overwhelmed her. "What kind of gift are you looking for Mr. Braxton-Worth?"

"Miles," he corrected her, gently. Maribel nodded and flushed again. There was really no reason for her to know his name except for the fact that *all* the sales girls knew who he was—from the perfume counter to the fashion accessories to the cutlery and dishware departments. But for Maribel, there had been only that one interaction with him, so many years ago, when he had spoken to her briefly to give her condolences for her mother's death. It was a moment she had never forgotten, an unexpected gesture of kindness from a complete stranger who shouldn't have even known about her mother's illness. He gazed at her now the same way he had gazed at her then, his enchanting blue eyes searing a silent moment of connection between them, as if nothing in the world mattered except for the way that he was looking at her.

Under the weight of his unwavering stare, Maribel felt the urge to curtsey, and she would have tried, if she wasn't wearing lady bug bedroom slippers. There was no way she could bring herself to call him 'Miles'—not when he was dressed up in a Valentino merino wool suit and sporting a gold and diamond Rolex Masterpiece wrist watch. She had been fortunate enough—once—to sell and receive commission on the female version of that watch, so she knew it was at least a thirty-thousand-dollar purchase.

"Is it a personal gift or professional one?" Maribel asked.

"That's a good question," Miles answered, as if he hadn't considered the meaning he wanted to convey behind the gift. "Unfortunately, I wish I knew…" He eyed her. She wondered if he noticed the chipped paint on her fingernails. She hadn't had time in days to manicure them herself. "You see, I don't know what the right approach is for this gift, so it's a bit of a challenge. That's why I'm hoping you can help me."

"I see…" She hesitated before turning towards the designer watches, still distracted by the clarity of his blue eyes and the beauty of his own manicured hands.

"I suppose it could be perceived as both," he finally decided. "But I want it to be a symbol—a symbol of pursuing something…mutual."

It was an intimate confession—one that surprised Maribel. "I see, so perhaps something a bit more delicate." She moved towards the bracelets. She was careful not to look up at him. She could smell the scent of his cologne and envision his impossibly handsome profile and enchanting eyes, though she wasn't sure she had the confidence to face them or allow them to settle upon her.

"Yes, delicate," he repeated, lowering his gaze to her wrist. She was wearing a diamond tennis bracelet with a sterling silver setting. It was a fake, clearly. Maribel had scooped it up on the clearance rack in the costume jewelry section when it was seventy-percent off.

"But also perhaps something that conveys a message," he offered.

She wanted to ask what kind of message, but she didn't dare pose the question. She glanced over at his ring finger. It was bare. She had never heard about a 'Mrs. Braxton-Worth' from the other sales girls, but the absence of a wedding band wasn't a sure sign of anything. She had served countless men who had chosen not to wear their wedding bands simply because they found it to be restrictive—both on their hands and in their extracurricular pursuits.

She needed another cue. Miles sensed her needs.

"Inviting, but not too forward."

"I see…earrings?" she suggested.

"I'm not sure…" He laughed, as if the joke was on him. "It's probably a typical mistake to assume all women are born with the ability to wear earrings." He grinned with self-deprecation, as if he was betraying a rare weakness—his inability to ever know perfectly the opposite sex.

"Better not to assume," she said sympathetically, turning away from the earrings. *Someone he doesn't know well…* she gathered. *Not a current girlfriend or a wife, but someone new.*

She smiled in return and they both relaxed. Now, they understood each other and were joined in their mutual quest.

"Well… I don't think you can go wrong with a necklace," Maribel finally said after surveying all the cases and carefully considering all their options.

"A necklace," he repeated as a confirmation. "Which is your favorite?"

The question caught her off-guard. The necklaces were five hundred dollars—minimum. She never dared to consider which one she might enjoy herself. Miles slid his fingers along the surface of the glass case, as if to coax her to follow him.

"They're all so lovely," she said, almost as a whisper. "You really can't go wrong with a solitaire diamond pendant…" There was hesitation in her voice.

"But…?" he nudged.

"But perhaps something less conventional."

"Yes, exactly," he agreed.

She finally found the courage to look up at him. He was staring at her with his radiant eyes, as if her answer was perfect. Simply perfect.

She exhaled with relief. She had helped so many men who didn't want to take risks; they preferred to stick with safe and traditional. Maribel, on the other hand, always preferred jewelry pieces that flashed with their own unique aura.

"That one." Miles nodded, his eyes falling upon a one-carat siren red ruby pendant with a checkerboard cut face. It glimmered with brilliance the moment Maribel lifted it out of the case and rested it on the glass countertop. It was crowned by three round-cut diamonds and accented by a border of petite white sapphires, all mounted in a contemporary platinum setting.

"Breathtaking," she said, acknowledging the fact that it was indeed the most beautiful pendant she had seen all season—and the most expensive piece in the case. "In some parts of the world, rubies are even rarer than diamonds. This one is set in platinum, which I always prefer over yellow gold settings."

It wasn't her standard sales pitch. It was all true. When she looked up, she expected to see him scrutinizing the necklace. But he wasn't. He was gazing at her.

"Not a fan of yellow gold, huh?" he said with smirk.

Of course, how foolish, she scolded herself. *He's wearing a thirty thousand dollar gold watch.* "Yellow gold settings are always elegant, of course," she corrected herself. "I just mean...with a gorgeous stone like this one, I think it should be the center of attention. The cool patina of platinum best accentuates the ruby's radiance."

"I see..." He studied her, resolutely. "Would you mind?" Taking up the necklace into his hands, he sought out a deeper intimacy between them. He wanted to see it—worn.

Maribel blinked, completely surprised. She had modeled pieces for her male customers in the past. But only the watches and rings—easy pieces to slip on and off, especially when she sensed there was indecision about whether or not it was truly the right purchase. But she had already determined that Miles Braxton-Worth was a man of decision. Every word, every glance, every moment of reflective silence told her that he knew exactly what he wanted even before she suggested it.

Slowly turning away from him, she swept up her long black hair, revealing the bare nape of her neck. With precision and delicacy, he draped the sparkling chain down her neckline and fastened its clasp. The touch of the ruby pendant set her olive skin aflame as she flushed with modesty.

Stop blushing, stop blushing, stop, stop, stop... she scolded herself, but the harder she tried to stop the warm blood from rushing into her cheeks, the faster it tingled down her neck and shoulders. His firm fingers wisped against the nape of her neck; they did not stumble with the clasp. Clearly, he had done this a hundred times before. But not her. For Maribel, it was her first time—being adorned with precious gems by a handsome distinguished man. And very likely, it would be her one and only time.

When the full weight of the necklace settled against her skin, she rotated around to face him. He was staring at her—not the necklace, or the ruby, or the full view of the piece on a woman—but *her*. And now, the only thing that mattered was the intensity of their connection, and the fact that she was the one who chose to break it.

"Rubies symbolize warmth, fire, vitality, and passion," she commented, desperate to shift his attention away from her and back onto the piece. "I think she will be more than happy with your choice. It's a lovely gesture." She said it as if she meant it—without envy or longing. She simply wanted to help him find the best gift for another woman.

When she attempted to turn away, he seized her hand. "Thank you. I'll take it."

She glanced down at his hand grasping her own. It was strong, but warm, and she noted the absence of a wedding band. After a moment, her eyes petitioned him to release her so she could move away to the register, prepare the gift box, and ring up the sale. Mechanically moving to the register, she attempted to remove the necklace herself, but her fingers fumbled. She was trembling. It was hard to give up being the center of his attention, despite the fact that she knew the whole time he was simply using her to remind him of another woman.

He slid his black credit card across the countertop, and she felt the intimacy of their interaction slipping away. Everything was back to business. She understood. She charged his card and watched as he penned his sweeping signature across the receipt before she handed over the petite shopping bag. He nodded curtly and disappeared out the revolving doors of the Grand Lobby and into the bleak cold of the winter night.

Crystal suddenly rushed over to Maribel. "Oh my God…You just made a sale to Miles Braxton-Worth. What did he buy? How much did it cost?"

Maribel heard her, but did not respond. It was the most expensive sale she had made all year; her commission would easily be more than she had made all week. And yet, she still felt sad—even dejected—deep inside. She couldn't stop thinking about his eyes and the way they had settled upon her, as if she was truly as unique and special as the necklace. She watched regretfully as the revolving doors came to a halt. Sometimes it was better to remain Cinderella, the quiet modest maiden, than to be granted the opportunity to attend the ball with the Prince and enjoy it for only a brief fleeting moment.

* * * *

It was nine fifteen when Maribel finally prepared to clock out of her shift. There were only a few other girls on the floor: Crystal was folding and re-folding the sweaters; Samantha was re-stocking the cosmetic counter; and Roberta was re-organizing the shoe displays. When the final lingering customers finished their purchases and exited the store, Thomas, the assistant store manager, locked the revolving doors and killed the instrumental shopping music.

"Happy Valentine's Day weekend, girls," Thomas called out with sing-song glee. "Kick off those heels and let's zip through closing so we can get the hell outta here."

"My thoughts exactly," Roberta cried out.

"Amen and hallelujah," Crystal rejoiced.

The signature boom-boom-boom bass of one of Thomas' many favorite hip hop artists filled the Grand Lobby. Throwing up their hands into the air, the girls smarted off with sassy expressions of relief and grooved to the beat. Thomas uncorked a contraband bottle of champagne. Everyone screamed with delight. Soon they would be home, relaxing for the night, until they had to return tomorrow afternoon and do it all over again. But for now, there was only hip hop, free liquor, and freewheeling jubilation.

Maribel smiled to herself and carefully locked up all her jewelry cases. She tapped her ladybug slippers to the heavy *boom-boom-boom* of the music, and accepted a paper daisy cup filled with champagne. Thomas pulled Crystal away from the sweaters, and together they danced and mouthed the rap song's swear words directly into the view of the security cameras. They tried to wrangle in Maribel, but she hid behind her register. Sipping champagne from her little paper cup, she watched her co-workers living it up in the Grand Lobby of the department store. *Perhaps it wasn't so bad, after all,* she thought with a smile, *not being a princess invited to the ball.*

Chapter Three

WHEN MARIBEL LEFT THE department store, it was almost ten o'clock. She walked out with Thomas and Crystal, and they all screamed when a gust of wind chilled them to the bone. Maribel was always prepared for the cold Chicago nights and had bundled herself up in her black wool coat, earmuffs, scarf, and snow boots.

"Girlfriend, you gotta let Crystal help you find something more stylish than those *thangs*."

Thomas always made fun of her earmuffs, but she didn't care. They protected her ears from the biting wind and kept her long hair out of her face.

"Better than hat head," she sassed, tossing a glance over to Crystal.

"Don't you know it," Thomas agreed.

"Bi-aaaaatches," Crystal countered, adjusting her rabbit fur cap and matching gloves.

"You takin' the train?" Thomas asked Maribel.

"Yes."

"Wanna catch a ride?"

"No."

"Damn, girl, why can't you be as independent as Maribel," Thomas chided Crystal.

"Because I'm a moocher," Crystal confirmed. "And I'm wearing heels."

Crystal extended her leg to compare her stilettos to Maribel's snow boots. It was a valid point.

"Wanna come over tomorrow, Maribel?" Thomas offered. "Patrick and I are having a V-day parteeeee. He's making the red Jello punchbowl spiked with a whole lot of orgasmic berry Schnapps."

Maribel smiled. "Maybe."

"No, I want to hear a yes outta you. Don't go spending tomorrow night alone. It's Valentine's Day, for heaven's sake. I'll even let you make out with me, if you don't find someone better at the party."

"*Ouuuuuwwww!*" Both Maribel and Crystal squealed.

"I'll close my eyes and pretend you're Matt Damon," Maribel joked.

"*Prrrrr...* although I much prefer the tall, dark Ben Affleck type," Crystal added.

"I'm just sayin'," Thomas said, defending his offer. "Don't go choosing to be all by yourself when you don't have to be."

Everyone knew how Maribel preferred to spend her free days—home and alone. She had been alone for so many years that she forgot what it was like not to be alone.

Maribel waited to see if Crystal would mention her interaction with Miles Braxton-Worth to Thomas. But it had already been forgotten and she decided not to bring it up, as if keeping the memory to herself could better preserve it.

"What about me, Thomas?" Crystal whined. "Do I get to come?"

"Excuse me, honey bunny? You're working tomorrow night. Didn't you look at the schedule?"

"Well, that doesn't mean I can't come after."

"And what? Bring that Frank-Sinatra-karaoke-lovin' manwhore again?"

"Hey, I'll have you know that I've got an even better manwhore now," Crystal said with pride. "And he sings Boy George flawlessly."

"Hm. Tempting," Thomas eyed Crystal before turning back to Maribel. "Seriously, think about it. Ta-ta..." Thomas and Crystal waved her goodbye as they parted in opposite directions.

Maribel approached the street corner and heard the cheery "Happy Valentine's Day" greeting of a homeless man. A cardboard heart was draped around his neck over his ripped coat. She glanced into her wallet. She had three dollars and she needed two for the train ride home. She handed him her last dollar, guilty she didn't have more cash to offer him. He nodded with appreciation and wished her a safe night as she crossed under the "L" tracks and into the empty downtown streets. *Yes, it had already turned out to be a pleasant start to her Valentine's Day weekend*, Maribel thought as she mounted the steps of the elevated train station, and indulged in the memory of her interaction with Miles Braxton-Worth.

* * * *

Maribel trudged up the staircase, three flights to her studio apartment. She wondered if her used books—ordered last week from her favorite online retailer—were waiting for her outside her door.

The door across from her apartment suddenly swung open. "Late, late, late… Little Miss Maribel Martinez," Emma Jean scolded her.

"Did I worry you?"

"Hell, yes," Emma Jean said with serious concern. "Work, work, work, that's all you ever do."

"That's because I don't have a fabulous Sugar Daddy like you who pays my way."

"Carl? Oh, he's history. Never liked his moustache, anyway. Working on securing me a new one. When are you gonna work on that for yourself?"

"Tomorrow," Maribel replied with sarcasm. "I have the day off. And it is Valentine's Day. Hey, did you pick up a package for me? I was hoping it would come today."

"Books?"

Maribel perked up. "Yes?"

"*Nada*," Emma Jean shot her down.

Maribel frowned, exhausted and disappointed. The only thing she truly looked forward to all day was curling up in bed with her newly-purchased used books.

"Well, good night, Emma Jean," Maribel sighed, unlocking her apartment door and flicking on the lights. 'Thanks for staying up and worrying about me."

"Come over tomorrow, sweet pea," Emma Jean's voice chased after her. "The whole building is going to celebrate like we're *Melrose Place*. Sort of an official Valentine's Day bash. We're wearing name tags and role-playing our favorite characters. Eddie from the second floor is going to be bad boy biker, Jake. Raul is going to be Matt, the token gay. And I'm going to be that devious doctor, Michael Mancini."

"That sounds dangerous."

"Damn straight. You can be my sweet innocent neighbor, Alison Parker. I know it's *such* a stretch for you."

"Is she the one who Heather Locklear always was trying to sabotage?"

Emma Jean winked. "I knew you were a closet *Melrose Place* fan. Party starts at eight. There's going to be free wine, deviled eggs, and several eligible divorcés. Don't sit around all day reading books, sweetheart. We're allowed to be alone and lonely all year-round—just not on Valentine's Day."

Maribel watched Emma Jean slam shut her door. She sighed with relief. Finally, after a long, long, long week, she could slip into the solitude of her own cozy studio apartment, peel off her work clothes, rest her blistered feet, and ignore the rest of the world for an entire day. It was nice that she had friends who invited her over to celebrate with them, but it was also nice that she could choose to disappear into her own little blissful haven of peace and not be bothered by anyone or anything.

Buuuuuuuzzzzzzzzzzzzzzzzzzzzzzzzzzzzzz.

Her buzzer rang out like a hornet in a tin can. *It was Friday night. Who on earth could be buzzing her door bell at this time in the evening?* Clearly, they had the wrong apartment. Suddenly, Maribel was inflated with unrealistic hope. She forced herself out of bed and moved to the window. Her heart raced when she saw the white van parked along the curb with its familiar *Express Delivery* logo. Maybe it was her package of used books, and they had been delivered after all. She quickly pressed the intercom button and called into its speaker.

"Yes?"

"Express Delivery for a Miss… Maribel Martin?"

"Martinez? Yes, please… I'll meet you downstairs."

She rushed to throw on her fleece jacket, pajamas, and slippers. She shuttled down the staircase and ran into the delivery man as he bounded up to meet her.

"Here you go," he said, handing her a gift box, wrapped with a silk red ribbon.

"Oh," Maribel said with confusion, signing for the package. "Are you sure this is for me?"

The driver referenced his delivery slip. "Maribel Martinez, 4892 Paulina St?"

"Yes…but…?"

"Then, it's definitely for you. Happy Valentine's Day."

The delivery man turned away and jetted down the stairs.

"Wait!" Maribel called after him. "Let me at least get you a few dollars for tip." Then, she remembered she was completely out of cash.

"No worries," he called back. "It's already been taken care of."

As she slowly started back up the stairs, she paused, half-expecting to see Emma Jean throw open her door again and interrogate her about the package. But the hallway was quiet. It was late on Friday night. Everyone was either out on the town or huddled up watching TV in their own private seclusion. Maribel entered her tiny apartment, closed the door, and placed the gift box onto her kitchenette table. For a brief moment, she admired its elegance before tugging on the red silk bow and lifting up the lid. There, resting in a bed of pink tissue paper, was a silver ornamental jewelry box and a small pink calling card. It read:

A less conventional gift for a less conventional woman. See you tomorrow for brunch. Will pick you up at ten. Miles.

It was his sweeping handwriting. Maribel recognized it immediately. It matched the confidence and flare of his signature on the credit card receipt. Her hands trembled as she creaked open the hinges of the ornamental case. The ruby pendant necklace glinted at her, flaring with fire and ice. She swept up the necklace into her hands and rushed to the bathroom mirror. With trembling fingers, she fumbled to undo its clasp before draping the pendant down around her neckline. The diagonal crack in her mirror disjointed her reflection, but still, she could see the full view of the ruby pendant and feel its extravagance resting against her bare skin.

Oh my God, oh my God, oh my God. She could barely think. She had *so very much* wanted the necklace—so much more than she cared to admit it. The commission was certainly nice, and for that reason alone, she had resisted the temptation to yearn for more. Even so, she had felt an uncontrollable pang of envy for the mysterious woman who was special enough in his eyes to receive it. Without truly knowing why, she had wished to be *that* woman. During the train ride home, she had fantasized that there had been more to their connection than just superficial attraction, and she wanted to believe that he felt it, too. Now, it was no longer a hopeful fantasy; it was a certainty—Miles Braxton-Worth had noticed her. He had believed that she was someone special. And he had bought her the most expensive necklace in the jewelry case—just to prove it.

Chapter Four

THE NEXT MORNING, MARIBEL awoke early, consumed by a mixture of anticipation and dread. She had worn her ruby necklace to sleep and it was the first thing she felt the moment she awoke as the sun shone through the blinds. *Valentine's Day*, she remembered. She had been prepared to spend the whole day by herself—lounging in the comfort of her bed and pajamas while reading, watching TV, and indulging in the discounted box of chocolates she had bought from Conchita in the candy department. But now, as she slipped out of bed, she considered all the possibilities the day offered. Then, she considered what to wear. She settled on something simple, casual, but fashionable. If working at a department store for the past ten years had taught her nothing else, it was how to be both comfortable and stylish. Knit tights, black skirt, and mohair shell pink sweater with a scoop neckline. It would accentuate her new necklace while hiding her perspiration marks. No matter how nervous she knew she would be, she didn't want to sweat in front of a billionaire.

Abruptly, her buzzer rang. She glanced over at her oven clock. It was 10 a.m.—sharp. She smiled with relief. Just like her, he was punctual.

She called into the intercom.

"Hello?"

"Driver picking up Miss Martinez."

A driver…? Maribel felt a wave of exasperation. She didn't even own a car, so she certainly hadn't expected to be picked up by a private driver. *But of course, his driver. He's a billionaire. He probably has ten drivers.*

"Yes, be right down." She tried to sound assertive, but she was shaking. She slunk down along the edge of her bed to calm her nerves. Now, she forced herself to stand in order to put on her winter coat, boots, scarf, earmuffs before gathering up her purse. She exhaled and left her apartment, fully aware she was trading the security and certainty of her cozy bed for the insecurity and uncertainty of a date with a wealthy man she barely knew and who barely knew her.

It was all so crazy, she thought as she pushed open the foyer door. Immediately, she spotted the black Mercedes and its driver, waiting for her along the street curb.

"Good morning, Miss Martinez," the driver said, crisp and attentive. He whisked open the rear passenger door, allowing her to slide across the beige leather seats. He closed it and slipped into the driver's seat to start up the engine.

"Here you are." He turned, passing off a powder blue bag. "A gift from Mr. Braxton-Worth." The driver didn't wait for her response. Instead, a panel of tinted glass rose between them, and before Maribel knew it, she was sealed up in the back seat like precious cargo.

She gazed down at the blue bag, recognizing it immediately. Its familiar black block logo stared back at her: TIFFANY & CO.

Her heart raced. She started to sweat. *Stop sweating, stop sweating, stop sweating.* It was useless. Whatever was in that bag was a symbol of his expectations, which suddenly overwhelmed her. Maribel considered how long it had been since she had been on a formal date—much less a date with a man who actually interested her. She usually only met immature men at Thomas or Emma Jean's outrageous parties, where on the very rare occasion she would consent to a one-night stand, just to justify staying on the pill. But it had been a very, very long time since she had a suitor, although Miles Braxton-Worth wasn't the first customer who had been interested in seeing her again after she had helped him with a special purchase. But unlike Miles, those men had been significantly older and already married, *and* they assumed Maribel was the type of girl who would understand that and still accept their invitations for drinks and dinner. They were wrong.

As for dating men her own age, she had invented every excuse in the book for why she was never destined to find the right man. Crystal had tried to convince her that online dating was the only way to meet a good guy, but in a world of smartphones and tablets and ebooks, Maribel felt impossibly old-fashioned. She didn't have any social media accounts. She still preferred to read paper over any digital screen. And she needed to *see* a man in person—hear his voice, look into his eyes, assess his manners, feel his sensitivity towards her—in order to judge whether or not spending her one free afternoon a week with him was better than spending it in her apartment, sipping hot chocolate and reading a romance novel from the library.

Maribel looked down at the gift bag. She was already wearing the ruby pendant necklace. *What else could he possibly have bought for her?* She sifted through the ruffles of white tissue paper with care, as if she was peeking inside a gift intended for someone else. There, under billows of white, was the corner of a powder blue box with white ribbon. *Yes, it was the real thing—an authentic piece of jewelry from Tiffany & Co.* Maribel sat back in her seat and peered out onto Lake Shore Drive. They were approaching Michigan Avenue's Magnificent Mile, where she often strolled during her lunch hour and window-shopped all of the finest retail jewelers—Cartier, Harry Winston, Georg Jensen, Bulgari—but none of them captivated her more than Tiffany & Co in the Peninsula building. And yet, she never entered the store. She knew that store attendants were trained to immediately assess the net worth of potential customers; Maribel would be dismissed by them as a having the net worth of a gnat. As merely a high school graduate, she had worked her way up into the fine jewelry section of the department store and she was proud of it, but she also knew her place in the world. Stores like Tiffany & Co. were sophisticated sanctuaries reserved for the wealthy elite. They were havens that Maribel admired from the outside without daring to dream that one day she would be invited in. Now, Miles Braxton-Worth was sending her an invitation—a crisp white gift card attached to the bag's silk rope handles. It read:

Thanks for the tip about the earrings. I checked. Miles.

The suspense was unbearable. *What did he mean?* She quickly dug into the bag and found the signature mint blue jewelry case. She flipped it open. Two dazzling tear-drop ruby and diamond earrings twinkled back at her. Their checkerboard cut face and platinum setting matched her ruby pendant necklace. Maribel touched her ears. *Thanks for the tip about the earrings, I checked...* She never even noticed him looking to see if her ears were pierced. In fact, she often had forgotten her ears were pierced because she wore the same cubic zirconia studs every day. They had been an early graduation gift from her mother, and she had never considered wearing anything else.

Jewelry—*any jewelry*—from Tiffany's easily cost five figures, much less pieces with decent-sized diamond and rubies. She fretted, suddenly reconsidering everything. This was not her; it was not her world. And it suddenly felt like a total and complete mistake. But it was too late. The car dropped below street level and into an underground parking garage. Their destination was near.

She unfastened one of the ruby earrings from the case and held it in her hand. It caught the flare of the garage's fluorescent lights and throbbed in her palm like a glowing ember. She swapped out her mother's earrings for her new gift. The teardrop earrings grazed her skin just below her ear lobes. She felt like royalty as the Mercedes rolled up in front of a ramp and stopped in front of a private garage door.

The driver lowered the tinted window and called back to her. "Almost here," he confirmed, and leaned out his window to enter a keycard into the security pad. The garage door rumbled open, and he navigated the Mercedes up the ramp and into the private parking garage. There was a white Bentley, two sports cars—a red Ferrari and a vintage black Corvette—two motorcycles, and one silver Tesla. The driver parked next to the Bentley and quickly opened the door, offering his hand for assistance. "Please…"

Maribel stuffed the Tiffany's bag into her purse and reluctantly slid out of the car. She followed the driver up a flight of concrete stairs and through a heavy door that opened into an opulent lobby with marble flooring and a crystal chandelier. Glimpsing out through the brass revolving doors, she recognized Michigan Avenue, its familiar boulevard and crowds of tourists were a relief. *A skyscraper along Michigan Avenue*, she thought as she followed the driver through the main corridor and past the doorman's podium. The driver greeted him while the doorman acknowledged her with a curt nod of his cap.

"Miss…" he said with formality.

Maribel smiled in return.

The driver led her towards the elevators and into the center cab, its doors already open, awaiting her entrance.

"Mr. Braxton-Worth is waiting for you," he confirmed, then pressed the button marked "68", allowing the doors to slide shut between them. Suddenly, the elevator cab accelerated upwards with a whirl. Her stomach butterflied, feeling the sensation of speed.

Forty-five, forty-six, forty-seven, forty-eight… Maribel heard the ping of every floor chime. *Dear God, it was endless. Fifty-nine, sixty, sixty-one, sixty-two…* She had never been in an elevator with this many floors, not even as a tourist to the top of the Hancock Building or Willis Tower. Finally, the elevator cab slowed to a stop as the final floor bell chimed. The doors shimmered open. She stepped out into the receiving area of an elegant, but empty restaurant. She was greeted by a pleasant man in a tailored waiter's uniform.

"Miss Martinez?" He asked.

"Yes…"

"Right this way."

He led her through rows and rows of vacant tables, dressed with crisp white table cloths and decorated with crystal vases of freshly-cut pink rose buds. Immediately, she spotted Miles, seated in a secluded corner of the restaurant. *My God, he was so impossibly handsome*, she thought with a sigh. All her uncertainty vanished when she saw him sitting there, flanked in sunlight and deep in thought. He looked relaxed and young, his dark hair and Mediterranean complexion glowing with warmth. He wore a charcoal suit and stark turquoise tie that flattered his piercing blue eyes, which seized upon her. And in an instant, she knew she would no longer be content with her former life—as a woman who had never craved the attention and desire of a man because no one had ever made her feel completely desirable with one penetrating gaze....until now.

* * * *

Earmuffs.

Miles Braxton-Worth had been gazing out at the immense skyline, considering his life and all the responsibilities he needed to address with every one of his buildings, when he caught a glimpse of her out of the corner of his eye. He had been surveying all his properties along the Gold Coast beachfront and the crystal waters of Lake Michigan that he could see—*one, two, three, four...* but none of it mattered when she crossed into view, striding through the empty white tabletops in her black coat and black earmuffs like a bounding rabbit cutting through snowdrifts.

Earmuffs, he thought again. *No one in the business world wore earmuffs*, Miles pondered, trying to contain his smile as she approached him. Her dark eyes immediately caught his gaze as he rose from his seat and circled around to greet her.

"Allow me," he said, offering to remove her coat. She consented with ease. He guided her into the leather high-back chair across from him. While catching the faint scent of her perfume, he noticed the way her shell pink sweater scooped along her graceful shoulders. And there, twinkling down along her attractive neckline, was the ruby necklace. *Earmuffs*, he thought again, hiding another smile. *Curious and endearing, just like her*.

"Javier," Miles said, passing off her coat to the waiter. "Wine for Miss Martinez, and then the starters...please."

"Very good, sir." Javier jetted away to fulfill the request.

Maribel flushed, as if she realized she was still wearing earmuffs. She quickly pulled them off and stuffed them into her purse. She didn't notice the way Miles admired her unassuming beauty. The sunlight streamed through the floor-to-ceiling windows and highlighted her long black hair, full lips and olive complexion. She was so naturally gorgeous, it was hard to look away. He took up his wine glass and released a warm smile, waiting for her to settle into the environment before attempting to make conversation.

"I wasn't sure you would come," he finally said.

"I wasn't sure either." She laughed in relief, signaling the release of hours and hours of anxiety and anticipation—and it made them both grin a little wider than either of them expected.

"You look lovely," he said.

"Thank you."

They fell into pensive silence; his patient gaze told her that he didn't want her to feel pressured to say or be anything she wasn't.

"I have to confess something…" she paused and looked down into her lap. "I'm very nervous."

"Don't be…it's just brunch." He noted the change in her face, as if she was disappointed. "So far…" he quipped.

She smiled. "Yes, and several very expensive pieces of jewelry."

Amused, he studied her and sipped from his wine glass. "Do you like the earrings?"

"Yes, of course."

"I had them open the store for me late last night—after my purchase at the department store."

"They opened it—late last night? Just for you?"

"Yes," Miles acknowledged, realizing he had said too much. He smoothed down the table cloth with his palm, attempting to return to the casual nature of their connection. "I know the owner well. I'm a regular customer."

Maribel suddenly frowned; he had done more harm than good. *She appreciated honesty*, he thought, *not pretense*. "I wanted something to match the necklace. I told the store owner it was for a special woman on a special occasion. You don't get any more special than Valentine's Day. Happy Valentine's Day."

She stared at him, as if she didn't understand why he would consider her special. "I guess I should thank you for getting me out of the house today. I was planning to just hang out all morning in my pajamas."

"And ladybug slippers." He couldn't help it. He had to zing that one at her for fun.

She paused, her train of thought interrupted, "Oh, no…please tell me you didn't see those."

"I didn't see those," he repeated, his smile betraying otherwise.

She covered her mouth and laughed. "Oh, no…that's horrible. I thought I'd gotten away with it. But my feet hurt so badly and I was standing in heels the entire day before and—"

"I know, I saw you then, too."

She fell silent, absorbing the fact that he had noticed her—more than once. That time, Miles was certain he had betrayed too much. He had noticed her wearing fishnet stockings and high heels while working in the lingerie department the day before, and he had thought about her all day and night—more than he intended to admit.

"And this restaurant?" she asked. "Did you have them open it this morning—just for us?"

"Yes," he said matter-of-factly, as if he was confirming the weather and the temperature. "I simply had to coordinate it with the wait staff and the chef."

"That sounds like a lot of effort."

"No effort at all," he countered. "I own this restaurant. And the building."

Obviously intimidated, Maribel sank in her seat.

"Here you are, Miss Martinez." Javier placed a glass of red wine on the table.

"Thank you so much," she glanced up at Javier as he refilled their water glasses, and waited until he left before she spoke. "Perhaps your wait staff would have preferred to have the day off?"

Miles looked at her curiously. She was more worried about his wait staff than herself.

"Don't worry. I pay them well. How's the wine?" Miles asked.

"I'm not sure…" she peered over its rim.

"You don't drink wine, do you?" he asked, noting how Maribel held her wine glass like it was orange juice.

"It's that obvious?"

"Yes." He laughed, delighted by her honesty. "At least try it," he encouraged her. "It's a vintage Pinot Noir that costs more than your ruby necklace."

Stunned, she gazed again into the glass. "I have to tell you that I am very flattered by all your gifts, but I can't accept them. I mean…they're lovely—no, *gorgeous*—but they're too much, obviously…and—"

"And?" He waited for her to find the courage to say what they both knew was true.

"And…you don't even know me."

Miles sat back in his chair and settled his hands in his lap. "You still haven't tried the wine."

She cautiously took a sip.

"Yes, it's true." He laughed again. "You definitely don't like wine."

She smiled with embarrassment and forced herself to swallow it.

"Look, let's be clear," he said, leaning into the table, determined not to say too much. The last thing he wanted to do was make her feel obligated to him. "The necklace is non-negotiable. You like it and it looks stunning on you." His eyes fell upon her neckline, admiring her natural ability to wear fine jewelry. "So please, no more talk about not accepting it. It was my pleasure."

He tried to keep the tone of his voice level, but firm. The idea that she might return his gifts truly pained him.

Perhaps it was the determination in his voice that made her blush. *Like a Renaissance painting*, he thought, with her soulful brown eyes and black locks of hair coiling down one side of her exposed shoulder. He felt certain there was no woman in the world who deserved rubies and diamonds more.

"Thank you," she whispered, honoring his request not to push the point.

He nodded in acceptance. "The earrings on the other hand, well…" He paused and wavered, noting the teardrop rubies. *How much should he say?* He wasn't sure. "I will confess something to you. I did consider the fact that you might not want to wear something other than your diamond studs."

Maribel touched her ears, as if she was surprised he had remembered what kind of earrings she was wearing before she changed them.

"Yes, I've had those studs a long time."

"Sentimental value," he acknowledged. "I understand."

She stared at him, as if he had read the deepest emotions within her heart.

He stared back at her, hoping it was enough for now. "The earrings can still be discussed. But they looked fantastic on you as well. So we may just need to shake hands and call it a draw. Agreed?" He intended to make her feel like she deserved it—every bit of it.

Extending his hand across the table, she reluctantly shook it. It was all so silly and juvenile, and yet, that was the spirit of their connection—casual and spontaneous.

"Agreed," she nodded.

They both smiled. Miles was used to shaking hands with women who had long painted nails, sharp diamond rings, and even sharper attitudes. In contrast, Maribel's hand was soft and tender. No acrylic nails, no flashy rings. There was nothing artificial about her. When she finally attempted to withdraw her hand, he held it a little longer than necessary.

"And so long as we're laying all of our cards on the table, I have a confession to make to you," he announced. "I thought that you might be planning to spend Valentine's Day alone, so that's why I invited you here to spend it with me."

Maribel's long eyelashes opened wide. "Were you planning on spending it alone, too?"

The insinuation surprised him. It was a perceptive question, one that probed whether or not Miles had betrayed more than he wanted. They were abruptly interrupted by the ring of his phone, lying on the table.

He glanced down at its screen. G-I-L-L-I-A-N.

It was a convenient interruption. He didn't want to take the call, but he didn't want to admit that he *had* planned to spend the most romantic day of the year—alone.

"Excuse me, business," he said. "Yes," he answered and shifted away from the table.

"You're avoiding me," Gillian asserted.

"No, it's Saturday."

"Since when do you *not* work over the weekend, Brax?"

"I answered your call, so let's cut to the chase."

"Oh, I see…all business, are we?" Gillian's voice grew aggressive. "Fine. My client wants seven-percent escalation, thirty-year lease term, and a twenty-percent share of common elements expenses, or the deal is off."

"Fine. The deal is off."

Maribel winced, as if she heard the sharp voice of another woman on the other end of his phone. Her eyes met his own, searching out the reason why there was now an edge in his voice, a distinct change away from his cheery quips and their upbeat conversation. But he knew nothing about "the deal is off" sounded good. Regretting taking the call, he shifted his weight in his chair and gazed out the window. Their lunch together was about escaping from his world of greed and artifice, not about dragging Maribel into it.

"Brax—" Gillian reprimanded him. "You're not blowing off a thirty-five million dollar deal. I know you. You're impossibly pigheaded and arrogant, but you're not stupid."

"Okay, thirteen-percent rent escalation, twenty-year lease term, and twenty-five percent expense share."

Javier returned with two white china ramekins and endive salads, and placed the plates in front of Maribel. "Here you are, Miss Martinez."

"Thank you so much."

Miles' phone suddenly went silent. "Oh, I get it," Gillian said, slowly. "You're not alone."

"No," he confirmed. He knew *that* would help get Gillian off his back, and it worked.

"Thirty-five millions dollars, Brax. To blow off thirty-five million dollars, she must be someone *very* special."

He gazed over at Maribel. She smiled at him with compassion. "I'm fairly certain she is."

It was the wrong answer. Gillian zinged back with her original offer. "Seven-percent escalation, thirty-year term lease, and we're not giving up the sublease contingencies—"

Miles cut her off. "Here's what I want. I want you to call me tomorrow."

"Brax," Gillian rushed to keep his attention. "She sounds too young, even for you."

He considered hanging up on her, but that's what she wanted, and he was tired of rewarding bad girls for their bitchy behavior. "Happy Valentine's Day, Gillian."

Silence filled the line before she ended the call for him. Miles tossed his phone onto the table.

"Business?" Maribel asked, her sympathetic brown eyes letting him know that she didn't expect him to discuss it if he didn't want to.

"Always." He sighed, relaxing under her gaze, trying hard not to think about tomorrow. The call had threatened to disrupt their brunch together, but in the end, he had chosen her over work. "You're not eating," he noted.

"I guess I'm not hungry."

It was a lie and Miles knew it. *It was her inability to hide how she truly felt,* he thought, *that kept him engaged and wanting more*. "Too hard to eat something black on Valentine's Day?" he joked.

"Maybe," she admitted, investigating the ebony soup. "What is it?"

"Octopus cooked in its own ink."

She shivered with disgust. He laughed and lifted up two tentacles with his fork. *That's what was so different. There were no games because she had nothing to hide.*

"They're good, I promise," he said, letting the tentacles jiggle on his fork before popping them into his mouth.

She wasn't convinced. *Gaining her trust,* he considered, *might be harder challenge than he had thought.*

Javier returned to offer more wine, but Maribel declined. She waited to speak until after Javier tidied their table and disappeared back into the kitchen. "Maybe we shouldn't stay here too long. Everyone deserves to have a day off from work." Her eyes fell down upon his phone. "Even billionaires."

It was true. He had been selfish to ask Javier and the rest of the wait staff to work that morning. He was paying them handsomely for it, but he never considered that they preferred to be at home with their families. He leaned into the table, his mind churning with possibilities. "What do you have in mind?"

"Something a little less…informal."

"You mean less stuffy."

"Casual," she corrected him.

He smiled, slyly. "Less pretentious."

"More *relaxing*."

He glanced down at her untouched meal and smirked. "Less inky."

"Maybe." She eyed his white ramekin with its giggly wiggly black octopus tentacles.

"Maybe," he repeated with a laugh of pure enjoyment. He had learned her language now and he knew maybe meant she wasn't completely rejecting him—and all his superficial attempts to impress her and gain her trust. At least, not yet.

"Javier…Miss Martinez would like her coat," he called out into the open room, then turned to her with a wink. "You're absolutely right. Let's go get some fresh air."

Chapter Five

HOT DOGS. FULLY LOADED. Now, *this* was perfect. Miles glanced down at Maribel, who seemed to think it was perfect, too. They both indulged in the steamy, juicy hot dogs while watching the ice skaters at the outdoor rink in Millennium Park.

Maribel took another gluttonous bite. A mixture of ketchup and mustard dotted the tip of her nose. Miles reached out with his napkin and wiped it off with care.

"Slow down, or I might have to buy you a second one."

He was used to dining with women who ate like birds and pretended they could barely eat dessert. But not Maribel. She consumed her hot dog without apology and smiled widely when he suggested they go for seconds.

"It's just so delicious."

"Better than octopus cooked in its own ink?"

"Please, don't remind me."

He laughed. *Sassy when relaxed and well-fed*, he thought. He could live with that.

"I have a confession to make…"

"Another confession?"

"Yes, a zinger this time," he quipped. "This is usually where I come to eat my lunch during the week."

He turned around and leaned against the rink's railing, taking in the full view of the city and its immense skyline. "That's my penthouse over there," he said, nodding towards Randolph Avenue. "I usually work from home in the mornings, then come down here for a quick lunch break before heading over to the office in the Fields Building."

Maribel followed his gaze to the top of each building. "It must be exhausting, living life at the top all the time." She chomped down on her hot dog. Ketchup smeared her cheek.

Miles fell silent. Her perceptive comments disarmed him. *It was exhausting. Lonely and exhausting.* He gazed at her ketchup smudge and black earmuffs, and realized she was the first person in a long time who made him want to betray his emotions. "Yes, it can be. That's why I make sure to come down to the street every day. To keep everything in perspective."

She finished her hot dog, then dodged his playful advance to wipe her face again. She wiped it herself, then turned back to admire the skaters, circling the rink with their brown rental skates and imperfect balance.

"I think that everyone is living their own private lives of pain and isolation, you know? And we're all trying to find ways to come together to enjoy ourselves—if only for brief fleeting moments. Then, we wake up the next day and struggle to do it all over again."

Pensive, Miles chewed on his hot dog and studied her. Her cheeks blushed from the cold air, and condensation escaped from her lips when she spoke. *She possessed such sophistication and maturity for her age*, he thought, *so authentic, inside and out.* It made him want to stare at her without restraint, waiting to discover a new angle that would charm him even more. He already knew she had the ability to be down-right sexy—images of her in high heels and fishnet stockings while she worked in the lingerie department had been permanently seared into his memory. But he wasn't prepared for her to be so genuine, nor was he prepared for their connection to be so intimate.

"Thank you for coming down here to join me for lunch," he said. "I mean it."

Something in his voice caught her attention, and she flushed red. "Now, I'm the one who has a confession to make," she said.

"Shoot."

"I am very grateful that you invited me. It's been years—*years*," she stressed, less to him and more to herself, "that I've spent my Valentine's Day with anyone other than Keats and Tolstoy."

"*War and Peace*, really?" He flashed a smile. "I much prefer Stephen King."

"On Valentine's Day?" She truly seemed horrified. He laughed and grabbed her hand. He tugged her towards him, but resisted the urge to kiss her and taste her sweetness. It was too soon, and he knew it.

Suddenly, his cell phone rang. Maribel looked down at his vibrating pocket. Their gleeful banter dissipated as she waited to see if he was going to answer it.

Miles glanced at its screen, noting the name of the caller, and exhaled into the cold air with bitterness. He answered the call. "I'm here."

"You're not going to blow this deal, are you?"

Miles clenched his teeth, drifting away from the loud, cheery gaiety of the ice skaters in the rink.

"Thirty-five million dollars, Brax, and you're making them wait on the details, just so you can get your nuts off with some call girl—"

"Enough, Gary—" Miles cut in. "Gillian called you, fine, I get that. But the rest is personal, so fuck off."

"Okay, okay, whatever you say. I'm just your lawyer, not your shrink. But maybe you need a visit to your shrink to have your head examined if you think it's a good idea to blow off a thirty-five million dollar deal."

"Look…it's Saturday—"

"I'm a lawyer, Brax. We don't acknowledge the difference between the work week and the weekend. They're all billable hours."

"We're too far apart on the lease terms."

"You're not *that* far apart," Gary insisted. "And that's what I'm here for. Tell me what you want, and if it gets shot down, then let me be the one who carries the surrender flag. No ego lost on your part."

Miles shook his head. *Ego, everyone always thought it was about his ego.* He considered spewing out the acceptable lease terms to Gary, then reconsidered. He had escaped—for a few brief hours—and now they were circling him like ravenous vultures.

He turned and suddenly spotted Maribel behind him. "Hot chocolate," she mouthed and proudly offered up two paper cups, steaming and frothy with their cocoa delight.

He gazed at her and slowly smiled—a thirty-five million dollar deal or hot chocolate on Valentine's Day with a sassy, spontaneous, sexy woman who he had always wanted to get to know better?

"Marshmallows," she mouthed again, sweetening the deal.

Oh, Maribel. He rubbed his face and peered down at the white dots, bobbing in the hot chocolate. She made difficult choices seem so simple.

"I'll call you tomorrow, Gary."

"Don't, Brax—" Gary rushed to keep his attention. "Don't do this. You blow this deal, and you'll quickly become the hard-ass megalomaniac real estate tycoon who nobody—and I mean nobody—is going to want to do business with."

"Well, that sounds better than just being known as an asshole."

Miles ended the call, regretting his decision to answer it in the first place. *Crude and rude.* That's how they provoked him to act because that's what they expected from him. It was a vicious cycle and he hated it. The sun drifted behind the thick winter clouds. The frigid wind lashed through their coats and pushed them close together.

Maribel shivered against his body. "Trade," she offered—the hot chocolate for his phone. He accepted the drink, but wavered on giving up his cell phone.

"C'mon on," she nudged, opening up her purse. "At least until we've finish our hot chocolates."

It was a fair compromise and a concession he was willing to make—more than she knew.

"I'm a wanted man, Maribel," he joked, depositing his phone into her purse. "My mug shot is all over the wires."

She shrugged. "You're a billionaire. Everyone will always want something from you."

Everyone—except her. She didn't seem to want anything from him except to share an uninterrupted moment on a brisk winter day to enjoy their hot dogs and hot chocolates until a gust of wind swept through the city like an invisible hand pushing them off of the street and out of the cold.

Miles considered inviting her up to his penthouse. It was right there, three buildings up on Michigan Avenue. They could escape from the weather and relax by his fireplace; he could give her a tour to make her feel comfortable, then scrounge something from his refrigerator and attempt to make them dinner. It would be a pleasant way to finish Valentine's Day, and at the end of their evening they could decide together whether or not she wanted to spend the night. He gazed down at her. She looked up at him. She was too good for him, too good for his greedy, superficial world—and she deserved better than to be corrupted by it.

Snowflakes glazed her hair and earmuffs like sugar. He wanted nothing more than to pull her into his body and kiss her, but he knew he hadn't earned the right.

"It's cold, too cold to spend any more time outside," he finally said. "We should think about getting you home."

Chapter Six

IT WAS A LONG DRIVE back to her apartment on the North side. They sat in silence. Maribel felt the tension between them and assumed he was thinking about work. When the Mercedes rolled up to the curb, the driver lowered the tinted glass panel and acknowledged their arrival. Before she knew it, the driver threw open her door and extended his hand to assist her out of the car. But she didn't accept it. Instead, she gazed back at Miles. They had barely spoken since leaving Millennium Park.

"Thank you so much. I had a lovely time."

He smiled—a reluctant, uncertain smile that kept Maribel in her seat. Silence lingered between them.

"It was wonderful spending time with you, Maribel."

She understood the flatness in his voice. It *had* been a wonderful way to spend Valentine's Day, but it was time for them to part ways. They came from different worlds, and now they needed to return to them—separately. He touched her hand briefly before pushing her out of the car with his distant gaze. She forced a smile before accepting the driver's hand.

"Maribel!" a voice cried out from the building. "Is that you?"

"Yes, Emma Jean." Maribel glanced up at her neighbor who was dangling precariously out of her third-story window and wearing a red feather boa and festive headband with two bobbing hearts. Music and laughter filtered down from her apartment like invisible confetti floating through the wind.

"What are you doing out there in that fancy ride?" Emma Jean called back, inebriated and squinting past her near-sighted vision. "And who the heck is that?"

Miles slowly lowered the tinted windows of the Mercedes and peered up at Emma Jean.

"Well, hello there, Mr. Handsome Mystery Man." Emma Jean waved and blew Miles a kiss. "The party's up here. C'mon up…"

Maribel noted Miles' designer suit, dark complexion, and hardened expression. It looked like she had been kidnapped by the mafia.

"And you, Miss Martinez. I've got your name tag already. I've been waiting for you all afternoon. We can't have a *Melrose Place* Valentine's Day party without our sweet, sensitive Alison Parker."

Maribel glanced back at Miles who was still attempting to make sense of her drunk neighbor.

"*Melrose Place*—it's a '90s-Aaron-Spelling-primetime-soap-opera-melodrama-TV-show-themed-party," Maribel tried to clarify, then shook her head. "Don't ask."

"C'mon up, already," Emma Jean drawled at Miles. "I'll make you a name tag, too. That suit is just perfect. You can be Jack Wagner/Dr. Peter Burns—my nemesis."

There was a crash from inside the apartment. Emma Jean pulled herself back from the window's ledge and called inside. "Are you all catfighting, Heather Locklear-style? Or just being clumsy?" Her inebriated laughter trickled down upon them.

Uncertain, Miles shifted his eyes to Maribel.

"You wanna come up?" she offered with a shrug.

"Nemesis?" he asked, his eyebrow arching with curious amusement. It was the first time the ice had thawed between them since escaping the bitter cold at Millennium Park.

"You billionaires indulge in octopus cooked in its own ink and expensive wine. The rest of us have *Melrose Place*. Are you up for it?"

He hesitated. It was the first time she had seen him betray indecision. She tried not to seem impatient, but billionaire or not, she didn't want him to come up if he wasn't going to enjoy himself. Finally, he got out of the car, emerging with a black duffle bag and his black dress coat.

"Take the rest of the night off, Andre," he said to his driver.

"Sir?"

"Don't worry. I'll take a cab home. Take the night off."

Andre smiled and nodded. "Thank you, sir." Quickly, the car peeled away from the curb, leaving Maribel and Miles to face the unpredictability of Emma Jean's party—together.

Maribel led him through the heavy front door of her apartment building. He trudged up the carpeted stairs behind her, and she wondered how long he would last at the party. *Five? Ten? Maybe fifteen minutes, if Emma Jean had a decent bottle of imported rum or whiskey.* As they reached the second floor, the swelling music and nasal crooning of Meatloafs' *I Would Do Anything For Love (But I Won't Do That)* overwhelmed them.

Five minutes. Definitely five minutes—max. Maribel was certain.

When they arrived at the third floor landing, she pointed out her apartment door across the hallway. "That's my apartment. You can leave your things there in the corner."

He surveyed Maribel's snow boots next to her porcelain gnome, dressed in beachwear—both resting atop a pink rubber floor mat. He didn't seem convinced.

"Don't worry…everyone in this building is poor, but we don't steal."

"I'm more worried about the rats," he admitted.

She eyed him, searching out the tease in his voice. He broke into his sly smile and settled his things onto the floor.

"What's in the duffle bag, anyway…stacks of hundred dollar bills?"

"Pajamas."

Maribel hid her smile. It was impossible to read him, but she knew one thing for certain—their playful connection was back.

"Let's do this already." He cracked his knuckles and nodded at her neighbor's half-open door.

They slipped through the door into Emma Jean's two-bedroom apartment, its entryway and living room crowded with guests, all sporting Valentine's Day hearts on their foreheads or cleavage, and all animated by the whirling strobe of a silver disco ball hanging from the ceiling fan. They passed a card table; its barren food trays and empty punch bowl signaled that they were late to the party. There was a burst of jovial laughter and a physical jolt of bodies as someone pushed Maribel and Miles towards the half-empty couch. An older couple sat on its opposite side, lip-syncing along to the music with a spatula and a cheese grater. Emma Jean rushed up to Maribel and Miles, and slapped them each with a name tag.

"Peter and Allison… I'd like you to meet Donna, a.k.a tough-talking, but emotionally wounded Jo Reynolds and her biker hottie boyfriend, Jake Hansen."

Miles dropped down next to them onto the couch and shook hands with the overweight man wearing an Ozzy Osborn T-shirt, black jeans, and black leather biker vest.

"Dr. Peter Burns," Miles introduced himself without a beat. "And this is Alison Parker," he said, referring to Maribel's name tag before sweeping her into his lap.

"Oh, you're a devious one, Dr. Burns," Donna gasped over her miniature bottle of cooking wine. "They brought you into Season Four to stir up trouble at the hospital."

Overweight biker Jake rolled his eyes. "Like there wasn't already enough trouble."

"Because of *moi*, Mr. Satan himself." Emma Jean returned from the kitchen and handed tumblers to Miles and Maribel.

Miles leaned in and read aloud from Emma Jean's name tag. "Dr. Michael Mancini?"

"Call me, Dr. Michael." She flirtatiously puckered her lips. "I steal your job as director of the hospital, and in return, you throw me out a window. Look at him, Donna. Isn't he the perfect Jack Wagner/Peter Burns with those dreamy blue eyes and everything?"

"I always loved Jack Wagner from the *Bold and the Beautiful*," Donna agreed.

Miles winked at both women and threw back his tumbler.

Maribel noted its sharp scent from over the rim. "What is it?" she asked Emma Jean.

"Girrrrrl, what's left!" Emma Jean cried out with a cackling smoker's cough, and disappeared back into the kitchen.

Skeptical, Maribel glanced at Miles, who crunched on his ice. "C'mon, Miss Parker. Don't be such a goodie-goodie." He bounced her on his knee, encouraging her to drink up.

"Oh, I like him already," Donna nudged Maribel. "But don't tell Dr. Michael."

Maribel wasn't convinced. She knew Emma Jean would happily serve rubbing alcohol if it was the only thing left in her apartment. She sipped from her tumbler. *Wow, it was strong—impossibly strong*. Miles, on the other hand, emptied his glass like it was water and relaxed his head against a fluffy pink pillow in the shape of a piglet. He looked over at Maribel. His lap was firm. He supported her back with his strong hand. But his gaze was flat and fading. Emma Jean was right. He did have dreamy blue eyes, and for a moment, she wished he would whisk her up into his arms and carry her out the door.

Without warning, a champagne cork exploded.

"Just found another bottle behind the dog food bag!" Emma Jean announced. All her guests applauded with cheers. Donna and Biker Jake rose and teetered into the kitchen.

The commotion caused an enormous Great Dane to glide along the base of the couch, seeking shelter from the uproar. She greeted Miles with a friendly whiff.

"Hey, girl," Miles said, nuzzling the dog with reassurance.

"That's Petunia," Emma Jean said, making the introduction while handing off miniature paper cups of champagne. "You must be *very* special because she normally doesn't kiss strangers. But she does have a soft spot for dreamy blue eyes—just like me."

Miles downed the champagne and relaxed more. His gaze drifted over to Maribel.

"I have dogs. Three," he confessed regretfully. "But I pay a professional to take care of them because I don't have time to ever see them."

He let Petunia lick his face with a generous kiss before she departed in search of her favorite squeaky mouse. "I pay professionals to do everything for me," he added with bitter laughter. "Except be me. Hopefully that's still worth doing myself."

He seemed so vulnerable and wounded. Maribel ran her fingers across his hair. He took her hand into his own and held it. His eyes fixed on her with intensity. She recognized that look—she had seen it when she modeled the necklace for him in the department store, and when the snowflakes fell upon them at Millennium Park. Slowly, cautiously, he leaned forward and wrapped both his arms around her waist, securing her in his lap. Then, he pulled her entire body against his chest and kissed her lips. His strong hand ran over her knit stockings and down her calves, then back up to her face as he held her cheek and covered her mouth with his own, kissing her fully, completely, without apology or restraint until she submitted herself to him—not because he forced her to acquiesce, but because she hoped for more…

"Can we go to your apartment?" he whispered, his forehead dropping against her shoulder, yearning for something only she could grant him.

"Yes," she heard herself whisper back as he lifted her into his arms with a strength that made her realize there was no turning back.

Carrying her through the crowded living room and into the stairwell, he released her in front of her apartment. Slipping off her coat, he kissed her earlobe, his hot breath exhaling down her neck, his nose tracing the edge of her pink scoop neck sweater. She sensed what he wanted—he wanted her completely. She unlocked the door, but dropped her keys when he embraced her and whisked them inside the dark shadows of her apartment.

Should she turn on the lights or leave them off? Her window blinds were always drawn, darkening the room by twilight. But Maribel barely had time to consider it before his hands swept off her sweater to expose her black lace bra.

Off, her mind repeated, *off, off, off, off, off* as she returned his advances, kissing him deeply and loosening his tie while he pulled off his coat. *Off, off, off,* she thought as she attempted to unbutton his dress shirt, but stopped, distracted by the sensation of his smooth chin and tongue flowing across her bare shoulders, down and around her belly button, and back up over her cleavage. She ran her fingernails through his dark hair as he slipped down the straps of her bra before delving his mouth deep into its cups to suck on her nipples. Maribel closed her eyes and accepted his mouth with a submissive exhale. She couldn't remember the last time she had invited a man into her apartment, much less allowed him to strip off her sweater, peel down her bra, and suck her dry, as he was sucking her off now. But she didn't want to remember anything, except the exhilaration of being devoured the way he was devouring her now.

Unclasping her bra, he flung it across the room, exposing her breasts to the massaging caresses of firm hands.

She sighed and tried hard not to consider what could be next. There had been so few men who she had dared to let touch her the way he was touching her—his hand sliding under her skirt to invade the soft lining of her knit stockings. There had been so few men who were willing to seduce her the way that he was seducing her tonight. She didn't know what to focus on more—her own insecurities about his intentions or the erotic sensation of his fingertips, probing her crotch, making her relinquish all her inhibitions and preparing her for his next request.

"Can I undress you?" he petitioned her.

He unzipped the back of her skirt without waiting for her consent. He already knew he had it. It slipped down her hips. He massaged her backside and exhaled against the nape of her neck. She unfastened the final buttons of his shirt, freeing it from his chest. Even within the darkened room, she could still see his bare muscles and feel the strength of his flexing biceps as he lifted her into his arms and placed her onto her bed. *Rosebud sheets*, she thought. She remembered buying them on sale in the department store, thinking the obnoxious pattern didn't matter because she would be the only one who would ever see them. Now, he spread her out like a five-point star and peeled off her tights, stopping only to release the straps of her shoes.

"You're so incredibly gorgeous, Maribel Martinez," he said, admiring her. Only her black lace panties, ruby pendant and ruby earrings remained.

She closed her eyes and savored how he said her full name. *Maribel Martinez*. When she opened her eyes again, she focused on how his sculpted chest loomed over her. He wasn't staring at her bare breasts or her jewelry. He was gazing into her eyes. The absence of his warmth against her body pricked her skin and nipples with anticipation. He circled his hot breath over her belly before whispering his lips between her breasts and over her tits. Then, his hand glided up her inner thigh and stopped over her panties.

"I want to feel inside you—deeply inside you."

She heard him clearly, but her mind replayed it in a daze. It had been so long since she had accepted any man into her body, but now she wasn't sure she could deny him—or herself. He slowly took hold of her panties in his teeth and stripped them down off her legs. She exhaled—an attempt to relax as he spread her bare legs wider for him. His fingertips probed her soft nest of hair and she tingled with every caress of his invading touch. It had been over a year since she had been fingered by someone other than herself, and he massaged her deeper and deeper with beating strokes. She sighed again. *God how she wanted this…*

She was gushing now, his confident fingers fondling her G-spot and priming her for more. Kicking off his shoes and unzipping his pants, he removed his boxers. He was sleek, hard, and gleaming like a chiseled marble statue.

"I want to be inside you." It wasn't a request, it was a plea.

She nodded, closing her eyes and giving in to him. She should have considered all the consequences before responding, but he considered them for her. Lifting it out of his discarded pants' pocket, he cracked the foil and sheathed his cock. Her tiny mattress forced him to mount her, smothering her body with the strength of his own. He placed the tip of his cock between her legs and tongued her with powerful, consuming kisses before penetrating her wetness. She moaned, breathless. *God, how she yearned to be wanted like this…*

Wrapping her arms around his strong shoulders, she arched her back, shifting him deeper inside her. With a hungry mouth and craving heart, she inhaled his breaths. He thrust into her, grinding his pelvis against her clit and heaving out each pant. Pausing to restrain himself, he hovered his hard chest over her breasts as his slick cock lingered between her legs. Brushing back her hair and glancing into her eyes, he confirmed what they both wanted from each other.

He accelerated his rhythm, pushing himself inside her—again and again—seeking out a way to melt all the barriers between them. He was no longer a billionaire; she was no longer a shop girl. He was no longer a wealthy aristocrat who barely knew her. They were simply two people who had chosen to spend Valentine's Day together—rather than alone—and now they had chosen to satisfy their carnal need for each other.

He pressed the full weight of his body against her chest. The ruby pendant dug into her skin with pain and pleasure. She throbbed and released, throbbed and released. Vibrations swept through her body as he increased his pace towards his final climax, burying his mouth between her breasts and suffocating her inner core with his need to capture her heart. But it was too late—he had already captured it hours and hours ago—and now, it was only a matter of when and how he would release it.

Chapter Seven

MARIBEL AWOKE TO THE sound of rushing water and the smell of smoldering coffee grounds. Her apartment was a vintage studio—one room with a kitchen sink, refrigerator, and gas stove along one wall, her full mattress and box spring in the corner, a second-hand couch along the courtyard windows, a large walk-in closet, and a small square bathroom—so it was impossible to do anything inconspicuously. She stretched out across the bed, naked and alone, half-covered by the thin rosebud sheets. The pattern glared back at her, even more obnoxious in the full glory of the morning light. She spotted his leather dress shoes, suit, and tie strewn across the floor and entangled with her own disheveled sweater, skirt, and tights. Settling back under her sheets, she heaved a sigh of relief. Her night with him wasn't just a faded fantasy; it was a reality. And it wasn't just a one-night stand. He hadn't left without saying goodbye. He was still there, and still willing to at least spend the morning with her.

The shower, she thought, noting the sound of spraying water.

Maribel quickly dressed. Normally, she would throw on her favorite flannel pajama pants, faded Madonna T-shirt, and hooded sweatshirt. But that was when she was alone, not when she was with a sexy, sophisticated man with whom she had just had the most amazing sex of her life. She scrounged through her closet for her yoga pants and spandex top. *Bra? No bra? Bra? No bra?* She wasn't sure.

"Hello out there?" His deep voice boomed off her shower tiles. "Is that Cupid's little helper?"

"Maybe? Who wants to know?" Cracking open the bathroom door, she called back over the rushing water.

Miles peeked over the shower curtain rod, revealing his wet black hair and sparkling blue eyes. "Someone who wants to be hit with another arrow."

She rolled her eyes. He chuckled and turned back into the steamy shower. "I made us some coffee."

She moved to the counter of her kitchenette and checked the wafting coffee pot. He had forgotten to change the filter and add new coffee grounds. Clearly, it had been awhile since Miles had made his own coffee. She dumped out everything, then poured in two cups of water and started up the machine. Next, she considered breakfast. Popping two pieces of bread into her toaster, she set out a fresh stick of butter onto a plate and searched her refrigerator for something other than eggs, but came up empty. It had been days since she had been to the grocery store. *Scrambled eggs and oatmeal cookies*, she considered, wondering how much longer Miles would be in the shower.

"Roxanne," he suddenly belted out, "You don't have to put on the red light/Those days are over/You don't have to sell your body to the night."

She smiled. At least for a few more refrains.

Suddenly, Miles' phone rang with a low muffled chime, and it took her several seconds to realize that it was still in her purse, where she had forced him to deposit it the previous afternoon.

"Miles, your phone's ringing," she called to him.

"Roxanne," he sang out, "You don't have to wear that dress tonight/Walk the streets for money/You don't care if it's wrong or right."

She smiled. He either didn't hear her or he didn't care because he was enjoying his alternate reality as Sting, the lead singer of the Police. She rushed to her purse and fumbled to secure his phone, planning to bring it to him. Abruptly, she heard the sharp raspy voice of the woman, questioning her on the other end. "Brax? Brax?"

Maribel had accidentally touched its screen and answered the call. She considered hanging up until she heard the woman's demanding voice: "Are you fucking kidding me, Brax? You don't even have the balls to say 'hello'?"

Maribel answered with an official air. "Receiving calls for Mr. Miles Braxton-Worth, how may I assist you?"

It worked. The woman fell silent, then hostile. "Oh, precious…now he has a personal assistant answering his phone calls, does he? Well, you tell Mr. Miles Braxton-Worth that Ms. Gillian Cartwright needs to speak with him today about our multi-million dollar deal, or else my clients are going to sign a lease with his competition at the Amory Building. Did you get all that, cupcake?"

The woman said 'cupcake' like she was slapping Maribel through the phone.

Calmly, Maribel counted to ten and restrained the urge to verbally slap her back. Her years of working in retail had trained her well. "I will be sure to relay the message," she answered, curtly. She immediately wanted to hang up the phone, but knew she had to wait until bitch-queen hung up first. *Click.*

Gillian. Maribel remembered that name and Miles' reaction to her call during their brunch. She shivered and set down the phone on the kitchen counter. No wonder Miles was avoiding her. Multi-million dollar deal or not.

Without warning, Maribel felt the warm tickle of kisses fluttering down her neck.

"Good morning, good morning," Miles said between nibbles. "Whatcha makin'?" he asked, peering over her shoulder. He was half-naked, dripping wet, and wrapped from the waist down in her pastel pink bath towel.

"Toast, scrambled eggs, and oatmeal cookies," she said, popping the butter and brown sugar together in her mixer. The mixer had been a gift from her mother, and she always loved making something fresh and homemade with it on Sunday mornings.

"Really? Yum, yum… Deeeelish."

She smiled, shrugged off his chin from her shoulder and searched her cabinets for the oatmeal. He fell backwards onto her bed, a gesture of relaxation. She eyed him as he stretched his long, strong arms into the air and exhaled—the promise of a good day. Last night, within the murky shadows, she had been consumed, devoured, and dominated by the strength and masculinity of his hard, naked body. Now, in the honesty of the sunlight, she finally had a chance to take in the full scope of his athletic form, smooth chest, and tapered waist. Beads of water clung to the smooth contours of his bare back. Every muscle was sculpted and defined, every movement was deliberate and determined, and he watched her—watching him—with a complete lack of inhibition. *He was so impossibly handsome*, she thought, *but it was his carefree confidence that was the sexiest part about him.*

"In all my years as a man, I never realized the way into a woman's heart was through her rosebud sheets," he joked, and spread his palms across her mattress.

"Who said you've gotten into anybody's heart?" she sassed back.

He rolled onto his elbow and gazed at her, assessing the challenge. "*Touché*." His crystal blue eyes were inescapable.

She finally broke away to pour two cups of coffee and stopped the whirling blades of her mixer to rebalance the batter with the spatula. Then, she glanced over at his phone on the counter. *Gillian*, she thought, *a thorn that threatened to pop each bubbly exchange between them.* He was in such a good mood; she didn't have the heart to dampen it. When she turned around, he was sitting at the three-piece dining table, legs crossed at the knee and dressed in a tight marathon training shirt and matching athletic pants.

"What's that?" she asked.

"My pajamas." He wagged his foot and studied her carefully.

"No," she said slowly, her eyes acknowledging the familiar powder blue box that he had placed in the center of the table.

"Why don't you come over here and find out?"

"Miles," she said, exasperated, and set down the coffee mugs in front of him.

He smirked and drew her into his lap. She gazed at the box—it was long and rectangular. Clearly, it was not something small and inexpensive.

"Don't look at me like that," he replied, pecking her on the lips.

Maribel kissed him back, silencing her protests. *The last thing she wanted was to say something that sounded ungrateful.* But she wasn't certain she wanted him buying her any more expensive gifts. What he had already given her was enough. *More than enough.*

"I knew I wasn't going to win with the earrings," he finally said. Maribel touched her ear lobes. In the middle of the night, she had awoken to use the bathroom and replaced his ruby teardrop earrings with her original cubic zirconia studs.

"It's nothing against the earrings, Miles. I loved them. But it's just that…"

"They're sentimental," he repeated her words from yesterday. "A gift from your mother."

She withdrew from his lap and curiously stared at him, replaying yesterday's conversation in her mind.

But he quickly confirmed that he knew more than he should. "Your mother bought them for you—as an early graduation gift—because she was certain you would finish school, even though she knew she wouldn't be there to celebrate it with you when you did."

Maribel studied his steady eyes, searching to understand how he could possibly know the details about one of the most important relationships in her life. His gaze revealed nothing, other than a calm persuasion that he could be trusted. She paused for an internal moment of silence and waited for him to explain himself.

"I have another confession to make…" But he trailed off, judging his words with care. It was as if he was reading her, waiting and watching until the connection between them signaled he could say more. "I used to hear stories about you—stories about you and your mother."

She slowly approached the table as she processed his words. "How?"

"From my aunt, Mrs. Strauss."

"Mrs. Strauss from the department store?" she repeated with shock before sinking into the adjacent seat. "Your aunt was Mrs. Strauss?"

Miles nodded. "Towards the end, your mother and my aunt were both being treated at the same dialysis clinic. I used to pick up my aunt every other day and she used to tell me stories of who she saw there and who she had spoken with that day. She often told me stories about your mother, and her stories about you."

Maribel looked away. *At the same clinic.* God, how she had hated those days at the clinic, where the only hope for her mother was a new kidney, but the new kidney never came. She hated the smell of decay and chronic illness. She hated the flickering fluorescent lights and the droning murmurs of the TVs. And she hated witnessing her normally vibrant mother withering into a sodden, listless ragdoll, barely kept alive by machines that cleaned her blood.

"I went there, too—every other afternoon after school," she finally said. "Then later, when I started working part-time at the department store, I went there after work."

She stopped and brushed welling tears from her eyes, reflecting on the past while trying to keep her nostalgia from overwhelming her. She had never spoken about that time in her life with anyone because she had tried so hard *not* to remember those days. Those impossibly long, exhausting, hopeless days—going to high school in the morning, then rushing afterwards to catch the "L" downtown to arrive early for her part-time position at the department store before doubling back to pick up her mother from the clinic. When all her friends were worrying about buying their homecoming dresses and passing driver's ed, Maribel was fitting in work, school, laundry, grocery shopping, cooking, caring for her mother, and sleeping during any free moments that were left. She worked every day at the department store—evenings and weekends—so she could afford to live on her own as an independent sixteen year-old and care for her sick mother rather than be swept into the dysfunctional foster care system.

"Yes, I remember seeing you at the clinic," he confirmed. "You were just a high school student then....me, on the other hand, I was a ridiculously self-absorbed, newly-minted billionaire who at least had the good sense to take care of his favorite aunt when she needed it most. But I remember seeing you at the clinic, picking up your mother. And later, I remember noticing you when you came to work at the department store."

"I remember going to the interview and thinking it was a complete waste of time," she confessed, regaining her composure. "I was only sixteen and I knew nothing about working in retail."

"Yes, I know. I was the one who set up the interview for you."

"You?" she whispered. She had always believed that it was her mother who had secured her the interview through her relationship with Mrs. Strauss, a life-long Marshall Field sales clerk who was being forced to retire due to her chronic illness. Her mom had met Mrs. Strauss at the clinic, and she was so relieved when Maribel had gotten the job. Part-time work for teenagers usually meant slaving behind a fast food counter, not behind the upscale sales counters of Chicago's most beloved department store. And it paid well—a decent hourly wage plus sales commission. With her mother's savings and Maribel's new job, she had a chance to make it through high school on her own, even if her mother couldn't be there to help her.

"But why? You didn't know me, and I was just an inexperienced high school student."

Miles laughed as if she had stuck a chord. "Because my aunt told me to do it. It was an easy favor and my aunt knew it. At the time, I was trading phone calls with the CEO of Marshall Field's on a regular basis. They were selling themselves to a larger commercial department store chain, and I was brokering the deal for them to turn over their lease agreement with me as the landlord to their new commercial buyers who wanted to remain tenants in the building. And if there was one thing, and one thing only, that has been constant in my life—it's that I've never said no to Phyllis Matilda Strauss."

The light shifted in his eyes. It was the softer, more sensitive side that he had shown her last night.

"I owe my aunt everything. She's the one who kept me grounded when I made my first million, which quickly snowballed into billions. I was young at the time—too young to really handle what was happening. Without her, I would have been totally consumed by my own narcissism and false sense of sophistication. I would have surrounded myself with sycophants who were willing to perpetuate the myth that I was God—just because I had more money than 99.99% of the population on earth and I wasn't afraid to spend it. But not Phyllis. Phyllis made me feel like the immature, inexperienced, twenty-something kid of privilege that I was. She saved me—and my soul. In that way, you remind me of her—down-to-earth and grounded. And I need that again in my life."

His long, steady gaze conveyed his private thoughts that words could not express. There were no longer any barriers between them. They were simply two people, sitting at a kitchen table over coffee, contemplating the circumstances of their mutual connection.

"Thank you," Maribel finally said, finding her voice under a blanket of repressed emotions. She rarely spoke of her mother—or of those dark days when she knew her mother wouldn't make it and she would be left alone to fend for herself. Her father had long since left them, and there was no friend or relative who knew Maribel better than her own mother. But now, for the first time since those difficult years, she didn't feel completely alone. With only his soulful eyes and earnest confession, Miles made her feel like they were united. "I don't know what else to say except—thank you."

Miles cut his hand through the air to stop her. "There's nothing more to say. There's only what not to say, and that's not to apologize for not wearing the ruby earrings because I understand. I remember my aunt telling me all about those studded cubic zirconia earrings, the ones Mrs. Martinez picked out for her daughter's high school graduation gift. Phyllis was so impressed with how real they looked. It stuck in my mind—still sticks in my mind—because it was one of the last conversations I had with my aunt before she passed."

Maribel picked at her chipping fingernail polish. "That was shortly after I started working at the department store. I remember it well because I remember how I never had the chance to properly meet your aunt. Everyone knew Mrs. Strauss and talked about her so often, especially to me since I was the one who replaced her."

"Yes." He nodded. "And so, when I see you wearing those diamond studs, they remind me of her. And they remind me that there are still a few sacred things in life that cannot be bought or replaced. So instead, when I was there at Tiffany's the other night, I made sure I had a Plan B."

He slid the new gift towards her. Maribel's gaze fell upon the blue box.

"No, Miles, I can't. This is all too much."

"Please," he insisted, as if her rejection was a personal rejection of him. "At least, open the box. After all, it is still Valentine's Day weekend." He winked, coaxing her to accept it. "Happy Valentine's Day."

Happy Valentine's Day. She had never expected to receive anything special this weekend, but it was the fact that he wanted to please her that felt like the most unexpected gift of them all. And deep down, Maribel was still holding back her most vulnerable emotions—in case the fairy tale suddenly ended at the stroke of a tolling clock, and everything reverted to the way it was before Friday.

She pulled the box towards her, untied its white satin ribbon, and lifted its lid. She spotted the light blue leather pouch. She drew it open and slid out the slinky diamond tennis bracelet into her palm. Its scintillating double row of baguette diamonds flashed in the sunlight.

She quickly stood up and handed it back. "No, Miles, I can't... absolutely not."

"You must," he countered, anticipating her every word. "Your other one is a cheap knock-off, and you deserve to wear the real thing."

He unfastened the clasp and encircled her wrist with the sparkling link bracelet. She had seen the price tags of similar bracelets in the windows of the high-end luxury jewelers. Almost always, they were high five figures or more. "No, it's too much," she petitioned, noting its elegance, the heavy weight of its authenticity pressing on her wrist and heart.

He pulled her body into his own and wrapped his arms around her waist, nudging her for a kiss. "A priceless gift for a priceless woman."

The sincerity in his voice melted her into his embrace. His strong arms pulled her forward, and he kissed her with such passion that all her feelings of inadequacy dissolved into burning sensations of desire. She desired his touch, his tongue, his lips, his hands—and his uncompromising insistence that she was worthy of more than she believed was even possible for herself. He swept his mouth down her neck, kissing her supple skin and the tender muscle along her collar bone. She relaxed into his embrace and yearned for more, but he pulled back with a mischievous smirk.

"Brown sugar?" he said, noting the taste in his mouth.

He had caught a smudge of it along her shoulder where she had accidentally dabbed the creamed butter and sugar from the mixer. He placed his lips against her neck and nibbled it again. Maribel felt the grit of sugar and the warmth of his breath against her skin.

Without warning, he took her up into his arms and balanced her on the kitchen countertop. He reached into the mixer with his finger and streaked another gob of creamed brown sugar along her neckline. His lips devoured it, and she cried out with laughter at the sensation of his mouth sucking the confection off her skin. He swept off her spandex shirt and surveyed her bare breasts. She had decided on no bra. He dotted each nipple with more brown sugar, then lowered his mouth over them, drawing out a deep tingle between Maribel's legs with every wet flick of his tongue. She ran her fingers through his hair, encouraging each alternating lick and gluttonous suck. The heavy weight of the diamond tennis bracelet slipped up and down her wrist, and the scratch of his sandpaper stubble brushed against her skin.

"I need you," he uttered with yearning. "God, I need you more than you know."

He lifted her again into his arms before pressing her against the refrigerator and tugging down her yoga pants and lace panties with one swipe of his confident hand. His tongue lapped her tits with ravenous kisses while he cupped her crotch and fingered her slit. Maribel opened her mouth with a silent gasp. The force of his strokes overwhelmed her. He took up her knee into the crook of his arm and pinned her bare ass against the cool vinyl surface of the refrigerator.

She wrapped her arms around his shoulders as he lowered his athletic pants and settled his cock between her thighs. They both heaved in unison with the first penetration—a mutual release of physical tension and repressed emotions, signaling that something had changed between them. She dug her fingernails into his shoulders, enduring the seething burn of his hard erection. He exhaled against her neck and groped her bare backside, then thrust himself into her a second time—a long heavy plunge that threatened to suffocate her with his desperate need to consume her. He covered her mouth with his own and kissed her with fury until they broke for breath and accepted their mutual surrender. He steadied her weight against the refrigerator, lunging himself inside her, building her up with pulsating waves that no one had ever made her feel—not even herself.

God, yesssssssssss, she heaved. Miles pressed up her knees, spread her wider, and thrust himself deeper.

"Can I come inside you?" he begged her.

Yessss... She moaned her sigh—a plea for him to liberate the rippling vibrations within her as she turned over her trust. She wanted to climax from the intimacy of his warm, bare cock releasing all her inhibitions, knowing she was protected and that she would be safe with him.

His determined fingers thumbing her clit and massaging her with forceful strokes while he accelerated his pace. She quaked and cried out, unable to control a primal scream that swelled within her. It was so different than anything she had ever felt—so acute and intense—that her instinct was to fight it. *God, how he filled her so completely.* He secured her body, steady, and pumped harder into her, forcing her to free what her body was trying hard to suppress. They surged simultaneously as she came—a combustion of euphoria that flushed across her skin and throughout her head as his warmth invaded her core. Then, it was over as quickly as it began. She relaxed as everything faded to black and her limp weight settled into his arms, relinquishing every part of her heart and soul to him.

He kissed her with affection and gazed into her eyes. Nothing needed to be said; everything was conveyed through the intimacy of their embrace. He lowered her feet to the floor and gathered up her yoga pants and panties as well as his own pants. It had been an unexpected exchange of memories and emotion, attraction and desire, and now, they both smiled, fingertips clinging to each other, wondering what more they would offer each other.

Maribel's eyes drifted to the wall clock. She was the first to pull away. "Oh my God, it's almost one o'clock?"

He laughed, clasping her hand. "You slept in this morning, Sleeping Beauty. You didn't know?"

"No," she fretted. "I thought it was still early. I have to be at work in fifteen minutes. It takes me forty minutes to get there by 'L'. Twenty—even if I took a cab. I can't be late. Thomas, my manager, will kill me. I'm the only one who is trusted with keys to the jewelry cases. When I'm not there, Thomas has to fill in for me. I can't be late."

Her mind in a whirl, she pulled away from Miles and scrounged through her closet for fresh clothes and her coat as she tried to determine what she needed to do and the best way to do it—fast.

"Stop," he seized her by hand again.

"No, Miles. I can't...you don't understand." She flashed a glare at him.

"Maribel, stop." He glared back, halting her with his firm tone. "My car is outside. I texted my drivers an hour ago to drop it off here for me. I'll get you there in ten minutes."

She frowned, annoyed by his calm demeanor.

"Okay, fifteen minutes—max," he corrected himself.

"How?" she challenged him.

"Speed."

Chapter Eight

MILES AND MARIBEL FLEW down Lake Shore Drive in his red Ferrari, accelerating as fast and furious as a bullet—a straight shot down the highway lane. The race car whirled against the pavement, and cut around the North Beach curve with precision. Inside the machine, the rushing wind was only a whisper and the Ferrari's revving engine was a muted buzz. Maribel glanced up at all the skyscrapers whizzing by her in a blur. *80, 90, 100, 110…* She tried hard not to look at the speedometer. It was measuring their acceleration in kilometers; she truly had no idea how fast they were traveling and she preferred not to know. She glanced over at Miles who shifted into fifth gear and hurled them towards downtown. He was focused and confident in his ability to blaze past every car on the highway, and the Ferrari's tinted windows and smoky leather seats made Maribel feel like an heiress entitled to speed above the legal limit because of her eminence.

Her fantasy of superiority quickly faded when Miles peeled up to the department store and killed the car's engine. She was fifteen minutes late—no one was going to bow down to her for that. She gathered up her purse, dress shoes, and coat, and rushed to open the car door.

"Don't—" Miles caught her hand. "Don't leave like this."

She was frazzled and he saw it. His strong hand calmed her.

"I want to see you again tonight—spend the night with me. After work."

"Miles, I can't. I don't have any of my things."

"We'll buy you new ones."

Maribel rolled her eyes. He had answers for everything.

"Please—" He tipped his head back against the headrest, and pleaded with longing. She felt the sting between her legs and the warmth of his strong hand. She acknowledged her own desire to spend the night with him again, but she wasn't certain if she was ready to commit to spending the night with him—in his own bed.

"Don't worry. I'll buy some rosebud sheets. You'll feel right at home."

It was as if he could read her mind. Maribel smiled. "We can talk about it later. I have to go now…" But she did not pull away from him; instead, he drew himself across the stick shift and stole a kiss like he was stealing away her heart.

"I finish tonight at nine," she heard herself say before dashing out of the car and through the revolving doors of the department store. She glanced behind her, just to check if anyone she knew had seen her exiting his red Ferrari. But there was no one. She shuttled across the Grand Lobby towards the fine jewelry counter, where she saw Thomas, waiting for her.

"Youuuuuuuuuuu're laaaaaaaaaaaate," he sang out, like he was greeting her with praise.

"I know, I know… I am so sorry." Maribel removed her coat and scarf, and traded her snow boots for her dress shoes. She stuffed her belongings under the register's cabinet.

"I tried to have Crystal fill in for you, but then she asked me what the difference was between regular gold and white gold, and if white gold was painted white, and that's when I said to myself, 'Hello, Houston…? We have a problem.'"

Maribel smoothed down her skirt and presented herself to Thomas; she was ready for the day. "I am really sorry. But don't worry. I'm here and it won't happen again."

"It's okay. I clocked you in ten minutes ago 'cause I knew you'd be here. And I won't write you up, even though you completely dissed me by not coming to my Valentine's Day party…. Holy crazy hell, that's some bling-bling you got there."

Thomas zeroed in on Maribel's diamond tennis bracelet.

"It was a gift," she quickly explained, sweeping her long black hair across her shoulder to cover her ruby pendant necklace.

"From who? George Clooney?"

She tried hard to sound convincing. "To myself."

Thomas eyed it again. "Damn, that's one fine knockoff, girlfriend. Don't go spreading the origins of *that* around. That kind of fake ice could put us out of business."

She covered the bracelet. Thomas knew fine jewelry—possibly even better than she—and she knew if he had the chance to scrutinize it, he would only interrogate her more.

"So…what did you do with your day off? I want to know since you avoided me like the paparazzi." He dropped his voice and glanced over her shoulder. "Holy sugar snaps. Don't look now, but we've got a seriously drool-worthy customer coming right towards us."

She followed his gaze as Miles strode up to the counter. He was still wearing his marathon training shirt and matching athletic pants, but his handsome face and confident smile were impossible to miss.

"Hello, Mr. Braxton-Worth. So nice to see you here. Welcome to our store," Thomas greeted him with embarrassing glee. "Can I help you with anything?"

"No, thank you," he said, his eyes settling onto Maribel. "Just browsing."

"Of course, of course. Well, we're always happy to help. Just let us know."

"Actually, I think I would like to purchase something," he abruptly said, peering down into the jewelry cases. "I'd like to take a look at your women's luxury watches. I have a friend who has a hard time keeping track of time. She's supposed to come to my place for dinner tonight, but she wasn't sure if she could get there before…ten? I thought maybe I'd buy her something—to help with her punctuality."

No… Maribel protested with her eyes. He smiled back with his own. He had absolutely no intention of stopping.

"Of course, of course." Thomas glided over to the appropriate case, keyed open the door, and lifted out several designer watches with leather bracelets and rose-gold face plates.

"This one," Miles said, ignoring Thomas' suggestions and tapping the glass to point out the most expensive watch in the case.

"Perfect choice, Mr. Braxton-Worth. Clearly, you have spectacular taste." Thomas pulled out the platinum bracelet watch and rested it on the countertop like a fragile museum relic. "Delicate mother-of-pearl face with scratch resistant sapphire crystal, double row of diamonds framing its round border, and diamond dot accents for each numeral." Thomas recited the sales pitch like a programmed robot. "Swiss two-hand quartz movement, and last—but not least—diamonds detailing every other link along its watchband."

"I'd like to see it on. Just to be sure," Miles insisted.

No… Maribel mouthed to him. He ignored her.

"Of course." Thomas acquiesced and turned to Maribel, draping it around her bare wrist without her consent. The sleekness of platinum glided around her arm, and the glistening diamonds caught the light in Miles' eyes.

"Perfect, I'll take it."

"Perfect!" Thomas sang out and turned towards Maribel.

Ohmygod, ohmygod, he mouthed to her. Thomas wasn't used to making a five-figure sale in less than a minute. But if there was one thing consistent about Miles Braxton-Worth, it was his taste for luxury.

“Maribel will ring it right up for you,” he said, sweeping her towards the register.

“Please charge it to my rolling account.”

“Of course,” Thomas replied, all smiles.

Maribel paused. “I’ve never charged a rolling account before,” she whispered, uncertain.

“Box and bag,” Thomas directed her. “I’ll do the rest.” He dialed the proper key code into the register. Then, he turned back to the counter with the receipt and handed him the purchase. “Here you are, Mr. Braxton-Worth. She must be one very special woman.”

Miles swept his bold signature across the receipt before resting his eyes upon Maribel.

“She is one incredibly special woman. Someone with whom I’ve had the pleasure of watching for years, but only recently have been given the opportunity to get to know better. And the way she makes me feel—the way I feel when I look into her eyes—is more priceless to me than any piece of jewelry I could possibly buy for her.”

Maribel stared at him. The intensity of his gaze and the sincerity in his voice made her feel like they were alone again—just the two of them—indulging in a connection that neither one of them truly understood, yet knew they couldn’t deny.

“Well, *pah….leeeeease* let us know if we can be of further assistance.”

“I certainly will… Thomas,” Miles said, noting his nametag.

Thomas and Maribel watched him stride away towards the revolving doors and exit without glancing back.

“Oh my God, we are totally splitting that commission, girlfriend!” Thomas cried out, fanning himself with the receipt as if he might faint. “*Phew.* After that, I’m not sure I can just settle for selling cashmere scarves.”

Circling out from behind the counter, Thomas darted away towards the accessory department, shouting out across the Grand Lobby. “Crystal! You are *never* going to believe who I just sold a luxury women’s wrist watch to!”

Maribel looked down at the receipt. She recognized Miles’ handwriting below his familiar signature. *Miss you already. See you on your lunch break.*

She smiled. Not only was he impossibly attractive, sensitive and sentimental; he was also impossibly determined—determined to have her, all to himself.

Chapter Nine

MILES BOARDED THE ELEVATOR, pressed the call buttons, and relaxed as the cab whirled upwards to his penthouse condominium. He leaned his shoulders and head against the elevator's gold-toned interior and clenched the shopping bag in his hand. With his eyes closed, still able to taste the flavor of sugar and salt from Maribel's skin, he reflected on their morning together, and the night before. In past years, he had been obligated to spend Valentine's Day with whichever woman he was sleeping with at the time. This year, he had planned to spend it alone—that is, until he had spontaneously decided to pursue Maribel. Now, he didn't want their time together to end.

Unexpectedly, it had been the perfect weekend—the kind that hinted at the possibility of enjoying something deeper in his life beyond just wealth and work. He had drunk hot chocolate, sung in the shower, slept on rosebud sheets, and awoken next to a woman who had wanted nothing from him, except for him to stop buying her luxury gifts. Now, as he still tasted her in his lips, he already missed her sensitive brown eyes and gentle touch, but it was the sense of companionship that made him want to share every moment with her that he missed most of all. It had been a long time since he had felt this way about a woman, and certainly, it had been an even longer time since he felt determined to commit to it.

The final floor chimed. The mirrored elevator doors shimmered open. Miles stepped out, not into a hallway or a private lobby, but directly into his penthouse suite. He snapped his fingers twice. The lights switched on, illuminating the spacious condominium—and his unexpected guest.

"Gillian." Miles said her name without surprise. He *should* have been surprised to see her there, lounging in his favorite lounge chair and sipping wine from a glass—no doubt one of his rare vintage bottles that she had opened without his permission. But with Gillian, he had long since learned that she had no sense of boundaries and nothing was beyond her. *At least she had her clothes on*, he thought, and tossed his car keys across the granite countertop of the kitchen island that separated him from her.

"Hope you don't consider it an intrusion," Gillian said with a purr.

He leaned against the island and confronted her with his glare. "To enter a home without an invitation?"

"Oh, come on now, Brax… we've never been *that* formal with each other and you know it. In fact, some of our best days were when we were a lot less formal with each other."

She stood up from the chair. She was wearing a tight red dress and a black mink shawl coat. "In fact, I'm fairly certain that one of our best negotiations was done while I was wearing nothing more than this mink coat."

Miles didn't need the reminder. He remembered buying it for her as well as the way she had modeled it for him and the "business" transaction that followed. That's all his life had amounted to now, and that's all Gillian expected from him now—a series of shallow, mutually beneficial transactions. At least with her, he had never failed to wear a condom.

The urge to put her in her place and cut to the chase swelled with his annoyance. But that's what the "old Miles" would do. The "new Miles"—the relaxed, amorous Miles from this weekend—was less interested in combat and more disciplined about avoiding it. Instead, he simply crossed his arms and stared at her—waiting.

She sauntered towards him and offered him a glass of wine. "It's one of your favorites: *Château Lafite Pauillac* 1990."

"Are we here to enjoy wine together, or do you want something specific?"

She threw back her head with laughter. Miles noticed her red lips, her bleached teeth, and her short blonde hair, freshly cut and styled. Then, he noticed how the veins in her neck bulged through her powdered pale skin and how her overpowering perfume poorly masked the staining scent of cigarettes.

"Brax, I really don't understand why you seem so determined to make this difficult on both of us. We want the same thing." Her fake red nails clicked against the granite island before gliding their way over his shoulder and behind the nape of his neck. She was close enough that he could see the pale green glints in her muddy eyes and smell her breath. "Let's find a way to come together, and close the Olson & Anderson deal," she whispered, "and then we can move onto more important things—like celebrating."

Like a vampiress, she touched his hand with her claws. She had sucked him dry so many times, and he went along with it because it was easy and automatic. But the outcome was always the same—nothing remained afterwards except emptiness and an executed business deal.

Miles remembered Maribel. The shopping bag burned in his left hand. He relaxed and set it on the counter.

Gillian angled her head, noting the change. Her gaze lowered onto the sleek gift bag—with its department store logo and "Fine Jewelry" tagline.

Reaching out to accept the gift, she tittered. "Brax, I'm speechless. You shouldn't have…"

"I didn't," he tossed back, sliding the bag away from her grasp. His strength pushed Gillian backwards and she faltered on the heel of her stiletto. It was a physical gesture of hostility. Her hazel eyes flashed at him. The game had changed. And they both knew it.

"Ahhhh, I see…you haven't been avoiding me. You've just been busy conquering new lands and pillaging their women."

He narrowed his eyes at her. *Juvenile and crude.* It was how their exchanges always had been, but now, he faulted her for failing to realize he wanted something better from her—and from himself.

"Well, since my phone call to Gary and my message to your assistant have all been lost in translation, let me put this in a way that everyone can understand." Gillian paced back to her purse and pulled out a contract.

"What assistant?" he asserted.

"Your newest cupcake," she countered with a flick of her tongue. "It's a bit tacky having her answer your phone, by the way. Wouldn't make a habit out of that." Gillian slapped the contract down on the island.

"This is a contract with Harvey Zale," he said, surprised. He quickly thumbed to its final page to see if it had been executed. No signatures yet—which meant it could all be for show, or it could be the official final draft, ready for execution.

"You sound genuinely shocked," Gillian replied. "I gave you fair warning. I'm not that cruel. But clearly, your cupcake is horrible at relaying urgent messages. Looks like you need to hire better help."

"Have they verbally agreed to these terms?" Miles paged through the contract, skimming the numbers and calculating the lease escalations, cost per square foot, rental expenses, and subsequent profit margins in his head.

"I spoke to Harvey yesterday. He wants my clients in his Amory building—and he's very motivated to do a deal. By the way, he told me to wish you a Happy Valentine's Day."

Miles gauged her sincerity. Since she was a woman who was rarely honest, it was impossible to parse out the lies from the truth. Harvey Zale was Miles' biggest rival, and he knew Zale would love nothing more than to steal the Olson & Anderson deal away from him. His competitive streak seeped into his blood like a mood-altering drug. He was fine with losing the deal. But he wasn't fine with losing it to a double-crossing, client-stealing leech of a building owner like Harvey Zale. And clearly, Gillian knew it.

"I suppose that I could call my clients and ask if they would like to give you one last try to make it up to them," she offered. "We're old friends, Brax, after all. And I'd hate for there to be bad blood between us. The last thing I want is to disrupt our current arrangement."

Their current arrangement, he thought, and considered how much damage altering their "current arrangement" would inflict upon him. They had an understanding: she would always bring him her best clients first before shopping them to his competition. Now, one thing was clear—that arrangement was in jeopardy. Miles could sign the deal that Gillian wanted for her clients; he'd just lose out on a few hundred thousand dollars per year along with a chunk of his pride. But he'd make up for it on all the other potential tenants she would bring him. He looked down at the contract and clenched his jaw. He hated to lose, but he hated being cornered even more.

Gillian edged closer and touched his cheek with her fingernails before slowly arching against his body like a pampered cat. She was tall and slender, and her red lips met his own. It was an empty, insincere kiss. She pressed deeper into him, attempting to slip her tongue into his mouth. The bitterness of nicotine and ash marred the sweet taste of Maribel that he had been savoring all morning. He was not the kind of man to shove away a woman—not even Gillian—but he no longer felt the need to placate her. Abruptly, he brushed her aside in a way that surprised them both. She glared at him, mouth gaping wide, expecting an explanation. There was only callousness in his eyes.

"Do the deal with Zale," he finally said, his tone simmering with anger as he stuffed the contract back into her hands, calling her bluff. "I'm no longer interested in maintain our 'current arrangement.'"

"Oh, Brax…" She forced a nervous laugh, as if she recognized the rage in his eyes. "You're always so dramatic about these things." She attempted to spark a friendlier mood, but it was in vain. He was done with her games and he was done with her.

"If you're looking to fleece someone, then it looks like you've found your match. Good luck getting good customer service from Harvey Zale. Now, get the hell out of my apartment."

Shifting her weight onto one heel, Gillian glared at him before rifling through her purse and tossing a gold-toned elevator access card onto the island. Then, she took up the contract into her hands and announced one final challenge. "You'll regret this Brax. I'll personally make sure of it."

"Maybe." He shrugged, certain she would make good on her threat. "But you'll find that Harvey Zale's a lot rougher and dirtier in bed."

Gillian smirked and sashayed into the open elevator. Miles did not look back. He only heard the *click, click, click* of her fingernails against the call buttons and the finality of the door chime, signaling he was shutting her out of his life for good.

Yes, juvenile and crude. It was always the same. That's what Gillian inspired in him, and that's what his materialistic world—a world of narcissistic negotiations and vengeful power-plays—expected from him. Money and power. Domination and control. Conceit and ego. Moral corruption and bitter emptiness.

Miles picked up the elevator access card and tap it against the countertop. Then, he glanced at his watch. He would have to wait patiently for another three hours before he would have the chance to see Maribel again. And then, he wanted nothing more than to put everything out of his mind except the anticipation of the newfound joy in his life.

Chapter Ten

MARIBEL DIDN'T MEAN to end up in the lingerie section of the department store during her lunch break. She drifted there unintentionally when she was wandering through the aisles, wondering about whether or not she was going to see Miles tonight. *Was she prepared to spend the night with him—in his bed?* She wasn't certain. One moment, she trembled with excitement and anticipation. The next moment, she worried that everything was moving too fast, and perhaps it would be wiser, simpler, more sensible to return to her apartment to let things cool off. She didn't even have any extra clothes with her, and now, she realized her black nylons were snagged along the ankle. The discovery forced her to the hosiery rack in the lingerie department where she noted the matching bra and panty sets that she never considered buying for herself—until now.

Maribel had never worn underwear in any color other than black and white. She always had admired the other colors, especially the sensual violets, coral pinks, and crisp fuchsia bra and panty sets. But for Maribel, shopping for lingerie that no man would ever see wasn't fun—it was discouraging. She generally avoided the whole section except when she was asked by Thomas to fill in for Crystal. Now, as Maribel lifted up a packet of black nylons, her gaze wandered over the colorful collection of revealing silk chemises, leopard print push-up bras, and French-cut panties. Her eyes settled on a siren red strapless corset and matching garter thong. She never would have thought she'd have the desire or confidence to wear something *that* risqué in front of anyone—not even her own reflection. Today, however, was different. Today, she imagined herself in each alluring color combination, submitting herself to Miles' strong hands and powerful embrace within his own bed.

"Ohmygod, ohmygod—"

Maribel frowned at the interruption. Thomas was coming straight at her.

"Guess who just ordered one of every women's apparel item in size six and eight!"

She could barely comprehend his words. She only felt the grip of his hand, squeezing the hard metal of her diamond tennis bracelet into her wrist.

"Miles Braxton-Worth!" He jumped up and down like he was the winning contestant of a game show. "Crystal is over there, right now, trying to sort through her notes from his phone call—if she doesn't hyperventilate first. He wants everything in all the major designer brands: tops, tanks, sweaters, pants, jeans, jackets, dresses, skirts, mini-skirts, mini-mini-skirts," Thomas nudged Maribel and winked. "Whoever his lady friend is, I hope she realizes the coin he's dropping on her." He shifted his eyes down onto the packet of nylons in Maribel's hands. "Shopping during your lunch break?"

"Snag," she confirmed.

"Bummer," he replied. "Anyway, Crystal sent me over here to find a pajama set. Would you believe it? Miles Braxton-Worth wants a pair of old-fashioned flannel pajamas. Rosebud print, of all things. Maybe he and his girlie don't even do anything naughty. Maybe they sleep in separate beds and eat pancakes together in the morning."

Maribel smiled. *Flannel pajamas.* Her shoulders slowly relaxed, releasing all the tension from imagining what more Miles expected from her tonight. Maybe he didn't expect anything more… Maybe he simply expected more of what she had already given him.

"My Lord, how should I know which ones to buy!?" Thomas groaned, shifting aimlessly through a rack of fleece and flannel top and bottoms.

"Here," she offered, lifting up a white set with small pink roses from the rack.

"Are *those* rosebuds?" Thomas eyed them, unconvinced.

"I'm sure they'll be fine. And look, 'medium'. So you don't even need to get two different sizes."

"Better get both a small and a medium—just to be safe. The last thing I want is to be the guy who screws up on the pajama fetish request from our building owner."

"Yes, you definitely don't want to go down in sales history for that."

"For sure." Thomas nodded with a snap before running away towards the shoe department. "Roberta, Roberta, I need six pairs of black leather boots and dress flats, pronto!"

Maribel watched Thomas race across the Grand Lobby. There was a flurry of activity in the women's apparel department. In contrast, the lingerie section was empty and quiet.

Pancakes—pancakes and sticky syrup. That sounded just perfect. A warm sensation of comfort washed over her heart. A rush of anticipation returned as she pondered spending the night at Miles' apartment. Maribel eyed the siren red corset and thong set. Motivated by a burst of spontaneity and self-confidence, she lifted it from rack and slipped into the changing rooms. She picked the dressing room farthest from the entrance, closed the door, and quickly undressed without looking at her body in the mirror. She had always been self-conscious about her body. She was petite, but curvy. *Too curvy*, she often thought. Miles had judged her size accurately. She was normally a size eight—courtesy of her round thighs, short torso, and full chest. With the help of the right underwire bras, fitted tops, and nylons, Maribel knew she could pack it all in and squeeze into a size six. Compact and shapely. She had long since accepted her body. *That's what your late-twenties were all about.* She wiggled into the red garter thong and fastened herself into the red corset bra. *But had she accepted her body—bare and buff—without the help of tummy-hugging panty hose and thigh-smoothing skirts?* She wasn't sure, especially now as the three-way mirror revealed every angle of her tummy and every fat dimple on her thighs.

"Wowzers…"

Startled, she whipped towards the voice. Miles' mischievous blue eyes peeked over the rim of the door into the dressing room.

"Is that a gift for me?" he said, tugging on the handle.

"What are you doing here?" Maribel's pulse raced with horror.

"I'm stalking you, of course. And waiting for you to change into *that*."

"It was supposed to be a surprise." Maribel gathered up her skirt—a feeble attempt to cover her bare legs and backside from his view.

"It worked. I'm surprised. Now, open this door, and don't even think about getting dressed."

Their eyes locked. His intoxicating blue eyes fixed on her. They made her want to trust him—even when she doubted his intentions and feared the consequences. She obeyed, unlocked the door, and allowed him to slip inside the dressing room and seize her into his arms.

"We can't, not here," she cautioned him.

Miles swept his tongue into her ear and down her neck.

"Shhhh…I've got the entire department store working on putting together a full wardrobe for you. They'll be busy until close. And there's no possible way I can control myself when you're wearing that."

He gazed down at her, taking in every angle and curve she had just cursed and scorned.

"Miles, you don't need to buy me every women's apparel item. And really, truly, we can't do this. Not here, not now."

"What you don't need is an excuse not to come to my apartment tonight."

Maribel pulled away from his hands, trying to resist him. But it was impossible. He looked powerful and sophisticated in his tan sharkskin designer suit, white shirt, and glacial blue tie. And he smelled amazing—fresh from a shower with the scent of aftershave still lingering on his smooth jaw and chin. The strength of his masculinity and commanding embrace overwhelmed her with a pang of tingling arousal.

"God, you look so hot and taste so amazing." He lowered his gaze onto her exposed cleavage—accentuated by the red strapless corset—and swiped his tongue over their buxom arcs.

"Miles..." It was her final protest before she wilted in surrender. He was sucking deeply on the tender nape of her neck, indulging in her weakness that he had discovered last night. Sucking harder, he ran his firm hands over her bare thighs, groping her ass and tugging on her red thong with a teasing snap. He fed on her, deeply, lowering his lips along her collar bone and dropping his chin between the plump curves of her breasts. Dipping into the bra cups, his mouth searched out her nipples, alternating between flicks and sucks. Her whole body ached for more as she glanced at their reflection in the three-way mirror. He looked handsome and debonair in his suit and tie. She was sexy and provocative in her red corset and garter thong. He followed her gaze. They both watched in the mirror as his fingers nudged past the flimsy silk protection of the thong and invaded her wetness, forcing her to gasp with the sensation of pleasure as she watched—and felt—him stroking her deeper and deeper.

"No, we can't..." she moaned.

"Yes, we can."

Slowly, he lowered himself to his knees and wrapped his hands around her backside.

"We shouldn't," she whispered, steadying her hands on his shoulders and sighing when he circled his hot breath over her crotch.

She gazed back at their reflection and watched as his tongue slipped past the thin silk strip of her thong and between her legs. Maribel exhaled and closed her eyes, relaxing her knees and thighs, granting him access. *Was she really doing this? Was she really going to let him taste her...here and now?* She had always been so proper and restrained. She had barely managed to have sex once a year, much less have *this kind of sex* in a private corner of a public place—her work place. She moaned as the tip of his tongue flicked over her clit. Her head dropped backwards; she released a soft groan that encouraged every lap of his velvet tongue.

Naughty and disgraceful. Dirty and taboo.

She finally found the courage to open her eyes, looking into the mirror—her knee was propped over his shoulder, his face was buried between her legs, his firm grasp encircled her ass locking her in place. *How would she ever be able to face him afterwards*? She didn't know and she didn't care. The sensation of his tongue penetrated her deeper and deeper...She pressed on his head and nudged him for more, watching in a euphoric daze as he sucked her off while genuflecting in his designer suit, as if it were she who was dominating him.

He paused, stealing a glance at their reflection.

You make me want to let go of everything, her eyes confessed to him in the mirror.

He held her gaze. *And you make me want to have every part of you.*

He pushed her knee higher and fingered her deeply before delving back into her with his tongue and hot breath. Maribel gushed for him, unable to believe the way she wanted him—*needed him*—to taste every drop of her. Just when she thought she could bear no more, his steady hand stripped down her corset below her cleavage, exposing her full breasts and maroon nipples. His fingers pierced her tits, one at a time, with unforgiving force. The prick of pain eased the swelling desire between her legs. In response, she slipped his fingers into her mouth and sucked them the way he had returned to sucking her.

"I want you inside me," Maribel whispered down to him, as if she was granting him permission to dominate her without restraint.

Miles rose from his knees, swept up her leg into the crook of his arms, and pinned her against the mirror. The cool surface of the glass stung against her thighs as she watched him unzip his fly and settle his firm cock between her legs. With her corset torn down below her tits and her thong stripped down around her ankle, she felt dirty and disheveled—at his complete mercy—as he manhandled her like a possession. He knew what she wanted, but he was making her wait for it. Shifting their weight off the center panel of the three-way mirror, he ran his hands around her exposed ass and led her gaze to their side reflection. They both watched as his index finger slipped between her cheeks and probed her most tender spot. Maribel's mouth opened with a silent gasp. She had never let anyone touch her there before, and she sank deeper into his caresses, full tender strokes that massaged her with tenderness. *God, how he owned her...daring to seduce her like a sexual goddess not just a mortal woman.* The hot tip of his cock teased her slit, priming her for something deeper. Every illicit touch made her ache for him to come inside her. She wrapped her arms around his smooth silk shirt and whispered for him to take her now—and take her completely.

Miles rested his forehead against her heart and sighed, as if she had just alleviated his suffering by surrendering to his single determined thrust. They exhaled in unison, like they were breaking through a barrier, fighting for air. The friction. The pressure. The penetration. Maribel could do nothing else but relinquish herself to him.

He braced her bare ass against the cool reflective glass and thrust upwards again, kindling a burning sensation of ecstasy deep within her. It started low in her G-spot, then rose through her pelvis with a trembling quake. She was climaxing, spiraling waves of pleasure rushing deeper and faster in a way she had never experienced before. She felt the rush of blood to her head, a flush sweeping over her face and neck. Gyrations—steady and unyielding—coursed through her entire body as he rode her hard like she was a saucy, naughty, thong-wearing vixen, one she barely knew or recognized. The force of his thrusts shuddered into one orgasmic spasm that released all of her tension and inhibitions, including every criticism and fault she had ever harbored about herself.

They clung to each other with a gasp, then indulged in the relief of their simultaneous release. *God, that's what it felt like to have an orgasm. A truly boundless orgasm*. She thought she had always known—until now.

She relaxed into his embrace, sharing the whisper of their breaths and the contractions of their chests. And within those precious moments of shared silence, Maribel no longer worried about the imperfect contours of her naked body or her waning self-confidence. She only concentrated on her feelings of sexual satisfaction—the blissful fulfillment of being ravished and conquered, a fulfillment which only Miles—and her red siren thong and matching corset bra—had unleashed in her.

Chapter Eleven

IN THE BITTER COLD and under the hazy illumination of a street lamp, Miles stood on the downtown street corner and waited for Maribel. Four hours—it had been four long hours since their escapade in the dressing room. It felt like an eternity. He had returned to his penthouse, but he felt nothing but emptiness without her. Now, the anticipation of seeing her again—or not seeing her—was unbearable. If she decided to see him again tonight, they agreed he would wait for her across the street from the department store and she would meet him there at the end of her shift. She seemed hesitant about spending the night with him when they parted ways earlier that day. They had moved so far, so fast—maybe it would be better if they spent the night apart. Her suggestion had crushed him, and he pressured her with a firm grasp of her hand before she slipped away from him and scurried back to the jewelry department. He didn't *want* to pressure her, but their session in the dressing room had proven to him how much he needed her. *Craved her like an obsession*. And he hoped that he had proven it to her.

Miles blew air into his cold hands and paced along the street corner like a caged animal. Suddenly, she emerged from the department store's revolving doors in her black coat and black earmuffs. *God, how those earmuffs made him smile*. He grinned and nodded to her, but noted the reluctance in her smile. Maribel wasn't ready to go public with their 'relationship'—if that what it was. Miles didn't know what 'it' was—he only knew he was determined to see her again. A gust of wind rushed against her back and pushed her across the street towards him. He gazed at her, realizing the only thing that mattered to him was right there in front on him. The sight of her shining brown eyes, endearing smile, and those black earmuffs was the only thing that mattered. *Yes, she had become an insatiable craving because he was falling in love with her.*

Snowflakes swirled down through the evening sky and passed under the misty beams of light from the street lamps. Miles held out his hand. She grasped it. He swept her into his body and greeted her with a tender kiss, vowing to himself that he would never let her go. *Her lips, her smile, her flushing cheeks. The taste of her body, her breasts, her nipples, her whole being…* He had waited four hours. It had been too long. And he would not give her up again.

He smiled and she smiled wider. "I'm glad you came."

"I almost didn't," she confessed. "But then I peeked out through the doors, and saw you standing here, looking so cold and miserable, and you're not even wearing gloves." She took his hands into her own. That was Maribel—always filled with tenderness and concern.

"Ahhhh, I see—the sympathy card. Noted. Next time, I'll be sure not to wear a coat."

"No, please, don't do that. Freezing to death is *not* a very romantic way to woo a woman."

"True. But warming up next to a fire definitely has its merits." Miles spun her into his body, pressing her tightly against his wool dress coat and stuffing her own hands into his broad pockets. "And I'm fairly certain that even without a fire, you would be able to warm me up."

Maribel rolled her eyes and tried to pull away. But he pinned her closely and laughed—a loud, spontaneous release of happiness that reminded him of why he loved being around her.

"Let's get you out of the cold," he said.

He turned and squinted across the street. For a moment, he thought he had heard his name before realizing he had only heard the sharp horns of traffic and the shouts of cabbies and street vendors. But the sensation of being watched was still there. A cautious reflex made him scan the sidewalks. There, he spotted her—*Gillian*.

She was watching Miles and Maribel. *Her. Them.* For how long, Miles didn't know, but the bitter glint in Gillian's eyes told him long enough. She stood at the end of the block in front of the Amory building, which was kitty-corner to his Field's building. Miles recognized Gillian's clients, Don Olson and Greg Anderson. They were all there, smoking and waiting for something. He wasn't sure what. Perhaps they had just signed the deal with Harvey Zale. Perhaps Miles had just lost thirty-five million dollars.

Gillian glared at him as she took a drag from her cigarette and smiled—a sly, vindictive smile through a puff of smoke that told him this was just the beginning of the end. *Et tu, Brute?* Then, the corners of her smile faded like melting ice as Gillian's scornful glare fell onto Maribel. Miles enveloped Maribel against his chest before guiding them across the street and away from the Amory building. *Thirty-five million dollars he could bear to lose,* he thought as he led them under the 'L' tracks along Wabash and towards his penthouse condominium on Michigan Avenue. But the possibility of redemption—the renewed passion for life and its ultimate meaning—he could not.

* * * *

Miles led Maribel by the hand into the opulent lobby of his high-rise condominium building. Her gait next to him felt light, happy, and trusting. They had stopped along the way for deep dish pizza and root beer—something he hadn't bothered to enjoy in years. Business meetings in fancy five-star restaurants and wine bars had long since replaced the casual experience of a ten-dollar meal eaten without utensils. He nodded to the doorman, who greeted them and held open the elevator doors. Miles escorted Maribel into the elevator cab, then slipped his gold-plated access card through the card reader. The doors shut and the cab shuttled upwards. They ascended in silence—not awkward elevator silence, but natural, meditative serenity. He squeezed her hand; it was warm and relaxed. She had chosen to be there with him. There was nothing more either of them needed to say.

When the elevator cab arrived to the top floor, the door chimed and opened directly into his dim penthouse suite.

"We're here," he said, encouraging her.

Maribel slowly entered into the darkness. He waited by the entrance as she navigated through the shadows of the open floor plan, lured deeper inside by the natural illumination of the full moon, shining through the floor-to-ceiling windows. Miles drifted to the fireplace and switched on the gas to ignite the spark. A burst of flaming orange reflected off the surface of the black leather sofa and granite island countertop before receding into a low, smoldering glow. He wandered through the living room and towards Maribel, who had settled her hand against the cool glass of the panoramic view.

"It's amazing up here. You can see everything," she whispered, almost like a prayer.

Lake Shore Drive blinked with rushing headlights. The black waters of Lake Michigan were dotted with the sleepy lights of sailboats. And along the Northern horizon, Navy Pier looked like a twinkling pixie fairyland.

"And look at the moon," she softly exclaimed. "It's so close. I feel like I should be able to reach out and touch it."

Miles had long since taken it all for granted. Now, he scanned it with fresh eyes and admired Maribel's profile in the moonlight.

"If you close your eyes, sometimes it feels like you're floating towards it." Moving behind her, he held out her hand and covered her eyes with his palm. She relaxed and smiled, like she could imagine the sensation.

"I think if I lived up here, I'd never leave. I'd stay here all day, reading books, drinking hot chocolate, and enjoying the feeling of never having to struggle through another day."

"It's an amazing thing to be able to live here, yes…" He nodded, his thoughts drifting far out across the black waters of the lake. "But it also gets lonely at the top of the world."

He laughed, realizing he was betraying weakness. Maribel turned to him, her soulful eyes shining with the moonlight.

"Miles, you have so much. So much wealth, so many expensive things. Cars and apartments, and entire buildings. You even have your own private view of the moon. But you always sound like they're nothing to you except a burden."

She raised her hand and touched his cheek. He closed his eyes. *God, he loved that.* It was a gesture of compassion, an endearing act of intimacy that casual sex with dozens and dozens of women had never brought him. Maribel, on the other hand, delivered it to him time and time again. It was what made him want to envelope her in his arms and own her in every way. He lifted her hand and kissed it.

"I do have more than almost everyone in the world," he acknowledged. "But it only brings me happiness when I can share it with someone else who deserves it. Someday, I'll take you out there on my yacht. We'll spend the night far out along the horizon where there's nothing but a veil of darkness—just the moon, the wind, the sound of the lapping waters, and an inescapable silence that forces you to consider what really matters in your life."

Slowly, he draped the freshly-purchased luxury watch around her bare wrist.

"Miles—" Maribel protested.

"Shhhh… We're past all that now," he reminded her, noting the diamond tennis bracelet on her other wrist. "There's nothing that gives me more pleasure than having you here with me. Thank you for coming."

Maribel admired the watch's regal elegance. "Thank you, Miles. It's lovely."

"You're welcome. C'mon now." He nudged her to follow him. "I have something else to show you."

He directed her away from view of the cityscape and down a corridor that flowed through the spacious penthouse. She suddenly stopped in her tracks, eyeing the aquamarine glow of the sixty-gallon saltwater fish tank.

"Sharks?" she asked, incredulously.

"Only small ones." He smiled.

"To keep you company at the top of the world?"

He laughed and relaxed his grasp on her hand. "Something like that."

Together, they drifted through a private hallway towards the dark seclusion of the master bedroom. Miles considered the fact that he hadn't slept there since Friday, and how he had vowed not to sleep there again without her. Her eyes settled on the master bed, wrapped in white untouched sheets and suspended on a platform like a floating iceberg. It dominated the space. He turned back into the hallway and whisked open a door. She peeked inside, but she could see nothing in the darkness.

"Lights," Miles directed into the air.

The lights suddenly flicked on, revealing the enormous walk-in closet with rows and rows of freshly-pressed clothes from the department store—women's blouses, sweaters, jeans, skirts, and dress pants. Below them, organized along gold-toned racks were dozens of shoes in every shape and color—high heels, flats, leather boots, fashionable sneakers. There was even a pair of white and pink bunny slippers. Miles watched as Maribel gazed down upon them.

"They didn't have ladybug ones," he quipped. "I asked."

Then, he nodded over her shoulder. There, displayed on a solitary hanger, were the white rosebud pajamas.

"I thought you might want something more comfortable. It can get cold here at night, even with the warmth of another person next to you."

She stared at the clothes in silence. He watched her, preparing for her protest. He knew she would claim that it was all too much—that he had done too much for her, and that she only needed her own clothes in her own apartment. It was true. And that's what he loved about her. That's all she needed. But that wasn't all he wanted to give to her.

But Maribel did not protest. Instead, she slowly reached out to touch the lilac cashmere sleeve of one of the designer sweaters.

"I've always wanted this sweater," she confessed, almost to herself. "Every paycheck, for the past two paychecks, I thought about buying it for myself… " Her voice trailed off as she realized that he had bought it for her in three different colors.

"Well then, let's try it on you," he encouraged, touching her waist and feeling her consent. He removed the lilac sweater from the rack, unfastened its shoulder buttons, enameled with mother-of-pearl, and tugged it off its hanger. Together, they peeled off Maribel's drab gray cotton top. She did not resist when he unhooked the clasp of her black bra with a whispering kiss along her shoulder. It dropped to the floor. He slipped the sweater over her bare torso like he was dressing a queen. Brushing aside her long black hair, he refastened the buttons of its rounded neckline. The soft, natural fabric clung to her full breasts and tapered her waist. He touched his nose against her collarbone, like he expected to smell the scent of flowers. Then, he rotated her towards the full-length mirror and admired her reflection.

"You are so gorgeous. But there's more..."

He turned to a lingerie chest, nestled in the corner, and pulled open its top door. They both saw the red corset and garter thong from earlier that day. He brushed past it and fished out a pair of white silk panties, trimmed with lace.

"I want you to be comfortable," he whispered.

He moved behind her, cautiously unzipping her pencil skirt. She did not resist when he slipped it down over her black nylons and removed her flats. He rose again and glanced at her in the mirror. *She was so beautiful, so genuine, so sacred and sexy.* He outlined the full shape of her legs, glazed by her stockings, before peeling them below her backside and thighs. He wanted to liberate her completely from her old clothes and her old expectations of who she was when she was with him. Now, she stood before him—wearing only the lilac sweater and her usual black panties. He lowered himself to his knees and looked up at her. He wanted her approval. She placed her hands on his shoulders and allowed him to remove her black underwear, one leg at a time, before redressing her with her new ones. With a worshiping stroke of his palm, he smoothed the white silk fabric over her curvy ass.

He paused and rested his forehead against her thighs—her warm supple thighs—and indulged in the sensation of her fingernails, stroking the nape of his neck.

"Miles, you've done so much for me—the jewelry, the clothes, all this attention—and it's not that I'm not grateful, but it's so much, so fast."

He waited. He knew she was expressing her greatest fears and he didn't want to overpower her.

"I'm just not certain I know what it all means, or what we can really ever be to each other."

It was true. He had already pondered whether or not Maribel was just another woman in his bed, another sexual conquest, a convenient distraction from his stressful life. He had pursued those types of relationships—many, many times—and Maribel was perceptive enough to know it. He understood why she was hesitant because he knew that he had not expressed everything that had been raging in his heart. But from the very beginning, she had made it all different for him. And now, he wanted her to know it.

"Maribel, I know nothing I can say will express what I've been feeling these past two days. But I want you to know that this connection between us is something different for me, something I can't completely explain with words—not even to myself. And yes, it's only been two days since we've formally met each other, but I feel like I've known you my whole life and now you're finally a part of it in a way that feels right. I can't claim to know what it all means or what we can be to each other, but I'm willing to find out..." He searched her eyes—those beautiful brown eyes that promised him nothing but a chance to save him from himself. "Are you?"

Slowly, she took up his hand and urged him to his feet. She loosened his tie and let it drop to the floor. Button by button, she unfastened his dress shirt. He moved his hands around her waist, preparing to draw her into his body and consume her. But she stopped him. Now, it was she who wanted to undress him. He dropped his hands and relaxed with a sigh, savoring how her fingers brushed over his shoulders before freeing his arms from each sleeve. The cool air of the apartment pricked his skin. She softened the chill with a kiss on his pecs. He exhaled and tried to run his hands under her new silk panties, but again, she stopped and resisted him. Her hands unfastened the gold buckle of his belt, sliding it out from each pant loop. Her release of its taut leather unleashed a pang of desire in him—a basic instinct to embrace her, smother her with his body, and force his way inside her. But he quelled the urge to dominate her. Instead, her eyes arrested him—as if he could only hear her thoughts.

Yes, she was willing to try, but only on her terms.

He clenched his jaw as she unzipped his fly, and watched as she lowered herself down to the floor, stripping him of each dress shoe, sock, and pant leg. She rose again and gazed at his reflection in the mirror. Only his black silk boxers remained. Her soft cashmere sweater feathered against his back before she moved in front of him and lifted his hand and moistened his thumb and forefinger with her warm lips. He exhaled with restraint. He wanted to claim her, slip his wet fingertips under her white panties and fondle her.

But it was she who lowered his boxers below his thighs and knees. The contour of her breasts grazed against his bare erection. He throbbed for her—hard and impatient, coursing with blood and emotion. The muscles in his chest flinched. Like a reflex, he placed his hands on her head to guide her mouth downwards. But she removed them, and circled her hands around his backside and between his cheeks, her fingers caressing him the way he had caressed her that afternoon. He exhaled and closed his eyes. She probed him deeply, then licked the slick tip of his erection, letting the sensation linger until he opened his eyes to meet her own. He had never stood naked in front of any woman without exerting his ability to overtake her. Now, swollen and yearning, he stood naked and vulnerable in front of Maribel, allowing her tongue to pleasure him without his direction.

"Maribel, I need you..." He clasped her wrists, seeking a signal that she was willing to let him be more to her.

"Why?" she whispered, rising from her knees and locking eyes with him. "Why do you need me so much?"

He hesitated as her question drove into the core of his soul. "Because you make me want to be a better man."

The sincerity in his confession disarmed them both. She gazed into his eyes, weighing his words before the lights in the closet suddenly flicked off. They stood in the darkness, the sound of their breath their only gauge of each other. Miles listened for her response. He heard her remove the luxury watch and diamond tennis bracelet from her wrists. They dropped onto the hardwood floor, clanging like broken chains.

"My love is free, Miles. Promise me you won't forget that."

Her body relaxed as he drew her in for a kiss. "Not free," he said with a hush, and cradled her head against his own. "Priceless."

She sighed and released herself to him, accepting the full weight of his tongue flowing over her own, then down her neckline. He heaved an emotional sigh into her ear and consumed her with tender commitment. She lifted her hands, allowing him to slide off her sweater and taste her nipples—*his sweet and salty Maribel.* His mouth dug between her breasts like she was offering up her soul.

Miles noticed the change in her body. Slowly, she pressed her silk white panties against his firm cock, squaring her pelvis against his own. It was the signal he had needed—craved—and now, it was filled with ravenous desire. He swept her up into his arms and carried her to his bed, crisp and fresh, waiting to be christened with their passion for each other. He spread her out across its sheets, admiring her in the soft light of the moon. She lifted his thumb and forefinger and sucked them with luscious flicks, which hardened his cock and energized his determination to satisfy her. He slipped down her white panties over her smooth legs. She exhaled from his touch and butterflied her knees as his fingers nestled between her legs and thumbed her clit. He moaned his hot breath against the softest part of her belly and raised his eyes to meet her own.

I love pleasuring you, he told her with his unwavering gaze. Her lips parted and eyes closed, absorbing the palpitations of his sensual touch.

Cupping her sex, his fingers massaged deeper and deeper, stimulating her G-spot with rhythmic strokes and encouraging her to give in.

Yes, yes, yes… she nodded.

Yes, yes, yes, he confirmed with the force of his fingers, taking in the view of her mouth, breasts, and legs—slackening with arousal.

He lowered his tongue to her slit and licked her—once. She shuddered and heaved. He lowered her own hand between her legs to calm her inhibitions, settling her fingers within his own and penetrating her—together. Their fingers established long, repetitive beats that assuaged her insecurities and relaxed her inner thighs.

"God, Maribel. You're so beautiful."

She was gushing and glistening for him. He lowered his chin and licked her again—first a teasing flick over her clit—and then, indulging deeply in her sweetness. Her body quivered, then quaked. He accelerated his flicks until she could no longer control her need. She tried to draw him in. *No, not yet, not yet...*his firm hand commanded her. He quickly shifted their position, drawing her up into his arms and into his lap, wrapping her legs around his hips. He spread open her backside to fondle her with his forefinger.

She lowered her head against his shoulder with a submissive exhale. "Don't stop, don't stop...."

Miles had no intention of stopping. He massaged her in circles, priming her open with her own wetness. Then, he shifted his cock behind her and explored her with ginger tucks—slow, coy pressure from his tip that tested her tautness and glazed it with his own slickness without fully breaking through.

Within the darkness, Maribel's panting fell silent. He sensed her anticipation. He knew she assumed it was what he wanted, and she was willing to give it to him. He simply sought to stimulate every part of her body and arouse every part of her being. She encircled his wrists and braced herself for him to take her—completely.

Deeper?

Yes, deeper.

They both sighed as he slowly penetrated her, forging past the friction with one forbidden thrust. Her head dropped backwards as her mouth opened with an inaudible gasp. She arched her back and accepted him deeply.

I'm going to fall in love with you, Maribel Martinez...

Miles wasn't sure if he said it aloud or not, but he knew he could no longer deny it. They exchanged breaths through their heavy, consuming kisses. He embraced her with all his strength and drove inside her, again and again, wanting her to feel the physical consequences of his stolen heart. There was nothing in the world more important to him in that moment than his quest for her unconditional trust. Then, as if they had traded hearts and minds, they shuddered in unison with a fervor before falling back together against the stark white sheets of his bed. It had been the most intense two days of Miles' life—and yet, he knew it was only the beginning of his love for her.

Chapter Twelve

MILES AWOKE TO THE SMELL of pancakes. *Vanilla*, he thought and rose from the bed in search of the source of the sweet scent. Maribel was there in his kitchen, dressed in her rosebud pajamas and bunny slippers, manning a skillet and spatula over his massive stainless steel stove.

"Good morning." She smiled, her eyes tracking him to the island, where he slipped onto the black leather stool and watched as she flipped the bubbling pancake. He rubbed his face, half-awake, and admired her in the natural sunlight. Her black hair fell over her shoulders and her face was fresh and invigorated—blushing cheeks, full lips, shining eyes. It was the same woman he had sought to please last night, and now she was seeking to please him by making flapjacks.

"I missed you this morning." His eyes lingered on her.

"Sorry, I wanted to surprise you with breakfast."

"I am surprised. But I still missed you."

Maribel smirked, tender but sassy, as if she pretended not to believe him. She flipped the pancake with her spatula, then opened his refrigerator.

"You have everything in here. I snuck into your kitchen this morning, expecting it to be empty. Instead, I discovered a fully-stocked refrigerator. Milk, eggs, fruit, butter, cheese." Maribel closed his refrigerator and opened the sleek modern cabinets. "Even your pantry is stocked with baking ingredients."

"Courtesy of Fang Ji, my housekeeper."

"You even have whipped cream."

"Yummy. For later," he joked and circled around the island to steal a kiss. She shrugged him off and poured syrup onto his flapjack. Then, she guided him back to the island with a place mat and utensils.

"It will get cold," she said.

Settling into his seat with ease, he eyed her. "Delicious."

She slid around his red Brazilian hardwood floor in her bunny slippers like she was skating on ice. After pulling out the butter and cream from the refrigerator, she removed two mugs from the wall hooks. He loved watching her. It had been a long time since he had woken up with a woman who made him breakfast. Not only did he look forward to spending the whole day with Maribel, he looked forward to never letting her go.

She poured him a cup of black coffee and offered him cream. He shook his head and accepted the mug. He smiled and relaxed his bare chest against the edge of the island's granite countertop. He was completely naked, but comfortable as the morning sunlight basked against his bare back.

"You're spoiling me with your baking." He drank from his mug and endured the sharp heat of the coffee.

"Somebody needs to spoil you," she answered, looking at him over the rim of her mug.

"You spoiled me last night," he countered.

She lifted her brown eyes and sipped from her coffee, but she did not respond. Instead, her eyes shifted to his ringing phone, buzzing in front of them and interrupting their peaceful morning.

G-A-R-Y. The name flashed across the phone's screen.

"Answer call—speaker phone," Miles said to the device. Gary's obnoxious voice blared through its receiver. Miles noted the look of disappointment in Maribel's eyes as she turned away and poured more pancake batter into the skillet.

"Brax, where the hell have you been? I've been trying to get ahold of you all fucking morning."

"I've been busy," Miles replied, drinking from his mug, "eating pancakes." He winked at Maribel, who pretended not to enjoy the attention. "By the way, Gary, don't swear so early in the morning."

"Fucking blue balls, Brax... have you lost your fucking mind? I'm trying not to lose you a hundred million dollars, and you're telling me to stop swearing while you're eating pancakes on a fucking Monday morning?"

Miles stopped smiling. He registered the uncharacteristic alarm in Gary's voice, took up his phone, and switched off its speaker.

"A hundred million dollars is an over-statement, Gary. The Olson & Anderson deal is only worth thirty-five million."

"Fuck the Olson & Anderson deal. The Olson & Anderson deal is dead. They've signed with Zale at his Amory building. I'm talking about Faber and Orsolini."

"What about them?"

"She's taking them. Gillian's taking them all away."

Miles weighed Gary's words, trying to piece together their implications.

"She can't. We've got letters of intent."

"Screw the letters of intent. There's no signed leases. Are you planning to drag them into court with only letters of intent?"

Miles' mind raced as he calculated the potential loss of both lease deals. "Maybe," he hit back. "Or maybe I'll sue Gillian for breach of fiduciary duties, just to shake her up."

"Brax, this isn't the time to play revenge within your personal life. If you've been banging Gillian, and now she's pissed off at you for not calling, then *call* her, and get these deals back on track. Then, dump her after the ink is dry. But don't blow her off now."

Miles looked over at Maribel. She was organizing and re-organizing the kitchen, peeking into cabinets and drawers and surveying all the cookware and kitchen utensils that hadn't been touched for months. She pulled out the eggs from the refrigerator, cracked them into a bowl, and whisked them with milk. She was preparing scrambled eggs. He loved scrambled eggs.

"For fucksakes, Brax… who the hell is doing all that banging? Your cat?"

"I don't have a cat. Just a small mouse."

"Some fucking mouse."

Miles pulled the phone away from his ear. Gary's swearing was grating on him. Miles wondered if he used to sound that way. He felt the urgency to change.

"Look, Gary…if Gillian wants to fuc—" he stopped, and reconsidered his words carefully. "If she wants to kill all my deals, then so be it."

Gary suddenly fell silent. "Brax, I don't know what's gotten into you lately but we're talking about a lot of time and money here. These deals have been in the works for months. You piss away these deals and you're not going to be able to replace that kind of income overnight. Especially in this economy. We're talking about a big hole in your bottom-line. And for what? Because you've got a new itch that needs scratching and you've decided *now* is a good time to trade up for a younger, prettier pus—"

"Gary—" Miles sternly cut in. "Shut your mouth and stay the hell out of my personal life." He wanted to hang up on him. Every muscle in his body fought the urge to end the call and completely abandon his life.

"Okay, okay, fine." Gary backed off. "I'm your lawyer, not your conscience. But we're talking about over a hundred million dollars, and that's just the three deals Gillian can guillotine now. That's not even all the future business she'll drive to your competition."

Miles traced the same sparkling shard of quartz, embedded in the counter. "It's been easy money for too long, Gary," he finally said. "Time to make a change."

"Ahhh, fuck me, Brax. I hate it when you say that."

"Well, good… then you're used to it."

"Brax," Gary said, giving it one last kick at the can, "Gillian's acting like a scorned woman. And a scorned woman is nothing but a bitch-on-wheels. I don't know what happened or what you did to her, but just make sure you know what you're doing."

"I always do."

"Yeah, okay." Gary laughed with sudden relief because they both knew it was true. "And Brax…she must be some fucking stellar special mouse."

Miles smirked, watching Maribel cook scrambled eggs in her rosebud pajamas and bunny slippers. "She is, Gary. She is."

He hung up and flipped over his cell phone, face down on the countertop.

"Work?" she asked.

He nodded, but didn't offer more. Instead, he gazed out across the crystal waters of Lake Michigan, trimmed with ribbons of floating ice like frosting. It was going to be a beautiful, winter day. He tried hard not to think about all the ways he was going to lose millions of dollars.

"I have to go into work at one o'clock," Maribel reminded him. "Maybe we could go to the library before then. I love wandering through their exhibit halls on the ninth floor. We can even sneak into the Winter Garden. Its skylight atrium is amazing. Plus, it's the perfect day for it."

"The library?" Miles arched his eyebrow.

She narrowed her eyes at him. "Yeah, you know…a big public building where poor people congregate and borrow used books."

"Ahhhhh…I see," he softened the edge in his voice and moved around the island, attempting to heal her wounded pride with his embrace.

"You might even find something that you like there," she said.

"I already found something I like," he whispered in her ear with a kiss.

She tried to shrug away, but he refused to let her go. He nibbled her earlobe before covering her mouth and kissing her with long, intense petitions for forgiveness—until he was certain she would no longer flee from him. Then, he looked down at his plate of perfectly prepared scrambled eggs.

"The library, huh?" Miles tried to remember the last time he had read anything for pleasure. It had been years. He nudged her another kiss. "Sounds perfect."

Chapter Thirteen

MARIBEL SPENT THE FIRST hour of work reorganizing all the jewelry cases and daydreaming about Miles. It had been hard to stop thinking about him. They had spent the entire morning at the downtown public library—one of her favorite places in the Loop. They admired a few post-modern paintings and peeked into the Winter Garden before ending up on the seventh floor, drifting through the language and literature resources section while holding hands and silently leafing through stacks of literary classics. They had only been together three days, but already she felt like she couldn't wait to see him again. Before last night, she had been anxious about staying overnight at his apartment. She didn't want to move too far, too fast into something that could be over before she even had a chance to understand it. But after their night together—last night—everything changed for her.

From the beginning—from the very first moment he spoke to her three days ago—Miles made her feel like she was the only thing of value in his life. And when he undressed her... *God, yes, when he undressed her...* he made her feel like she was the only one who held the power to satisfy him. She had tested him last night, holding herself back because she needed reassurance that it was all more than just sex to him. He had sensed her reservations and let her take the lead. Now, she couldn't stop thinking about all the way he had pleasured her last night—the way he massaged her breasts and sucked her nipples; the way he had encouraged her to touch herself in front of him while he licked her most private parts and let her gush for him; the way he fingered her from behind, spreading open her backside and sliding his erection between her cheeks, stimulating her with his slick tip. The way she felt herself dilate with every tuck, slowly opening, then closing with heavy anticipation; the way he groped her thighs and backside before penetrating her. She still burned with the searing sensation of his firmness, and considered how he drove deep—

deeper than she ever thought possible—inside her and liberated all her defenses.

Last night, Miles had sealed their connection with the deepest intimacy she had ever known. But most importantly, he had articulated it with his whispering confession—*I'm going to fall in love with you, Maribel Martinez.* She tried hard not to dwell on whether or not he would. For now, she simply wanted to replay in her mind all the ways he had demonstrated it might come true.

No, she couldn't stop thinking about him—or his intimate touch. She could only mindlessly rearrange all the jewelry pieces in the cases, and fix her eyes on the luxury watches, considering every minute that ticked, ticked, ticked by…every moment which brought her closer to another night with him.

"Hello, I'd like to buy some jewelry."

The woman's sharp voice interrupted Maribel's thoughts. *Mink coat. Diamond ring. Alligator skin purse.* The woman was a serious customer.

"Yes, of course." Maribel quickly closed the case and turned to assist the woman. "How may I help you?"

"What's your most popular item?"

"Well, we have so many lovely pieces to choose from… it simply depends on your tastes and preferences."

"Gold." The woman laughed with abrupt candor. "And expensive."

It was almost a hiss. Maribel noted the woman's bright white teeth and shining smile.

"Gold," Maribel repeated. "Yellow or white?"

"Yellow, of course," the woman cried out, as if it was obvious. Then, her feline eyes dropped down onto Maribel's wrists.

"Although I must say… those are very nice. From here?"

"The tennis bracelet, no. But the watch, yes."

"Lovely," the woman nodded. "And that…?" Her eyes flicked at Maribel's ruby pendant.

"Yes, from here as well," she answered slowly. "Would you like to see our necklaces? We have a wonderful selection."

"Why not?" the woman laughed again, clicking her red fingernails across the top of the glass counter with a *rap, rap, rap.*

Maribel carefully considered all the options, then pulled out three choices and set them out onto the countertop. "Each of these necklaces is stylish and sophisticated, but each has its own specific flair—a short modern choker with Japanese pearls; a long braided chain with a twist diamond pendant; and a gold cable link chain with multi-colored gemstones…"

"I'll take all three," the woman said without a beat.

Maribel paused, replaying the woman's words to be sure she had heard "all three" correctly. The woman gazed at her with confidence. There was something about her that made Maribel feel inferior. The woman's impatience. Her bossiness. Her ability to know exactly what she wanted without even needing to weigh all her options. There was no hesitation in her voice; there was only chilling certainty.

"Okay, yes… wonderful."

"Separate boxes, of course."

"Yes, of course."

Then, the woman slipped her credit card across to Maribel.

Maribel lifted each necklace from the counter, turned to the register, and scanned the tags. *$4,556.51*. She couldn't believe the total. She double checked the screen, then confirmed the description of each item. *Almost five-thousand dollars*. Maribel had been certain the woman would purchase a necklace…or maybe even earrings. She never expected she would purchase all three. When Maribel returned to the counter with the printed receipt, she noticed the woman gazing down at her ladybug slippers.

"Comfortable?"

"Yes." Maribel flushed. "I have to stand all day, so heels can be a little much."

The woman squinted at Maribel, sizing her up. "You're really very modest, aren't you?" she snickered, as if it was the funniest observation in the world. "It's a good thing you've got such sparkling jewelry to spice you up."

Maribel suddenly felt uneasy. "Just your signature," she replied, returning to the register to finish the gift boxes.

"You know, I don't usually shop here. I prefer Tiffany's or Gucci. This is a bit low-end for me."

Maribel felt the sting of the comment, but kept focused. "We try to cater to all tastes and budgets." Her hands trembled as she clipped off the tags and rearranged the first necklace under tissue paper.

"Yes, I can see that," the woman hissed through her white teeth. "Unfortunately, I think I've changed my mind." She slid the signed receipt back across the counter. "I'll only take the pearl choker and multi-colored gemstone necklace. You can credit the third as a return without any trouble, I'm sure."

Almost five-thousand dollars. Maribel knew it had been too easy. She pulled the diamond pendant necklace out of its gift box—the most expensive of all three necklaces—and returned it to the case. Then, she re-scanned its clipped tag, and swiped the woman's credit card to produce the refund receipt.

"I'll just need your signature again," she said, offering the woman the remaining two necklaces, boxed up in a sleek shopping bag.

"Oops, looks like I've changed my mind again." The woman's sly eyes glazed over Maribel. "Won't be needing this one either."

The woman removed one of the boxes from the bag and pushed it back across the counter, then scrawled her signature across the first refund receipt. Maribel stopped and looked down at its illegible writing. *Why had she thought this woman was a serious customer*? Now, Maribel couldn't remember. She took back the second box and moved to the register. She processed the second refund and slid its receipt into the woman's red lacquered fingernails.

"Oops, changed my mind again… looks like I won't be needing any jewelry after all."

"Gillian—" Miles' voice cut across the Grand Lobby. Maribel spotted him, charging towards jewelry counter and the woman.

Gillian. Maribel had remembered the name and the way Miles' expression changed every time he answered her phone calls. The woman swiped back her credit card and the shopping bag, and turned to greet him.

"Fancy meeting you here, handsome," Gillian touched Miles' cheek with her hand, but he resisted it and glanced over at Maribel.

"Don't—" he warned Gillian, his voice stern.

They know each other well. Maribel tried hard not to stare.

"Just finishing up a little shopping. We're closing the Olson & Anderson deal with Harvey Zale, and I wanted to treat myself to something special. But then I realized I prefer a more upscale experience." Gillian finished her words like she was finishing a dry wine. "Really, Miles…I expected more from you." Her flat hazel eyes flicked over at Maribel.

"And I expected nothing less from you," Miles' shot back.

Gillian smirked and touched his tie. "When you get bored, give me a call."

Miles clenched his jaw and let her walk away without another word.

"Who is she?"

"My ex-real estate broker."

"Is that all?" Maribel pressed him. She wanted him to know it was true—she was modest, but not stupid.

Miles approached the counter and tenderly took up her hand. Cautioning him with her eyes, she attempted to pull away. *Someone might see them together…*

I don't care, he told her with his confident blue gaze and secured her hand.

"We're meeting again tonight." It wasn't a question.

"I don't know… perhaps it's better for me to go home tonight."

Their eyes locked.

"Don't—don't do this," he petitioned her, entwining his fingers within her own, as if he knew her pride had been wounded. "I'm sorry you had to deal with Gillian. She's my headache, not yours. Please tell me you're coming back to spend the night with me. Please…"

It was impossible to resist his earnest gaze, promising her that he would make it up to her. He was dressed in a shale grey, pinstriped suit and periwinkle blue shirt and tie. His hair was slick wet, fresh from a shower and shave, and his complexion radiated with warmth under the glare of the department store lights. He always looked so powerful and handsome during the work day. It was hard to say "no" to him.

"What's for dinner?" she asked with a reluctant smile.

"Soft tacos and fried ice cream."

He smiled at her. She grinned wider. It was her favorite and he knew it.

Chapter Fourteen

Savoring its cold sting against her skin, Maribel inhaled as the frozen ball of vanilla fried ice cream balanced itself on her tummy. They had eaten dinner in his penthouse, and then moved onto dessert: fried ice cream. She had finished hers in a matter of minutes, but he had saved his serving—until now. He had turned off all the lights in the kitchen and moved to undress her—sweater, bra, skirt, stockings, panties—by the light of the moon. Then, he undressed himself—shirt, tie, shoes, pants, socks, boxers—before spreading their naked bodies across the cool hard surface of the granite island. She was his sacrificial offering and he planned to indulge in her.

Miles slid the fried ice cream ball across her bare tummy and down to the tip of her pelvis. She shivered with anticipation, feeling the sleek polished granite against her arms and back, the sting of the fried ice cream between her legs, and the warmth of his hands, snaking her closer and closer towards him. He dangled her knees off the edge of the island and exhaled his hot breath between her legs. Maribel sighed and relaxed, just like he wanted. *Yes, she kneeeeeeeeeeeeeew him now...* She knew how much he loved the challenge of lowering her defenses, arousing her until she gushed, before priming her with the introduction of something sensual and forbidden.

The cool stream of ice cream drip, drip, dripped down over her crotch and she pressed her palms against the hard granite. Then, she felt him slowly lick her—cautiously, sensually, making sure not to enter her too fast until she consented it. *He always secured her consent.* She had fantasized about him all day, owning her in this way. When he was certain that she would not push him away or refuse more, he lowered his chin again and delved deeper, devouring the combined sweetness of the melting ice cream and her gushing wetness. She shuddered with each hot flick of his tongue.

God, he knew her body so well, better than she knew it herself.

He lifted his eyes in the darkness and told her what he wanted—*to bring her to climax with just his tongue.* Until their whirlwind affair, Maribel had rarely experienced an orgasm that she didn't produce herself. But that was Miles' secret, he made everything sensation feel natural and effortless. Miles dropped the ice cream ball between her legs and ate away part of its crust, then touched its stark velvet cream against her clit. She shuddered again, sparked by the nip of polar ice, before surrendering to the rushing warmth of his mouth, pleasuring her deeper, and deeper, and deeper than ever before.

She exhaled and raised her arms above her head, nodding to herself. *Yes, yes, yes, yes…she would try…how could she not try*? He took her cue, kneeling before her, raising her feet—one at a time—onto the curves of his bare shoulders before shifting her whole sex deeper into his mouth. *God, yessssssss…* She dug in her heels and arched her back. He spread open her cheeks and savored her. *God, yessssssssssss….* She fell into a daze and gazed over at the moon. It illuminated their ghostly reflection in the panoramic glass. It was as if she was watching someone else—someone prettier, sexier, naughtier—submitting to the dizzying euphoria of pure sexual domination. She could feel him, fully consuming her now—licking her clit with his tongue, then lapping her wetness. Her whole body quaked with the rhythm of his stimulation. She groaned, releasing control of every aspect of her femininity with a primal heave. Miles secured her ass into his hands and delved deeper with one final attempt to unleash her. She shuddered with vibrations, unlocking her climax in a way that made her whole body spasm with violence before an overwhelming sense of relaxation rushed through her inner core.

Miles enveloped her body and guided them over to the broad leather cushions of his couch.

"Fire," he called into the shadows. The gas fireplace automatically blazed on and he massaged her with warmth—her breasts, nipples, and backside were chilled from their exposure to the drafty air and the cool surface of the island.

Maribel savored the heat from the fireplace and how its warm glow complemented Miles' handsome profile. He lowered his lips and kissed her mouth. His sensitivity disarmed her—it always disarmed her—and it inspired her confession. "I'm always so reluctant to give myself over to you. But then, you always find a way to make me feel like I can't resist." The crackling fire comforted her with a sense of peace and security.

"Why are you so reluctant?" he asked. His chin nestled over her shoulder and his body draped over her like a blanket.

"Because I'm afraid of what happens when you realize I'm not as special as you think I am."

Miles pushed himself up onto one hand and gazed down at her, the light from the fireplace blazing in his eyes. "Maribel—" he asserted. "Every day we spend together, I find out you're more special than I had ever imagined."

She rolled her eyes. He laughed. "What? You don't believe me?"

His warm cock rested against her thigh. She playfully nudged him away. "No, I don't."

"Maribel," he suddenly grew serious. "This isn't just about sex for me."

She shifted her eyes to the fire. He had just named her most intense fear, but she wasn't ready to admit it to him. Even if it was just about sex, she didn't mind because they had been the most intimate, passionate three days of her life. She just didn't want it to end before she had a chance to know—somehow—if she was truly different to him than all the others.

"Maribel," Miles repeated with firm command, "this isn't just about sex for me."

"But we barely know each other..." she whispered, look away through the panoramic windows at the black night.

"No, you're wrong," he countered, pressing his body tighter against her own. "I've been watching you every day since you were sixteen, every day since I helped you get your job interview. I fully expected you to fail, so I kept my eye on you—every day. In the beginning, I expected you to show up late to work, call in sick, or simply quit—pushed out by the demands of working retail. I was convinced that I had made a mistake in appeasing my aunt and recommending you as a new hire—convinced that somehow it would come back to bite me. So every afternoon, I came down from my office, just to prove to myself that I was right. You know what...? It was you who proved me wrong because you never missed a day of work—not once."

"I didn't realize you had even bothered to notice me."

Maribel looked up at Miles. His eyes were locked on hers, and he held her in his arms like she was his most prized possession.

"And I didn't realize how determined you were," he admitted. "That was the first thing I learned about you."

She listened to his confession and settled into his embrace. Her mind drifted back ten years to those early days. "I wasn't sure that I was going to be able to do it all—work and continue going to school every day. But I knew I didn't have a choice, and I was so grateful to be able to make enough money to take care of my mom and pay our rent. And yes, I was terrified of being late. I actually got permission from my high school to leave early every day, just to make sure I could get to work early. I knew from my mother that I was taking over Mrs. Strauss' position as a sales clerk. I knew she had been there for forty-five years, and that everyone knew and loved her, so I had to make a good first impression. But I didn't know you were watching me."

"I was watching you—carefully. Every afternoon, when I boarded the elevator, I told myself that I was checking on you to appease my own pride, but really, I was checking on you because I had become interested in you. You were so young, but already mature beyond your years. I remember overhearing you greeting the customers. You were always so polite. '*Is there anything I can help you with today*?'" He mimicked her soft voice and sincerity. They both laughed with ease. Maribel attempted to push him away, but he refused to let her go.

"And that was the next thing I learned about you—your understated sense of composure and grace, which intrigued to me because I was so different. I was a self-centered, arrogant, twenty-something bachelor who didn't care about anyone or anything other than making money and proving to the world that I was a force to be reckoned with—just because I had bought a bunch of downtown properties, I expected the world to answer to me."

"You did seem a bit arrogant," she betrayed with a smile. "You used to stop in the middle of the Grand Lobby and finish your business calls before heading into the elevators. I remember I could hear you talking sometimes—all the way in the ceramics section."

Miles flopped his head into her chest with shame. She giggled and stroked his hair. "Don't worry. All the sales girls loved it. You were quite the topic of conversation during our lunch breaks."

"But you knew better, I'm sure."

Maribel shrugged. "I was too young and too busy to involve myself with those kinds of things."

"Yes." His eyes fixed on her. "I always saw you on Saturday nights and wondered why you weren't out with your friends or boyfriend. Instead, you were always there at the department store, folding underwear and arranging socks. You didn't have much of a chance to be young and carefree, did you?"

Maribel fell silent. There was no sense in feeling sorry for herself then—or now. She turned the question back onto him. "What were you doing at the department store on a Saturday night? Didn't you have better things to do?"

The contour of his chin shifted in the darkness, and his heavy legs and warm chest released his weight from her body.

"Keenly perceptive." Miles leaned back against his arm. "I've come to learn that about you as well." He suddenly grew pensive, as if he was gauging the emotional gravity of what he was about to say to her. "Those months after my aunt passed away, I would stay at the office for hours after it got dark, usually drinking and feeling sorry for myself. My mother died when I was young. My father and I hadn't spoken in years. My aunt was the only person in my life who knew the real me, knew I was just a lonely, insecure kid with too much money and too little sense to know what to do with it. So those days after she passed were some of the hardest days of my life. That's why every night, I would come down from my office and walk through the department store, just to kill time so I wouldn't have to come here—alone. And it became a routine for me, a comfort, because I knew I would have the chance to see you, and somehow, that made everything a little more bearable."

"I had no idea..." Maribel's voice faded as she watched the light from the fireplace reflect the emotions deep in his eyes. She didn't know he had lost his own mother at a young age, nor did she realize the pain he endured with the passing of his aunt. She suddenly felt the need to reveal something painful of her own. "I remember how one night, you made an effort to come up to me and acknowledge my mother's death. I was careful not to ever tell anyone about her illness because I was scared that someone would report me to the State. So when she finally passed, the grief was like a secret that I had to hide. It's one thing to suffer, but something even worse when you have to suffer in silence. But I remember how you came up to me and touched my shoulder and said—'Maribel, I'm sorry to hear about your mother. She was a special woman who cared about you very much'—before striding away. I barely knew who you were, or that your aunt and my mother had been sick together, and yet, those few simple words of condolence meant the world to me."

"I didn't realize you remembered that."

"How could I ever forget it?"

Their eyes locked. He suddenly kissed her—longer, deeper, more penetrating than ever before. It was more than just a kiss, and they both felt it.

"See? How can I resist you when you kiss me like that?" Maribel laughed through the darkness. He was invading her heart and she knew there would be consequences. "What if it's all too far, too fast?"

"Three days of sex doesn't make a relationship, Maribel. I won't deny that because I know it's true. I've had more casual relationships than I care to admit, and that's how I know that this is different for me."

"What do you mean?"

"I mean, it's usually just a game to me—a game of power and control, a way to prove that I can have anything I want—even things money can't buy. I've never pursued the sexy receptionists, or the pretty assistants, or flirtatious wives whose husbands I wanted to fuck over in a business deal. I've always pursued the bitchiest woman—the hard-ass M&A lawyers, the uptight accountants, even the catty clients who claimed to hate Chicago and my buildings because they didn't have the prestige and glamour of a Park Avenue address—just to see if I could get them to relinquish their ice queen personas by getting them flat on their backs."

There was a somber moment between them, as if they were both absorbing the significance of his confession. Maribel sensed that he wanted to tell her more, so she fell silent and let the sound of the crackling fire help him gather his thoughts.

"But it's been a shameful way to waste my time—and theirs—because it brought me nothing but misery and taught me nothing except that I've been acting like a narcissistic bastard who only cares about reaffirming his own shallow ego. So I understand your concerns, and why you think this might just be all about sex for me. But nothing could be more different because you couldn't be more different."

"Is that how you know Gillian?" Maribel was careful with her question; she heard the caution in her own voice, as if she wanted to know, but was afraid to hear the answer. And she heard the hesitation in Miles' answer.

"Gillian is one of those relationships that I regret…yes," he finally confirmed.

"And now?"

"And now… she has the power and the ruthlessness to try to destroy as many of my business deals as she can. And I'm fine with that. I'm fine with the monetary loss—even if it's millions of dollars—if it means regaining a bit of my soul. But I'm not fine with her trying to destroy the trust between me and you." His strong arms drew the warmth of her body back against his own.

"What we have between us is something that I can't explain and don't want to understand. I only want to protect it because it's the only thing making me feel like I'm happy to be alive. And I can't change the past. I can't change all the mistakes I've made, but I can strive to be a better man—now and in the future. And I can strive to be a better man with someone like you by my side."

She sensed that he was waiting, waiting for her to meet his eyes to prove how much he was willing to give to her—how much of himself he was willing to share. When she finally found the courage to look at him, he was staring at her with such intensity that it dissolved all of her insecurities about his motives and intentions. They had stripped themselves physically and emotionally bare, and now there was nothing left between them except the inevitability of losing themselves completely to the other. Miles kissed her deeply, then lapped his lips over her belly, breasts, and neck. He did not seek to overpower her, like so many times before. This time was different. He rose to his knees, permitting her to stroke his erection and fondle his sack, closing his eyes and releasing his tension. He rarely granted her the opportunity to touch him, but now, he released a sigh that revealed he was making himself vulnerable to her. He cradled her head and kissed her again—and again—and again. Then, he stopped and stared into her eyes, and confessed from his heart what his gaze had already requested.

"I want to make love to you, Maribel." His request filled her with a hush of silence. He grasped her hand into his own. "Will you let me make love to you?"

She held his gaze, steady. Their fingers entwined. She kissed him with longing, giving him the answer.

He guided her to the couch and sought out her lips, his tongue ravenously seeking out her own—luscious sweeps that entangled their breaths. Her arms crossed over his shoulder as he mounted her and slipped his firm erection between her legs, settling it where they both wanted it most. Maribel closed her eyes and submitted herself to the heavy weight of his powerful body.

He cupped her chin and stroked her cheek. *Was she ready to accept him?*

She had never been more ready.

She raised her hips, inviting him in. He accepted, entering her with slow deliberation.

Yeeeeeessssssssssssssss… Maribel gasped, feeling the initial burn of friction before it bled into pleasure.

"You feel amazing," he exhaled and thumbed her clit.

God, how he always made her feel so amazing. She arched her back, absorbing the firmness of his cock and the stimulation of his fingers. Every part of her body ached to submit to him in every possible way. Then, with a guarded thrust, he drove into her again, his cock searing deeper than before. Maribel embraced his chest and accepted him with silent yearning for forever. He hugged her in return—a simple admission that something had changed between them. She sensed the change and relaxed wider for him. He shifted himself deeper inside her and caressed her cheek. She prepared herself for the full force of his desire as he accelerated his pace with a determination to unite them in a way that neither one had anticipated, but could no longer repress. They both groaned. Miles halted his thrust, controlling his urge to climax before her. He wanted them to feel it together.

Maribel understood. She wanted it, too. She lifted her arms and relaxed, allowing him to slip out his cock and slip in his fingers, building her up with every sigh. *He had come to know her so well,* she moaned, *so…so…well…* He slid his free hand under her backside and groped her cheeks, loosening her inhibitions and encouraging her to contract and release her wetness around his fingers.

"Yes, that's it. I can feel you changing," he whispered, and they savored her quivers while alternating between kisses of affection and passion. She gave into every stroke, letting him build her up with the promise of an intimacy between them that she had never experienced with any other man. His hot cock throbbed—hard and swollen—against her thigh, but still, he was holding off until she was flushed and ready to release herself to him. Suddenly, she seized with a spasm of arousal. He pacified her with a hush, and lowered his lips to suck her nipples, listening to the change of her every breath. *Yesssssssssssssss…* the force of his hot mouth over her breasts and the rhythm of his stroking fingers between her legs finally ignited a series of trembles and quakes that only he had ever produced. Primed and shuddering, she reached out for him and drew his ear to her lips.

"I'm ready for you."

Miles pressed his forehead against her own—acknowledging the worth of her unconditional trust. He pulled her up from the couch and steadied her against the couch's back rim. His tongue swept into her ear and washed down her neck. Cupping her breasts with his hands and pressing his pelvis against her backside, he spread her stance with his knees and penetrated her from behind—a long enduring thrust that consummated the sincerity of their union with one decisive lunge. He accelerated his pace and pumped inside her again and again, over and over, faster and faster until she could no longer deny what he was determined to prove to her with his masculine force and strength. They surged in unison, the warmth of his undulating ripples coursing inside her. Maribel collapsed into Miles' embrace. He spooned her body and wedged them into the leather cushions with a sensitivity that she had never known. The sound of the crackling fire consumed their thoughts and slowed the rhythm of their respirations—panting, emotional breaths that acknowledged what had changed between them. Maribel had never been in love before. And now, she was certain that she never wanted it to end.

Chapter Fifteen

SOOTHED BY THE MORNING sun shining in through the sweeping bedroom windows. Maribel awoke alone in Miles' bed. The distant murmurs of conversation traded back and forth, and the distinct aroma of breakfast wafted through the air. She spotted her pajamas, carefully folded and lying at the foot of the bed. It was a signal for her to get dressed and come find him whenever she was ready.

She wandered through the long open hallways and found Miles in the kitchen, doing battle with a skillet and a pan full of bacon. The grease and meat crackled, like the reception of the voice coming through Miles' speakerphone, resting on the countertop.

"It's still on the table. The Olson & Anderson deal is *still* in play, but he can't get the deal done because you've been M.I.A. since Friday."

Maribel sat down on a barstool at the island. Miles turned and greeted her with his eyes; they were bright and inviting. He looked fresh from a shower, his dark hair slicked back and his skin smooth from a shave. He was wearing his matching athletic shirt and pants, which accentuated his tall form and well-toned chest.

He mouthed to her—*Good morning.*

She smiled and mouthed it back. He leaned over the island for a kiss and passed her a mug with more cream and sugar than coffee. *He had been paying attention,* she thought as she sipped it. *He knew exactly how she liked her coffee.* She glanced at the island and thought about last night. It felt like they were newlyweds, embarking on their first morning as an official couple.

She looked down at his phone. *His lawyer*, she noted, recognizing his abrupt voice and the context of their conversation. Miles was right; they weren't going to leave him alone—even if he wanted them to.

"Gillian's been pissing down our backs and telling us it's raining, Brax. But I just talked to Olson. He still wants in at your Field's building—and in on your terms. "

Miles winked at her. He seemed relaxed and playful. Swapping out the spatula and skillet for plates and forks, he arranged each setting on the island. He was in control of their breakfast destiny—everything else could wait.

"Hello? Hello? Have I lost you? Am I talking to myself here?"

"I heard you, Gary," Miles answered him. "I'm just not certain that I care anymore."

"You—don't—care?" Gary repeated, slowly. "Boy, Brax, you're either playing hardball as punishment or you're seriously hung over—or both. I truly have no idea what you've been doing for the past four days that could possibly make you *not* care about closing a thirty-five million dollar deal."

"I'm making bacon," he replied, flipping over a sizzling strip before lifting it from the skillet and onto a plate. "And if you were here, Gary, I'd share some of it with you, and we'd take a moment to simply sit back and enjoy the finer moments of life." Miles chomped down on the bacon, then offered a taste to Maribel. She accepted. *It was delicious.*

"Oh, fuck me, Brax. Have you gone completely Zen Hippie Hare Krishna on me? Please tell me you haven't shaved your head and that you're fully dressed."

"Haven't shaved my head—yet," Miles quipped. "And Hare Krishnas don't eat meat, by the way. Clothes, on the other hand, tend to be optional around here."

"Ugh," Gary crowed. "TMI, Brax. T-M-I."

Miles snickered with juvenile delight—the same amusement that Maribel had often seen when he teased her.

"Well, you've left me with no choice." Gary sighed. "I've invited Don Olson here for dinner tonight and told him that you'd be here to ink the deal."

"Gary—" Miles suddenly warned him, as if he had pulled this trick before.

"Look, Brax, I'm your lawyer, not your maid. I'm here to close your deals, not clean up after you when you've pissed everything away."

"Maybe I have other plans tonight."

"Other plans? Like what?"

"Like ice skating and hot chocolate."

"Brax, what the hell is going on with you? Have you completely lost your mind?"

"Probably."

"Okay, I get it. You don't want to waste any more time. Message received loud and clear. So let's get to the bottom-line—I've got a final contract here with every single one of your original lease terms, and Olson is ready to sign when you're ready to sign. So just get into that fancy helicopter of yours and get here tonight, and then go back to living in your fucking merry winter wonderland—thirty-five million dollars richer."

Miles looked at Maribel.

Helicopter? she mouthed.

He shrugged, widening his pinched fingers. *Just a small one.*

"What's for dinner?" Miles suddenly asked.

"Whatever the fucking hell you want, Brax. Just tell me what will get you here."

"You, Gary—promising to cease your usage of the f-bomb for at least twenty-four hours."

"Oh, for fucksake," Gary snapped back.

"I mean it," Miles countered. "And…" he stalled until he had he came up with the perfect request. "Tacos and fried ice cream."

"Oh, holy hell…Are you completely high? And I suppose you expect me to wear a fuc—freaking sombrero and hire a goddamn mariachi band?"

"Sure, why not?"

"Great, just great. Tacos, fried ice cream, sombrero, mariachi. Anything else, El Capitán?"

"Nope. Just put me down for one." Miles smiled and winked at Maribel. "Plus guest."

Chapter Sixteen

WHOOSH, WHOOSH, WHOOSH, whoosh, whoosh, whoooooooooosh…Through her protective headphones, Maribel heard the gyrating pulse of the helicopter blades through the air and the pilots in the cockpit reciting their navigation calls. Miles swung his arm around her for comfort as they lifted off the helipad on the rooftop of his condo building and suspended high in the middle of the twilight sky. *It was terrifying and exhilarating.* She shivered with fear and delight as the chilling wind beat against the helicopter's doors. Maribel tracked the helicopter's shadow, slinking across the rooftops of skyscrapers until they eventually reached the shoreline. Cruising faster and faster across the vast open waters of Lake Michigan, the jagged city skyline soon became only a distant memory. It was a beautiful evening, made more beautiful by the promise of what was yet to come. By tomorrow, Miles's business deals would be closed and he would be a free man who intended to whisk her away on his yacht—just the two of them—and make love to her in the serenity of the moonlight.

And then, as quickly as they jetted into the sky and across Lake Michigan, they slowed their pace and descended to the earth. *They were there already.* The helicopter cleared the rocky bluffs before touching down onto the expansive green pasture near the edge of the lakefront estate. Miles pushed open the door and spotted the co-pilot waiting to receive Maribel into his hands.

Swoooooooosh… The gusting draft from the helicopter blades whipped them away from the machine and through the garden terrace towards the glowing lights of the Prairie-style mansion. Miles slowed their pace as he led them up a stone stairway and into the open patio, as if it were his own residence.

Several couples mingled near an open pit fireplace with cocktails and rowdy laughter. They turned and greeted Miles with familiarity.

"You just can't arrive in limousines like the rest of us, can you, Brax?" one of the women exclaimed.

"It wouldn't be Miles Braxton-Worth any other way," her date replied. "Glad to see you finally made it. Gary said you've been tied up with extracurricular activities. Can't wait to hear all about them."

"Nothing to tell, Pete," Miles answered. "Business as usual."

"Which means he doesn't kiss and tell, Pete," the woman said with a flirtatious shrug of her bare shoulder.

"Well, neither do I—officially," Pete countered, flashing his wedding band.

The woman rolled her eyes. It suddenly was clear to Maribel that she wasn't Pete's wife. The woman was dressed in a sleek ivy green dress and vibrant purple stiletto heels. She sipped from her martini and eyed Maribel. *Women always know how to size up other women*, Maribel thought, as she locked hands with Miles who seemed intent on guiding her through the sliding screen doors and away from the couple, avoiding introductions. She knew he hated the idea of returning to his former life—so soon after escaping it—but he especially hated the idea of directly exposing Maribel to it.

"Brax, I'm starting up a new hedge fund in China, we should talk…" Pete called after them.

Miles nodded while ushering Maribel into the house without delay. She glanced back at the woman whose eyes flicked up and down her. Maribel suddenly felt self-conscious in her silver sequined cocktail dress and shearling coat that Miles had chosen for her to match his ivory Italian suit and lavender shirt.

"You look stunning," Miles reassured her, as if he had read her thoughts. His compliment relaxed her. He always had that effect on her, despite the fact that she was clearly the newcomer—the novelty—who commanded everyone's attention the moment they entered the mansion and into the grand living room. Live mariachi music bounced off its glass-paneled walls and cathedral ceilings. Guests mingled near the elegant mahogany bar and lounged around a billiard table. Maribel caught the inviting draft from the freestanding fireplace, suspended in the middle of the room, burning like a cyclone of modern art.

"Brax—" a voice boomed over the trumpets and maracas.

Both Maribel and Miles turned towards a tall, handsome man jetting towards them. He wore a tailored navy suit with matching vest and a ridiculously large black sombrero.

Miles immediately shook his hand. "Impressive," he said, noting the guests, live band, catering staff, and finally his friend's ostentatious sombrero.

"I am both a man of the law and a man of my word," Miles' friend replied, throwing back his tumbler and crunching on the ice.

Gary, Maribel thought. She always envisioned Miles' foul-mouthed lawyer as a short, pudgy, bald, exceedingly ugly man. But instead, he was fashionable, tanned, and beautiful—like all of his other guests.

Gary fixed his eyes on Maribel. "I wasn't certain you were going to show, and now, I understand why. Please tell me this is the little mouse whose cheese you've been stealing the entire weekend and all shall be forgiven." Gary moved behind Maribel and politely removed her coat.

Miles smirked with mischief. Clearly, they were old friends who knew more about each other than they cared to share. Maribel expected Miles to officially introduce her, but Gary cut in first. "Congratulations, Brax. You've got everyone chasing their tails. No one expected this deal to be postponed for this long." Apparently, Gary was focused on business this evening.

"I'm not the one who decided to shop it."

"But you were the one who decided to put a freeze on it all weekend long. So are you here to close it or not?"

"That depends. How much am I supposed to give up?"

"I have the seventy-page contract on my desk in the den." Gary lowered his voice and gnawed on his last ice cube. "They've included every single deal point except the escalation. They're keeping it at eight. But you've got him by the balls because Olson doesn't want to be in Harvey Zale's palm… Hello, Marzena, lovely as always." Gary suddenly took the woman's hand and swept her close for a side kiss on the cheek.

"Thank you, darling," she slurred with her heavy Slavic accent. "I love the Mexican *hor d'oeuvres* and the margaritas." She lifted up her empty glass.

"Yeah, requested by the man of the hour." Gary nodded at Miles.

"Nice to see you, Brax." The woman held out her hand for Miles to touch it, just as she was slinking away to the bar. "It's been such a long time."

"Marzena, tell him to be nice to me tonight," Gary teased. "I'm on his side."

Marzena pouted on cue. "Don't be too much of a meanie tonight, Brax. It's still so early. Do whatever Gary wants, then come have drinks."

The woman never once looked at Maribel and Maribel noticed it. She also noticed how Miles' eyes lingered on the woman's fishnet stockings and how it was she who finally pulled away from his fingertips. It was as if everyone had forgotten Maribel was even in the room, including Miles.

"Escalation at eight percent is bargain for them." Miles flipped back to business. "I asked for thirteen."

"Don't be a stubborn son-of-a-bitch, Brax. Olson's here to do the deal, and I can probably get him to nine. But he's ready to sign, and the contract has the escalation set at eight. He's been waiting for you the last freaking hour. If you blow up the deal tonight, all bets are off."

Miles scanned the grand living room. His eyes rested on a group of laughing guests near the decorative champagne waterfall.

"What's she doing here?" Miles suddenly asked.

"Who, Gillian?" Gary followed his gaze. "She's with them. I know you dropped her on her ass, but she's still their broker on the deal. Plus, you know Gillian better than anyone. She's a canine bitch—her jaws won't open until her teeth meet."

Maribel glanced over at the group. There was an older, stout man in a tan suit. Standing beside him and touching his elbow was a mature woman with bleached hair and heavy make-up. *The wife*. Then, Maribel spotted another blonde woman, holding a margarita with a pink umbrella. She threw back her head with grating laughter from her full red lips. Maribel recognized her from the department store, but more importantly, she recognized the way Miles was glaring at her. Miles slowly loosened his clasp of Maribel's hand—a signal that she was losing him to them.

Miles nodded over to the group. "Are you going to bring Olson over or do I have to do everything?" he snapped at Gary.

Gary grinned with a glint in his eye. Stopping a server in a black catering uniform, he lifted two glasses of white wine from his tray and passed them to Miles and Maribel. "Take the edge off first. I'll see if I can warm him up before getting you two in the same room."

Gary stole a tray of *hor d'oeuvres* from another server, then swaggered over to the group and greeted them with exuberance. Maribel glanced at the server—dark eyes, dark hair, olive skin. She seemed lost without her catering tray and purpose in the room. The woman did not make eye contact with Maribel; she simply scurried across the hardwood floors and up the stairs. Maribel scanned the guests and the rest of the catering staff. At any other time in her life, under any other circumstance, she would only be allowed to attend the party as part of the wait staff, not as a guest. She suddenly felt like an imposter at a costume party.

Maribel looked over to Miles for comfort. They were alone—their first moment of privacy since they had left the city. She waited for a word of encouragement from him, a gentle touch of his hand or a tender smile. But instead, he downed his wine and gazed over at Gary, who was schmoozing the group with boisterous conversation, pulling off his sombrero and slapping his own backside like he was a rodeo rider.

"Gary can be such an asshole," Miles muttered, almost to himself. His eyes fell back onto the intense glowing helix of the fireplace. Clearly agitated, he clenched his jaw while his blue eyes hardened like stone. He was the one in charge. He was the one who called the shots. Everyone needed him now. And yet, he was the one who seemed trapped, unable to let it all go.

"I must have the honor of meeting your gorgeous date…"

The smooth voice came from behind Maribel. The attractive man immediately held out his hand to her and introduced himself. "Timothy."

"Maribel," she said. He was the first person to introduce himself to her.

"Pleasure to meet you." Timothy released her hand with a nod, then turned his attention to Miles. "Gary didn't think you would show. He accused me of not properly doing my job."

"You can only manage my money, Timmy. You can't manage me."

"Well, that's certainly true, Brax. I suspect your new lovely friend has learned that lesson as well." Timothy's eyes twinkled at her. They were friendly and unpretentious, and she finally felt at ease in the conversation.

"Brax—" Gary abruptly called out across the room. "C'mon over here so we can draw swords and fight to the death."

Miles reluctantly smiled.

"There you go." Timothy nodded, sipping from his brandy. "Leave it to Gary to force all the enemies in one room, just to see how much blood they'll draw."

"Five minutes. And then we'll go outside to look at the stars," Miles promised her, attempting to sound reassuring. She knew he was there to do the deal, but she also felt her heart sink when he turned to leave her behind. "Take care of her for me," Miles instructed Timothy.

"If she can handle you, Brax, I'm fairly certain she can take care of herself."

Maribel forced a smile. She wasn't a child. She could hold her own.

Miles patted Timothy on the shoulder; nothing more needed to be said. He winked at Maribel before crossing the living room and joining Gary and the Olson group. Authoritative like a naval officer in his ivory European suit, Miles immediately commanded their attention, as if he was ready to do battle and win.

"You all have known each other for a long time, haven't you?" Maribel noted.

"Fraternity brothers from college. Except Brax—he got kicked out of the frat house after his first year."

"Really, why?"

"He slept with the fraternity president's girlfriend." Timothy suddenly laughed and softened his voice. "Don't look too concerned. The president was a real prick and his girlfriend deserved better…and got it. Brax fell in love with her and treated her like a queen. They got engaged within the year."

It sounded like the Miles she knew—sweet, romantic, devoted—and yet, it was a part of his life that he had never dared to share. "What happened?"

"Life." Timothy replied. "Brain aneurysm. She didn't even make it to the hospital. Too bad, too. She was a great girl. You know…you look a little bit like her, if you don't mind me saying."

"No, I don't mind," Maribel said, her voice trailing off in thought.

They paused in silence and gazed into the mesmerizing plasma churn of the fireplace. Suddenly, the Olson group burst out with laughter. Miles was their center of attention. It was hard not to notice how easily he seemed to fit in with them.

"I was a Finance major. Gary—Pre-law. Brax—Calculus… But Brax dropped out after Cristina died. Then, within six months, he had made his first million. That's when Gary and I knew he was someone to stay close to."

"He never told me how he made his money."

Maribel's eyes followed Miles. He was heading up a flight of stairs, but stopped to look back at Gillian who lingered behind him. They were staring at each other, as if they were the only ones in the room, and it suddenly made Maribel flush with jealousy.

"Yeah, Brax prides himself on being an enigma. See that guy?" Timothy nodded over to the man hunched on a stool at the bar. "That's Brax's former business partner. They started working at the Chicago Board of Trade at the same time. Brax created a proprietary trading algorithm and Mitchell sold it to one of the big pension hedge funds for a ninety/ten split. That was the last time Brax ever let someone sell him short in a deal, I guarantee you. A year later, Brax created a second trading algorithm and sold it himself. Five years later, Brax was buying his first downtown Chicago building while Mitchell was fighting foreclosure on his North Shore home. It was Brax who bailed him out. Paid off the debt and brought Mitchell back into the fold to manage their own hedge fund together. That's the difference between owning your own destiny versus selling out someone else's. It's not a business strategy for Braxton, it's a way of life."

"I couldn't agree more," the sly female voice said from behind them.

"Hello, Gillian," Timothy politely greeted her.

"Hello, Handsome," she countered, reaching out her long red nails to adjust his tie. "Babysitting?" She glanced over at Maribel.

"Getting acquainted," he corrected her. "Shouldn't you be in the war room?"

Gillian shrugged. "War is for men. Clubbing each other over the head isn't exactly the way women go about getting what they want. Am I right?" Gillian lobbed the question to Maribel.

"I think I'm going to freshen up my drink," Maribel replied, searching for a diplomatic escape.

"Oh, that's what Timmy is for." Gillian swiped Maribel's wine glass from her hand and passed it to him.

"Chardonnay?" he asked Maribel.

"Yes, that's fine, thank you," she answered with quiet dread. Her mind was quickly considering some way she could accompany Timothy rather than being left alone with Gillian.

"And you, my dear?" Timothy asked her.

"Whatever she's having," Gillian flirtatiously tossed back, outlining his chin with her fingertip. "Thanks, love. You're always such a doll."

Timothy hesitated, as if to convince himself that Gillian would behave herself before returning to the bar. When the two women were finally alone, Gillian sneered at Maribel, noting her luxury watch.

"Well, isn't that romantic. You two must really be hitting it off."

Maribel had been bullied in elementary school on the school bus; she knew stoic silence was her best defense. But she could still feel Gillian's glare, burning into her.

"Let me guess," Gillian continued, her sickly green eyes trailing down Maribel's neckline. "The ruby pendant necklace was first. Brax does always like to start modest. Can't set expectations too high from the start, or else the Tiffany jewelry won't seem like such a stunning surprise."

She reached out and gripped Maribel's wrist, rotating the diamond tennis bracelet into full view. "See what I mean? I'm sure he bought you *that* lovely thing after you agreed to sleep with him the first time. Although I'm surprised he settled on platinum. He always chose yellow gold for me. Then, again…he never offered me anything other than jewelry. Oh, and great sex. But in some ways, that was enough. He does have an irresistible way with food, doesn't he?"

Maribel felt her cheeks flush red. She glanced over at the bar. Timothy was still waiting for their drinks. She looked around at all the elegant strangers—no one offered her sanctuary. Maribel felt herself trying not to frown, but instead, she frowned more.

Gillian lowered her voice and sighed. "Or maybe he simply thinks you're special. I'm sure he's told you that already, am I right? It's one of his favorite lines. Although it looks like he's forgotten the earrings. Maybe *that* will be his surprise gift tonight after he closes the Olson & Anderson deal. He always bought me something grandiose whenever we closed a deal. Although Brax is also good at getting whatever he wants for as little as possible. Maybe he figures a shop girl at a department store isn't that hard to please, and he can get away with giving nothing extra at all."

"You couldn't be more wrong about him," Maribel spat back, abruptly countering with a flash of anger.

"Ahhhh, so you do have a personality? Not just a pretty face," Gillian surveyed her. "I was wondering what your appeal was to him. But I see it now. Brax does always like a good challenge. Watch out for that granite island in his penthouse... it's one of his favorite places to get you flat on your back."

Maribel tried, unsuccessfully, to control the waver in her voice. "Perhaps it was all about sex for you. But it's different between us," she asserted, feeling desperate to defend Miles as well as their relationship.

"Really? I don't think so, cupcake. I'm sure it feels like 'love' now—that's how they *all* get us to submit in the beginning, and convince us to spread our legs open and often. But I've known Brax for years. You and Brax have only been together less than a week, am I right?"

Maribel's eyes swam with emotion. "How would you know that?"

"Because he only broke it off with me a few days ago," Gillian confessed, like it was a dark secret. "Unless…of course, you think he's been double-dipping."

Maribel suddenly felt nauseous. Gillian's hissing voice and the smell of her cigarette breath was simply too much to bear. She turned away and bumped into Timothy, who had returned with their wine.

"Excuse me," she said, pushing past him and out of the main entrance. Timothy called after her, but it only motivated her to rush out the door where she spotted several parked limousines and their drivers, smoking and loitering in the circular driveway.

"Please, could one of you drive me back to Chicago?" Maribel rummaged through her purse. "I have forty dollars. Please, anyone?"

"I can drive you back."

Maribel glanced at the source of the voice. The man looked like he could be her younger brother. He didn't give her any clue as to how or why he was able to leave the party. Perhaps he knew he would be waiting on his clients all night, and figured he could get to the city and back before dawn. Perhaps he noticed the mascara streaming down her face, or the fact that she was shivering uncontrollably in the winter night air without her coat. Perhaps forty dollars was simply worth the three-hour round trip drive. Regardless of the reason, the driver swiftly blunted out his cigarette with his boot, saved the remainder in his pocket, and opened the passenger door of his limousine for her.

"Thank you," she said softly, wiping black streaks from her cheeks while trying hard not to look at him again. She slipped across the limo's black leather seats and bit her lip. With trembling hands, she removed the ruby pendant, tennis bracelet and luxury watch that Miles had given to her and passed them to the driver as he started up the limo and cruised out of the driveway.

"This is your tip."

The driver slammed on the brakes. "Wow, for real?"

Maribel nodded listlessly, then settled herself into the back seat—out of sight of his rearview mirror. When the limo accelerated again and the mansion estate drifted into the distance, she finally gave herself permission to weep, vowing it would be the last time she would pretend to be part of a world that was not her own. A fairy tale was a fairy tale for a reason—because in real life, Cinderella didn't always get a spot at the ball. And the wealthy, charming man who asked her for a dance wasn't always her faithful, happily ever after prince.

Chapter Seventeen

MILES CAST HIS GAZE across the room at Maribel and Timothy. She looked stunning in her sequined dress—the same one she had modeled for him before they made love that afternoon. *Maribel would make any woman jealous in that dress*, he thought. There was no way he was going to get the deal done with Gillian in the room, and there was no way he could leave Maribel alone at the party if he knew Gillian was acting like a shark, waiting for the perfect moment to sink her teeth into her. But in the safety net of one of his best friends from college, he knew Maribel would be taken care of. *She was in good hands with Timmy*, he thought before calling out to the Olson group—Don Olson, his wife, Annabelle, their lawyer, Wendell, and Gillian who suddenly threw her head back with grating laughter. He had come to hate that laugh.

"Good evening, gentlemen. Nice to finally have a chance to meet face-to-face without the counter-productive meddling of our lawyers and brokers." Miles shook Don Olson's hand and kissed his wife on the cheek, but he was careful to exclude everyone else in the group from acknowledgement, including Gillian.

"Hey, that counter-productive meddling is called 'negotiating,'" Gary corrected him.

"And I'm here to make sure that my client always knows all his options," Gillian jumped in, anticipating Miles' strategic maneuver to alienate her.

"I'm pretty sure at this stage in the game Olson doesn't need his broker to act like his babysitter. That's what Wendell is for." Miles eyed Olson's lawyer.

"If you think you're throwing me out of my own house, Brax, you've clearly forgotten who has the key to the liquor cabinet." Gary pulled out a small antique key from his vest pocket.

"I'm fine with just legal counsel," Olson said with his Southern drawl. "So long as they keep their mouths shut and provide free Scotch."

Miles glanced at Gary. "Asking Gary to keep his mouth shut is like asking a dog not to bark at a squirrel." Everyone laughed. Gary knew it was his job to take the joke and run with it. He feigned shame and pretend to lock his own mouth. "Ruff, ruff…you're still paying me by the hour," he muttered.

"Trust me. I see all your bills," Miles added for show. "I pay you by the minute."

The group laughed again. Miles waved them all up a half-flight of stairs towards Gary's den. "Shall we, gentlemen?"

He said it with intentional chauvinism. He was boxing Gillian out and she knew it. Their eyes locked, but it was Gillian who finally broke the stalemate. When he was certain she wouldn't attempt to fight him, he ascended up the stairs and followed the group behind closed doors.

Gary's den was an expansive room, offering an unobstructed view of the jagged bluffs and sandy shoreline from the second level of the estate. With its angled ceiling and walls of glass, the den was both spacious and secluded—the perfect place to execute business without worrying about formalities. Miles settled himself into one of Gary's leather club chairs and gestured for Olson and his wife to do the same. Wendell, their lawyer, circled around the Italian conference table and surveyed the seventy-page contract, lying on its tempered glass. Miles already knew they had been through it—page by page—but still, Wendell paced around it like an anxious bulldog. *They were still uncertain about something*, Miles noted, even though he felt anything but uncertain.

As promised, Gary moved towards the impressive cherrywood liquor cabinet, unlocked it, and swung open its broad doors.

"Jura Vintage 1977 Single Highland Malt Scotch Whisky," Gary recited, lifting up the unopened bottle from the cabinet. "And that's before anyone signs anything." He pulled tumblers from the stemware rack and poured out the drinks.

He passed the first serving off to Olson's wife, and the second to Olson.

"That's a fine aroma," Olson complimented. "Real fine."

"Only for the finest occasions," Gary confirmed, handing off a drink to Miles and Wendell before serving himself and savoring his own drink.

"You still never told me why you didn't bother to do the Zale deal," Miles asked.

"Came close to it," Olson snapped. "But then Gary called me directly and said he could get me in the room with you if we still wanted to be in your Field's building. I figured it was worth one more kick at the can. Your buildings are premium properties, Braxton. The only thing Zale's got is plain vanilla skyscrapers—just a bunch of lofty floors of concrete and glass. I like personality. And I like vintage. But I don't like being yanked around like a half-dead hog tied to a pickup truck, so I'm glad to see that we finally want the same thing. Otherwise, Gillian was right. You were leaving us with no choice but to shop the deal."

"Well, there's no need to shop it anymore," Gary interjected. "We all want to close it—tonight."

"Have you looked at the contract?" Olson asked Miles.

"No," he replied with a cavalier disinterest that made Olson shift in his chair. "That's what I pay Gary to do."

"Then you know we're holding firm at eight percent for the annualized rent escalation."

"Yes, and I'm not happy about it."

"Well, you realize eight is market."

"Sure, on Zale's plain vanilla properties. But not on classic vintage properties with unparalleled history and irreplaceable architectural flair." Miles rotated his tumbler, letting the light reflect off its amber Scotch. "The Field's building has an antique stained glass ceiling dome designed by Louis Comfort Tiffany. It has a historic Edwardian walnut-paneled tea room that spans the entire seventh floor. It has one-of-a-kind terra cotta ornamentation that brings in foot traffic, just by its sheer natural beauty and stunning elegance. That's the power of style and class. It gets noticed without even trying, and that's the secret to knowing the difference—not between market and premium—but between premium and priceless. One is worth paying for and one is worth fighting for."

"I'm not interested in fighting any more, Braxton," Olson said, tossing back his drink and throwing down his hand. "So you let me know now if we've got a deal. Otherwise, Marge and I will call it a night and be on our way."

"How 'bout we split the difference, gentlemen, and settle on nine percent," Gary cut in, refreshing Olson's tumbler. "That's a healthy bump of a few hundred grand over the twenty-year lease."

"Three hundred eleven thousand, four hundred and eighty-two dollars," Miles countered, calculating the spread in his head. "Just to be exact."

"Calculus major, casual genius, annoying show-off," Gary joked with a nod at Miles. "Let's all agree on nine percent—an acknowledgement that Brax is offering you the best of the best in Chicago downtown rental space."

"I can live with that," Miles said, tossing the choice to walk away from the deal back onto Olson.

"Nine percent," Olson chewed on the new terms. "What do you think, Wendell?"

"I think the longer we stay here, the more we give up."

"Damn straight," Olson confirmed. "Alright, boys. Let's sign this puppy before I finish my drink and change my mind."

Olson rose from his club chair and eyed the contract on the glass table. He watched Gary adjust the escalation clause by hand, and pointed out where Olson needed to initial and sign to formally execute the deal. Miles followed behind him.

Freedom, he thought. *Finally, he would be free of all of them*. Gary would get off his back and Miles could disappear with Maribel for a few weeks on his yacht without anyone demanding anything from him. Miles scanned through the seventy-page contract—pages and pages of indemnification clauses and financial legalese. Instead of relief, he suddenly wondered if thirty-five millions dollars was enough? Was it enough to commit him to a life of real estate deals and petty negotiations about rent escalations and expense charges for the next twenty years?

Then, they all heard a disruption at the doorway and turned towards it.

Miles eyed Timothy, panting and flushed at the top of the stairs.

"Sorry to interrupt, Brax…" His eyes fell onto the business contract and backpedaled, realizing his intrusion was ill-timed.

"What is it, Timmy?"

Timothy wavered. Miles frowned and searched his friend's face, filled with distress.

"She's gone, Brax. Maribel's gone."

"Ah, the mouse," Gary said with a tease. "Don't worry, Brax. After you sign the contract, you can go back to hoarding cheese."

Miles stared at Timothy. *Gone…? He couldn't possibly mean 'gone'*.

"Brax," Gary leaned into him. "The contract?"

"It can wait." Miles tossed down the pen onto the table and shoved him aside.

"Brax, don't do this—" Gary lowered his voice with caution.

"Are we going to finish this thing or not?" Olson insisted, the ink of his full signature still wet on the contract's final page.

Miles glared at Gary, then Olson. Then, he shifted his eyes back onto Timothy.

"Where?" Miles demanded, signaling to everyone in the room that his priorities had changed. Beckoning Miles to follow him, Timothy retreated down the stairs. Without warning, Gillian crossed into their path and pushed against Miles like a cat looking for a scratch.

"What's all the rush? You can't leave without saying goodbye."

"Get out of my way, Gillian—"

"What's the matter, Brax? Did your little schoolgirl leave already?"

Miles glared at her. "What did you say to her?"

"I just made her aware of how much we have in common."

"You have nothing in common with her. Nothing."

"Don't be so dramatic. She's barely legal and you're acting like you're in love with her."

"Get out of my way, Gillian, before I push you across the room."

She sang out with a nervous laugh. "My goodness, Brax…tell me it isn't true. You don't *really* think you're in love with that girl?"

"And you don't really think you know how the first thing about me," Miles seethed, cornering her against the wall and wrapping his hand around her wrist. "Because you don't, Gillian. You can't. You want to know why? Because the only thing we shared was our inability to love anyone but ourselves. And you want to know the really sad part? For years and years, I was fine with that because I was incapable of love. Totally, completely shut down to it until I met someone who wasn't. Someone genuine and caring—someone who only wants to love and be loved, and I realized there's nothing more important in my life than that, and no one—especially not you, Gillian—can take that away from me now."

Miles backed her against the wall and tightened his grip around her wrist until her artificial smile betrayed pain.

"Miles—" Timothy said, pulling him back.

Miles released his grasp, but not his threatening gaze. When he was certain she wouldn't follow them, Miles abandoned Gillian in the corner and raced behind Timothy to the front door and out into the circular driveway.

"Has anyone seen a young woman leaving the property?" Miles called out.

All the limo drivers stopped their chatting and stared at him. They dragged on their cigarettes and kicked the curb. Their unified silence confirmed they weren't interested in helping him.

"Maybe she followed the terrace pathway into the gardens," Timothy offered. "Or maybe she started down the road herself. We can take my car…"

Miles stopped him and surveyed the motley crew of drivers.

"Let's try this again," he insisted, pulling out a roll of cash out from his pocket and peeling off five one-hundred-dollar bills from it.

"Has anyone seen a young woman leaving the property?"

Suddenly, all the drivers raised their hands—eager to assist.

Chapter Eighteen

MILES LOOKED OUT THE limousine's window as Maribel's apartment building came into view. *This is where they had spent their first night together—this is where it had all started.*

It had been a long drive back to the city. Along the way, Miles realized he didn't even have Maribel's phone number. They had spent almost every moment together since Valentine's Day. He had picked her up and dropped her off from work and she had slept in his bed for the past three nights. And yet, he never bothered to ask for her number. He hadn't needed it.

Now, as the driver rolled up to the curb, Miles jumped out of the limo before it stopped. He was not going to let it end like this—not before they had a chance to truly explore what was growing between them. He charged up to the front door and buzzed Maribel's intercom button. It was almost midnight and the entire building was quiet with slumber. He stood back, searching for a sign—any sign—that she was there, waiting for him.

Desperate, he shouted up to her third floor window. "Maribel! Maribel!"

"Jesus, Mary, and Joseph!" Emma Jean threw open her window. Her hair was webbed with a net and her face was smeared with nighttime cream. "What the heck are you doing? Trying to get arrested?"

"Please, have you seen Maribel? I need to talk to her." Miles called out again, projecting his voice past Emma Jean's window. "Maribel!"

Emma Jean hushed him. "Jeepers. Stop your hollerin' for chrissakes, and come up to talk to me like a normal fella."

The vibration of the buzzer unlocked the foyer door. He passed into it and ran up the stairs to the third floor landing, then pounded on Maribel's apartment door. "Maribel, please… please open the door." He was only greeted with silence.

Holding her robe shut with one hand, Emma Jean cracked open her own door and peeked out at Miles.

"I truly don't think she's there, honey. I haven't seen her since the night of my party. And if you weren't so handsome and charming, I'da called the cops days ago. I just assumed she finally found true love and was making the most of it. Is everything okay?"

Miles held his head, shutting out Emma Jean's raspy voice. *Think, think, think…* he tried to remember their conversations, somewhere else she might go, the name of a friend, a favorite bar, a special spot in the city. He only remembered the library. *The library.* And at this time of night, it was closed. But maybe in the morning, he would find her there. And if not there, surely she would be back at work tomorrow afternoon.

"Please, if you see her, tell her to call me." He patted the front of his suit jacket. He had a solid gold pen, but no paper. Instead, he pulled out a hundred dollar bill and scribbled out his phone number. "If you see her, tell her to call me. Please…" he pleaded, his voice cracking, his eyes begging for mercy.

"I sure will, love," Emma Jean nodded empathetically, accepting the hundred dollar bill and slowly shutting her door.

Crushed by hopelessness and dread, Miles trudged down the stairs. He knew he was not a perfect man. He had made many mistakes in his life and there were more indiscretions in his past than he cared to remember. But Maribel had made him believe in the possibility of change—a change in his life which had already brought him four days of happiness—simply by being with her.

Now, as he slipped back into the limousine and turned to watch as the apartment building rolled away from sight, that happiness vanished, leaving only a churning anguish in the pit of his stomach and a salty lump in his throat. In those four short days, he had grown used to her in his life, and just as quickly, he had lost her. It was an ironic punishment for all those years he had dismissed love and spurned countless of women in the process. But he realized there was nothing more important in the world than a woman's love, especially a woman who wanted nothing from him except to be loved in return. *No, Gillian was wrong—he didn't think he was in love with Maribel; he knew he was in love with her.*

* * * *

Maribel sat huddled on Emma Jean's couch and listened to Miles hollering her name through the window. She knew he would try to come find her there. She also knew she wasn't strong enough to resist him. She had been a fool—*such a fool*—this whole time. She had fooled herself into believing there was something more to their "relationship" than just sex. She had fooled herself into believing they had shared a bond through their mutual loss of her mother and his aunt. She had fooled herself in believing she could assimilate into his wealthy world without paying a price. But she had paid a price, and now, she recognized that price was too high for her to bear. She had lost herself along the way, handing over her mind, body, and heart to a man she barely knew—simply because he had asked her to. *Yes, her love was free. But her dignity was priceless.*

"He's going to wake up the whole neighborhood," Emma Jean whispered, peering out at Miles from their dark apartment.

"I can't see him, I can't," Maribel insisted, closing her eyes. "I feel like a fool."

She cringed as he repeatedly called out her name. He wasn't going to stop until he had his way. Stubborn. Relentless. Selfish. She had fooled herself into believing that she motivated his determination. Now, she realized he was always motivated to have whatever he wanted.

"Jeepers—" Emma Jean warned him from her open window. "Stop your hollerin' for Chrissakes and come up to talk to me like a normal fella."

When Maribel heard Miles bounding up the staircase, she snatched Emma Jean's sofa quilt and snuggly wrapped it around her revealing sequined dress. She hadn't been home yet. Seeking sanctuary and companionship, she had come straight to Emma Jean's apartment. Emma Jean had let her cry for hours, allowing her to release her tears of humiliation. Now, Maribel rubbed the black smudges of mascara off her hands. She was too weak, too fragile, too emotional to face Miles. She was counting on Emma Jean to protect her. Both women shifted their eyes to the hallway as Miles banged on Maribel's apartment door, calling out her name. There was suffering in his voice—as if he truly missed her. *A fool*, she thought, *a silly naïve fool.*

"Don't say a word," Emma Jean instructed Maribel before cracking open the front door.

Maribel caught bits and pieces of their exchange, but the only thing she registered clearly was the sound of pain beneath his final plea—"If you see her, tell her to call me. Please…"

"I sure will, love," Emma Jean said, accepting the bill and slowly shutting the door.

Maribel spotted the money in her hand. *Typical*, she thought. In his world, everything could be bought. Everything had a price.

As they listened to Miles' footsteps descending the staircase and out through the building, fresh tears flooded Maribel's eyes. *He had given up already.* Emma Jean locked the deadbolt and sat down beside her.

"Honey, he sure knows how to drive a hard bargain." She grabbed her cigarette lighter and tossed the hundred dollar bill into an ashtray. It curled as it caught fire. Maribel forced herself to watch it burn. For four brief days, she had believed she had fallen in love with a man who could have any woman in the world he wanted, but had chosen her. Now, she realized she had fallen for a man who could have any woman he wanted, and just as easily, could abandon her.

"Do you want to sleep here tonight?" Emma Jean offered. "I can make up the couch real comfy, and you can borrow a pair of my flannel pajamas."

Maribel stood up from the sofa and dropped the quilt behind her. "Thanks for everything, Emma Jean, but I just want to sleep in my own bed tonight."

"Don't give up on love," Emma Jean encouraged her. "Lord knows I never found it and I'm a cynical old hag because of it. But you're still young and beautiful, and you've got a sweet caring heart that deserves to find it."

Maribel nodded in appreciation, not because she believed Emma Jean, but because she knew it was a lovely sentiment that was true for someone else.

As Maribel unlocked her apartment door, it was as if she was returning to the home of a stranger. Everything was untouched in the darkness, like she had fled her life, lured by the promise of a better one. But now, she wanted nothing more than the simplicity and security of what was rightfully hers. Stripping off her sequined dress, she stumbled across the floor and into her bed, smothering herself under the covers and indulging in the faint scent of his cologne that still lingered on the rosebud sheets. Maribel caressed herself the way he often caressed her. *It had been a lovely four days, but it had all been a foolish fantasy.* And like every fantasy, there was the stark truth of reality, lurking below the gaiety and infatuation, waiting to bring everything to an abrupt, sobering end.

Chapter Nineteen

MARIBEL EXHALED WITH a sigh of relief. *Back at work.* She had always loved her job, loved the department store, loved working as a sales clerk. She took pride in the fact that she had advanced from folding socks and underwear to manning the fine jewelry counter where she cared about every piece of jewelry and every sale as if it was an expression of herself. She arrived early and left late every day because her job was the one thing that gave her a solid feeling of security. It was the one thing that was truly hers. The department store depended on her to be there each day, and Maribel liked feeling needed. It wasn't just a paycheck for her. For ten years, it had been her life.

As she walked through the Grand Foyer, it felt different now. Sadness and disappointment weighed heavy on her heart. She passed by the lingerie section and tried to forget her tryst with Miles in the dressing room. It suddenly felt like a shameful lack of judgment. Crystal was there, restocking packages of nylons into the shelves.

"Good morning." Maribel forced a smile, then noted how Crystal failed to return her greeting. *It was early. Crystal probably hadn't had her morning coffee.* Instead, Maribel noticed Crystal's eyes tracking her as she slipped behind the jewelry counter. She glanced across the Grand Foyer and noted that most of the girls were looking over at her. *Had they heard about Miles and her? Did they all know...somehow?* With dread, Maribel considered the possibility of everyone finding out about her affair with Miles. She knew it wasn't a matter of *if* Miles would come to see her there. It was a matter of *when*.

She moved to the register and attempted to clock into her shift. Her employee code failed to work. Maribel tried again. ERROR.

"Good morning, Maribel."

Maribel looked up. "Thomas, perfect timing. My employee code isn't working for some reason…could you clock me in?"

Maribel pulled off her coat, scarf, and earmuffs and settled her purse under the register's cabinet. She swapped out her snow boats for her extra set of dress flats. When she finished, she turned to begin her routine inspection of the jewelry cases, but stopped when she realized Thomas had failed to clock her in.

"Thomas?" she said with concern. He was staring at her with grave eyes.

"I don't know how to say this, Maribel, so I'm just going to say it…" his trademark glee was absent from his voice. Later, Maribel would only remember the foreboding look on his face.

"The department store is investigating a series of charges from your register during your shift. A customer made a formal complaint that she viewed several necklaces, but decided against purchasing them. Apparently, the items were rung up on her credit card and never properly credited."

Maribel felt the blood slowly drain from her cheeks. *Gillian.* Her mind whispered the name, but she could barely recall the interaction.

"There must be some mistake," she floundered. "She purchased two… no, three necklaces, but then returned all of them. I remember refunding all three purchases."

Maribel stopped, suddenly wondering if she had made a mistake and failed to properly refund the final necklace. She couldn't remember. It had only been a few days ago, but so much had happened since then. Maribel held her head.

"There were two refunds, but the third purchase was never credited. The customer claims she never purchased the third necklace, but the charge was still authorized on her card and the necklace is out of inventory."

"What!?" Maribel exclaimed. She rushed to the counter and surveyed the necklace display. The multi-colored gemstone necklace was gone. How had she missed that? She suddenly felt sick.

"It must be some kind of mistake," she repeated, unable to offer a better explanation.

"I know it must be, honey." Thomas moved to touch her hand. "But this kind of thing is serious. So you can't come back until they've formally investigated the complaint, reviewed the security camera videos, and put you in the clear. I'm sorry, but you'll have to pack up your things."

"Thomas? What do you mean?"

"The department store has placed your employment on temporary suspension. I have to send you home."

Maribel stared at Thomas, then shifted her eyes across the Grand Lobby. All her co-workers were watching her from afar. Everyone already knew, but no one had warned her. No one had pulled her aside before she arrived at the jewelry station to prepare her for the devastation. For ten years, the department store had been her second home—her family, her life. But not today. Today, they were all cutting her loose like a frayed string. She was disposable, expendable, despite the fact that her commitment to them had been constant and dependable for the past decade.

Numb with shock, Maribel obeyed Thomas and quietly packed up her things—her extra pair of flats, her hair brush, her tooth brush, her ladybug slippers—then put on her coat, scarf, snow boots, and earmuffs. Thomas escorted her through the Grand Lobby like a criminal under armed guard. Maribel was careful not to look at anyone and no one said anything to her—not a small word of consolation or even a silent wave goodbye as she pushed through the revolving doors and back out into the unforgiving winter cold.

The overcast skies dampened the city's verve. A harsh gust of wind whipped through her coat and clothes, deepening the sting of being completely betrayed and abandoned. Maribel had lost many things in her life—her mother, her own youthful carefree spirit, her ambitious dreams for her future—but she never lost her pride because she had worked hard every day since she was sixteen and she given herself everything she had. But now, in that moment, everything she had accomplished was suddenly gone and the only thing that remained was the crippling sensation of meaninglessness and injustice.

Chapter Twenty

MILES FLIPPED HIS GOLD PEN against the glass top of his desk, wondering why he bothered to come to work each morning. *Because he had nowhere else to go*. He owned nine downtown properties, and yet, he felt like he was an aimless wanderer passing along unfamiliar streets. He was restless and incomplete. Even his own penthouse apartment no longer provided him refuge. It was filled with nothing but the tastes, smells, and memories of her. Miles flipped his pen again. It caught the edge of his desk and bounced onto the floor. He gazed at it without picking it up. He had waited three days before going to see her at the department store. He wanted to give her space. Let her come to him. But he had misjudged her. *Three days had been too long*. When he finally worked up the nerve to visit her, she had already left her job. *Personal reasons*. He had been given the vague answer without any hints of her whereabouts. She had simply disappeared. Disappeared from his life. Four magical days of happiness after an entire decade of watching her from afar. Now, she was simply gone, and none of his wealth or properties or connections could bring her back to him.

He finally reached down to retrieve his pen, but stopped when his cell phone rang.

G-A-R-Y.

Miles shifted his gaze out the window at all the impersonal adjacent skyscrapers. Miles had avoided Gary since the party. He knew he had pissed away the deal with Olson, but he didn't give a damn. None of it mattered. Not Gary. Not Olson. Not Gillian. Not his damn buildings. The only thing that mattered was something he couldn't have, and it consumed him every minute of the day and tortured him every moment of the night. What had started with flirtatious curiosity—his first interaction with Maribel on the Friday before Valentine's Day—had turned into a mission to prove his self-worth. *And he had failed.* Miles retrieved the pen and flipped it again. He had never failed at anything in his life until now. And now, his failure to prove himself to her—his failure to redeem himself to her—threatened to overtake his every thought and his very soul.

His cell phone rang again and displayed the anonymous caller. U-N-K-N-O-W-N.

It could be Gary, trying from a different line. Or maybe it was Don Olson. Miles considered both possibilities, and watched as the screen blinked with each ring. Suddenly, he felt inflated with hope. *Maribel.* He grabbed the phone and answered in anticipation. Then, he fell silent and flipped his pen as he recognized the caller's voice.

"Yes, tell me what you've found," Miles directed him.

"Sorry Mr. Braxton-Worth. Just checking in. Still nothing new to report."

"I see." Miles sighed, disappointed.

"I've been watching for her at her home address, but she hasn't been in or out of there in days," the man continued. "Plus, the cell phone number that I dug up for her was disconnected three days ago. She's got no other family or relatives in the area that I can track down."

"I understand," Miles said, his listless gaze falling onto his cuff links and discarded tie that he had removed hours ago.

"Do you want me to keep looking?"

"Yes, keep looking," Miles ordered him. "Send me the bill at the end of this week, regardless of what you find. But if you find her, I'll pay double."

"Yes, sir…all right then."

Miles hung up. It had been his last hope—the private detective he had hired to find her. At the very least, he had hoped he could return to her apartment and meet her there—one final time. But all the signs—quitting her job, disconnecting her phone, avoiding her apartment—signaled the same thing: Maribel didn't want to be found.

He swiveled in his chair until something metallic pricked his skin through his silk dress pants. Reaching down into his pocket, he withdrew the tear-drop ruby earrings. Frowning, he recalled his brunch with Maribel, and later, how she returned the earrings after their first night together. The earrings had clung to the lining of his suit pocket like two stubborn lovers, unwilling to surrender or separate themselves from each other. Miles contemplated the earrings in his palm. *He would not surrender either.*

Motivated by a new sense of urgency, he picked up the phone and dialed his long-time friend with haste, then confirmed the hour with his Rolex watch. It was almost lunchtime, and he was in the mood for a hot dog—fully loaded.

Chapter Twenty-One

FOR THE FIRST WEEK after her break-up with Miles and after being suspended from her job, Maribel hid from the world in bed. She wore her pajamas and only left her apartment in the evening, skulking across the landing and entering Emma Jean's apartment for a home-cooked meal and a shoulder to cry on. Then, she would return to her bed and lie there for hours, watching the shadows shift across the ceiling with the glow of the moon as she tried to forget everything that had happened in the past few weeks. Occasionally, she would hear a bump in the hallway or the accidental buzz of her intercom, and secretly wish it was Miles, seeking her out one last time. She would replay the fantasy of a reunion with him over and over again in her mind. *If he truly loved her, he would come...* She would lie awake for hours until darkness and disappointment lulled her into a reluctant sleep. Miles never came, which only confirmed everything she had feared was true about him—and about them.

Now, Maribel drifted down Michigan Avenue like a candy wrapper caught in the wind. She floated forward and backwards, browsing all the window displays of the luxury jewelers the way she always had done during her lunch hour. Her black wool coat and earmuffs protected her from the bitter cold, and she zigzagged along the sidewalk, avoiding the patches of ice.

It had been several weeks since she had been forced to leave her job, but in that time, Thomas had called and left the message that she could return to work—if she still wanted her job back. The security camera footage had proved that Gillian had taken the necklace with her, and the store's receipts confirmed that Maribel had properly charged her for it. *It had all been a terrible misunderstanding*, Thomas had casually laughed while recording his message, as if he was simply calling to hear about all the fun things she did while she was away on her "vacation".

A terrible misunderstanding, Maribel clarified in her mind—one that had tainted the way she viewed her former job and co-workers. No one had bothered to call her during her suspension. No one had tried to reach out to her to find out her side of the story. And no one formally apologized to her for making her the scapegoat. And so, it was easy not to bother to call Thomas back. Instead, she disconnected her cell phone and her cable TV, and relinquished her dreams of buying a microwave. She had two thousand dollars in savings—just enough to cover rent and minimal expenses for the next two months, and she was prepared to use it all. Because if there was one thing that Maribel had learned, it was how to survive the worst situations in her life with her pride and dignity intact, and "terrible misunderstandings" were no exception.

HELP WANTED.

She spotted the inconspicuous, hand-written sign in the corner of a storefront window. She looked up and recognized the iconic clock entrance and revolving door, crowned with elegant beveled gold lettering—TIFFANY & CO. The HELP WANTED sign called out to her. She would clean bathrooms and mop the floors if it offered her the chance to move up into a sales clerk position at the most premier jeweler in the world. *Maybe, just maybe…* Maribel had never dared to step foot inside the store, but now, she took in a deep breath and pushed through its revolving doors.

The bright airy interior lured her deeper into the first floor showroom, lined with oversized glass cases. Maribel cast her eyes onto the stunning jewelry; there were dozens of intricate diamond necklaces and bejeweled designer bracelets from some of Chicago's most preeminent estate collections. There was even a scintillating gem-studded tiara, fit for a queen. They were showy pieces, intended to lure and awe potential customers and prepare them for the glamorous sales experience that awaited them.

"May I help you?"

Maribel turned towards the voice, as if she had been caught trespassing. The grey-haired gentleman peered at her through his bifocals from behind the counter. Wearing a dark grey suit and silver bow tie, he eyed her modest coat and earmuffs and waited—less for an answer and more for an explanation.

"Hello, I'm looking to speak with the store manager. I saw your HELP WANTED sign outside, and thought that maybe… Well, I wanted to inquire about the position."

"I see." The man arched his brow. "You can speak with me."

Unprepared, Maribel suddenly flushed. "Uh, um…hello, sir. Nice to meet you."

"Likewise," he said, his eyes fixed on her earmuffs. Maribel read his mind and quickly removed them.

"Do you have any retail sales experience?"

The question surprised Maribel. "Well, yes, of course. I used to work as a sales clerk in the fine jewelry section of the department store in the Field's building."

The man's eyes flashed, as if he had dismissed Maribel before quickly reconsidering her. "I see… for how long?"

"Ten years total…eight years in the fine jewelry department."

"And now?"

Maribel hadn't prepared herself to answer that question. She fumbled for a response, then simply settled on the truth. "I've moved on, and now, I'm looking for a change."

The man stroked his silver goatee, as if he was assessing Maribel's age and manners.

"Well, I must tell you…you're in luck, young lady. I'm looking for a new sales clerk to start immediately. We're understaffed at the moment, and unfortunately, I cannot spend my own time manning the jewelry counters. When can you start?"

Maribel wondered how best to show she was eager, but not desperate. "Tomorrow?"

The man nodded; it had been the right answer. "Allow me to gather up the proper paperwork in the back. You may fill it out here, and we'll try you out now—today—to see how it goes. My name is Charles."

"Maribel… Maribel Martinez."

Charles nodded. "Nice to meet you, Maribel. May I take your coat?"

Maribel couldn't believe how fast everything was happening. She flushed and considered what she was wearing before removing her jacket. *Thank goodness she had decided on a skirt and knit tights rather than jeans*! Something about venturing downtown always made her dress up more than usual. *Oh no!* Then, she remembered she was wearing her vintage Madonna T-shirt under her black cardigan sweater. She handed off her coat, earmuffs, and purse to Charles, who settled her belongings behind the counter and turned to disappear into the back room. Maribel used the opportunity to button up her sweater and smooth down her hair before Charles returned with the application and placed it on the glass countertop in front of her. She couldn't believe her luck; she was actually applying for a sales clerk position at her favorite jeweler in the whole world.

"It looks like you have your first customer. Let's see how you perform in action."

The man nodded to a heavyset woman who pushed through the revolving doors, and charged up to Maribel. Maribel dropped her application and pen under the counter and felt herself start to perspire. *How was she going to navigate unfamiliar jewelry cases with luxury pieces, brands, and price tags that she had never seen before?* Maribel had no idea.

"Excuse me, do you have bathrooms here?"

Maribel exhaled. *This*—she could handle. "No, no public bathrooms here, but just two doors down, you'll find public bathrooms in the corner drugstore."

"Oh, thank you, thank you." The woman heaved with relief and hurried out of the door.

Maribel glanced at Charles, who had returned his attention to his inventory sheet. "Not every interaction is as glamorous as you might expect."

Maribel smiled. She liked Charles. She liked his calm demeanor and his smooth voice. It was such a change from Thomas' dramatic personality and the chaotic energy of the department store. She straightened her posture and waited for the next opportunity to show Charles why she was the right fit for the job.

Her eyes glanced down upon several diamond tennis bracelets. She immediately spotted a double link baguette diamond bracelet, similar to the one Miles had given her, and then as if in a dream, she heard his confident voice, greeting her.

"Hello, Maribel."

She raised her eyes to see him standing before her. It wasn't a dream; it was a surreal reality. Everything around her went strangely silent as his blue eyes seized upon her with his intoxicating gaze. He looked impossibly handsome in his navy pinstripe wool suit and crisp white shirt.

"What are you doing here?" Maribel quietly insisted, attempting not to draw Charles' attention onto them.

"I'm looking to find the right gift for someone," he replied cautiously, his voice filled with cool restraint.

From the corner of her eye, she sensed Charles noting their interaction, waiting to see how she would handle a serious buyer.

Suddenly, Maribel remembered that Miles was a regular customer. *Someone new. He's already shopping for someone new.* What horrible luck that she was there, now.

"How may I assist you?" she said, digging deep inside to keep her composure to pull off the persona of a polite, attentive sales clerk. *Asshole.*

"Well, I don't know the right approach for this gift, so it's a bit of a challenge."

Maribel gritted her teeth. The irony was too cruel. It had been a script—all of it—and now, he expected her to assist him with the purchase of a new gift for his next conquest.

"Something personal or professional?" Maribel tossed at him. She wanted him to realize—at the very least—that she was only playing along for show.

"Personal. Deeply personal."

"I see..." Maribel said, barely controlling her anger and trembling hands. "Well, you can't go wrong with earrings." She started forward, seeking a way to distance herself from him, then she fretted, wondering how she was going to make it through the next minute, much less an entire sales transaction.

"Earrings," he repeated. "I don't think that's an option."

"No? Pity." She was less than sympathetic.

"Perhaps something less conventional and more unexpected."

She glared up at him. "Sometimes conventional is just fine. In fact, sometimes it's better than spontaneity, which never seems to last."

He nodded. "Yes, I can understand why you might believe that to be the case. So perhaps something that also conveys a message."

She sneered at him. She hated his games. "And what might that be?"

"A symbol of pursuing something...intimate and long-term."

Bastard. It had only been a few weeks, and she had already been cast aside for someone he was willing to commit to in a way that he couldn't commit to her.

"Intimacy can be fleeting and misleading," she said with bitter eyes.

"Yes, until it's gone and you finally realize that you can't live without it."

Their eyes locked. Maribel glanced over at Charles. She wanted the job, badly, but she refused to let Miles mock her with his "feelings" for someone else. "I see that you're a bit undecided," she announced, intentionally raising her voice. "Perhaps you might be interested in browsing our fashion accessories. I believe that's on the second floor."

She dismissed him, pushing him away with her glare. He needed to leave and he needed to leave now. She was no longer his possession. She no longer felt the desire to submit herself to him. And she no longer was interested in investing her emotions in a man who bought fine jewelry for every woman he courted, but failed to realize that sincerity was more meaningful than seduction.

Charles suddenly appeared next to her. "Is there something I can assist you with Mr. Braxton-Worth?"

"Yes." Miles nodded, shifting his attention to Charles. "I'm certain now of what I'd like to buy." His long arm stretched out across the adjacent glass jewelry case.

"Very good, sir. Any one in particular?"

"Yes, this one," Miles pointed to a gorgeous two-carat diamond ring in an elegant white gold setting.

"Excellent choice." Charles nodded and opened the case with his keys.

Maribel stared at Miles, hatred in her glare. He mildly smiled back at her. "I'd like to see it worn. Would you mind?"

He waited for her consent. She refused with defiant eyes.

Breaking the awkward stalemate, Charles took her hand and slipped the diamond ring onto her finger. "Please," he encouraged her.

Maribel looked down at the ring—it was stunning, and breathtaking, and so obviously meant for someone else that a wave of renewed heartbreak overwhelmed her. *Don't cry, don't cry...not now, not here, not in front of him.* She cleared her throat and channeled all her frustration and humiliation into her glare. Finally, she lifted her hand and flashed the ring at Miles, as if she was giving him the finger.

Miles recognized the gesture and smirked. Then, unexpectedly, he seized her hand and drew it to his chest and against his heart.

"Maribel, I miss you more deeply than you can possibly comprehend because I can't comprehend it myself. I'm begging you to please give us another chance. What we have together is more precious than anything I could ever buy for you—more precious than the most expensive diamond or the rarest gemstone. And I can't claim to be a perfect man...God knows, I have made serious mistakes in my life, but I can strive to be a better one with you in my life. Maribel, please...I'm not asking for you to let me commit myself to you in the future. I'm simply asking you to let me commit myself to you—here and now."

Maribel gazed at him, unable to process his words and all the emotions raging behind his eyes.

"Well said, Brax," Charles interjected. "It almost makes me want to kiss you myself. You've clearly made an indelible impression on him, my dear." Charles reached out for Maribel's hand and snipped off the tag from the diamond ring.

"I asked Charles to put up the HELP WANTED sign," Miles explained, "hoping you would eventually stroll by and see it."

"You're the store owner?" Maribel asked, suddenly remembering the ruby teardrop earrings Miles had purchased from him.

"Yes. Brax is both my best and worst customer," Charles confirmed. "He's been calling me twice every hour. He's terribly miserable without you, and as a result, he's resorted to making me terribly miserable as well." Charles chided Miles with an irritated smirk. Then, he shifted his eyes onto Maribel. "And I shall be happy to grant you a more formal job interview, my dear, after you have a chance to sort out whether or not you wish this madman to remain a part of your life. But for now, my job is done and I shall retreat to the backroom until one of you decides you'd like to purchase more jewelry. I'll put the ring on your tab, Brax."

"Thank you, Charles."

Charles circled around the jewelry cases and drifted behind parting curtains.

Maribel slowly looked up at Miles with swimming eyes. He held her hand like he had no intention of ever letting her go.

"I've been trying to track you down for a week, but you've been impossible to find. You left your position at the department store and disconnected your phone. And you never called. This was the only plan I could come up with to find you, and possibly persuade you to give me—*us*—another chance."

Maribel passed her finger over the diamond ring, unable to deny its significance. "I don't understand…why this, why now?"

"Because you're all that matters to me now. You're the only reason I'm happy when I wake up in the morning and content when I go to bed at night. You're the only person who can make me laugh when I haven't smiled in days, and the only one who offers me tenderness and compassion when I'm alone. And you're the only person in years who has made me feel like I want to live my life for someone other than myself. Ever since those very first days of watching you overcome one of the most tragic circumstances of your life, I've always known you were someone rare, someone special, but now it's only been in the past four days that I've finally realized how rare and special because I've fallen in love with you."

Miles pressed the palm of her hand against his chest, allowing her to feel the weight of the diamond on her finger and the furious beating of his heart.

"I'm in love with you, Maribel Martinez. Please say that you'll have me back again. Please tell me that you believe, the way I do, that what we've shared together is more precious than anything else in the world. Please say you'll give us another chance."

Maribel gazed at his earnest eyes and wounded expression. She no longer had the strength to deny the way he made her feel and everything they had shared together. He was right. It was more precious than anything else in the world, a bond that couldn't be bought or sold. It could only be discovered like a priceless treasure.

"What's for dinner?" Maribel sassed, slowly relaxing her hand within his grasp.

Miles slowly grinned. "Seafood."

Chapter Twenty-Two

MILES KISSED MARIBEL with longing, holding her naked body between his arms and settling his chest against her own as they cuddled inside the triangular berth within his yacht. They had sailed far across the black waters of Lake Michigan to a secluded spot where they could no longer see the blinking lights from distant shores. Maribel relaxed her head inside the crook of his arm as they gazed up through the boat's ceiling hatch at the flawless night—every star in the sky twinkling just for them. The gentle rocking of the boat settled her mind, and the rhythmic pulse of his heart made her nestle herself closer into his body.

He had swept her away on his yacht, just as he had promised, and made love to her in the serenity and peace of the silent night. There were no longer any barriers between them; nothing had been left unsaid; no part of their bodies had been left untouched. And there were no longer any expectations beyond their desire to remain physically and emotionally vulnerable to each other.

Suddenly, Miles' cell phone rang.

Dismayed, Maribel dropped her head against the cushions. "You actually get reception out here?"

"Satellite," he confirmed, rolling over to reach the phone. "But don't worry. This will be a short conversation. And I want you to hear it." Answering the call, he set it on speakerphone. "Tell me the good news, Gary."

"Good news and only good news, Brax," he confirmed. "The deal is done. Zale signed the contract. The building is all his. Congratulations, you're a free man."

Miles dropped his head onto the pillows and turned to catch Maribel's expression of surprise.

"And here I was," Gary continued, "being an asshole extraordinaire, worrying about how you were pissing away the Olson deal when really you were negotiating behind the scene to sell the whole damn Field's building to Harvey Zale. Never saw that coming…"

"Neither did they," Miles replied, stroking Maribel's hair and gazing deeply into her eyes.

"Yeah, we all thought you were just stalling on the lease terms. Never realized you were using the contract as leverage to get Zale to buy the whole property for a premium. And here I was, trying to keep you from losing thirty-five million dollars while you were busy making triple that."

"We can't all be perfect, Gary," Miles quipped.

"No, just you, Brax. Just you."

Maribel rolled her eyes. Miles retaliated by nibbling at her earlobe. She shrugged him off with a laugh.

"Is that your little mouse, I hear?"

Miles coaxed her to answer.

"Hello," she said reluctantly, settling her ear against Miles' smooth chest.

"Well, hello to you, too," Gary purred. "Make sure Brax buys you some extra special bling-bling for your part in all of this. That disappearing act at the party was Oscar-worthy. Best excuse ever for Brax not to sign the lease contract."

"She's already wearing it, Gary," Miles confirmed.

Maribel's gaze lowered to her diamond ring and savored the feeling of Miles' fingers caressing the small of her back.

"And just for the record, Gary, she hopes she never has to hear from you again."

"Wouldn't be the first time I've heard that, Brax. Wouldn't be the first time." Gary sighed. "Okay, love birds, I'll let you two roll around in your bed of hundred dollar bills without my fuc—," he paused and reconsidered his words, "without me ruining your night. Take care, Brax and little Miss Mouse, and call me when you're ready to sell your other eight properties."

"Already in the works," Miles said, smiling at Maribel.

"Love that. *Ciao*."

Miles hung up the phone and searched out his own reflection in Maribel's dark eyes.

"Why didn't you tell me you were selling the Field's building?" she asked.

"Because I'm not particularly proud of it. At first, I was motivated by deal fatigue. I was looking for an easy way out from all the greed and drama that had been slowly killing me from the inside out. So I called Harvey Zale right before Gary's party and quickly realized how interested he was in buying it. Then, everything fell apart between you and me, and you disappeared, and the sale suddenly became more about getting even than just getting out."

"Getting even? With who?"

He looked away, as if it pained him to say her name. "Gillian."

Maribel guided his chin back towards her own face. "But why?"

"Because I'm used to playing dirty and she almost ruined the only thing that mattered to me in my life. And now that the sale of the Field's building has closed, she'll have to start all over negotiating Olson's lease with Harvey Zale. And Zale won't think twice about pissing away the deal the moment Gillian grates on his nerves. And if Zale and Olson don't agree on a deal, then there's no commission for Gillian."

"But trying to get back at someone only hurts you more than them—ultimately."

Miles gazed into her eyes, as if she had just expressed the genuine core of her soul that he had come to love. "It's true. Even when I knew Zale was going to buy the Field's building and it would disrupt everything for her, it didn't make me feel any better because I still didn't have you back and I knew you still thought the worst of me."

"No," Maribel whispered, shaking her head and fiddling with a loose thread on the silk sheets. "Nothing she said made a difference to me in the end. It didn't change my feelings for you because…" she hesitated, gauging whether or not to take the leap. "Because I had already fallen in love with you."

Miles waited for her to raise her eyes to meet his own before nudging her for a kiss—a long sensual pledge of his desire to prove his own love for her. But he didn't need to prove anything anymore. He simply needed to hold her closer, drawing her entire body over his own. His strong arms nestled her into his embrace, his hard chest pressed against her breasts, and his firm cock slipped between her thighs, igniting a yearning ache to express her love and receive his love in return.

Her mind drifted through everything they had experienced together—a lifetime of change made in only a few weeks. "Is it really true that you're selling all of your properties?" she suddenly asked through their exchange of breathless kisses.

"Yes, definitely." He rolled her beneath him, sweeping his tongue down her neck and over her tits, sucking them hard and erect before teasing them with gentle nips. "I want to make sure I have time to be around." There was playfulness in his voice.

"Around for what?" Maribel sighed, enjoying the sensation of his lips as he dropped lower and lower along her belly until he finally circled her midriff and kissed it with tenderness.

"Babies."

THE END

Devotion

Aria Hawthorne

Devotion - Book Summary

For the past five years, Isabel Alvarez has dedicated herself to her work, determined to prove her worth to her British billionaire boss, Phillip Spears, the only man willing to hire her—a pregnant, college dropout—when no one else would. So when she receives a mysterious bouquet of long-stemmed blush pink roses at the office, she assumes it must be a mistake until she reads her own name on the card's envelope and its enigmatic inscription: *"This is only the beginning..."* An alluring succession of seductive gifts follows, and soon, Isabel must decide whether or not to jeopardize the security of her professional career in order to submit herself to the forbidden fantasies of her persistent secret admirer. Could he simply be Phillip's competitor, wooing her as a pawn in a dangerous game of greed? Or could she really have an impassioned suitor, determined to conquer his own insatiable desires while satisfying her own?

Mysterious and guarded, British real estate tycoon, Phillip Spears, has mentored his executive assistant, Isabel Alvarez, for the past five years without daring to cross the formalities of their professional relationship. But when his direct competitor courts Isabel for his own gain, her loyalty is tested, and Phillip must decide whether or not he will reveal his most guarded secrets to maintain her allegiance. Will he risk losing his most important employee to preserve his own stubborn pride? Or will he engage in his own strategic game of charades to keep her at all costs?

Chapter One

"OKAY, WHO PUT THE FLOWERS on the wrong desk?" Isabel announced the question into the air, fully expecting to hear an immediate answer, but no one responded. She had arrived late to the office while everyone was already in the full swing of their work morning and no one looked up to acknowledge her question. She gazed at the gorgeous bouquet of three dozen long-stemmed, blush pink roses, freshly cut and perfectly arranged.

Pink—her favorite color. Then, the brief whisper of romantic hope faded from her imagination. *Giselle*, she thought with an impatient sigh, searching for the card. *Clearly, they were for Giselle.* All the men—bike messengers, delivery men, business colleagues—who came to the office were smitten with her, and why shouldn't they be? Giselle was tall, thin, blonde and beautiful, an overly eager woman of twenty who liked to wear tight Victoria's Secret skirts and fuchsia bras that showed through her low-cut ivory silk blouses.

"Go-o-o-o-od m-o-o-orning, hot stuff," Tami sang out while striding up to Isabel with an iced Frappuccino in hand. "You're late and incredibly desired by your British boss in the War Room."

"The War Room? Already?" Isabel sighed, mentally rolling through Phillip's morning schedule from memory. "But it's not even nine o'clock yet."

"Yeah, must be something B-I-G and extremely hush-hush. Phillip told me to stay out and send you in when you arrived. Jett's already in there as well as Phillip's hotter-than-hell lawyer. What's his name again?"

"Gary."

"See, you've noticed, too. How can you go to dinner with him all the time and not end up being his dessert?"

"Because I don't want to lose my job." Isabel removed her coat and smoothed down her cashmere sweater and black skirt. She had spent the whole night caring for her son who was sick with a fever. She barely had a chance this morning to consider her clothing options, much less grab a shower or even style her hair. Just lots of perfume and a French twist with a hair barrette. She definitely felt like she was one notch above struggling single mom, but a dozen notches below powerful executive assistant. She knew her black hose had a run along her ankle, and Aidan's virus was already making her congested. And now, she was needed in the "War Room".

"So what's the deal with the flowers?" Tami suddenly asked.

"They're certainly not for me," Isabel replied with disinterest, picking through her scattered desk for her pen and notepad. "Did you ask Giselle? I'm sure they're for her."

"You mean, Giselle?" Tami pretended to flip back her imaginary long hair over her shoulders and smack her gum with an overextended cheerleader smile.

Isabel eyed her. "Tami, let's try to be nice. Giselle is helpful—on occasion."

"Only when she's bent over at the copy machine, entertaining Jett with her backside so I can steal a few minutes to post a status update on my Facebook account. So are they from Giselle's boyfriend, or just somebody she bangs on the side?"

Isabel frowned. "Come on, now. Don't be so mean."

"Mean? Of course I will be mean. That's what I'm here for…" Tami adjusted her librarian glasses. "I'm the office's honorary sexless spinster secretary. *You're* the senior executive assistant peacekeeper. Phillip pays you more than anyone to take care of everyone, including our clueless interns. The only things Jett pays me to take care of are his phone calls, emails, and dirty laundry. And trust me, Isabel. Half my salary is just to stomach Jett's dirty laundry." Tami shivered and slurped to the bottom of her Frappuccino.

Isabel spotted a white envelope buried within the stems of the rose bouquet. She carefully reached out to retrieve it from its plastic card holder stake. "Tami, can you at least tell Giselle to pick up her flowers from my desk while I'm in Phillip's office?"

Isabel glanced down, expecting to see Giselle's name on the envelope, but instead, she felt a jolt through her heart when she read her own name: *Ms. Isabel Alvarez.*

"I'm fairly certain she's in the bathroom, applying more neon blue mascara."

But Isabel barely heard Tami. A hush passed through her chest as she gazed at the blush pink roses, absorbing the surreal fact that they were actually meant for her. All thirty-six of them. She reached out to touch one of their velvet petals. *Who would bother to send them?*

Isabel glanced around the office, thinking she might find a hint. But it was just the girls—the regular office assistants seated at their desks, lost in their own insular worlds of typing out emails, fielding phone calls, sipping their coffee and peeking at their phones, engaged in their personal social media *du jour* while they still had the chance.

Isabel removed the card from its envelope and scanned the inscription:

This is only the beginning...

Crisp white card stock with masculine cursive, confident with a flair of artistry. Isabel studied the enigmatic message, intrigued by what it could possibly mean.

"I have an idea," Tami offered. "Why don't we just lie and say they're for me?"

"Never mind," Isabel lowered her voice and stuffed the card back into its envelope. "They're for me."

Tami sneered at her through her glasses. "Bi-a-tch. Don't steal my idea." She swiped the envelope away from Isabel, then returned it when she saw her name typed across it. "Wow, you're serious. They are for you. From who?"

Isabel protectively cradled the card in her palm and feigned indifference. "Just a 'thank you' from a client."

Tami whistled. "That's some 'thank you'. What did you do? Help convince Phillip to give the guy a million dollars?"

"A million dollars wouldn't even pay for light fixtures in most of these development deals," Isabel replied, feeling her hands tremble as an unnatural flutter rose up from her voice. "And usually, it's the other way around. They're trying to impress Phillip and me with their wealth so they can invest in one of Phillip's real estate deals."

"Like how? Telling you all about their yachts and gold-plated urinals?"

Isabel paused, considering last night's business dinner. She had dined with Phillip and one of his business suitors, Stu Lofton, who wanted Phillip to partner with him on a mixed residential and commercial development deal on the Northside. Isabel had received gifts from Phillip's business colleagues in the past, but never luscious long-stemmed roses and never with an unsigned card. And if there was one truism that Isabel had learned from her five years of working for Spears & Associates, it was that wealthy businessmen never did anything without receiving credit for it.

"Last night's dinner was all about Stu's adventures in Africa, hunting big game animals."

Tami rolled her eyes like she was being stabbed. "Gag me." Tami was a vegan, after all. "I never thought I'd say this—but thank God I work for Jett rather than Phillip." Tami glanced back at Phillip's office door and eyed Isabel's boss, swiveling back and forth in his seat, looking displeased with life and everyone around him. "Especially when Phillip has that stern frown permanently etched on his face."

Isabel glanced into his office, and rushed to gather her belongings. "It's harder than you think, Tami. Being in Phillip's position." She tried to sound diplomatic.

"Harder work for *you*. You're the one being forced to schmooze with African safari killers and dealing with four surly men in the War Room."

"It's just part of my job." Isabel shrugged. "Especially the surly part."

Both women giggled before Isabel noticed Tami's concerned gaze and followed it through Phillip's office door, ajar with a direct view of Isabel's desk. Phillip's marble blue eyes seized upon them. Isabel acknowledged his gaze with a subtle nod; she knew it well. It seared into her heart with its stark reprimand, summoning her into his office—immediately.

"I'll be in Jett's office, if you need me later," Tami said before darting away. "You know…to detox from testosterone overload."

"Thank you," Isabel mouthed in appreciation, whisking up the card and envelope from her desk and hiding it in her skirt pocket. She didn't want anyone in the office to discover the card and assume she had somehow been inappropriate with one of Phillip's colleagues. Plus, keeping it physically close was a way to extend the sensation of excitement, tingling throughout her body. It was, after all, an enchanting surprise—the idea that someone, someone who knew her well enough to know her favorite color, was courting her with flowers, and perhaps, courting her for reasons not related to business at all.

Isabel entered Phillip's spacious executive corner office and shut the door behind her. The morning light cascaded through the high rise windows and bathed her boss in its beautiful beams of gold. Phillip looked immaculate in his favorite Valentino suit—sharkskin grey with an iceberg blue shirt and tie that complemented his winter complexion and glacial blue eyes. He always looked immaculate in the morning. *Showered and freshly shaved, which meant he had already been to the gym. Fencing…good.* Isabel knew Phillip was always in a better mood whenever he had the chance to attack an opponent with a sword before arriving at the office.

"There's no way to get out of it now. It's already in motion, and you can't change horses in the middle of a race, Phil," Gary said.

Isabel waited to see if Phillip's eyes lifted to meet her own, but he did not look up. Instead, he looked grim, concentrating on whatever bad news Gary was doling out. Everyone's attention was squarely focused on Gary, who was circling the office like he was holding court. Jett, Phillip's commercial broker, sat in front of Phillip's desk, and Norton Harrington, Phillip's eighty-year-old actuary, leisurely reclined across the full length of the black leather mid-century sofa.

"Well, thank you, Bella, for joining the party," Gary announced, putting the spotlight on Isabel. His eyes tracked her as she crossed in front of him.

Isabel dismissed his flirtatious use of her nickname, trying not to notice how handsome he looked in his tan suit and silky buttermilk tie. *Confident and commanding.* No one enjoyed being the center of attention more than Gary.

"If I have to repeat myself one more time, I'm going to slit my own throat," he quipped. "If you could please convince your boss that breach of contract is *not* the way out here, I'll happily take you out to dinner tonight to the only six-star restaurant in Chicago. Best chocolate lava cake in town."

With a routine flick of the cord, Isabel adjusted the sleek silver blinds, muting the flood of light sweeping across Phillip's aristocratic profile. Phillip preferred subtle shadows over the bold morning light, and she knew it.

"Well, at least you remember how much I love chocolate, Gary," Isabel sassed back.

"Dark chocolate," Gary added.

Their eyes locked. She had done both drinks and business dinners with Gary and Phillip more times than she could remember, usually whenever they were on the brink of closing a major real estate deal. At the end of the dinner, Phillip never ordered dessert, but Isabel and Gary always shared each other's *crème brûlée* or chocolate *soufflé*. Gary was a serial bachelor—even a self-professed womanizer—but he definitely knew how to treat a woman to fine dining. And maybe even long-stemmed roses.

"Then, there's no other choice," Phillip interjected like an intentional interruption of their camaraderie. "Kill the Amway deal."

Isabel stared at Phillip. He never bluffed about pulling out of a deal. When he decided to cut the cord, he meant it.

"Phillip, we can't go blowing up the deal now," Gary countered. "If we pull out today, they'll sue us."

The sharp angles of Phillip's face darkened as he glanced away, toying with his gold pen in cold, unpleasant silence.

"Screw 'em," Jett pushed back. "Cut off their balls, and let them whine about it in court. I'll personally countersue them for my broker's commission."

Phillip raised his eyebrow at Jett. Gary was the litigation expert and they all knew it. But Jett's crass bravado and affinity for confrontation were characteristics that Isabel knew amused Phillip.

Phillip shifted his gaze out of the window at the sweeping panoramic view of downtown Chicago—lost in a moment of private thought. "We can't move forward under the current lease terms, Gary. I'll never agree to sell the Amway building to Zale, knowing he plans to reassign the deal to my ex-business partner."

"They've got you by the balls, Phil," Gary countered. "According to the contract, the current owner can reassign the deal to whoever the fuck they want unless you pull out now, and pulling out now is going to get you nowhere except a litigation blood bath."

Isabel watched Phillip's silent disapproval harden his expression like stone. She knew Phillip's old-fashioned sense of propriety made him despise it when Gary dropped the F-bomb in front of her, but he hated even more that he was being told he was trapped.

Isabel watched Phillip's merciless eyes, staring Gary down. She knew that he never surrendered—ever.

"Gary, let me make this bloody crystal clear," he said, his anger melting through his English reserve. "I'm not staying in a deal that reassigns my property to Symeon Colovos. Whatever the cost."

"It's a set-up," Isabel suddenly offered.

Everyone turned their attention to her. She cleared her throat and smoothed down the seam of her skirt. During Phillip's business meetings, she had long since grown accustomed to being the only woman in the room, but that didn't mean she didn't feel self-conscious whenever she had to speak her mind in front of Phillip's colleagues. After all, she wasn't one of Phillip's business partners; she was his executive assistant. She never stopped feeling like she had to prove herself to every man in the room, every time.

"It's been a set-up from the beginning," she insisted, settling her gaze on Phillip. "That's why they wouldn't budge on the re-assignment clause when we negotiated the contract in the first place. Remember, Gary?"

"Yeah, yeah... right," Gary pondered aloud in agreement. "I do remember."

"Symeon is trying to ruin you, Phillip—revenge for running him out of the firm. But he knows you. He knows you'll never sell anything to him after the way he handled himself here, so he's set you up from the beginning. He's been going through Harvey Zale this whole time to make the purchase on his behalf."

Skeptical, Jett challenged her. "What's in it for Zale?"

"Money," Phillip offered with stale disgust. "Zale is a ruthless greedy wanker and Symeon is likely paying him a premium to reassign our deal to him."

"No, Phillip," Isabel respectfully cut in. "I don't think so. I think Harvey Zale is playing Symeon the way Symeon thinks he's playing you. Harvey Zale wants something from you, and he's going to try to leverage the reassignment deal to get it."

"I love it when Isabel starts imitating Nancy Drew," Jett smirked, throwing his weight back into his chair and bracing his hands behind his head. "Sexy," he snarled with sarcasm, chewing on his gum like he was a teenager in high school. And just like a teenager, Jett Watson loved to publicly provoke Isabel—loved it a little too much.

Isabel sensed Phillip watching her, waiting for her to fire back at Jett. She could handle herself and Phillip knew it. But this time, she chose to ignore him. Deep down, she was thinking about the flowers. *Notre Dame graduate. Fraternity president. Football junkie.* It was hard to imagine Jett giving her anything except a reason to report him to Marcy, the human resources director, for sexual harassment.

Instead, Isabel locked eyes with Phillip. He was still giving her a chance to prove her point. She knew she had to make the most of it.

"We should have seen this from the beginning, Phillip. Harvey Zale usually doesn't purchase vintage commercial properties like your Amway building. Zale likes government buildings. Political statements. Power plays. Harvey Zale is threatening to reassign the Amway building to Symeon Colovos because he knows it's exactly what you *don't* want. That way, he can turn around and squeeze you for something he really does want."

Phillip fixed his arresting blue eyes on her. She knew he was reading her confidence and assessing the merits of her theory.

"What do we have that Zale would want?" Norton's ancient voice suddenly floated up from the couch like a ghost in the room. Like a supportive grandfather, Phillip's eighty-year-old actuary often lent his support to Isabel during their meetings. Whenever she had to go up against Phillip or Jett, Norton took her side without fail. "The Mercantile?" he offered.

She shook her head. "Too lucrative, Norton. Harvey Zale knows Phillip would never sell a cash cow like the Merc."

"40 South LaSalle?" Gary jumped in, playing the game.

"There's nothing powerful or sexy about the Federal Reserve Building," Jett snarked. "Sure, they print billions of dollars, but they don't know how to spend it." He winked at Isabel, shifting his gum from one side of his cheek to the other.

"City Hall?" Norton guessed again.

"Phillip would gladly pay Zale to take a pain-in-the-ass tenant like the Mayor off his hands," Gary cawed. "Am I right, Phil?"

But Phillip didn't respond. He was lost in thought, as if he had disappeared from the room. Then, Isabel realized he was peering at the pile of mail on the edge of his pristine glass desk.

Suddenly, a rubber band whizzed into Phillip's chest from across the room. Jett tittered like a school boy, and for a brief moment, they all laughed as if they had forgotten they were fighting a losing battle. There was an awkward return to silence when no one else offered up any other suggestions.

"The Old Main Post Office." Phillip stated it with uncharacteristic resignation. He leaned forward from his chair and picked up the rubber band from the floor, then tossed it into the trash can. He peered over at Isabel, supporting her theory. "Harvey Zale wants The Old Main Post Office."

Isabel nodded, as if they were reading each other's minds. "Yes, it's the perfect play."

"A vulture play," Phillip confirmed. "Completely Zale's style."

"But everyone knows that property has been tied up in federal red tape for years," Jett said, shooting another rubber band directly into the trash can.

"And that's exactly why Zale wants it," Isabel replied. "Everyone has left that building for dead because they assume it's worthless—everyone except Phillip."

"Four thousand feet of premium riverfront property," Phillip stated dryly. "It's clearly worth more than anyone has given it credit for…"

"And completely your style," Isabel offered in consolation. "Your style is to revitalize downtown Chicago—one vintage building at a time."

He gazed at her, his eyes softening. "Let Zale have any of my other properties to keep him from selling The Amway to my bastard ex-business partner. But not The Old Main Post Office. The Old Main Post Office is not for sale."

"It's going to take millions of dollars to renovate it back to its former glory," Jett interjected. "You should just dump it, Phillip."

"Three hundred and fifty million dollars—to be exact," Norton verified, rising from the couch like he was awakening from his mid-morning cat nap. "That's why you've owned it for twenty years, Phillip, and even you still haven't bothered yourself with it."

"You're wrong, Norton. Renovation of its historic main lobby is almost complete," Phillip shot back. "And Zale will take it and turn it into a shopping mall. A tasteless tourist attraction. Or worse—a parking garage."

"Yes, but at least he's too cheap to tear it down completely," Norton countered, his sunken eyes challenging Phillip like a father. "He'll keep the exterior. But it's true, he'll likely gut everything else, including its Beaux-Arts marble lobby."

As if he had lost interest in the fight, Norton shuffled towards the door, preparing to exit. "Know your own intentions, Phillip. Some things are worth fighting for, but many, many, *many* more things are simply a display of one's own stubborn pride."

Isabel watched Phillip absorb Norton's words. Norton knew the history behind every Chicago downtown real estate deal since The Great Depression, and his uncanny ability to assess risk had kept Phillip from chasing deals that had bankrupted several of his competitors. If there was one person who could alter Phillip's opinion about how to deal with Harvey Zale, it was Norton Harrington.

Phillip's phone intercom suddenly buzzed. "Mr. Spears?"

"Yes, Lucy?" Phillip called to the receptionist.

"Harvey Zale is on line seven for you."

Phillip looked down at the blinking light on his phone receiver, then glanced over at Isabel. She nodded without indulging in her victory. She had been right, but now it meant that Phillip would likely be forced to forfeit The Old Main Post Office to keep Harvey Zale from reassigning the Amway deal to his ex-business partner, Symeon Colovos.

Isabel gazed at Phillip's troubled blue eyes, offering up her support in any way she could. But it was out of their hands now, and they both knew it.

"Thank you, Lucy," Phillip answered, defeated. "I shall take the call."

"Don't blow his brains down to his balls, Phil," Gary warned.

"No," Phillip replied, turning away his Roman profile towards the windows, allowing the muted sunlight to warm his smooth face. "That's what I pay you to do, Gary. And fortunately, I have an incredibly savvy executive assistant who has warned me not to blow out his brains—not quite yet."

Phillip glanced over at Isabel. She smiled in appreciation.

He waited, his finger hovering over the blinking light on his phone until Jett and Gary filed out of his office. Isabel turned to follow them, catching a glimpse of Phillip as she prepared to close the door behind her. He lifted the handset to accept Harvey Zale's call while his gaze fixed on her. *He would need her again after the call. She shouldn't go far.*

She understood him. They always understood each other.

"So Nancy Drew…that was some sexy sleuthing in there."

Isabel shut Phillip's office door and turned towards Jett, his devious eyes tracing the scooping neckline of her sweater. His eyes were always fishing, and he never attempted to conceal it. "Maybe you need to stop by my office sometime and we can try to unravel the mysteries of some of my real estate contracts—together."

Isabel rolled her eyes. But it was hard to take him seriously when his breath smelled like bubble gum.

"The alphabet's a little too much for you these days, Jett?"

He snuffed out through his nose and cracked his gum. "Maybe. Or maybe Phillip's not the only one who should be entitled to a sassy executive assistant."

"Good, because that's what I'm here for…" Tami said, appearing behind him, holding up an iced latte in one hand and Jett's phone messages in her other hand like a crushing full house.

"Simon called. Angie called. George Barnes called. And your mother called—twice. If I were you, I'd call your mother back first, since she's the only one who thinks you're not an offensive, juvenile beefcake. Is that sassy enough for you?"

Jett chomped down on his gum, baring his bleached teeth at her, as if he despised the interruption. "*Très*," he shot back with a glib smile, plucking all of the phone messages out of Tami's fingers.

"*Merci*," Tami answered curtly. "Now get back to your office and start your work day," Tami ordered him like she was the boss, and Jett was merely her assistant. "And spit out your gum. No one wants to hear the sound of your smacking tongue, I can guarantee you. Not even your mother."

"Are you sure about that?" he said, passing his nose over Isabel's bouquet of flowers. Isabel eyed him for a sign. *Had he been the one?* Was it even possible that Jett Wattson—the immature, inappropriate real estate broker—had a clandestine romantic side?

"Very." Tami challenged him with her open palm. Jett rolled out his cotton-candy pink wad of gum into her hand with a long, gagging display of his stained tongue. Tami held her ground without flinching.

"Try not to miss me while I'm gone." Jett winked at Isabel before sauntering off with glee, stopping only to steal a loose sheet of paper from Tami's desk to make a free-throw shot clear across the office into the saltwater aquarium tank. The tropical fish crisscrossed each other in explosive fright. Jett threw up his arms in victory and disappeared into his corner office. Clearly, he was the champion.

Tami rolled her eyes and turned back to Isabel, dumping Jett's distasteful gum wad into her trashcan. "Neanderthal. How does he even figure out how to put on his underwear the right way every morning?"

"He probably just goes without."

"Ugh," Tami retched, adjusting her black-rimmed glasses. "Let's not even speak of it."

Tami was the only executive assistant who had lasted longer than three weeks working for Jett, and now, Isabel calculated that it had at least been two years. Phillip tolerated Jett's juvenile behavior because he was used to it from their days together at Harvard Business School. Also, Jett knew every banker, broker, and billionaire in the city and had an uncanny way of sniffing out the most desirable real estate deals before they hit the open market.

Tami, on the other hand, tolerated Jett's behavior because she had five older brothers and she was the only other woman in the office, besides Isabel, who had figured out that Jett was an adolescent puppy constantly seeking a titillating scratch.

Both women turned and saw Gary, standing alongside Isabel's desk, waiting for his chance to gain her attention.

"That was brilliant in there, Bella. How did you sense what Zale was really after?"

Isabel shrugged, downplaying his compliment. "Sometimes, things are more obvious when you're pushed against a wall and forced to consider what the other person truly wants from you."

"I think sometimes things are less obvious when you're not ready or willing to acknowledge them." Gary shifted his briefcase from his right hand to his left, and traced the edge of one of the rose petals with his finger. "Phillip is very lucky to have you."

He kept his steady eyes on her. Gary had shown his interest in her before, but never with such unguarded intensity as he did now.

"From a secret admirer?" he suddenly asked, as if he was noticing the bouquet for the very first time.

Isabel gazed at him, searching for a sign that he was its sender, but Gary betrayed nothing more to her. Instead, the light in his honey-glazed eyes fell flat as he scanned the flowers before turning away with a polite nod. "Looks like someone has upstaged us all with his admiration."

He headed down the corridor towards the glass doors. "I meant what I said about treating you to that six-star dinner. We can share dessert."

"I usually prefer my own," Isabel lobbed back.

"Noted." Gary glanced back with a flirtatious smile and cavalier salute before disappearing through the office's double doors and into the lobby.

Tami slurped on her latte and followed Gary out of the office with her eyes. "Holy hot-litigator-on-a-popsicle. What the heck was that all about?"

Isabel lowered her smile and nodded to the flowers.

"Ge-e-e-e-et. O-o-ut!" Tami sucked down her iced latte like a caffeine junkie trying to stabilize the highs and lows of her addiction. "You told me they were from a client!"

"Shhhhh," Isabel silenced her again. "I don't know…I mean, maybe."

Isabel hesitated before pulling out the card from her skirt pocket and handing it over to Tami.

"*This is only the beginning…*" Tami read aloud. "*Ouuuuhhhh*, totally crazy witchy mysterious." She shivered, as if she finally had absorbed the chill of her iced latte, then peered enviously at the roses. "I kinda wish I had somebody sending me flowers. Or expensive chocolates. Hell, at this point, I'd even settle for some scented hand lotion and a naked selfie."

"Now *that's* creepy."

Tami shrugged. "Not for me…I'm old and desperate."

"You're thirty-four, Tami. That's hardly old, and I seriously doubt you're that desperate."

"You're completely missing my point, Miss Long-Stemmed Roses. I am absolutely that desperate because I've got exactly zero prospects. Count them—zero. You're barely thirty and at least you've got flowers."

Tami touched one of the rose petals like she was truly heartbroken.

"Well, you're not completely out of luck," Isabel teased. "Jett gives you nice gifts on a weekly basis."

"What, like basketball tickets? Oh, no…you must mean the Hilary Clinton bobblehead," she snorted sarcastically.

"It's his way of showing his professional affection for you."

“To hell with professional affection. I’d gladly settle for some non-professional affection from someone, anyone—*trust* me. I’m telling you: hand lotion and a naked selfie. He doesn’t even need to include his face.”

The sound of sudden banging filled the office. Giselle, the intern, was at the copy machine, attempting to unjam the jam.

Tami rolled her eyes. “Oh, good Lord, she’s beating the copy machine again.”

“Go help her…please.”

“*You* help her, Isabel…I’m just the crotchety sexless secretary spinster, remember?”

“Tami—please.”

But Isabel knew it was fruitless. Tami had already spent every shred of civility dealing with Jett. She couldn’t be forced to be nice to the helpless intern, too.

“Look—” Tami nodded into Jett’s office. Both women spotted Jett, adjusting his position in his swivel chair in order to gain an unobstructed view of Giselle at the copy machine—and her over-extended backside.

“Facebook time.” Tami typed through the air and skated back to her desk like she was the busiest assistant in the office “Thank you, thank you, thank you, clueless sex-pot intern Giselle.”

Bang, bang, bang.

Isabel watched Giselle open and shut trap doors on the copy machine—again and again. Her tight skirt stretched over her curvy backside as she bowed forward and peered between the drums and rollers like she was investigating under the hood of a car. Isabel spotted Jett, leaning back into his swivel chair, enjoying the show.

Neanderthal. Isabel quickly swept into Jett’s doorway and closed his door, shutting out his voyeuristic view. Then, she walked over to Giselle and offered her assistance.

“Here, you usually have to open the lid and lift up this.” Isabel flipped up a small lever and pulled out a crumpled piece of jammed copy paper.

“Oh my God, thank you so much. How did you know to look there?” Giselle peered into the drum spool like she was expecting to see a magical gnome pop out.

“Years and years of practice.” Isabel closed the lid and restarted the machine with a vibrant purring hum. “There, all better.”

“Thank you, Miss Alvarez.”

Isabel looked at Giselle, disarmed by the formal use of her surname. “You’re welcome, Giselle. Anything else can I help you with?”

Giselle hesitated, her eyes glancing back at Phillip’s closed door.

“C’mon, don’t be shy. You’re still new here and I would be happy to help you. What is it?”

"Well, it's just...Mr. Spears told me this morning that I slouch too much and that I needed to practice my posture."

Isabel tried hard not to break into a smile. "Giselle, try to remember that Phillip is English. If he had his way, everyone would be forced to stroll around the office on their tippy-toes, balancing copies of the *Encyclopaedia Britannica* on their heads."

Giselle released a burst of laughter from her glossy pink lips. Isabel noted her blue neon mascara and low-cut blouse. She was so young, so incredibly naïve and so inexperienced, it was almost too painful. At least Isabel had the benefit of being in her mid-twenties when she had started working at Spears & Associates. In her mid-twenties—*and* pregnant. She silently cringed, remembering how hard it had been for her, too.

"Anyway, Phillip's just testing you," Isabel reassured her. "He does that with everyone. When I started working for him, he told me I needed to cut my hair because I was always playing with it."

Giselle's crystal eyes widened with horror. "Oh my God. I would have died. What did you do?"

"I left the office during my lunch hour, walked into the nearest salon, and got my hair cut past my ears. It was the worst haircut of my life. The next day, Phillip said nothing about it—*nothing*. Instead, he gave me a raise and promoted me from my position as the office copy clerk to his executive assistant. It took me almost two years to grow my hair back, and Phillip has never dared to ever say anything about it since."

Giselle touched her long blonde hair, as if she feared it might face the same drastic fate.

"Don't worry," Isabel said, noting her concern. "Here's the secret to working here—just focus on being professional and try not to let anyone intimidate you."

"Okay. Thanks so much, Miss Alvarez. Oh, and by the way...I love the bouquet of flowers you received this morning. Those Chihuly vases are my favorite." Giselle eyed the iridescent blown-glass vase shaped like a swan, complementing the beauty of the blush pink bouquet.

Isabel peered at Giselle with curiosity. "You're familiar with them?"

"Oh sure. They're a signature thing from the flower shop just down the street on Washington Avenue. I worked there all last summer as a flower arranger. The Chihuly vases are in limited supply—only available to customers who purchase three-hundred-dollar bouquets. Somebody must be sending you a really special message."

"Isabel—" Phillip's stern voice called out of his office.

All the assistants looked up from their work and turned their attention to Isabel while Giselle shot her a glance of concern.

"*Encyclopaedia Britannica*," Isabel reassured her with a playful wink before whisking down the hallway. "Coming…"

Isabel slipped into Phillip's office. "You rang?" she chirped, knowing she was going to have to compensate for his foul mood after his phone call with Harvey Zale.

"Close the door."

She obeyed and took a seat across from him.

"Sooooooo… how did it go?"

"Better than he expected," he replied without offering more.

"Really?" There was surprise in Isabel's voice. Phillip noted it with his cool blue glare.

"Yes. Zale expected me to tell him to piss off the moment he offered the barter—taking The Old Main Post Office off my hands in exchange for not re-assigning the Amway deal to Symeon Colovos."

"And…you didn't?" Isabel was fishing; she wasn't expecting to see that familiar victorious glint in Phillip's eyes that told her he hadn't lost.

"No, I did not. I told him to go ahead with the reassignment. And then, I agreed to sell him The Peoria as well."

"The Peoria?" Isabel repeated in shock. "But why?"

"Because you are right about my ex-business partner. Symeon Colovos is getting his revenge against me. The Amway building was our first purchase as business partners. He's maneuvered himself into the Amway deal because he's sending me a message—we're no longer business partners; we're competitors."

"He'll never be your competition, Phillip, because he doesn't have your integrity."

Phillip stared at her, momentarily distracted by the unexpected compliment. "Perhaps. But in the end, it doesn't matter because he's going after something that I've decided I no longer care about—winning at any cost. Norton is right. There's a cost to engage in the fight, Isabel, and I'm no longer interested in paying the price."

Isabel watched Phillip shift his gaze away from her and out the window. Like a Roman statue, he sat powerful and motionless in his Valentino suit—a man who had built up an indomitable real estate empire, and yet, his distant eyes were filled with discontentment. She rarely saw him express anything other than measured propriety and British reserve, but in that moment, she sensed things had changed. He was a different man with different priorities.

"Gary is right. Symeon Colovos will get The Amway through the reassignment from Zale. There's no way around that now," Phillip said, flat and emotionless. "But it doesn't mean I have to be a pawn to his rook."

His gaze fell onto the marble chessboard resting on the edge of his desk. Isabel knew he loved the game of chess because he loved games of strategy. But everything seemed different now, and there was no reading him.

"But I still don't understand why?" she pressed him, carefully. "Why not just get rid of The Old Main Post Office to keep Zale from reassigning The Amway to Colovos?"

Isabel watched the light shift in his eyes with disarming honesty.

"Because The Old Main Post Office has great sentimental value to me. It was my very first commercial purchase after I graduated from university here in America. And I'm not ready to give it up—yet." Phillip lowered his voice, as if his confession made him vulnerable and uncomfortable. "Perhaps I am simply a hopeless romantic, but I have recently come to realize that there is only one truly valuable ideal in life and that is kindling something productive, something meaningful—perhaps even something priceless—from nothing more than a hope that has long since been discarded or abandoned."

When he finally looked up at her, he held her gaze to ensure that she heard him. *Truly heard him.* This was not a conversation with the same unyielding, competitive man who she had known for the past five years. This was an introspective conversation with a conflicted man who seemed to want to convey how much he needed a change in his life.

Without warning, he suddenly sat straighter in his seat and sharpened his British accent, as if he realized he had let his guard down too much. "The Old Main Post Office is a classical piece of history, and it deserves a better fate than to be gutted out by some real estate wanker like Harvey Zale seeking discounted riverfront footage. When I look at something like The Old Main Post Office, I see a lost treasure, marred by the greed of modern life threatening to destroy it. In a world that values so little and disposes of so much, there are few untouched gems like The Old Main Post Office left in the world. And I am determined to protect it."

"I think it's a worthy endeavor, Phillip. I had no idea that The Old Main Post Office meant that much to you."

He circled his finger along the surface of his glass desk, his voice dropping to a whisper. "Many things mean more to me these days than I dare share."

He rose from his chair and paced across the polished hardwood floors. "The Amway deal will go through with Zale as planned, and he will reassign it to Colovos. But Zale will also buy The Peoria from me, and then, he will turn around and flip it to Isbon, or McCallister, or Weiss, or any one of the other sharks looking for their next meal in the pond. Any of them will be more than willing to overpay for a prestigious building like The Peoria, and in turn, *they* will compete against my ex-business partner for potential tenants. But not I. I'm tired of the misery of it all. Let them all be miserable together. I simply want a bit of peace."

Phillip stuffed his hands in his pockets and turned his angular jaw towards the windows.

"I know what you're thinking," he confessed softly. "That I'm simply giving up without my usual fight." He looked down, pretending to be preoccupied with his diamond-studded cuff links.

"No," Isabel said cautiously, realizing he was revealing a rare glimpse behind his steely façade. "No, not at all. I think you should do whatever you feel is right for you."

Their eyes locked. She wanted him to know that she understood him. Nothing more needed to be said.

"By the way," Phillip said slowly, hinting at his desire to change the focus of their conversation. "Lucy told me you called in late because of Aidan. How is he?"

"Sick. Fever. I apologize for being late."

Phillip cut his hand through the air like no apology was needed. "Our business dinner last night with Stu ran later than both you and I expected, and I imagine you were up well after that caring for Aidan. Is it serious?"

"He's four, Phillip. And I'm his mother. So every illness seems serious."

Phillip nodded and allowed an unspoken moment of connection between them. They rarely discussed their personal lives. As a matter of routine, he preferred to maintain a cold professional detachment as part of his British formality. So whenever Phillip made a conscious effort to inquire about her son, he always disarmed her.

"Is he still interested in dinosaurs?"

"And airplanes. Right now, his dinosaurs and B52 bombers trade off eating one another."

"Brilliant." Phillip mused, waiting to hear more.

"Then, at the end of the day, they all make up and are fast friends by bed time so they can all sleep together under his pillow."

Phillip's eyes danced with delight. "As they should." Then, the light quickly faded and his tone grew serious. "Unfortunately, Isabel…I need you again tonight."

"The Watercross gala?"

He nodded. "I would like you to accompany me." He gazed at her cautiously, as if he was preparing for her refusal.

Isabel grew silent. She knew about tonight's gala. She knew that Phillip had always planned to attend—just not with her. And now, she assumed there was a high probability that Phillip's ex-business partner *and* Phillip's ex-fiancée would both be there—together—although she knew better than to acknowledge it.

After a long pause, she nodded with a smile. "Don't worry, Phillip. My mother can watch Aidan tonight. I will be there."

"Thank you," he whispered, subtle appreciation of the connection between them—a professional bond of loyalty and trust that had developed during the time she had worked for him. She did not refuse him because she felt eternally indebted to him. He had been the one to hire her as his office copy clerk when she was only an inexperienced college dropout, pregnant and recently abandoned by Aidan's father. Without her job at Spears & Associates, Isabel shuddered to think how much different—*harder*—her life would be now, especially as a single working mother.

"Well, I suppose I should get back to my desk," Isabel said, rising from her seat. "You've just sold a second property to Zale. We're going to need to get working on that as soon as possible."

"Zale said he'll send over the letter of intent. You can forward it on to Gary."

"I'll talk to him about preparing all the due diligence documents for The Peoria, and then I'll have Giselle make copies so we can circulate them."

"Giselle?" Phillip suddenly questioned her.

"Yes, the new intern."

He scoffed. "Is that her name? You mean like the ballet?"

"No, probably more like the supermodel."

"Well, she is a bit of a tart, isn't she?"

"Phillip..." Isabel paused, muting her urge to scold him. "Try to be a bit easier on her. She's only a college student."

"No, she's a Spears employee."

"You shouldn't comment on her posture."

"Did she complain?"

"I wouldn't call it complaining."

"Well, she *was* slouching."

"She's terrified of you, you know."

Phillip snorted like he was truly amused.

"Just like I was," Isabel added. "When I first started working here."

Phillip gazed at her with interest. "Terrified, were you? Of what? Of me?"

"Of everyone. And yes, of you."

Phillip held her gaze longer than necessary. "Well, you certainly grew out of that, didn't you? And now I can barely get you to bring me my afternoon cup of tea."

Isabel opened his office door. "Phillip, you are more than capable of getting your own tea."

"*Touché*. It's true. I am." He eyed her in the doorway. "Terrified, really?" he repeated with a mischievous glint in his eye. Then, he suddenly laughed. It was only the second time all morning that he allowed himself the luxury of expressing an unguarded emotion. "Well, you needn't have been, Isabel. You were exceedingly bright and quick-witted, despite your age and your situation."

"You mean despite being unmarried and pregnant," she clarified.

"Despite *not* being enrolled in university, unlike our newest supermodel, Miss Giselle, who only seems to know how to walk in stilettos."

"*Shhhhh*," Isabel hushed him, partly closing his office door. "Please, Phillip. I'm simply asking that you go a bit easier on her."

Phillip sat down at his desk, crossed his hands, and swiveled in his chair. His handsome face indulged in a playful smile. "For you, Isabel—I will do anything."

His valiant gaze seized upon her, conveying what was often left unspoken between them—he appreciated her more than she knew, and certainly more than his own sense of business professionalism would ever allow him to openly betray. But Isabel didn't need him to express anything more to her. He was her boss; he paid her a six-figure salary and treated her with respect because she did her job well. That was enough for her.

She turned, preparing to leave, but he called after her, as if he wasn't ready to let her go. "So you will start the ball rolling on The Peoria?"

"Yes, I'll start on it right away."

"Good." He nodded with satisfaction. "Oh, one more thing…" His voice dropped just as she was on the brink of abandoning him. "You received roses this morning?"

Isabel stopped and glanced back at him.

"Yes."

"From whom?" There was almost a hint of envy in his voice.

"Just an old friend," she slowly said, feigning disinterest.

"I see…"

It was a lie, and his searing eyes told her he knew it. A blunt chill of distrust cooled the warmth between them.

"I shall pick you up tonight at eight o'clock sharp."

"Yes, of course, Phillip. I will be ready."

Chapter Two

ISABEL STOOD IN FRONT of her dressing mirror within her bedroom, struggling to decide what to wear for the gala. Without knocking, her mother pushed in through the doorway. "*Estás preparada*?" Mrs. Alvarez asked with her sharp Castilian accent, as if she expected Isabel to stop dressing and come downstairs immediately. "Aidan is finished with his bath, and now, he is asking for you."

Isabel looked down at herself in her dressing mirror. She was only wearing her beige slip and pantyhose. "Mother, I still need a few more minutes."

Mrs. Alvarez leaned into the doorway. "Are you certain you really have to go out again tonight? You went out last night for work. I think it is time that you tell this wealthy boss of yours that your son needs you more than he does."

Isabel glanced up at her mother's displeased expression in the mirror's reflection. It was the same glare that her mother gave her whenever she wanted Catholic guilt to weigh on Isabel's soul. Isabel lowered her gaze and picked through her makeup bag, a preoccupation to avoid her mother's black judgmental eyes.

"Mother, please don't do this. You know how demanding my job is—"

"I believe it is time that you start telling *him* how demanding your job as a mother is."

Isabel sighed and lowered her mascara wand onto her dressing table. It was the same conversation they always had, but every year it grew more and more frequent. The more trust and responsibility Phillip gave her as his executive assistant, the more dinner meetings, fundraisers, and opening night galas she was expected to attend with him. And every year, her son, Aidan, grew more interested in spending time with her rather than just her mother. The pressure of juggling both her personal duties as a mother and her professional responsibilities as Phillip's assistant was starting to weigh on her—weigh on all of them—and Isabel knew the only choice she had was to promise her mother that things would be better tomorrow in a desperate attempt to skate by another day before having to make good on her promise.

"It's only one more night. One night, Mother. And after tonight, I'll be home by six o'clock for the rest of the week."

"It is not me who you need to promise. It is your son. He knows that his mother should be here, but instead, she is choosing not to be here."

"I'm not choosing anything. I'm doing my job—a job that pays for us to live in this amazing house and in this affluent neighborhood, and send my son to a prestigious preschool, and allow his grandmother the chance to enjoy her retirement, spending her free time with him. Without this job, you and I would still be cleaning houses. Except we'd probably be dragging Aidan along with us because we wouldn't be able to afford childcare. *That's* what this job means to me—to us."

A dose of her daughter's quick temper silenced Veronica Alvarez. Through the mirror's reflection, Isabel watched her mother absorb the sobering realization that she was right—painfully right. She knew her mother's inability to read and write English was a handicap that had kept her a house maid for the past thirty-five years. And she knew her mother had expected everything to be different for Isabel until a foolish college romance with an Italian foreign exchange student and an unexpected pregnancy changed that.

Mrs. Alvarez eyed Isabel's silk slip. "I hope you plan to wear something warm tonight. The wind downtown will be strong."

She closed the door. Isabel felt empty and heartless. What Isabel *hadn't* said was that they would be forced to drag Aidan along with them while cleaning houses the same way her mother had dragged her around when she was young. Isabel had refrained because she knew her mother was proud of what she had accomplished as a mother and as a widow in a foreign country. *It's so ironic how life repeats itself*, Isabel thought, reflecting on how perhaps it was an act of miraculous fate that she had ended up where she was now, or perhaps it was simply a repetition of history—her own stubborn determination to succeed at all costs for the sake of her son. Either way, Isabel knew exactly what she would *not* have without her job at Spears & Associates, and she knew the only person who had truly given her the opportunity to provide them all with a better life was her boss, Phillip Spears.

The doorbell rang.

His driver.

Isabel looked at her reflection. She barely had finished her make-up or curled her hair. She quickly finished her blush and lipstick before sweeping up her long brown hair into a French twist and securing it with an ornamental gold-plated hair clip that she reserved for special occasions. She heard voices downstairs. Aidan's bashful voice, talking to someone at the door. Then, she heard her mother's reprimanding tone. *Phillip's driver and her mother. Together without her.* Isabel sighed. She needed to get down there—and quick. She threw open her closet; she was prepared to dress in her favorite black evening dress before realizing it was still at the cleaners. Her mother spoke louder, as if she was summoning her daughter to descend the stairs with every word. *Yes, stop talking, Mother. I'm coming...* She turned to her fitted ivory dress. Could she wear ivory in October? She couldn't remember the fashion rules—but she knew she had worn it only once on an impromptu date with her dentist. *Yes, a moment of weakness.* Dating the dentist didn't last, but she still loved the dress. And at a black-tie gala hosted inside a glitzy ballroom with chandelier lighting and sapphire blue tablecloths, Isabel would stand out like a white dove passing through the night.

She glanced at her bouquet of pink flowers. She had avoided her mother's inquiries regarding where she had gotten them and had placed them in her bedroom where she could secretly admire them. And yes, she still felt an unexpected sensation of curiosity and flattery every time she surveyed their elegance. *He might be there*, she thought, as she stepped into the ivory dress and slipped it over her hips with a cautious exhale. Its hem was shorter than her black cocktail dress. Its neckline, less conservative. Perhaps she *wanted* to send him a message. She slipped on her champagne pink heels to finish off her ensemble. *No earrings.* Just the same simple diamond pendant necklace she always wore. *The dress will speak for itself.*

Yes, she confirmed with an approving nod at her reflection. Tonight might be the night in which she decided whether or not this was truly the beginning.

She followed the sound of her mother's raspy voice to the top of the staircase and peered down from the banister.

"Phillip?" she called out with surprise. She saw him at the base of the stairs waiting for her in the foyer. In the five years that she worked for Spears & Associates, it was always Phillip's driver who rang the doorbell to retrieve her. Now, Phillip gazed upwards, staring at her—and her dress—and she suddenly grew self-conscious about her choice. *Should have stuck with black or charcoal grey,* she mentally scolded herself. An ivory dress was likely too much of a departure from her usual attire, and too much of a departure for Phillip, who preferred consistency and dependability over the capricious whims of trendy fashion.

As she started down the stairs, his gaze remained on her. She suddenly considered how long he had been waiting for her. As usual, he looked handsome and distinguished in his black tuxedo, especially in contrast to the informal decor of her house—a welcome mat with polar bears, worn tennis shoes and snow boots piled in a corner of the entryway, an assortment of puffy winter jackets and hats lining the coat rack. Isabel had just shoveled the driveway after returning home late from the office, and the shovel was now dripping dirty salty water across the hardwood floor near Aidan's random rock collection.

She arrived at the base of the stairs and stared at Phillip with a mixture of embarrassment and discomfort. He had never seen the inside of her house, and it felt like an awkward intrusion. She preferred Phillip to believe that every aspect of her life was under control with the same professionalism that she asserted every day in front of him at the office, and she preferred not to grant him a voyeuristic glimpse into the constant disarray that was her household.

"Are we late?" She glanced up at her wall clock and noted the defensive tone in her own voice. Phillip noted it, too, and his response turned hard and assertive.

"No, I simply felt that it was a necessity to drop off something for my friend."

Phillip revealed a small gift from behind his back and presented it to Aidan, who was lurking in the fringes of the living room. Isabel watched her son. He had only met Phillip a handful of times when she had brought him to the office, and now, she wondered if Aidan remembered him. But the wrapped gift was too much to resist. Aidan swooped out from his hiding place, grabbed the gift from Phillip's hands, and tore off the wrapping paper, revealing a battery-powered helicopter.

"Whoa, cool!" Aidan exclaimed, watching its headlights flash and its blades swoosh in circles, all with the touch of a red button.

"Phillip, you shouldn't have." Isabel studied the helicopter. She always arranged all of Phillip's gifts—even for his own aging mother who had since passed away. *This time, Phillip had taken the time to shop for the gift himself.*

"Yes, it was obligatory. Your son has been kind enough to lend me his mother—two nights in a row. Minimally, that sacrifice deserves a new helicopter."

Suddenly, he presented a bow-tied box of chocolates to Isabel's mother. "It also deserves a gift for his grandmother as well."

Mrs. Alvarez eyed the elegant box with skepticism, but deep down, Isabel knew her mother wanted to accept the truffles more than she wanted to maintain her icy glare. How Phillip knew her mother loved Godiva chocolates, Isabel didn't know; but she also wasn't completely surprised. He always performed his due diligence in order to strategize the best angle to negotiate a business deal with anyone—including Isabel's own rigid mother.

"Thank you, Mr. Spears." Mrs. Alvarez nodded politely. "You will have my daughter home by midnight?"

"Mother—"

Mrs. Alvarez ignored her daughter and challenged Phillip with her brooding Spanish eyes. He smirked and lowered his voice like a teenager escorting Isabel to the prom. "Yes, of course. Midnight. I promise."

Isabel rolled her eyes. *Impossible.*

"Mommy, can I eat some toast before bedtime?" Aidan suddenly asked.

"Yes, of course," she said, kneeling down to her son and reaching out to him for a hug. "Nica will help you make it. I have to go now, but I'll be back soon."

Aidan flew his fancy helicopter into Isabel's arms, allowing her to kiss his cheek. "Can I wait up for you?" Mimicking the sound of sputtering blades, he cut his toy through the air.

"No, honey. Be a good boy and go to bed with Nica and don't wait up for me. I'll see you in the morning."

The disappointment on his face was almost too much to bear, and for a fleeting imaginary moment, Isabel envisioned herself telling Phillip she couldn't leave her son tonight—not again. Instead, she pushed down her guilt and pushed out her whisper. "I love you."

"I love you more," he replied, completing their special routine. "Can I bring my helicopter to bed with me?"

"Yes, of course…say thank you to Phillip for bringing it."

"Thank you, Phillip, for bringing it," he recited with bashful eyes before disappearing through the kitchen's swinging door and out of sight.

Her mother watched Isabel suppress her swelling emotions. "*Estás segura que quieras dejarnos otra vez*?"

Isabel ignored her mother's clandestine Spanish. Whenever she was forced to leave Aidan behind for work, Isabel was always conflicted about her choice, and her mother knew it. But this wasn't about what Isabel wanted; it was about what was expected of her because Phillip needed her.

"Goodnight, Mother. Don't wait up, either. I will be home late—and likely *after* midnight."

She locked eyes with her mother until her mother conceded.

"*Buenas noches*," Mrs. Alvarez said curtly to Phillip while guarding the chocolates in her arms.

Isabel watched her mother disappear into the kitchen. She would have preferred that he not witness how she struggled to sacrifice her personal life on a daily basis to make everything in her professional life seem flawlessly executed. She opened the side closet door and rummaged for her half-length natural mink coat. It had been a gift from Phillip for occasions like this… an unspoken gesture of what he expected from her in terms of public presentation. She was a symbol of his wealth and success. Faux fur was not an option.

"Allow me," Phillip suddenly offered, slipping behind her to assist with her coat.

Phillip, always the gentleman.

She felt the confidence of his touch, guiding her hands through the silk lining of the sleeves. The firmness of his chest brushed against her back as she leaned back to accept the coat's plush collar over her shoulders. The heavy weight of its authenticity disarmed her whenever she wore it. She sensed Phillip's chiseled profile passing behind her ear. She had decided at the last moment to wear perfume, something she rarely wore while working at the office. Now, she wondered if Phillip had caught its scent. *Was it too overpowering*? Isabel perspired beneath her dress as he lingered behind her—a brief moment longer than necessary—before pulling away from her.

"Thank you." She lifted her beaded purse from the hall tree. When she turned, she caught Phillip gazing at her face. *Had she put on too much blush*? She noticed his black tuxedo tie, imperfectly formed and canted to the right. *Phillip never quite got his ties right*. She reached out to adjust it. His body stiffened and his jaw flinched as she worked closely against his body.

"Better," she said with a tender smile. It was a familiar routine and they both knew it.

"Much," he agreed, eyeing her proximity.

An uncomfortable silence settled between them. Phillip turned and opened the front door, allowing her to pass through it while following her steady gait to his midnight blue Bentley parked in her driveway. Phillip's driver, Param, exited the car and assisted with the door.

"Miss Alvarez," he greeted her.

"Thank you, Param," she said, taking in his warm reassuring smile while slipping into the sleek vanilla cream seats. She never took for granted how the sensation of luxury always relaxed her—the smooth Italian leather against her thighs, the regal glints of gold-plated trim, the sensual warmth of the climate-controlled interior that immediately buffeted her from the brisk evening wind. Phillip glided into the adjacent seat and Param closed the door for him.

"You look lovely tonight," he said, filling the silence while there was a moment of privacy between them.

Isabel dropped her eyes, feeling herself flush. Phillip rarely commented on her appearance, and she wasn't used to his attentive gaze or the way he refused to release it until they were no longer alone. Param whisked open the driver side door and immediately started the car's powerful engine.

"Thank you for bringing the gifts for Aidan and my mother. My mother *is* very grateful for everything that you have done for us. She just has a hard time expressing it." Isabel stroked the pelt of her mink coat with preoccupation.

"Sometimes it's hard to express our emotions," Phillip acknowledged, lowering his tone and shifting his gaze out the car window as they merged onto Lake Shore Drive and shuttled past the black, expansive waters of the lakefront towards the twinkling lights of downtown Chicago. "Like an unbridled amorous love." Phillip eyed Isabel, then broke into a sly smile. "For chocolate."

Isabel laughed. "Yes, you definitely have discovered my mother's weakness. Although she's way too proud to ever let you know it."

"I understand." He nodded and tilted his head back against the headrest in an uncharacteristic gesture of relaxation. "There are many times when I wish I could convey my gratitude, but instead, choose to refrain from expressing it. Perhaps it is stubbornness or pride, or perhaps it is simply a cynical belief it is more prudent to remain silent rather than endure the consequences of betraying one's most intimate emotions."

"Like what, Phillip? Like your own carnal love of chocolate?" Isabel teased him.

He settled his head deeper against his seat, indulging in the casual moment between them.

"Yes, something like that."

"Well, Phillip, there are consequences for everything. All we can do is try our best to be honest with ourselves and with those who we care about most."

He stared at her, as if she had spoken a secret buried within his heart. But rather than acknowledge it, he shifted his eyes out the window at the dark meaningless void across the lake.

He straightened himself in his seat and she sensed the change within him.

"Is there an agenda for tonight?" she asked.

"The same agenda as usual." His tone was flat and filled with disinterest. Flaring across the windows, the light from the street lamps streaked past them. "I imagine news has already been bandied about regarding our intention to sell The Peoria. That will likely start the sharks circling, and where there is blood, there is always a feeding frenzy."

Isabel caught sight of Phillip's steady gaze, peering at her in his window's reflection.

She nodded. It had taken her years of experience and professional grooming to be granted the opportunity to swim in the tank with Phillip and his business colleagues, and there was always a chance of getting bitten. And with the recent news of Symeon Colovos' departure as well as Phillip's recent break-up with his fiancée, Isabel knew she would have to navigate through the evening with more caution and diplomacy than usual.

As they passed over the Chicago River and headed south towards the Loop, she glanced up at the skyscrapers, illuminated with accents of neon white, yellow, orange, green, and red like cosmic rockets, preparing to soar into the black veil of outer space. She counted three of Phillip's buildings among the parade of towering skyscrapers along the riverfront. The others were owned by his competitors—a handful of powerful men holding the deeds to seventy-percent of Chicago's downtown real estate, and almost all of whom would be there at the gala tonight.

Their Bentley cruised up to the curbside of the Watercross Tower, the newest addition to Chicago's skyline and the tallest residential complex in the city. Isabel waited for Param to exit and assist her out of the car. Guiding her to the curb, he passed her off to Phillip, who enveloped her hand within the crook of his arm and led her through the building's revolving door. She had accompanied him to functions in the past, but the intimate clasp of her hand and the matching pace of their gait towards the elevators told Isabel that Phillip was interested in keeping her closer to him than usual.

"There's a private casino at the top level," Phillip said, nodding to the tacky décor of the elevator cab's interior, trimmed with blue neon lights reflecting off the flashy metallic panels of brushed gold. He peered up at the conspicuous security camera, encased in tinted plastic in the corner of the cab. "Only a megalomaniac bastard like Eliot Watercross would exploit the only loophole in the City of Chicago's ban on downtown casinos by building it above the City's official air space rights."

Phillip pressed the call button for the ninety-ninth floor. The glittering metallic doors closed and the cab shuttled them upwards to the top of the world. Isabel knew that Eliot Watercross was one of Phillip's biggest competitors. Phillip valued original and vintage—form follows function—while Watercross preferred modern and ostentatious—the tallest and most expensive building wins. But unlike Phillip's real estate empire, which had been built upon partnerships of investment equity and solid cash flow from commercial lease deals, Phillip suspected Eliot Watercross had built up his entire real estate empire on pyramid schemes of leveraged debt. And pyramid schemes—no matter how flashy and impressive—always led to bankruptcy.

The elevator chimed and its doors slid open. They were immediately greeted by men in black catering suits. The younger one with an attentive boyish face approached Isabel.

"May I take your coat, Miss?"

She complied and slipped off her mink coat. Phillip removed his own black trench coat and passed it off to the second attendant. Then, he offered Isabel his arm as they crossed the grandiose sky-level casino, its sweeping reflective ceilings and vibrant illuminated floor panels reminding Isabel of her son's favorite carnival ride at the zoo.

Phillip surveyed the surreal atmosphere of purple neon lights and bubbly inebriated cheer. "It's a perilous pair of Jacks he's passing for a flush at the poker table, and one day, someone is going to come along and call his bluff."

Elegant men huddled over the blackjack and roulette tables, waiting for their next capricious win between their boisterous exchanges and bursts of laughter.

Isabel unexpectedly felt a hand slip around her waist and force her away from Phillip.

"Hello, lovely lady. You might just possibly be the most attractive thing in the room."

Isabel relaxed in his embrace. "Good evening, Gary." She was relieved to see it was a familiar face rather one of Phillip's more presumptuous business colleagues.

"Good evening" he playfully purred at her while releasing her from his grasp. "Are we going to get some business done tonight?" He eyed Phillip before sweeping up two champagne flutes from the tray of a server darting by them and handing off the first flute to Isabel with flirtatious chivalry. "My lady."

"There's definitely no shortage of egos here," Phillip remarked, accepting the second champagne flute from Gary while scanning the casino.

"Yeah, I'm fairly certain every man, woman, or child who owns a building east of LaSalle Street is here tonight," Gary confirmed.

"And Watercross?" Phillip asked.

"Negative," Gary replied, attempting to adjust the asymmetrical cream pocket square accentuating his royal blue Brioni suit. "Watercross is the only businessman I know who waits until everyone is drunk before arriving at his own party."

"Here…let me help you with that," Isabel offered, passing her flute off to Phillip before moving in front of Gary to unfold and re-fold his pocket square with origami precision. "I'm glad to see it's silk. I thought it might be just a cardboard cut-out."

"I'm not very good with arts and crafts," he said, peering down at her, openly admiring her face and eyes. "But you, Miss Alvarez, make everything seem so easy."

"I've had plenty of practice," she replied, glancing over at Phillip's tuxedo tie while tucking the silk square perfectly into Gary's breast pocket.

"Cheers to you," Gary announced, passing back Isabel's champagne and stealing a martini from a passing tray. "Phillip, I hope you know you're a lucky, lucky man."

Isabel caught the strange hint of jealousy in Gary's voice, and glanced at Phillip who was eyeing her reaction. She had always casually sidestepped Gary's subtle innuendos, which often crossed the professional line between them. But from the very beginning, Phillip had warned her about Gary's "affection" for women—all women—and she soon learned that he loved a good challenge even more. And Isabel certainly offered Gary a challenge.

"Where's your date tonight, Gary?" Isabel asked, calling him out on flirting with her when they all knew that Gary never attended a party alone.

"There..." Gary sighed, sucking on his olive. "By the champagne water fountain."

Blonde, Isabel noted. Gary always picked blondes.

"Well, at least she looks older than the last one," Phillip remarked.

"I try to stay above the drinking age."

"It doesn't look like it's helping." Isabel observed the blonde woman's imbalanced sway.

"She's already had three flutes," Gary admitted. They all watched her stumble towards the open bar. "Looks like that's my cue."

He quickly downed his martini and handed it off to Phillip. "Phil, always a pleasure. We're going to bag that Peoria deal. Call me in the morning—just not too early." He winked and patted Phillip on the back before glancing at Isabel. "From now on, you're going to redo all of them." He tapped his pocket square. "This is only the beginning..."

He waved goodbye with a two-fingered salute and gazed at her with searing intensity, as if he intended to leave her with those haunting words.

Feeling the color drain from her face, Isabel watched Gary stride across the expansive casino.

"Does his womanizing bother you?"

Isabel turned to Phillip, realizing she had been lost in her own private thoughts. Gary had stopped briefly to shake hands with Carlton Weiss, a serial divorcée who married and divorced women like he bought and sold properties—over and over again.

"Who? Gary or Weiss?"

Phillip smiled, knowing she was avoiding his question.

"I can handle myself, Phillip. You know that."

"Oh, yes," he replied, finishing his champagne and handing it off to a nearby waiter. "I definitely know that." He smirked, taking her hand into his own. "Come now...let's see if I can be inspired to mimic your diplomacy."

He intentionally led them towards Carlton Weiss, the man who had attempted to punch Phillip in the face at the last gala they had attended together. Weiss had failed. He had been drinking, and Phillip anticipated the throw. Weiss' fist ended up on the other side of a pane of decorative Tiffany glass. Isabel remembered everything about that night—Phillip had Param drive Weiss—and his bloody, shredded fist—to the emergency room.

Now, Phillip led her directly towards Weiss, who had moved near the seafood appetizer tower, lined with chilled caviar and oysters on the half shell. Phillip wasn't the type to avoid conflict. He was always willing to challenge it—head-on.

"How's the hand?" Phillip announced to Weiss, as if they were the only ones in the room and there was no need for formal greetings. Phillip dished up the imported black fish eggs onto the Russian blini and offered the first serving to Isabel.

"Still hurts," Weiss snapped with his blue-collar Chicago accent. "Heard you're selling The Peoria."

"News travels fast."

"Your lawyer just told me. He's got a big mouth"

"Yes, he does. That makes him very good at his job."

"I hate lawyers."

"I know," Phillip replied as he prepared a blini and offered it to Weiss. "You hate a lot of things."

Weiss glared at the blini before finally accepting it. "So cut all your fancy talk and tell me, why would you sell a premier piece of real estate like The Peoria in a pocket deal to Harvey Zale?" Carlton shoveled the delicacy into his mouth.

"Because I want to sell it fast, and you and I both know that Zale will buy anything fast."

"Anything at a discount," Weiss muttered through crumbs and caviar. "Is it a done deal?"

"Letter of intent."

"Then there's still room for a competing offer."

Phillip's answer was in his silence.

"Why are you selling?" Carlton pressed the point while wiping down his grey mustache.

"To raise capital," Phillip answered flatly. "I'm moving forward with the redevelopment of The Old Main Post Office."

"That ol' junk space?"

Phillip's blue eyes flashed like a snake preparing to strike.

This was how it happened last time, Isabel thought, *two men sparring over their egos through the reputations of their properties*. But this time, Weiss seemed more interested in making money than physically bruising Phillip's smug smile and air of British superiority.

"Taking on business partners?"

"No, it's going to be a solo project."

Weiss whistled. "Then you're gonna need more than what Harvey Zale is offering you for The Peoria." Weiss suddenly slipped his business card into Phillip's breast pocket and offered a handshake. "Call me tomorrow and let's hammer out something before you give it away to Zale. But I want to talk to *you*," he warned. "Not one of your fancy henchmen."

"You mean Jett, my broker."

"And not your chatty lawyer, either."

"I'm flattered." Phillip nodded in agreement with a mixture of sincerity and sarcasm.

Weiss paused, carefully weighing Phillip's fancy Oxford accent and whether or not it was mocking him. "Because at least with you, I know you aren't gonna kiss my ass and tell me it tastes like ice cream."

"No, certainly not," Phillip replied.

Isabel watched Phillip and Weiss shake hands like they were best friends again. She waited until Weiss crossed the room before she narrowed her eyes at Phillip.

"You're going to move forward on the full renovation?" There was an edge of accusation in her voice, and they both heard it. "You *intentionally* want the word to spread as fast as possible about The Peoria in order to help you sell it. You want to use the capital for the renovation of The Old Main Post Office."

Phillip arched his eyebrow. "What was it that Jett called you the other day?"

"Nancy Drew."

"Ahhh, yes. Nancy Drew," he repeated with amusement. "I'm more of an Agatha Christie fan. But really, you're too young and lovely to be compared to frumpy old Miss Marple."

"Phillip—" Isabel insisted, realizing she was foolish not to have understood his intention all along. "Are you really selling The Peoria to fund the full redevelopment of The Old Main Post Office?"

Phillip released a sly smile before moving closer to whisper in her ear. "Slowly, carefully," he instructed her. "Look around the room and notice how many guests were watching us, wondering if Weiss was going to throw another punch at me. Instead, they saw him give me his business card and shake my hand. That's the beauty of our industry. The best marketing tool for making a sale is still an old-fashioned one—gossip."

Isabel fixed her gaze onto Phillip's sparkling eyes. His mood suddenly grew cheery and she realized she had just witnessed her boss do what he always did best—manipulate everyone to his advantage.

"You've been planning to sell The Peoria all along in order to raise capital to renovate The Old Main Post Office, haven't you?"

He repressed his smile without responding. No response was needed. Isabel knew he loved playing chess, and he never sacrificed a rook without laying a trap to catch a Queen. Being "cornered" by Zale into selling The Peoria was simply an opportunity he intended to use to his advantage.

"I've told you many times before that some things—things that are precious and irreplaceable—deserve to be nurtured and preserved. But I think you've underestimated my commitment."

Phillip moved towards the panoramic views of the city he had come to love. Shrouded by a veil of darkness, the lights along the cityscape blinked with endless promise. He cast his gaze to the south branch of the Chicago River and settled his eyes on The Old Main Post Office, an expansive rectangular building along the riverfront.

"And now, I have decided it's simply time to finally do something about it." He shifted his gaze to Isabel and held it with determination.

"It's not that I underestimate you," she replied. "It's that I'm less of a romantic and more of a cynic who worries it might not all be worth the risk."

Her eyes drifted over The Old Main Post Office's expansive footprint, dominating all the other buildings around it like a fortress. *Three million square feet, a daunting amount of space to lease*, she considered. *And three, possibly four, rounds of renovation.*

"But it does offer so many incredibly exciting possibilities," she finally acknowledged, recalling his pledge to create a public park across the building's rooftop—a recreational garden in the summer and a public ice rink in the winter. "And no, I would never underestimate you, Phillip. If there's one thing I've learned over the past five years, it's never to underestimate Phillip Spears."

Together, they peered out through the glass, their gaze holding steadfast on the soot-stained terra-cotta walls of the historic landmark.

"Still wasting your time pining over old buildings that no one cares about, Spears?"

Isabel turned to the commanding voice—*Eliot Watercross*. She tried hard not to notice how handsome and domineering he looked in his navy Neapolitan suit. *Tall and dashing*. He handed over two glasses of white wine to Isabel and Phillip.

"Better than wasting my time constructing garish new ones," Phillip slung back with his trademark British bite.

Phillip was referring to the completion of the Watercross Tower. Watercross had outbid him for the purchase of landfill rights at the mouth of the Chicago River, and Isabel knew Phillip was still sore over it. Not since the eighteenth century, when Chicago's moguls intentionally reversed the flow of the Chicago River, had anyone fundamentally altered the city's natural waterway in the manner Watercross had when he dumped three million tons of sand and stone into the river to create the manmade foundation for his newest development. Nothing served more of a threat to Phillip's self-imposed mission to preserve Chicago's history and vintage icons than the slash and burn modernization of Watercross Capital.

"Why save it when you can tear it down and build something better for half the cost, that's what I always say." Eliot's jade eyes flashed as they settled on Isabel and her ivory dress. "You look amazing as usual, Bella."

"Thank you, Eliot." Isabel didn't dare shift her eyes to see Phillip's reaction. She already knew how much Phillip despised Watercross, but she knew he hated Eliot's presumptuous use of her nickname even more.

"Well, you've certainly made your mark on the city," Phillip said with an undercutting tone. "So that years from now, they will no doubt declare Watercross Tower as the most demonstrative example of twenty-first century consumerism."

"Better than not discussing it at all."

"Better is a matter of opinion."

"No, Spears—it's a matter of fact," Eliot sharply asserted, the annoyance in his voice rising above the sudden brass melody of lively big band music. "This project cost me seventy-five million to build and we've already sold out all the limited-edition condominiums for almost double that."

"Really?" Phillip peered at him with skepticism. "I heard at last tally, you were liquidating the remaining dozen units at auction." He sipped his wine, but his cold blue eyes challenged Eliot's claim—and his integrity.

Isabel watched Eliot's reaction. No one was more masterful than Phillip in his ability to know everything about every business deal in the city. But it was Phillip's desire to uncover the personal agendas behind every real estate transaction that made him truly a dangerous competitor. Isabel knew Phillip thought that Watercross was lying about the profitability of the development, and now, Phillip clearly wanted Watercross to know it.

Watercross chewed on his challenge before unexpectedly removing the wine glass from Isabel's hand and passing it off to Phillip.

"Shall we...?" he said, noting the swelling sway of a Viennese waltz. He didn't wait for her response or acknowledge the hesitation in her eyes. He simply took her by the hand and led her across the burgundy wooden dance floor.

From the corner of her eye, Isabel saw a crowd of bystanders exchange whispers. She suddenly felt self-conscious in her ivory dress, beaming beneath the bright lights from the stage. He encircled her in his embrace, allowing everyone in the casino to take notice of them as the sole couple sliding in unison to the rhythm of the waltz.

"I'm surprised you picked such old-fashioned music for such a modern event," Isabel said, attempting to persuade him to release her from his grasp.

"I knew you would be here, and I knew that the waltz is your favorite."

Isabel remembered the last time they danced together at the recent gala in the Cultural Center's Tiffany ballroom. Eliot had learned then that she loved to dance—and that Phillip hated giving her up to him. She suddenly thought of the flowers with a cold sense of dread.

"But somehow," she offered carefully, "dancing to a waltz feels more appropriate under the canopy of Louis Comfort Tiffany's 1897 mosaic glass dome rather than—"

"The interior of a glitzy, glamorous skyline casino?" he countered, his gaze falling upon her with intensity. "I'm a man of many dichotomies, Bella. I value stylish beauty wherever and whenever I see it." He slowly pulled her through the closure of the waltz and held her with a pause. "You should know that by now."

She did know it; he made sure of it.

"Then you understand Phillip's passion for historic preservation." The sudden tensing of her body made it clear she was on Phillip's side—always. It was one thing to enjoy the occasional ballroom dance with Eliot Watercross at a public event, it was another thing entirely to accept romantic advances from her boss' mortal enemy.

"The only thing I see is your employer's philosophical crusade to get in the way of anything that I am determined to claim for myself." Eliot's voice dropped as he embraced her tightly, making it clear that she should reconsider her allegiances.

"Eliot," Isabel whispered, resisting the innuendos behind his touch.

Usually, Phillip's business colleagues brushed her aside, or worse like Carlton Weiss, ignored her completely. But not Eliot Watercross. Eliot Watercross always made her feel like the most important person in the room. It had been a very long time since anyone had held her the way Eliot Watercross held her whenever they danced together. Powerfully seductive. *It had been long…too, too long.*

She stopped his lead and collected her composure. "Thank you for the dance, but there are so many people I still need to see tonight. "

Watercross did not attempt to draw her back to him. Instead, he outlined the platinum strand of her necklace with the tip of his finger. The delicate sensation along her neckline silenced her protest.

"Lovely, but too modest." His finger lingered over the diamond pendant, the first Christmas gift that Phillip had ever given her.

She gazed into his jade eyes and attempted not to betray how Eliot's seductive touch made her yearn for more. Working for Phillip and raising her son had dominated every aspect of her personal and professional life for the past five years. There was no room to enjoy anything or anyone else—especially not the possibility of an intimate romance, and especially not one with a man like Eliot Watercross.

"I'm sure you don't mind my cutting in—" Phillip's voice asserted.

The waltz had come to an end and the band quickly rolled into a popular swing tune. Phillip guided Isabel towards him; Eliot relinquished her from his arms and surrendered her without a fight.

"It was my pleasure." He bowed. Isabel watched with disappointment as he disappeared through the fresh mix of couples that flowed onto the dance floor, and turned his attention towards a group of Chinese business investors who had just arrived.

Phillip gazed at her frown. "Don't tell me you're smitten with Watercross?"

Isabel glanced back at Phillip; she had been both foolish and careless. The music bounced with an upbeat tempo, but Phillip did not lead her through the steps. Instead, he guarded her in his arms as if he expected an answer.

"I'm always smitten with Eliot," she casually tossed back. "He dances the waltz like an expert—almost as well as you." She tried to nudge Phillip into the dance, but he resisted.

"I see…so you're easily impressed."

Isabel challenged his gaze. "Women like to be wooed, Phillip. It makes us feel like we're *actually* women. Are you jealous?" She fully expected him to sneer at the suggestion.

Instead, his cool blue eyes stared at her with disarming conviction. "I don't want him recruiting away my most important business asset."

"He'd have to pay me double what you're paying me," she teased. "Plus, I like my bosses to be British and surly. So I think you're safe for now, Phillip."

Isabel feigned a smile, urging him again to start his lead. But he held her a moment longer than necessary. Suddenly, she regretted the entire exchange. She knew he depended on her on a daily basis, and the insinuation that she might leave his company or become romantically involved with one of his direct competitors wasn't something to joke about.

Without warning, Phillip pulled her against his chest, closer than he had ever embraced her before. Maybe she imagined it or maybe he was simply more attached to her tonight because of her own behavior.

"Never safe enough…" he whispered into her ear, betraying a hint of rare vulnerability. Phillip's unforgiving embrace rotated her body, allowing her to gaze across the casino at Symeon Colovos and Marlow Sheffield, who strode out of the elevators—together.

Phillip's ex-fiancée, she noted. *How long had it been since Phillip last saw her*? Isabel wasn't certain. Marlow looked stunning in her full-length evening gown and black opera gloves. Phillip steadily watched Marlow. Isabel watched Eliot move past the poker tables to greet them. He bowed and embraced Marlow's gloved hand with a flirtatious kiss. Like a silent movie star, Marlow threw back her red painted lips with animated laughter. She had always been the center of attention whenever she accompanied Phillip, and in that moment, she continued to be the center of attention because she commanded it.

The swing tune ended and the band shifted the tempo into the melancholy jazz ballad, *My Funny Valentine.*

"C'mon," Isabel encouraged Phillip, attempting to draw his attention away from something over which neither of them had any control. "This is one of my favorite songs, and you're my favorite dance partner."

She confessed it with sincerity, hoping it would help him dismiss the distraction. It worked. Phillip relaxed his shoulders and drew her against his chest. His cheek, smooth and freshly shaven, brushed against her own. She noted the familiar scent of his cologne—a European old-world fragrance with a hint of citrus. Its familiarity made her settle into his arms as he led them across the ballroom floor. She closed her eyes; the soft, brooding melody overwhelming her senses. She always loved dancing with Phillip. She never had to think about anything other than where he wanted her body to flow, and it made her trust him—unconditionally. Publically, in front of the office staff and his business colleagues, Phillip was always her stern, demanding boss. But on the dance floor, without anything between them except their mutual desire to unite their swaying movements, he made her feel like his equal. He led and she followed. But together, they were always one.

"Hello, Phillip." The abrupt interruption of the female voice disrupted the harmony of the connection between them. Isabel opened her eyes. She saw Marlow, radiant in her lava red dress, in the arms of Phillip's former ex-business partner, Symeon Colovos.

"Marlow..." Phillip nodded. Isabel felt his body stiffen as the conclusion of the song drew Marlow away from Symeon and closer to Phillip.

Marlow did not acknowledge Isabel. She never did.

Isabel noted Marlow's lush wet lips. *Siren Rogue.* She recognized the lipstick color because she had been the one who had bought it for her when she discovered that Phillip had forgotten Marlow's birthday. Isabel had scrambled during her lunch hour to find something suitable for him to present to Marlow over dinner. She had chosen it because she knew Marlow could pull off flaming red. But now, Isabel gazed at her lips—and the way Marlow was flaunting her new relationship with Symeon—and only saw the color of poison.

"Hello, Marlow...Symeon," Isabel acknowledged Phillip's ex-business partner. It was the first time she had seen Symeon since his explosive departure from the firm. He looked freshly tanned, back from a recent vacation to a tropical location, and his bald head reflected the lights from the stage like a Greek god. But his dark black eyes settled on Phillip with aggression. Uncharacteristically avoiding the conflict, Phillip turned Isabel away from them.

"Running away already?" Symeon called after him, circling Marlow into his arms, flaunting his possession over her as the live band started up their lively introduction to a new dance number. Isabel knew that neither Marlow nor Symeon knew how to dance. It was a deliberate attempt to position themselves in front of Phillip.

Phillip stopped and glared back at him. "I'm English. I don't dance the jive."

Symeon snorted like it was the funniest admission in the world. "Then I should take this opportunity to let you know that we'll soon be neighbors. I'm buying the Amway building."

"Yes, congratulations on successfully purchasing it through Zale's reassignment of our deal to you," Phillip said dryly. "Quite a masterful maneuver of cunning deceit."

"Hard not to claim what's rightfully mine, Spears."

Phillip shifted his glance to Marlow. "You've always been one to take what you can get via any means possible."

Marlow eyed the mounting tension between them, as if she enjoyed it. She pulled away from Symeon and slid her long, feline figure between Isabel and Phillip.

"It looks like neither of you has figured out that this is a party, not a cockfight. And we women *much* prefer parties."

Wrapping her ballerina arms around Phillip's neck, she smoothed down the lapels of his suit and asserted their former familiarity and intimacy. Then, she turned and flashed her fierce eyes at Isabel. "Why don't you go and get us all some drinks."

It was a standard Marlow maneuver, reducing Isabel to the status of subservient employee whenever possible.

"I'd be happy to." Isabel forced a smile. She had never enjoyed Marlow's melodrama, and she wasn't about to indulge in witnessing it now.

"No—" Phillip halted her.

Marlow glanced at Isabel, then back at Phillip, who punished her with his callous glare. She released a nervous laugh and outlined his angular cheek with her fingertip as a moment of understanding lingered between them, which even Symeon noticed was prolonged.

"Symeon, did you tell Phillip the good news?" Marlow pulled herself away from Phillip and reclaimed her status as Symeon's possession. "Symeon is going to partner with Eliot Watercross on his next project."

For a brief moment, Phillip's eyes clouded with uncertainty. It was obvious to Isabel that he hadn't heard the news—which was rare for him. He processed the new information with silent reserve, but deep down, Isabel wondered if he was considering all the ways a romantic relationship between Marlow and Symeon—much less a business partnership between Eliot Watercross and Symeon Colovos—made him vulnerable.

"Exactly what I expected," Phillip finally said. "Now, you'll excuse us."

He took Isabel by the hand and led her towards the elevators. Isabel glanced back at Marlow as she draped her arms around Symeon's neck and clung onto him like a buoy in the open sea. What was it about her that made Isabel feel so inferior? Was it her heiress background? Her ability to assert Isabel's social status as beneath her own? Or perhaps it was the constant reminder in her presence that no matter how deep Isabel believed her connection was with Phillip, it would never rival the fact that Marlow had once been his fiancée. As they entered the elevator in silence, Isabel glanced at Phillip and followed his distracted gaze, still fixed on Marlow and Symeon far across the casino. Perhaps that was the answer—she had just witnessed the reason why Phillip had invited her to accompany him to the gala, and she was unable to ignore how it made her feel like an outsider amongst them.

Chapter Three

Within the dark car, Phillip and Isabel remained silent. Param cut through the moonless veil of midnight like a speeding demon. Phillip kept his eyes fixed out the window—a conscious attempt to avoid conversation. Isabel took his cue and reflected on the people and events of the evening. She occasionally replayed her interaction with Eliot—flashes of his suggestive words and alluring glances. But each time she returned to them in her thoughts, she quickly dispersed them from her mind. *This is only the beginning…*

Tomorrow, she would throw away the flowers. If they were from Eliot, there was no reason to keep them because she could no longer indulge in the fantasy of a romantic relationship between them. The "beginning" of *any* sort of relationship that Eliot sought to initiate between them had to be swiftly and decisively ended before it even started. She considered whether or not she had given him mixed signals. *She was sure she had…* But now, she reflected upon the fact that her sole priority was taking care of her family by maintaining her professional career, which meant maintaining her loyalty to Phillip. Her emotional needs—and her needs as a woman—would simply have to be put on hold for a few more years. It had been a wonderful night of dancing, conversation, and flirtation. But Isabel had swiftly been reminded that she was only invited to these galas as Phillip's assistant to further his professional agenda, not to advance her own personal life by entertaining the flirtatious advances of her boss' competitor.

She glanced over to Phillip, whose profile was shrouded in darkness. His expression was stern and unflinching, like a marble statue of a Roman emperor. But the accents of his wealth—his gold Rolex watch, his diamond cuff links, the shine of his polished Italian leather shoes—glinted every time they passed under the rolling lights of the street lamps. His tailored black dress coat made him look like a man who feared nothing—other than the consequences of allowing others the privilege of coming too close to him.

"You're very quiet, Isabel. Have you regretted your decision to come with me tonight?" His deep Oxford accent unexpectedly disrupted the invisible wall of silence.

Isabel peered at him in surprise. "No, not at all."

His eyes were obscured by shadows, but the tenderness in his voice revealed he wasn't consumed with thoughts about business; he was concerned about her answer.

"Of course, I wish sometimes I could spend more time with Aidan," she confessed, smoothing down the folds of her dress along her legs. She felt his eyes, following her nervous preoccupation, and she raised her hand back into the slope of her lap. "But I understand that you needed me there tonight, and I was happy to accompany you."

He unexpectedly reached out and touched her hand—both a gesture of gratitude and affection. "Thank you for coming. It was above and beyond the call of duty, and I want you to know that I deeply appreciate it."

Isabel felt herself flush. Phillip rarely expressed affection, and she had long since grown used to his British reserve. Even when they danced together, he led her with his expertise, not his touch—the delicate, flowing motions of a master in synchronization with his muse. Now, his hand lingered over hers before pulling away and Isabel suddenly realized that he was reaching out to her as a friend rather than a boss.

"Was it difficult for you?" she cautiously asked. "With Symeon and Marlow there—together?"

Phillip fully shifted his gaze towards her. The deep shadows receded from the angles of his face and Isabel sensed the indecision within him—a rare moment of hesitation, as if he wanted to express something more to her, but refrained because he was uncertain about whether or not it was appropriate.

"I am not generally one who has many regrets," he finally said. "But I cannot deny that recent events have persuaded me to evaluate the past choices in my life—choices that now seem conspicuously flawed and negligent."

Isabel listened to Phillip's bitter confession, searching out the deeper meaning beneath it.

"Are you concerned because you shared confidential details about the business with Marlow?"

Phillip winced, as if a hammer had cracked through the sculpted lines of his frown. "Good God, no." He snorted with amusement. "I quickly learned—early on—the only thing worthy of sharing with Marlow was my bed. And even now, I realize my error behind that choice."

Isabel smiled. She couldn't help it. Marlow was young, beautiful, and seductive. But she was also rude, spoiled and capricious—completely different than Phillip in every way. Isabel knew very little about Phillip's childhood, but she did know that he had used his love of books and schooling to ascend the ranks of his class in England and attend Harvard Business School on scholarships; Marlow, on the other hand, was a privileged heiress who partied her way through college on Daddy's dime, knowing she would never have to work an honest day in her life.

Two years ago, Phillip met Marlow at a charity ball. Isabel had always assumed Marlow had been the one who pursued Phillip because he never seemed fully committed to her—or their relationship. Phillip's abrupt announcement of their wedding engagement last year forced Isabel to admit to herself that she didn't know her boss as well as she thought. In fact, the only news that seemed more shocking than their sudden engagement was the news that Marlow had broken it off—just as suddenly—in order to pursue a relationship with Phillip's ex-business partner, Symeon Colovos.

"And Symeon?" Isabel pressed him.

"No, Symeon Colovos wasn't smart enough to attempt to understand the structure of the company or its financials. You're the only one, Isabel, who knows as much about the company as I do."

Isabel stared at Phillip, attempting to comprehend his words. Over the years, he had slowly entrusted her with access to all the financial documents of his investment properties as well as his firm's balance sheet and his billionaire net worth. But she was surprised to hear that she was the only one in the company—other than Phillip—who knew any of the confidential details.

"Phillip," she said, choosing her words with precision and care. "I want you to know that I take my job working for you very seriously. I do not take your trust in me for granted, and regardless of anything I might have said or done tonight…" She stopped, suddenly pained by her own careless actions. "I want you to know that I am fully committed to you—always."

Phillip looked at her, as if her words pierced through his armor of guarded emotions and lanced his most private thoughts and desires. His eyes weighed private thoughts that could not be expressed through words.

"Yes… thank you." His voice was raspy with restraint, and he glanced away through his window as their car approached Isabel's house. His silence told her that nothing more needed to be said, and the rare intimacy between them faded into the darkness. It had been a long, long night; now, it was time to leave everything behind them and part ways as usual.

"Good night, Phillip," she said softly, lingering in the darkness before Param pulled open her door and led her out by the hand.

She did not hear Phillip greet her goodbye in return. Instead, she only heard the eerie creaking of her house, settling in its foundation as the wind rushed against its wooden siding and pushed her along the pathway up to her dimly lit porch.

"Isabel—"

Phillip's commanding accent forced her to stop and turn back towards the Bentley. He had called out to her through the car's lowered window. She checked to see if she had left behind her purse. *No, she had everything with her.* She peered back at him with an uncertain pause.

"Be sure to spend tomorrow morning with Aidan. We'll manage at the office without you. Your son, no doubt, needs time to show off his new helicopter to his mum."

Without waiting for her response, the tinted window slowly rose, but not before Phillip's blue eyes glinted with his trademark devilish charm. Isabel smiled and nodded. She unlocked the front door and pushed into the security of the foyer as the car peeled away from the curb and raced away into the distant night.

Thank you, Phillip. Thank you for everything.

She navigated through her house with care, quietly bumping into a series of Aidan's cars, trucks, and plastic jungle animals lined along the foyer's stairs like a barricade.

Aidan had been playing there, waiting up for her…

She saw her son's dirty clothes, tossed haphazardly in a pile on the floor. She lifted up the clothes and smelled Aidan's familiar scent—a mixture of gravel dust, mud, and boyish perspiration. She smiled. Everything about him was still so precious.

Ascending the staircase, she heard her mother's nasal snore filtering out of the master bedroom. Isabel quietly closed her door and silenced her. She entered into her own bedroom. Kicking off her heels and peeling off the stockings from her legs, she undressed in the darkness. *God, how she hated pantyhose.* She replaced her ivory dress with a pair of yoga pants and ragged T-shirt that made her feel like a teenager again. She glanced over at the bouquet of roses, perched on her dresser, and admired their majestic silhouette. She closed her eyes and inhaled their scent. *They made her bedroom smell like expensive perfume.* Whoever sent them to her knew exactly what she liked and how much she would enjoy them. Her gaze lingered on them, indulging in a final moment of fantasy before reaffirming her plan to throw them into the garbage the next morning.

She slipped out into the hallway and crept into her son's bedroom. Aidan stirred under the train pattern of his sheets. She had bought a double bed for him, knowing that there would be many nights when he would ask her to sleep by his side, and she would be unable to refuse. But when she had been away from him the whole day and night, it was she who often sought to sleep by his side. She peered down at him, admiring his sweet heart-shaped face and acknowledging to herself how little time she had spent with him over the course of the past two days. She slipped next to him with a cuddle, vowing to him—and to herself—that tomorrow would be different. His shallow breaths whispered against her cheek as her mind replayed a drifting collage of images from the day—the rush to the office, the sound of Gary's brash voice, Tami's animated expressions, Giselle's naïve gaze, the soft shell pink color of the roses, Aidan's joyful acceptance of his new helicopter, her mother's disapproving glare, the flashing neon lights of the casino, Eliot Watercross' tiger green eyes, Marlow's Snow White red lips… but ultimately, it was the sway of being in Phillip's confident arms and the melancholy echo of her favorite song that eventually put her fast to sleep.

Chapter Four

ISABEL WALKED OFF THE platform of the "L" train and descended the stairs down to the street level. She loved not having to rush in the morning. She was always running late for work, trying to balance her need to spend a few extra minutes with Aidan over getting out the door and catching the train to downtown. Her mother couldn't understand why she just didn't drive to the office.

"That demanding boss of yours pays you enough to have an expensive car and you never drive it," Mrs. Alvarez complained every morning.

But Isabel hated fighting the morning rush hour, and preferred riding the elevated Brown line train, where she could relax with her coffee and contemplate life and everything around her while winding through the city's buildings and brownstones. This morning, she had woken up next to her son, whose green almond-shaped eyes and elfin smile beamed back at her.

"Good morning, Mommy. I love you," Aidan said with such sincerity that she wished he would stay four-years old forever.

"I love you more."

"I stayed up last night for you, but you never came home."

"I know, honey. I had to work. But now, I'm here the whole morning, and I'm going to make pancakes."

"With syrup?"

"Lots and lots."

"Yummy. Let's go downstairs together, Mommy…" He grabbed her hand and led her out of bed in a rush for the kitchen.

Eating pancakes and spending time with Mommy—such simple joys, she smiled to herself as she strode along the harsh pavement streets and past dozens and dozens of anonymous faces. She took comfort in the fact that it was Friday, and she had no other plans or commitments that weekend except spending time with the most important person in her life—her son.

When she arrived at the lobby of the office, Lucy greeted her with a beaming smile.

"Heard you got the morning off. Looks like you enjoyed it."

Isabel stopped in front of Lucy's receptionist desk. "Pancakes with Aidan."

"Ummm, hmmmm. Sounds good," Lucy clucked. "You worked late last night?"

"Gala with Phillip. Opening of the Watercross Tower."

Lucy chewed on the end of her pen and eyed Isabel. "You mean Eliot Watercross? Doesn't Phillip hate that man?"

"Yes," Isabel sighed, sipping her coffee. "But we still have to go and work the room."

"That's Phillip…all work, work, work, and no play, play, play…"

Suddenly, the phone rang. Lucy answered it, touching the side of her headset and changing over into her smooth receptionist voice.

"Phillip Spears & Associates. Yes…May I tell him who's calling?" She paused and shifted her eyes up to Isabel. "One moment, please…" Lucy placed the caller on hold, then dialed the extension. "Phillip has been asking about you all morning."

"Has he scheduled an unexpected meeting?"

"No, girl…he just can't do anything without you."

Isabel rolled her eyes. "Men love to pretend they're helpless when it gets them what they want."

Lucy nodded. "You know that's true. Unofficially—he wants you to know that he hasn't been asking all morning if you've arrived yet. Those are *my* words. Officially—you should take your time. *His* words. I found him this morning, staring at the copy machine, trying to find the START button."

Isabel smiled, indulging in the image of Phillip in front of the copy machine, or anything mechanical. "I told him yesterday that Giselle is scared of him, so he likely didn't want to ask for help."

"Well, I rescued him. But I think he would have preferred you over me. Phillip's got his pride. You know how it is."

"Yes, I certainly do. Thanks, Lucy."

"No problem."

Isabel passed through the double glass door and strode through the open office towards her desk. She set her coffee and purse down while peeking into Phillip's executive suite. *On the phone—as always.* She stalled a few more minutes, contemplating entering his office to greet him. Instead, she slipped off her coat and rolled through all her phone messages while logging into her computer. Then, she noticed it. There, partially obscured by a freshly copied lease contract, was a sleek gift bag adorned with a white satin ribbon. Isabel glanced around the office. The other girls were on the phone or typing on their keyboards. Isabel felt her heart flutter as she sank into her chair, reached out for the bag, and secretly slid it into her lap. She peered down through its tufts of white tissue paper and spotted the oxblood red box with its distinct gold engraving: *Cartier.*

Isabel touched her forehead. She was perspiring. *This is just the beginning…*

She recalled the inscription from yesterday's flowers. Determined to avoid the flood of conflicted emotions she was experiencing right now, she had thrown them out with the garbage this morning, despite their full bloom and luscious scent.

Close the bag and don't explore what's inside it…

She closed her eyes and paused, considering all her options, including leaving the gift untouched in her purse until the end of the day when she would carry it home and deal with it—and its consequences—in the privacy of her own bedroom. Her eyes fell upon the pink miniature envelope, just above the jewelry box. She quickly unsealed it.

With the same strong black penmanship scrolled across a white calling card, it read: *Tonight, I will treat you like a Queen.*

Isabel stared down at the card, her eyes passing over the words without repeating them—except one: *Queen.* A paralyzing silence overcame her as she lifted the red leatherette jewelry box out of the bag and creaked open its lid.

"Holy mother of God, what the hell is that?"

Startled, Isabel shut the box and looked up at Tami, attempting to scoot under her desk to conceal the gift. But it was too late.

"Seriously, did I just see what I think I saw?" Tami adjusted her glasses and leaned in for an uncomfortable view of Isabel's lap.

"*Shhhhhh*—" Isabel pushed her away and glanced into Phillip's office. *Still occupied with his phone call.*

"Don't *shhhh* me," Tami slung back. "I freaking know Cartier when I see it, and holy mother fucking bananas, *that* is some amazing Cartier bling-bling."

Tami and Isabel looked down at the necklace and its five brilliant oval-cut sapphires, surrounded by round-cut diamond studs in a platinum setting. Elegant, regal, and easily worth more than either of them made in an entire year.

"You look like you're going to throw up," Tami suddenly said.

"I might." Isabel stood up and searched for her trashcan.

"No, no…" Tami rushed around her desk and consoled her. "No, don't…especially not on the bling. Just sit down and breathe and try not to—"

Isabel handed off the card to Tami, who grew silent the moment she read it. "My God…"

"Sapphire is my birth gemstone," Isabel added, looking up at her. "Whoever sent it knows my birthdate, and he knows my favorite color is pink."

"And he knows you're in need of a really good fuck," Tami added.

Isabel glared up at her, unappreciative. "Thanks."

"Okay, you win. It's wicked weird, *but*—" Tami countered, trying to muster up enough empathy to win back Isabel's attention, "—you and I both know you've been off the market for way, way, *way* too long, and so does your secret admirer. Maybe this is just his way of telling you it's time. Maybe tonight, it's time to just let it all hang out."

"No, absolutely not." Isabel tried to control the horror in her voice. "And definitely not without knowing who he is before I let anything 'hang out'."

"Well, who do *you* think it is?"

Isabel felt the blood rush from her cheeks. She lowered her voice and traced the gold lettering of *CARTIER* on the leatherette box. "I can't be sure, but I think it might be…" Isabel paused then made the leap. "Eliot Watercross."

Tami gasped and covered her mouth. "Phillip's mortal enemy?"

Isabel nodded. "I saw him last night. We danced together in front of three hundred of his guests. Phillip was not happy with me."

"Clearly, Eliot Watercross was *more* than happy with you." Tami licked her lips and shimmied her body.

"How can you not find this all a bit unnerving?"

"Because it's like you said: he's someone who *knows* stuff about you. Plus, there's no creepy stalking sicko in the world who could possibly afford that kind of bling, which is why if you're not going to let him woo you, worship you, and then fuck you, you should direct him to me. I've got serious needs and they most definitely are going unfulfilled."

Isabel rubbed her face and tried to avoid her own thoughts. "I just can't deal with this right now."

"I think you can and you should," Tami encouraged, lifting up the box and putting it back in Isabel's hands. "You *deserve* to be treated like a queen, even if it's only once, and even if it *is* by Phillip's mortal enemy."

"Tami!" Jett suddenly bellowed from across the hallway. "I can't find my nose hair clippers and I've got a one o'clock lunch date with Fifi Litzker."

Tami rolled her eyes. "Such a Neanderthal."

"And my nasal spray!"

"Coming—" she hollered back and started towards his office. "Seriously, Isabel…just go along with it for once in your life. Whatever Mr. Billionaire Mystery Man wants from you, give it to him—even if it's only one night. But if not, text me, and I'll gladly show up for you—sporting that amazing necklace and nothing else. Maybe he'll never know the difference."

Tami winked and rushed away into Jett's office. Isabel glanced into Phillip's office. His eyes were fixed on her. He had ended his call and motioned for her to enter. She collected her pen and notepad and placed the Cartier box back into the silver bag before slipping it into her purse. She had no intention of following Tami's advice, but unlike the roses, a diamond and sapphire designer necklace wasn't something she could simply throw away.

When she entered Phillip's executive suite, she saw Norton Harrington, lounging casually in a side chair near the windows with his eyes closed. Isabel stopped and studied him—Norton was eighty-some years old. His face and hands were withered like prunes and his frail frame sank beneath his grey suit. For a brief paranoid moment, she studied him to ensure he was still breathing.

"Norton and I are discussing The Old Main Post Office," Phillip said and nodded for her to take a seat.

"Phillip is discussing it," Norton retorted, sunning his face with the rays streaming through the window, completely uninterested in the topic. "I've already told him he's a damn fool for wanting to restore it. And now I'm being tortured by our merciless employer."

Amused, Phillip grinned and rolled his fingertip across the glass surface of his desk. "Norton, you're only one of a dozen people in the city who actually remembers it during its glory days."

"And I prefer to take those secrets to my grave," Norton said, ominously lifting up one eyelid.

"Rubbish. If that were true, you would have retired ten years ago."

Norton closed both eyes again. Despite his age, Norton was one of the sharpest, most knowledgeable actuaries with expertise in assessing development risk for vintage properties. At any other firm, he would have been forced to retire when the booming real estate market favored investment in contemporary developments over historic preservation. But at Spears & Associates, Norton was one of Phillip's most trusted colleagues, and one of his most valuable employees.

"Norton has seen the plans for its redevelopment—the ones we drafted last year. I've asked him to have a look again to render his opinion."

"And…?" Isabel turned to Norton.

"And I think Phillip is mad as a hatter—as usual."

Phillip swiveled in his seat, clearly amused. "But what do you think of the budget?"

Norton opened his eyes and shifted his listless gaze across the cityscape.

"You paid two hundred thousand dollars for the property twenty years ago when the government officially shuttered its doors and put it up for auction. You've already spent approximately fifty million dollars renovating its Beau-Arts marble lobby. And now, you plan to spend three hundred million dollars more to fully redevelop it."

"As a mixed commercial and residential development—with both retail boutique shops and affordable condominiums with the full amenities of expansive roof-top gardens, underground parking, and riverfront views. An urban mecca of vintage living."

"Hogwash," Norton shot back. "It's a three-million-square-foot blight on your balance sheet."

Phillip let out a soft laugh. Isabel knew Phillip secretly liked the fact that Norton was the only one in the office willing to challenge him at every turn. "Your expertise is not required to appraise the current value of the building, Norton. Your expertise is needed to evaluate the budget for its redevelopment in relation to the investment risk."

Norton lifted one piercing eye at Phillip before shutting it again with resentment. "Extremely high," he punctuated. "A three million dollar budget is sufficient, but grossly imprudent. And you've already spent fifty million dollars restoring its grand marble lobby."

"The building is a one-of-a-kind historical landmark," Phillip cut in. "Which arguably makes its restoration value...priceless."

Norton conceded Phillip's point. "It's true. Its structural wooden beams are sawn lumber—solid prairie oak timber of a grade that would cost one hundred times current market rates for lumber if an exact replica was built today because trees of that size and density simply no longer exist. In addition, trains no longer deliver the mail the way they did when The Old Main Post Office was the major continental hub of postal transportation. But the railroad tracks beneath the belly of the building are still fully accessible and connect to the existing modern commuter rail system, allowing for instant accessibility by hundreds of thousands of residents and tourists."

"And retrofitting for current safety codes?" Phillip prodded him.

"My estimation is that the regulators would have minimal additional requirements upon inspection of the restoration," Norton replied, as if it pained him. "If a fire broke out today, it would smolder out on its own because The Old Main Post Office was constructed to withstand infernos like the Great Chicago Fire. In short—the building is a perfectly preserved historic fortress, and your budget for its restoration accounts for every single aspect of preserving its vintage integrity. Whether or not spending three hundred million dollars to make it useful to modern-day society is worth the risk is another matter entirely. I still contend that it is not."

Phillip rubbed his jaw, absorbing Norton's negativity with displeasure.

"There's still the question of the bureaucratic red tape, Phillip," Isabel jumped in. "Our zoning application and redevelopment plans still need to be approved by the city."

"Then we shall host a grand gala at The Old Main Post Office and invite all the city officials we need in order to expedite zoning approval."

Norton snorted. "An old-fashioned Chicago ball to grease the palms of our old-fashioned Chicago bosses?"

"Precisely." Phillip nodded. "It's a federal landmark. We'll appeal to their sense of patriotism as well as their affinity for campaign contributions."

"That, my dear boy, is a hornet's nest beyond my expertise." Norton rose from his seat and nodded to Isabel. "And unfortunately for you, young lady, I sense that Phillip is about to delegate a new project onto your plate. Be sure to ask for a raise."

Isabel hid her smile and waited until Norton hobbled out of Phillip's office before confirming its truth. "A grand gala at The Old Main Post Office?"

Phillip lifted up his gold-plated pen and flipped it across his knuckles. "An ambitious project for an equally ambitious woman."

Isabel brushed off his compliment. "And I suppose you have an equally ambitious timeline to pull off this sort of thing?"

"The faster, the better. We'll hire whoever you want to assist with the event coordination."

"Of course." She nodded, trying not to think about all of the long evenings she was going to spend orchestrating a grand gala. "And a guest list beyond city officials? It's our opportunity to showcase the property to the community, you know."

"You mean showboat it—the same way as Eliot Watercross?"

Isabel heard the spite in his voice. "I simply mean that Eliot has a way of gaining media exposure for his properties that garners him significant notoriety."

"Yes, notoriety," he repeated as if he was drawing out the oxygen from the room. "I shall leave it to you to do whatever you deem best."

Their intimate connection from the previous evening was completely gone. Now, Phillip seemed like nothing more than a callous real estate tycoon who expected his priorities to be received and executed—regardless of the cost. She stood up and turned away, realizing his eyes were pushing her out of his office.

"Oh, and Isabel…" his stern voice stopped her in her tracks. "Did you find the gift bag that was delivered to you this morning?"

Confused, Isabel glanced back at him. "Yes…" she heard herself whisper.

"Good. I was the first one in the office this morning, and so I was the one who signed for it from the messenger." He glared at her, distrust shadowing his face. "Another gift from an old friend?"

Their eyes locked. She knew what he was thinking; exactly what she had tried to avoid thinking herself—that it was a gift from Eliot Watercross. She quickly replayed the physical details of the gift bag in her mind. *How much had Phillip seen? The card?* No, it was sealed when she opened it. *Had he seen the Cartier box below the white tufts of tissue paper?* Perhaps—if he had dared to allow himself the indiscretion to investigate inside it.

"Yes, something like that," she finally answered. It was a cold, mechanical response, one intended to convey that it was none of Phillip's business because it was nothing—truly nothing at all.

Chapter Five

FOR THE REST OF THE DAY, Isabel remained at her desk, placing phone calls, drafting emails, and preparing a game plan for organizing a grand gala at The Old Main Post Office in the shortest amount of time possible. She knew Phillip would expect her to have answers for him by the end of the day—a full invitation list, a tentative date, an estimated budget, and even a theme for the ball.

Elisa, the office coordinator, breezed up to Isabel and handed off the mail. "Phillip seems kinda grumpy today," she whispered. "Everything okay?"

"Phillip is English," Isabel replied under her breath while typing out an email. "The more interesting question is when is he *not* grumpy?"

"Gotcha," Elisa sympathized. "Are you staying late tonight? Since it's Friday, most of the girls are doing happy hour up at the bars in River North."

Isabel stopped typing and sighed. "God, I'd love a cocktail right now, you have no idea. But I can't. I've been out late for the past two nights, and Aidan needs me home at a decent hour."

"Totally get it. So that means you're not allowed to stay past five tonight."

Elisa glanced up at the wall clock.

Almost four-thirty. Isabel sighed. "How does that happen?" The whole day had escaped her and she had barely made any progress at all.

"It happens because you spend too much time at your desk—actually working." Elisa giggled. "You need to lower your standards and waste more time with the rest of us, gossiping in the bathroom and making homemade Frappuccinos in the kitchen."

Isabel glanced towards Phillip's office door. "Not even a possibility."

"It's true. You are a slave to the master. And you protect the rest of us."

"For better or worse…" Isabel quipped and resumed typing.

"For better *and* worse," Elisa corrected her.

Suddenly, the women silenced themselves as Phillip exited his executive suite, wearing his formal black overcoat and carrying his leather briefcase.

"Leaving early today," he said curtly to Isabel. "We'll touch base over email this weekend about the gala."

Phillip did not make eye contact and there was no formal goodbye. He simply turned and strode down the long office corridor.

Isabel fumbled in confusion. She quickly glanced at her phone, scanning their shared calendar—no happy hour drink or early dinner meetings had been scheduled with his colleagues or investment partners.

"Good night, Mr. Spears," Elisa called after him. "Happy Friday."

Phillip nodded, but he did not glance back. Like a phantom, he disappeared through the double glass doors and out of sight.

"Someday, I'll get him to say goodbye to me," Elisa asserted, like it was her own personal challenge. "Do you think he'd fire me if I openly addressed him as Mr. Grumpy Pants?"

"Yes." Isabel tried not to smile—too freely. Her official title within the company was "senior executive assistant," and everyone knew she was ultimately responsible for overseeing the office conduct of all of Phillip's staff. "Go tell the girls to get out of here a bit early and enjoy your drinks. It's been a long week for everyone, including Phillip. Happy Friday."

"Awesomesauce," Elisa exclaimed. "Thanks, Isabel. We'll toast a cocktail to you in your honor. Oh, I almost forgot…" she said, doubling back to Isabel's desk. "This just came for you."

Elisa placed a glossy white box onto Isabel's desk. Isabel glanced down at it, then at Elisa. "From who?"

"I don't know…I saw the bike messenger waiting at the reception desk for Lucy. But she was away from her desk, using the bathroom, so I signed for it. He said it was for you."

Isabel studied the box. It was larger than a shoe box, but light as air. There was no marking or brand on its exterior and no card.

"Quitting time ladies," Tami suddenly hollered, flicking off her computer monitor, and jumping up from her seat. "Last one to the bar has zero chance at sleeping with Raul, the hot Peruvian bartender!"

Tami whisked up her coat and purse and raced down the corridor and through the double glass doors while Marcy, Jenna, and Grace all rushed to follow her. "Lucy, hold the elevator," Tami shouted. "We're free at last!"

Elisa quickly distributed the last pieces of mail on the remaining desks before rushing after them. "Gotta go, Isabel. But if you change your mind, come down and find us. Something tells me we're gonna need help keeping Tami from sexually harassing every eligible bachelor in the joint."

She disappeared through the glass doors. Isabel stopped and listened to the eerie emptiness. Phillip and Jett had both left for the day. All the assistants had cleared out with Tami. And now, she only heard the subtle click of typing in the far corner office. *Likely Norton.*

She stared down at the glossy white box. Then, she rose from her desk and whisked herself into Phillip's office. She closed the door and sat down on the mid-century leather couch. She could feel herself trembling although she didn't know why. She had done nothing wrong. She had made no inappropriate gestures or remarks that would ever lead any of Phillip's business colleagues to assume that she was interested in anything more than a professional relationship. *Except, perhaps, last night's dance with Eliot Watercross.*

Isabel settled her hands across the box's sleek surface and slid open its lid. Folds of shell pink tissue paper were sealed shut with a golden heart sticker. Tucked along its crease was a white calling card; the same strong, but elegant black penmanship swept along its surface.

The Peninsula Hotel. Ten o'clock. The Duchess Suite.

Isabel held her breath and lightly tore through the golden heart sticker to reveal the mysterious gift. But she sensed what it was before she saw it. There, presented like a silent invitation, was a black bustier with garter straps and matching French cut thong, both embellished with fuchsia lace, and a pair of sheer black Cuban heel seamed stockings.

Suddenly, the office door swept open, and Phillip strode through it. He stopped when he saw Isabel. Startled, she rose from the couch. His fierce eyes fell down onto the box in her hands. She had covered it with its lid—just barely.

Their eyes locked and Isabel paused with hesitation before she spoke. "I'm sorry to be an intruder within your office. I simply needed a quiet place for…a moment to myself." His blue eyes flashed at her like gemstones, reflecting the streaming rays of twilight.

Phillip stared at her with uncertainty before pushing past her towards the windows. He adjusted their blinds, cutting off the unforgiving light and focusing the dark contrasting patterns onto Isabel's flushed face.

"Yes, of course," he said softly, attempting to refrain from distressing her more. "Anything that is mine…is yours."

He peered at her with quiet conviction. "I simply came back to retrieve a file that I had forgotten."

But Phillip did not move towards his desk. Instead, his eyes searched out the unmarked white box in her hands. "I shall leave you now." He nodded and passed through the door, closing it behind him with a gentle tug.

With a heavy sigh, Isabel dropped onto the couch and tossed the lingerie box onto the coffee table. She rose from the couch to gaze out at the city's skyline. *Watercross Tower*, she thought, studying its neon blue antennas, beaming up into the hazy stratosphere like a launching spacecraft. She pressed herself against the cold glass of the window and peered up to its top floor. Flickers of strobe lights flashed through the panoramic windows of the casino. Eliot Watercross had built the tower as if it was a reflection of himself—garish, domineering, and impossible to ignore. He had successfully cajoled city officials into granting him unprecedented landfill rights along the Chicago River to build the foundation for his behemoth tower, and he had garnered the sole permit to operate a casino within the downtown city limits. There seemed to be nothing that he couldn't obtain through sheer persuasion and charm, and as a result, he always got exactly what he wanted—whenever he wanted it.

As Isabel stared out at the jagged skyline, owned by a handful of powerful men who she could name on both her hands, she wondered if any of them, besides Eliot Watercross, was bold enough to send her roses, luxury jewelry, and lingerie to her office. Were any of them bold enough to send them without revealing his mysterious identity while *still* expecting her to accept his seductive overtures by agreeing to meet him tonight at the Duchess Suite of the Peninsula Hotel?

No one was bold enough except one man—Eliot Watercross.

Isabel glanced back at the lingerie box. She needed to put an end to this. Whatever *this* was, it had to stop. She could no longer sit back and silently endure the romantic advances of one of Phillip's competitors. She had to make it very clear to her admirer that any expectation of a sexual relationship between them was both unprofessional and unrequited. Her sole commitment was to Phillip. *There was no other choice—absolutely none.*

Fueled by renewed commitment and conviction, she left Phillip's office, shut off her desk lamp and computer monitor, and slipped the lingerie and Cartier necklace into her purse. She retrieved her coat from the closet and flicked off the main lights, but stopped when she heard the soft flutter of typing down the hallway. Slowly approaching the doorway of Norton's corner office, she peeked inside.

"Giselle?" Isabel said, surprised. "What are you still doing here so late?"

Beaming with enthusiasm, Giselle looked across the wide screen monitor. "Hello, Miss Alvarez. I hope it's okay. I'm working here late on a project for Mr. Spears. He asked me to create a social media campaign for a gala that he's hosting at The Old Main Post Office. Have you heard about it? "

Isabel stared at Giselle, unable to comprehend her words. "Yes, of course."

"Well, I just got so excited about it," Giselle gushed, "that I started working on it right away and I haven't been able to stop."

Isabel stared at her. Isabel was Phillip's most trusted employee; he rarely delegated anything off her plate unless it was with her consent. Plus, the orchestration of The Old Main Post Office gala was her official project. She assumed every detail would be entrusted into her care—until now.

"I have a meeting with him first thing Monday morning about my progress. I don't want to disappoint him." Giselle typed furiously.

Isabel gazed at Giselle. Phillip despised social media. It was modern society's way of valuing instant gratification over strategic calculation. Isabel noted Giselle's flowing blonde hair, freshly powdered skin, penciled eyeliner and shiny lip gloss. Even from the doorway, Isabel could almost see down her low-cut blouse, something she regularly dismissed. But now, she realized how many times all the men in the office—including Phillip—had taken the opportunity to indulge in the view the way she was doing now. And Giselle was young. *So very young and inexperienced*, thought Isabel. And yet, not much younger than she had been when she first started working for Phillip, and certainly not too young to be professionally groomed and mentored in the same way Phillip had groomed and mentored her.

A pang of jealousy swept through her heart. It was a ridiculous swell of envy, of course. Giselle was an intern. Isabel was Phillip's senior executive assistant. But the news that Phillip had reached out to her without Isabel's consent suggested Phillip was driven to accomplish his goals and priorities at whatever cost necessary—and without Isabel's exclusive assistance.

Isabel forced a smile. "Well, try not to stay too late. Phillip would let you work all weekend long on his projects if you're willing to..."

Her own advice echoed in her ears. How many times had she given up her weekends or nights to draft last-minute proposals or attend late-night dinner parties? So many times that Isabel had lost count.

"Don't worry. I don't have much else to do anyway this weekend. I'll be sure to lock up and set the alarm. Lucy taught me how since I'm usually the first one in every morning. Good night, Miss Alvarez."

Isabel glanced back at Giselle, who resumed her concentration on the screen and clicked away as if Isabel had already left the room. *Not much else to do on a Friday night? No boyfriend? No college parties? No girls' night out with friends and roommates?* There was only conviction and determination within the fury of Giselle's typing. Isabel gazed at her as if she was staring at a former image of herself.

"Good night, Giselle," she said slowly and exited Norton's office, striding through the main glass doors into the reception lobby. As she waited for the elevators and listened to the dull hum of its ascent to the top floor of the building—Phillip's building—she wondered if all these years she had actually been as naïve and submissive as Giselle seemed to her now. It was a sobering realization—one that lurked within the deepest part of her heart—

because she no longer felt the privilege of being irreplaceable and indispensable. Instead, she felt the sharp reality of sacrificing too much of herself—too much of her entire life—than perhaps was truly necessary.

Chapter Six

IT WAS ALREADY NINE-THIRTY when Isabel made the spontaneous decision to call a cab and leave her house for the night. She had spent the entire evening with Aidan and her mother. They had cooked dinner and eaten together for the first time in weeks. Despite her mother's disapproval, Isabel and Aidan constructed an enormous fort across the living room furniture with sheets, pillows, and her mother's favorite quilted blanket, and relocated all of Aidan's dinosaurs, trucks, airplanes, trains, stuffed animals and even their dessert—strawberries with whipped cream—under the expansive fortress for a night of indoor dragon hunting and flashlight puppet theater. Together, they encouraged Nica to go to bed early while mother and son dragon-slayers stayed up extra late to protect the castle and discuss the difference between good dragons and bad dragons, and all the magical reasons why they were both fire-breathing and invisible. Then, after promising Aidan that they could do it all over again tomorrow morning, she coaxed him up the stairs and into bed where she lay next to him until he fell soundly asleep; but not before he let her know she was the best mommy in the world and his very bestest friend.

When she left his bedroom, she heard the routine sound of her mother's snoring. Isabel slipped into her bedroom and closed her door. After arriving home from the office, Aidan had barely given her a chance to deposit her purse in her room, much less allow her to change out of her work clothes. Now, she sighed with relief as she peeled off her skirt, pantyhose, and silk blouse, and released her hair from its French twist bondage—*safe and conservative*. Even when she dressed up for fancy galas, like the one last night, she rarely wore her hair down. But as she peered at her own image in her dressing table's oval mirror, she allowed her long brown hair to cascade below her bare shoulders. Isabel always felt so much older than her twenty-nine years. *Almost thirty.* Ever since deciding not to terminate her unexpected pregnancy and choosing motherhood over college graduation, she felt like she had skipped over her carefree youth and skidded past the prime of her life. Now, as she stared at her own reflection in the dim light—her black spandex bra, her bare shoulders, her flowing locks of hair—she silently accepted the possibility of an alluring woman staring back at her. It was an image she generally ignored or dismissed because there was no reason to entertain it. But now, her eyes fell upon the Chihuly swan vase and its single dried rose, its petals curling with resignation. It was the lone remnant of the blush pink roses that she had discarded earlier that morning, and the solitary reminder of the fact that someone else wished to admire her the way she secretly hoped someone would—as an attractive, passionate woman who yearned to be more than someone's mother, daughter, or executive assistant. An attractive passionate woman capable of experiencing desire and reciprocating it.

Isabel turned to her purse and fished out the red leatherette Cartier box. She creaked open its hinges and settled her eyes on the stunning sapphire and diamond necklace resting inside the black velvet interior. It was the first time she truly allowed herself to admire it as her very own. In the privacy of her own bedroom—without the oppressive office politics and her own conflicted feelings of obligation influencing her every glance and thought. Isabel indulged in the necklace's scintillating brilliance as she gently removed it from its case. She lifted up her hair and slipped it around her bare neck, its sleek platinum setting and majestic gemstones pressing heavy against her skin. Fastening its sturdy clasp, she relaxed her shoulders and submitted herself to the cool touch of its elegance. How her admirer knew her birthstone, she had no idea. But only a man who had studied her with silent adoration could calculate how perfectly the necklace would adorn her neckline and accentuate the flashing spitfire within her smoldering Spanish eyes.

Passionate. Sexy. Seductive. They were all aspects of her personality that she was forced to suppress on a daily basis because there was no place for personal emotions and desires in her professional career or around her family at home. *Passionate, sexy, seductive*—they were emotions that kindled inside her as she touched her own bare shoulder and imagined what it would feel like to be caressed by a man determined to express his own desire for her. She glanced down at the white lingerie box that rested on her dressing table, then turned towards her closet and quickly pulled out her favorite black dress. She wrapped it around her torso and tied its sash across her hips. The simple cocktail dress hugged her figure with sophistication, but its plunging neckline suggested something more than just modesty and grace. Isabel had never had much cleavage, but the dress insinuated that she had just enough to spark a second lingering glance. *It was the perfect dress for the night,* she thought, adjusting the sapphire and diamond necklace along her neck. It was the perfect dress to accept his invitation, pretending she was the woman he wanted her to be—if only for a brief few hours—before she intended to return the necklace and decline any additional offers to reunite again.

Quietly, Isabel called for a cab while jotting a note for her mother. She exited her bedroom and crept down the dark staircase, stopping at its base to leave the note on the hall tree while retrieving her full-length winter trench coat and fuchsia silk scarf from the closet. *Just a touch of color and flair*, she thought as she slipped out of the house and into the idling taxi, fully anticipating she would return less than two hours later—before anyone would notice she had ever left.

* * * *

The cab turned onto Superior Street and Isabel spotted the Peninsula Hotel. She glanced at the clock on the taxi's dashboard—*9:55pm.* As the taxi driver pulled into the circular driveway, she surveyed the hotel's regal front entrance and clutched her purse, considering the implications of her arrival. The doorman, dressed in a forest green suit with gold lapels, opened her door and extended his hand. She paid the cabbie and exited the taxi.

Isabel knew very little about The Peninsula, except that it was known for its luxury rooftop spas—some of the most revered sanctuaries of relaxation in the world. But more importantly, she knew The Peninsula Hotel was a conspicuously neutral location. The building was owned by an Asian investment firm who had no other real estate properties in the city, so there was nothing that hinted at a connection to any of Phillip's colleagues or his direct competitors, nothing to dissuade her from entering through the broad revolving doors and into the hotel's luxurious lobby—nothing except her own inhibitions.

"The Duchess Suite?" she asked the doorman.

"Of course," he said with a nod, as if he had been expecting her. "Take the elevators to the nineteenth floor. It's the private suite at the end of the hall." He rolled open the revolving door, assisting her entrance.

A private suite. Isabel took in a deep breath. *Was she really doing this...?* She touched the diamond and sapphire necklace hidden under her silk scarf. *Yes, she was. She really was...*

As Isabel entered the grand lobby, she strode across its white marble floors and under its scintillating chandeliers while turning her attention towards a lobby attendant, stationed near the elevators. He curtly greeted her with a smile and waited for her instructions.

"Hello, The Duchess Suite on the nineteenth floor."

"Of course," he nodded and pressed the elevator's call button for her.

She entered the elevator cab and watched as the lobby attendant allowed its doors to slide shut, shuttling her upwards without warning. Isabel glanced at her own reflection in the gold-plated doors. Her black trench coat and modest heels revealed nothing about the anticipation that overwhelmed her heart. Years of dinner meetings and after-hours drinks with wealthy, powerful men had taught Isabel how to appear calm and collected, especially when so often she was the only woman in the group. But now, she felt an urgency to stop the trembling of her hands despite the fact that it was true that she didn't know—for certain—the identity of the man she was going to meet once she stepped out of the elevator. She had crossed paths with so many men over the years—so many lawyers, real estate brokers, building owners, property managers—who had insinuated their attraction for her through sexually-charged quips and lingering glances. *It could be any one of them.*

Her anxiety was heightened by the fact that it had been years—years—since she had shared a bed with *any* man. She had long since accepted the fact that her life as a single mother and a workaholic prohibited her from indulging in life as a sexual woman. Plus, her pool of options was limited to the men she met at work, and her desire to prove herself professionally meant she had to make careful choices about her personal life. *Yes, he could be any one of them.* It was impossible to know who might want to seduce her in such an intimate, enigmatic way, but the sudden hush within her soul confirmed a certainty within herself—she was willing to take the personal and emotional risks to find out.

The elevator slowed to a stop. Its chime rang as the doors glided open, allowing Isabel to cautiously exit the cab. She surveyed the floor; it was quiet and empty. There were no other hotel rooms and no other guests. There was simply a long private hallway ending with a dark mahogany door, propped open like an alluring invitation, beckoning her through it.

"Hello?" she called out faintly while creeping farther down the hallway, catching glimpses inside the luxury suite—modern accents of Asian décor, a churning cylindrical fireplace, a stately leather sofa. But it wasn't until she fully passed inside its interior that Isabel spotted the contemporary glass dining table, dressed with a full bouquet of stunning magenta pink roses, their sweet scent perfuming the air and relaxing her senses. There were two full glasses of white wine, paired next to each other, and a silver-plated bucket chilling the bottle. Then, Isabel spotted something else resting on the table, something unusual and unexpected, something that quickly told her that she had not fully calculated all the expectations of her mysterious suitor…she saw a black silk blindfold. It was draped across a silver serving tray, positioned like a conspicuous offering at the head of the table. Isabel stared at it, taking in all its implications, until the stern command interrupted her thoughts.

"Do not look behind you."

She froze, sensing his lurking presence drifting behind her; then she heard the heavy weight of the suite's door clicking shut with finality.

She stared straight ahead of her at the panoramic windows, attempting to garner a glimpse of his reflection in the black canvas of its floor-to-ceiling glass. *But of course, he had considered that.* She could see nothing more than city lights refracting back the images of the adjacent commercial stores and skyscrapers, flanking the broad boulevard of Michigan Avenue.

"Take a drink of the wine." It was an order, not an offer.

Isabel shifted her gaze to the dining table and noted the bottle's label: *Riesling—her favorite.* Her memory swam over all her recent dinner meetings and evening cocktails. *Someone who knew her favorite wine, her birthday, her favorite color. Someone who knew her better than she even thought.* Isabel approached the table and downed half the glass.

"Take off your coat," he said firmly, his voice pushing in closer.

His voice—his voice should reveal his identity. Isabel floundered. Instead of confirming his identity, it confused her more. Well-educated and perhaps a trace of a New England accent? Merciless and forceful, but also smooth and seductive.

"I'm not certain that I'm going to stay..." She lifted her chin and slightly adjusted her head, testing the boundaries he had suddenly placed on her.

Her suitor responded by moving directly behind her, placing his possessive palm on her shoulder, tempering her instinct to defy him. When he felt certain she would not betray him, he secured his strong hands along the belt of her trench coat and stripped it out from its loop holes, spreading open the lapels. He cautiously edged it off her shoulders, revealing her black dress and sapphire diamond necklace.

"Are you wearing it?" His hot breath lingered next to her ear.

Isabel's mind spun in a whirl. The familiarity of his voice was hard to place, made even harder by his deliberate attempt to mask it through sparse exchanges and whispering breaths.

"No, it's in my purse."

Like an answer to her challenge, he snaked his domineering hand around her waist and pinned her body against his chest. The hard metallic buttons of his shirt pricked against her spine, and the smooth silk of his dress pants brushed against the back of her calves. She closed her eyes and felt herself consciously exhale, attempting to quell her internal protest as he passed his hand up the hem of her skirt along the seams of her Cuban heel stockings and flicked the garter straps against the back of her thighs. *Punishment for lying to him.* At the last moment before exiting her house, she had doubled back into her bedroom and replaced her casual black bra and panties with his gift, surprising herself with how sexy it made her feel while simultaneously denying to herself how much she secretly hoped she would have the chance to reveal it to him.

"You will stay," he whispered, the strength of his assertive embrace making it clear she was no longer in control of her own body. "Because it is what we both want, and you know it."

To be seduced without apologies or excuses? Yes, yes… perhaps it was. Isabel closed her eyes again in surrender. His fingers wisped across her collarbone and glazed over her necklace. The confidence behind his every action persuaded her to relax into his touch. She exhaled with a deliberate release, feeling the desire to obey. Then, she sensed the tip of his nose skating over her collarbone, savoring her perfumed skin.

"I love your scent."

It was the same perfume she wore every day.

She indulged in the warmth of his breath passing over her exposed shoulder before everything suddenly went black as he slipped the blindfold over her eyes with certainty that she would accept it.

Darkness. Sheer, complete darkness. She held up her hand, seeking out reassurance. He rescued her, sweeping her into his arms and whisking her through the expansive suite, passing by the fireplace as its flashing burst of heat warmed her world of darkness before he ushered her into the seclusion of a private space. *The bedroom.*

Isabel sensed the immediate change in the temperature; she could still feel the low, even blush of heat from a more intimate source, its flames crackling in sparse intervals as she barely sensed its golden flicker beneath the rim of her blindfold. She could still hear the sounds from the city through the window panes, but the blinds or shades were fully drawn, muting everything into distant reminders of a world that they sought to escape—together—if only for a few brief hours.

Cautiously, he laid her on the bed. Within her sightless private world, she suddenly took in the soothing mink pelts beneath her and the sweet, undeniable aroma of something beautiful—*rose petals.*

"I'm going to undress you now…" his low, indistinguishable voice whispered through the darkness.

Isabel felt the tug on her sash. Anticipation pricked her skin as he slowly peeled open the folds of her dress, fully exposing the front of her bustier, which stopped just above her hips. *Was he silently admiring her?* She could see nothing beyond the blackness of her blindfold, but she sensed he was staring at her, taking in the boosting bra cups, accentuating the arcs of her cleavage. She waited for his cue, his next advance, his next expression of desire. The bustier's unforgiving constriction punished her every inhale, but still, she savored his silence as she imagined him taking in the full view of her wearing his gift. In that moment, within the secrecy of darkness, she was someone else;

someone naughty and desirable; someone worthy of his masterful seduction and forbidden desires; someone who was willing to submit to him without protest—not because of the taboo thrill of being dominated by a mysterious suitor, but because of the unexpected sensation of the unconditional trust that settled between them.

Slowly, he slipped off her dress, stripping it along the silky texture of her stockings before finally allowing it to drop to the floor. Now, she was half-naked, wearing only her bustier, stockings, and racy black thong, barely guarding her wetness.

"So, so lovely…" he said with a hush before exhaling—a deep masculine release of yearning that suggested he could no longer repress his physical need to claim her.

Without warning, he spread her body out across the king-sized mattress like a sacrificial offering. She heard the *click, click, click* of the beads snaking along the mattress before she felt him wrapping each silky strand around her wrists. *Pearls*. Symbols of her fragile bondage to him—and their tenuous bond to each other.

"I want to be sure that you won't resist me."

She felt the sudden constriction of her wrists, tied to bedframe with the precision of a sailor's knot. Suddenly, she was completely at his mercy, gushing with her own desire to receive everything he intended to gift to her—fully and without apologies.

With her hands secured over her head, she was forced to focus only on the sensation of his fingers, peeling down the strapless bra cups of her bustier, fully liberating her breasts to the rushing wash of cool air. His palms massaged her with force. She tilted back her head, indulging in the circling caresses of his every stroke. His hot breath drifted over her nipples, each tit aroused by the lushness of his tongue and the intentional nip of his lips. *Hot, then wet. Painful, then pleasurable.* The plushness of mink pelts against her skin and the fragrance of rose petals—sweet, velvet rose petals—invited her to relinquish all her inhibitions within the security of the altar that he had prepared for her. She could not push him away or rotate away in protest. She could only yearn for more, the mounting burn throbbing between her legs every time his mouth sucked her like his submissive. He was reining her in, gaining control over her senses, fueled by the masterful balance between pain and pleasure, and preparing her for his next conquest.

Then, she felt it. She relaxed her head and released an involuntary moan as his fingers slipped under the taut protection of her thong and tested her wetness. She tugged on the restraints of pearls, wanting to resist the temptation of yielding herself completely to him. But she was his captive now, and there was nothing she could do except endure the sensual heat of his breath, whispering across her bare hips before exhaling between her legs. *Yes, she was gushing for him now.* He stroked his finger over the damp silk of her crotch band; he wanted to be inside her, and he wanted her scent to confirm how much she wanted it, too.

Suddenly, she sensed him pull away from her, as if he planned to leave her—bound and vulnerable and panting—spread out across the bed. The flipped-down cups of her bustier exposed her bare breasts to his full view. The thin strip of her black thong barely covered her glistening slit. And now, slowly, she felt him unfastening the garter straps and rolling down her Cuban heel stockings with his fingertips. His hands worked to undo the clasp of her heels before tossing them onto the floor with a subtle thud.

A smothering silence filled the room.

"I want to watch you come," he finally said, low and brooding.

She shook her head before she could utter her protest—"No."

"Yes," he insisted.

*She couldn't. It wasn't a possibility, even if she tried...*she lowered her hand as if she thought she might persuade him to stop. He had no intention of stopping.

"Isabel..." he whispered her name like she was his seductress. "I want to watch you come and if you resist me, I will stop, walk out, and never acknowledge my admiration for you again. Do you understand?"

His voice was stern. She thought she had placed its cadence, but she pushed its familiarity out of her mind and nodded in agreement. *Yes, she understood.* She waited, expecting to hear him unbutton his own shirt and remove the buckle from his pants. Instead, she sensed his presence above her, releasing her wrists from the bedframe by slackening the strands of pearls. Then, his presence shifted to the foot of the bed. That's when she felt it—his possessive grasp around her ankles, pushing her bare heels towards her backside, encouraging her knees to drop open and grant him access to the part of her that he craved most.

There was a pause—a deliberate pause—before his angular chin lowered itself between her thighs. She gushed with anticipation before the tip of his tongue slipped under the thin strip of her thong and flicked her tingling slit.

She moaned and rotated her hips away. *No, it was too much, too fast...* It had been five long years since she had accepted a man into her body, but even longer since she had allowed anyone to pleasure her in such a compromising way. But he clasped her ankles like a warning—he had meant what he had said—*he would stop and never openly admit his admiration for her again.*

Isabel closed her eyes and exhaled. *God, how he knew what she wanted...knew her so, so, so very well.* Without the anonymity of the blindfold and his lingering threat to end it all, she never would have consented to being stimulated in such a risqué way. Forceful, domineering intercourse would have been so much less personal—so much less *vulnerable*—than spreading open her legs and permitting him to *taste* her like he was tasting her now. He fondled her clit and teased her slit with his fingers, arousing her even more, but it was the agility of his forbidden tongue that she ultimately craved. She tilted up her pelvis and gasped, raising her breath above the surface of lapping waves that threatened to drown her in sexual gratification. *He was determined to pull her down, down, down with him.* His tongue slid inside her again, building her up with full circles, forcing her to shudder with an exhale. *Yes, yes, yes...*she rhythmically chanted with staccato breaths while lifting her backside, offering him to strip off her thong and remove the last barrier preventing him from accessing her completely. But he did not accept her offer. Instead, he countered it by placing his calming palm on her midriff—a command to slow the rapidity of her accelerating breaths. A moment of stillness settled between them like a private acknowledgment of his determination to make her climax and her willingness to grant herself the permission to enjoy it. *Every minute of it.*

Isabel waited, gazing into the endless darkness while absorbing the sound of his respirations, moving closer to her face. *He was lying next to her now.* Carefully, he secured her wrist and positioned her fingers underneath her thong, guiding her to finger herself, slowly, repeatedly, aided by his confidence and experience. Isabel had tried to have an orgasm so many times before—by herself, alone in the midnight solitude of her bedroom, and only when she was certain her household was fast asleep and no one would interrupt her. But every time she had tried to masturbate, she never allowed herself to betray her deepest fantasies—not even to herself—and so, it had been five long years since she had experienced anything like the start of what he was building up within her now. He paused before repeating the strokes, as if he was watching her touch herself beneath her naughty thong, waiting for her to accept the fact this time was going to be different.

She sensed his shifting weight, lifting himself from the mattress and moving to the foot of the bed. His strong palms slipped between her knees, butterflying her open. Slowly, he peeled back her thong and ran her own forefinger along the full length of her slit before guiding her deeper to explore her G-spot with unwavering repetition. Isabel heaved with a sigh, feeling his hot breath exhale between her legs before his tongue slipped inside her, mimicking her own rhythmic motions as he devoured her with hungry, lustful swipes that unleashed years and years of longing. Isabel shuddered with every lick as an elusive wave of gratification ebbed and flowed across her body, grounding itself into the base of her pubic bone before swelling into a violent tremble of ecstasy that made her cry out to release it.

But she could not release it—she was at his mercy to release it for her. He responded by bracing her ankles and burying his chin deeper against her flesh, forcing her to accept every expression of his sinful yearning into the very core of her being until her body confirmed what her mind had tried so often to deny—that she had craved to break free from the repression and austerity of her professional life.

Isabel threw back her head against the mink pelts and raised her pelvis, stroking herself like she wanted to prove to him that he was her only motivation, and inviting his mouth to overtake her with every palpitation of his penetrating tongue. Just before it was all too much to bear, she seized up from the bed and convulsed with an uncontrollable spasm that climaxed into a rushing arc of sexual heat and fury. She collapsed, absorbing whooshing satisfaction flushing her cheeks and rolling across every inch of her being. And then it was over.

As she rolled to her side, she sensed his presence shifting from the foot of the bed to the surface of the mattress as he lay down behind her. The full security of his masculine body, still fully clothed, spooned her. Slowly, he removed her bustier and the blindfold, heightening her sensation of liberation. She curled up into his body and settled her drifting mind onto the shadowed patterns of the fireplace's receding flames. There was only one caressing kiss along the nape of her neck that she would remember…every moment after that would be clouded from her memory by the protective gesture of his embrace and her own internal ethereal bliss that plunged her into a euphoric haze of slumber.

* * * *

The bleeping of the alarm shot through Isabel's heart. She rose up from the bed and glared at the red neon numbers on the clock: *6:00AM*. She reached to shut off the alarm and shivered. The chill in the air pricked her bare skin. Like a Greek goddess, she wrapped the flowing white sheet around her naked body and pulled herself out of bed. In the full unforgiving glare of early morning light, she saw all the details of the room that had been obscured from the night before—the king-sized platform bed with a Japanese painted-silk headboard, contemporary bay windows adorned with floor-length sheer curtains, and the wall-mounted gas fireplace. The rose petals, strands of pearls, and mink furs were gone, but the perfumed scent in the air and the sensation of luxury against her skin lingered with her like a lyrical dream. She paused in front of the glass French double doors leading out into the suite and noted the stark silence beyond them, confirming what she already knew—she was alone.

She turned back and glanced at the clock. He had set the alarm for her, early enough for her to return to her house, perhaps even before her mother and Aidan awoke and discovered that she was gone. Her clothes and coat, including the lingerie he had bought for her, had been slung carefully across the back of the white leather sofa chair. Her shoes and purse were arranged in front of its ottoman. Then, she noticed something else on the decorative nightstand—something red and familiar, something that made her drift towards it as the bed sheet trailed behind her like a bridal gown's train. Isabel lifted up the red leatherette box and brushed her thumb over its signature gold embossed trim—*Cartier,* she thought before glancing down at the white calling card and taking in the confident cursive inscription:

Alone—but not abandoned. My devotion is now boundless. See you tonight. Monroe Harbor. Ten o'clock.

Isabel lifted the bed sheet to her nose, searching out a reminder of his masculine scent. *His devotion.* She could still feel the persisting burn of his invading touch between her legs and the indelible memory of her rushing climax at his hands. It had been a night of unrestrained carnal passion—one that neither of them could truly claim they had shared as a couple—and yet, it had been one of the most intimate experiences of Isabel's life, despite the fact that she didn't even know with whom she had experienced it. *His devotion.* Yes, she had felt it, his unwavering commitment to please her—unconditionally. Without allowing her to know who or why, her admirer had succeeded in making Isabel *feel* his desire to satisfy her with every flick of his tongue and every stroke of his fingers. And yet, it wasn't just about the sex; it was about his promise of fulfillment—a fulfillment he had only just begun to offer her.

Isabel gazed down at the classic red Cartier gift box, its two doors sealed by a fitted button. She unsnapped the button and flipped open the doors like a miniature treasure chest. Two diamond and sapphire studded earrings sparkled back at her.

Complements to her necklace, she thought as she touched her neckline. Her diamond and sapphire necklace was the only thing he hadn't removed from her body last night, and she noted how quickly she had grown used to the conspicuous weight of its extravagance. *Like a queen.* For one night, he had worshipped her like a queen, and now, it was as if he wanted her to know that she had deserved every bit of it. She unclasped them from the white velvet palette and brushed back the sheer curtains of the bay windows to view her reflection. Isabel rarely wore earrings. She was always rushing to get out the door in the morning, so stopping to change into a fresh pair of chandelier or tear-drop earrings was something she hardly had time to do. Studded earrings, on the other hand, could more easily be worn day after day. And his gift to her—Cartier diamond sapphire gemstone studded earrings—were breathtakingly worthy of being worn day after day.

Isabel fastened the earrings within her ear lobes and gazed at her own ghosted reflection like she was staring at an unfamiliar image of a mythical high priestess, cloaked in white and adorned with jewels. Something had changed within her and she sensed it…something serene and divine. She had been granted the permission to release the most authentic core of her being—her sexuality—in a safe and fulfilling way. And she had been rewarded for it.

She lowered the gift box in her hands and heard something hard and metallic shifting within it. She glanced down and tilted it in her palm. Again, she heard the subtle click of metal against the box's edge. *Could there possibly be more?* She carefully pried up the white velvet earring palette. There, beneath it, was a silver-toned key, waiting to be discovered like an alluring secret. She slipped out the key and guarded it in her palm. It was flat and smooth, and yet, Isabel knew from her real estate experience that it wasn't a door key. It was too small to fit most building entrances or interior doors. She rotated its smooth side towards the window; it glinted like a precious artifact with the rising rays of the sun. She caught sight of an engraving across its tiny handle and squinted hard to make out its letters—*TRUST*.

Isabel closed her eyes and pierced the sharpest part of the key into her heart until its penetrating sting confirmed it wasn't all just a tantalizing dream. What he had planned for her tonight, Isabel wasn't certain. But she was certain of one thing—he had secured her trust, and now, she was committed to finding out what he intended to do with it.

Chapter Seven

When Isabel returned back to her home, it was almost seven-thirty. Aidan was already awake, watching cartoons, and waiting for her. It was a relief. The idea of having to sneak back into her own house seemed ridiculous in the clarity of daylight. She was an adult woman who had the right to spend the entire night—one private, blissful night—away from her family, away from her role as dutiful mother and daughter without apology or explanation.

But now, the sound of her son's gleeful cheer filled her with warmth; she was home.

"Mommy!"

Aidan bolted around the living room corner and attacked his mother's legs with a bear hug. She lifted him into her arms and plopped them both down onto the sofa.

"Mommy, I missed you this morning."

"I missed you, too," she said, kissing his forehead and smoothing down his matted hair.

"Nica and I looked for you in your bed, but you weren't there."

Isabel sensed her mother sliding quietly into the living room behind them and her disapproving frown settling upon her.

"Well, that's because I was out." Isabel consoled him with another kiss. "And I got these!" She suddenly revealed the bag of donuts like an unexpected prize. Aidan squealed and slapped his own cheeks. "Chocolate-glaze?"

"*And* powdered," Isabel added.

"Powdered, too!" Aidan flopped off the couch like he had just heard the most joyous news ever.

"C'mon—" She rose from the couch and encouraged him to follow her. "Let's go to the kitchen, get some milk, and see if we can stack all the donuts higher than last time."

"Last time was the highest high donut tower ever, Mommy. Like a hundred feet."

"Really, a hundred feet high?" Isabel said with exaggerated thought. "Hmmmm…Well, maybe this time, we can make it *two* hundred feet high."

Aidan slapped his face again. "*Two* hundred feet! That's like…infinity plus one DONUTS!" he belted out before catapulting himself through the swinging kitchen door. Isabel started to follow him but stopped when she was met with her mother's stern glare.

"*No dormiste en tu cama anoche*?"

Veronica Alvarez always succeeded in making Isabel feel like she was a disrespectful teenager again, especially when she interrogated Isabel in her native tongue. Isabel brushed past her mother and intentionally avoided removing her coat. Clearly, it was no secret that Isabel had spent the night somewhere else. Early this morning, Mrs. Alvarez had likely discovered Isabel's note. Now, Mrs. Alvarez scanned her daughter's pantyhose and high heels and confirmed her own suspicions.

"Aidan is waiting for me in the kitchen," she replied, attempting to disengage from her mother's judgmental glare. "Please don't ruin our morning, Mother."

Mrs. Alvarez shifted her weight onto her good leg and held her hands in front of her stocky torso like she was preparing to say a prayer to save Isabel's soul.

"I am leaving for the morning to have my hair done," she announced in English. "I hope you will finally have a chance to spend time with your son."

"Mommy!" Aidan cried from the kitchen. "DOOOOONUTS!" he demanded.

Their eyes locked before Mrs. Alvarez relented by turning away and silently traveling up the staircase. With calm restraint, Isabel watched her mother as she disappeared into the master bedroom, but the sting of the comment flushed her cheeks with anger. It had been true: Isabel already had spent two evenings that week away from home—working. But not last night; last night was different. Last night had been an impromptu indulgence for her—and solely for her. And allowing herself the rare, selfish pleasure of indulging in what she had experienced last night was something she knew her mother would never—*could never*—possibly condone or understand.

"Mommy!"

Isabel swung through the kitchen doors and tried to shake off her resentment. It melted away when she saw Aidan, settled on the smooth linoleum floor, transporting powdered donuts on the bed of his tow truck.

"Are they broken?" she teased, pulling out an unopened carton of milk from the refrigerator.

"No, but they need to go get fixed at the car shop."

"Really, why?"

"To get dusted up with more sugar." He smiled, knowing his mother's next response.

"Well, I'm pretty certain they have plenty of sugar. C'mon and drink some milk."

She poured two glasses and set out plates for them.

"Mommy, can I have a chocolate one and a powdered one?"

"Maybe," Isabel said, placing a chocolate-glazed donut in front of him. "Eat one first and finish your milk. Then we'll have to see…"

"No, Mommy, I *need* to eat both," he pleaded with a high-pitched insistence that boys only maintain while they were sweet and young. "Otherwise I won't be able to know how to fix them."

Isabel eyed him. "I'm pretty sure they'll be fine without more sugar."

"Well…we'll have to see," he repeated her phrase and shrugged, as if he believed everything that his mommy said simply meant that she loved him.

Suddenly, Isabel heard her phone ping with a text from the pocket of her trench coat. She pulled out her phone and read it with confusion.

Emergency meeting this morning at the office. Mandatory attendance required.

It was from Phillip, but he rarely sent her texts, nor had he ever called an "emergency meeting" at the office on a Saturday morning. Sure, there had been urgent business issues that came up over the weekend, and he often expected her to assist him with them. But they were never issues that required face-time in the office, and certainly never anything that couldn't be discussed over the phone or reviewed and discussed through ongoing emails. She glanced at the clock. It was barely 8:00AM. She stared at the text and hesitated. She didn't want to text back that she had no intention of coming to the office *now*, much less later this morning, so she considered her words carefully.

With Aidan now. Mother away. Perhaps calling in would be better?

Isabel hit send and waited. She never used Aidan as a scapegoat for work. In all the time that she had worked for Phillip, Isabel had only missed one meeting to take her son to the ER when Aidan believed he was as invincible as Superman and slammed his own finger in the door jamb—just to prove it. Every other sick day, evening work night, dinner party, weekend gala, Isabel had always relied on her mother to watch Aidan. And Phillip knew it. She listened to her mother's heavy footsteps creaking along the wooden floorboards above them. *No, it would be impossible.* This morning, there was absolutely no way she could ask her mother to take care of Aidan, and there was no way that Isabel could bear the disappointment in Aidan's eyes if she told him she had to leave him—again.

Ping…

Isabel glanced down at Phillip's response: *MEETING AT 9AM. BRING HIM.*

Isabel laughed aloud—the way people inappropriately laugh at funerals—before covering her mouth to collect her thoughts. She glanced over at her son, his face and fingers smeared with chocolate-donut glaze.

"Mommy, can I have another one?" he asked earnestly, as if it was the most natural request in the world.

Sure, Phillip…bring my four-year-old son on a sugar high to your emergency business meeting. Isabel exhaled and dropped her phone onto the table as she watched Aidan sneaking a second and third donut into his greedy hands. Clearly, Phillip had barely spent any time with children.

Chapter Eight

"Mommy, can I press the button?" Aidan squeezed his mother's hand, as if he was hoping beyond all hope that his mother would say yes.

She looked down at him. She had warned him that he would need to be on his best behavior. It was their first trip to Mommy's office in over a year, and Isabel had prepared an entire tote bag of Aidan's toys, coloring books and sticker collection—just to keep him entertained. But she failed to consider how visiting Mommy's office was going to be more interesting than anything in her tote bag, and the glee in his eye as they boarded the elevator was reminder enough that a four-year-old boy could be entertained with the simplest of things.

"Go ahead." She nudged him forward. "Number sixty-five…can you reach it?"

Aidan stepped forward and pointed at the button marked 'thirty-five'. "This one?"

"No…" Isabel guided his finger several rows higher. "Here."

"Whoa, up there?" He lifted himself on his tippy-toes and pressed the proper button and watched as the elevator doors closed on command.

"Up, up, up…" she sang, raising his hand as the cab shuttled upwards with the sound of Aidan's gasp.

"Cool," he exhaled, overwhelmed.

The simplest of things. Isabel smiled down at her son with a moment of nostalgia. Aidan's first time coming to the office was also Isabel's first time when she arrived for her interview with Phillip while she was six months pregnant—far enough along that it was impossible to hide it, and yet, still early enough to think that she would be able to do everything the same way she had done before. *Naïve and inexperienced*, she thought to herself, squeezing her son's hand as he dutifully watched the floor chimes rolling upwards in succession. How different she felt now with five years of experience under her belt and a professional salary that had never left her—or her son—wanting for anything, except perhaps…more time together.

Phillip. He had taken a chance on her. He had been the sole reason why she had survived that first year of hardship after being abandoned by Aidan's father. When no one else would hire her, Phillip offered her a position as the office copy clerk, including a healthy salary and full-benefits, simply for making copies all day long. *Copy clerk*, she smiled, knowing now that she had been the first and only copy clerk ever hired. But like everything with Phillip, it was a game—a challenge to see how she would navigate such a mundane, unglamorous position—a test through which he expected her to persevere or fail. *One of many, many, many tests*, she thought, looking down at her son and anticipating their arrival as the elevator cab slowed to a halt.

Ping…

"Mommy, we're here!" Aidan enthusiastically led the charge out of the elevator.

Isabel followed her son through the lobby to its glass doors, swiping her access card and punching the security code into the keypad. Whenever she entered the office after-hours, Isabel always experienced a rush of exclusivity, like it was a private space that only she was permitted to use whenever she wanted. But she slowed her pace when she heard the voices. She had expected Phillip to be waiting for her, but only him. Instead, as she rounded the corner and peered into Phillip's office, she traded glances with Jett, casually dressed in an athletic shirt and running pants. He swiveled in his chair like an impatient schoolboy and seized his eyes on her.

"The duchess is here," he announced, rotating gleefully in his chair.

Isabel halted and glanced over to Jett. *Duchess*, she repeated in her mind. She suddenly thought she recognized the hint of a New England accent in his voice. He had, after all, gone to Harvard Business School with Phillip. She scanned the executive suite. To her surprise, everyone was already there, waiting for her—Jett, Tami, Norton, and Phillip; they all silently held her gaze to acknowledge her arrival.

"Good morning, everyone," she said, but her mind replayed Jett's greeting. *Duchess… No, it was impossible…not Jett.* She shivered off the thought, then shifted her glare to him, as if she expected it to all be her imagination. His Cheshire smile beamed at her while his strong jaw chewed on his gum like he was savoring her discomfort. "You're looking dashing as always, Bella."

Jett stood from his seat and offered to remove her trench coat.

"No, thank you," she declined, quickly remembering she hadn't had time to change her dress and shoes from last night. Phillip's cool eyes studied her as she quickly ushered Aidan to the opposite side of the office. Her stomach churned as her mind raced through the implications of last night.

"And who is this little guy?" Jett asked with a sharp snap of his gum.

Aidan frowned and moved behind his mother.

"Oh, leave him alone, Jett. You'll scare him with your bad breath," Tami snarked.

"Impossible. Fresh stick of gum," he countered with pride, stringing the wad out of his mouth—just to prove it.

Tami rolled her eyes and looked over at Isabel. *Please God, help us both…*she conveyed with her feisty glare made more severe than ever by her rushed application of black eyeliner.

"Phillip," Isabel petitioned him. "I understand that this is an urgent meeting, but I'm concerned that my time is somewhat limited." She glanced down at Aidan, who was clinging to her hand, betraying his sudden shyness.

"Mommy, can we go now?"

Phillip's eyes did not meet her own. Instead, he gazed at the boy. "Aidan, come here, please. I have something I'd like to show you." He made no attempt to soften his stern English accent or smile at the child who clearly didn't want to leave his mother's side.

Isabel glared at Phillip, certain there was no way he was going to persuade Aidan to come to him, especially when he sat behind his glass executive desk like an unforgiving schoolmaster in his white business shirt with French cuffs and classic navy blue silk tie.

Phillip's eyes tested Aidan's resolve. "Come here, please," he repeated.

The room fell silent, watching the stand-off. Then, as if by a magical spell, Aidan slowly detached himself from his mother's leg and crossed over to the opposite side of the room.

"Do you like games?"

The boy nodded, his eyes flashing with delight.

"Good. Then take this." Phillip handed off his gold-plated phone. "Look here…you will have to match each alien to its proper flying saucer."

Aidan grinned, swiping its screen and immediately understanding the game's objective. He turned and beamed up at his mother, but Isabel hesitated with concern.

"Phillip, I don't know if that's such a good idea…" Her voice trailed off, eyeing his expensive phone in the unpredictable hands of her four-year-old son.

Phillip dismissed her and watched Aidan settling himself into the sofa, completely consumed by the device. "You and I both know I hate that phone. And if it keeps him content, then we shall simply be grateful to Giselle for showing me a few new tricks on it this morning."

"Giselle?" Isabel repeated her name without hiding the surprise in her voice. Phillip stared at Isabel with his steady blue eyes.

"Good morning, everyone." The cheery voice rang out behind Isabel. She turned and tracked Giselle as she brightly bounced into the office, carrying Phillip's favorite coffee mug and passing it off to him.

"Thank you, love." He nodded, accepting the mug with appreciation.

Isabel glared at Phillip. *Thank you, love.* It was one of his British colloquialisms, something he had occasionally said to her, but only in rare, private moments when he desired to acknowledge his esteem for her—and all her hard work—after a long day. She always silently accepted it, as if it was nothing more than an unguarded expression of his professional affection. But in that moment, Isabel heard the words with envy. She shifted her gaze to

Giselle, dressed in her standard tight pencil shirt and flowery low-cut blouse, just like it was any other normal business day. But it wasn't any other normal business day. It was nine o'clock on a Saturday morning and Isabel knew that Giselle had stayed late the night before.

Isabel surveyed Phillip's perfectly pressed shirt again and noted his strong, freshly shaved jawline that gleamed in the morning light. Both he and Giselle were impeccably dressed, well-rested, and even united, as if something else—something deeper last night—had happened between them.

"Shall we get this meeting underway, Phillip," Norton called out, asserting his seniority.

"Yes, of course." Phillip nodded, then addressed Isabel. "With your permission, Giselle will take Aidan into the conference room to keep watch over him."

But before Isabel could respond, Giselle greeted Aidan with the warmth and familiarity of a regular babysitter. "Hey there, Aidan. My name is Giselle, but my friends call me Gigi. Wanna come with me? I'm gonna go check to see if there's any hot chocolate in the kitchen."

"With marshmallows?" Aidan asked.

Giselle laughed. "Of course! You can't make hot chocolate without marshmallows."

Aidan cradled Phillip's phone in his hands and looked at Isabel for reassurance. "Can I bring this, Mommy?"

"Yes," she reluctantly said as her son slipped his hand into Giselle's before she closed the office door and disappeared with Aidan.

"Now, we may commence," Phillip announced. "As you all know, we have decided to move forward with plans for the redevelopment of The Old Main Post Office; however, we still require the building permits from City Hall before we can break ground." Phillip shifted his attention to Jett. "And it has now come to our attention that we will have increased competition."

Jett stepped in, taking his cue from Phillip. "My broker buddies have told me they've heard that Eliot Watercross and Symeon Colovos are forming a joint business venture to actively petition City Hall to grant them a permit for a site development along the Chicago River."

"What kind of a site development?" Isabel asked.

"A riverboat casino." Jett snapped his gum, his cocky smile daring her to test him again.

"A casino boat on the Chicago River would attract more tourism for the city while circumventing the state's ban on gambling developments within city limits—on land," Phillip added. "But on water, there's always been that possibility."

"But Phillip," Norton challenged him with his low, sonorous voice, "City Hall has always rejected proposals for riverboat casinos in the past. How is this any different?"

"Because this is Eliot Watercross," Phillip replied. "And instead of simply proposing a cruise ship or even a luxury yacht, he is proposing a permanent Las Vegas-style resort with three five-star restaurants, a luxury heated swimming pool, international upscale retailers, and a mineral spa."

"Using water from the good ol' Chicago River?" Tami teased.

"Nope. Imported from the melting snow caps of the Artic," Jett corrected her—dead serious. "And I'm hearing that the entire structure will be designed in the shape of a floating iceberg."

"This all must be some kind of a joke," Isabel exclaimed.

Phillip shot her a glare; the severe glint in his eye expressed that he didn't appreciate the insinuation. Her eyes challenged him. She didn't appreciate being forced to come to the office on a Saturday morning to hear about Eliot Watercross' floating iceberg.

"They aim to make it a top tourist destination in Chicago," Phillip clarified with bite. "And they aim to station it along the riverfront at 400 South Wacker." He held her glare, ensuring that she fully understood the full severity of the situation.

"Directly in front of The Old Main Post Office," Tami exclaimed. "What total son-of-a-bitch assholes."

"If Watercross and Colovos secure their permit before we do," Phillip warned, "then it's unlikely we'll ever be able to gain development approval for restoration of The Old Main Post Office."

"So what does this all mean, Phillip?" Norton called out like the ghost in the room.

"It means we no longer have the luxury of time because we are now in direct competition with my ex-business partner," Phillip stated gravely. "Jett, I will need you and Tami to begin due diligence on securing potential tenants interested in leasing space within the remodeled Old Main Post Office. Use the current CAD drawings of the proposed renovation to help sell the space. We need a well-known name."

"Like a luxury hotel chain, or an upscale spa and salon, or a luxury European retailer," Jett rolled through the options like he was reading Phillip's mind. "Preferably elite and trendy, right?" he clarified for Tami, who was furiously jotting down notes.

Phillip nodded. "Anything to bolster our own case for attracting tourists."

"You got it, Chief," Jett confirmed, standing from his chair and flicking his rubber band across the office, landing it directly into Phillip's trash can. He glanced over at Isabel and winked.

"Isabel," Phillip said, securing her attention. "We must plan our gala as soon as possible. Next weekend—"

"Next weekend?" she interrupted with exasperation. "Phillip, don't be ridiculous."

There was impertinence in her reprimand. Everyone heard it and shifted their gaze to Phillip, his piercing blue eyes glaring at her with censure. Isabel quickly realized her error. It was one thing to speak her mind—even complain openly to Phillip—behind closed doors. But it was another thing entirely to criticize her boss—and challenge his expectations—in front of his most trusted business colleagues.

"It will happen next weekend," he insisted, his jawline flinching with restraint. "Saturday evening, to be precise. We'll offer Mario double his normal rate to expedite the event coordination, and if you personally need more assistance, I will have Giselle help you as well. I have already met with her this morning about running basic errands for the gala, so you should be consoled that some of the coordination has been taken off your plate."

He said the word "plate" with a snap of his teeth that conveyed to Isabel that he would not endure another word of protest. She glared at Phillip, enduring his punishing tone, intended to put her back in her proper place. She was, after all, his assistant—not his business partner or his equal. *Something had changed between them.* His stormy glare and clenched jaw confirmed it. Rather than their usual fluid conversation and amiable cooperation, there was nothing but an undercurrent of tension and conflict.

"Okay—" Tami interjected, snagging Jett by the spandex of his running shirt. "Jett and I will hash out some more leads for you, Phillip, and get right back to you with as much information as possible by Monday."

She turned towards the door and mouthed her sympathy to Isabel. *Oh my God, good luck.* Then, she called out to Jett to follow her. "C'mon, I'll order breakfast from Eduardo's. I need to drink at least three Bloody Marys to get me through an entire Saturday of working for you."

Jett followed Tami towards the door, passing Isabel with a snap of his gum. "Love the new cat-fight attitude, Bella. *Meow.*"

He held her gaze longer than necessary before snickering and striding out of the office with a holler. "Tami, let's get you as many Bloody Marys as it takes you to get drunk. I'm in the mood for a good time."

Isabel tried to shake off the gleeful insinuation in his voice as she shut the office door and turned back to meet Phillip's eyes.

"Eliot Watercross is our competition," Norton called out, reminding Isabel and Phillip of his phantom presence. "But only because you treat him as such." He slowly rose from the sofa and hobbled across the office, opening the door and signaling the end of the meeting.

"As for our dear Isabel…don't be such a tyrant, Phillip. She's a mother with a young child. Leave her a bit of peace this weekend and have dinner with me instead. We can pick out china patterns for your precious gala," he offered with lofty sarcasm before exiting the office without a backwards glance.

Phillip circled the translucent surface of his glass desk with the tip of his fingernail and waited for the absence of everyone in the room to change the dynamics between them. Finally, he raised his eyes and fixed his gaze upon her with authority.

"You and I shall meet tonight to confirm all the details of the gala in order to make additional arrangements," he stated, leaning back into his executive leather chair like it was an undeniable fact.

"Tonight?"

"Yes, tonight," he asserted, as if there was no other choice.

Isabel's lips parted in silent protest as her body flurried through all the passionate sensations of last night. The bite marks on the tips of her nipples still stung beneath her dress and the quivering burn of her own invading fingers was more than just a faded memory. She constricted the lapels of her trench coat, as if she worried that Phillip could read the physical change within her body as well as her yearning desire to fulfill her needs again. She was expected to show up tonight at Monroe Harbor—and if she failed to arrive, then she knew she risked signaling to her admirer that their affair was over.

"No, I'm sorry…I can't meet tonight, Phillip," she said with resistance.

Their eyes locked. It was the first time since working for Phillip that Isabel had ever declined his request for her to work after-hours. "I have other plans. I'm sorry. It will have to be tomorrow."

An awkward discomfort between them ensnared her like an invisible net.

Then, like a welcomed distraction, her cell phone rang. She pulled it from her trench coat's pocket and looked down at the screen: WATERCROSS CAPITAL. She hesitated, feeling the prickling sensation of dread coursing through her heart.

"It's Eliot Watercross," she announced like an intentional challenge to Phillip's control over her. She watched his expression harden like cement. "I extended an invitation to him to the gala—before I knew he was our direct competition."

"Watercross has always been our competition," Phillip replied with skepticism. "Only recently has he found a way to compete with us so…directly." He pushed out his words, as if he was implicating her misconduct. Like a threat, her unanswered phone rang in her hands.

"Confirm his attendance," he finally relented, bitterness filling his mouth. "Next time, you will have to conduct yourself more carefully with him."

She glared at him, silently wondering if he was the real enemy rather than Eliot Watercoss.

She turned away, answering the call. "This is Isabel."

"Bella…" Eliot Watercross' confident voice called through her receiver. "I've missed you."

Isabel felt the hush in her heart. *I've missed you.* She repeated the phrase in her mind and glanced up at Phillip, certain he had heard Watercross' flirtatious words through her phone. Confirming her fears, Phillip's distrustful glare pushed her away towards the walls of windows.

"Got your message about Phillip's gala at The Old Main," Eliot continued. "Sounds like quite the lavish affair. I assume you'll be attending?"

Her pulse raced as she attempted to compare the strong cadence of each word against the husky whispers of her seducer from last night.

"Yes, of course," she confirmed. "However, the date has changed. We've pushed it up to next weekend—Saturday night."

"Even better," he said with sly delight. "Count me in."

Isabel studied his silence and hesitated. "Shall I put you down as plus one?"

"No, just me, Bella. Just me. And while I'm there, I'll expect you to grant me a private tour. See you soon."

He lingered on the line, waiting, listening, studying the pace of her anxious breath before ending the call. She shivered, the smoothness of his arrogance sliding down her back like a forbidden chill. *See you soon…* He had said it with an alluring magnetism that forced her to consider its implications, and yet, she had confirmed nothing and everything. It was impossible to believe that she had allowed herself to be seduced by the one man who could ruin her and her career; but it was impossible to deny the fluttering palpitations within her own heart.

"He plans to attend, I presume," Phillip finally said.

Isabel nodded, turning to meet his gaze. "Yes. And I apologize, Phillip. Next time, I will be sure to gain your approval regarding the invitation list."

His crystal blue eyes stared at her, as if he expected her to surrender to the silence. She waited to see if he would keep her there or release her, but he did neither. Instead, he gave her the choice—and for the first time in a long time, she chose her own personal needs over the demands of her professional life. She broke from his gaze, gathered up her briefcase and Aidan's backpack, and moved to exit his office, pretending that none of it mattered until Monday. But Phillip's commanding voice trailed after her.

"New earrings?"

She halted in the doorway and touched the gemstones. *Nothing ever went unnoticed with him.* She touched the matching sapphire and diamond necklace around her neck—a physical reminder of how much she had been desired and coveted only hours before.

"Yes," she whispered, directly meeting his searing eyes. "A gift."

He stared at her, judging the tension between them.

"Lovely," he remarked, as if he was taking in the way their shining brilliance framed her high cheekbones. "Your birthstone," he added, lowering his eyes and fingering a loose paperclip across the glass surface of his desk. "A gift from someone who must know you well."

Isabel peered at him, her dark eyes challenging him—and his assumptions of her. "Yes. Sapphires symbolize devotion."

"That's very…telling."

She held his gaze before confidently exiting his office.

It was her final act of defiance. He had treated her with callousness, even disdain, during the meeting, but she wanted him to realize the fault was his own. If Phillip expected Isabel to always remain the dutiful assistant—completely subservient to him—he was the one in the wrong. Last night, she had experienced the ecstasy of being satisfied and pleasured as a woman and lover, and as a result, something untamed and ravenous had been unleashed within her.

She strode out of Phillip's office and down the open corridor, searching for Aidan. But Tami peeked out from Jett's office and intercepted her along the way.

"What the heck has gotten into Phillip?" Tami said under her breath, keeping pace with Isabel as they headed for the kitchen.

"You mean…something more than his usual obsessive, demanding, surly bastard self?"

Tami snorted. "Totally. I mean…does he think you are seriously going to work non-stop for the next week to plan that gala for him?"

"Yes, he does." She squarely turned to Tami. "And no, I'm not because tonight, I have other plans."

Tami stared at her, noting the glint in Isabel's brown eyes.

"Oh my God…you did it. You met up with Mr. Mystery Billionaire Man last night."

Isabel hid her smile and entered the kitchen.

"Oh my God, oh my God!" Tami pawed at the sleeves of her trench coat, dragging her back. "Don't you dare walk away like that? Who was it?"

"I don't know," she whispered, as if she was surrendering someone else's secret. "He made me wear a mask."

"He what?!" Tami almost shouted before muting her own horror. "You mean like a weird Smurfette fetish Halloween mask?"

"Shhhhh—" Isabel grabbed Tami's elbow and hushed her with reprimand. "No, like a blindfold."

Tami pushed up her librarian glasses, unable to decode the unusual expression on Isabel's face. "Wow, seriously kinky," Tami said, chewing on the idea like invisible gum. "And you actually did it?"

Isabel answered with silence. Tami's jaw dropped.

"Wowzas. And so…*what*? Did you actually *do* it with him? While blindfolded?"

Isabel looked out across the open floor as Phillip exited his office. His eyes immediately met her own, and she challenged his piercing gaze.

"I'm meeting him again tonight," she punctuated.

"Holy hell, it was *that* good?"

But Isabel barely heard her. She watched Phillip, tracking her and Tami as he crossed the hallway and disappeared into Norton's office, shutting the door behind him.

"Yes," she stated, like she was a new woman, and turned towards the glass doors of the kitchen.

Tami trailed after her. "Geez, please tell me this guy has some single friends?"

Isabel and Tami halted inside the kitchen, spotting Aidan and Giselle sitting at the kitchen table, playing with a stack of poker cards. Aidan was completely enthralled by his new babysitter.

"You can't pick another card!" Giselle suddenly exclaimed. "You already have *five*. Look, one, two, three, four, five."

"Hee, hee, hee…" He deviously snuck another card out from the center pile of cards. He flipped it over and showed it to Giselle, who dropped her head in dramatic shame. "Oh no, not again. You win!"

"I win!" Aidan bellowed with delight, sweeping all the cards into his chest and hoarding them like a windfall of poker chips.

Isabel gazed at Giselle, who pretended to cry. When Aidan gazed at her in concern, she popped up with a smile and tickled his belly.

Aidan giggled and pushed all the cards towards her. "Let's play again!" he squealed and waited as she gathered up all the cards and dealt him a fresh hand. It was obvious that they were playing a made-up game. Isabel had seen her mother's attempt to teach Aidan how to play "Go Fish" with painful results. In contrast, Giselle's silly faces, sound effects, and willingness to follow Aidan's lead invigorated him with joy and delight. Clearly, the problem was not entertaining him; it was how she was going to tell her son that it was time to say goodbye.

"Look," Giselle suddenly said, shifting their attention on Isabel. "Let's tell your mommy which card is your favorite."

Aidan glanced over at her. "The King of Spades."

"Really, why?" Isabel asked, surprised that Aidan even knew what "spades" were.

"Because he's so grumpy!" Aidan cried out.

Both Aidan and Giselle slapped their foreheads and laughed like it was the most hysterical joke in the world.

Tami glanced at Isabel, then gazed at Aidan and Giselle's mugs. "Please tell me you didn't give him any of the Vodka that was in there."

"Nope, just silly juice," Giselle giggled.

"Silly juice, Mommy!" Aidan exclaimed and burst out in laughter.

Isabel peered into his cup. It was hot chocolate.

She glanced at Giselle; she peered back at her with earnest blue eyes, outlined with neon-blue eyeliner. Her blonde flowing hair, blushing skin, and generous smile reminded Isabel of how young Giselle was.

I was only a few years older when I got pregnant with Aidan, she thought as she watched Aidan and Giselle drinking from their mugs, pretending to be kitty cats. *Just a few years older.*

And yet, it wasn't the stress of her job or being a mother that made her feel so much older now; it was the premature sacrifice of her carefree youth. In Phillip's office, Isabel had experienced a flash of envy towards Giselle, fearing that somehow she was being favored by Phillip over her. Now, Isabel realized it wasn't that she was envious of Giselle; she was envious of her gaiety and spontaneity—traits that Isabel had somehow lost in herself along the way.

"Giselle, would you like to come over to our house this evening for some babysitting?" Isabel suddenly asked. "It would also give us a chance to discuss the gala. We have to map out our strategy to make it happen by next Saturday."

Giselle grinned at the offer. "Definitely," she said with an enthusiasm that made Isabel remember a time when she would do anything to be included at the company.

"Great." Isabel nodded, certain of her plan. "You can come to the house around six and join us for dinner. We'll order Aidan's favorite—Hawaiian pizza."

Chapter Nine

ISABEL GLANCED AT THE WALL clock in the hallway. It was nine fifteen.

It had been a good night. Giselle had come over to the house on time and had stayed for dinner. They traded ideas back and forth about the gala while building Lego towers for Aidan to torpedo down with his Nerf football. In three short hours, they had successfully created a wish list for the gala's theme, décor, appetizers and spirits menu that they could pass off to Mario, their event coordinator, as well as a list of preferred vendors for Mario to call on Monday morning. Ultimately, Isabel knew the biggest challenge wouldn't be the preparation of hosting a spectacular party; it would be the successful showcasing of Phillip's development project to the City Hall politicians who had the power to grant or deny him the renovation permits. Isabel had enough experience to know that she could spend thousands upon thousands of dollars on the most extravagant hors d'oeuvres and champagne fountains, but none of it mattered if the most influential aldermen in the city didn't attend the event.

Isabel glanced up at the wall clock again. Nine twenty. She had called for a cab for Giselle, who had left just moments earlier. Now, as she stopped in the hallway and listened to the sound of silence, Isabel finally felt confident that Aidan was asleep. Her attention shifted to her mother's bedroom. Mrs. Alvarez had retired upstairs the moment Giselle arrived and had not emerged from her bedroom since—not even for dinner. Isabel knew her mother—and her anger. They had barely exchanged words since this morning. She knew she wouldn't be able to leave again without telling her mother that she intended to be out late—possibly out the whole night—but she also knew that she didn't feel obligated to tell her mother anything more than was absolutely necessary.

There was a faint knock at the front door. Isabel paused and frowned. *Did Giselle forget her purse?* Isabel quickly scanned the living room's sofa before whisking open the front door.

But it was not Giselle. It was a driver, dressed in a black chauffeur's uniform and a matching black cap, tilted downwards across his mirrored sunglasses.

"Miss Alvarez?"

"Yes?"

"I'm here to take you to your destination."

The tone of his voice was deep and ominous, and she struggled to identify his foreign accent. *Turkish? Persian?* Isabel glanced behind him and spotted the black stretch SUV limousine, idling along the curb of the street. It was a bold, pretentious luxury limousine with a flashy chrome grill and glaring white headlights—certainly not a ride intended to carry her away quietly into the night.

"Monroe Harbor?" she asked.

"Yes, of course." The chauffeur nodded and extended his hand, clad in black leather.

"But I'm not even dressed…"

She glanced at her own image reflecting back in his sunglasses. Ponytail and T-shirt. She looked down at her torn jeans and flip-flops. At least her toenails were freshly painted pink.

The chauffeur grinned, as if he anticipated her question. "Everything will be taken care of," he said, his gloved hand steady in its resolve to draw her out from the security of her home.

"Trust," he suddenly said, like a secret password.

Isabel gazed at him, repeating the word in her mind. *Trust.* She touched her ears; she was still wearing the sapphire earrings, and hours ago, she had wedged the mysterious silver key snugly underneath the underwire of her bra cup—a physical reminder of her intention and commitment to reunite herself with him tonight, whatever the personal or professional cost.

She quickly turned into her hallway and saw her mother, dressed in her nightgown. She stood in the shadows of the staircase, gazing upon Isabel with her silent disapproval.

"You're leaving again tonight," Mrs. Alvarez stated in English. It wasn't a question; it was an accusation.

Isabel glanced back at the chauffeur, waiting to lead her into the unknown night. Then, she met her mother's embittered gaze—the same gaze that punished her with disappointment years ago when she confessed she was dropping out of college because she was pregnant.

Isabel flipped open the closet door and pulled out her trench coat, then rifled through her purse to ensure she had her wallet, cell phone, and keys.

"I will be home before Aidan wakes up," she replied, turning out of the door to accept the chauffeur's hand and her uncertain fate. "Goodbye, Mother."

* * * *

Isabel entered the limousine and heard the chauffeur's voice behind her.

"We shall arrive at our destination in approximately twenty minutes, Miss. Alvarez. The contents of the closet are yours to wear."

He shut the door before she could answer him, sealing her up within the limousine's dark interior. Accents of lunar blue light glowed along the trim like a cosmic spacecraft. She perched herself on the edge of the curving leather bench seats, taking in the beveled mirrored ceiling, a crystal wine bar, and high-definition television screens. But it was a miniature aquarium with jellyfish that caught her attention. She had often taken Aidan to the Shedd Aquarium, deliberately stopping for their snack on the basement benches, where they could sit in front of the jellyfish exhibit and admire the translucent creatures, tumbling in slow-motion through the thick nectar of salt water. *He knew about her private love of jellyfish,* she thought as she reached across the limousine to touch the aquarium's sleek panel of impenetrable glass. Their pulsing tentacles spun around in circles like wet strands of cotton candy. Slowly, the blue lights dimmed within the limousine's interior as she felt the vehicle pull away from the curb.

Twenty minutes. Isabel shifted her eyes onto the long, narrow closet door, camouflaged by its black reflective paneling that mimicked the surface of the adjacent mini-fridge and cocktail cabinet. She approached it and outlined its chrome keyhole, confirming it was just the right size. Without hesitation, she unbuckled her trench coat, slipped out the key from underneath her T-shirt and bra cup, and slid it into the keyhole—a perfect match.

A sudden sensation of anticipation filled her as she turned the key with a *click.* Immediately, she paused and glanced around the limousine, wondering if she was being watched through cameras. When her paranoia waned, she popped open the door and peered inside.

There, dangling from a pink satin hanger by its spaghetti straps, was a shimmering rhinestone-studded, sequined cocktail dress. The closet's mirrored interior reflected its iridescent beading like sparkling diamonds. Next to it, draped along a second hanger, was a silver fox fur shawl. Isabel stroked its luxurious pelt and took comfort in its heavy weight. *Protection from the marina's evening breeze.* There was nothing understated about the ensemble. It was unapologetic with its sexy, abbreviated hemline and seductive cut-out back, and it immediately made Isabel forget everything about her day—up until now.

She slipped off her trench coat and slowly watched herself undress in the closet's mirror, leaving everything about her ordinary self behind. She removed the sequined dress from its satin hanger before sliding her arms and torso through its silky stretch bodice that clung to her every curve. Its hemline stopped just above her knees, and its plunging neckline settled like a whispering kiss between her bare breasts. *No bra, no panties—that was the intention.*

Beneath the closet was a drawer with another key hole. Isabel slipped out the key and tested it. It popped open with a resistant *click.* She slid open the drawer and spotted a pair of silver shoes with ankle straps and lacquered high heels—size nine and a half. *Exactly her size.* She strapped them on and admired how they accentuated the long contour of her exposed legs. Then, she slipped the fox fur shawl from its hanger and draped it around her shoulders, tempering a shiver of anticipation. She gazed at her image in the closet's reflection, barely able to recognize the woman staring back at her. She was no longer constrained by her own clothes and her own inhibitions. She was now someone else—a provocative enchantress willing to assert the power of her sexuality and her right to claim and indulge in it.

Slowly, something caught her eye; it glinted at the bottom of the drawer—another miniature silver key. She flipped it on its side and read the engraving along its reflective surface—FORBIDDEN.

Suddenly, the momentum of the limousine came to a halt. *They had arrived.*

Isabel glanced out the tinted windows and cradled the key in her palm. Even under the dark veil of night, she recognized the carousel of moored boats in the harbor, their furled sails bobbing up and down in alternating unison. She looked inland and saw the rushing headlights of traffic along Lake Shore Drive and the magnificence of Buckingham Fountain exploding its streams of illuminated water into the night like aquatic fireworks.

The chauffeur whisked open her door and extended his gloved hand to her. His strong grasp guided her out of the limousine. *Like royalty*, she thought, securing the protective pelt of fur over her shoulders while he escorted her towards their destination—a black luxury yacht concealed along the dark waters of the harbor, like a stealth protector offering an escape. As they approached the vessel, Isabel spotted the scrolling white inscription of the ship's name along its fiberglass hull—*THE DUCHESS.*

Two men, the yacht's captain and his first officer, attentively stood at the edge of the boarding ramp. They were dressed in formal uniforms and they greeted her with deferential nods of their caps. The chauffeur passed off her hand to the first officer, who embraced it and accompanied her up the boarding ramp. Isabel glanced back at the skyline of skyscrapers, their towering shadows adorned by glowing antennas and white beacon lights. *Was she really going to do this? Yes…*She exhaled with certainty while silently bidding farewell to the city that defined all her routines and roles within her conventional daily life.

The first officer supported her across the yacht's threshold onto the promenade deck. Isabel had the sensation of being watched. She glanced up to the balcony of the upper deck. Beyond its tinted windows along the steering bridge, a silhouette shifted deeper into the shadows as her gaze focused on the familiarity of its form. *He was waiting for her.*

With anticipation, she followed the first officer through an access hatch that led into a wooden-paneled passageway. He stopped in front of a cabin door and opened it, allowing Isabel to pass directly inside. They exchanged no words. He simply nodded before closing the door, as if he was following a series of pre-designated orders to deliver her into the safety of the compartment before returning to the helm of the ship to shuttle her away into the open, unforgiving waters.

Isabel glanced around the stateroom, taking in its lustrous wooden paneling and elegant décor. The soft sheen of a crystal chandelier reflected off the surface of the Baroque mahogany dressing table. In its oval, ornamental mirror, she watched herself remove her fur shawl and drape it across the French antique settee under the stateroom's only porthole. She approached it and peered out into the moonless night. Without warning, the ship's engines roared, propelling the vessel forward through the sleepy waters of the harbor and into the crisp lapping waves of Lake Michigan. She clenched the key against her heart as the yacht pulled her away from the luminous Chicago skyline—and away from everything that was familiar and certain.

Her attention shifted across the room to the antique walnut armoire, inlaid with mother-of-pearl ornamentation. She studied it carefully—and its tiny keyhole. She closed her eyes, held the key in her palm, and concentrated on the furious beating of her own heart. Whatever he expected from her tonight, she intended to grant it to him. She turned back to the armoire, inserted her key in its keyhole, and swept open its double doors. Hanging on pink satin hangers was her second wardrobe—a black corset gown, its tight strapless bodice and billowing tulle train hinting at the forbidden expectations of the night. As if she was watching another woman—a stranger—in the dressing table's oval mirror, she slowly pushed the straps of her sequined dress off her shoulders. It fell to the floor like a casual goodbye. Naked and vulnerable, she reached out for the black gown and unclipped its cinching hooks before stepping through the open bodice and slipping the black tulle train over her exposed legs. The cascading folds settled just above her bare hips and backside. *A noir bride preparing for her master.* She fastened each metal loop along the corset's front closure, sealing the stiff bone ribs of bondage along her torso before latching the final clasp—just below its lacy burlesque cups. Isabel inhaled and exhaled, the constriction of each breath transforming her into another woman—a seductress with an hourglass figure, arcing cleavage, and long siren legs.

Her gaze shifted onto an ornamental silver box, resting on the lower shelf within the armoire. She exhaled before raising the lid and discovering the familiar white calling card inside it:

Everything forbidden between us during the day shall be unleashed in the secrecy of the night.

She touched the strong, scrolling inscription with her fingertips as her eyes absorbed the significance of the object beside it—a black Venetian mask, its elegant plume arching upwards like a crown and rhinestone trim glinting in the chandelier light. She lifted the mask into her hands and slipped it over her face, disguising her innermost fears with the mystique of a temptress. A flushing tingle of passion burned between her legs, igniting her deepest desires. She knew what he wanted because it was what she wanted for herself—to unleash the burden of every repressed emotion and physical inhibition and allow herself the permission to become his unbridled fantasy.

The roaring engines of the yacht suddenly stopped and glided across the surface of the lake before slowing with the rolling pace of the waves. Isabel crossed to the porthole where she gazed out into the black waters. There was no moon, no lights from the shore, nothing except the privacy of her isolation. Slowly, the chandelier dimmed to darkness, casting everything into shadows. Overwhelmed with anticipation, she held her breath and paused, listening to the lapping waters and the oppressive sound of solitude. A soft vibration buzzed inside her stateroom as the sleek wooden-paneled wall disengaged and slid open like an invitation. Isabel peered into the dark companionway, studying the half-flight of fiberglass stairs, flanked by mirrors, reflecting the vision and masquerade of herself as she ascended to the upper interior deck.

Was that the whispering rush of her palpitating heart, or the sound of waves licking the sleek ebony surface of the ship's hull? Enveloped by darkness, she pushed up the narrow passageway's final step and entered into the master suite, seamlessly sculpted in the shape of the yacht's aerodynamic bow.

The rolling waves churned like a murmur, summoning her towards the French double doors of the private veranda. Her high heels tapped along the dark fiberglass floors past the Empress platform bed, wrapped in navy satin sheets. Stepping out onto the balcony, Isabel took hold of the stainless steel railing, overlooking the celestial sky and starry waters of Lake Michigan. Inhaling the misty midnight air, she indulged in how the moisture seductively glazed her cheeks and bare shoulders. Then, like a premonition, she sensed his dominating presence behind her. Slowly, his strong forearms wrapped around her waist like an anchor, mooring her into his assertive embrace.

With authoritative control, his fingers secured her chin and lifted it upwards like a cherished possession, as if he was admiring her masked profile in the shadows.

"My muse," he whispered, his hot breath exhaling into her ear as his hands constricted around her cinched corset.

She attempted to confirm the cadence of his voice, but quickly abandoned the effort. Tonight wasn't about revealing their true identities. It was about exploring their deepest, darkest desires, shrouded in the fantasy of the night.

"You punish me for it," she whispered back, closing her eyes and taking in the warmth of his chest against her shoulder blades. He was naked. The stark, unexpected sensation of his bare skin against her body titillated her.

"Not as much as you punish me." His nose passed over the nape of her neck, taking in her scent.

She felt him shift his pelvis against the tulle train of her gown. He was hard and erect, ready to dominate her with the strength of his masculinity. She sighed and gripped the railing, expecting him to mercilessly overpower her. But he was making her wait for it. He wanted to make sure she was ready in every way.

"Close your eyes," he commanded.

She obeyed, relinquishing herself to the euphoric sensuality of the night.

He braced her like a submissive doll, drawing back her head by her hair, signaling his expectation for her full consent. His smooth cheek grazed against her mask as he lowered his lips to her throat and kissed it with tenderness.

Yes...she sighed, savoring the sensation of his wet mouth running down her collarbone as he secured her torso against his firm pecs and groped her cleavage with savage desire. He stripped down the ruffled cups of her corset, exposing her bare breasts to the chilling air. Her tits tingled as his hands slipped under her gown and followed the inner contours of her thighs until they reached her bare crotch. He tested her wetness, proving she had no choice—she could not defy him or deny herself.

"You inspire every forbidden desire within me," he betrayed in his low hush. "I can no longer endure it."

Pressing the full weight of his chest against her shoulder blades, he restrained her again. She gripped the railing and submitted to his domination, allowing his determined hands to peel back the sheer netting of her gown and expose her backside to his view. She sensed he was admiring the vision of her—masked and forbidden and fully surrendering herself to his command. She sighed deeply, absorbing the firmness of his hand, traveling along the curve of her backside. He massaged her cheeks in circles, loosening her defenses while exhaling his longing into her ear. His sharp chin pinned itself into her shoulder as his mouth sucked her neck with indulgence. He passed his fingers in front of her body and cupped her pubic bone, coating his fingertips with her wetness. She was gushing now. Slowly, he parted her slit and stroked her into submission, coaxing her stance wider and wider with her every moan. She clung to the railing, pushing herself deeper against his touch.

Yes...she exhaled, granting him permission to explore her, and granting herself permission to enjoy it. She relaxed her weight into his embrace, his probing fingers diminishing all of her defenses. She wanted him inside her—

wanted him to ravish and conquer her with the full force of his masculinity because he had succeeded in making her believe that she was the only one who could satisfy him.

Then, she felt his hot cock replace his fingers. She arched into it, accepting the firm pressure of its tip. He cupped her breasts, steadying her body against his chest while testing her tautness.

"Tell me you want this," he hushed past her mask into her ear.

"Yes." She nodded, anticipating his initial breach.

"My naughty vixen." He exhaled his desire through his nostrils, subduing his own instinct to dominate her without restraint.

She sighed, gazing upwards, seeking out the dark contours of their silhouettes in the reflective glass of the suite's ceiling panels before he whisked her into his arms. Carrying her to the Empress platform bed, he spread her, face-down, across its satin navy sheets. She gasped with the sudden jolt of his hands, violently ripping apart the tulle netting of her gown, exposing the supple curves of her backside to his full view. She clenched the sheets, feeling the stain of her arousal christening them as his hot breath dropped behind her, his tongue seeking out her slit.

"I love tasting you," he confessed.

She muted her protest against the mattress, his teasing licks traced the contours of her backside before bringing her to the brink of an unbearable groan. *Forbidden.* She shut her eyes, accepting her role as his submissive, allowing him to draw her up onto her hands and knees, and granting him full access to her. She arched her back, savoring the taboo satisfaction of being fully penetrated by his invading tongue. *Yes, yes, yes*, she was his dirty mistress. *Such a dirty mistress*, she sighed, allowing herself to be lapped so submissively. *Would she ever be able to face him—and his true identity—in the daylight*? She didn't know and she didn't care. She only wanted to endure the quivers of excitement rising up through her pelvis every time he nipped her clit and flicked his tongue deeper and deeper inside her slit. Within the security of the darkness, his anonymity made her feel like another woman—a sexual goddess—willing to relinquish herself completely to him.

Slowly, he withdrew his tongue and shifted behind her, slipping the hot tip of his cock against her slickness, hinting at his invasion. He coaxed her stance wider and braced her hips with his strong grasp, pinning his pelvis against her flesh and preparing to seduce her in the most sacred of ways. She heaved out a sigh, signaling her desire for him to breach the glistening spot that they both knew he wanted most.

There, yes…

She gasped, like she was surfacing for air, as he pushed the full length of his cock past the initial friction of her slit. He filled her completely, the strength of his erection kindling a throbbing ripple of relief. He ran his palms around her cinched corset, gauging her need for him by the intensity of her breath, before slowly withdrawing himself and searching out her desire for his second thrust.

Deeper, she sighed, aching with satisfaction; she wanted nothing more than to feel him inside her, accelerating his pace from behind her. But he was making her wait for it. *Beg for it.* His fingers slipped in front of her body, teasing her clit with precision, building her up with ebbing waves of stimulation, reminding her of the sexual gratification he had delivered to her the night before. She lowered her head against the mattress and gushed for him. *Wetter and wetter.* He stroked her ass and fondled her slit like he was her master. *Yes, yes, yes,* she chanted, petitioning him to overtake her—ride her harder, rougher, deeper. *Yes, yes, yes, she repeated. His dirty, naughty vixen.*

Slowly, confidently, he pulled her back onto her knees, cupped her exposed breasts, and drove the firmness of his cock into her, challenging the limits of intimacy they both had imposed on themselves. She opened her mouth, shuddering with the vibrations humming within her, mimicking the rhythm of his accelerating penetrations.

God, don't stop, don't stop, don't stop…Her private petitions for more echoed through her mind before escaping her lips like guilty sins.

"Say you will accept me—fully."

Yeesss, she sighed as his thrusts raided her every inhibition, heightening her gushing desire to be conquered and punished like his divine whore. *His muse, his temptress, his enchantress, his mistress*—she had fantasized about being all of them, and now, he had offered her the opportunity to become them in the security of their charade.

She heard him groan from behind her, a warning that he could no longer withhold his own need to come. He grasped her shoulders and shifted into his final acceleration. She arched her tailbone, absorbing the domineering strength of his pelvis against her backside, forcing her to accept his unyielding rhythm. She fondled her own clit, searching out relief from the seizures of ecstasy he was building up within her, before drawing back her head with a heave—on the brink of her climax—as he surged with his final thrust. His flowing warmth coursed through her, initiating her simultaneous release with a flush of rushing heat that radiated a rippling wave of satisfaction throughout her body that only he had the power to unleash within her.

When it was all over, they fell into the dark flowing sheets, drowning in their own panting breaths. *One forbidden night.* She felt his hands unclasping the loops of her corset, fully liberating her body and breath. She curled her knees against her own chest as he removed her mask and spooned her with his protective embrace, confirming his devotion behind their mutual masquerade. It was no longer a question of whether or not they had both yearned to break free from their sexual repression. It was only a question of how they would face its consequences within the raw candor of the morning light.

* * * *

Isabel opened her eyes to the sound of roaring engines.

She sat straight up in the bed before fumbling out of it, half entangled in the sheets, as the yacht moored against the harbor's buffering tires with repetitive thumps.

What time was it? She glanced out of the veranda's double doors at the timid sun, rising across the endless horizon of Lake Michigan.

Oh, thank God—dawn.

Quickly, she gathered up her clothes—T-shirt, yoga pants, tennis shoes—arranged with care at the foot of the bed—and hastily dressed, barely considering how they got there. She could only focus on how the vessel's revving engine steered its hull against the waves and how its undulating rhythm mirrored the lingering sensations of what had transpired last night. She surveyed her surroundings, realizing how ordinary everything appeared to her now—the tousled bed sheets, the dull black floors, the muted ceiling mirrors reflecting the suite's emptiness. The only proof of his domination—and her submission—was her own surreal memories of their lustful night.

Then, she spotted it on the corner of the nightstand—a red leatherette jewelry box. Beneath it was the familiar white calling card. She retrieved it and read its bold inscription:

Beneath the fantasy of last night lies my fidelity to you.

Her pulse quickened as she peered at the jewelry box, attempting not to allow herself to hope for something grander than what she had already received—a gorgeous necklace, beautiful studded earrings…*what more could he bestow upon her now*? She unfastened the red button clip and opened its double doors. Then, she heard a gasp. It ricocheted through her mind before escaping from her lips. She gazed at the awe-inspiring ring, its two-carat sapphire centerpiece glinting like a mythical nautical treasure. Her fingertip swiped over its diamond-studded platinum setting, taking in its full beauty and significance. Isabel never wore rings; they had always been too restrictive and distracting on her hands. But now, she peered down at the ring and savored its sleek sensation of extravagance on her finger, wondering if perhaps she had adopted a physical aversion to rings to reinforce her own private belief that she would never find love—and certainly never *fall* in love—ever again.

There was a soft knock on the door. She turned towards it, waiting for him to enter the suite.

"Miss Alvarez?" the voice filtered through the locked door.

"Yes?" She started forward before halting with hesitation. The sound of his voice was polite and official, but unfamiliar.

"We're docking now. I've been instructed to accompany you ashore where a driver is waiting to escort you home."

Chapter Ten

ISABEL STROLLED THROUGH the office on Monday morning like a new woman. It was a fresh, crisp autumn morning and everything about her felt different. Without knocking, she passed through Phillip's executive office and strode across its gleaming hardwood floors.

"Good morning," she offered brightly, approaching the silver-toned blinds and filtering out the golden morning rays that streamed through the expansive panoramic windows. In his tailored Royal Oxford white shirt and glacial blue silk tie, Phillip sat at his glass desk like a man who had both endless amounts of money and time. He stroked his chin and contemplated the positions of the miniature pieces along his marble chessboard.

"Lovely day," she asserted with confidence.

"Yes, it is," he replied, studying the chirpy edge in her tone. Isabel passed behind his desk in order to adjust the second set of blinds. *Phillip, always shrouded in darkness*. When she circled in front of his desk, she sensed his gaze tracking her—the same way his eyes always tracked her in the morning—silently anticipating the content of the conversation she intended to present to him.

"You'll be very pleased," she said with a broad smile. "I've got great news. I've already received thirty-five RSVPs to Saturday's gala and more than half of them are city officials."

Phillip crossed his hands and shifted his weight back into his swivel chair. Isabel watched the light in his eyes change from guarded grey to muted blue.

"Alderman Orsollini?"

"Confirmed."

"Alderman Donovan?"

"Confirmed."

"Fitzpatrick and Ginozi?"

"Yes and yes."

Isabel sat down on the leather sofa with an exhale—a long, deliberate sigh signaling victory. Phillip toyed with his black rook and muted his smile, as if the heavy sound of her relaxation amused him.

"Well, of course, I cannot say that I expected anything less from you," he finally said, overtaking a white horse from his imaginary opponent.

"Of course not," Isabel tossed back.

Phillip stroked his chin and watched her, watching him. There was a casual air of comfort between them—a connection of trust and cooperation—and one that was notable because it had been absent in recent days; now, they both seemed to be indulging in its return.

"We're going to get your permits, Phillip. You'll be able to start the redevelopment before the end of the month."

"Let's hope so," he said, lowering his eyes and guarding his emotions.

"Coffee?" Isabel asked. It was a rare offer and they both knew it.

Phillip nodded. "Please…"

Isabel turned and left his office with the same confident stride she had when she entered it. She headed through the open hallway and greeted the other office staffers—Elisa, Marcy, Jenna, Grace—with enthusiasm before rounding the corner of the kitchen and bumping into Tami and her super-sized homemade iced latte.

"Good morning, and wow…tell me that's not your second breakfast?" Isabel asked, watching Tami slurping down her creamy concoction through her straw.

"Third," Tami admitted, her voice saddled with Monday morning depression. "It's the only way I've been able to function all weekend. Jett has been on my ass non-stop since Phillip's meeting on Saturday. He even made me go to a hockey game with him on Saturday night, so he could dictate messages to every single one of his commercial broker buddies who hadn't returned his call from the morning. After three straight hours of texting, I finally decided that I couldn't be held responsible for making typos like 'thongs' instead of 'things'."

"Don't worry…that probably made Jett's texts sound more authentic."

"Totally," Tami emphasized with a noisy slurp. "Jett will probably promote me to executive sexting assistant. Anyway, how was your weekend? I bet you had it even worse than me. Phillip was literally calling Jett every hour to see if we had secured any viable tenant leads for him."

But Isabel didn't hear her question. She was busy riffling through the cabinets for Phillip's favorite mug while humming the theme song to one of Aidan's favorite cartoons.

Tami narrowed her eyes at her—and her inappropriately misplaced chipper Monday morning attitude. "You little slattern whore. You didn't work all weekend like me. You got laid."

Isabel whirled towards her, horrified. "Tami!"

"Don't –Tami – me, Isabel. I can recognize the afterglow of an awesome fuck when I see one, and you definitely are glowing like a freaking Christmas tree."

Isabel stared at Tami, who crossed her arms and stared back at her. It was a stand-off.

"It wasn't sex…exactly," Isabel finally conceded, turning away and pouring coffee into Phillip's mug. "It was more like…liberation."

"I knew it!" Tami exclaimed like she had won a game show. "You whore, you frickin' skanky whore…so it *is* true!"

Isabel rushed to the kitchen doorway and peeked out into the office; she lowered her voice, attempting to minimize Tami's expectations. "It's not what you think."

"So enlighten me!" Tami sucked down her iced latte with anticipation.

"It was more like…a forbidden affair."

"An affair? You mean he's married?"

"God, I hope not," Isabel sighed and placed the mug on the counter to collect her thoughts. "No, I mean…I don't know what it was exactly," she finally confessed.

"What do you mean 'you don't know'?" Tami replied, adjusting her glasses.

"I mean…I don't know because it was dark and we never really…we just sort of..."

"Snogged?" Tami offered, seeing Isabel struggle for the right terminology.

"More," Isabel said, leading her like a charades partner.

"Lewinskied?"

"No, the opposite."

"Tangoed in Paris?"

"Well, not exactly that *scandalous*, but it certainly felt that fabulously scandalous."

"Holy hell-ooooo," Tami exhaled, absorbing Isabel's confession with a long incredulous slurp. "Totally in the dark?"

Isabel nodded. "*And* on his yacht."

Tami wavered like she might faint. "And you never even saw him?"

"No, not really… " Isabel paused, her mind suddenly replaying the shadows and sensations of the night. "He was behind me the whole time."

"That is ri-DUNK-ulous, Isabel. You know that, right?"

"I know," Isabel said, fidgeting with the sapphire ring on her finger—*his* gift to her. "But somehow, it was exactly what felt right."

"Damn straight!" Tami cried out, pawing at Isabel's stunning new piece of jewelry for a better look. "Especially if he gave you that...holy motherfucker."

Isabel fell silent. There was nothing more about the night that she wanted to disparage or betray. Tami tossed down Isabel's hand in disbelief. "Seriously, Isabel...someone is either out to marry you or out to totally ruin you." Tami suddenly shifted her attention out into the office. "Holy hell..."

"Hello, ladies!" Symeon Colovos hollered out with his Greek bravado. "Did you miss me?"

Tami and Isabel watched as Phillip's ex-business partner glided through the office corridor in his flaring trench coat and black pinstriped suit. He carried an oversized black umbrella, slung over one shoulder, despite the fact that it was a sunny autumn morning. With his shaved head and fierce Mediterranean features, Symeon looked like a Spartan warrior preparing for battle. It was the same disruptive way he used to greet the office staff every morning when he worked there while carrying in pastries from the nearby Greek bakery. But now, his grandiose enthusiasm was only met with awkward confusion. All the girls stared at him in silence, as if they were replaying in their heads the day he left Spears & Associates and never returned. It was a day that none of them would ever forget because it was the only day they had ever heard Phillip raise his voice beyond the walls of his executive suite to a threatening level of rage.

"Holy moly hell," Tami repeated, shifting her gaze to Symeon's handsome companion strolling behind him with a Cheshire smile. Isabel's eyes settled upon him, too. *Silver grey vested suit. Lavender shirt with white scalloped collar. Midnight purple tie.* With his playboy insouciance, tanned complexion and commanding stride, Eliot Watercross never failed to make an entrance without attracting everyone's attention—especially of all the women in the room. But in that moment, his tiger green eyes seized Isabel's gaze and conveyed it was her attention—and only her attention—that was the prize he aimed to claim.

Without warning, the men entered Phillip's executive suite and closed the door behind them.

"What the hell is that meeting about?" Tami turned to Isabel.

"I have no idea," she replied, fumbling to check her phone and Phillip's calendar for the day. "It's not on the calendar and they never cleared it with me. They've come completely unannounced."

Isabel strode out of the kitchen. She clenched Phillip's hot coffee mug in her hands, hoping the searing burn against her skin would calm her trembling hands as the implications of Eliot's lingering stare weighed heavy on her heart.

Tami chased after her. "I wonder if Jett knows about this?"

Suddenly, Phillip's British accent filtered through the speaker on Isabel's desk phone.

"I'd like you in this meeting, Isabel," he said with stern expectation, then ended the call without waiting for her reply.

The girls all stared at Isabel who glanced at Tami. Tami read her mind.

"Just try to keep them from mortally wounding each other until I can text Jett and see how fast he can get back here. Go—"

Isabel nodded, rushing to open Phillip's office door before shutting it behind her.

Phillip sitting at his desk. Symeon circling the room. Eliot perched on the arm of the sofa. Isabel noted the position of each man in the room as she strode across the office, overwhelmed by the heavy sensation of masculine glares on every part of her body.

"Good morning, Bella," Eliot was the first to greet her.

Phillip shot him a glare. It was a deliberate use of Isabel's nickname in front of Phillip, and she knew it was only the beginning of trouble for her.

Symeon twirled his folded umbrella over his shoulder and eyed Isabel as she handed off the coffee mug to Phillip. "Well, well, well…how things have changed. I've only been gone for four weeks, and already Phillip has trained you to bring him his morning coffee."

"I would have brought *all* of you coffee," Isabel replied, "if you had bothered to contact me about scheduling a meeting with Phillip rather than showing up unexpectedly."

"I'm Greek, Isabel," Symeon countered with a snarl. "I do everything unexpectedly."

"Which is exactly what we've come to expect from you, Symeon," Isabel sassed back, sitting down in front of Phillip's glass desk. She chose her position strategically—turning her back on Eliot Watercross while maintaining direct eye contact with Phillip. And yet, she could feel Eliot's searing eyes watching her.

Isabel glanced up at Phillip. *They were both watching her.*

She smoothed down her skirt and straightened herself in her seat. Phillip's expression hardened as he addressed the room without vigor.

"You have arrived unannounced, but not without a purpose."

"To discuss business, of course," Symeon said with glib enthusiasm.

"Of course," Phillip repeated.

"We've heard you're moving forward on the redevelopment of The Old Main Post Office," Symeon prodded.

"And I've heard that you have already confirmed your attendance for our opening gala this Saturday." Phillip lifted his voice, signaling he was addressing Eliot Watercross rather than Symeon.

"Wouldn't miss it for the world," Eliot confirmed, rising from the edge of the sofa's armrest, as if he intended to assert his physical dominance. Eliot Watercross was tall, taller than most men, but it was the way he carried his rugged physique under his trendy, modern suits and fashionable silk ties that made him seem bold and brash beyond comparison. "Especially since half the real estate investors in Chicago are likely to be there."

"Unlikely. Capital has already been raised," Phillip replied. "It's simply a matter of gaining the city's approval."

"Really? No investors?" Eliot pressed the point.

"No investors." Phillip glared at him with conviction. "I'm funding it myself."

"Ahhh, that's right, Eliot." Symeon circled the room like a ringmaster announcing the next attraction. "We're forgetting that Spears is selling The Peoria to Harvey Zale—at a *discount*."

Isabel watched Symeon relish the genius of his own slight against Phillip, but she heard Eliot's steady voice dismiss it.

"Whisper number is three hundred million dollars," Eliot noted, his brow arching with skepticism. "Discount or not, that's a lot of cash, even for you, Spears."

Phillip challenged him with his steady blue gaze. "I like control."

"Well, we're moving forward on our own new development project," Symeon blurted out, as if he could barely contain himself.

Phillip deliberately remained silent. Symeon crossed the room and flopped down onto the sofa, as if he still worked there.

"Yes, I've heard. You're proposing to construct a floating iceberg in the middle of the Chicago River," Phillip replied dryly.

"News travels fast," Symeon grinned with obnoxious pride. "A floating iceberg with a casino, spa, upscale boutique shopping center, *and* a three-story hotel."

"I didn't realize that icebergs could be so luxurious," Isabel chimed in. Phillip glanced at her. She couldn't help the dig and he knew it.

"Luxurious *and* lucrative," Symeon stressed. "That's why we're seeking investors."

Phillip's eyes flicked upwards. Isabel recognized the sudden spark of interest.

"So you are here to discuss business after all," Phillip said evenly, guarding his thoughts.

The room suddenly fell silent—and waited. Isabel watched Phillip's eyes, tracking Eliot Watercross as he drifted to the expansive windows and peered out at the impressive view of the city and lakefront.

"Water recreation is big business in Chicago, Spears," he said. "And if there's one thing that this town has plenty of…it's water. Montrose Beach. North Beach. Monroe Harbor. And then, there's the Chicago River, winding through some of the most influential downtown buildings. During the summer, this city's waterways are like passages of gold that everyone aims to mine."

Eliot turned his gaze out towards the massive cityscape and sprawling lakefront. "But during the winter, everyone's love affair with Chicago's lakefront and riverfront fades away like a cruel lover after a one-night stand."

Isabel shifted her gaze behind her, catching sight of Eliot from the corner of her eye. He turned into the streaming sunlight, which accentuated his tanned skin and green eyes. "There's only one way to find true love—true enduring love—for Chicago's waterways, and that's through year-round courtship."

"Courtship," Phillip interjected, "although romantic and alluring, does not guarantee a faithful heart."

"But it does guarantee an invitation to explore the possibility of something more," Eliot challenged him. "And that's what we're going to be offering to the City of Chicago. A winter wonderland fantasy experience along Chicago's magnificent waterways—year-round."

"Except in the summer months," Phillip countered with bite. "When your iceberg will melt."

"Already got that covered," Symeon gushed, like he couldn't contain himself. "We're working with naval engineers on CAD plans to turn the whole thing into a convertible riverboat casino during the summertime. It's going to be an aquatic recreational tourist attraction—on steroids."

"Sounds like true love," Phillip punctuated, keeping his valiant blue eyes squarely on Watercross.

Watercross smirked and noted the chessboard on Phillip's desk. "You're a man of limited time and patience, Spears. So we'll jump right to the heart of it. We're seeking investment capital in exchange for partnership equity—preferred stock. It's going to be a very elite investment group—one that makes allegiances or divides them."

"Yes, I can only imagine. A floating iceberg has the potential to be supremely divisive."

Isabel heard the sarcasm in Phillip's tone—a mixture of blatant mockery and disgust. She glanced back at Eliot. His Cheshire smile sharpened with malice.

"So you claim to have the capital for the renovation of The Old Main Post Office, but not the approval from the city officials. Not yet, anyway. It would be a shame not to be able to move forward with the redevelopment simply because one alderman received a large campaign contribution from your competition for wrapping up your permits in bureaucratic red tape."

"It's a risk I'm willing to take," Phillip lobbed back, impervious to Watercross' veiled threat.

Eliot laughed with a spontaneous burst of confidence. "Which is why I like you so much, Phillip. You're determined to get exactly what you think you deserve—whatever the cost. Just like me."

Suddenly, Isabel felt the pit of her stomach constrict as Eliot's looming presence drifted behind her chair.

"We're proposing 400 South Wacker as the site for our new development. Right across the river frontage of your development. I would hate to be forced to encroach upon your territory…" Slowly, Eliot placed his domineering hand over Isabel's shoulder. She blushed as her entire body acquiesced to the sensation of his possessive palm, mastering her with the force. It told her that she would not be able to liberate herself until he chose to release her.

Isabel lifted her eyes to Phillip, his gaze studying the flush of her cheeks and her uncharacteristic submission to Watercross' touch.

"I have come to expect that from you, Eliot," Phillip stated with a subtle frown. "And I am willing to simply govern myself accordingly."

"Well, then…" Eliot suddenly said, casually abandoning Isabel's shoulder as quickly as he had claimed it. "We should plan to discuss it more over drinks this Saturday at your gala."

He pushed forward towards Phillip's desk and studied his chessboard, pompously taking a turn by sweeping up Phillip's dark queen with the white rook. He strode towards the door, signaling the end of their meeting before turning back with a sly glance.

"Oh, and one more thing, Spears—" Watercross abruptly called out, whizzing the chesspiece at him like a baseball pitch. With flawless precision, Phillip caught the queen in his palm, but did not replace it back onto the chessboard. "Be sure to mark Symeon down as one plus guest." His eyes flicked to Symeon.

"Marlow can't wait to attend," Symeon confirmed. "She loves your galas and wouldn't miss this one for the world."

"See you soon, Bella. Save a dance for me." Eliot winked before opening the door.

"Gentlemen—"Jett announced, bounding into Phillip's office like an Olympic track star, dressed in a red and grey jogging shirt and matching athletic pants. "What's going on? No one invited me to the party? I'm truly heart-broken."

Jett extended his hand to greet Eliot and Symeon like dear friends.

"And truly in need of a shower," Symeon joked, accepting his handshake while wafting away the scent of his sweat.

Isabel watched Jett round up the men and offer his own office as their next stop. *Jett—the perfect politician.* He never missed a networking opportunity, not even with the competition, and that was the reason why he was one of the most connected commercial real estate brokers in the city. Jett always followed the scent of money, not the stench of the men behind it.

Isabel waited to speak until she saw the door completely close behind them, trapping her within the invisible walls of Phillip's reflective silence. She shifted her gaze onto him, waiting for his eyes to meet her own.

"Phillip—" she petitioned him, an attempt to console the disquiet darkening his aristocratic profile. But he did not acknowledge her. Instead, he tilted up the marble chessboard with one surrendering hand, allowing all the pieces to haphazardly scatter off its checkered base.

He did not speak, and she knew better than to press him. Slowly, she rose from her seat and escaped behind the familiar civility of their professional relationship. "I'll send you the current invitation list for the gala, and we can arrange a time to meet about approval of the final details…at your convenience."

She turned away to the door, but stopped when she noted two chess pieces at her feet. She retrieved them—the bishop and the Queen—and laid them carefully on the surface of Phillip's desk.

"You are the object of desire, Isabel."

She turned and stared at him, unable to comprehend his words. Phillip's gaze remained fixed on the empty chessboard, but his words addressed her, unwavering and firm. "You are the object of Eliot Watercross' desire. And he's willing to obtain you at any cost."

Isabel parted her mouth to protest, but only felt the chilling freeze of fear escape her lips. "I don't understand…"

She watched Phillip pause—a long, grave moment of silence before he swiveled away from her and rose from his seat, revealing the clean lines along the tapered waist of his Royal Oxford shirt, glistening white in the sunlight. Silent and pensive, he gazed out through the windows, as if he was considering all the ways he had fought to preserve a city he considered his own. His eyes settled on the iconic Willis Tower—one of the tallest skyscrapers in the world.

"The Sears Tower—one of Chicago's most iconic symbols of financial power—was renamed the Willis Tower, simply because the Willis Group moved in and leased more than sixty percent of its commercial space. In this world—*our* world of commercial real estate—you are only as successful as your last business deal and only as powerful as the size of your bank account."

He turned his elegant profile to Isabel and allowed the sunlight to glint off his cerulean eyes and cool winter complexion.

"Eliot Watercross needs capital. I have always suspected that his real estate deals were built upon fraudulent financials, and one bad loan leveraged upon another bad loan does not build a real estate empire. It builds a garish, but fragile house of cards. When Watercross forged a business venture with Colovos, he believed—falsely—that he had secured all of Spears & Associates' financial information, including access to our investors. Now, he finally knows the truth."

Phillip's gaze shifted onto Isabel. Their eyes locked.

"The only other person—besides me—who has an intimate knowledge of our balance sheet and the equity partnerships of all of the real estate investors within all of our properties is not Symeon. It is you."

Isabel stared at Phillip, attempting to absorb the gravity of his confession.

"And that confidentiality has been something that Symeon has always resented, but I realized early on that he could not be trusted. And it was the main reason why I forced him out of the company."

Isabel peered at him in disbelief. "I always assumed that Symeon left Spears & Associates because of his relationship with Marlow."

"Marlow?"

"Yes, of course."

"No, not at all. Marlow was simply a casualty, not the cause." Phillip slipped his hands into his pockets and circled around his desk. "When I first started Spears & Associates, I offered Symeon a minority equity stake with the agreement that it would be re-evaluated after five years of service. Five years came last month. Symeon is a brilliant architect, but an exceedingly reckless business partner, and as a result, I refused to offer him a greater portion of equity ownership in the company. Rather than make him a full partner, I bought his equity stake and forced him out. That's how he was able to turn around and purchase the Amway building from Harvey Zale—a complete squandering of his wealth because he grossly overpaid for the privilege of exerting his revenge against me."

Phillip peered out far across the cityscape at its skyscrapers of concrete and steel, as if he was considering whether or not it was all worth it.

"Bringing Symeon Colovos into Spears & Associates as a minority equity shareholder was a mistake from the very beginning. Fortunately, I realized my error early in our partnership, and restricted his access to the company's most confidential contacts and financial statements. Instead, I slowly began sharing that information with you. And now, Eliot Watercross has just given me an ultimatum—either become an investor in his…floating iceberg," Phillip punctuated with disdain, "or prepare to defend myself."

"Defend yourself from what?"

"His conquest of you."

A hush of silence whispered through Isabel's chest. She felt the sting of passion, still lingering within her body, and considered whether or not she had already been conquered.

"Phillip, you know I would never intentionally betray you."

Isabel heard the word "intentionally" echo through her mind and suddenly fell silent with guilt, wondering if she had just promised more than she could honor.

"Yes, I believe that. And yet, I cannot protect you from Colovos and Watercross, who are determined to make you a pawn in their ruthless game of greed."

He looked away as a flash of pain spread across his face. Isabel knew very little about Phillip's personal upbringing or family, except that he had lost his father at a young age; but she suspected that his steely exterior and guarded emotions stemmed from a childhood fraught with instability and distrust. It was rare for Phillip to betray anything but stoicism, but now, she could see him struggling…struggling to wrestle with his swelling emotions.

"Isabel…" He suddenly said her name like a request for mercy. "I fear that I have unwittingly exposed you to the egos of powerful men willing to compromise you at whatever the cost."

Isabel rose from her seat, motivated by the disarming petition for forgiveness in his eyes. She approached him at the window, determined to assert her own strength and independence.

"Phillip, you have given me—and my family—a level of comfort and security that would never have been possible without your willingness to allow me the chance to prove myself to you. I do not fault you in any way for bringing me into this world. I only fault you for believing that I can't handle it myself."

He peered at her, acknowledging the truth behind her words.

"You are a smart, experienced, savvy, and dare I add, highly desirable woman, Isabel," he confessed, almost in a hush. "There is absolutely no reason why Eliot Watercross shouldn't attempt to recruit you into his camp the way he successfully recruited Symeon. There is only your own willingness not to be courted."

The intensity within his gaze drew her closer to him, closer than she expected.

"Courtship, Phillip," Isabel replied, "although romantic and alluring, does not guarantee a faithful heart."

He betrayed a smile and peered at her with a vulnerability that expressed more in that moment than he had expressed in the entire time she had worked for him. She stared at him, taking in the elegance of his British profile, the sophistication of his propriety, and his desire to protect her from the sins and corruption of men—all around them.

She gazed at him, disarmed by the gentle tone of his voice and the sensitivity in his crystal eyes. She no longer felt like his employee; instead, she felt like his salvation.

"Sometimes it does all feel like a fragile façade," she whispered, sensing his desire to close the space between them. "And the only person who knows that better than me is you."

Phillip nodded, brushing his hand against her arm without apology. "You are the only person who reminds me—above all else—what is genuine and irreplaceable in my life."

Isabel gazed up at Phillip, finally glimpsing the man behind his embittered pride. She thought she felt him securing her hand, seeking the acceptance of his intimate touch; but then, it all ended when the abrupt knock on his office door erased the certainty that he had ever reached out to her at all.

"Mr. Spears?" Giselle peeked inside the office with hesitation.

He shifted his profile without addressing her, signaling his displeasure.

"I'm sorry to interrupt," Giselle quickly apologized, "but there's a woman here, waiting to see you…"

Marlow suddenly pushed past Giselle, waltzing into the office as if she was Phillip's wife, and not his ex-fiancée. "And I certainly shouldn't be kept waiting all day." But she halted when she saw Isabel and Phillip, standing near the window with a proximity that produced a combative flash within her feline eyes. "Especially since I know how your sense of propriety would never allow you to intentionally slight a lady."

She held out her hand with expectation, intending to draw Phillip away from Isabel, as if she expected to be treated like royalty. Phillip circled around the desk, took her hand, and kissed it with politeness.

She had won. Marlow always won.

Marlow stroked the otter fur lapel of her turquoise bolero jacket and intentionally ignored Isabel's presence, as if she was merely a servant in the room.

"I'm here to meet Symeon for lunch," Marlow sang out. "We're going downtown to the Russian Tea Room, but when he sent me a text, saying he was here, I decided to stop by…we were all such good friends—once."

She punctuated "*once*" with her pouty red lips as her long slender fingers playfully outlined Phillip's strong jaw. Isabel watched him accept Marlow's touch without censure or rejection. No matter how Isabel personally felt about Marlow, it didn't change the fact that she was Phillip's former lover. They had been engaged, which meant she had succeeded in capturing Phillip's elusive heart—*once.*

"Relationships are easily lost and discarded," Phillip confirmed, his eyes tracking Isabel as she moved to the door, preparing to exit. "But less easily replaced."

"Exactly," Marlow said, adjusting his tie like a cat playing with a ball of string. "No need for everyone to have such hard feelings, especially when you and I always have had such a familiar way with each other." Marlow shifted forward, brushing up against him with suggestion. Was it her stylish flair—her fitted black vintage secretary dress, her bolero jacket, her heeled leather boots, and her blatant disregard for boundaries—that made her so alluring? Or was it her capricious youth and flirtatious smile? Isabel didn't know, but it seemed that Marlow always had the ability to maneuver past Phillip's British reserve like it was nothing more than an amusing challenge. And despite their recent separation and Marlow's new romance with Symeon, in that moment, it was clear something still endured between them—some kind of mutual understanding, frozen in time—something that granted Marlow the freedom to act like Phillip's mistress simply because they had once shared a bed. Isabel watched Phillip entertaining Marlow's advances like it was a social obligation. *Had Marlow betrayed and abandoned Phillip, or had he intentionally pushed her away?*

Isabel turned to the door, but glanced back, sensing the weight of the unresolved history between them. She forced a smile, trying not to acknowledge the sting of being displaced. "I will send you the update on the gala, Phillip."

"Yes, the gala," Marlow repeated. "Symeon told me about it yesterday. You know how much I just *adore* a grand vintage ball, especially when you always look so dashing at them, Phillip." She traced the starched collar of his Royal Oxford shirt with the tip of her lacquered fingernail. "I've already placed a rush order on the most perfect vintage designer dress. You're going to love it."

"Let me know if you need anything else," Isabel added, announcing her exit.

"A bottle of Pelligrino would be lovely…"

Marlow's request hung into the air like a lofty command. Isabel stopped in the doorway without glancing back. She considered ignoring it and continuing on, or worse, responding with a catfight glare. But Phillip took the dagger away from her.

"Isabel," he punctuated, lowering his voice with authority, waiting for her to turn and meet his gaze. "Please send in Giselle whenever it's convenient."

"Of course," Isabel replied. "I'm sure she would be happy to fetch whatever you might need."

Good grief. Isabel closed the door and exhaled with relief, barely making it past the water cooler before Tami rushed up to meet her.

"*Ohmygod, ohmygod, ohmygod…*" Tami hyperventilated, grabbing Isabel by her elbow and guiding her to Isabel's desk. "You are never going to guess who I saw putting *that* on your desk five minutes ago."

Isabel gazed down at the powder blue bag with white satin handles and its black block trademark: TIFFANY & CO.

"Eliot Watercross," Tami blurted out.

Isabel glanced around. Several of the other girls looked up from behind their computers but Isabel quickly hid the bag behind her purse.

"Eliot Watercross is Mr. Billionaire Mystery Man. You totally called it. You're officially sleeping with the enemy."

Isabel suddenly felt her heart constrict with dread. She peered down into the sleek gift bag. There was no note. No card. Nothing to confirm Tami's claim except what Isabel sensed in her bones. She rummaged through the folds of tissue paper and pulled out an oblong powder blue box. She handed it to Tami. "Please tell me it isn't more sapphires."

Tami flipped open the lid, her jaw dropping as she drew out the triple-strand South Sea pearl bracelet, stunning with its silver overtones and smooth uniformity. "It isn't more frickin' sapphires," Tami repeated, wrapping it slowly around her own wrist. "Oh. My. God."

"This has to stop," Isabel said, unfastening the clasp and taking back the bracelet.

"No, please—" Tami pleaded, mourning the loss of luxury from her wrist.

"Did you see him leave?"

"I saw him head for the elevators, but seriously, Isabel…wait." Tami clawed at her. "Stop and really *think* about what you're doing." Tami stroked the pearls like she was vicariously living out her own fantasy.

"I know what I'm doing. I'm putting an end to the games. I'm not going to be a pawn on anyone's chessboard."

Isabel strode down the hallway and pushed through the lobby doors. Eliot Watercross was waiting in front of the elevators doors. His eyes dropped down onto the pearl bracelet, dangling from her fingers.

"I should have known you were too smart to let me get away with it for long," he said with his trademark slyness.

Isabel held out the bracelet to him. "I'm sorry, but we have to end this. Phillip is my employer and you're his competition. It's really that simple."

Eliot slowly accepted the pearls with a curious glint in his eye. "I think the only thing simple is that you look stunning wrapped up in pearls."

He pushed forward with merciless determination and ensnared her wrist, clasping the triple strands around it. She gazed down at the bracelet, transfixed by its silky sensation of bondage. The elevators doors chimed open, but Eliot did not release her.

"Eliot, what do you want from me?"

He leaned into her, deeper, like he was savoring his new possession. "Come work for me."

"That's impossible," she replied, resisting his firm grasp. But he was stronger—and more resolute—and they both knew it.

"No, it's not impossible and you know it." He drew her in, his jawline flinching as his lips searched out what she refused to grant him.

"As your assistant?" she scoffed, feeling her shoulder brushing against the familiar strength of his hard, flexing chest beneath his vested suit. He smelled like cedar and pine, and his tanned skin and green eyes shone down on her like they had played this game before—and he had won.

"No," he countered, his gaze flashing with desire, "as my partner."

"Eliot—" she said, wincing before he finally released her. "You don't mean that."

He stared at her before pressing the call button for the elevator.

"You're a smart woman, Isabel. You've known me long enough to know that I'm a man who says *exactly* what I mean. My lawyers are drafting the final paperwork for our newest business venture. I'll grant you a ten-percent minority ownership stake in exchange for bringing in no less than forty million dollars of investment capital. I'm a modern man with a modern vision, Isabel. I need business partners who are willing to seize upon an opportunity when they see one." He advanced towards her and stroked her cheek like he was admiring her stubbornness. "Everything else is just an added bonus."

Isabel turned away from his touch, letting the haunting cadence of Eliot's voice sink into her soul. "Phillip warned me that's what you wanted from me. You're courting me because you want me to tap into his investor base."

"No," Eliot challenged her, closing the distance between them. "Phillip is wrong because he only uses you as his old-fashioned secretary. That's the difference between Phillip and me, Isabel—I don't need you to be my Girl Friday who plans my precious parties and organizes my dry cleaning. I need you to be by my side—as my rainmaker—and I'm willing to share my wealth with you, just to prove it."

The truth behind his sarcasm stung more than she wanted to betray.

"What makes you so certain I can raise forty million dollars?"

"I'm not certain. But I'm certain it's a risk I'm willing to take," he said, indulging in the scent of her perfume. "Are you?" He lowered his chin and grazed his lips across her ear and neck.

"No," she asserted. "You're asking me to betray someone who has professionally invested in me for years."

"Admirable," he countered. "Except your loyalty is misplaced because I'm offering you more now than Phillip ever has—and ever will."

"No." She shook her head, battling the war waging within her own heart. "You're wrong about that, Eliot. Five years ago, I was a single, pregnant college dropout with almost no professional work experience. Phillip was the only person willing to give me a chance."

"And now, ask yourself," he lobbed back, closing the gap between them. "Is that how Phillip still sees you?"

The chime of the elevator cab interrupted their conversation. Isabel pushed away from him—and his hurtful words—like she was resisting the fear that they might be true.

With his sly smile, Eliot turned to the elevator and strode through its shimmering gold doors. "It's nice to play hard to get, Isabel. But ultimately, that's just a game, too. I've already shown you—without question—what I want. Now, it's time for you to decide if it's what you want."

"I already have," she replied, unclasping the pearl bracelet and liberating it from her wrist. She stepped across the elevator threshold and handed it back to him. For a brief moment, she saw herself in its mirrored walls, as if she was watching someone else force the finality of her decision upon them.

Eliot gazed down at the bracelet, draping it across the forearm of his silver grey suit like a flag of surrender rather than a rejection. He pressed the lobby floor button and casually leaned against the mirrored wall of the elevator. "Phillip's a lucky man, Isabel. The only thing he has to do to secure your loyalty is to pay you the right price."

"That would make me his whore," she punched back with resentment. "And I'm nobody's whore, Eliot."

The sound of his laughter ricocheted off the metallic interior of the elevator cab. "Then prove it," he dared her with an arching brow.

Slowly, the elevator doors rolled shut, removing Eliot Watercross from her view, but not from her mind. She exhaled and held her head. *Had he been right*? Had she allowed Phillip to limit the role she played within his company to just his secretary? She gazed at the elevator doors, fighting to shake off Eliot's snickering laughter and the nagging sense of distrust and disloyalty it inspired within her. Then, the unnerving sensation of being watched settled into her soul. She turned and shifted her eyes through the glass doors of the lobby. There, she saw Phillip and Marlow standing at the end of the hallway. Phillip's piercing blue eyes seized upon Isabel. *How long had he been standing there, watching her and Eliot?* She didn't know, but the stormy glare in Phillip's eyes warned her that perhaps he had seen more than he should have. Isabel watched Marlow's red lips reciting words into the air like floating bubbles. *Long enough to watch Eliot draw her close into his body and almost kiss her lips?*

Marlow clung to Phillip's sleeve like a forlorn lover postponing her farewell. Again, the whispering question returned to Isabel's mind: *had*

Marlow willingly abandoned Phillip, or was it he who had cast her away? His eyes challenged Isabel—challenging him—before drawing Marlow past the doorway and out of sight.

Isabel slowly exhaled, a deliberate release of tension, as Phillip's confrontational stare lanced into her heart. Unexpectedly, she questioned her relationship with the man who had granted her the opportunity to become a professional woman, rather than just a house cleaner and a single mother. Had she actually achieved all of her success because of Phillip's mentoring? Or had he been the one who intentionally held her back from achieving even more? Had he intentionally kept her in her place as merely his assistant in order to satisfy his own needs without considering her own?

Isabel gazed back at the elevators, fighting the urge to call a cab and chase after Eliot Watercross. Instead, she turned and forced herself to draw open the glass doors of the lobby and pretend that she was re-entering the office exactly as she had left it. Eliot Watercross had not successfully recruited her away from Spears & Associates, but he had successfully placed uncertainty in her heart, which could actually be more dangerous.

Chapter Eleven

IT HAD BEEN A LONG, hard day before Isabel finally reached her house and settled in for the night. She had attempted to shake off Eliot Watercross' conversation and move forward with the final preparation for Saturday's gala. But his searing eyes and alluring touch looped in her mind like an unsettling revelation. He had always been so flirtatious in his interactions with her that it seemed easy to dismiss his public advances as nothing more than a disingenuous display of power. Eliot was Phillip's rival, and she was Phillip's assistant. Plus, everybody knew that Eliot Watercross was invigorated by a good challenge. But within the inexplicable moments of magnetic attraction between them, it was hard to deny his insistence that she was worth more to him than she realized—or that she allowed herself to admit—and his assertion that she had unwittingly accepted her role as Phillip's submissive servant rather than his equal partner weighed heavy on her heart.

Could Eliot offer her something even more? For the past five years, she had been given more responsibility under Phillip's mentoring than she had ever dreamed possible...*but now, was it no longer enough*?

She shook her head and tried hard not to let her mind dwell on it during her dinnertime with Aidan.

"Mommy, did you know that police officers came to school today to talk to us during circle time?"

"No, honey, I didn't know that." Isabel aimlessly picked at the peas on her dinner plate.

"They showed us their pincher things that they use to catch the bad guys." Aidan clapped his hands, like he was squashing a bug in the air.

"Pincher things?" Isabel asked with a strained spark of curiosity.

"These silver metal pinchers."

"You mean, handcuffs?"

"Yeah, to catch the bad guys and throw them in jail."

"Did the police officers tell you that?"

Aidan lowered his chin, bashful. "No, that's what Jeremiah said."

"Ohhhhhh, I see…Jeremiah." Isabel nodded to her mother, who was listening from the kitchen counter while preparing the salad. Aidan had told both Isabel and Mrs. Alvarez on several occasions that Jeremiah knew everything because he was five.

"The police officers just showed us their handcuffs and their big black flashlights and their *guns*," Aidan whispered, his eyes widening.

"They. Did. Not," Isabel punctuated.

"Okay, it's true. They didn't." Aidan stuffed his mouth with his pizza. "But they did tell us they don't have to shoot anything very often. Mommy? Do you know what? The police boss man is called the chief."

Suddenly, the doorbell rang.

Mrs. Alvarez dropped her knife onto the cutting board and wiped her hands on her apron.

"*Quién crees que está llamado*?" she said to Isabel before passing out of the kitchen's swinging door.

"Mommy, mommy…" Aidan tugged on his mother with excitement. "Maybe it's a policeman."

"A policeman? Why would they be here?"

"Because they think we're hiding the bad guys."

"Or maybe they're here to see if you've eaten all your dinner," Isabel teased, nudging Aidan to take another bite of his pizza.

"Isabel—" Mrs. Alvarez suddenly called out from the living room with the same threatening tone that she used to use whenever Isabel was a disobedient child.

Isabel rose from her seat and peered out of the kitchen. She spotted her mother, struggling near the front doorway, overwhelmed by the weight of three dozen long-stemmed red roses in a pink crystal Chihuly vase. Isabel rushed to help her mother navigate the massive bouquet onto the nearest end table in the living room. Aidan heeled after them, like a puppy enchanted by their perfumed scent.

"Flowers, Mommy…Flowers!"

Isabel looked at her mother for answers.

"*No tengo ni idea*." Mrs. Alvarez shrugged. "It was just the delivery man."

Her mother reached out for the white envelope within the center of the bouquet and handed it to Isabel, who slipped out the card and read it with dread.

WAITING… ~EW

Isabel re-read the card, noting the uniform typesetting of its printed inscription. Then, she studied the Chihuly glass vase and spotted the glinting highlights of a foreign object submerged in its water like a lost treasure. She carefully pulled up the thorny stems and fished out something painfully familiar—the triple-strand pearl bracelet.

Damn him, she cursed under her breath, rolling the sodden, slippery pearls between her fingers. It was so *him* in every way. Just when she thought she had escaped him—and every lingering forbidden thought about him—he had reclaimed her attention and demanded a response. Like a shot through her heart, the doorbell unexpectedly rang again.

"Don't, please…" she said to her mother, who started to the door. Isabel shut her eyes, fighting the urge to break down in tears. It had been such a long emotional week, and she didn't know if she could face him again.

Mrs. Alvarez gazed at her daughter, heeding the pain in her voice. She nodded and stepped away, beckoning Aidan to her.

Isabel exhaled and calmed her trembling hands before opening the door. Immediately, she fell silent when she unexpectedly saw Phillip, pacing along the landing of her porch.

"Phillip?" she whispered in shock.

He turned to look at her, as if he had heard the echo of his name without the certainty that she had actually said anything at all. He was dressed in his long wool trench coat, and the chilly October evening wafted his breath into the air.

"Please, I need to discuss something with you." Without waiting for an invitation, he pushed past her through the doorway and entered the house.

"Of course," she replied, watching him stop suddenly at the sight of Mrs. Alvarez and Aidan, who stared at him like an unwelcomed intruder.

Aidan quickly broke away from his grandmother's hand and rushed up to Isabel. "Mommy, do you have to work tonight?" He slipped behind his mother and eyed Phillip with a mixture of curiosity and annoyance.

"No, I don't think so…" She turned to Phillip for an answer. His searing blue eyes settled on the boy—weighing the consequences of his visit and actions—before finally insisting on a private moment between them. "Please, may I speak to you—alone?"

Isabel nodded, recognizing the gravity in his face. "Aidan, go back now with Nica into the kitchen and finish your dinner. I'll be there shortly."

She encouraged him with a smile, but Aidan had other plans. He held up his hand to Phillip and shouted at him. "I'm the chief of police. And I'm going to get all the bad guys, including you. You're under arrest!" He laughed like he was inflicted with madness, and burst through the swinging kitchen door with a wail. Isabel locked eyes with her mother, who glared at Phillip, then back at the flowers before reluctantly drifting into the kitchen.

When she was certain they were alone, Isabel glanced back at Phillip. "The police officers visited his school today. He's a little bit excited by it all."

Phillip nodded, then turned away from her, as if something about her made him uncomfortable. Suddenly, she realized what she was wearing—bright pink yoga pants and a frayed, cut-off T-shirt with the slogan "Mama's Gonna Knock You Out." Her hair was tossed up in a careless ponytail, and she remembered that she was no longer wearing a bra. It was her favorite "after work" routine—stripping away the formality of her work clothes to make her feel like she was truly herself again.

But for Phillip, she sensed it was an awkward moment of informality between them. He was used to addressing her in his office—where the professional boundaries of boss and assistant were clearly defined. Now, Isabel waited, feeling the burden of his heavy silence before he cleared his throat in an attempt to address the reason behind his visit and the severe look in his eyes.

"It is with great reluctance that I have forced myself here…" he started in a low, apologetic tone, then paused, as if the words proved difficult to pronounce. His piercing gaze and sharp profile turned away from her before swaying back with firm resolve. "Upon many difficult hours of reflection, I have come to the conclusion that I can no longer maintain my silence, and instead, feel the most urgent need to openly express my…"

Phillip abruptly stopped his confession. The undercurrent of suffering beneath his tone waned as he caught sight of the bouquet of long-stemmed red roses in the living room. Without permission, he brushed past her to inspect them, as if she was a stranger in her own house.

"Phillip—" she said his name like she intended to stop him.

He scanned the bouquet, dropping his eyes onto the calling card resting on the surface of the end table. But ultimately, it was the alarm in her voice that directed his attention to the sleek pearl bracelet, dangling from her hand. He stared at Isabel with cold detachment, processing its significance.

"I understand that I have come too late…in the evening. I was hoping that perhaps you would be available for dinner tonight. But now it is clear that I have interrupted your personal time with your family and…" he paused, stumbling through his thoughts, "with others who you may hold dear. It is my mistake, and one I shall not commit again. Good evening and good night."

Phillip turned away without waiting for her reply and passed out of her house. Isabel rushed to the threshold of her front door and watched his dark hair and black trench coat completely disappear into the cold dark night. It was as if he had never been there, and yet, Isabel knew his assumptions—and their consequences—threatened to haunt every future word and glance between them.

"*Todo está bien*?"

She heard her mother emerge from the kitchen behind her.

"I'm not sure," Isabel answered, her gaze on the pearl bracelet, cradled in her palm.

Her mother's black eyes fell upon it and arched her brow. "Do you have to work tonight?"

Isabel slowly shut the front door and shook her head with a regretful heart. In so many ways, it would all be so much easier if the only thing she had to worry about *was* whether or not Phillip needed her tonight for work. *How had it all grown so complicated*? She looked at the pearls again, savoring the silky elegance of the pearls. There had been so few times in Isabel's life when she had dared to allow herself the pleasure of believing that she was worthy of another man's affections. She had been so busy—simply struggling to provide for her family—that everything beyond work seemed inconsequential and unimportant. Now, she had been introduced to the possibility of something more, which threatened to disrupt everything she had worked so hard to achieve—perhaps even disrupt the entire stability of her life.

Was it worth the risk? Isabel handed the jewelry to her mother like she was relinquishing a chain from around her heart. She didn't know, but she definitely wasn't going to waste time thinking about it. It was dinnertime, and she wasn't interested in squandering the rare, precious chance of eating dinner with her son.

* * * *

It was almost eleven o'clock when Isabel finally locked up the house for the night. During the remainder of the evening, she had put everything out of her mind, consciously making the decision to dedicate herself to her role as Aidan's mother rather than the melodramatic fantasy of being a desired woman. Isabel hated melodrama. It was the reason she had enjoyed working with Phillip all these years—together, they sought to solve problems, not create new ones. And now, after giving her son a bath and putting him to bed, she realized the only thing that truly mattered was what she already had. Everything else—the flowers, the jewelry, the lingerie, and yes…even the great sex—had simply been an unsustainable fantasy. It was time to bring it all to an end and pretend that none of it had ever happened. Isabel knew her priorities, and she knew that being the object of desire was nothing more than a dangerous masquerade of courtship that had preyed on her repressed emotions and starved sexuality. The courtship had been appealing while it lasted. But fundamentally, it was still just a forbidden fantasy—and Isabel was no longer willing to sacrifice everything for a charade.

Flicking off the final light in the living room, everything fell into shadows, and for a brief moment, she indulged in the foreboding silhouette of Eliot's roses. Then, like an unwanted temptation, her phone vibrated from inside her purse.

Isabel shuffled through the dark foyer to retrieve her phone, glancing down at its screen:

Waiting…It read.

She glanced at the phone number of its sender: UNKNOWN.

She held her breath and froze, as if she felt the need to hide within the darkness. But she could not hide—not from him—and she knew it. Her phone suddenly vibrated again.

Waiting for you…

Isabel shook her head, defiant.

*This must end…*she texted back, then hit send. She held her breath, like she was anticipating the most important message of her life. Without hesitation, her phone buzzed.

Then choose for it to end.

Isabel exhaled, preparing to text back her final refusal—and terminate everything that had been initiated between them.

Buzzz. Isabel glanced down at her phone.

I choose you.

Isabel stared down at those three simple words—*I choose you.* Unapologetic and undeterred. A rush of emotions swelled within her heart. Her hands trembled. Her breath accelerated. Such tiny simple words, and yet they were enough to bring her to tears. She glanced up into the silence of her sleeping house, vacillating between the safety and security of her life now and the temptation of being lured into the future of a new one.

She cradled her phone against her chest and felt it vibrate with his final command: *180 N ASTOR PL*

180 North Astor Place? The address was in her neighborhood, only a few blocks away. Isabel rushed to her bay windows and peeked out into the black night. For a fleeting moment, she was sure she glimpsed his elusive shadow passing through the darkness. A sweeping sense of urgency quickened her pace. He *was* there, waiting for her…

She gazed down at her yoga pants and T-shirt. There was no time to change and no options for her. Everything was upstairs in her bedroom. She rummaged through the foyer closet. *Trench coat.* She slipped it on and pulled her house keys from her purse, slipping them in the pocket of her coat. She stripped the rubber band from her hair, unleashing her long brown hair, and gazed at herself in the hall tree's mirror. Hesitating, she glanced down at her phone before texting back her definitive response.

Soon…

She dropped the phone inside her purse and abandoned everything that identified herself as "Isabel Alvarez." *Would it all be a mistake?* She shut her eyes, confirming the answer before rushing out onto her front porch like a fugitive relinquishing herself to the consequences. The cold night air stung her lungs; she exhaled, attempting to force out the fear and anxiety from within her heart. Wisps of condensation furled into the air and disappeared underneath the illumination of the harvest moon. Before rounding the corner of her block and liberating herself completely, she surrendered to the sudden pang of obligation and glanced back at her home, just in time to catch sight of the curtain flapping shut along the window of her mother's bedroom.

Isabel raced along the sidewalk and through the bulky shadows of elm trees lining the historic streets of Chicago's Gold Coast. It reminded her of how far she had come from being a pregnant single mother—overwhelmed with finding a job, having a new baby, and providing for both him and her mother—to being a professional career woman able to afford her own house in one of Chicago's most affluent neighborhoods. It had been no accident. There was only one reason, and that reason had been one man and one man alone—Phillip Spears. She shivered, the drafty breeze cutting through her sleeves, and listened to the swaying bristle of dried oak leaves, mimicking the murmuring secret within her heart. *It had only been because of one man…*

She scurried along Astor Place and glanced at the numbers, checking each three-story brownstone and high-rise apartment complex. But she already knew her destination—The Wilder Mansion. She had passed it countless times while riding bikes with Aidan through their neighborhood. The Wilder Mansion had been constructed as a symbol of power and prestige by Thurston Wilder, one of Chicago's wealthy stockyard barons. Now, as she approached the red masonry fortress, she was reminded of the history behind its original owner, who had wheeled and dealed his way into power after the Great Chicago Fire of 1871, and apologized to no one for it.

Isabel cautiously climbed up its sleek sandstone steps, flanked by lion statues, and arrived in front of a massive solid walnut door. She tested the bronzed door latch. Immediately, the heavy door clicked open, guiding her inside the cathedral foyer, its Victorian opulence obscured by darkness, except for the distant hint of flaming light glinting along the varnished banister of the grand interior staircase.

He was waiting for her upstairs.

Drawn forward by her own curiosity and anticipation, Isabel climbed the imposing staircase, following the seducing warmth and crackling sound of a fireplace, its flickering shadows dancing against the amber mahogany walls of the narrow hallway that ended at the entrance into a secluded chamber. *The master bedroom.* Ajar with a silent summons, she pushed against the door and spotted the fireplace within the vaulted stone mantelpiece. Its undulating glow cast moody, irregular patterns along the chamber's Persian wall tapestries and ornate Oriental rugs. She shivered as a natural draft cut through the room, threatening to extinguish the sole source of light. It was a reclusive sanctuary within an enigmatic fortress that offered no escape, and one single, overpowering piece of furniture filled the chamber like a symbol of domination—an Emperor canopy bed.

"Take off your coat."

She recognized his terse voice, directing her from the shadowed corner behind her, as if he expected everything from her without the promise of giving her anything in return.

She paused, repressing the reflex to spin around and confront him. But it was a test—a challenge of her allegiance. She closed her eyes and inhaled the scent of burning pine. He had texted her to choose, and her decision to come to him tonight confirmed that she had made her ultimate choice: *she would not betray him.*

Slowly, she unfastened the belt around her trench coat and slid it off her shoulders. It dropped to the floor, its metal buckle clanking against the carpet. *He was waiting and watching her.* She sensed his presence behind her, like an invisible force, anchoring her in place and preparing her for his next command. She noticed the heavy antique bear rug, spread across the canopy bed, wondering if he planned to spread her naked body across it like a hunting prize.

"Undress."

One simple word—*undress*. And yet Isabel felt her pulse race as she considered the consequences of surrendering to his order. He did not raise his voice or shift out of the shadows. He simply expected her to expose herself completely. She obeyed, pulling her T-shirt over her shoulders, and exposing her bare breasts to the glow of the fireplace. She paused and waited for his next command, but she only heard his muted exhale—an audible betrayal that he was stroking himself. Isabel closed her eyes and sighed, stimulating her nipples with her own fingertips, releasing the unbearable tension that had built up between them throughout the day.

"More…"

He whispered it like a wish. With every sensual twist and pluck of her own tits, she heard him pleasuring himself in turn. In that brief moment, she was now his captor. She fixed her eyes on the wafting flames of the fireplace, imagining how its reflection flickered off her bare skin as she submitted herself to his voyeuristic gaze.

When she no longer heard his moan, she placed her fingers over the waistband of her yoga pants and deliberately teased them off her hips, luring his eyes over the string bikini band of her black French-cut thong—the same one he had given her as a gift. She had never intended to reveal that she had worn them since their first night together. They were a nostalgic reminder of the passion he had unleashed in her, a memory which she reflected upon during the most unexpected moments of her work day and with a frequency that felt like a dirty addiction—one she wasn't prepared to admit to anyone, not even to herself. Now, she felt an overwhelming need to expose it to him like a guilty confession. *No matter the sacrifice or cost, she had not wanted their first night together to be their last.* She could no longer pretend that he was the only one who wanted what he offered her. *Now, he knew everything.*

With stealth and precision, his footsteps shifted along the floorboards as he slipped behind her and sucked the nape of her neck. She moaned in acceptance before his hot breath traveled down her shoulder blades and along her spine. *God, how desperate she was to feel his lips moistening every part of her naked body.* His hands wrapped around her waist and pinned her against his smooth, broad pecs. His pelvis pressed against her backside. He was naked and ready for her. His firm erection brushed against her cheeks, and she reached behind her—a spontaneous desire to pleasure him. But he evaded her touch; instead, he pressed his hot breath against her neck and secured her in his embrace, ensuring she should not attempt to glance behind her. Isabel closed her eyes and swallowed her gasp as his fingers slipped under the silky panty line of her thong and indulged in her wetness.

Yeeeessss...

He pinned her tighter against his chest, stroking her slit and fingering her clit, eliciting her groans and relaxing her stance into his embrace. He ensured her ultimate surrender by cupping her sex and rousing her with undulating waves of pleasure until he could no longer wait for what they both desperately yearned for...

Suddenly, the entire chamber plunged into darkness. The rushing draft washed across her bare skin before snuffing out the final ember of warmth in the room, leaving her with only the cold aftershock of foreboding silence. She opened her eyes as his shielding body swiftly released her, but she could see nothing within the chamber—nothing except her memory of the heavy velvet curtains masking the arcing windows and the thick stone walls shutting her inside his protective fortress. Then, unexpectedly, she felt his fingernail tracing over the tips of her erect nipples. *He was in front of her now...directly in front of her.* Isabel's pulse quickened as she waited for her eyes to adjust to the suffocating absence of light and settle upon his shadowed face. But still, she could see nothing—nothing beyond the prison of darkness suppressing all her senses, and she could anticipate nothing—nothing except his intention to seduce her the way she had come to secretly crave. His demanding hands tore down her thong, abandoning them at her knees. Then, she felt his tongue sliding between her thighs, teasing her clit with a flicking lick. He waited for her moan before bracing her backside and coaxing her legs wider, testing her wetness. Even within the absolute darkness, he could read her most forbidden desires. How many times had she fantasized about his tongue lapping over her again and again? *Too many times.* She folded forward, supporting her own weight against his sculpted shoulders and gushed for him, confirming what he had already discovered during their first night together—her buttoned-up professional persona was a façade. Beyond her routine of civility and diplomacy within her work life, there was an irrepressible sexual goddess who yearned on a daily basis to submit herself to his carnal lust.

Yeeessss…

She sighed, releasing all the tension between them as he invaded her deeper, tasting her within the darkness. His hands massaged her supple backside, spreading her open and uninhibited, while he hummed heat and desire into every erogenous part of her body. Her knees and thighs slacked with arousal as his rhythmic vibrations swelled inside her like tides yearning to break against the shore.

With agility and strength, he rose from his knees and swept his lips over her tits, sucking her like a punishment before pressing the heat of his firm cock between her legs. She pushed back against his domination, but he refused to relent. Tonight would not be like their previous nights of seduction. Tonight, he wanted to prove to her that she meant something even greater to him than she had allowed herself to believe.

He abruptly swept her into his arms and spread her out across the plush mattress of the canopy bed. The rough bear pelt grazed against her thighs and backside as she sensed his erection drifting over her navel. He was listening to her respiration in the darkness, waiting for her to settle her racing breaths before lowering his mysterious whisper against her neckline.

"Tell me you want this..."

His chin dug between her breasts as the tip of his erection, hot with fury, lowered between her legs, seeking out an intimacy neither one of them had been willing to concede. His burning cock pushed against her sex, throbbing to come inside her. Suddenly, doubt and uncertainty flooded her senses. Was she willing to spread herself open and accept him—despite the lingering threat that everything might change between them? Isabel pressed her fingers into the strong arc of his smooth back, signaling that she was ready to risk everything for the pleasure he was about to give her.

The moment he made direct contact, she heard herself gasp—an involuntary reflex after so many years of sexual repression. His hand cupped under her backside, tilting her pelvis upwards, easing the friction of his first, resistant thrust. Her moan signaled how much she yearned to endure the raw, primal power of his desire pushing inside of her.

"I choose you," he repeated like a vow.

In the past, he had spoken to her like a submissive and treated her like his possession. Now, with only the palpitating of his beating heart against her breasts, she heard the distinct change within his voice and that difference was tenderness.

Yeeesss, she sighed, signaling her acceptance of his next penetration—chafing deeper. His smooth, bare chest pinned against her body, forcing out her apprehension like air from a balloon. She opened, slick and shuddering, as he sought to build her up with the intensity of his accelerating pace.

"Tell me how much you want this…" he rasped into her ear, as if he would not be satisfied until he fully satisfied her.

But no words could escape her lips, only an inaudible cry, choked with unbearable need—he filled her so completely, so intimately, that she could not contain the sensations that raged inside her. She wrapped her legs around his hips and dug her fingernails into the hard bones of shoulder blades, allowing the swelling waves of stimulation to ebb and flow throughout her body without trying to repress them like she had always done in the past. Even with Aidan's father, she could never release herself completely—there had always been a hint of distrust, a wisp of immaturity within their intimacy that prevented her from experiencing what she was experiencing now. Now, she only concentrated on how he cradled her in his arms and untied them with unrelenting devotion.

She shuddered again, the uncompromising veil of darkness allowing her to focus completely on her own liberation. She nuzzled her nose along his smooth cheek, savoring the intoxicating scent of his noir cologne. She groaned, enduring the smothering constriction of his embrace and the uncompromising drive of his cock. Raising her chin, she gasped under the crushing weight of his chest and the uncontrollable spasms within her pelvis, resisting his efforts to unleash her scream.

But she was no longer able to contain herself.

Drawing back her head, she begged him not to stop until the vibrations rose up from within her core. He thrust his cock harder, faster, deeper until her plea became a repetitive chant. At last, like a flaring spark, his final thrust ignited a seizure of ecstasy that threatened to shatter her into a thousand unrecognizable pieces unless she grounded its shuddering quake and accepted its flushing heat.

In that moment, he covered her mouth and kissed her fully, bracing her wrists above her head as she submitted herself to the fury of their simultaneous climax. They traded panting breaths in the darkness like lovers desperately exchanging the last bit of oxygen in the room. Then, with reluctance, he withdrew from her without untangling his body from her own. Warmed by the heat of their passion and soothed by the sound of their own labored exhales, Isabel tried—one futile time—to search out his eyes within the smothering darkness. Perhaps she even whispered his name, or perhaps she simply confessed it within her mind like a secret within her own heavy heart. Then, lulled by soft breath against the nape of her neck, she slipped away into the undertow of slumber, tethered only by the security of his embrace.

Chapter Twelve

ISABEL HURRIED THROUGH the open corridor of the office while carrying her coffee and briefcase. Earlier that morning, she had awoken to the streaming rays of sunlight on her naked body. He had left her alone, sleeping and undisturbed, in the Emperor canopy bed—just as he always had in the past—only this time, there was no jewelry box on the mantelpiece as a gesture of reassurance. There was only the meticulous way he had folded her clothes and draped them over the claw-footed arm chair with a torn leaflet from an unknown book resting atop of them. At the top of the page, inscribed in mid-century typeset, was the first stanza of a poem:

Lady, i will touch you with my mind/
Touch you and touch and touch/
until you give me suddenly a smile, shyly obscene.

And beneath it, Isabel saw his personalized note in his familiar sweeping cursive: *Tonight, the gala…*

She studied the massive French Empire bookcase and opened its glass doors, immediately spotting the lone spine disrupting the uniformity of all the other books on the shelf. She drew it out—a poetry anthology by E.E. Cummings—and easily flipped to its missing page, marked by a dried pink rosebud nestled within its center crease. The haunting remainder of the poem was still there for her to view.

After dressing herself, she slipped the anthology into her purse before leaving the chamber. She noted the eerie silence within the mansion, as if it had been completely abandoned. Scurrying down the grand foyer staircase and out the mansion, she returned home, just as the rising sun glittered through the fog like a misty dream.

Yes, the gala. She understood. Everything would be different after the gala.

Now, Isabel breezed into the office with a bounce in her step that caught the attention of Lucy, the receptionist.

"Somebody's got that good ol' lovin' feeling."

"Good morning," Isabel said with a smile, pulling back the glass door of the lobby entrance and gliding through it.

"Don't go being too chipper—" Lucy called after her.

But Isabel didn't wait to hear the rest. Instead, armed with the confidence that today was going to be a good day, she strode to her desk. With the taste of his tongue still lingering in her mouth and the burning sensation of his lust between her legs, she felt like a different woman—a woman who was rushing towards her new life instead of slowing to a halt in the middle of her current one. She rounded the corner of Phillip's office, fully willing to endure his reprimanding glare for entering it without invitation or announcement. But she halted in the doorway and noted his barren, untouched desk while absorbing the eerie atmosphere of frozen time clinging in the air.

Then, like a haunting phantom, she felt a whispering breath behind her ear. "I'm still waiting…"

Isabel whirled around to see Jett's mischievous eyes glistening at her.

"Waiting for what?" Isabel awkwardly pushed past him towards her desk.

"Waiting for you to thank me for last night."

She turned and narrowed her gaze onto his playboy smile. *Play it cool, play it cool.* Meanwhile, her heart raced with a rush of paranoia. "Excuse me?"

"Go ahead…Thank me first." Jett edged closer, lowering his voice.

Isabel glared at him, attempting to unravel the riddle behind his cocky grin.

"Last night, I had dinner with one of the most elusive public figures in all of Chicago," he finally explained, "and scored you one of the most preeminent tenants for The Old Main Post Office, which means you'll have a sensational publicity announcement for your grand gala tonight."

Jett downed his coffee and waited for the news to relax Isabel's glare. But she was more focused on his basketball star build and the fragrance of his flowery sandalwood cologne—and the fact that neither of them matched her memories from last night. Slowly, she exhaled, unknotting the pang of anxiety in her chest.

"Who?" she asked, feigning interest, because the truth was, in that moment, nothing else mattered except for the fact that she had not mistakenly had heart-stopping sex with Jett last night.

"Guess," he prodded her.

Isabel frowned. Why couldn't Jett ever have a conversation without turning it into a trivia game?

"Oh, for fricks sake, Jett. Just tell her or I will."

Isabel turned and sighed, relieved to see Tami sweeping in to her rescue. "Good morning."

"Apparently, it's Jett *Jeopardy* hour this morning at Spears & Associates," Tami snarked.

"More like *Wheel of Fortune*," he corrected her. "Especially since the correct answer is: Augustina van der Meer's Royal Jewel collection."

Isabel gazed at Jett in disbelief. "What?"

"I told you I was waiting for you to thank me."

"But how?" Isabel said, glancing at Tami for confirmation, but Jett was determined to capture the spotlight. "Because Yours Truly got wind that the loan of her entire collection to the Field Museum was up at the end of this month without any plans to renew it. So I made some phone calls—"

"*I* made some calls," Tami overrode him. "You just sat in your swivel chair, eavesdropping on me while pounding down your Doritos."

"My mom always told me it was rude to talk with food in my mouth."

Tami rolled her eyes. "Anyway, *I* confirmed that Madame van der Meer was indeed seeking a new permanent home to display her private jewelry collection—one of the most infamous jewelry collections in the world."

"Infamous? How is it infamous?" Isabel asked.

"Because it's been the target of more attempted thefts than even the *Mona Lisa* in Paris." Tami slurped down to the end of her Frappuccino.

"And because Madame van der Meer's own mother smuggled the collection out of Nazi Europe by stuffing it inside her cat who had died from starvation," Jett added, looking to provoke both women with the gory imagery.

Containing her shiver, Tami ignored him and turned to Isabel. "Her mother escaped their Amsterdam estate with all thirty-five pieces of jewelry, just days before it was raided and pillaged by the invading Germans—"

"Poor little Fluffy," Jett cried out with dramatic despair.

"Including the diamond choker necklace that King Henry the Eighth gave his second wife, Anne Boleyn—before he divorced her and sent her to the Tower."

"Well, at least he had the good sense to keep the necklace before cutting off her head," Jett sniped.

Tami glared at him with disdain. "You *do* realize the reason why you're still single is because you're disgusting. You understand that, right?"

"But I'm also amazing in every way," he flung back. "It's called a paradox."

"It's called stunted puberty," Tami coughed back.

Isabel slipped between them. "Does Phillip know?"

Jett relented and smoothed down his silk tie. "Phillip is the one who arranged the dinner last night and convinced Madame van der Meer to permanently display her collection in the renovated Old Main."

Last night? Isabel gazed down at her phone, quickly thumbing through her texts and emails, wondering why she had been kept out of the loop on such an important development. Then, a slow burn of dread seeped into her soul as she reflected on Phillip's arrival at her house early in the evening and his agitation when he saw the flowers from Eliot Watercross.

"Apparently, Norton and Madame van der Meer are old friends. I'm just the bloodhound sniffing out the leads and collecting the six-figure commission." He grinned with pride, baring his overly-bleached teeth at Tami.

"And purchasing your ridiculously dedicated executive assistant a new car lease as her bonus for working a hundred and fifty hours this week," Tami reminded him before seeking out advice from Isabel. "I'm still trying to decide between the MINI Cooper—hot pink convertible—or the sassy, sexy silver '*I have arrived*' Mercedes Benz with leather interior."

"MINI Cooper, hot pink convertible. No question," Isabel confirmed.

"It is more me."

"Once the deal is *signed*," Jett reminded her.

"So nothing's been signed yet?" Isabel pressed him.

"It's all with the lawyers now, but Madame van der Meer herself gave us the green light to make the announcement tonight—at your precious gala. In fact, she's even letting us showcase several of her jewelry cases as artistic centerpieces within the Grand Atrium."

"What?" Isabel exclaimed with alarm. "Who's setting it up? When are they arriving? Does Mario know about this?" She couldn't help revealing her exasperation and annoyance at hearing this all second-hand.

"Chill, Duchess, chill..." Jett sighed, stretching his long, basketball player arms behind his head. "It's all been arranged. Apparently, that hot little intern of yours is good for more than just being delicious eye candy."

The women followed his lascivious gaze across the office to Giselle, who was typing with fury on her computer's keyboard. The high slit of her cigarette skirt exposed her fishnet stockings and the sensual black seam running up the calves of her crossed legs.

"Neanderthal." Tami jabbed Jett with her elbow. "Go away. You're worse than dried-out, expired chocolate. Except we can actually *tolerate* dried-out, expired chocolate when we're really desperate."

Jett handed his coffee mug to Tami, just to prove who was really in charge, and headed towards his office. "Try not to miss me too much. Going out for breakfast with the Mayor's daughter-in-law—her treat. She's got a fundraising project and she's looking for donations. I told her we're looking to accelerate our building permits. Nothing like doing business in Chicago."

"Please, Jett," Tami called after him. "Don't do or say anything that could be recorded and get you arrested."

He disappeared into his office and returned with his suit coat, slipping it on before returning to Tami for a final appearance check.

"How about do or say something that could be recorded and break up a marriage?" He snickered, impressed with his own cleverness.

Tami tightened his tie like a punishing noose before brushing powdered sugar and donut crumbs off his suit lapels. "I've decided—MINI Cooper. Hot pink convertible. And an upgrade: turbocharged engine."

"*Vrrroooooom*," he confirmed, pulling away with a wink and heading down the corridor to the elevators. "Tell Phillip I'll see him tonight at the cocktail bar," he called back to Isabel. "I'll be schmoozing with Fifi Litzker to sign up her new luxury, boutique hotel chain as our next tenant in The Old Main. It's a tough life being so desirable with the ladies. A tough, tough life."

Tami chewed on her straw, watching him stroll through the glass lobby doors. "Sometimes, I wonder how I can possibly be so desperate to stay working for such a juvenile beefcake? And then I imagine myself in my new, hot pink, turbocharged, convertible MINI Cooper and I remember why I secretly love him so much."

"How long have you known about the van der Meer jewelry collection?" Isabel suddenly asked, betraying the insecurity in her voice. "How could Phillip not tell me about it?"

"Only since this morning, despite the fact that all this gala-gaga garbage is the only thing I've been working on this week. No offense."

"None taken."

"And then there was this mad flurry to get Madame van der Meer to dinner last night. I just assumed you already knew because you were already there with them."

"No, I wasn't there," Isabel replied, quietly, reflecting on the visceral reminders of last night. "I didn't know anything about it."

"So typical," Tami snipped. "Should we really be so surprised? These are *our* bosses we're talking about. They expect us to be mind-readers and make everything perfect at the eleventh hour. By the way, do you have any idea how hard it was to secure a last minute seven o'clock dinner reservation at Tru? I can't remember the details, but I'm pretty sure I bartered away my ninth virginity to Boris, the general manager, for an all-inclusive one-night fling." Tami bit her nails in reflection. "God, I hope he's at least a 3 on the hottie scale. And not short. I hate short."

Tami adjusted her glasses and suddenly focused onto Isabel's ashen face. "What's wrong with you?"

Isabel gazed gravely at Tami. "I think Phillip is stonewalling me."

"Stonewalling you? What? What do you mean? Why?"

"Because…he came to my house early last night, I guess to tell me about the dinner with Madame van der Meer, but then he didn't tell me anything. I think because he saw the flowers."

"What flowers?"

"The flowers…from Eliot Watercross."

"What!?" Tami yelped like a bus had just run over her foot.

A few of the girls glanced up from their computers.

Isabel hushed her with a killer glare.

"C'mon…in here—" Tami bullied Isabel inside of Phillip's empty office.

"No, we can't," Isabel resisted.

But Tami elbowed her past the threshold and slammed the door. "You do realize your master and commander is gone for the day."

Isabel stared at her. "That's impossible." She gazed down at her phone again.

"Let me guess," Tami said. "He didn't tell you."

Isabel shook her head, feeling the blood draining out of her cheeks.

"Well, I heard it from Lucy," Tami said, flopping down onto the mid-century sofa and kicking up the red soles of her heels onto its leather armrest. "Phillip called in early this morning. Something about personal business, *blah, blah, blah*…He's out the whole day, *blah, blah, blah, blah*…don't forward any of his calls."

"See…he *is* stonewalling me. It's not like Phillip to keep me out of the loop like this unless he's doing it intentionally."

"Well, what did he say when he saw the flowers?"

"Nothing."

"Ugh…" Tami sighed. "So Phillip."

"I know." Isabel nodded, aimlessly circling the office. "But I'm pretty sure he saw the pearl bracelet. Which is almost worse because I think he also saw me yesterday when I gave it back to Eliot."

"Don't remind me," Tami held up her hand, truly pained. "Okay, so maybe you're right. Maybe Phillip *is* stonewalling you."

Isabel dropped into Phillip's executive chair and held her head. "That's the reason why I wasn't there last night at the dinner with Madame van der Meer. Phillip thinks I'm betraying him."

"Well, you *are* sleeping with the enemy."

"I don't know… I guess. Maybe." Isabel folded forward and cradled her body like she was going to be sick. "God, it's all such a big mess."

"Hell, yes. It really is." Tami gazed at Isabel like she was watching her turning into stone.

"There's more…" Isabel finally confessed.

"More? What is this, an E! Hollywood True Story?"

"Eliot wants me to come work for him. He's offered me an equity partnership in his new business venture."

"He did what!?" Tami threw down her heels and jumped to her feet.

Isabel nodded. "He's offering me equity partnership in his next deal—the same one that's competing with The Old Main Post Office."

"Frickin' hell, Isabel. And what did you say?"

"I didn't say anything, or at least…I tried to say no by giving back the bracelet and ending everything, but you know Eliot. No is not in his vocabulary. So then he sent me flowers with the pearl bracelet—again—and then Phillip came over and saw them, and then I got this mysterious text to meet, so then I went—"

"Wait, wait, wait, just wait—" Tami held up her hand like she could hear no more. "Slow down…no, wait…forget that. Speed up. Speed WAY up. You had sex last night—again?"

Isabel covered her face, filled with shame. "And now I've got the gala tonight, and a million things to confirm, and Phillip is gone and not talking to me, and Eliot is coming tonight, and I don't know what to say to him."

"You say, hello sexy, hot cock, but good-bye."

Isabel shot Tami a glare. *Not helpful.*

"Don't look at me like that, Isabel. There's *no* way in hell I'm letting you take a new job as a partner somewhere and leave me alone here to toil as Jett's office assistant, watching my face and boobs sag with every passing year. I'll never forgive you. Not even while sitting in my new hot pink, turbocharged, convertible MINI Cooper. I'll tell the whole office that you slept your way into that position."

"Tami!"

"Okay, sorry. That's terrible. But I *would* hate you forever."

"And I would deserve it because I'm such a horrible, disloyal person."

"Don't, Isabel. Don't go there. You're not horrible. Just horny as hell, and we've all been there, so you're forgiven. But what are you going to do now?"

"I have no idea. I have to get through this gala tonight, and then…I'm hoping that everything will just magically fall into place."

Tami snorted. "Good luck with that, Cinderella. Just remember not to lose your heel at the ball. Or your panties."

There was an abrupt knock at the door. Both women jumped from their seats and turned to the visitor.

"Sorry to interrupt…" Giselle's bright bubblegum pink smile peeked in through the opening. "But I was hoping to meet with Isabel this morning to touch base about the gala tonight."

Isabel nodded. "Yes, of course."

Giselle exhaled with relief and entered the office with her tablet. "Okay, well…first is the flower arrangements. I've talked to Mario about scheduling their arrival for two o'clock, but he also has the caterers coming at the same time for set-up and prep, so I guess I'm wondering if that's okay, and how are we planning to coordinate the arrival of the band and the staging…"

Isabel watched Giselle launch into her long list of concerns; she couldn't help but notice her sparkling lip gloss and fresh buttermilk skin, flattered by the morning light. Giselle always wore high heels and tight skirts to accentuate her perfect figure, and she always let her long blonde hair flow freely over her shoulders. But it was her earnest attempt to prove herself that was most disarming—the way she stood in the middle of the office and recited her to-do list with such dedication. Suddenly, Isabel was reminded of her herself—five years ago.

"And then, there's the arrival of Madame van der Meer's collection. Phillip said it was going to be accompanied by four security guards, so I guess I'm concerned about how everyone is going to be moving in and out of the freight elevator at the same time…"

"You already know about Madame van der Meer?" Isabel interrupted her.

Giselle paused, recognizing the edge of displeasure in her question. "Yes…Phillip told me when he called me this morning."

"Phillip called you this morning?" Isabel asked.

"Well…yes…" Giselle fumbled like she had committed an unintentional slip. "Phillip called me to talk about the gala, and then he apologized because he said he had a personal emergency and wouldn't be able to come to the office and he said he was likely going to be out all day."

Isabel gazed at Giselle. The familiar, casual way she said "Phillip" filled Isabel with a sickening envy—she *was* being replaced with a younger, more innocent version of herself.

Tami suddenly jumped in. "Look, Gigi. You're doing great. Major overachiever award here. First place winner. So now, let's let Isabel have a chance to get to her desk, take off her coat, drink some coffee, and settle in before we all vomit out our every concern about the next twenty-four hours."

Giselle flashed a fluttering smile. "Oh my God, you're totally right. I am *soooo* sorry. Of course, of course. It's just that…this is my very first gala, and I'm *soooo* excited, and I want everything to go perfectly. I even spent the entire weekend shopping for what I plan to wear. I bought four different outfits because I know we're supposed to wear something with vintage flair, but I can't decide on what!"

"I'm planning to wear my grandmother's knit, mothball-ridden cardigan," Tami quipped. "That's vintage."

"Oh, that's number forty-four on the list of things to tell you," Giselle suddenly said to Isabel, scanning her tablet. "Your wardrobe has been arranged. It's being delivered to your house this afternoon."

"Arranged? By who?"

"Well, by me," Giselle replied. "At Phillip's request."

Tami snorted through her nose. "That's seriously ridiculous. The only thing Jett has ever 'arranged' for me to wear is one of those monster-sized foam fingers at the Bulls game."

Giselle referenced her tablet. "Phillip also wanted me to let you know that his driver will to pick you up at eight o'clock—sharp."

Isabel and Tami exchanged silent glances. It was impossible not to feel unnerved by the display of power and control Phillip was asserting over her—even in his absence.

"Thank you, Giselle. But I expect that I'll talk with him before that."

"Well, I don't think so. He really seemed to be certain that he would be out-of-pocket until tonight."

"Yes, maybe, Giselle. But I've been Phillip's assistant for a long time. And when I need to get in touch with him, I can and will."

Both Giselle and Tami noted the edge in Isabel's voice.

"Of course…I apologize, Miss Alvarez." Giselle lowered her gaze and shut off her tablet.

Isabel frowned and moved towards the windows, pretending to survey the clouds over the cityscape. *Was it all really worth it?* After five long years, was it worth losing her position as Phillip's most trusted employee for the sake of exploring something that threatened to risk everything between them?

"Giselle, why don't you go and get ready now," Isabel finally replied as she studied one of Phillip's favorite Art Deco buildings in the city—the Chicago Board of Trade, crowned by the faceless stone statue of Ceres. "We'll head over to The Old Main Post Office now to check in on Mario and the status of all the arrangements, and we'll stay until we're certain everyone and everything has been coordinated. I want everything to go perfectly as well."

"Great," Giselle grinned in relief, bounding to the door like a puppy dog with a fresh bone. "Can we finish running through numbers twelve through forty-two on my list on our way there?"

Isabel forced a smile. "That sounds great."

Tami watched Giselle rush out of the office, scanning her fishnets and tight skirt with a judgmental glare.

"God, if I could have her tight, little body for just one day, I think I would actually try to get laid in the elevator. I've always wanted to have sex in an elevator."

Isabel barely heard her. "You see what's going on, don't you?"

"She's your very own Mini-Me," Tami confirmed. "And Phillip's your very own Dr. Evil who's grooming her as your replacement. Not even Jett has done something that stupid to me, and Jett is the King of Stupid."

Isabel slid down into Phillip's executive leather chair and eyed his marble chessboard. "It's really that bad, isn't it?"

"Look, Isabel…" Tami paused, adjusting her glasses and replacing her irreverence with sincerity. "I don't know what's going on with Phillip, but I do know one thing: Phillip can't afford to lose you. His break up with Symeon Colovos was bad, but if you leave the company, the heart and soul of his entire business goes with you. So if I were you, I'd figure out how to get Phillip on the phone and make him aware that *you're* his senior executive assistant—and no one else. Unless, of course, you're planning to accept Eliot Watercross' offer, in which case, all I ask from you is that you don't make me find out by reading your resignation email. We've been friends for five years, Isabel, and that's just lame, and if you're going to leave for something bigger and better, I want to be the first one to congratulate you."

Isabel looked up at her friend with appreciation. "Thanks, Tami. That really means a lot to me."

"No problem." Tami nodded. "Bi-a-tch."

* * * *

After a long moment of silence, Isabel finally picked up the handset on Phillip's desk and dialed his cell phone. *No answer.* She paused and considered leaving a message before hanging up. Then, she listened to the desperation in her own heart before slowly dialing an alternative number—his personal cell phone.

Since working for Phillip, there had only been three times that Isabel had dialed his personal cell phone to reach him: the first time—when he had traveled to England to attend his mother's funeral; a second time—during his two-week vacation to Italy with Marlow to celebrate their engagement; and now. She held her breath and listened to the distant ominous ring. *Eight, nine, ten,* she counted as the phone rang without connecting to his voice mail. *Probably better,* she thought, preparing to hang up. She had no intention of leaving a message.

"Yes?" The dark brooding timber of his voice caught her off-guard.

Isabel hesitated before speaking into the receiver. "Phillip?"

"Yes." His voice softened, recognizing her immediately. He paused, waiting for her to speak first. She choked up with silence, completely uncertain about her original intention for calling.

"It's me. I'm sorry for the interruption, but I wanted to check in with you." She paused, gathering her thoughts while wrapping the phone cord around her finger like a tourniquet. "You know, the gala's tonight and there's still so much to discuss…"

Like Madame van der Meer's Royal Jewelry Collection, she wanted to say, but instead, she only heard the waver in her own voice. She suddenly glanced down, pricked by pain. The constriction around her finger had changed it from fleshy peach to stark white.

"Yes…I know," Phillip said coolly, failing to reveal more. "But there is no way that I can be there today. I trust you are able to coordinate everything in my absence."

Isabel listened and waited. There was no rush in Phillip's voice, which she took as her cue to push forward. "Yes, I'm about to go there now to be on-site to help Mario coordinate all the vendors. But, of course, I was surprised to hear about the van der Meer Collection…"

Isabel's voice trailed off as she stopped to listen to the long beat of silence on the other end of the line.

"Yes, it's a fortunate development from last night." His voice dropped, as if he was regretting the absence of communication between them.

"Yes, everything I know about it I've heard from Jett and Tami. And of course, Giselle."

"I expect that they should be able to fill you in—fully."

Silence smothered the line. Isabel paused and held her breath, wondering how much else she should say, or if it would be better to just initiate an end to their conversation. Without warning, Phillip initiated its end for her.

"Is there anything else, Isabel?"

He asked it with a sensitivity that disarmed her, almost as if he was willing to hang onto the line forever until she was ready to express exactly what was in her heart. She suddenly noticed the scent of his cologne on the surface of the phone's receiver, and for a moment, it physically connected them as if they were standing in the same room.

"No, I hope I didn't disturb you."

Then, a strange sound of gurgling filled the background of Phillip's location, followed by the rustling of blankets and the soothing words of a female voice. Isabel pressed the phone to her ear, both certain and uncertain that she heard a child-like whimper of discomfort.

"I'm sorry, Isabel. But I must go now," he said in a rush, his first betrayal of agitation during their entire conversation.

Concerned, she struggled to identify the strange noises. An abrupt slurp of suction? Tiny gasps for breath? Encouraging whispers of a woman?

"Yes, of course," Isabel whispered, fully expecting Phillip to hang up without saying goodbye.

"Isabel?" he quickly added, clinging to her silence.

"Yes?"

"I look forward to seeing you tonight," he said with haste. "Especially in your new gown. It will complement your eyes."

Click.

Isabel paused, waiting for the droning buzz of the disconnected line to confirm the end of their call.

I look forward to seeing you tonight.

Formal and polite. Subtle and sincere. Why had she called him on his private line in the first place? She suddenly couldn't remember. Phillip's even tone and his natural command over their conversation made all of her insecurities seem petty and irrelevant.

Maybe the fault was her own? Maybe it was she who had seemed disloyal and he who had simply guarded himself against it. But Phillip was always so guarded—walled behind evasive expressions and impervious glances—that it was impossible to ever know what he was thinking or feeling, much less his intentions for maintaining a sudden distance between them. And despite all the countless hours they had worked together, Isabel suddenly reflected on the fact that she knew absolutely nothing about his private life. She had never seen his personal home. She had never met any of his personal friends. She had never heard him talk about his extended family or his life outside of work. In fact, she had consciously avoided inquiring about any of it because she knew that he considered it an intrusion. Not even his separation from Marlow—his fiancée of more than two years—was ever discussed until yesterday. And even then, it had been barely addressed, then dismissed like a fleeting error of judgment, never to be repeated again.

That had always been Phillip's way of navigating their relationship, and one of the main reasons why she had gained his trust over the years; she never assumed it was her right to know more than he intended to share with her. Now, Isabel pondered his mysterious absence and the final moments of their conversation. She reflected on the unidentifiable noises in the background as well as the distraction in Phillip's voice and contemplated his decision to end the call without waiting for her good-bye. Was this the same Phillip who she had come to know over the past five years? Or was there something he was deliberately hiding from her? She hung up the phone and stared far out at the faceless statue of the goddess Ceres, looking down upon a city born from her strength. *Yes, it was true...*she whispered to herself. Perhaps she had seemed disloyal, but perhaps it was because it was difficult to maintain loyalty to a man who challenged her devotion at every turn while unveiling so little about himself in return. Suddenly, she no longer felt certain about anyone or anything in her life. In fact, the only thing that seemed certain was that everything would come to an uncertain end tonight at the gala.

Chapter Thirteen

FLASHING BURSTS OF WHITE exploded like stars. Isabel reached out and accepted the masculine hand, drawing her out from the pearly white Bentley and escorting her past the barrage of flashing cameras. The photographers.

Isabel shielded her eyes and face. Mario, the gala's event planner, insisted that every Spears & Associates' grand opening merited no less than a dozen reporters and photographers. Dressed in her scarlet evening gown and natural mink shoulder-wrap, she clearly had been mistaken for someone more press-worthy, like the Mayor's mistress or one of the Litzker heiresses. Her escort whisked her up the Persian red marble staircase of The Old Main Post Office and ushered her towards its grand Art Deco entrance. In the stark daylight, the three-million-square-foot building spanned the entire city block of Van Buren Avenue like an imposing fortress, supported by the classical repetition of its towering entryways, each with a golden revolving door. Now, in the chill of the evening night, strategic spotlights spliced upwards along the building's bold vertical lines and its rigid granite symmetry. Isabel's escort deposited her in front of one of the revolving doors, its cylinder of polished bronze and glass twirling her into the lobby like a time machine.

Isabel pushed out of the revolving doors and lifted her eyes through the soaring iconic Grand Atrium. *Breathtaking.* The exterior spotlights poured in through the grandiose, three-story window panes and flared across the Italian Carrara marble floor, pristine like a sheet of ice. Her eyes scanned the gold-foiled walls, glistening with rejuvenated glory.

He knew how gorgeous it could be, she thought with a subtle smile. Even when she doubted him, Phillip never deterred from his vision of how spectacular it could be. And she knew he had one mandate for the project from the very beginning—every original detail of the dilapidated lobby would be researched and restored, regardless of the cost. He had started its restoration just after she started working for him, treating it like his secret passion that he rarely discussed, but that she knew always lingered there in the background, awaiting fulfillment. She saw the drafting proposals, the budgets, and the expenses receipts. And finally, just days after her first work anniversary, he brought her there to reveal his ultimate vision for it.

It had taken four more long years... Her eyes traced the regal bronze emblems of the postal service—air, land, water, rail, and even pony express—mounted above the clerk stations. She remembered each one's corroded surface and lackluster patina and questioned Phillip's ability to restore them.

"Symbols of the American spirit to endure," he had replied with his British sarcasm while his sparkling eyes and wry smile hinted at his secret affinity for romanticism.

He had endured, and he had been right. Everything was beautiful—stunningly beautiful.

"Isabel!"

She turned and saw an unfamiliar woman rushing towards her.

"Holy Moly, sexy lady, look at you!" the woman cried out, gawking at Isabel's crimson gown with its mermaid silhouette and sweeping train.

"Tami?!" Isabel exclaimed, noting at her heavy makeup, rhinestone hairpiece, and beaded purple and black flapper dress. She had never seen Tami without her glasses, much less wearing cherry red lipstick and dressed in anything that revealed her cleavage. "What happened to your grandmother's vintage cardigan?"

"Jett told me if I tried to wear it, he would fire me," she replied, rolling her eyes. "So instead, he took me to that crazy expensive clothing boutique, *Gatsby*, and told me to pick out the most expensive dress I could find. Look at me, I feel like I want to dance. " She shimmied the beaded fringe of her dress back and forth. "Which would seriously be the most embarrassing thing ever, but whatevah. Oh my God…is *that* the dress Phillip picked out for you?"

"Yes," Isabel said, tracing over the raspberry sequins embedded into the silk tulle of her gown. "Have you seen him?"

"Negative. I thought he was coming with you?"

"No, he sent the dress to the house with a note saying he would meet me here." Isabel quickly scanned the crowd, expecting to spot Phillip's distinct profile. She noted all the familiar faces of her guests as the swirling decorative lighting ebbed and flowed with the rhythm of the live jazz band. But Phillip was nowhere in sight.

"Where's Jett?" Isabel asked.

Tami led Isabel's gaze across the lobby to the hors d'oeuvres table. "Schmoozing with every politician that he can and using Giselle's tight, little ass to lure them in—completely baseless and deplorable, but unsurprisingly effective. That, and the temptation of these amazing stuffed crab and sausage mushrooms. Delicious, by the way." Tami brushed away the crumbs remaining on her lips. "I've already stuffed my face with four."

"My word," Isabel exclaimed, pawing at Tami's gloved hand for a closer look at the square-cut green stone on her ring finger. "Is that from Jett, too?"

"Negative. It's from Madame van der Meer's collection. I know, can you believe it?" Tami bragged, wiping her thumb across its broad emerald. "I just met her—totally my fairy godmother in every way. She was wearing it and she saw me drooling over it, so she offered to let me borrow it for the rest of the night. I promised her that if I dropped it into the chocolate fountain I would fish it out. Madame van der Meer laughed. Jett turned bright red like he was about to have a coronary. Have you seen the rest of the collection?"

Isabel shook her head. "The security guards still hadn't arrived with the display cases when Giselle and I were here this afternoon. Mario sent me home early to get ready, promising me he'd take care of everything."

"Well, wait until you see it. She's even got a bejeweled fan that was owned by Marie Antoinette. " Tami clasped Isabel's elbow and guided her down the lobby towards the jewelry display cases, mounted atop the former postal clerk counters and lighted from above like priceless museum artifacts. "Everyone's buzzing about the fact that it's a brilliant tourism draw. Jett even got Fifi Litzker to agree to lunch tomorrow with her lawyers. Fifi said that she wants to settle on an exclusive tenant agreement to build out her new spa & hotel chain on the second and third floors. If Madame van der Meer is a part of the project, Fifi Litzker wants to be in, too."

"Fifi Litzker is exactly the type of elite tenant that this building needs." Isabel peered inside the nearest jewelry case at its royal coronation tiara, matching diamond necklace, and petite ruby scepter. "Mario did a great job displaying everything. No one does lavish better than Mario."

"Seriously true." Tami nodded. "Have you seen the fourteen-tier cheesecake at the other end of the lobby? Too bad he's gay or else I'd force him to marry me, just so that I don't end up being forty without someone planning me a ridiculously extravagant wedding."

"Gay and taken," Isabel confirmed.

"Aren't all the good ones?" Tami sighed.

"Not this good one," the masculine voice purred from behind them. "Hello, lovely ladies."

"Hello, Gary," Isabel replied, exhaling with relief that it wasn't one of the presumptuous politicians on her guest list. Phillip's lawyer she could handle.

"And heeeelloooo lovely dress." He eyed Isabel, scanning her up and down, taking in the full view of her gown and its strapless cinched bodice.

"Thank you. It was a gift."

"Well, someone certainly knows how to make you look delicious."

"From Phillip," Isabel clarified, raising Gary's chin—and his gaze—back to her face. "But thank you. You do always know how to make a woman feel special."

"In more ways than one." He smiled, his flirting amber eyes drifting down her bare shoulders again because he knew he could get away with it.

"Gary, you do realize that good in this context does not mean 'manwhore.'" Tami downed her champagne and handed it to Gary. Her filter was waning—fast.

"I'm a lawyer, my sassy little friend. I've been called much, much worse."

"*Touché*," Tami lobbed back at him, pulling his tuxedo bow out of alignment before stumbling away from him. "Speaking of manwhores, I better go back and check in with Jett before I insult any more of his colleagues. Isabel, if you see me passed out in the corner, rescue me before I end up making out with someone embarrassing."

"Not to worry, Tami," Gary interjected, calling after her. "I'm only interested in one woman tonight." He settled his gaze onto Isabel.

"I'm flattered," Isabel said. "But I know you prefer blondes, and I don't double date."

"Tonight, I prefer brunettes," he corrected her, admiring the way she re-tied his tuxedo bow with perfection. "And you'll be comforted to know that I'm flying solo." He swept his arm around her waist and ushered her along the sleek marble floors like her personal escort. "Direct orders."

"Direct orders? From who?"

Gary smiled with amusement. "Who do you think?"

Isabel confirmed her suspicion with silence.

"He asked me to meet you because he was coming late." Gary surveyed the room, noting the obese man near the dessert table, who was laughing loudly and drinking heavily. Gary nodded at him in acknowledgment. The obese man raised his tumbler in return.

"Ahhh, I see…" Isabel replied. "Phillip still hasn't forgiven me for throwing a drink in Alderman Madison's face last year at the Mayor's Christmas party."

"I'm fairly certain Phillip has forgiven you. It's more a question of making sure that Madison doesn't get the opportunity to get that close to you again—as well as a few less desirable guests."

Shielding her like a bodyguard, Gary drew Isabel against his chest as if he was protecting her from something or someone. But she resisted his embrace when she heard the charismatic laughter from the man in the conspicuous white tuxedo—*Eliot Watercross*. He was chatting with Norton and a stately elderly woman dressed in a black empress dress, its bustle accentuated with peacock feathers. She wore a black beaded shawl draped over her drooping shoulders and an Egyptian-inspired diamond tiara on her head. *Madame van der Meer*. Eliot's lion green eyes shifted away from the conversation and seized onto Isabel like he was calling her to him.

Isabel attempted to circle away from Gary's encroachment. "I'm going to have to work the room, Gary, especially in Phillip's absence."

"The room is working itself," he countered. "Why not relax and enjoy the atmosphere. And the company."

His protective embrace suddenly felt familiar—too familiar. Isabel glanced up into his light brown eyes, remembering that he went to Harvard Law School. She pushed back against him, seeking refuge from their private corner. His chest was hard and toned; Isabel suddenly noticed his athletic build and his desire to contain her.

"Gary, is this really about protecting me? Or is there something else going on here?"

He confronted her distrustful gaze until he could no longer defy her direct challenge.

"What do you think about the van der Meer collection?" he suddenly asked.

"I think it's lovely, but I was completely kept out of the loop about it."

"The deal isn't completely closed, you know. I'm still working on it with her lawyers, and already, we're hearing that a rival has made her a competing offer."

"A competing offer?" Isabel repeated. "From who?"

Gary glanced across the room to Eliot Watercross, who whispered something into Madame van der Meer's ear, which she accepted with a touch of her hand on his arm like she was receiving assurance from a favorite nephew.

"It's all cheery smiles and fairy tale parties now," Gary said, lowering his voice and turning to the display cases. "But at the end of the day, it's a dangerous game; if Phillip loses the van der Meer deal after publicly announcing the partnership tonight, he'll never recover the momentum it's generating to secure other high-profile tenants like Fifi Litzker who will drive the second and third phases of the renovation. Three million square feet is a lot of space to fill, and if you're Phillip Spears, you can't fill it with big box retailers and parking spaces."

"Sounds like a big dilemma," the voice cut into their conversation.

Isabel turned squarely into Eliot's chest. His green eyes flashed with the overhead lights. He eyed her over the rim of his glass of brandy while crunching down on the ice.

"Perhaps Phillip should rethink renovating a postal factory with zero historic and architectural significance," Eliot said, taking in Isabel's revealing neckline. "Good evening, Bella. You look ravishing tonight."

Isabel lowered her eyes, feeling the blush in her cheeks match her crimson dress.

"Nice to see you, Gary," Eliot said flatly. "But I hope you're not supposed to serve as an acceptable substitute for the man of the hour. Fashionably late to his own party, I presume? Taking a cue out of my own playbook because it takes a special blend of balls and arrogance."

"Spears isn't lacking in either, and he'd be the first one to admit it." Gary countered in Phillip's defense.

"Yes, he would, wouldn't he?" Eliot slyly glanced over at Isabel for confirmation. "Gary, you've forgotten your manners, by the way. Our breathtaking hostess is missing a drink."

"You both forget it's a work night for me," Isabel cut in, attempting to diffuse the mounting tension between the men.

"One drink, Isabel," Eliot insisted. "It's a gala, after all. Not a funeral. Although it does feel like a mausoleum in here, doesn't it? Still, the woman deserves to enjoy her own party."

Pressing the point, he narrowed his eyes at Gary and threw back more ice with a calculated crunch.

"White wine, Isabel?" Gary interjected, cupping Isabel's elbow and preparing to lead her to the open bar. But she unexpectedly resisted his lead.

"Go ahead, Gary. I'll come in a minute and you can introduce me to Madame van der Meer."

Gary's face grew serious. "I think it would be a better idea if you accompany me."

"Why don't you go get us *both* drinks," Eliot asserted, brushing Gary aside by handing off his empty tumbler. "Then you can come back and rescue our fair maiden from the Big Bad Wolf. Two minutes isn't enough time to corrupt her too much. Just enough to make things interesting."

Eliot challenged Gary with his impressive height and build. Both men were tall and imposing, but Eliot Watercross seemed more willing to use it as a threat.

Again, Isabel slipped between them, dismissing Gary's concern with her calming eyes. *It's all games and showmanship.* "White wine would be fine."

But underneath her silent communication was the cold hard fact that she was making a conscious decision to stay with Eliot rather than accompany Gary—a fact that Gary acknowledged with reluctance before turning away and striding towards the open bar.

"Apparently, Phillip thinks you need a babysitter," Eliot said, tracking Gary's departure.

"They think you're intentionally trying to derail our redevelopment of The Old Main."

He smirked in delight. "What do you think?"

"I think men love competing for the sake of competing."

He reached out his hand and followed the pleasing curve of her bare shoulder with his fingertip. "Except, in this case, the prize isn't just a gold-plated trophy. There's much more at stake."

She gazed into his eyes, and for a moment, she lost herself in her own reflection. "What do you think of the restoration?" She consciously shifted away from his touch, redirecting his attention.

"I think it's very Phillip."

"Yes, it's true. Classic and refined, almost disarming in its strength."

"I was thinking more along the lines of old-fashioned and outdated."

Isabel censured him with her glance. He grinned like a mischievous child, as if he had gotten what he wanted—her attention.

"I have to admit that I was skeptical, too. He first took me here years ago, when the ceiling paint was peeling and the window panes were so obscured by city pollution that they barely let in the sunlight. He even restored the original chandeliers. When I saw them, they were aged, seemingly cracked beyond repair. Even then, it was Phillip's vision to bring it back from disrepair. No matter what you think about vintage architecture versus modern construction, you have to admit that he succeeded."

"He's succeeded in restoring a flashy Art Deco lobby. The rest of The Old Main is three million square feet of factory warehouse space that still needs to be leased *and* renovated. And there are a lot more interesting alternatives available for potential tenants than a blighted architectural albatross."

"You mean alternatives like your floating iceberg casino directly across the river at 400 South Wacker?"

"Well, I wouldn't be a very compelling rival without offering competition." He pushed forward and grasped her hand. "You're not wearing my bracelet," he said, drawing up her wrist and feathering its inner fold with a presumptuous kiss.

"I'm not wearing any jewelry." Isabel attempted to pull away, then surrendered when she felt the familiarity of his strength guiding her back.

"Did you like my flowers?" he said, closing the space between them.

"I generally prefer pink ones."

"But they persuaded you just the same…" His hand snaked up her arm and caressed it in a way that felt forbidden.

"I'm not sure I've been persuaded into anything."

"Does that mean you're no longer considering my offer?"

Cautiously, Isabel tested him. "Perhaps it simply means I'm still trying to decide on whether or not I prefer sapphires over pearls."

"She prefers sapphires," the stern voice asserted behind them as Isabel unexpectedly felt the sensation of a heavy gemstone choker draping around her neck.

"Phillip…" Isabel's voice wavered with surprise.

"My apologies for being late," he whispered into her ear and clasped the necklace with finality.

She outlined the oversized gemstones with her fingertips; they felt like cold heavy ice cubes against her skin.

"It's the sapphire and diamond necklace that Napoléon Bonaparte commissioned for his mistress, Joséphine, who eventually became the Empress of France. It's a loan from Madame van der Meer for the night," Phillip explained. "She's waiting for us."

Eliot studied the necklace. "Good evening, Spears. Glad to see you finally found time for your guests."

Isabel gazed at both men—equal in their confidence and prowess, but neither could be more different in their personalities and their professional ambitions. Phillip—stern, reserved, with his unflinching porcelain complexion, flawlessly manicured black hair, and classic black Armani tuxedo. Eliot Watercross—tanned and glowing, the perfect symmetry of his face and body relaxing her inhibitions. With the confidence of a movie star, he vainly wore his starched white tuxedo and black tie through the sea of dark winter gowns and evening suits.

"My guests are here to see the grand opening of the restoration. I am the least exciting part of the evening, I assure you." To prove his point, Phillip shifted his eyes back onto Isabel, taking in the full view of her crimson sequin dress paired with the scintillating sapphire necklace. "You look lovely tonight," he said, encircling her hand with his own and drawing her back from Eliot like a stolen possession.

"I'm afraid I haven't had much of a chance to work the room," she admitted.

"I've already spoken with Jett," Phillip confirmed. "He's spoken with Alderman Chase and Alderman Fitzpatrick and received their assurances that we'll be granted the proper zoning entitlements."

"That's an impressive accomplishment," Eliot cut in. "That must have cost a fortune."

Phillip shot a glare at Eliot; it was an insulting insinuation of bribery and they all knew it.

"It cost nothing more than my integrity and my word. Empty promises, on the other hand, are expensive, especially when they're backed by unsecured loans and shadow investors."

Isabel quickly jumped in, attempting to diffuse their silent stalemate.

"Phillip, I think Madame van der Meer is waiting for us." She nodded to a small group of guests who had settled underneath the glittering gold canopy that billowed through the towering ceilings like celestial arcs denoting royalty. With her hawkish eyes and peacock face, the elderly matriarch of the group was watching Phillip and Isabel from afar.

"Yes," he acknowledged, his voice low and severe. "Shall we?" He swept Isabel towards the center of the grand lobby, its white marble floors glazed with winter crystal lighting like a serene wonderland. But his glare zeroed back onto Eliot Watercross—a warning not to follow them.

"I'm glad you had a chance to make it."

"Were you worried?" he asked, barely turning to face her.

"No, just uncertain."

"Yes…spending time alone with Eliot Watercross seems to produce those kinds of feelings in you."

Isabel recognized his trademark sarcasm. She suddenly stopped and faced him. "I'm not certain Eliot Watercross is the one to blame for my uncertainty."

"Interesting. Because I'm fairly certain he is to blame for mine." Phillip's cold blue eyes challenged her.

"Isabel!" Mario rushed up to them. "You're finally here and looking spectaculious."

Mario greeted her with double-cheek faux air kisses, but Isabel was still replaying Phillip's enigmatic reprimand in her head until Mario forced her back into the present moment

"Whoa…I've just been blinded by the most ridiculous bling-bling ever!" He shielded his eyes and backed away from her. "Where on earth did you get *that*?!"

Isabel glanced at Phillip and touched the sapphire necklace. He avoided her gaze. Its heavy weight suddenly felt like a punishing leash, inspiring nothing in her except the desire to detract attention from it. "You've done a brilliant job, Mario, with everything. I barely recognize the lobby from this afternoon."

Mario dialed down his enthusiasm in front of Phillip. "Good evening, Mr. Spears. Dashing in Armani, as always. I hope you like what we've done with the menu and the décor…"

"I defer to Isabel. I know she trusts you implicitly."

"Wonderful!" Mario clapped his hands and donned a sugary smile.

Phillip suddenly released Isabel's hand. "Excuse me, I must go ahead now. You'll meet us shortly." He nodded to Mario, then drifted off to greet Madame van der Meer.

Mario tracked his departure, murmuring through his frozen smile. "He's impossible, you know. I don't think I've ever received a direct compliment from him. And trust me, I've *fished* for it."

"And you won't," Isabel exhaled, releasing the tension from her body. "Try not to take it too personally. It's just Phillip's way. Impossibly impossible."

Mario sighed, fanning himself. "Honestly, if that disciplining English accent of his wasn't so freaking sexy, I *would* be insulted. But those stern, hot, punish-me-now Mr. Darcy eyes get me every time. *Whewwwww*. Okay, meet me near the seafood pyramid after the publicity announcement. We'll compare notes about the hors d'oeuvres and play *which-guest-is-too-drunk-to-drive-home-alone*."

Mario blew her a kiss before disappearing through the crowd. She turned and started towards Phillip, but stopped when a cold, thin hand intercepted her wrist.

"Don't rush away just yet." Marlow slurred, then suddenly swayed sideways.

Isabel reached out to steady her. "I'm glad to see you're enjoying the gala, Marlow." She caught Marlow's empty cocktail glass, slipping from her fingers. "Where's Symeon?"

"With Eliot, discussing all the ways they intend to lure away Madame van der Meer from signing the deal with Phillip."

Isabel peered at Marlow. *Was she simply drunk or dead serious?* From across the lobby, Isabel spotted Eliot with Symeon as both men approached Noah Spiegel, one of Phillip's most prominent business investors and ushered him towards the opposite end of the corridor.

The heavy sensation of guilt constricted Isabel's chest. That would be *her* courting Phillip's investors if she dared to accept Eliot's offer to become one of his business partners. She would have to play the role of rainmaker, doing exactly what Symeon and Eliot were doing—capitalizing on Phillip's investment connections and attempting to influence them to invest in Eliot's newest real estate venture over Phillip's redevelopment of The Old Main Post Office.

"It all bores me to tears," Marlow drawled. "I much prefer dancing and drinking. That was something that Phillip was always good at when we were together—making me feel like a proper woman." She zeroed in on Isabel and her sapphire and diamond necklace. "How does it feel to be his favorite pet?"

"I'm not anyone's pet, Marlow," Isabel replied, guarding her anger. When Marlow was Phillip's fiancée, Isabel was forced to silently endure her snotty elitism and catty remarks. But now, even without the duty of diplomacy hanging over her, Isabel didn't feel the need to zing sarcasm back at Marlow.

She just felt the need to abandon her in her own inebriated haze of self-pity and dejection. "Excuse me, my guests are waiting for me."

Isabel attempted to brush past her, but Marlow seized her arm again and dug her fingernails into the tender part of Isabel's wrist.

"The hair, the eyes, the same height," Marlow hissed through her smeared lipstick. "I'm a bit thinner, but still, I should have known all along that I was just a pitiful substitute.

Isabel stared at Marlow, attempting to discern the meaning behind her intoxicated words. "You're drunk, Marlow."

"No, I'm simply disposable," she seethed, her shiny red smile slowly drooping like the frown of a sad clown. "You really have no idea how much he's played us both."

The searing pain of Marlow's nails finally forced Isabel to twist away. Marlow hiccupped with a scoff before stumbling away, dragging off the tablecloth from the nearest table with her. The crystal centerpiece reeled off the edge with an explosive crash.

Isabel rushed to retrieve the scattered roses off the floor—an impulsive attempt to tidy up the mess until Mario swooped in and pulled her away from the inquisitive glances of all the guests.

"You're expected elsewhere," he warned below his breath, nodding over to Phillip, who briefly stopped his conversation with Madame van der Meer to survey the disruption. "Let me handle the clean-up with the catering staff. Go—" Mario shooed her forward, encouraging her to arrive beside Phillip with a gracious smile.

"Good evening, I apologize for my delay," Isabel greeted the group.

"Madame van der Meer, this is Isabel Alvarez," Phillip said, offering the introduction.

No title, Isabel noted as she formally extended her hand to Madame van der Meer. Normally, Phillip introduced her as his executive assistant, sometimes even his business manager. But tonight he avoided offering any title with her introduction.

"It's such an honor," Isabel said, controlling her impulse to curtsy. "It's wonderful that you're going to be showcasing your collection here permanently. And thank you so much for allowing me to wear this tonight."

"Ahhh, yes…the Bonaparte necklace." Madame van der Meer cast her grey eyes upon the glittering necklace. "It's one of my favorite pieces. Napoléon commissioned it as a gift for Joséphine before they were married."

Isabel touched the necklace. "Well, it certainly feels historic—and heavy," she laughed. "I wonder if I'm really the right person to be wearing it."

"I insisted," Phillip said abruptly.

Isabel glanced over at Phillip, who gazed at her like a curator admiring a priceless painting. Marlow's bitter warning haunted her. *Was she just a marketing tool for him? A way to help appease Madame van der Meer and secure the lease deal?* She challenged his gaze.

"Phillip saw the piece in the catalogue and said there was only one woman in the world who could possibly wear it," Madame van der Meer clarified. "Even in spite of its controversial history."

"That sounds exactly like Phillip," Isabel replied. "He's certainly never one to shy away from controversy."

"Joséphine was ultimately unfaithful in their marriage," Phillip slung back. "Some historians question whether or not Joséphine married Bonaparte for love, or simply to secure her status within society after her dramatic divorce."

"What do you believe?" Isabel asked Madame van der Meer, attempting to ignore Phillip's searing gaze upon her.

"I believe it's one of the many reasons why I never married," Madame van der Meer offered with a knowing smile. "To love a man of ambition is a lesson in humility, Miss Alvarez. And for many of us women, humility is too high of a price to pay." Madame van der Meer flipped open her stunning fan, hand-painted and bejeweled with gemstones. Isabel remembered Tami mentioning it was from the estate of Marie Antoinette.

"Perhaps Joséphine's betrayal wasn't calculated," Isabel suddenly offered. "Perhaps she felt driven away by the painful realization that she would never be as important to him as conquering all of France."

"Bonaparte loved Joséphine more than any other woman in his life," Phillip stated, as if the conversation had grown tedious to him. "And he wrote her the most expressive love letters—just to prove it."

"But he also loved to hold a grudge," Madame van der Meer eyed him. "And he never wrote her another love letter after her betrayal."

"Perhaps he was too wounded." Phillip adjusted his diamond cufflinks.

"Or too proud," Isabel simply added.

"Or too much of both," he intentionally challenged her.

She endured his gaze. "Sometimes loving a woman is more about vulnerability than it is about conquest."

The lights slowly faded with the rhythmic jive of the band, and Jett emerged from the crowd with a microphone in his hand. Everyone redirected their attention onto the open lobby as the spotlights twirled lyrical patterns of Caribbean blue across the pearly marble floor like waves in the sea.

"We're about to make the official announcement...Please excuse us, Madame."

"My pleasure," she nodded in return.

Phillip secured Isabel's reluctant hand and pulled her through the natural aisle of the parting crowd.

"Ladies and Gentlemen," Jett's confident voice boomed through the microphone. "On behalf of all of Spears & Associates, thank you so much for attending the grand opening gala of The Old Main Post Office."

The crowd clapped in acknowledgment. Jett paused as the applause faded into a polite simmer. "Ladies and gentlemen…there is only one man in Chicago who could possibly view an abandoned government building as something potentially glamorous, and of course, that one man *has* to be British."

The crowd tittered and shifted their attention onto Phillip and Isabel. She felt the strength of his hand, tightening his possession over her. He knew she hated public speaking, and the grip of his hand signaled he had no plans of allowing her to escape.

"But that one man," Jett continued, "has a reputation in Chicago of being more than just a profiteering Brit—he has a reputation of being a loyal benefactor of this city's rich cultural history and architectural heritage. And so, without further ado, I present to you the man of the hour, Mr. Phillip Spears."

Like thunder, a second wave of applause rolled throughout the echoing lobby as Jett beckoned Phillip and Isabel out from the crowd and into the spotlight.

Phillip released his possessive grip of Isabel's hand as Jett passed off the microphone to him. She shielded her eyes and squinted out into the crowd; she could see nothing beyond their shadowed faces. She closed her eyes, unnerved that she was being watched by all of her guests, including Eliot Watercross. Instead, she settled her gaze onto Phillip. Mario was right; as always, he did look elegant in his classic black tuxedo, its lapels accented with a pink rose boutonniere. The spotlights reflected off his slick black hair as his Roman profile surveyed the crowd. Even in front of a crowd of one hundred guests, Phillip was poised and self-assured.

"Good evening, everyone…" he said with a deliberate pause. "Thank you for coming this evening to witness the unveiling of a labor of love."

He scanned the lobby's soaring ceilings and white glacier floors, as if for a moment, he was the only person in the room able to admire it. "As many of you know, I am a man of few words…but still, I would like to take this opportunity to say something about this project—and all it represents." He paused again, taking full command over his own thoughts and the attention of his guests.

"There is value…value in caring for sacred things—things that cannot easily be reproduced or replaced. There is honor in celebrating them to ensure that they will be properly preserved and restored. And there is an urgency to protect them when they are threatened with disrepair or destruction. Tonight, I am pleased to see so many of our friends and colleagues supporting our efforts to restore the incomparable beauty within this building—a reminder that beauty exists even in the most unexpected of places."

Suddenly, a voice heckled Phillip from out of the dark crowd. "Especially places where you're willing to spend over three hundred million dollars."

The crowd stirred before growing quiet. Beyond the piercing lights and obscurity of darkness, Isabel searched out the faces; but it didn't matter. She recognized his mocking tone—*Eliot Watercross.*

"No," Phillip casually replied, barely turning his head towards the direction of the heckler. "Four hundred."

Phillip stated it like a challenge, as if he was raising the stakes at a poker table. The crowd murmured with a hush and waited for the heckler to respond. Everyone, including Isabel, listened to see if the banter between the two men would escalate. But Eliot Watercross uncharacteristically fell silent.

"Four hundred million dollars makes this party look like the cheapest part of the renovation's budget," Jett called out from the edge of the crowd like a pandering clown.

"Yes…unless we account for the priceless historic jewelry," Phillip added, turning towards Isabel to draw attention to her sapphire and diamond necklace. "We are, indeed, most fortunate to have arrived at an agreement with Madame van der Meer to permanently display her collection here in the grand lobby for years to come. Thank you, Madame van der Meer."

The crowd quickly applauded. It was a flawless segue—one that redirected everyone's attention back onto the celebratory grandeur of the night. Eliot's tall silhouette shifted deeper into the shadows of the huddled guests. Isabel watched him disappear with heavy disappointment in her heart. Then, as if it was a cruel punishment, Phillip settled his gaze upon her and ended his time in the spotlight with a nod in her honor.

"At this time, I would like to thank my business manager and our incomparable staff for making tonight a reality. And thank you all for joining us. I wish you a lovely rest of your evening."

The spotlight lifted and morphed into pale celestial swirls across the lobby floor as the jazz band picked up its cue. Persuaded by the swaying ragtime beat and the festive atmosphere of ballroom dancing, the guests crowded into the center of the room, surrounding Phillip and Isabel and blocking their exit.

"Shall we?" he said, offering his hand to her, as if she had no other choice.

She reluctantly accepted, allowing him to draw her into his arms. But the sting of their recent exchange prevented her from relaxing into his lead, and Marlow's resentful words echoed through her mind. *You really have no idea how much he's played us both…*

"The necklace was a brilliant marketing tool," she said, holding back her weight.

He eyed her resistance to his lead. "Simply celebrating beauty within beauty," he said in an unemotional tone.

Isabel stared at him, her heart coursing with suppressed resentment and fear. "Phillip…why didn't you tell me about the van der Meer deal?"

"Why didn't you tell me about your personal interest in Eliot Watercross?" he shot back. It wasn't a question. It was an accusation.

"Because there's nothing to tell." They both noted the insincerity in her voice.

"Isabel, I wish we could be more open with each other."

"I have never lied to you, Phillip."

"And yet, you have lied to yourself—about us."

She stared at him, unable to endure his relentless gaze searing into her heart, unleashing every fear and insecurity she had tried so hard to contain.

"Lady, I will touch you with my mind," he whispered, obscuring his strong Oxford accent behind the mysterious cadence she had come to know so intimately. "Touch you and touch and touch, until you give me suddenly a smile, shyly obscene."

But Isabel did not smile. The blood drained from her cheeks as she processed all that had transpired between them. "You…" The accusation escaped from her lips with faint regret.

He anticipated her protest and locked her body into his embrace. She immediately recognized the strong, athletic contours of his chest. He molded her hips into his own, dominating every part of her body in the same way he was controlling every emotion within her vulnerable heart. The physical intimacy between them bled into her soul, so natural and familiar, and yet, she scrutinized him as if he was a stranger, a man who had inspired her most thrilling yearnings of desire without daring to admit his quest to inspire them.

"But why?"

He broke his gaze and drifted his lips into her ear. "Do you really need me to answer that?"

"Yes." She nodded with conviction, attempting to pull back from him, unnerved by the hint of sarcasm in his reply. *Yes, she did.*

She fixed her swimming eyes onto him like a challenge. In all the years she had worked for Phillip Spears, she had never known him to hesitate as long as he was hesitating to answer her right now. She waited, uncertain what she expected as an answer; perhaps she needed him to openly express in words what she had imagined had been conveyed during their passionate nights together—the most intimate and vulnerable moments of her life. But instead, she was only greeted with his frown of silence, forcing her to accept the insecure hush within her own subconscious, asserting her own answer as the one and only truth.

"You used me." She pushed out the words like painful breaths. "You used me like you're using me now. For your own gain—on your own terms."

"They were our *mutual* terms," he flung back, defensiveness creeping into his stern voice. "And there was never a moment when I thought that you weren't fully complicit in our...arrangement. Never a moment until...last night, when I saw that you were accepting the advances of another man. And not just any man, but my direct rival."

Their eyes locked. Phillip's jaw flinched, holding back a flood of his own scorn and pain, as if he hated the fact that she was forcing him to confront her sense of loyalty.

No— Isabel swallowed hard, searching out the ember of truth flaming within her own heart. "I never betrayed you," she replied, unable to accept that he believed otherwise. "But I was also never certain..." Her voice trailed off, struggling against the sound of her own desperate denial. Had she deceived herself—even in the smallest of ways—in order to lessen the shame of willfully allowing herself to be sexually dominated by her boss? Or had he been the one who deceived her so completely?

Phillip narrowed his eyes, challenging her. His hands constricted around her waist and pressed her body deeply into his own—an unspoken reminder of every forbidden touch and view she had permitted him. "You were never certain?" he mocked her. "Perhaps because you preferred it that way."

Without warning, Isabel drew back her hand and slapped Phillip's chiseled cheek.

Bastard.

The sound of the impact cracked like thunder. Phillip clenched his jaw, absorbing the sting of her rage without raising his eyes.

"What I prefer is not to be turned into your casual whore."

She raised her hands to the sapphire and diamond necklace, clawing to remove its noose from around her neck, and flung it into his hand before rushing off the dance floor. But Phillip was faster and stronger. He seized her wrist and pulled her back into his body—one final time.

"Isabel...do not do this." His voice dropped with rigidity, attempting to control her as his own emotions surged within his raging heart. "Do not leave like this or it will be the end of everything." He asserted it like a threat—a warning that she was jeopardizing more than simply her pride.

"The end of everything?" she repeated, her eyes storming like a gale across black waters, threatening to sink them both. "You mean the end of my employment with you? The end of our efforts together to restore The Old

Main Post Office? The end of everything that we've worked on together for the past five years?"

"The end of everything...between us." He pinned her wrist against his chest.

"And what is that, Phillip?"

She waited again, gazing into his struggling eyes. She just wanted him to say something, anything that would alleviate the anxiety in her heart. Instead, his stoic silence confirmed everything she feared most—that the passionate nights that had transpired between them meant more to her than it did to him.

"It is not the end of anything between us because there was never a beginning," she muttered with cold brutality. She tried to pull away again, but like so many times before, he forced her into submission. Their eyes locked as the uneven noise of the chattering crowd and the swinging beat of the live band fell to a surreal hush.

As if he was testing her resolve, Phillip lowered his chin along her neck, taking in her scent as his lips grazed her skin. In bitter protest, Isabel shut her eyes and turned away her cheek, attempting to dismiss the physical intimacy that they had shared. He could physically force her to submit to him, but he could no longer force her to make eye contact with him, just as he could no longer force her to believe in their perfectly manufactured charade. Suddenly, Phillip tossed down her wrist and backed away with a resentful glare, surrendering to her contempt by allowing her to abandon him.

Overcome by her impulsive need to flee, she strode off the dance floor as bitter waves of injustice coursed through her heart. The swirling lights distorted her vision and filled her with nausea.

"Isabel!"

She stopped and spun around defensively when the male voice hollered out her name like a battle cry. With his coat draped over his arm, Eliot Watercross emerged from the shadowed wings of the lobby.

"I'm just about to head out, but I certainly can't leave without saying good night to the most important woman in the room." He approached her; his greedy green eyes passing over her body. "It looks like you're preparing to rush away like Cinderella into the night."

She averted her gaze and shivered, as if an invisible draft swept through the cavernous lobby. He responded by slipping his heavy wool coat over her bare shoulders, capturing her like a prize. She feigned a smile in appreciation and gazed at the shimmering gold revolving doors, wondering why she didn't push forward and complete her escape.

"My car is waiting outside. I'll give you a ride." His finger flirtatiously lifted her chin, calling attention to her teary eyes and quivering lips.

Had he seen her interaction with Phillip?

"No, thank you. I'm fine." Neither one of them was convinced that she meant it. Presumptuously, he reached out and traced her neckline down to the tip of her breastbone. "Perhaps sapphires aren't your favorite gemstone after all."

Isabel closed her eyes, accepting his touch. But she only felt doubt.

The sensation of being watched tingled across the nape of her neck. She glanced back at the inebriated laughter of all her guests and spotted Phillip surveying her from the distance. His searing eyes seized onto Watercross, then back onto her. She held his gaze, waiting and waiting and waiting…testing if Phillip would try to stop her from leaving through the revolving doors, testing if he would try to stop her from leaving him.

Phillip stared at her, coolly, impassively, telling her she was free to come and go as she wished. His pride would never allow him to make a public scene in order to keep her there. He made no effort to chase after her or assert his feelings or emotions, not even when Eliot Watercross placed his forearm around her waist and guided her to the doorway. *No, he would never admit it.* Not even in that moment was she anything more to Phillip than an expendable guest.

"Thank you, Eliot," she said, allowing her embittered gaze to confirm Phillip's worst assumption about her. "I would be happy to accept a ride."

Eliot nodded and ushered her into the grand revolving door, forcing her decision to leave with the one man who had desired to ruin everything true and honorable about the night.

Chapter Fourteen

PHILLIP SPEARS AIMLESSLY gazed out of his office window on Monday morning—certain that his life had changed forever. Seated at his desk, canted towards his unobstructed view of downtown Chicago, he stared out at the ornamental peaks of all the skyscrapers, noting all of the properties he had intentionally purchased to restore to their full historical glory. They were symbols, not only to his dedication in preserving some of the most influential architecture in Chicago, but also symbols of his success as a self-made man in a foreign land.

It all meant nothing in the end.

His buildings, his reputation, his passion for a city that had been his adopted home for the past twenty years, none of it mattered—*none of it*—unless she chose to walk into the office.

Phillip settled his gaze onto the statue of Ceres, the Roman goddess of fertility. *Faceless*, he thought. She had been erected atop one of the most iconic buildings in the center of downtown Chicago's financial district, but sculpted by the artist without a face, just so wealthy, egotistical men who observed her from the adjacent skyscrapers could imagine whatever expression they wanted her to possess.

Lecherous men like him.

He pitched forward in his chair as a debilitating ache throbbed throughout his chest. Paralyzed, silent, and barely breathing, he waited for the surge of regret to release its constriction on his heart.

He glanced at his watch. *Fifteen minutes late*. He gazed at his office phone. She still hadn't called.

He had considered calling her. Every hour, the impulse swelled in him to dial her home phone number. But he had resisted every time. He had already played the role of intruder. Now, he was forced to accept the role of penitent, forced to accept his punishment—he would have to wait and see if she would choose to come to him.

He cast his eyes to his office door, bidding it to open. Over the weekend, he had played out all the possible scenarios in his mind. Her anger and contempt for him he could handle—would handle—even console, if she would allow him a moment of forgiveness. Her deliberate absence, on the other hand, he would not be able to endure.

Open, open, open…the wait was killing him; the wait and the uncertainty that she would possibly choose to stay away from him—possibly and intentionally. He pushed the fear from his mind, but regret bled into his heart like a seeping sickness, slowly crushing his desperate fantasy of a reconciliation between them.

He anxiously stood from his chair, stuffing his hands into his pockets. He had endured many hardships in his life, but not seeing her again, not having the chance to express everything that raged in his heart was more than he could bear. He shut his eyes and reflected on some of the hardest moments in his life, attempting to summon the inner strength he needed to quell his emotions. They included the endless struggles as a young man growing up in the poor, industrial town of Jarrow, England: the premature death of his father in a mining accident, the despair of his mother and her inability to provide for him and his younger brother, and his subsequent decision to leave school at the age of fifteen to go work in the mines to earn a living wage for them. Sometimes, he still felt the invisible, haunting sensation of coal grime under his fingernails, inspiring the recurring memories of his childhood, fraught with poverty and despair. For two long years, he worked underground for eight hours a day, six days a week, with nothing more than the weak glow of his helmet light. *That's where he had developed his unnatural affinity for darkness*, he thought, turning down the blinds and reducing the sunlight within his office.

When the mines closed, he was forced to scrounge for odd jobs at the shipyards, eventually making a name for himself as a rigger for any captain willing to take him onto his schooner. It was there that he quickly learned what separated leaders from modest men. Captains were revered not only because they knew more than anyone about their ships, but also because they commanded the fidelity and dedication of their crew. It was not the high wages or fancy words that turned sailors into mates. It was their love of the sea and their love of their captain who united them.

Loyalty and devotion, he reflected. And it was that spirit of brotherhood that kept Phillip sailing with the best shipmasters until they encouraged him to go back to school to become the captain of his own schooner. *Couldn't be a master of men without a proper degree from the Queen*, they all told him. Had it not been for the captains at the shipyard who were willing to take him under their tutelage, it was a certainty that he would still be stuck in Jarrow—without worth or wage.

Loyalty and devotion.

Phillip paced around his office like a man caged by his own remorse. Had he betrayed her loyalty and devotion to him? Or had he simply attempted to honor her in the only way he knew she would accept him? He aimlessly gazed down at the polished figurines upon the marble chessboard on his desk.

In the end, she had felt deceived by him. And to her, that was all that mattered.

Had he merely been a lecher and Isabel his whore, then he could accept her contempt for him. *But had that been his intention?* Perhaps initially—when he first chose to send her the pink roses and initiate their meeting at the Peninsula Hotel, when everything was unknown and uncertain, and his years of yearning and unbearable repression clouded his judgment and overpowered his guilty conscience. *He could not risk her rejection.* And so, he invented a way to achieve her consent—at any cost. And yes, he had deliberately altered his accent like a con artist, perpetuating a myth of himself. *It was more natural to seduce her behind the myth of her mysterious admirer*, he thought, *than behind the myth of her stern, reserved boss.*

Her stern, reserved boss. Yes, that was equally a myth because there was nothing reserved about the fantasies and desires he had harbored for her every day for the past five years.

And yes, it was true. He had consciously changed his accent, and in her eyes, that made him guilty of misleading her. But it was not the first time he had altered his accent to hide the real version of himself. It had been the same at Newcastle University, where he had taught himself early on how to hide his lower-class roots, learning to manipulate his own speech by suppressing his working class Geordie accent and elevating his cadence to proper Queen's English. But *he* never really changed; he simply learned how to become a chameleon, mimicking his classmates and their privileged lifestyles and mannerisms.

Even back then, he was a charlatan.

Beyond economics and calculus, university taught him how to master the art of impersonating someone else for the sake of gaining respect and prestige. He had learned to discipline every spontaneous gesture of the teenager who had toiled in the mines and shipyards, and in turn, successfully converted himself into a cautious, reserved, educated, and exceedingly insular imposter. There were no rewards for a slip of the Geordie tongue or an off-color sailor's remark; there was only awkward judgment and aspersion which simply taught him the merits of repressing everything…even the core of his own soul. Slowly, every natural mannerism of his body and every inflection of his voice receded from the forefront of his persona, a subservient shadow bowing behind his new identity—the ambitious university graduate from Newcastle who went on to receive a Fulbright scholarship from Harvard Business School, and eventually made his fortune investing in real estate in America.

The American Dream...Phillip Spears had lived it without being an American and he never forgot that fact because it still felt like a shameful secret—his grueling life of poverty before America. After Harvard Business School, there was no reason to embrace anything except his ambition—an ambition that led him to Chicago and into various real estate ventures during the booming years of the hottest real estate market in a century. Buying properties and flipping properties over and over again until he was eventually able to purchase his first downtown skyscraper. After that, everything changed. His net worth quadrupled, his network of colleagues turned from wealthy to elite, and he was forced to reaffirm—again—the myth of a man who flawlessly belonged among them. And soon, it became easy to pretend he had never been a man without means because Phillip Spears—the billionaire real estate investor—was truly the only persona that ever seemed to matter.

Except to her.

While closely working together as employer and employee, business owner and assistant, Isabel never questioned him about his background or his net worth. She simply showed up every day, determined to prove her own worth by doing her best job for him. During the day, she attended every business meeting, accompanied him to inspect real estate leads, and served as his gatekeeper, shielding him from everyone who wanted his time and attention. At the end of the day, she was often the last one in the office, reviewing his emails, returning phone calls on his behalf, scheduling his appointments for the following week. And often on the weekends, at his urging and insistence, she accompanied him to business dinners and fancy galas, and soon, whether either one of them chose to acknowledge it or not, it became almost impossible to maintain a perfect separation between their personal and business lives.

And slowly, she saw through him. He felt certain of it. She had been the only person who had sensed there was more to him than he ever cared to admit. She was the only one who noticed that he preferred a simple beer over a four-hundred-dollar bottle of wine; or how he often used the wrong forks at the wrong times while dining at the most prestigious five-star restaurants; and how he rarely swore—not because he didn't have it in him, but because his loss of control made his English accent cruder in a way that seemed curiously different.

And he felt certain she had sensed how he was smothering himself with his own protective pride. But an unspoken understanding had grown between them. Beyond their guarded glances and business banter, he knew she respected his privacy, and in turn, he had grown accustomed to revealing that he was a man of self-worth beyond his net worth through private moments—moments while sitting together in his office, dancing together at a gala, or traveling together in his car. He knew there had been moments when he captured her curiosity and inspired her long inquisitive glances, especially when he betrayed his appreciation for her, fueling the undercurrent of unity between them—an intense connection that neither of them was willing to name except through silent glances of allegiance.

Her loyalty and devotion to him—it was the only authentic relationship he had left in his life, and now, he could not bear the thought of being forced to surrender it. Especially forced to surrender it by her deliberate absence.

He stared at his office door. *Open, open, open...*

He pressed the intercom button on his phone's handset.

"Lucy, has Isabel arrived yet?"

"No...still not yet, Mr. Spears."

He cut off the line. It had been the third time he had checked in with Lucy this morning. He was growing impatient—and desperate.

Without warning, his office door flung open.

Norton stopped short inside the doorway. "Good Lord, Phillip...please try not to look so exquisitely disappointed to see me."

Phillip rubbed his face and slowly exhaled to relieve the pain in his chest. He turned away and fumed while gazing out the window at the cityscape, a preoccupation intended to hide his pain. "No, it's not you, Norton. I assure you." His voice was flat and unconvincing.

Norton advanced into his office without an invitation and followed the dull swath of light seeping through the blinds and encaging the floor with prison bars. "Well, I've come to congratulate you. The gala was an impressive success."

Phillip nodded, but his mind was clearly elsewhere. *Yes, it was true.* He had gotten everything he wanted out of the gala. Everything except the most important thing to him—*that, he had lost.*

"You're waiting for her, I presume."

Phillip glanced up at Norton who removed his shoes and leisurely reclined across the couch. As an actuary, Norton was brilliant at assessing business risk. But as a man of eighty years who had fought in a World War and buried not only a beloved wife, but also an adult daughter stricken with cancer, Norton had endured the joys and sorrows of life in a way that made him perceptive beyond compare. Phillip had forgotten how well his longtime friend was at reading people—and their private emotions.

"I presume you saw the slap," Phillip replied.

"Many of us saw the slap," Norton repeated, stretching his long frail legs out across the sofa like he was relaxing within the comfort of his own living room. "It was hard to miss, and yes…I had an enchanting view of it from the front of the flaming fondue tower." Amused, he scanned Phillip's cheek. "I'm surprised she didn't leave a mark."

Phillip touched his jaw. "It would have been well within her right."

"Truer words have never been spoken." Norton closed his eyes, taking in the dimness within the office. "I also saw that she left with Eliot Watercross," he added cautiously.

Phillip did not respond. Instead, he stood from his seat and paced around his desk, exhaling all the words he could not express any other way. He moved to the panel of windows farthest from his desk and drew up the blinds—an action she always performed whenever she entered his office. He cast his pensive gaze across the magnificent lakefront that had always comforted him. "I've made a mistake, Norton. Several mistakes, perhaps. And now, I fear that I've driven her away."

There was a long pause as both men reflected on the merits of their own private regrets. "Mistakes are never permanent, my dear boy. They can always be rectified based on our own admission of them."

"She may not grant me the opportunity, Norton."

"The soul of a woman is not leaden like yours, Phillip," Norton mused. "You simply need to make it known to her that you recognize the error of your ways."

"What if that's not enough?"

"Phillip—" Norton insisted, rising from the couch like a father challenging his son. "Within matters of business, it is true that money and titles cure all differences. But with matters of the heart… " He hesitated, as if he knew he was treading across fragile terrain, "there is only one cure—and that is the admission of one's willingness to change."

The sharp buzz of the phone's intercom interrupted them.

"Mr. Spears…she's on her way into the office now, and she's coming to see you."

Phillip locked eyes with Norton. "Thank you, Lucy," he called to the intercom.

"Don't let your pride supersede your need for others," Norton cautioned him. "For us men, it's a difficult balance, but the rewards far outweigh the risks."

Norton slipped on his shoes and hobbled towards the door like he intended to avoid a tempest. But as he reached for the doorknob, Isabel threw it open for him. It was the first time in five years that she hadn't knocked.

"Norton?" she said with surprise.

"Good morning, Isabel. Wonderful gala. Congratulations on all your efforts."

Her eyes shifted onto Phillip, who held her gaze.

"Thank you," she whispered, like it was a painful memory.

"I shall leave you two now," Norton said, connecting them both with his foreboding voice. "I can only imagine that you both have much to discuss…"

He closed the door behind him, filling the office with inescapable silence. Phillip stared at Isabel; he had waited all weekend for this moment—just to see her, just to settle his eyes upon her and have her return his gaze with her dark Spanish eyes.

Dignified and beautiful.

Even after the distress and heartache he had inflicted upon her, she stood before him and held herself like an indomitable queen. *Always so formal in her black pencil skirt and white button-up Oxford shirt.*

He could tell it was her blatant attempt to keep things all business and dismiss everything that had happened between them. *But he had no intention of dismissing it.* He fixed his eyes on her, wanting her to know it was impossible for him not to look at her now without reflecting on the night they shared on his yacht—a night of pure passion and vulnerability. She had allowed herself to become the fantasy he never dared to indulge in, not even in his most private moments within the darkest parts of his soul—until that night, when she submitted to his conquest and sealed his fidelity to the one woman who had become the most important person in his life. *And she would not leave today until he made her realize it.*

Isabel edged away from his desk, as if she was gauging whether or not to confront him or simply turn and walk out.

He would have to be the one to speak first…he *should* be the one to speak first.

He lowered his eyes and acquiesced. "Isabel," he said, hearing how his own voice dropped an octave. Within his mind, he had rehearsed every word, every glance that he intended to exchange with her; now, that script faded away from his lips as he noted she was conveying her own message through her physical distance: *it had all been a shameful mistake.*

"Phillip—" she cut in, then paused, as if she, too, had rehearsed her own script, and needed a moment to mentally consult it before making the leap and pushing out the words. "I've come this morning to…deliver my resignation."

He his eyes fixed upon her. Like a masterful chess player, he had considered all her possible moves, including what he would say if she attempted to resign. He knew it was a possibility, and over the weekend, he had checked his phone and email every hour, anticipating the worst with dread. But he was unprepared for the way her rejection of their professional relationship—and everything else they had mutually shared together—would overwhelm his sense of pride.

He searched her fierce challenging eyes. Was there really nothing between them? Nothing worth salvaging? Nothing worth resolving through conversation or even silence? Was she really ready to dismiss the past three weeks of intimacy that had been mutually shared, but never verbally expressed?

"Effective immediately," she asserted.

Motivated by a flare of impulsive anger, he pushed back with aggression.

"Surely you must reconsider…your mother, your son—both depend on you and your employment."

Phillip stopped, feeling himself reeling out of control. Nothing about their exchange resembled what he hoped to convey to her. He had slipped behind the persona of the surly, unforgiving billionaire boss, and it filled him with both security and disgust.

Isabel accepted his disdainful glare, as if it fueled her motivation to forge ahead. "I've accepted a position with Watercross Capital," she punctuated with finality.

Phillip shut his eyes, as if he had just been shot. In his youth, he had known a good friend who had caught a stray bullet while hunting in the fields. His friend described it as a blunt assault to the body, paralyzed by surreal shock. The actual sensation of pain didn't come until minutes after…when the sight of blood made the disbelief a reality.

"Did you spend the night with him?" he suddenly asked like an accusation.

She glared at him with defiance; her silence confirmed the worst.

Furiously, he swept his hand across his chessboard, scattering the marble pieces like pellets of ice across the hardwood floors. He saw her flinch, then hold herself firmly in place, deliberately absorbing the full force of his rage. He clenched his jaw and tightened his fist, tempering his instinct to punch his hand through his glass desk—just to diffuse the searing pain within the depths of his heart.

Five years of their working relationship—his direct mentorship of her career and training—had meant nothing to her. *Nothing*. And three nights of their mutual passion and intimacy had meant even less. He glared at the indifference within her expression, its detachment turning her into a callous stranger. She was not only rejecting their professional relationship; she was fully and completely rejecting him.

"Please get your things and leave." His raspy voice was the only evidence of his inability to speak.

He turned away from her, searching for a distraction to cage the fury within him. Flicking open the blinds, he allowed the flood of light to shower upon them as he listened to his own accelerating breath. He waited and waited and waited for her response while scanning the skyline. *Her merciless, punishing silence*. It seemed to last an eternity before her heels clicked across the floor and approached his desk to deposit something on its surface.

"The rest of your jewelry I put into a box and left with Lucy. But this…I wanted to give back to you personally."

He heard her pause, as though she was waiting for him to turn to face her. But he refused. Instead, he caught her wounded gaze in the reflection of the window; it was filled with hesitation and penance, as if she was suffering—even more than he was—because it was she who was choosing to inflict punishment upon them.

"And no…" she said flatly. "I didn't spend the night with him."

Only when he heard the sound of the door, closing behind her, did he drop his head and shut his eyes, as the surge of adrenaline trembled his hands.

He. Had. Failed.

He scanned his desk and spotted the familiar sparkling cord of platinum and its modest solitaire diamond—his Christmas gift to her after her first year of working as his assistant. *A careful, calculated choice*, he remembered. S*omething simple, but elegant. Something beyond friendship, but just short of romantic*. It had been purchased as a gesture of gratitude—he had convinced himself at the time—for all the long hours she had granted him that year, when so often they were the last ones to leave the office and the first ones to arrive in the morning. He remembered how she gazed down upon it, even turning away from him, as if she might refuse it. Then, like a light that illuminated his shadowed heart, she had smiled, offering him the honor of draping it around her neck. It was the first time she had ever granted him such close proximity to her—close enough to indulge in the scent of lavender in her hair and hint of perfume beneath her shell pink sweater. *Even back then, she loved blush pink.* His fingers had wisped across the nape of her neck, briskly, confidently, feeling the velvet tenderness of her skin and the way her sloping shoulders relaxed with his touch. *She trusted him.*

Every day after that, she had worn it like an acceptance of his appreciation. And every time he looked at her, it served as a reminder of her unwavering commitment to him. During his most grueling days, filled with endless conference calls of legal negotiations and threats of lawsuits, he would peer at her from across his desk and take comfort in the way she gazed back at him, donning the necklace like an unspoken symbol that she was dedicated to him until the bitter end.

Loyalty and devotion.

Phillip gripped the necklace in the palm of his hand and dug the hard surface of its diamond into his flesh.

No, he would not fail.

"Isabel—" he suddenly called out, rushing to the door and throwing it open. "Isabel—" He scanned the desks of his employees. They stopped typing and looked up at him with concern, noting the uncharacteristic alarm in the tenor of his voice.

"She went…that way," Elisa dared to offer, pointing to the elevators.

Phillip nodded and strode down the hallway, pushing through the glass doors into the reception lounge.

He locked eyes with Lucy, who frowned, sensing their conflict.

"Out there," she said with a nod.

He shifted his wild gaze out through the final set of glass doors and spotted her waiting for the elevators. This time, he called after her with ferocity. "Isabel—"

She glanced back at him with shining eyes and hesitated as the chimes of the elevator rang. Then, she slipped through the shutting elevator doors like a fugitive fleeing from her captor.

Phillip bolted after her, jamming his hand through the final sliver of space. The elevator shuddered with violence as he forced his entrance. She pressed herself against the farthest wall, daring him to close the separation between them.

His eyes and furious heart accepted her challenge—*he would not let her go so easily, not this time.*

"If you truly have no feelings for me—for us—except hatred and regret, then, yes…I shall accept your resignation and release you from my life forever. But if you are doing this to punish me…" his voice grew guttural and raw, choked with an uncontrollable surge of emotion, "punish me for the way that I…used you—as you believe is the case—then you are not only punishing me, but you are also punishing yourself."

The elevator doors closed behind him, forcing his physical proximity to her. He seized her arm, an insistence for her surrender. She protested, shutting him out of her view like she intended to shut him out of her heart, refusing to grant him what he wanted—a signal that she needed him as much as he needed her.

He slowly drew her body against his own; she did not pull away from him. He grazed his nose along her ear, exhaling his desire for every part of her that she had once permitted him to touch—and pleasure. The graceful slope of her neck, the tender crease along her collarbone, the sensual curves of her breasts, the supple taste of her lips, the inviting rotation of her hips…Their three nights of passion had been the most intimate, sacred experiences of his life; and perhaps now, she simply needed him to openly confess it.

"If you truly no longer want to accept me in your life, then I shall bid you goodbye and all shall be forgotten. But if there is a part of you, Isabel…a part of you that I believe consented to—and desired—everything we shared, then know this…" He pinned her against his chest and pressed his promise against her ear. "I shall not surrender you so easily."

He grasped her wrist. She looked up at him with a plea in her eyes—*please…*

It was a plea for mercy, a plea to accept that things had irrevocably changed, as if the corruption of their professional relationship was a casualty too acute to bear.

The floor chime rang and the elevator doors rolled open to the forty-fifth floor. She pushed away from him, seeking asylum from his intensity, and waited for another person to enter the elevator. But there was only breezy emptiness in the hallway. As the doors rolled back, Phillip pounded the red emergency STOP button, halting the cab.

"Come to me tonight," he insisted. "One final time. And if you still feel as if you cannot accept me, accept us—in spite of everything—then I will accept that it was all a mistake—a pitiful, regretful mistake—and I shall let it all go." He looked at her wet black eyelashes, shutting him out of her mind and soul.

She shook her head in protest. "No. It's impossible. I'm taking care of Aidan. My mother is gone tonight. "

"Then let me come to you," he whispered, desperately seeking her acceptance.

"No—" She shook her head again. "There is no chance for us, Phillip." Finally, she found the strength to look at him, impressing the certainty of her rejection.

"You must give this a chance…give us a chance."

"Phillip—" She petitioned him, exhausted by his smothering persistence. "My life is my family and my work. The rest was just…" she hesitated before attempting to make the truth known between them—once and for all. "Just a fantasy."

He searched her eyes, struggling to accept how easily she was willing to dismiss the most personal and vulnerable moments of his life.

"Yes, our nights together may have been a fantasy, but the emotions you stir inside me, the desire to know you, see you, touch you—every day in every way—are nothing short of real. I assure you."

He pushed towards her with a familiarity she could not deny, yearning to kiss her to prove the sincerity behind his pledge; but he stopped short, confirming what they both knew was the truth—he had lost the privilege of her unconditional trust, and now, he was fighting for the right to earn it back. He brushed her lower lip with his thumb, an artist admiring his muse, and he persuaded her to meet his gaze. Her Spanish brown eyes, which had filled with compassion and empathy for him so many times before, now welled with suffering. *Suffering because of him.*

"Please…let me come to you tonight."

The emergency bell rang out with piercing desperation. She glared at its unidentifiable source, petitioning him to end it—end everything. He studied her resolution, her determination to deny his every advance. Finally, he caved, disengaging the emergency stop button and releasing her from his possession—and his life.

She wiped her eyes and smoothed down her shirt and skirt, attempting to regain her composure as the elevator spiraled down, down, down like a diving bell plunging them into the depths of uncharted physical and emotional separation.

Ping. Forty-five floors passed by in an instant.

Such a simple sound, Phillip thought, foretelling her imminent goodbye.

She adjusted the strap of her purse, then pushed forward the moment the elevator doors rolled open and abandoned him without any lingering hope for their future. He watched her glide away across the marble floors of the Beaux Arts lobby and pass through its bronze doors into the bustling energy of the city. Watercross Tower was only a few blocks north along the river. She could easily be traveling there now to meet him. Phillip shut his eyes, pushing the possibility out of his mind; instead, he dwelled on how the softness of her lips still lingered against his fingertips. He closed his palm to guard its memory. *No, she hadn't verbally agreed to see him tonight*. But the consent of her body fueled his desperate hope that he had not lost her—not forever.

Chapter Fifteen

PHILLIP PRESSED THE doorbell and waited, reflecting on how many times he had arrived at her house…*Had it really been all for business? Or had he used business as his excuse to spend time with her?*

His mind waited for his subconscious to answer, knowing the truth, and expecting a lie. But he was beyond lying to himself and to her. Tonight, he only wanted to confess everything that he had avoided admitting for the past five years in order to salvage whatever trust and intimacy remained between them.

The house was silent. He hesitated, second-guessing his impulse to ring the doorbell again. Then, fear swept through his heart. She wasn't home at all—or worse, she was intentionally choosing to avoid him.

Abruptly, the door whisked open, but it was not Isabel who greeted him.

"Uhhhhh-ahhhhh," Aidan whined, slumping with disappointment. "You're not the delivery man."

"No," Phillip replied, eyeing the boy's honesty and cruelty. "Do you remember me? I'm a friend of your mother's."

"No, you're not. You're her boss," Aidan corrected him. Phillip peered at the boy, noting his knack for precision and honesty. *Clearly, a genetic gift from his mum.*

"May I still come in?"

"I guess…" Aidan sighed, turning away and abandoning Phillip in the doorway.

"And your mother?" Phillip insisted, peering into the house without fully entering it.

"She's here," Isabel answered coldly, stopping halfway along the staircase, as if she was reluctantly weighing whether or not to tread all the way down to meet him. "We were upstairs, brushing teeth. It's bedtime, you know."

"Yes," he replied, suddenly absorbing the reality of the situation—it was not the most convenient time or place to continue whatever it was he had fantasized about all day. He noted her yoga pants and T-shirt. Her hair was tied up in a casual ponytail, and she was barefoot. He had seen her dressed up like a queen and naked like a mistress, but somehow, none of it mattered because in that moment, the only thing he wanted from her was the simplest thing she could grant him—an invitation to stay.

"Well, perhaps it's too late then to offer this…" Phillip withdrew a sleek red bag from behind his back and passed it off to Aidan.

"Mommy, hot chocolate!" He presented it to his mother like a prize.

"Dark truffle chocolate," Phillip confirmed. "Your mum's favorite."

He fixed his eyes on her, wondering if it would be enough to lure her down the staircase. Phillip had learned early on that it wasn't tea or coffee that powered Isabel throughout the day—it was several mugs of gourmet hot chocolate, especially during Chicago's long bitter winters.

"Aidan, we *just* finished brushing teeth."

"Pleeeeeeeeease, Mommy. Pleeeeeeeease."

Isabel sighed, annoyed and exasperated, as she drifted down the stairs. "It might be Mommy's favorite, Phillip, but clearly you've never given sugar to a child before bedtime."

The comment cut into Phillip more than he was willing to admit. He paused and guarded his instinct to correct her. "No, I admit to never having the pleasure." He noted the sound of his own voice, wounded and raspy. When he glanced back up at her, he saw her ice queen persona thawing into an expression of uncertainty.

"Mommy, pleeeeeease…just one cup." Aidan rushed to his mother and tugged on her hand.

"I see he's already quite the masterful negotiator," Phillip said.

"Yes…like most of the men in my life."

She sat down on the final step and held Aidan's chin to meet her eyes. "Fine, but only one—one cup," she insisted. "One."

"Yes!" Aidan exclaimed, celebrating with an awkward jumping jack and turning to Phillip like a winning teammate. "Did you hear that? She said we could have one cup!"

"Sounds lovely." Phillip smirked, resting his gaze onto Isabel. He knew that look. He had seen it a hundred times before whenever they clashed over work issues. It was the look of begrudging concession. Whenever they had a disagreement at the office, Phillip rarely lost, not because he was her boss, but because he was more skilled at finding the pressure point that persuaded her to surrender. Now, they both silently acknowledged that he had scored the loyalty of her son. But still, he needed her permission to stay.

"You'll be forced to clean your own mug," Isabel said flatly.

"And put it in the dishwasher," Aidan chimed in, reiterating a rule that he had clearly been reminded of a thousand times before. "Mommy hates it when we leave dirty dishes on the countertop."

"No dirty dishes." Phillip nodded with quiet gratitude.

She gazed at him with resistance. Her eyes conveyed what he knew she always wanted him to know—*he had won this time, but don't expect such an easy win the next time.*

Isabel followed Aidan through the kitchen's swinging door.

"And no putting your feet on the table," Aidan suddenly called back to Phillip.

"Really?" Phillip stopped and feigned shock. "No putting my feet upon the table?"

"No," Aidan wagged his finger. "It's very bad manners and it makes Mommy very angry."

"Well, we shan't make your mother cross, so I shall be sure to keep my feet to myself. In fact, I'm certain that's one way I can make her happy..."

Suddenly, the sight of something on the kitchen countertop—something familiar and scarring—jarred him into silence and dashed their camaraderie.

"Even if, perhaps, there are very few other ways..." His voice trailed off as he approached the bouquet of Watercross' long-stemmed red roses and noted their freshness, perfectly preserved with diligence and care.

He lowered his eyes and internally retreated, attempting to quell the bleeding fear that he had made another critical error in judgment. Perhaps her acceptance of a position with Watercross Capital wasn't merely a punishment against him for his deception; perhaps it was simply an indication of her own preferences and desires. Perhaps she had already made her choice. *And her choice was not him.*

"My mother's been taking care of them," Isabel said, observing his sudden frown. "She loves flowers, and we rarely have them here at the house, so she's been committed to changing their water twice a day."

"Of course," he said slowly, taking in the number of place settings that Isabel had set at the kitchen table. *Three.*

"Here, let me hang up your coat," she offered, holding out her hand to him.

He nodded and removed it like a burden, feeling the weight and constraints of his professional identity slipping off him. Isabel accepted it and disappeared from the kitchen. He loosened his tie and sat down next to Aidan at the table.

"That's a vampire's coat," Aidan stated with conviction.

"Really, a vampire? I always thought it was more like the monster in *Frankenstein*."

Phillip suddenly outstretched his hands, gaped open his mouth, and growled his best monster impression.

Aidan slapped his forehead. "That is reeeee-diculous."

"It is," Phillip whispered to him like a guarded secret as Isabel passed back into the kitchen.

"Are you boys behaving?" She eyed them, moving to the stove and stirring the milk in the saucepan. She turned off the gas and distributed it between the three mugs.

"We were just discussing the best way to catch a tiger in the jungle." Phillip winked at Aidan.

The boy's eyes lit up. "You've caught a tiger?"

"Not one. Three."

Isabel narrowed her gaze at Phillip, as if she was trying to assess which part of his claim was true. She served the three mugs onto the placemats and moved the can of hot chocolate into the center of the table. Aidan lifted to his knees, scooped up a spoonful, and dumped it into his mug. "Did they try to bite you?" he asked Phillip.

"Oh, yes…of course." He unfastened his cuff link and rolled up the sleeve of his shirt. He watched as Isabel scanned the searing pink scar along his forearm. He twisted his wrist, allowing his veins and muscles to bulge through his disfigured skin. Sometimes, he still felt the phantom burn from the boating accident about which he rarely spoke, and tried hard not to remember.

"Whoaaaaaa," Aidan said with amazement, lifting up to his knees for a closer inspection of his injury. "Look at that, Mommy."

Phillip shifted his glance onto Isabel with a small smile. For a moment, he wondered if she believed him. Then, like an overwhelming flashback, he remembered the sensation of her fingers, running curiously over the scar's jagged imprint during their passionate nights within the darkness. Their eyes locked. *She remembered it, too.*

Isabel turned away to the counter. Phillip cleared his throat and rolled down his sleeve.

"Tigers don't like to be surprised. You have to lure them in with bait."

"That sounds a bit unfair to the tiger," Isabel cut in, tossing the pan into the sink, drowning it with spraying water.

"Yes, perhaps it is. But tigers are quite independent. You can't just expect them to accept your advances from the beginning without some enticement."

"Maybe the tiger would simply prefer to be asked into the cage."

"And what if she refused?"

"She most certainly would have…and should have." Isabel shut off the faucet.

"She sounds like a smart tiger," Phillip conceded.

"Mommy, can we catch a tiger and keep it as a pet?"

"No, tigers are meant to roam free, not be trapped for a hunter's selfish gain."

Aidan ignored her and turned to Phillip for support. "I think we should catch it with a net and then put it in a cage with a gorilla."

"The poor gorilla would certainly be the unfortunate one," Phillip replied.

Aidan shrugged. "Yeah, but maybe they'd become friends?"

"I'd like to think so." He sipped from his hot chocolate, admiring the boy's innocence. "But I'm fairly certain the tiger wouldn't have him."

"Yeah—" Aidan cut in with serious thought and consideration. "I think I've changed my mind. I don't want a pet gorilla. Or a pet tiger. I want an anaconda."

Isabel shivered. Phillip remembered how much she hated snakes.

"Okay, that's enough scary, forest creature talk for one night. It's bedtime." She glanced up at the wall clock, signaling the end of the night—and the end of Phillip's visit.

He peered at her, understanding her impatience. *She was a mum, and that was her priority now.*

"Yes." He nodded, accepting her dismissal. He slowly rose from the table, trying not to reveal his disappointment. It had been a lovely moment of escape from the tension of the day—and the tension between them.

"But we haven't even had a chance to eat chocolate chip cookies," Aidan insisted, determined to prolong the night.

Phillip glanced down on the child, sympathizing with his perseverance.

"Aidan, we are *not* having chocolate chip cookies."

"Ugggghhhhhh," Aidan slouched and whined through his nose. "Well, it's not fair because I can't go to sleep now."

"And why not?"

"Because I'm too scared."

"Scared?" Isabel laughed. "Of what?"

Aidan smiled bashfully, like it was the only answer that came to mind. "Tigers?"

"Oh, I see…well, that's a good thing to be scared of because there are no tigers in the house, and certainly none in your bedroom. Now, let's go upstairs."

Isabel ushered him out through the swinging door and back into the living room.

"I have an idea!" Aidan cried out, stalling like a pro. "Mommy, let's sleep down here tonight." Aidan catapulted himself onto the sofa like it was a familiar negotiation. Phillip noted her laptop on the coffee table. He suddenly wondered how many nights over the years she had sat at that coffee table, working late into the evening while her son slept nearby on the couch.

"Maybe you can even spend the night, too," he offered to Phillip. "You can use my Batman sleeping bag. You know, if you want to?"

"I love Batman," Phillip replied.

Isabel shot him a stinging glare.

"Please, Mommy…Can we sleep down here tonight?"

"You—yes. Phillip—no, absolutely not. Go get your pillow and blanket. Quickly." She added an edge to her voice that spurred Aidan up the stairs.

Phillip watched the boy scamper up to the landing and disappear into his bedroom. He stared at Isabel. She stared back. An awkward silence fell between them. He had fifteen, maybe twenty seconds, to express something that could alter their destinies; but instead, his voice froze into haunting silence until she was the first to break away from their mutual gaze.

"I'll get your coat."

Phillip swallowed hard, resisting his urge to capture her hand. But the moment was lost when Aidan reappeared on the top of the landing and called down through the banister. "Was I fast enough, Mommy?" He scampered down the stairs with excitement, dragging his blanket behind him.

"Don't be so fast that you trip and fall down the stairs," she cautioned him while handing off Phillip's coat. Then, she took up Aidan's blanket off the floor and into her arms. "Where's your pillow?"

"Ugh!" Aidan slapped his forehead. "I forgot it." He started up the stairs again, but she secured him in her arms.

"No… Stop running around. Stay here and calm down. I'll go and get it. Say goodnight to Phillip."

"You're leaving?" Aidan asked him.

Phillip watched Isabel trudge up the staircase. "Yes, I believe so."

Aidan kicked the floor with disappointment. "Is that your monster coat?"

"Yes," Phillip nodded, slipping it on. "How do I look?" He outstretched his hands, set his jaw into an overbite, and moaned with menace.

Aidan giggled and spun away. "I think you look silly."

"I'm certain you're right."

"Are you sure you can't spend the night?"

Phillip glanced upstairs. "No, I don't think that's possible. Your mother needs her rest."

"Yeah, she's pretty sad. She cries a lot now."

Phillip eyed the boy. "What do you mean?"

Aidan shrugged. "She says it's her allergies."

"Okay, here it is—" Isabel called across the banister, waving Aidan's pillow. Phillip fixed his eyes on her. With her ponytail swinging side to side, she bounced down the plush white carpet like a teenager. *Bare feet and yoga pants*, he noted. *She seemed so carefree and happy.* Obviously, she had perfected the art of repressing her emotions as well as he had.

Aidan dove onto the couch and nestled into its cushions while his mother tucked him in. "Mommy," he whispered. "I asked Phillip if he wanted to stay and spend the night. But he said you need to rest."

"*You* need to rest," she insisted, kissing her son's forehead. "And yes, it's time for Phillip to go now."

"Can he come back and play another time?"

"No, I don't think so."

Phillip stared at her, absorbing the finality of her words.

"Then, this shall be our final good-bye?" he said, testing her.

She nodded. "Yes, I think so."

"It's a pity. After so many years of allegiance between us." He heard his own voice drop into bitterness.

She glared at him, recognizing his signature tone of displeasure. The expression on her face changed from hesitation to confrontation.

"Phillip, the fact of the matter is that it doesn't matter now. We cannot go backwards and we cannot go forwards."

"You say that as if you feel you are trapped."

"I am trapped, Phillip," she asserted, anger and resentment simmering just below her voice. "You were my boss. I was your assistant. I took great pride in that work—in working for you. And now…"

She stopped, but he pressed her. "And now?"

She lowered her gaze, collecting her words and thoughts. "And now…regardless of whatever was expressed in our moments of…weakness…I cannot continue to come into the office every day and stand before you as both your assistant and your lover. I'm sorry, Phillip. But you know that, too, because that is the truth."

He did know it, but her brutal honesty hit him harder than when he had endured her physical slap. From the very beginning, he sensed that she was not the sort of woman who would allow him to ever be more than her boss, and it was a fact that he admired like a virtue, and spurned like a prison sentence.

"So my loss is Eliot Watercross' gain," he said flatly, edging towards the door.

He had consciously avoided the topic all night, but now, in their final moments of candor and conflict, there was no reason to refrain from acknowledging the salted wound. The next time Phillip would see her, it would be during an opening night gala hosted by one of their mutual business colleagues, where he would be forced to graciously pretend that he had accepted Isabel's departure from his firm and publicly act as though she had meant nothing to him beyond the disposable relationship of a former employee.

"Phillip—" she said like a command, keeping him there rather than pushing him away. "It's true that Eliot has offered me a position as a business partner in his newest venture. But it wasn't true what I told you this morning. I haven't officially accepted his offer—yet."

He gazed at her, waiting for her to confirm what he feared most. "And will you?"

She held his gaze without betraying anything other than her silent strength.

Unexpectedly, Aidan's snoring interrupted them. It transformed itself into a sonorous wheeze that only a child could make sound endearing. Amused, Phillip peered at her. She ignored him, attempting to hold her ground without conceding anything to him until Aidan's snoring grew guttural, grossly offensive, and even comical.

"That's a brilliant trait," Phillip quipped. "Being able to fall asleep in the middle of an argument."

Finally, he registered her resistant smile, as if she was unable to ignore the innocence of her own flesh and blood. She circled around the couch to adjust Aidan's head on the pillow. He closed his mouth and rolled away, blissfully silent.

"It's the same almost every night," she said, gazing down upon him. "He's grown used to sleeping down here on the couch while I work late. He doesn't want to fall asleep upstairs in his own bed if I'm not up there with him. I used to be able to carry him up the stairs without waking him. But not anymore."

She lifted her laptop from the coffee table and pushed it back against the fireplace mantel. "I've learned that the best thing I can do is wear earplugs and grow fond of sleeping on the floor." She pulled off a folded quilt from the adjacent sofa chair and spread it across the carpet. When she shut off the lamp, it cast deep shadows across Aidan's face. She stopped and gazed down at her son, indulging in a moment of reflection.

"He has such long legs now. He gets them from his father. His height and his persistence. I used to look at him at night, when he was sleeping so quietly like that, and see the resemblance of the man who broke my heart. Now, I look at him and wonder if tomorrow will be the day when having only a mother won't be enough."

Phillip suddenly realized he had never asked Isabel about Aidan's father. "Does he know him?"

She shook her head. "No, not at all. He didn't want a baby. I didn't want an abortion. It's been more than four years since we've last seen or spoken to each other, but I still have his email address. I send pictures occasionally, but I never get a response—not even when Aidan was born."

"I didn't realize..." Phillip whispered.

Isabel looked away, flopping down a sofa pillow onto the floor. "It's fine because Aidan's fine, and the only thing I care about is his happiness." She paused, choosing her words carefully. "And you've helped me with that, Phillip. You gave me a job when no one else would, and the chance to provide Aidan with more than I ever thought possible. I will always be grateful to you for that. Always."

She stared at him—a confessional moment of gratitude that softened her frown and reminded him of so many times when they had found a way to understand each other through their unspoken connection.

Like a jolting reflex, Aidan kicked his leg, almost pushing himself off the edge of the couch. Isabel rushed forward, barely securing him in place. Phillip intervened and swept up the boy into his arms.

"Come now," he urged her. "Let's get him upstairs and into bed."

Gathering up Aidan's pillow and blanket, Isabel led them up the staircase and into Aidan's bedroom. Pushing past fire trucks and race cars littering the floor, Phillip navigated through the shadows and gently laid him down in his bed. He traded places with Isabel who tucked the blankets over her son with a final kiss goodnight.

She followed Phillip out of the room, shutting the door behind them. They both paused without movement, listening for the sound of stirring beyond Aidan's door. But there was nothing except heavy silence within the empty house.

Phillip gazed at her. She smiled, acknowledging their cooperative success. Then she turned away, preparing to lead them down the stairs until Phillip clasped her hand and drew her towards him.

"Isabel…" He said her name like a plea for their reconciliation. Then, he fell silent and waited, not for her response of encouragement, but rather for his own courage to push him forward—whatever the cost to his pride.

"Phillip…" she said softly, not with censure, but with a simple petition for him to remain silent. Moonlight streamed in through the bathroom window, reflecting off its vanity mirror and illuminating the indecipherable expression on her face.

But he could no longer remain silent. He had remained silent for five long years. Tonight was his final chance to betray the deepest, most painful secrets within his soul. And he would never forgive himself if he left her house without openly confessing what had always been present within his heart.

"If I have caused you pain or shame because of my actions, then I want nothing more than for you to know that I am truly sorry. But you must know, Isabel…you must be made aware that this distance…this distance between us I cannot endure."

He dropped his gaze, suddenly unable to face the consequences of his confession.

"And it is this distance that I feared all along if I openly admitted my affection for you, and yes…in that way, it was fear that perpetuated our lie—as you call it. But this distance, Isabel…this distance between us is rotting my soul because it is denying me the pleasure of one of the most sacred relationships in my life."

"Phillip—" she petitioned him again, tugging back on his hand.

But he would not relent—not until he had properly expressed in words what he had attempted to express through his passionate seduction of her.

"You claim that I am merely your boss and you are my assistant, but that, too, is a lie. Because when I look at you…when I look at you now, I do not see my assistant or even my temptress. I only see a woman who has graciously endured my selfish pride for years without challenging my surly attempts to remain closed off from her—and the rest of the world. I see a mother who has struggled to provide for her family through her dedication to her work, which often resulted in the sacrifice of hours and hours of her time because of the professional demands that I placed upon her. And I see a woman who has offered me her loyalty—every day for the past five years. A woman who I cannot bear to live without…"

He paused as if he could barely speak the words. "For the past five years, I have been sick with longing…longing to express my deepest devotion to you, all the while knowing that in doing so, I risked losing you completely."

He did not dare raise his eyes to meet her own. He simply focused on the subtle change in her body and the way her hand reluctantly relaxed in his grasp.

"If you truly regret everything that has transpired between us, then I will agree to pretend that it was nothing more than an unfortunate lapse in our judgment for which I must pay the ultimate price. But if some small part of you feels that there is something more between us—more than just the professional admiration between a boss and his assistant—then we have a duty to ourselves to explore it rather than simply abandoning it."

He finally found the courage to fix his eyes on her, like a man who was searching out the merits of his own soul within her acceptance or rejection of him. "Please, Isabel. Please do not deny us that." He stared at her with an intensity that mirrored the full force of his emotions. She did not avert her eyes or reject his gaze.

"You were only surly when you didn't get want you wanted," she unexpectedly whispered.

"And I cannot promise that I will ever change," he whispered back, sensing the absence of tension between them. "But for you, I shall strive to be a better man."

His gaze lingered on her as he reached out to stroke her cheek. She closed her eyes and leaned into his touch. For a silent, penetrating moment, their hearts were united. Then, she enveloped his hand and nudged him forward, leading him down the hallway and through a door. He stopped on the threshold and surveyed the modest bedroom—a queen bed crowded into the corner near the window, decorated with simple ivory shades knotted at their ends with a silver loop. There was a small dressing table, cluttered with personal items: hair brushes, makeup, tissue paper, and something unexpectedly familiar—the swan Chihuly vase, *his* first gift to her, and a single pink rose, dried and withered with nostalgia.

He stared at the vase and dried stem, then glanced at her. "You kept it?"

"I meant what I said at the gala. I was never truly sure," she admitted, lowering her voice. "And after our first night together—one of the most intimate nights of my life—I tried so hard to convince myself that it wasn't you because I didn't want to endure the risk of everything coming to an end."

It was a confession of her own, and he suddenly realized she had invited him into the most vulnerable space within her heart without restrictions or expectations.

"It doesn't have to end," he whispered through the darkness.

This time it was she who reached out to him, encouraging him to slip off his heavy trench coat before opening a drawer of her dresser and draping it across it. She lifted his hands, unfastened his diamond cuff links from his shirt, and set them aside on the corner of her dressing table. Slowly, she turned back to him, undoing the tortoise shell buttons along his neckline. *How many times had he imagined her undressing him? Too many to admit.* But he could never have imagined this feeling of serenity as he submitted himself to her, savoring the sensitive tug of her fingers against his chest that eventually brushed back the folds of his shirt, exposing his bare chest to the caress of her fingertips.

Carefully, he drew her closer, narrowing the separation between them, and folded himself against her shoulder like he was seeking out her forgiveness.

"Even when I was engaged, I only ever thought of you," he confessed, exhaling his burden into her neck as she consoled him, running her fingertips through his hair. It was, perhaps, his most shameful secret—using Marlow as his sexual surrogate to enact his forbidden fantasies for Isabel. Beneath the superficial emptiness of their relationship and the depths of his imagination, Marlow's height and stature, the length and color of her hair, the clothes he bought her to wear, all served as reminders of Isabel. Even her perfume—misty rain with a hint of lavender—was a fragrance that Phillip deliberately purchased for Marlow to mimic Isabel's scent. It had been an oppressive sin, one that filled him with bitterness and threatened to destroy his pride as a man and the integrity of his soul unless he called off their engagement and ended his fraud.

He had ended it, painfully, mercilessly, abandoning Marlow like a fragile snowflake caught up in the cruel winds of winter. It had been dishonorable and selfish, and he took full responsibility for perpetuating the myth of their engagement when she confronted him with the truth of what she had begun to suspect—that she was merely a proxy for the real woman who he craved with every thought and desire, but who he feared would never accept his desire for her.

Now, he closed his eyes and heaved a sigh—an emotional release of all the fear and heartache that had weighed on his every glance and gesture like punishing chains. *The tenderness of her body. The warmth of her breath. The supple curves of her breasts pressing against his heart. Her acceptance.* He had always been the one in control, forcing her surrender. But in that moment, it was she who was the one in control of liberating him.

She gently stroked his hair, as though she was absolving him of years of internal deception. He met her gaze, restraining his instinct to overpower her as a means of asserting his masculine pride. *He had done that so many times before…*Now, he wanted nothing more than to prove to her that he was finally willing to submit himself openly, honestly, because it was she who was the only person in the world who knew him—truly knew him—and still accepted him despite all his flaws and all his mistakes.

He concentrated on the sensation of her hands following the curve of his pecs. Fixing her dark eyes on him—those beautiful Spanish eyes—she sensed his deference to her lead, as though she was taking in the vulnerability of the new man who stood before her. She clasped the edges of her T-shirt and slipped it over her elbows and head, revealing her bare chest in the moonlight. There was no bra or corset to escalate his forbidden fantasy. There were only the natural contours of her breasts and the acceleration of her breath. He held her gaze—a gesture of honor—and reached out to her, drawing down her ponytail and catching the familiar scent of shampoo in her long hair. She guided his hand over her heart, allowing him to massage her. He exhaled with force—an act of restraint. During their previous nights of passion, he had dominated her like a vixen, suckling her tits as an expression of his insatiable desire. But now, everything was different as he watched her fully accepting his caresses, her steady gaze matching his own, granting him a boundless view into the depths of her soul—and everything about her that she was willing to offer him.

She loosened the buckle of his belt and tugged it through its loop holes before dropping it onto the floor like a clanking chain. He felt the tug of his zipper, drawing downwards across his throbbing erection. He clenched his jaw, enduring his swelling desires as her fingers grazed against it. Cautiously, she grasped the silk fabric of his dress pants and tugged them downwards, the sensual tickle of her nipples passing across his erection as she lowered herself and removed each pant leg. Then, he felt it—her lips deliberately kissing the tip of his erection, bulging through his boxers, before she drew them down, exposing his hard cock completely. He touched her hair, guarding his primal instincts and refraining from guiding her to take in more. Tonight wasn't about her pleasuring him. It was about him surrendering every aspect of his pride and masculinity to her, allowing her to accept them on her terms and in her own way.

She rose up and peered into his eyes. The serenity of the moonlight captured their unspoken exchange. Like an offering, she drew down her yoga pants and white cotton panties, matching his nakedness. There, face-to-face, she permitted him a long, lingering view of her body. During their sessions of passion, consumed by their charades and shrouded in darkness, it was a luxury he had not even granted himself; now, he was certain she was the most beautiful, authentic thing he had ever seen. He pushed forward and kissed the edges of her athletic shoulders. *Always asserting her independence.* His fingertips drifted across the soft curve of her midriff. *The sacrifice of being a mother.* His hands passed along the smooth contours of her backside. *The femininity of being a woman.*

He heard her sigh, savoring his touch. He had admired her physical beauty a thousand times before, but always at a distance—from across his desk, across the dinner table, across the seats of his car—never like this, never completely naked and vulnerable with the assurance that he would be accepted by her. Finally, like a silent answer to his petitioning gaze, he felt her full consent as she rotated her pelvis towards him, allowing his firm cock to brush against her sex and test her willingness for more. He buried his hot breath into the sensitive crook of her collarbone and kissed its tenderness with all his strength. He could feel her relinquishing her defenses, accepting his need to devour her with every nip. He feathered his lips up her throat, stopping short of covering her mouth with his own. He hadn't kissed her since their final night together in the mansion—but that was a moment of intimacy cloaked within secrecy and darkness. Now, he gazed into her shining eyes, confirming not only her desire for him in that moment, but the sincerity of her desire all along to be more to him than just his assistant.

He held her cheek and nudged her for a kiss, softly, gently. She accepted him, sweet and forgiving, as her velvet tongue entangled with his own, fueling his need to surge inside her. *How different she felt*...different than all their previous nights together when every touch and gesture served to lure her into his maze of seduction. Tonight, there was no undercurrent of apprehension holding her back from fully accepting his pleasuring mouth and massaging hands. There was only her willingness to share herself with him. She shuddered with anticipation as he sucked her nipples and cupped her backside. She exhaled as he ran his mouth along her throat, lapping her with his tongue, coaxing the rotation of her pelvis into his burning cock.

There, yes...He released a sigh, feeling her wetness, inviting him into her. Swiftly, he whisked her up into his arms and spread her across the bed, smothering her nakedness under his weight and edging his cock between her thighs. She raised her chin and gasped, pushing back on his imminent breach. But he tamed her, passing his hand under her hair, clenching it with a delicate balance between possession and tenderness, asserting his desire to pleasure her. His fingers slipped around her backside and stroked her slit; she gushed her consent like a gift and relaxed into his embrace. He secured her body into his arms, exhaling hushes of comfort into her ear before initiating his first penetration.

Yeeesss...

They traded groans and quivers of relief as he pushed past the friction and held himself steady inside her. *God, how often he yearned to feel her body like this*... The softness of her breasts and midriff, the caress of her fingertips along the nape of his neck, the warmth of her breath against his shoulder, the slickness of her arousal against his throbbing cock. Every part of her sensuality cured his isolation and soothed his bitterness. Within the darkness of the mansion, he had pushed into her with unyielding desire, determined to release his unbearable repression through his sexual conquest of her. But now, within the intimacy of her own bed, he savored their connection, gazing at her with the full intensity of his soul. He was no longer her billionaire boss; he was only a man desperate to make love to her.

"I need you more than you can ever know," he whispered.

"You have always had me."

He entangled her hand and drew it over her head, lowering his lips over her tits, stimulating her with the heat and suction of his mouth. He ground himself against her clit, watching her expression slacken as a sparking wave of arousal built up between them. He kissed her mouth with worship; their tongues melded together like their exchanging breaths. Bracing her backside, he shifted himself deeper. She moaned, an invitation for more. He thumbed her clit, heightening her arousal while accelerating his pace, and calmed her fragile sighs with whispers of adoration. Her tongue swept into his ear, yearning for him to complete her.

He accelerated his pace. *Harder, faster, deeper*. She shut her eyes and tilted back her head, seeking relief from his plunging cock. Her first shudder made her cry out for restraint. He relented and hushed her with affection, absorbing her heat and slickness as ripples of satisfaction ebbed and flowed between them. He cradled her head and petitioned for her consent for more.

Now...?

*Yeesss...*She nodded, digging her fingernails into his shoulder as he pushed deeper, uniting them like familiar lovers. *How many nights had he longed to unify them like this...*She was no longer simply his sinful temptation; she was his companion. *How many times had she looked at him and made him feel like the man he wanted to be*? Every day she had unknowingly challenged him at every turn with her own honesty—a sincerity that weakened his icy facade as her stern boss and slowly revealed an imprisoned man, struggling to accept the feelings of vulnerability and fondness she inspired within him.

She gasped, releasing her second shudder as his rhythm intensified, mimicking the coursing pulse beating within his heart. She quivered with every tremor, yielding herself to the escalating vibrations he produced with every thrust. He buried his exhale into her ear as his own climax threatened to surge beyond his ability to contain it. But he wanted to wait for her; he wanted to complete her.

He drew her up from the bed, straddling her over his lap and wrapping her legs around his waist like a hug, and replaced his cock with his fingers. He slipped past her wetness, fingering her deeply, building her up with fierce palpitating strokes that aimed to satisfy her very core. Her head dropped back with a silent exhale as she relinquished herself to him through her unconditional trust. *Trust.* It was a gift that he did not take for granted.

Yes, that's it...

He encouraged her with every beating stroke and ceased only to shift her off his lap and lower his lips down to taste her. His tongue flicked her with precision, unleashing her unguarded sigh of satisfaction that he had come to know so well.

She was ready for him.

Slowly, he laid her down across the bed, enveloping her body. She exhaled, embracing his chest as he united them with his burning desire. He drove deeper, muting her moans with his consuming kisses and trading breaths like they were sharing each other's deepest secrets. When he ran his mouth along her neck, her staccato panting grazed against his ear like a rhythmic chant for *more, more, more...* He cupped her backside and spread her wider, thrusting himself into her until it was too much for him to bear. He groaned, surging within her, and rode them together towards a shuddering apex of relief that radiated throughout their bodies and ended with her unbridled release. He braced her torso, absorbing her climax while simultaneously coursing inside her, his warmth and wetness mimicking her own until she fell forward against him. Her head and arms draped over his shoulders for support. He would always support her—no matter what.

I've fallen in love with you, Isabel.

The sentiment escaped from his heart as he guided her down onto the bed and molded their bodies together like two souls entwining into one. Every moment of every day, she had made him yearn to express his emotions of affection and adoration—emotions that only she inspired in him. Now, everything had been released, and he was left with only one certainty that consoled and fulfilled him—*she completed him.*

Chapter Sixteen

ISABEL ROLLED OVER in her bed, roused by the rays of sunlight across her face. She squinted and shielded her eyes until she could focus on Phillip's glinting gaze and register the fact that he had been watching her.

"Good morning," he said, as if it was the most natural thing in the world, waking up next to his former assistant in her own bed.

"How long have you been awake?" She drew the sheet over her naked body, absorbing the reality of what they had shared last night.

"Over an hour." He shrugged without apology. "I wanted to see if you were a snoozer or a drooler—or both." He shifted closer, attempting to wrap his arms around her waist.

"Neither." She nudged him away, feigning offense. He smirked and drew her into his possession, whispering a kiss behind her ear.

"Neither," he agreed. "You're perfect…even when you're asleep."

"You'll soon learn that's not true either."

"I can't wait," he mused, locking her into his strong arms and pulling her down against the pillows.

"Phillip—" She faintly resisted him as he fluttered his lips down her throat and across her breasts. "We have to be careful. Aidan will be up any moment and he'll come looking for me."

He relented and flopped back against the mattress, flexing his bicep behind his head while tracking her escape from the bed. She quickly slipped on her T-shirt and white panties, sensing how his eyes tracked her every movement like so many times before. But this time, she silently admitted to herself how much she secretly enjoyed it. So many times during their business meetings, she had noted to herself how attractive he looked in his tailored European suits without ever granting herself the permission to indulge in the thought. Now, as she slipped on her yoga pants and tied up her hair, she glanced back at his sculpted shoulders and smooth chest, unable to ignore the vision of him—naked and relaxed—beneath the sheets of her own bed. *Her boss—Phillip Spears.* It was both the most natural and surreal things in the world. Last night, he had offered himself to her with such tenderness that it was impossible to resist resolving the tension between them. And when he touched her...*God, how he touched her...*he lowered all her defenses and dissolved all the fear within her heart before making love her in a way that made her believe every expression of his devotion had been true.

But was it love?

She barely dared to repeat the word in her mind. It had been a long time since Isabel had been in love—an experience that ended in the birth of her son and the devastation of her heart. *Was she ready to open herself up to being loved again?* She wasn't certain, but she no longer could deny her feelings for the man who had offered her sanctuary when she needed it most. The man she had spent time with almost every day for the past five years. The man she had grown to know and respect more than anyone else in her life.

"It's a shame it's ending already," he said, noting how quickly she had dressed, transforming herself into the presentable mother he knew she had to be.

"It's not just me," she countered, eyeing the way he leisurely reclined in her bed. "It's a work day for you as well."

"Except I've lost my best, most desirable employee," Phillip replied. "You clearly have no idea how seeing you every morning served as my own personal motivation to come into the office."

His despondent gaze fixed on her, revealing distress that only she could relieve. She sat down on the edge of the bed and ran her fingers through his tousled hair. His expression of vulnerability disarmed her. *He seemed like such a different man now.* The phantom nips along her flesh and the burn between her legs were the physical reminders of his willingness to prove himself to her, but now, it was the way that he wrapped his arms around her waist and watched her—watching him—that made her feel like she had discovered a new uninhibited man beneath the formerly stern, cautious one.

"And now, this morning, I have the pleasure of seeing you without having to go into the office, which is why it's such a pity that it's ending already." He leaned in closer, nudging her for a sensual kiss within the security of his protective embrace. *She could no longer resist him—any part of him.* His desire would be forever seared within her. She kissed him back, reliving the sensations of how deeply he drove inside her with his need to claim her heart.

"Isabel—"

She heard her name called out beyond her bedroom door. *Her mother.* Mrs. Alvarez abruptly whisked it open and entered the room like it was her own.

Halting in the doorway, she frowned at her daughter—and her daughter's half-naked guest.

"Good morning, Mother," Isabel said, rising from the bed and adjusting her ponytail.

An unforgiving ray of sunlight fell across the lovers like a jailhouse spotlight. Mrs. Alvarez's silent disapproval seethed through the deep creases along her furrowed brow. She moved like a maid to the window, unclasping the knots of the shades and diffusing the sunlight through the sheer curtains, cutting off the harsh reflection along Phillip's smooth bare chest.

"Good morning, Mrs. Alvarez." He nodded, perfectly pronouncing her last name with its proper Castilian accent.

Mrs. Alvarez arched her eyebrow, surveying the full scene of their debauchery.

He gazed at her with mischievous glee in his eye, like a rebellious teenager who almost enjoyed being caught in the act.

"Aidan is downstairs with me," Mrs. Alvarez said slowly. "We are making pancakes. I will tell him that you will be down…shortly."

She shifted her censure to her daughter, who deflected it with her own glare. Mrs. Alvarez exhaled through her flaring nostrils, as if she had seen everything she needed to make her ultimate judgment. Then, with a ferocious slam, she shut the door behind her, conveying an unmistakable message.

Isabel sunk onto the edge of the bed and held her head. "She makes me feel like a teenager in my own home."

"That sounds sinfully devious," Phillip joked and kissed her behind her ear.

"It's been this way ever since I dropped out of college, pregnant with Aidan. It doesn't matter that since then, I've given her a beautiful grandson, a wonderful home, and a life free of the physical hardships that she endured when she was cleaning houses. It only matters that I somehow continue to disappoint her."

He gently traced his finger around her elbow and along the curve of her wrist before taking her hand into his own.

"Isabel, they are our parents. They are hard on us because they have come to realize—like we have—that they have very little control over our lives, including who we choose to become and what we ultimately achieve…and that lack of control terrifies them."

Isabel stopped and reflected on the fact that Phillip had attended the funeral of his own mother not less than a year ago. She knew very little about

Phillip's relationship with his mother, but when he had returned from England after her death, she sensed that he had buried a part of himself there with her.

"It's just that I don't want that for Aidan. I want him to know that I'll always support him in whatever he wants to do or be—no matter what."

Skeptical, Phillip narrowed his eyes at her. "Isabel, your son is four going on five. I will be sure to remind you of those precise words when he is fourteen going on fifteen and he arrives home with a piercing through his nose and the name of his girlfriend tattooed across his buttocks."

Isabel crossed her arms and shifted away. He laughed and embraced her with all his strength.

"You're going to be around ten years from now to remind me of that?" she tossed back.

"Yes," he answered with quiet conviction.

Isabel stared into his sparkling eyes and noted the way he cradled her with certainty. "Well, we'll have to see about that," she replied dryly, testing him and her own expectations for their future—together.

But he knew her now; she needed his unguarded expression of commitment as much as he needed her acceptance of it. He locked her in his arms, unwilling to let her go. "I always love a good challenge." He stared deeply into her eyes in a way that declared he had all the time in the world and desired nothing more than the honor of spending it with her.

"Come on, now…let's go get some pancakes."

* * * *

Everyone sat around the kitchen table in silence, except Aidan, who was thrilled at the idea that Phillip had spent the night in the end.

"Nica…Mommy said Phillip wasn't going to sleep over, but he did. Did you sleep in the astronaut sleeping bag or the green alligator one?" he asked Phillip.

Phillip raised his eyebrow at Isabel. "You didn't tell me I had a choice between astronauts and alligators?"

Mrs. Alvarez clanked her coffee mug down onto the table. Isabel glanced down at it. She knew Phillip wasn't used to her mother's silent wrath and her mother wasn't used to Phillip's dry British humor.

"And guess what else, Nica?" Aidan slurred, his mouth stuffed with pancake. "Phillip fought *three* tigers…Show her your scar."

Aidan tugged on Phillip's shirt sleeve. Isabel watched her mother casting her eyes over his half-unbuttoned shirt and wrinkled dress pants, clearly the same clothes he wore from the day before. She shifted her gaze to Phillip, who seemed unfazed by her scrutiny. Instead, he looked relaxed and content. He crossed his legs and wagged his socked foot while sipping from his coffee mug like his presence at the table was the most normal thing in the world.

"Aidan, I'm certain your grandmother prefers that I not remove any more of my clothes."

Isabel nearly sprayed out coffee through her nose.

Mrs. Alvarez narrowed her scornful black eyes and crossed her arms. "Mr. Spears, I know that you are a very important man, and I'm sure you are used to inventing many grand stories to impress all your important wealthy friends. But here, in this house, I much prefer that you not tell lies to my grandson."

"Mother—" Isabel sniped back, but it was too late. Mrs. Alvarez's icy comment settled upon the table like a sudden frost.

"It's not a lie, Nica," Aidan insisted, tugging again on Phillip's sleeve. "Show her, show her…"

Phillip reluctantly set down his fork and rolled up his cuff. Isabel looked away—an entire chunk of his forearm had been sheared off, leaving a jagged absence of flesh, deeply gnarled and unnaturally pink.

Mrs. Alvarez, on the other hand, stared at it without emotion. "Tiger," she mocked under her breath. "To me, it looks more like a motorcycle accident."

"Boating," he clarified respectfully.

"Tiger," she huffed, snorting through her nose. "*Increíble.*"

"Mother," Isabel insisted again, but Phillip silenced her with his gaze.

"Your grandmother is right, Aidan," he announced. "I shouldn't tell you lies. I received this scar not from a tiger, but while working on a fishing boat when I was just a little bit older than you. My family didn't have a lot of money, and so I went to work at the docks where I sailed on ships to earn my worth."

Aidan's green eyes opened wide. "You sailed on boats? Like a pirate?"

"In some ways…yes." Phillip nodded, glancing at Mrs. Alvarez, as if he was preparing for her to challenge him again. "Like a pirate, I sailed far away from home for weeks and weeks at a time, often with very little to eat or drink except stale bread and canned jams. One day, there was a storm—a fierce and terrible storm—and I was thrown overboard. I didn't know how to swim and I still don't. I remember swallowing more water than a whale until—by the grace of God—I felt the slap of the life preserver hit my shoulder. It bounced far away from me, but somehow, I managed to wind its cord around my arm, just before I fell unconscious." Phillip glanced down at his scar. "The scar you see here is from the rope that towed me back to the boat and saved my life."

Isabel stared at Phillip. She had never heard anything about his past except the fact that he had graduated from Harvard Business School—the same year as Jett. Sometimes she *had* noticed small details about him—the way he preferred that she always help him with his tuxedo's bow tie, or the way he used his steak knife like a crude saw, or the fact that he never sent uneaten food away from the table—that made her suspect that he came from a working-class family rather than an affluent life of leisure and luxury. But she never dared to inquire about his upbringing, and Phillip never betrayed anything about his past—until now.

He lifted up a napkin and carefully folded it into an origami boat, setting the gift in front of Aidan. "So you see, we all have secrets and stories to share…even us billionaires."

"Awesome!" Aidan grabbed the boat and held it like a prize. "Can I learn how to be a pirate, too?"

"Yes, perhaps someday you can sail on ships far, far away. But first, you need to learn how to swim." He dotted Aidan's nose with his fingertip.

"Mommy, can I take swimming lessons?"

She started to answer before her mother stood up from the table and cut in.

"Isabel, it's late. Aidan is due at preschool by nine."

"*Awwww*," Aidan whined. "Do I have to go to school today? I want to stay here with Phillip and make more boats." He grabbed another napkin and handed it off to Phillip.

Mrs. Alvarez glared down upon Aidan, taking in his sudden attachment to Phillip. Her accent grew thick with displeasure. "Mr. Spears, I will remind you that this is not just a house where you can casually come and go—but it is a family with many responsibilities."

"Mother—" Isabel cut in. "Phillip may not formally be a part of this family, but he is the main reason we have all benefited."

"Yes, you have been sure to remind me of it on a daily basis," she clucked in return. "Perhaps you are offering him more than necessary."

Isabel felt the heat rise up through her cheeks as her temper flared. It was one thing for her mother to be envious of Phillip's interactions with Aidan. It was another thing entirely for her mother to pass judgment on her private relationship with a man who had proven himself to be so much more to her than simply her boss. She pushed back from the table, preparing to stand in defiance, but stopped when she felt Phillip's hand embracing her own.

"I can assure you, Mrs. Alvarez," Phillip said, his voice dropping low with sincerity, "that I do not plan to come and go casually. I am very much in love with your daughter, and I have no intention of doing anything that would hurt her—or those around her. Delicious pancakes, by the way," he added casually, polishing off the last bites from his plate. "Much better than stale bread and canned jams."

He winked at Mrs. Alvarez, wiping his mouth with a napkin and reclining in his chair, fully satisfied. "Aidan, you're very lucky to have a grandmother who cares enough about you to make you pancakes from scratch."

Aidan slurped down his milk. "And chocolate chip cookies, too." He grinned.

"A rare devotion," Phillip answered.

Mrs. Alvarez's eyes scrutinized Phillip, but the deep wrinkles around her frown finally receded until she simply looked tired and worn. "Come, Aidan…you must go upstairs, brush your teeth, and dress yourself."

"Do I really have to, Mommy?"

"Yes." Isabel answered him with a kiss. "But I will take you to school myself this morning, so Nica will have a chance to have the morning to herself."

"*Cómo quieras*," Mrs. Alvarez huffed, then shrugged as if nothing mattered to her. "*Ven aquí*, Aidan. You must come now." She ushered him towards the kitchen's swinging door.

"If you come back quickly, maybe we can even find your superhero cape and you can wear it to school," Isabel called after him.

"Yes! Superman to the rescue," he cried out, flying away, leading Mrs. Alvarez after him.

An awkward moment of silence fell between Isabel and Phillip.

"I rather like your mum," he casually said, breaking the ice.

"I'm sorry about her comments to you."

"She's protecting her family. It's an admirable thing."

Isabel watched him scrounging up the last morsels of pancake off her plate before reclining in his seat as if it was all part of his new routine.

"Did you mean what you said?"

"Yes, absolutely." He wiped his mouth with his napkin again. "Your mum makes delicious pancakes."

"No, the other part." Isabel glanced down at her hand, as if his expression of love was still imprinted there.

The sharp angles along his face softened as he eyed her uncertainty. Slowly, he tucked a loose strand of hair behind her ear before cupping her cheek. "Yes, I am very much in love with you. And since I have already been reprimanded once by your mother for lying—I'm certainly not brazen enough to attempt lying twice." He leaned in to kiss her with an intimacy that filled her with assurance that he meant every word.

When he was certain she believed him, he slowly pulled away and held her hand like they were an old-fashioned couple enjoying their lazy breakfast. "The good news is that I think your mother is warming up to me."

"You're an optimist," she replied. "But you certainly have a knack for gaining the affection of four-year-old boys."

Phillip hesitated, as though he was unexpectedly disarmed by the comment. "What if I told you I have more experience around children than you might presume?" His question trailed off before he found the courage to look up at her again.

"I'd say I'd want to know more," she answered, treading carefully.

"Good. There's something I want to show you."

Chapter Seventeen

DRESSED IN HIS HEAVY black wool coat, Phillip led Isabel by the hand along the sidewalk of her Gold Coast neighborhood. They headed towards the lakefront as the oak trees swayed overhead with the October breeze. With his nose and cheeks flushed pink and elated that he was skipping preschool in favor of their spontaneous adventure, Aidan gleefully wove his bike behind them.

"Can we do this again tomorrow?" he asked, increasing his speed and shooting off in front of them.

"No, probably not. And don't go too far ahead," Isabel cautioned him.

It was a familiar routine—riding in a loop around their neighborhood and back again. Except this time, Phillip led them across Dearborn Avenue, detouring past their normal route and towards the ritzy historic mansions along Astor Place.

"Where are we going?" Aidan stopped and glanced back at his mother for reassurance.

"To see a haunted house." Phillip nodded ahead, encouraging him forward along the sidewalk.

"Which one is it?" Aidan pedaled ahead with fury.

"That one," Phillip directed him, pointing out the red granite fortress.

Aidan suddenly braked and skidded in front of the familiar mansion. Isabel stared at its broad granite staircase and imposing stone lions. It looked so much more untouchable and threatening in the daylight than in the tempting lure of darkness.

"Don't worry," Phillip said, pulling her forward by the hand. "It's not really haunted."

"You own it?" she asked, trying to reconcile the memory of their night of unbridled passion with the reality of how far they had come in less than a week.

"Yes," he admitted quietly.

"Have you lived this close to us, this whole time?"

"No, I don't live here." He scanned the mansion, his voice husky and remorseful. "Come on, let me show you."

* * * *

Aidan climbed the massive grand foyer stairs like he was hiking up the steps of an amusement park ride. "Mommy, look at this." He slung his leg over the polished banister, preparing to shoot himself down to its end.

"No—" Isabel caught him in the nick of time and pulled him safely back onto the steps. "Let's not start our day with a visit to the emergency room."

"No fair," Aidan whined, racing up the staircase.

She followed him, skating her fingers along the smooth polished wood of the banister, remembering the sensation of ascending its imposing stairs within the darkness. In the purity of daylight, she felt the security of Phillip's presence next to her. Objects that had been previously obscured by shadows glinted now like precious artifacts of opulence—a looming grandfather clock, a mahogany side chair with bear-claw feet, a French giltwood oval mirror, a stag head with majestic antlers. She paused with a shiver, overcome by a strange mixture of anticipation and memory. *Was there the same crackling of the fireplace from the master bedroom?* Instead, she noted the whistling draft and the house's museum silence, and how Phillip directed her away from the master bedroom towards the unfamiliar chamber at the opposite end of the corridor.

Passing ahead of her, he stopped in front of the imposing walnut door and knocked for entrance.

"Ada?" he called quietly. "It's Phillip. May I come in?"

Without warning or explanation, Phillip disappeared into the chamber before emerging again, signaling for Isabel and Aidan to follow him.

"Mommy, are we going to see a ghost in there?"

"I don't think so, honey," she said, hiding her own uncertainty. "Probably just a few dusty beds and hopefully not much else."

"Maybe a tiger?"

Isabel looked down into his earnest green eyes. "Maybe."

She held his hand and led him into the massive room. Sheaths of golden light streamed through arching cathedral windows, offering an unobstructed view of the lakefront from the mansion's second story. Gusting winds rolled waves across the surface of Lake Michigan. Isabel shivered again, as if she could feel the autumn chill rattling the window panes and hear the creaking sound of the house, settling on its foundation. Then, she spotted Phillip, huddled in the corner, partially blocking her view of something—or someone. Standing off to the side, an unfamiliar woman nodded to Isabel and Aidan. She was dressed in a white uniform, blue cardigan sweater, and white tennis shoes. Her inviting smile drew them closer until Isabel saw the unmistakable contours of a young boy supported within an electric wheelchair. His thin arms curved into his body from disuse while his head limply rested against a padded brace. An oxygen mask clouded over his china doll complexion while his absent eyes gazed out the sweeping windows.

Isabel stared at the child, listlessly bathing in sunlight. She peered down at Phillip, kneeling before the boy. Phillip looked up at her, sensing her confusion and discomfort.

"This is Ellison," he said, rising from his knees.

Isabel stared at Phillip, waiting for an explanation. But the resemblance of the boy's delicate profile and translucent blue eyes already whispered the answer in her heart before Phillip confirmed it.

"My son."

Isabel stared at the child. "I had no idea…" Her voice trailed off because she had no idea what else she could possibly say.

"Why would you? I've never told anyone about him—until now."

"But why not?"

He turned away from her, as if he knew his answer wouldn't satisfy her. But she could read him now—read the distress in the creases of his frown—and she knew he was trying to protect Ellison from a world Phillip viewed as hostile and unforgiving.

Slowly, she drew closer to Ellison, lowering herself to his eye level. "How old is he?"

"Almost five. His birthday is next week."

Isabel peered up at Phillip, attempting to contain her shock. *Almost five?* Almost the same age as Aidan, and still, she had never known anything about him nor had Phillip ever hinted at the fact that he had been in a relationship that resulted in a child.

"He was born only a few weeks before you came to interview for a position at Spears & Associates," Phillip added, sensing Isabel's need to understand more. "Prior to that, I had been in a relationship with a woman for over three years. We were in love, or so I thought. She became pregnant—unexpectedly. She didn't want to have the baby. I did. She conceded. But shortly after her first trimester, she began to experience complications with the pregnancy. Her resentment towards me—and the baby—quickly drew us apart, and in the end, she ended up delivering prematurely at twenty-five weeks." Phillip's gaze settled on the boy's wheelchair and his motionless expression. "We've all had an uphill battle ever since."

Aidan cautiously drew closer to Isabel's side. "Mommy, what's wrong with him?"

"Shhhh, Aidan," Isabel hushed him. "Be respectful."

Phillip winked at him with reassurance. "He's a bit more bashful than you, Aidan. But he likes the sirens of fire trucks, just as much as you, especially when they speed along Lake Shore Drive at night. That's always a treat for him."

Isabel studied Ellison's absent gaze. "Does he…know you?"

"I've been told he likely doesn't know much of what's going on around him. His vision is weak and his hearing is stunted. They tell me he only sees blurry faces and hears muffled voices, but beyond that, it's impossible to truly know. His lungs are incredibly weak. They've told me that he'll never walk. Never learn how to gain full control over his bodily functions. Never fully use his hands. Never speak. A physical therapist comes every week; she attempts to prevent the atrophy of his muscles with massage and small exercises, and she's also quite determined to teach him how to swallow solid foods, despite his stubborn resistance to eat anything beyond milkshakes—Oreo chocolate is his favorite flavor."

"That reminds me…" the unfamiliar woman said from the background.

Phillip glanced back at the woman who had begun tidying the room, replacing the bed's white sheets and swapping out the pillow cases.

"Isabel…this is Ada," Phillip said, formally providing the introduction. "Ada is one of five nurses who I employ to help me take care of Ellison around the clock. The nurses are much better than the doctors about keeping up all of our spirits." He gave Ada a meager smile of appreciation.

"I'll be back with his milkshake," she said, glancing up at the antique wall clock and moving towards the door. "We don't want to feed him too late."

"No, we mustn't," Phillip replied, as if they were sharing a mutual warning. "Ellison is quite punctual. And he does love his Oreo milkshakes." Phillip smiled down at Aidan.

"That sounds delicious," Aidan agreed, peering at the boy with curiosity.

"And Ellison's mother?" Isabel suddenly asked. "Does she see him?"

Phillip shook his head and moved away to the windows, attempting to shield her from the wounded expression on his face.

"It's just been myself and the nurses for the past five years. I stay at my downtown penthouse during the week. But on the weekends, I'm often here, just sitting with him, sometimes reading to him or simply confessing all the things that one thinks and feels on a daily basis, but rarely professes to anyone—not even themselves. And I will confess that he has heard much about you…and Aidan. Ellison's been a great confidant to me in that way."

Phillip glanced back at the boy who gave no indication that he heard, saw, or felt anything in the room except the streaking sunlight across his face. Phillip's eyes grew pensive and his voice haunted, as if he was forcing himself to betray his most painful secret.

"Sometimes, after weeks and weeks of unresponsive silence, he'll suddenly squeeze my hand, as though he's been paying attention to me all along. I'm told it's just a muscle spasm, but it's hard to simply dismiss it when it happens so infrequently and with such ferocity, like a vicious clasp of survival, reminding me that life must go on, that bitterness and anger provide no solace, and that there is no other choice but to wake up and try to live the best life that I can for myself—and for him."

Isabel circled around the wheelchair, inspecting the maze of tubes connected to the oxygen tank. "Do you ever take him out?"

Phillip nodded, striding forward towards the French double doors and opening them for fresh air.

"There's an incline that leads from the terrace down to the private garden where he loves to sit in front of the water fountain with cherubs shooting streams through their lips. Whenever we try to move him back inside, he grunts and whines, like he's overcome with a seizure of grief. Sometimes, Ada has to swaddle him with quilts until he falls asleep to the sound of percolating water. Occasionally, I've wheeled him down to the street level along the bike path towards the lake. Just father and son. But those occasions are growing rarer these days—especially as there are more and more complications with his health."

Phillip turned back to Isabel, making sure she understood him. "That's where I was on the day of the gala—at the hospital. Ellison had developed an infection in his lungs, and he had to be hospitalized that morning. There was a moment when I wondered if any of it mattered at all, trying to restore something like The Old Main Post Office that no one saw any value in except for me. And then I realized that I was doing it for him as much as for myself. A way to prove to the world that there is meaning in protecting things—things our society would rather just discard or cast out."

"Phillip, I'm so sorry…" Her voice dropped, flooded with guilt and regret. "I'm so sorry I made that night harder on you than you needed it to be."

"No, you made the night possible. And I never thanked you properly for it."

He moved across the room and clasped her hand. The revelation that he had carried the emotional burden of raising a disabled child all these years pained her more than she could express through words.

Suddenly, she noticed how Aidan was playing with a long peacock plume, snatched from the interior of a decorative bronze umbrella stand near the doorway. He dangled it over Ellison's head like a fishing line, tickling his forehead.

"Aidan, no—" Isabel scolded him, attempting to grab away the feather.

He spun away, guarding the plume. "Look, he likes it."

Isabel glanced back at Ellison. A strange expression spread across his mouth beneath his oxygen mask.

"Watch," Aidan insisted, lowering the tip of the feather to the boy's hand and tickling it with mischief. Ellison's hand twitched as his mouth gaped wider, just short of a recognizable smile.

"Phillip?" Isabel glanced over at him.

Phillip stared at Ellison's hand, studying the change in his expression. "Again, Aidan… Do it again," he whispered.

This time, Aidan lowered the feather to the boy's bare feet, tickling the top of their arches.

"See?" Aidan exclaimed when Ellison's foot twitched like a playful answer to his childish game.

Phillip swallowed hard and turned to the doorway. "Ada, come quickly please," he called out into the hallway before turning back into the room. Flooded with emotion, he watched from afar as Aidan continued to tickle Ellison's feet.

Ada pushed through the door. Phillip directed her to the scene; she stopped to watch—as Phillip and Isabel watched—and waited to see if there would be another spasm of movement.

Without warning, Phillip's cell phone rang from within the pocket of his trench coat. He ignored the call, hearing only Ada's soft gasp as they all witnessed Ellison gurgle with glee.

"Look, Mommy. He's laughing."

Ada rushed to clear the hissing sound from the oxygen tube. But the source wasn't a blockage; it was Ellison's own amusement behind the mask's plastic.

Phillip's phone rang with persistence; he ignored it. His attention seized on Aidan, who giggled and spontaneously reached out for Ellison's hands, forcing them to clap.

Unexpectedly, Isabel felt the vibration of her own cell phone within her purse. She glanced down at the text message from Jett: *Need to find Phillip. Big problem with Old Main.*

She hesitated, watching Phillip and Ada taking in the scene of Aidan and Ellison's childish interaction. Then, she heard Phillip's cell phone ringing again. He continued to ignore it. Her own phone buzzed again with another message: *Isabel, any idea how I can reach Phillip ASAP?*

She finally caved in and texted back: I'm with him now. I will tell him to call you.

She waited until Phillip strode towards her like a caged tiger, pacing in anticipation for Ada's assessment.

"I don't know what to think, Mr. Spears…maybe he's just been in need of someone his own age."

"Yes, indeed." Phillip studied Aidan, who had started spinning himself in circles along the Persian carpet. Gazing back at Ellison, he noted how he had fallen into silence without Aidan's prodding.

"Phillip," Isabel gently called to him. His attention shifted to her. She offered her phone and encouraged him to scan the messages.

He reluctantly took it, dialed Jett's number, and spoke sparingly into its receiver. "Yes, it's Phillip. What is it?"

Isabel waited. The expression of cautious optimism generated by Ellison and Aidan's interaction dissolved from Phillip's face.

"Yes, I understand. We will be there." Phillip ended the call and handed back the phone to Isabel.

"What is it?" she asked.

"The city has sent us an official summons. They're invoking eminent domain through condemnation of The Old Main Post Office. They're attempting to take it back into their possession as a government property and reassigning their own developer to the renovation project."

"What?" Isabel cried out. "Who?"

Phillip looked away, guarding his emotions. "Watercross Capital."

Chapter Eighteen

ISABEL FOLLOWED PHILLIP'S long strides down the office corridor towards his executive suite, pulling Aidan along with her like a flailing kite. Giselle caught sight of them from the kitchen.

"Well, hello there, handsome," Giselle greeted Aidan with a tickle. "Long time, no see."

"Giselle, please," Isabel exhaled, exasperated. "Would you mind taking Aidan into the kitchen and making him some hot chocolate?"

Both Isabel and Giselle glanced ahead at Phillip, who had stopped in the corridor and waited impatiently for her to meet up with him.

"Aidan, go with Gigi. I'll be back in ten minutes and then we can go to the aquarium."

"C'mon," Giselle said, coaxing him to trade his mother's hand for her own. "Let's see if there are any dry erase markers in the storage closet. We can go into the conference room and draw on the walls."

It was a proposition that Aidan could hardly refuse. "Cool!"

He skipped away with Giselle, allowing Isabel the chance to join Phillip when Tami bounded up to them.

"Oh, thank God, thank God, thank God, you're back." Tami feigned a sugar-coated smile and switched into her best *merrily-she-rolls-along* tone. "Good morning, Phillip."

"Good morning," he replied. "I trust that Jett is already here?"

"Just getting off the phone with Alderman Fitzpatrick now," she confirmed—all business.

"Good. Send him in as soon as possible," he started forward into his office, fully expecting Isabel to follow him.

"Isabel…" Tami grabbed her elbow, halting her by her desk.

Isabel studied Tami. Clearly, there was something weighing heavy on her heart.

"I'll be right in, Phillip," she reassured him.

In the past, his stern eyes would warn her not to take too long; he needed her. But now, the severe lines softened across his forehead as he accepted her delay with understanding. His eyes relaxed with calm trust, which filled her with an unexpected rush of comfort. Perhaps things *could* be different between them.

Tami waited until Phillip completely shut his office door. "Ohmygod…don't *ever* scare me like that again."

Isabel felt Tami's fingernails digging into her arm.

"Calm down, what's going on?"

"You tell me what the hell is going on? Jett gave me Monday morning off because I was still recovering from gala overload, but I heard from all the girls that you stormed out of Phillip's office. They all thought you quit. I tried calling and texting you, but you never answered me."

Isabel pulled out her phone from her purse, suddenly realizing she hadn't checked her messages since yesterday evening. Every moment since then, she had been with Phillip—re-discovering themselves and their relationship without the constrictions of their business lives impeding on them. Now, they were back at the office, falling into their same roles and routines, preparing to reclaim their professional personas as if nothing had ever happened.

"Phillip's here?" Jett rushed out of his office, pen in his mouth, phone in his hand, and his suit coat hanging off one shoulder.

"Yes, he's waiting for us in his office," Isabel confirmed.

"Good." He nodded. "Tami, hold all my calls, except from Ron Johnson, the city commissioner or his assistant, Rochelle."

"Your coffee." Tami passed off his mug. "Cream, sugar, and a pinch of salt. Just how you like it."

"Thanks. Wish us luck."

"Luck," Tami offered with sincerity as Jett disappeared through Phillip's office door.

"Wow…that was the most civil interaction I think I've seen you two have in years."

"We had sex," Tami muttered under her breath.

"You what? When?"

"After the gala," she moaned, drawing her lower eyelids down past her plump cheeks. "And then, again…this morning…in his office…on his desk."

Incredulous, Isabel peeked into Jett's office at his desk. "Really? Well…good for you. I guess that means you can stop complaining to me about growing old and undesirable."

"Isabel, I can't believe it. I mean…it's totally changed me. It's like I actually want to do my job better now—or at least, do it better until I can find a way to lure Jett into the storage closet."

"Oh, God." Isabel held up her hand to silence her. "Please don't tell me that. Giselle just took Aidan in there to find the dry erase markers."

"Okay, you're right." Tami pinched herself. "Horrible idea. Totally irresponsible. And completely unprofessional in every way." A smile spread across her lips. "But Isabel…I'm telling you, the sex is so awesome that I totally—don't—care. Jett could fire me tomorrow, and the only thing that matters to me is that he called me baby while he was banging my brains out. And I'm pretty sure he meant it."

Isabel shut her eyes.

Tami scrunched up her face. "TMI?"

"Just a tad."

"Understood. What about you? Did you ever confirm that Eliot Watercross was Mr. Billionaire Mystery Man?"

Isabel felt her cheeks flush as she considered everything that had transpired since the last time she saw Tami.

"No." She smiled and headed towards Phillip's office door. "I confirmed it was someone even better. Gotta go now."

Isabel swept into Phillip's office. He was standing behind his desk, scanning a leaflet of paper in his hands. Jett was on his cell phone. Norton rested on the couch, looking more grave than normal.

"Good morning, Norton."

"Good morning, Isabel," he replied, his pale face brightening with her entrance. "So nice to see you back here. Perhaps things aren't destined to be doomed and gloomy after all."

"How bad is it?" she asked him.

Norton eyed Jett, pacing vigorously in circles.

"I dare say, not good."

"Isabel," Phillip finally said, tossing the leaflet down onto his desk. She shifted towards it and skimmed its contents: *Official Summons from the City of Chicago. Notice of Condemnation of the Property Located at 433 West Van Buren Street…*

"Check—mate," he punctuated, peering out through the windows at the vast skyline of the city that had turned against him like a traitor. "The right of the government to expropriate private property for public use. It's the perfect strategic maneuver, claiming their right to seize the building for their own political interest. The building spans four thousand feet of Chicago River frontage and sits directly above six lines of federal railway."

Jett ended his call and exhaled with disgust. "That was my contact down at City Hall. He's the head of the City's Planning & Urban Development department. He said once the City has moved to reclaim a property through eminent domain, it's almost impossible to reverse the decision. And we can forget about getting any approval on any of our outstanding redevelopment permits. It's just a monumental circle jerk."

Jett ran his hands through his hair, then tossed his phone onto the couch beside Norton.

"And there's even worse news—Madame van der Meer's lawyers called this morning. Watercross Capital sent them a copy of the official summons, and now her lawyers have called off the tenant lease negotiations. And it's going to be the same with Fifi Litzker. Nobody is going to pursue lease deals with us without our renovation permits in place. And there's no way we're going to get permits when nobody knows for sure who owns the building."

"I own it," Phillip shot back with malice.

Isabel stared at him, absorbing his silent fury.

"Yeah, of course you do, Phillip," Jett conceded.

Realizing he had just assaulted one of his own, Phillip circled away to the far corner of his office. "Bollocks," he cursed, his accent growing brutally thick.

Isabel glanced at Norton, who encouraged her towards Phillip with a toss of his chin.

Carefully, she approached him, touching only the seam of his suit jacket.

"Phillip, we can fight this…let's attempt to fight this—together," she whispered.

"No," he sighed, his eyes gazing far out past the frigid panes of glass. "I'm tired of fighting. Let them fight—all of them." He barely shifted his profile away from the window. She glanced down, feeling the inconspicuous touch of his hand against her own. "I have other priorities now, and there are very few things worth distracting me from them."

"Phillip," she urged him. "This is your property, no one else's. We can't just allow them to take it from you." Isabel searched for hints of the man she had come to know and trust last night. The touch of his hand confirmed he was still there, buried beneath a stone wall of repressed anger and guarded emotions.

"Jett, call Gary…Tell him that I do not intend to challenge them. Let the courts settle the amount of compensation. It will take years, and my interests are occupied elsewhere."

"Phillip, are you sure?" Isabel pressed him.

"Phillip, c'mon," Jett insisted. "We can't just give up. We have to at least appeal."

"No. Let it go, mate," Phillip warned him. "You've never been fond of the building anyway, and I'll compensate you out of my own pocket for the loss of the van der Meer commission. There will be other projects. You always find us something."

"Let me call Gary then," Isabel insisted. "Let me investigate all of our options."

Amused, Phillip eyed her. "Isabel, I'm fairly certain you officially resigned yesterday."

She smiled. He was right; he was always right. "Well, perhaps this morning I realized how much I missed my job because it encompasses everything that I love."

Their eyes locked. Then, like an act of resolution, he fully turned to her and touched her cheek, as if he had forgotten where he was and who was in the room, or perhaps he simply no longer cared.

"Phillip," Norton's voice rose up from behind them, "to surrender so graciously to a man like Watercross is not in your blood."

"No, Norton, it's true." Phillip nodded. "But perhaps I am willing to lose this time because I've won something even more precious."

His eyes lingered upon her. How everything had changed, and yet remained completely the same. They were there in his office, working together like they had always done with a mutual allegiance that bonded them. Only now, there was an open acknowledgment of their union beyond just their professional lives and it gave them strength.

"Call Gary, Jett. Tell him we will not pursue an appeal."

Jett pushed back one final time. "Phillip, are you sure? I've still got a call into the city commissioner—"

But Phillip silenced him with his eyes. "It's over, Jett. Let them have it. They just saved me four hundred million dollars in renovation costs. We'll send them a Christmas ham as a thank-you gift."

"Butt end?" Jett quipped.

"Butt end, mate." Phillip chuckled.

"Ten-four, Chief." Jett saluted and backed away to the door and opened it, calling out into the hallway before disappearing into it. "Tami…get Gary on the line, and hold all the rest of my calls."

Isabel felt the security of Phillip's hand smoothing her heartbreak and bitterness over the injustice that they were being forced to endure. *Let it go,* he was telling her. *Just let it go. We are not giving up, we are simply moving on…*

She squeezed it back, a gesture of understanding. She indulged in the serenity between them, as if together they could conquer anything. Only when her phone rang from inside her trench coat pocket did she reluctantly pull away. She lifted it up and glanced down at its screen: WATERCROSS CAPITAL.

"Phillip," she whispered, showing him her phone.

His eyes hardened and his jawline flinched. "Do as you must," he said, offering her nothing but his unconditional trust.

She gazed down again at her phone, ringing like a threat before she surrendered to its persistence. "Yes…?"

"Bella," Eliot's smooth voice purred through the phone. "So glad to finally hear your voice. I've been missing you all weekend since you left me so abruptly after the gala."

The gala. Isabel rubbed her forehead and turned away from Phillip.

It had only been three days since the night of the gala when she had left with Eliot Watercross. He had driven her home in his Porsche Spyder, but only after she declined his offer to return to his penthouse at the top of the Watercross Tower. Within the speeding darkness of his sports car, whirling like a silent bullet down Lake Shore Drive, she had hidden the quiver within her voice and the tears within her eyes while piercing her own skin with her fingernails and counting down the minutes before they would arrive at her house where she could escape from him. When she was finally alone, in the solitude of her bedroom, she completely undressed and cried herself to sleep—long, bitter sobs that mourned for everything she knew she had lost—not only the stability of her job and the integrity of her professional career, but also her own self-respect, and her respect for the man who she believed had turned against her.

Everything was so different now…

Clasping her hand and luring her to him, Eliot had tried to kiss her before she slipped out of his car. His eyes captured hers as he touched her cheek like she was his prize. *She had escaped, just barely.* But she knew what he wanted, and she knew that he would not be deterred simply because she had declined him that night. *He would try again.* She had felt certain of it; and now, as she heard his seductive voice through her phone, she knew his intentions were clear—he intended to lure her back—and he would not be satisfied until she gave into him.

"I want to see you," Eliot said, determined. *No, there was never any hesitation with him.*

"That's not possible, Eliot."

"I seriously doubt that. And I'm still waiting…"

"For…?"

"For your answer to my offer."

"I'm fairly certain that I've told you no."

"A smart businessman can read a good bluff when he hears it."

"That makes me sound insincere."

"I prefer to think of you more as stubborn."

"I'm not sure if I should be flattered or insulted."

Eliot laughed, a sign he wasn't going to relent until he got what he wanted. "I assume you've heard the news by now?"

"Enlighten me."

"The City has condemned The Old Main Post Office under their right of eminent domain."

Her eyes settled onto Phillip who watched her in return. "Yes, we've all been informed."

"Then you know it's going to linger in the hands of the courts for years until they finally determine an appropriate amount of compensation before turning the redevelopment project over to the City. And to Watercross Capital."

"You say that as if you know that's all a certainty." She was fishing, feeling him out.

"Nothing is ever a certainty with these kind of deals," he replied slyly, tugging on her line. "This is Chicago, after all, and there's always room for negotiation." He fell silent, waiting, listening to her breath, wanting to ensure that she understood him completely. "Which is why, Bella…the only thing certain is that I need to see you."

I need to see you. Isabel broke her gaze with Phillip. *Yes, she understood him.* And she understood exactly what she could offer him in exchange for what he could offer her.

"Where?"

"Here, at my penthouse."

"That sounds a bit informal."

Devilish in its intentions, Eliot's laughter rang out.

"I'll leave the manners and formalities to gentlemen like Phillip. I'm fairly certain you and I prefer a different sort of interaction."

Click.

Chapter Nineteen

ISABEL ENTERED THE PRIVATE residential elevator and allowed the doorman to press the call button for her. She exhaled as the cab butterflied her stomach up, up, upwards—all eighty-nine floors to the top penthouse suite of the Watercross Tower. *The penthouse suite, of course. Eliot Watercross wouldn't have it any other way.*

Ping.

Had she arrived already? Isabel barely had the chance to contemplate her decision to come—and to come alone.

The sleek black elevator doors rolled open. She stepped out into the dim private hallway and noted the only door at the end of the corridor. She approached it, noting the absence of a doorbell. Instead, a security camera was mounted above its entryway.

Buzzzzzzz.

The heavy steel door clicked ajar, facilitating her entrance.

He was watching her, as always.

She slowly pushed across the threshold, drawn in by the sleek vinyl floors, black and reflective like mirrors amplifying the rays of daylight bursting through the duplex windows. White spherical walls churned and curled through the penthouse like a fun house playing games with her perspective. She wound through the penthouse, lured in by glimpses of trendy furniture and modern art carefully filling pockets of expansive space—*living room, dining room, kitchen island…*She stopped, suddenly uncertain about her desire to navigate forward, and yet equally uneasy about her ability to double back.

Pomp, pomp, pomp. She edged towards the rhythmic sound of blows against rubber, hoofs beating in succession. She slipped between two Miró statues leading her through a vortex of contemporary fused glass panes and emerged on the other side of its maze into the penthouse's exercise suite. She spotted him, shirtless like a boxer, his strong shoulder muscles flexing in unison with his accelerating breaths as he sprinted across the treadmill's running deck, embedded into the black vinyl floor. Gleaming in sweat, he snorted like a race stallion, pushing hard to break out of his own limitations. Above him, a checkerboard of video panels replayed her own entrance into the building—elevator, hallway, and finally, his penthouse. She halted, unnerved and captivated, by the eerie images of herself within the black and white security videos.

"In this day and age, there's always someone watching," he called to her, cutting the power on the treadmill and dismounting from its motorized belt. "Glad you made the right decision to come."

"The right decision? For who—you?"

He swiped his water bottle from the treadmill's shelf and took a swig while his menacing eyes fixed on her. The decelerating belt droned to a buzz until it finally cut off completely. "For both of us."

He reached out and stroked her cheek with the tip of his finger, a presumptuous greeting and the flirtatious invitation of something more. Their eyes locked as she attempted to keep her own gaze above his eye line, despite the temptation to follow the beads of sweat rolling down his shoulders, pecs, and abs before staining the waistband of his red boxing shorts. He chugged from his water bottle, studying her over its rim, as though he was assessing her strengths and weaknesses from his corner of their invisible boxing ring. He had intentionally drawn her deeply into the maze of his penthouse, trapping her within the intimacy and seclusion of his private lair with no offer of an escape, until he was satisfied that she had given him exactly what he wanted.

"So how many bribes did it take to get the city to condemn The Old Main Post Office?" she interrogated him, deciding her best defense was to go on the offensive.

"None," he punctuated, musing over her anger while downing the final half of his water bottle. "I simply had to propose the idea. Everyone else was more than willing to see the genius behind it."

"So you consider robbery genius?"

Eliot eyed her. "That makes you sound like your loyalty is still with Phillip." He circled behind her, slipping off her trench coat without permission. "Does that mean you're simply here to reject my offer?" His voice dipped lower into her ear. "I highly doubt that."

"I'm here to negotiate," she clarified, holding her ground. He was testing her, and she was willing to prove that she could endure it.

"Really? I'm intrigued. But first, I need a shower. Wanna join me?" He laughed, as if he fully expected to be refused; and yet, his swagger asserted that the power was in the offer, not in its refusal.

He sauntered away from her and crossed behind an expansive wall of frosted glass, a decorative partition cornering off the far end of the open suite. She watched his silhouette as he kicked off his shoes and stripped off his shorts before flicking on the steamy spray of the shower and drenching himself beneath it.

"Is this how you get ready every morning, showering in front of the entire city of Chicago?" She called to him, noting the exterior walls of panoramic glass and the unobstructed view of the city and lakefront he was afforded.

"Not in front of them, above them," he clarified, extending his muscular arm and retrieving a bar of soap.

"Is that what you're after? Putting the city beneath you?" she lobbed back. "Total domination of everyone and everything?"

He doused his head under the spraying water, running his hands through his hair before wiping his biceps and chest clean of all the suds. Isabel watched him, wondering if he had the bravado to exit the shower—wet and naked.

"Domination is just a means to an end, and I don't mind doing whatever it takes to get it."

She almost thought she saw him smile as he pivoted his body, revealing his profile before reaching out for his towel. Turning away, she moved to his bench press, inventing a distraction until she could prepare herself for her next move. She skated her fingers around the barbell's cold metallic weights; it was hard not to imagine him, lying across the bench and steadying two hundred pounds of weight across his chest before exploding it upwards with a single bursting exertion of strength.

When she turned back, he had already emerged from his shower, wearing only his white bath towel, wrapped around his tapered waist. He shook his slick dark hair with his hand and gazed at her, gauging her lack of discomfort.

"So what kind of negotiations did you have in mind?" he asked, encroaching upon her personal space.

She held her ground. "I want you to convince the city to revoke their condemnation of The Old Main Post Office."

"In exchange for…?" His finger traced her neckline.

She gazed into his green eyes. "In exchange for the names of ten investment leads for your iceberg project."

"Really?" He sounded impressed, even surprised. "Does Phillip know you're here?"

Her silence confirmed his suspicions.

"You still haven't answered my question." He sinfully pressed his bare chest and hard body towards her.

"Eliot..." Her hand pushed back on his bicep. "I'm not interested in becoming your business partner. I just want you to persuade your contacts to revoke the condemnation."

He reached out to fondle a wayward strand of her hair in a way that made her reconsider whether or not he was really the enemy—which made him even more dangerous.

"But I'm offering you so much more."

"I don't need anything more...more than what I already have."

"Everyone needs more, Bella. Don't kid yourself that you're any different."

"I'm not different. But I also know my own professional ambitions won't fulfill me more than what already makes me happy now—and that's my own personal devotion to the things that I hold dear in my life...And the people that I love."

He eyed her, sidelong. "That's a very pretty speech. But your loyalty is misguided. It's foolish to stand by something—or someone—who does nothing but hold you back. You're more than a secretary, Bella. And you deserve to be treated like more."

"As opposed to being treated like the ultimate prize in a competition?"

He smirked, confirming what they both knew was the truth.

"And such a lovely prize, indeed."

He touched her cheek, testing her acceptance. She challenged him with her eyes and held up a paper, forcing him to betray which prize he truly desired most of all.

"Ten," she insisted.

He held her chin between his fingers and leaned in, grazing his nose along her cheekbone, as if he was savoring the scent of powder and perfume on her skin. "It's a shame we couldn't find more common ground." His lips lingered, threatening to breach the boundaries of her allegiance, before he snatched the paper and pulled himself away from her.

Isabel shut her eyes and exhaled, watching him whip off his towel and disappear around the curling white corner. Phillip was right. She was just a pawn. A pawn in a game of egos between greedy men. And it was a game she was glad had finally come to an end.

* * * *

Isabel exited the Watercross Tower and approached the pearly white Bentley, idling along the curb. Its tinted windows slowly lowered, revealing Aidan in its rear seat.

"Hi honey," she said to him while approaching the passenger door.

"Mommy, can I tell you something?" he called out with excitement. "Phillip's car sounds like a dragon."

On cue, Phillip revved the Bentley's engine.

She got in the car and glanced over at him. "And I suppose you boys are the knights?"

"We prefer to be cowboys, don't we, Aidan?" Phillip glanced at him in the rearview mirror.

"Yeeeeehaaaaaaaw!" Aidan bellowed.

Isabel covered her ears. "You taught him that?"

"Naturally." Phillip nodded, tearing away from the curb. "It's every English boy's dream to be a cowboy."

"Yeeeeeeehaaaaaw!" Aidan hollered again, just in case his mother didn't hear him the first time. "Mommy, are we going to the aquarium now?"

"Yes, honey. Thank you for being so patient." Isabel smiled at her son, noting how snugly he fit into Ellison's car seat. "So what happens now, Cowboy?" she asked Phillip.

"Watercross took the list?"

"Yes. Everything happened exactly as you said it would."

"Good. Then, we do nothing."

"Nothing?"

"Yes, nothing."

Isabel frowned. Phillip glanced at her, then shifted gears, powering them into the fast lane along Lake Shore Drive.

"Watercross will contact our investors. He will most likely persuade them all to invest in his real estate fund for his miserable iceberg. And he may or may not persuade the city to revoke the condemnation of The Old Main Post Office."

"May or may not?" she questioned him. "Won't it be a stipulated contingency in the investment contract?"

"Surely not."

"Then, Phillip...?" She paused, attempting to understand the calm resignation in his voice. "Haven't we just given Eliot Watercross some of our best investment contacts without any assurance that he will help revert The Old Main back into your possession?"

"Yes," he replied, cutting across the highway towards their exit. "Except all ten of those investors are tied back to my investment hedge funds."

"*Your* hedge funds?"

"Yes."

"Which means…" Isabel's voice trailed off, realizing the implications of his strategy.

"Which means…no matter how much capital Eliot Watercross leeches from my minority shareholder partners, I am the one who has to agree to participate in order for capital to be distributed. So not only will I ultimately control the decision to fund Watercross' iceberg, I will also be the one who ultimately owns it."

"Oh, Phillip," Isabel sighed, barely containing her displeasure.

He pulled into the parking lot of the Shedd Aquarium—one of her favorite sites in the city—and parked along the Northside boardwalk, where the picturesque view of Lake Michigan and Chicago's downtown dominated their view.

"Don't worry. I won't let it melt completely." He cut off the car's engine and relaxed against his headrest, enjoying the way she censured him with her gaze. "I'll just let it get sloppy and soggy a bit—or at least until I get back The Old Main Post Office."

She eyed him. "I should have known."

"Yes, you should have." He smiled slyly, reaching out for her hand and caressing her wrist, admiring how well she wore his sapphire ring on her engagement finger. "But you don't think that way, devilishly, and that's what I love about you the most—your absolute sincerity."

He drew her to him for a kiss—a long, penetrating expression of devotion that he had been forced to suppress for years; but now, he made it feel like the most natural thing in the world.

"Yucky!" Aidan cried out, covering his eyes. "Boring! Can we please go to the aquarium now?"

Phillip glanced back at Aidan, then Isabel. "I'm glad to see he has your temper."

Chapter Twenty

FOUR MONTHS LATER

"AWESOME!!!!" AIDAN'S voice echoed throughout the warehouse, bouncing off the sleek concrete floors as he darted his bike through pools of sunlight streaming in through the two-story arching windows. Guiding Ellison in his motorized wheelchair, Isabel and Phillip trailed far behind him.

"Don't go too far," Isabel called after him, a routine warning that now seemed inconsequential in the vast interior space void of cars, crosswalks, and street lights. There was only the sensation of the boundless unknown, spanning the length of three skating rinks, which Aidan pedaled through like a speeding bullet in a vacuum.

"Has Fifi Litzker committed to all of it?" Isabel turned back and asked Phillip.

She stopped and surveyed the repetition of steel rafters bracing the ceiling, allowing the open space to be clear of any load-bearing walls or side beams. She cast her gaze at Phillip. He was studying Ellison, wearing his new thick-lensed glasses and circling his wheelchair through a puddle of sunlight with only the touch of his thumb against the navigation joystick.

"She's committed to leasing both the second and third levels," he confirmed. "This floor will be the day & evening spas, and at the far end, they will build out their trendy restaurant and bar. Above, on the third level, they will remodel the space to include their luxury hotel suites—each one with private terraces overlooking the riverfront."

He moved to the cathedral windows and peered out onto the South Branch of the Chicago River and the city's financial district, just beyond it. "Jett's still working to secure a deal with several European retailers to lease out space on the fourth floor, but even without that, Madam van der Meer's collection will help draw the tourists."

"It all sounds wonderful, but I'd be lying if I didn't say that some small part of me fears how much work it's all going to be..."

Her attention drifted off to Aidan and Ellison as she reflected on the blissful, carefree day that they had spent together as a family.

"Well, we're partners now. We'll get through it together."

"Partners?" She turned to him.

"Yes." He peered down at the sapphire ring she wore on her finger. "I've arranged for Gary to reallocate shares to you in the holding company that formally owns The Old Main. Twenty percent of my own equity stake. Consider it a tardy five-year bonus."

Isabel felt her lips quiver. Twenty percent of a four-hundred-million-dollar real estate development was more than Isabel could calculate in her head. "Phillip...I don't know what to say."

He consoled her with his steady blue eyes. "Don't say anything. I shall say it for you—thank you," he whispered, caressing her cheek and kissing her with reverence, reminding her that she meant more to him than anything that money could buy or share.

"Eww...yucky!"

Glaring at Phillip kissing his mother, Aidan skidded his bike to a stop and covered his eyes. "Gross! Mommy, what's he doing that for?" His childish disgust boomeranged off the concrete floors, which made Ellison stop his own circling and look up at them.

Phillip pulled away with a smile, allowing Isabel to field the interrogation on her own.

"Phillip just likes to share more than he should," she replied.

Aidan glared at Phillip, making sure he knew that he shouldn't share *that* much.

"Perhaps someone should put me in jail," Phillip announced and held up his hands like he was under arrest.

"Yeah!" Aidan squealed and sped around Phillip, mimicking the sound of a police siren. Ellison smiled, attempting to cruise behind Aidan. He accidentally nudged his wheelchair into Aidan's rear bike tire. The boys traded teasing thumps before knocking into each other with a jarring bang like bumper cars.

"No, Aidan—don't," she reprimanded him. "You'll hurt Ellison."

The boys ignored her and circled away, shooting down the sleek floor together like drag racers.

Exasperated, she glanced back at Phillip. "Boys."

Phillip shrugged and enveloped her hand.

"You don't seem concerned."

"No," he confirmed, tracking Ellison rolling through the unobstructed space, as if he was just like Aidan. "It's true, they're just being boys. And watching them act like that is making me the happiest I've been in years."

He lifted up her hand and kissed it with affection.

She eyed him. "You say that now, but just wait until one of them ends up in the emergency room."

He shrugged again.

She pressed her point. "Which means *you'd* be without your business partner—possibly for days—while she's tied up with the responsibility of taking care of reckless, injured children."

"We'll do it together." He drew her against his body and feathered his whisper against her ear. "Let's have more."

THE END

Acknowledgments

I would love to take this opportunity to thank all of my dedicated readers who have supported me through their reviews, word-of-mouth recommendations, and kind emails of praise and encouragement. Many of these readers are now part of my ARC crew, and without their enthusiasm—and fandom—early on in my career, I wouldn't have had the confidence to keep writing and producing my Chicago billionaire romances. I am a hopeless romantic at heart, and I often think my greatest fans must be hopeless romantics, too!

I would also like to thank the women who offered their editorial and proofreading services on many of my novels, including Jennifer López, Jan White, Anna Albo, Kerrie Bedford, and P.N. Stockwell, whose "killer kellar editing" is the main reason why you are reading this boxed set. I would also like to thank my son, whose eye condition discovered at the tender age of four years-old inspired me to explore Sven's blindness as both a challenge and a gift. And last, but far from least, I would like to thank my unwavering, committed Irish Catholic mother and my equally, strong-willed Spanish father whose unexpected five-month hospitalization inspired me to write *EXES* as a way to forge ahead through the darkest time in my life, and taught me the invaluable lesson of holding out hope at all costs and the importance of believing in that mythical Tiffany stained-glass window within all our lives.

Great word-of-mouth is the best advertising an author can hope for from her fans, and I am so very grateful for all of my readers who believe in billionaire loves stories and happily ever afters as much as I do.

smooch
very best, Aria Hawthorne

About the Author

Bestselling author Aria Hawthorne loves writing about billionaire men who lavish their women with expensive jewelry and ravish them like queens in bed. EXES - A Second Chance Billionaire Romance is her newest erotic romance, which Amazon UK named a Top 100 "Most Read" Kindle All-Star following its release and Ms. Hawthorne was named a Top 100 "most Read" Kindle author. Her billionaire romance novel, CLOSER, was also awarded this distinction by both Amazon US and UK after its launch. Once upon a time, she lived in the grand lakefront city of Chicago; now, like a forlorn lover, she simply yearns for the day when she can return to it. She can be contacted through her publisher, French Kiss Press. www.frenchkisspress.com

Website: frenchkisspress.com
Twitter: @frenchkisspress
Facebook: facebook.com/AuthorAriaHawthorne
Instagram: instagram.com/AuthorAriaHawthorne
Mailing List: frenchkisspress.com/join_mailinglist
Amazon Author Page: amazon.com/follow_ariahawthorne

Chicago Billionaires

Aria Hawthorne

Made in the USA
Columbia, SC
22 March 2019